The Darkness Within Trilogy Book Two:

Blood of the Lost

by JD Franx

The Darkness Within Saga:
Book 2

Blood of the Lost

Author: JD Franx

Joel Lagerwall and Stefan Celic

Editing by Casa Cielo

Createspace Design and Formatting

by Rachel Bostwick

ISBN 978-0-9953363-1-5

Dedication

To all my readers:

The dedication for this second book can really only go to you.

You are the reason I have worked as hard as I did to finish this book and have it ready for release six months after the first. The private messages, the emails, and even the comments on my Facebook page and posts all kept me writing, revising, editing and even proofreading in order to see *Blood of the Lost* completed.

Thank you to each and every one of you, wherever you may be. You have all been phenomenal.

Table of Contents

Dedication 3

Chapter One 9

Chapter Two.. 23

Chapter Three 43

Chapter Four 61

Chapter Five 77

Chapter Six 93

Chapter Seven.. 105

Chapter Eight 119

Chapter Nine.. 131

Chapter Ten.. 147

Chapter Eleven 157

Chapter Twelve 173

Chapter Thirteen 195

Chapter Fourteen.. 207

Chapter Fifteen 215

Chapter Sixteen 229

Chapter Seventeen.. 237

Chapter Eighteen.......... 253
Chapter Nineteen.......... 269
Chapter Twenty.......... 287
Chapter Twenty-One.......... 305
Chapter Twenty-Two.......... 327
Chapter Twenty-Three.......... 343
Chapter Twenty-Four.......... 355
Chapter Twenty-Five.......... 369
Chapter Twenty-Six.......... 383
Chapter Twenty-Seven.......... 407
Chapter Twenty-Eight.......... 423
Chapter Twenty-Nine.......... 437
Chapter Thirty.......... 453
Chapter Thirty-One.......... 471
Chapter Thirty-Two.......... 487
Chapter Thirty-Three.......... 505
Chapter Thirty-Four.......... 521
Chapter Thirty-Five.......... 537
Chapter Thirty-Six.......... 561
Chapter Thirty-Seven.......... 579

Chapter Thirty-Eight 595

Chapter Thirty-Nine 611

Chapter Forty 625

Chapter Forty-One 639

Chapter Forty-Two 659

Chapter Forty-Three 665

Acknowledgements 671

Preview 675

GLACIAL MOUNTAINS
TAI SA NEBAN
ANCIENT KINGDOM
WESTERN JAWS OF ICE AND ROCK
GAUNTLET PASS
BLACK HOLLOW PENINSULA
EASTERN JAWS OF ICY AND ROCK
DEAD STRAIT
KASTALBORG ISLAND
SEA OF THREE
TYR'S STRAIT
DRAGON ISLES
WHITEWYRM OCEAN
FREE LANDS
YUSAI
WOODS
SEA OF STORMS
FAE ISLANDS
CAULDRON'S WHITE CALM
BLACK CAULDRON OCEAN
THE NECK
THE NECK
QUY
MIDNIGHT CANOPY FOREST
DORMASAI
SALZARA
ELLORYA

Chapter One

"Talohna is home to some of the nastiest creatures that exist. And as a bard, minstrel, and writer, I have sung about and studied most of them. Weres, banshees, gorgons, and even the Mahala. Like every good entertainer, I have travelled far and wide in pursuit of myths and legends, real and imaginary, learning more about them in the hopes that inspiration would strike. The DeathWizard is probably feared more than any other magical creature, but they are ultimately extremely rare. On the other hand, Ella Navasha, the White Witch, is feared even more, mostly because she does exist in the here and now. To control the power offered by or stolen from an Angel is an amazing feat. But the thing is, with Ella the White, no one alive knows whether she was granted her power or whether she stole it. Some people even believe she killed an Angel to get its power, as disturbing as that is. I've often wondered myself, which version is actually true."

Garren Sallus, A Traveller's Codex, Vol. 2

ELLORYA, 5025 POST CATACLYSM
NORTHERN ELLORYAN FOREST

Fourteen-year-old Desiree Star tripped on a raised root, plunging head first into a stagnant, slow-moving creek. Pulling her face from the noxious green slime, she gagged as the taste of rot filled her mouth. Realizing it came from the putrefying human corpse half-submerged in the creek, her stomach rebelled, tossing nothing but bile from her empty stomach. A howl followed by the crash of something heavy racing through the forest behind her spurred her back to her feet and straight into another desperate run. Her legs ached with a constant throbbing and added more agony to the pulsating thump behind her eyes caused by a lack of sleep from two full days of running and fighting.

The apprentice Broken Blade assassin had known no fear until three days past. As the thought of what she witnessed bounced to the front of her mind, her legs trembled, making her stumble and cold fear flipped her stomach. Worse than either of those was that she was defenceless.

The creatures chasing her were relentless. Weres never gave up the hunt, but werewolves were so much worse with that canine nose. With both of Desiree's wooden dagger blades broken off inside of the massive alpha female, the great beast still pursued her. The weapon's natural poison only slowed the monster—it did not stop her. It would be almost an hour before the blades grew back, she hoped. The magic within the handles was efficient, but not perfect.

Another howl rolled across the valley behind her, bouncing off the mountain cliffs and dense brush, making it impossible to know exactly where the creature was. Desiree pushed harder, increasing her speed, dodging and slipping between the trees of the northern Elloryan Forest. Another howl, deeper than the female's, bounced off the rocks ahead of her and to the right. She stopped dead in her tracks. Holding her breath for a couple seconds, she could hear the female to her rear, racing through the forest. Even running on two legs, the alpha was nearly as fast as her. But there was something else bothering the assassin. She frowned and focused harder, but her advanced skills and senses were unable to pinpoint it.

Darting to her left, Desiree leapt into a roll, running the moment her feet landed as a dark-pelted werewolf crashed into the tree behind her. The savage growl and exploding bark lent her more speed a second too late, as a blaze of silver-white hair slammed into her side, knocking her to the ground.

She lifted her arms to defend herself as the alpha female chomped down on her left wrist. Trained from the age of four to ignore pain, Desiree ground her teeth as canine jaws crunched the bones in her wrist. Swallowing the tingle of fear creeping into her body, she smiled up at the growling beast. Jamming her right thumb into the monster's mouth, she forced it under the tongue and pushed with everything she had. The werewolf gagged, letting go of her wrist and pulling back. The assassin shifted her weight, pushing her waist up. Throwing her right leg over her left, she grabbed the female by the neck and pulled her closer, heaving both of their bodies to the left. The werewolf tripped on Desiree's legs, falling on its side and snapping its jaws. White teeth clicked, catching only air as Desiree mounted the creature, her good arm pressing down on the female's throat.

"Where is he? Where's your mate? Tell me, or I'll skin you alive!" she screamed.

The creature huffed and a distorted laughed crawled from her throat.

Desiree pressed down harder, cutting the laugh short. "Fine, I'll get him too if he keeps chasing me. So long, dog-bitch." Desiree spit, pressing down with all her weight, but a set of teeth clamped tight to her neck halting her kill. The pressure increased quickly, until both sets of canines pierced her flesh, stopping an inch deep in her throat. A growl rumbled from her captor's throat, vibrating the flesh of Desiree's neck and forcing her to release the female as the second werewolf carefully eased her off the pack leader. The white female snorted and pulled herself off the ground onto her hind legs, towering over Desiree as the male shook her neck, pressing her to her knees. The female bent over, looking into Desiree's pale blue eyes. Their noses almost touching, the female growled, her black lips curling away from six-inch long canines. The teeth in her neck eased and disappeared.

"If you wanted to find me so badly, why run from my family?" a male voice asked from behind Desiree only seconds after he released her neck. He shifted to Human-form a little too fast. Impossibly fast.

"Not exactly running from you, dog," she sneered.

"Ah yes. Your encounter with the mad alchemist. I caught the scent of vaporized assassin on your clothing. You must know by now that the crazy fool isn't chasing after y—" Desiree frowned and the creature clearly sensed it, though the voice remained behind her. "Of course, of course... You survived, but your mentor did not. So, you run from the Broken Blades then. Won't guild loyalty protect you?"

"Yrlissa Blackmist is dead. Guild law means little lately. For some," the assassin answered.

"So, you ran." The alpha male chuckled. "Not the smartest move, but the only one, I guess."

"You're smart for a smelly mutt, but I'm not... Wasn't looking for you, just passing through your territory..." Still nose to nose, the female alpha growled, bumping Desiree with her wet nose and huffing in her face. The nauseating stench of rotting meat made her eyes water, but she'd smelled much worse—swallowed worse only minutes ago.

"Yes," the male continued, finally walking into her view. She was surprised at his youthfulness, almost too young for an alpha. His black hair, tipped with flecks of white, matched the dark pelt covering his body earlier. White and Black, female and male; the perfect werewolf match, which further explained his youth when compared to the scarred, grizzled female; their brindle pups would be incredibly powerful shifters. "You're heading for DormaSai. You assassins really aren't the brightest bunch, are you? Most people in Talohna go out of their way to avoid us."

"Had no idea this was your territory, dog. Still wouldn't have stopped me. Merethyl has too many guild killers in the Southern Kingdoms these days. This forest is the only way out." The alpha male laughed, deep and throaty, but it was a female voice that answered, again from behind.

"This isn't werewolf territory, my dear Blade. It's mine." Desiree swallowed hard, her mouth drying with excitement. The points of her daggers gently poked the underside of her arms. The blades had finished growing, finally. "They merely guard the forest and keep the riff-raff away from my home. You should be more respectful to my friends," the voice carried on. "After all, they're just following my orders. Strangers aren't welcome here, killers least of all. You must have heard the rumours."

"I... have..." Desiree said. As her esoteric senses flared as a warning to what stood behind her, she pulled her tongue from the roof of her cotton-filled mouth. "Still didn't stop me. I believe I said that... witch."

"Your senses are well-honed. Though not many people would speak to me like that," the woman said. Desiree could hear the woman move, her footsteps light, balanced. Something she'd expect from a skilled fighter, not a witch.

The alpha male snorted. Desiree watched him carefully as he breathed deeply. As if not satisfied, he approached, kneeling at Desiree's side. Grabbing her dark ponytail, he pulled her head closer, breathing deep. Her skin twitched with revulsion as his nose nuzzled her ear and he inhaled her scent. "I smell no fear, Mistress," he said, releasing her ponytail and rising to his feet. "Only charred Elvehn flesh and organs."

"Of course you smell no fear, Torgo. A Broken Blade assassin fears only their own. You don't scare her, even that crazy alchemist didn't scare her, though he wasn't the easy target you expected, was he, my dear?"

"Obviously not," Desiree answered.

The woman stepped in front of Desiree, the alpha female relinquished her guard in order to make way. "I'll bet dear old Merethyl Bellas neglected to tell you and your mentor what you would really face in that glade. Am I right?" Desiree frowned, saying nothing. "Let me guess... Bring her some crazy old fool, an alchemist, and an easy target, not even a corpse. Bring him back alive, easy job, easy money. I bet she even dropped the guild's tax for this job. Yes?" Desiree's frown deepened. The witch's words were almost identical to what Merethyl had said during their contract briefing. "Your head council member didn't exactly have your best interests in mind, did she?"

"Not this time, witch."

"I promise you, my dear, Merethyl Bellas knew exactly what she was sending you into. So you must be a Yrlissa Blackmist loyalist then."

"My loyalty lies with the guild. Always."

"That's too bad for you, Desiree Star." Desiree frowned. Regardless of the rumours, there was no way this witch could know who she was. "Yrlissa Blackmist was my friend. If you knew her at all, you'd know my real name."

"Your real name won't frighten me either, witch." The moment she said it, the white werewolf laughed, and the rumours Desiree had heard around the guild started to drift back through the haze of exhaustion smothering her brain.

"We shall see, my dear." The witch leaned over. Desiree felt the woman's breath tickling the soft hairs by her ear. "I can see you struggling to pull my name from the depths of your sleep-deprived, exhausted memories, child. Let me help you." A spell slammed into her mind, the rumours and innuendo stormed back, as clear as the very first time she heard them, especially the stories Desiree had heard during her initiate years.

"Impossible..." she whispered, trailing off.

"Not so, my dear. My name is Ella Navasha. But most people call me Ella the White." Desiree turned, bravely smiling over her shoulder at the most powerful witch to ever live, doing her best to keep her bladder in check. The witch was young, too young for the experience within the voice.

Dressed in an immaculate long, white dress even though they were in a damp forest just seemed to match the rest of the impeccably proper-looking woman.

"Talohna's only angel-blessed witch..." Desiree breathed.

Ella's voice dropped even lower. "Because a witch has the power of the White does not mean she is blessed by an angel. Angels don't like giving mortals power unlike demons. What power an angel gives up is gone forever, but they can be tricked into surrendering it, or it can be taken when you kill one." More memories, rumours, myths, swirled inside Desiree's head, leaving her with the truth as her only option.

"If you really are Ella Navasha, then you should know that my dead mentor and myself were both trained by Yrlissa."

"But I do know that, my dear. Why do you think we're here? Merethyl already knows you're alive. You were branded a day ago. Look." The woman stepped around her and lightly lifted her left hand. Like all Broken Blade assassins, the black magical tattoo of two opposing daggers, one missing the blade and one whole, marked Desiree's palm.

"*Jafin Berr,*" Ella whispered, pressing her right hand to Desiree's left palm. A bright light flashed and searing pain followed.

"Dammit! What the fuck, witch?" Desiree cursed. Ella released Desiree's hand, her spell completed. The tattooed blades were broken in numerous places, as if shattered by a smith's hammer.

"You've been branded a traitor by your guild. Only those hunting you can see the brand. It is how the Broken Blades hunt their own so easily, how can a Blade run when they rarely realize their guild wants them dead."

"I... I didn't know..."

"Because you've yet to reach the rank of guild assassin, apprentice. You still should have known, Desiree Star. The magic imbued in that mark no longer works. Your heightened speed, reflexes, and stealth are all gone. A werewolf, even an extremely rare alpha like my dear friend here, should never catch your kind. You want me to believe your loyalty lay with Yrlissa? Come with me now and I'll make sure Merethyl never tracks you down. Not until we're ready for you to burrow that broken blade in the bitch's neck."

"How could you possibly offer such a thing? Even if all the rumours about you are true, it'll take me four hundred years before I could rival Merethyl as a killer, even she won't live that long."

"Oh, my dear, you have so much to learn. Come with me and have faith that my name carries with it *no* rumours." Truth seemed to layer every word, but still Desiree had doubts.

"Have faith?!" she yelled. "I'm marked for death by Talohna's best magical killers. Killers who don't have targets, but corpses, because a contract is only fulfilled when that person is dead—they never give up. Even Yrlissa Blackmist wasn't good enough to survive against Merethyl. Give me something now, Ella, or kill me. I'm not afraid to die!"

"Fair enough, Desiree Star," Ella said. Leaning closer once more, she whispered, "I trained Yrlissa Blackmist. So many years ago, you wouldn't even recognize your own guild."

The alpha female shifted back to her human form, muttering. "Fuck me." The transformation took mere seconds.

Desiree didn't know who to stare at, the werewolf who changed ten times faster than any other, or the witch claiming to be over several millennium in age, at least. The guild's only changes occurred during the Cataclysm over five thousand years ago. The guild had grown so large that the independent cell structure used no longer allowed for the guild to be efficient. After months of internal conflict, dissidents had been rooted out and killed, leading the way for the guild to be run by a senior council. It was the largest recorded change in the guild's history.

Finally, she found her tongue and asked, "Why? Why me?"

"Yrlissa's loyalists outside the guild who have already undergone your training don't exist. Blade initiates receive training unlike anywhere else. You were trained by Yrlissa, which means the months you suffered building poison and pain resistance are irreplaceable. Not every Blade initiate gets that. The years of agony you suffered learning to ignore your stealth skills and your magic so that you'd be that much better with them. Everything! The best way to kill Merethyl Bellas is from within, but a serious threat from outside her guild is the best way to keep her distracted..."

"A distraction," Desire said, spitting at Ella's feet. "Fancy word for a sacrifice. Stuff it, witch..."

Ella's hand snapped out, wrapping around Desiree's throat so fast she never saw the woman move. Currents of sparkling energy crawled under and along Ella's fingers as she chanted slowly. Little blue worms of lightening slid into Desiree's throat and cheeks. It tingled at first, but quickly surged with intensity. Her eyes popped open, beyond her control, as the current locked her teeth together, nipping the tip of her tongue. The scent of charred flesh drifting up her nostrils made her gag, but even her stomach refused to obey the commands of her mind as electricity invaded her entire body.

"Interrupt me again and I will fry you from the inside out. Show me such disrespect again and I will turn your entire body inside out while you remain alive. Am I clear, Desiree Star?"

The current tormenting her body lessened enough for her to nod.

"Good," Ella said. The current increased again. Every muscle in Desiree's body went rigid, aching from the pressure put on every muscle and nerve. "I don't sacrifice people for any reason, not any more. I was going to tell you that you'd have your chance at Merethyl, a distraction is useless if the threat it poses is not real. Yrlissa's faithful would be there to back you up should you need them. Do you understand?" Desiree nodded as Ella's spell lessened once more. "Now get up, we have work to do and you have a year's worth of training ahead." Ella removed her hand from Desiree's throat and she crashed to the ground twitching from the after effects of the spell.

Struggling to her feet, Desiree couldn't help herself. "What work?" Ella gave her a look that let her know she was pushing her luck, but answered anyway.

"I need your skills. We have to hunt someone down while you train to become an even better killer.

"Who?"

"Not really a who, my dear, more of a what."

"What then?"

"A DeathWizard. We are going to hunt Talohna's only living DeathWizard."

"No. Just kill me. I'm not going to die trying to kill a gods-cursed DeathWizard, my soul..." The alpha female's backhand came from nowhere, knocking Desiree back to the leaf-mold. The power behind the blow was incredible, even though she was in Human form.

"Respect, my dear," Ella said. "Second warnings are not something I normally give. Besides..." The witch smiled, helping Desiree back up. "We're not hunting him so we can kill him. We're going to help him, if we can find him in time."

WILDLANDS EASTERN SHORE

Kael floated on the white clouds and smoky haze that accompanied all subconscious wanderings of the mind, and yet for some reason, he knew he wasn't alone. A presence kept him company, a presence he knew well. Though the swirling miasma of white blurred her appearance as she drifted closer, he knew the form of his wife, Ember, as if she were a disconnected piece of his own soul. He would know her anywhere, even if she'd been dead for many months. He looked around to see where his broken mind had brought him, but his eyes saw nothing but the shapeless white. As his wife drifted within a few feet, he held up his hand for her to stop. The image created by his mind of the only woman he had ever loved was exactly how he had remembered her minutes before he saw her last.

"I know you're not real," he said, sadness layering every word. "This is a dream, but just let me look at you before the nightmare begins again. You can't imagine how much I miss you," he added, his voice heavy with regret and the guilt of her loss.

She smiled that perfect smile he remembered so well. "This is one dream I promise you will not turn into a nightmare. Please, love, let me show you." She stepped forward to take his hands, but he jumped back to avoid triggering the part of the dream where she died before his eyes again, for the thousandth time. The look of hurt nearly broke what was left of his tortured soul.

"Please, Kael, listen to me. I don't have much time. You have to help us, you have to help me. Take my hand and I will show you. I control this dreamworld, not those who have hurt you for so long. Please," she pleaded, reaching for him. Afraid of what had happened so many times before, he shook his head, taking another step back.

"You're not real. I watched you die inside the vortex, you and Max both. The king's man told me that he removed your bodies. I'm sorry, Ember. It was my fault, they wanted me, not you..." He coughed, as a tickle formed in his lungs.

"I know, babe," she said. "I know all of it, but we're not dead. Max is right here with me and we're in trouble, right now, here in Talohna. How would I know what this world is called if I weren't real? We need you. Take my hand, Kael, please. My strength is waning." Desperate to believe what she said was true, Kael closed his eyes and took her hand.

With a rush of what he knew could only be magical power, Kael smiled as the fog of white turned to darkness and after only a few seconds, the dark faded, transforming into a tropical forest. Ember and Kael glided into a camp of savage human beings as if they both had wings. She led him by the hand to a cage filled with people, all of whom had been beaten badly. Many of them still suffered from bloody, open wounds. Memories of himself and the others who had suffered for months at the hands of the Dead Sisters came rushing back to the forefront of his mind and the anger always just under the surface roared to life once more. Even in the dreamworld, the thorn-covered black vines covering his body jumped to life, growing through him.

He grunted from the pain, stumbling, until he saw his wife, bruised and dirty, laying beside a young Elvehn woman. Kael glanced back at the Ember holding his hand, confused and unable to comprehend what he was seeing.

"I don't have time to explain, babe. What you see is very real. We are both alive. The ones who told you otherwise lied. Look," she said, pointing to Max. Kael stumbled again, weakness washing over him, but as he looked at his closest friend, there was no doubt in his mind that it was Max. A once seldom-seen frown, a couple weeks of beard growth, and a set of nasty looking scars across his face were the only difference. Kael recognized the change in his friend all too well; it was what this world did to people who weren't born in Talohna.

"What happened to his face, Ember?" Kael winced, as he got a good look at the fresh scars. He wheezed, coughing a second time in an attempt to push the irritation from his lungs.

"A Wraithlord. We were trying to find you. He saved us the day that happened, like he saved us back home the night you were shot. You remember?" He nodded. "Don't you see? We're alive, Kael, and you need to save us. Please," she begged, yet again.

The tickle in his lungs grew stronger, turning to fire. He hacked, trying to expel the pain, but a racking cough took over.

"Where... ...are you?" He coughed and spit on the ground, but nothing came from his lungs or mouth. The burning worsened as he gasped, his breath failing.

Almost unable to breathe, he heard Ember yell, "I wasn't fast enough, Kael. I'm sorry." He continued to sputter, struggling for air as Ember closed her eyes, concentrating on something only she could see. When they snapped back open, she screamed with panic.

"No! Kael, listen to me, please. We're in the Wildlands, help us. The Wildlands, Kael, we're in the Wildlands. Help us. Please!" Doubled over and fighting for breath, he glanced up in time to see her fading from his sight, her arms outstretched, reaching for him.

Her voice reverberated inside his head as the fog of white returned, more like the beginning of the dream. "You have to wake up now. Wake up. Now, wake up, Kael!" She screamed a second time as an explosion of magic roared inside his head.

She was gone.

SEA OF STORMS

Kael jerked awake, inhaling a mouthful of salty water before he was fully conscious. Thrashing at the panicked sensation of breathing water and not air, a second wave slammed his face and body, lifting him further up the beach before it was clear he wasn't actually drowning. The panic subsided. He was no longer out in the ocean, drifting and lost. Lying face down on a beach with his head towards the incoming tide, he would have drowned had the realistic dream not woken him. Dizzy and disoriented, he pulled himself from the surf and fell to the beach, gasping for breath, utterly exhausted.

The dream about Ember and Max was crystal clear in his mind, but the rest of what had happened over the last couple days was a confusing mess of flashes and darkness. The dream felt so real; he wanted to believe it was. Had Ember not screamed at him to wake up and had the strange power inside his head not awoken him, he would have drowned face down in the sand and surf. With more than a little difficulty, he focused on remembering how he ended up stranded on a sandy beach.

His last clear memory was in the captain's cabin of the ship he and Kyah had stolen with Galen and Kalmar's help after escaping from the underground Dwarven prison of Arkum Zul. Like a light snapping on in his brain, it all came rushing back. He heaved into the sand, the rush of memories swallowing his mind in vertigo. Bile and sea water splattered the wet beach when he realized what he had done, the lives he ruthlessly took fighting to be free, and how he had outright murdered Arabella Ondoloth. The dream of Ember turned his stomach cold as he remembered his worst crime.

Like every other horrific memory he'd had since arriving in Talohna almost five months ago, the events of the past two days went all wrong after only hours of finally being free and finding some peace and quiet.

Chapter Two

"Officially, slavery is illegal in Talohna. That being said, the Free Lands located in the old Dwarven Kingdom have no laws against it and no recognized king has any power there. The seaport city of Dasal is home to the last slave market in Talohna. The area known as the Wildlands is another place where slavery flourishes. Home to fierce tribal natives, their entire society is built on the blood and sweat of slavery. The Wildlands of Talohna is the last place any sane man would want to find themselves. Ending up as a slave is the best possible option I can think of for someone who stumbles into that massive forest. Landing in one of the southern tribe's communal cook pots is probably the worst."

Garren Sallus, A Traveller's Codex Volume 2

NORTHERN WILDLANDS FOREST
TWENTY-NINE DAYS EARLIER

The Archwizard, Giddeon Zirakus, and the Northman, Kasik Blodhjorr, led their small group through the Wildlands' Northern Forest quietly and at a slow pace. Prepared and guarded against attack from any and all sides, Giddeon's daughter, Saleece, along with Ember Tollen-

Symes, and the magical assassin, Yrlissa Blackmist, rode twenty feet behind them, leaving Maxwell Soryn to guard their rear another thirty feet behind that.

For two days, they travelled beyond the Wildlands' Northern Peace Border with no sign from any of the tribes that called the Wildlands home. The group's presence was a direct violation of the peace treaty that had ended the last Wildlands War. Tasked by King Bale of Cethos to find his daughter, the princess Corleya, the group had no choice but to follow her trail into the land of Tribals and spirit magic.

Yrlissa managed to keep to the trail of Princess Corleya and Lady Alia, even though no one else had been able to make out the tracks for days. Max had been at the assassin's side most of the way, determined to learn everything he could and to spend as much time with her as possible. Like Ember and Kael, Max was another transplanted refugee from Earth, brought to Talohna by the Dead Sister witches and their dimensional vortex nearly five months ago.

Max, a retired U.S. Army Ranger Sniper, fit into Talohna's violent world seamlessly, unlike Ember had. After only five months, his reputation as an archer and warrior was quickly spreading, not to mention that garnered by his almost-mystical strength. His life back on Earth was just another memory. Still very shy towards Yrlissa, Max now at least managed to speak to her without stumbling on his tongue, even if it had taken months. His clumsy attempts had not gone unnoticed. Used to working alone, Yrlissa welcomed any offer of company he made.

Max and Yrlissa were off their horses, down on one knee, looking at the faintest impression of a shod horse's print when the first flight of darts from the Taktala blowguns hissed through the air. Yrlissa was the only one not hit in the first wave, rolling the millisecond she heard the sound of expelled air from the blowguns. Max was hit but didn't seem to notice. As everyone else fell from their horses unconscious, he ripped the dart from his neck and threw it to the ground in disgust. Kasik stayed coherent long enough to earn a second dart, again to the side of his neck, before he too fell from his mount.

Yrlissa suspected her best chance of escape would be up into the towering trees and their heavy cover. It took only a second before she was fifteen feet above ground and bursting through the lush leaves of the giant tree.

Bala Takma, the Taktala tribe's tracker and hunt leader, had specifically set the ambush to accommodate for the agile Elvehn woman and was waiting for her on the very branch where she stopped to catch her breath. Yrlissa saw Takma the moment she landed, but would never move fast enough to avoid his dart. Even her resistance to toxins would give her little protection against the savage's sleep poison coating the darts, especially with her heart pounding from exertion.

She cursed at him the second the dart hit her skin. "Bo'Chava," she barked, calling him a bastard in his own language. "You've just made a... big... mistake," she stuttered, falling from the tree barely conscious.

With strength well beyond what one might think possible, the tribal scout moved, grabbing her around the waist as he dropped from the tree without making a sound. As he landed, Yrlissa let out a delirious chuckle at the ridiculous, poison-induced hallucination of Max snorting like a bull and shaking his skin, dislodging three sleep darts that fell to the ground. Bala Takma barked in a guttural tone and a dozen more darts shot towards Max. Every projectile hit flesh and even his abnormal strength waned as he slowly dropped to the dirt, unconscious.

Ember was the first to wake, her natural Fae healing ability breaking down the sleep dart's poison faster than the others. It was late evening; she noticed all three of Talohna's moons high in the dark sky. Looking around the camp fire she could see that they were all bound and gagged, sitting back to back with one another. The three women had all been bound to one of the men. If one of the men tried to run it would cause incredible pain for the woman tied to him. She could feel Giddeon at her back and smiled to herself as she noticed Yrlissa had been tied to Max. A small group of the tribal natives sat around the fire, but she suspected there would be more guarding the camp from beyond the fire's light. It was clear they were in a lot of trouble, but worrying would get her nowhere, so she leaned her head against Giddeon and went back to sleep.

Ember woke again during the early morning hours as the tribe prepared to move the camp. They were fed twice a day while they travelled from sun-up to sun-down. Food was brought to them in the morning before they left and at night before they slept. The Taktala, as Giddeon called them, had plenty of experience with prisoners. All of Ember's group walked with their hands tied behind their backs, and their feet were tied together with each other at night. The heavy, braided vines tied to their necks were strung between their legs when each was secured for the night. Sitting back to back as they were, running was impossible. They hadn't been allowed to talk because of the gags, even if the gags were to prevent spell-casting, and not only talking.

During the hours of dark, two guards watched directly over them, neither dozing off nor becoming distracted during their duty. Ember suspected more guards were out of sight. On the second night, Giddeon succeeded in freezing his bindings so they would shatter and prompt an escape, all of which he did without speaking a single word. The ArchWizard's ability to cast silent spells had been passed down for generations for just such an occasion. It didn't help. He was hit with sleep darts the moment he tried to stand. The concealed blow-dart hunters high in the trees were the second line of guards overlooking the prisoners. It was clear there would be no escape, at least not for the time being.

It took the better part of two days to arrive at the Taktala's main camp. The evening meal was being served, so the tribesmen and their new prisoners arrived to cheers, shouts, and celebration from the rest of the tribe. Ember, Giddeon, and the others were taken to a caged area on the south side of the camp. There was no one else in the cage and they were shoved in after their hands had been released.

Food was brought immediately by several young slaves who were accompanied by four Taktala blowgun warriors. Wooden bowls were filled with a spiced meat and vegetable stew. Each prisoner also received two pieces of baked flatbread.

Max smiled as he wolfed down a mouthful of the rich food. "They always feed prisoners so much?" he asked. "We haven't eaten like this since we left Corynth."

Giddeon nodded as he dunked his bread into his bowl of stew. "We're not prisoners any more. We're slaves, and hungry slaves can't work properly."

Always the pragmatist, Max shrugged. "At least we'll eat well."

It wasn't long before the tribe's chief stopped by the cage to inquire about their capture while trespassing on his land. The leader of the Wildlands most civil tribe looked at Giddeon as if memories were struggling to surface.

"I am Chief Vattis Taktala," he said, in a stilted but good grasp of the common tongue. "You I know," he said, pointing to Giddeon. "You wish war with the forest tribes, defiler?" The ArchWizard's muffled grunt was unintelligible.

Giddeon quickly swallowed. "We talk, northerner, but defile your speak and all die, yes?"

Giddeon nodded and wiped his mouth on the sleeve of his robe.

"It is good to see you again, Chief. I am happy to see you healthy and still in power," he said.

The tribal chief snorted. "You be, yes. Others leave you gutted and rotting by this day, take only women."

"You're right, but we're not here to start war, Chief Vattis. We're merely looking for two young women from the castle in Cethos. They were just days ahead of us. They didn't know where your lands began; they are just foolish young girls, Chief, that is all. Let us take them home and we will pay for breaking the treaty. We can grant you more land if the tribes need it, or maybe supplies. Anything you need," Giddeon said, speaking as fast as he could while still making sure that Vattis Taktala understood his words.

"You are too late. The women you seek belong to others now, two days my Bala track them. They come deeper into Taktala land. We stop them. Now you come. The Taktala remember you, defiler. Your magic destroyed many innocent lives. Northern magic," he spat. "Defiles the spirits. Treaty states no entry to forest for no reasons. You should not have crossed Taktala land. Forget about foolish girls. Worry about all tribes gather in two moons to decide on war. You too late," the chief stated, matter-of-fact. Pointing to each of the prisoners Chief Vattis added, "At rise of new sun, you will be sold. Any that try to escape will bring punishment for all. Speak words to defile the spirits one time and you will lose tongues." He pulled a hooked blade from his belt as if to emphasize the threat. "Do as commanded, no more." With a spin of his long, dirty, fur coat, the Taktala chief was gone.

One of the guards untied all their feet, double-checked to make sure the cage was secure, and left.

Kasik looked around carefully as he ate. "We have six guards watching us, two are almost out of our sight in the trees. All have those damned blowguns, Giddeon. Getting out of here won't be easy."

Ember had other concerns. "What the hell did he mean by we will be sold at the rise of the sun?" she asked, looking from Giddeon to Yrlissa.

"Giddeon," Yrlissa said, her voice emotionless. "Tell us all you know of these people. I haven't had a lot of experience with them in recent centuries." Ember watched the ArchWizard closely. He sighed as if the weight of the world was resting on his shoulders, and she was positive he had aged a hundred years in the last two days alone. The guilt of triggering a fourth Wildlands war was eating at him.

Giddeon nodded at Yrlissa and backed himself up against the cage's woven-branch wall. Leaning against it, he took a couple of deep breaths.

"First off," he began, "some history, for Max and Ember. We have been to war against the tribes that live in this forest three times. I was in Ellorya and DormaSai during the first so I didn't fight during that one—it was about seventy-five years ago. Oddly enough, we were trying to avoid a war between those two countries in the south. As for the other two Wildlands Wars, I fought in both. Kasik was with us for the last one which ended twenty-five years ago. Cethos has always been the dominant power of the Blood Kingdoms, we came to aid Yusat all three times the Wildland tribes invaded their country. My predecessor, the ArchWizardess, Calladia Veht, was in charge of magic for that first war."

Ember swallowed the last bite of her food and set the wooden bowl aside. "Why did they invade?" she asked. "Surely they must have known they were outmatched."

"Slaves and land," Kasik replied. "Can't grow your tribe without land, and you don't gain power within the tribe without slaves. Believe me, they're not as outmatched as you might think."

Giddeon nodded and carried on. "Kasik is right. All of Wildland tribal society is founded around slavery, which allows the warriors to train, hunt, and fight from a young age because they have no other responsibilities. And the more land a tribe has, then the better they can hunt and forage, eventually increasing their numbers. When morning comes, we'll be sold to whichever tribe member has the most to barter with," he guessed.

Ember felt the blood rush from her face and fear gnawed at her stomach. "Wait. What the hell happens to us women if we get sold to someone who wants a wife? Or worse? What then?"

"I'm sorry, Ember. Those sleep darts will put us down before we get anywhere close to freedom. Even your jump spell takes time to activate, if you can even do it again. We'd be shot full of sleep darts before you finished the spell. For now, we have to do as we're ordered. Keep your head down and don't attract attention," Giddeon insisted. Ember shook her head as Yrlissa put an arm around her for support.

"Fuck, Giddeon, we really stepped in shit this time didn't we?" Max asked, though it clearly was not a question.

"We did. I would've bet a year's salary teaching at the Eye that Vattis would negotiate for more land and weapons or maybe even female slaves. I never thought he would be set on war so quickly. The Taktala are the most civil-minded of all the tribes, it doesn't bode well," Giddeon said, rubbing his face with his hands.

"What the hell changed then?" Max asked. "He doesn't look like a very forgiving man. I bet they don't make many mistakes when it comes to their slaves either. Their security is better than any terrorist camp I've seen back home. I'll keep an eye out, but I doubt they'll slip up enough for us to get away," Max said.

Kasik offered the only explanation to Max's original inquiry. "You have to understand, Max, these tribes suffered horrendous casualties during the war. Thousands of lives were lost on both sides, but they don't have the numbers that we do. Three of Vattis' sons died during the final battle, and it made him push the other tribes for a peace with us, in the hopes of saving more lives. My guess is that he's regretting his decision now."

Giddeon nodded. "Uh huh. That'd be my guess, too. Vattis, as well as these other tribes down here, all know that either side could have won the last war. They would've actually, had the Sartaq joined the war."

"The Sartaq?" Max asked.

"The Sartaq," answered Kasik. "Outcasts from all the tribes. Giddeon? You know the story better than most, from what I've heard."

Ember noticed a visible shudder strum its way through the ArchWizard's body.

"The Sartaq," he began once more. "That's a word I had dearly hoped to never hear again. It's a tribal word, means 'death-talkers'. Calladia told me that the ones they faced during the first war almost tipped the balance in favour of the tribals. I have... I... Well, let's just say I enjoyed the company of one of their witch doctors for a time. It was a personal matter—one I'd rather not repeat. The Wildland tribes hate and fear the magic we use; they call it defiling the spirits, and they refer to us wizards as Defilers. Their priestesses and shamans down here practice a type of nature or environmental magic. We don't understand how it works, but it's pretty weak compared to ours. The tribes won't let us get close enough to study it or find out anything about it. The Sartaq, though, they somehow manage to use both—a mix, but the two magics seem to corrupt each other, making a strange type of spirit magic. That's our guess anyway. The things they were capable of gave Calladia nightmares until the day she died..." His body shook with chills at the memories, and Ember could only stare in horror.

A commotion from the centre of the camp ended their conversation, and more guards headed for the caged compound, dragging two young women by their hair. The gate flung wide and the others could only watch as the two women, still in their teens, were tossed into the caged area like sacks of garbage. Kasik managed to catch the first and the second crashed into Ember and Yrlissa and all three tumbled to the ground. Ember was quick to regain her feet and carefully turned the young girl over.

Saleece gasped, catching them all by surprise. "Father, it's Princess Corleya!"

"Shh! They don't need to know that," he whispered, as he crept over to see how bad the king's daughter was hurt. As he bent over her to check, the princess' eyes popped open and the recognition of who she was looking up at lit up her eyes with what Ember recognized as desperate hope.

"Master Giddeon, is that you? Why are you here?" she asked, as a smile of disbelief showed on her face.

"We came to get a foolish young princess. Now we're slaves along with you, and the Wildland tribes prepare for war. I hope your decision to run from the castle was worth whatever you were trying to do. You've condemned the Blood Kingdoms to another Wildlands war," he scolded.

"I'm so sorry, Giddeon. I fled to save Alia's life. Father sentenced her to death for helping me train to fight. He's not the same man he used to be. You must have noticed the change in him."

"I've noticed, but he is still the king. Please forgive all our familiarity over the next while, but we can't let these tribes know who you really are. Understand?" he whispered.

"I do, and that's fine, but what about father? Do you know what is wrong with him? You said you've seen the change as well?" she asked, clearly hopeful that he would know something.

"I have, Corleya, but I don't know why. He seems less inclined to listen to council and just demands things to be done, even sending us here without listening to any other options and knowing it would start a war."

Corleya placed her hands on Giddeon's. "I'm sorry. This is my fault. I thought that if I could save Alia, and we brought the Kai'Sar to him, he would see that a woman could be Queen by leading her country, even in battle. The Bale monarchy has had many queens who have fought," she explained.

Giddeon's face paled with shock at the sheer stupidity of what the princess said. Ember shook her head. She knew that even as experienced as he was, having to face his son and the only living DeathWizard was a terrifying prospect. It was not something for a young princess to be playing games with.

"That is the most foolish thing I have ever heard come from your mouth, Corleya," he said. "There is a reason there are six of us hunting this wizard," he said, swiftly putting his hand up to silence Ember and Max before they said something. "And I don't believe for a second that all of us will survive the encounter."

"I... I... just assumed their power was an exaggerated myth. I didn't know. Gods, I'm so sorry," she cried, as she pulled her knees up and hid her face in her hands.

"It's all right. We cannot turn back what has been done, so we must do better in the future, right?" he said, offering soft words of scholarly advice. Without looking up, she leaned against Giddeon and nodded.

"I think we should all get some rest," Max said. With a touch of sarcasm, he added, "I'm told we have a busy morning coming up. And, Giddeon, might be better if everyone called her Cora, maybe? Something other than her princess name."

The ArchWizard nodded in agreement and everyone chose a spot on the bare ground to get some rest. Princess Corleya... Cora... never left Giddeon's side.

Morning came quickly when sleeping on the damp ground with no blankets to protect one from the night's chill. The Taktala guards had the prisoners up just after dawn. Corleya and Alia, were taken from the cage and sent to their owners. The rest were fed a mashed grain gruel that neither Ember nor Saleece could get down. The men, all of whom at one time had eaten battlefield rations or worse, devoured the food like a pack of hungry wolves.

After they finished the meal, they were dragged to the centre of the camp where a small platform five feet high and four times as long had been erected overnight for the sole purpose of selling the new slaves. Like all captured slaves or those not native to the Wildlands, Corleya, Alia, and the others would continue to be locked up at night and kept under guard until they were no longer considered a flight risk. Chief Vattis was in charge of the proceedings and none of the back and forth was in the common tongue. When

Saleece was chosen to be sold first, blades were placed to the throats of the other five and the chief spoke so they could understand.

"You fight and you die." He said nothing else before continuing.

The bartering for Saleece carried on for fifteen minutes as the leader of the party who brought them in, Bala Takma, and one of the female warriors were in a heated dispute over who wanted her the most. Though he could have taken her as his right in being track leader, Takma never took any slave they captured. Instead he turned them over so the bartering was fair for all. Every single person of the tribe respected him for decisions like that.

Finally, Takma was forced to back down as the price became too high. The other warrior cheered and danced in triumph as her mohawk-cut hair flopped back and forth and others with her hooted and hollered at her success.

With a blade still at Saleece's neck, the tribe's high priestess stepped up onto the platform and checked her over, chanting in their primitive tongue as she examined her. The priestess stopped behind the new slave and slipped a collar around her neck, locking it with a small flare of magic.

Saleece and Giddeon both recognized the collar. The Pogahna. A woven collar enchanted with tribal magic and designed to deaden a mystic's power. They worked well, but could be overcome with time and effort. The subtlest smile crept onto Giddeon's lips; one of the trials a master wizard must pass to become an ArchWizard was to circumvent a Poghana. It took him a week during his trials, but Giddeon was the only wizard to do it in almost a hundred years. Saleece had been practicing for over a year, even though she was decades away from her own master trials, but still hadn't been able to get by the collar's effects.

It was one more technique the Taktala used to reduce the chances of an escaped slave. It was the first mistake that Max said to watch for. Giddeon's smirk soon vanished though, as the winning warrior walked up the platform and dragged Saleece away by her attached collar, disappearing through the crowd. Ember feared what might happen to her. Kasik lost control, head butting the guard in front of him and leaping from the raised platform. Max was only a second behind the Northman, but both were hit repeatedly by sleep darts the moment they touched the ground. Max held out for a half minute longer, tackling one of the blowgun warriors. His extra weight and size made all the difference as he jumped to his feet and stomped the warrior repeatedly before finally succumbing to the sleep poison.

A guard punched Giddeon in the kidney and shoved him to the front of the platform. After Max and Kasik were dragged back to the platform unconscious, Giddeon was sold to the old man in charge of making the tribe's poisons. Ember stared incredulously as the ArchWizard shook his head at the irony. The sale went off without any problems. After his examination, the priestess attached a Poghana to his neck and the old poisoner led him away.

Max and Kasik were both sold to the grizzled warriors in charge of training the tribe's young fighters. After close scrutiny, the priestess shook her head at the notion of a Pogahna and a heavy leather slave collar laden with big rings was attached instead. Neither man stirred from their dart-induced slumber.

With only Ember and Yrlissa left, they were brought up to the front of the platform together. The hooting and cheering increased tenfold as every warrior in the tribe seemed to be there and ready to barter for the two women.

Ember shook with fear, but stood tall and stared defiantly at the crowd. Yrlissa smiled her way, nodding at her refusal to shed a single tear or break under the stress of the situation.

"If one of those men buys us," Ember whispered. "I'm jumping us out of here. I don't care if it kills me. I can't go to one of them. I won't. I've never been with anyone besides Kael. I won't allow it. I'd rather die than be used as a plaything every day. I swear to god, Lissa," she rambled.

"Calm down, *mai-nahlla*. Let us see what happens. There is more interest in us than men. You must be strong; you know your love is out there. You must live for him. Be strong for him, but right now, be stronger for yourself. The Fae have other ways to defend themselves."

The bartering began as the two talked back and forth, one by one the men dropped off as the price went higher and higher. The Chief put the two youngest looking women together to be sold as a pair because his daughter wanted both for herself. More men dropped out of the auction as the Chief's daughter bid aggressively, pushing the price higher, until no one else could pay what she offered. Vattis' tactic worked perfectly. The final warrior cursed and stormed off into the crowd as the cheering reached a fever pitch.

Ember looked at Yrlissa one more time. "What just happened?"

"I don't know, *nahlla*. It appears a young woman has bought us both," she guessed.

"Oh, thank you, God," Ember prayed as she fell to her knees in gratitude.

"Never let looks deceive you, *nahlla*. We watched Saleece get dragged away by a woman. It may not be so in this situation, but being sold to a woman in one of the cities that still have slavery could mean being bought by a madame, or worse, by some crazy Braiga."

"Braiga?"

"An insane wizard. That pleasant feeling when you get when you use magic, you felt it in the pass before you jumped us to Corynth?"

Ember nodded. "Yes, right before it kicked my ass and stopped my heart."

"Well, some wizards, very few, thank the gods, become addicted to the euphoria of magic and use it all the time, for everything. But when you do, that feeling weakens and so they use more magic, chasing the way it used to feel. It doesn't take long before they go insane chasing something that their actions are pushing farther away. They're dangerous and disturbed and they can't be reasoned with, and if you ever come across one, *mai-nahlla,* kill it and don't hesitate. Most can play with magic far more powerful than Giddeon's, or mine. Experience and time is what makes a wizard grow in power, but the insane are not bound by the same rules we are. Pain and exhaustion mean nothing to them, while such things limit our magic." Ember nodded as the priestess approached, hissing at them to be silent.

The Taktala high priestess placed a Pogahna on Yrlissa, but stopped when she came to Ember. Confused, she shook her head as if clearing a dizzy mind and then continued putting a Pogahna collar around her neck, pushing her red hair to the side.

Yrlissa smirked, whispering out of the corner of her mouth. "More than one way to defend yourself, *nahlla.*"

The Chief's daughter walked up the platform, slid a hook through the collars around Ember and Yrlissa's necks and led her new slaves away. As quickly as they had been captured, they were now slaves with even less chance of escape.

The first day passed at a snail's pace for all the new slaves. Giddeon spent the day under guard in the forest picking certain plants and fungus, but was not allowed to watch the poisoner mix any of his creations. Max and Kasik spent a very long day as practice dummies for the young warriors. They were only allowed to defend themselves with their bare hands while the younger students attacked with stick swords and poles. They were returned to the cage that night, bruised and bloodied. Max was also dealing with the intense pain caused by the whipping he received around midday for striking a relentless student. The barrage of attacks made him strike out on pure reflex, and the young recipient suffered a broken jaw. It was something he could never do again, a second offence would result in the removal of his hands.

Ember and Yrlissa had the easiest day physically, but still found themselves on the wrong end of slaps and curses when the chief's daughter thought they should know the Taktala customs and rituals. They also returned to the cage bruised and sore, but on a much lesser scale than Max and Kasik. Saleece spent the day in her new owner's hut, experiencing utter terror and pure hell, discovering quickly that her new master felt slaves were good for little besides venting her sadistic anger and desires on. Saleece returned for the evening in a worse condition than the others combined and on the verge of catatonic shock. There was no threat to her life because the punishment for killing any slave, regardless of the owner, was the removal of the killer's hands, but her mind and soul were in mortal danger after only one day.

Giddeon returned to the cage for the night, and his heart broke at what his group had suffered because of his decision to enter the forest. His eyes immediately sought out Saleece, filling with moisture at what he saw. Kasik held her tight as she shook with tremors and mumbled incoherently.

Guards escorted Ember to the prison cage only moments later. The chief's daughter kept her longer in an attempt to talk about her red hair but the conversation went nowhere fast because the chief's daughter couldn't understand that her red hair was natural and not dyed from the forest plants. Natural red hair was non-existent in the Wildlands, though an exotic assortment of red dyes were abundant and several of the tribe's women used them to colour their hair.

Ember noticed Saleece the moment she stepped inside the cage, realizing the young wizardess had lived the day with her own greatest fear. She sat in the dirt beside Saleece and Kasik. The Northman looked as lost as Ember felt.

"Help her," he pleaded. "You cannot leave her like this, and I... I cannot help her." Desperation radiated off the normally strong warrior. It was the first time she had seen him like that. Her heart ached for both of them. As if finally understanding her birth right and her people's intense hatred for injustice, an incredible strength of spirit filled Ember's very being. She took Saleece's hands in hers, placing both on the terrified girl's chest.

"Let me try, okay? Just keep holding her," Ember offered, closing her eyes. In only seconds, her right hand moved up Saleece's body, cradling her head.

Ember gasped at the overwhelming sensation of power flowing through her body. The euphoria of new magic not pushed beyond its limits—Yrlissa's words from earlier in the day finally made sense. It was her first time really experiencing magic without the devastating side effects of drawing on too much. The wall inside her mind had been holding back the memories of all she was, and a small piece broke off and tumbled away. There was so much more there—she could feel it—but what she needed right now was available to her, so she used it.

"I can help her, I think," she said. "But it will have to wait until later when the closer guards move further out for the night," she whispered. "Just hold her for now and she'll make it," Ember added quietly.

As they did every night, the inner circle of four guards moved their perimeter about twenty feet out from the cage, blending into the tropical brush and dark of night.

"It's to make us think we're on a lighter guard," Yrlissa offered. "To see if we'll try escaping. They are there; I can see and hear them." She smiled at Max's questioning frown. "The Elvehn are not Human, Max. We only look it. Kind of." He grinned back, shaking his head.

Ember waited another hour before Yrlissa nodded her way, letting her know the guards had moved even deeper into the utter darkness. Quietly making her way over to Kasik and Saleece, she could hear the young woman sobbing. She shivered at the thought of what she had been through.

"Everyone gather around," she whispered. "We have to be sure no one can see what I do. I don't know what will happen, but it seems like magic has to be bright and colourful in order to work. Come on, we have to hurry."

Clearly suspicious, Giddeon touched her arm. "What exactly are you going to do?"

"Help her, if I can," Ember replied, laying her hands on Saleece's head.

"How? You can't have circumvented the poghana already," Giddeon said, dumbfounded.

"It won't be a concern," Ember assured him. She could see it only added to his doubt. "I can't explain it, Giddeon. I can't feel the collar. It never affected my magic even when that priestess first put it on. It's a necklace, nothing more."

"Fair enough," he said.

Taking one last look around, Ember glanced at Yrlissa and received another nod as everyone held their blankets up in the hopes of blocking the light from Ember's magic. "Let's hope for her sake this works," she said. Closing her eyes, Ember opened her mind, focusing on the wall that was holding back what she hoped was more Fae knowledge. The wall crumbled a little more, giving her the words she needed.

"Amaeh Shalaness," she whispered. A warm, pink and blue glow came from both her hands and slipped into her patient's damaged mind. Like wildfire feeding on dry grass, it spread, flickering its way down her beaten and ravaged body. A second spell followed the words of the first as Ember shifted her right hand to the tortured woman's chest above her heart.

"Amaeh Naolass," Ember said with a sigh. The magic shifted, changing to blue and red, swirling as it infused Saleece with magic that would calm her mind and strengthen her soul. With her body healed and her mind quieted, Ember's senses returned to her own control. Saleece opened her eyes and stared at her.

"Thank you," she cried, as tears continued to roll down her cheeks. "You helped. It was foolish, if you were caught..."

"The risk was mine to take, Saleece. Our differences aside, I couldn't watch you suffer like that if I could help,"

Ember said, smiling. "Now listen, closely, please. I can offer you one more thing to help, but it will come at a price," she offered.

"What exactly are you talking about?" Giddeon demanded. Ember ignored his outburst and spoke directly to Saleece.

"I can place a protection spell around your mind that will keep you from having to endure your time with that she-monster. You'll have no memory of what happens to you."

Giddeon persisted with his questions. "You said there would be a price, Ember. What is it?"

"I'm not sure Giddeon, haven't exactly done this before... She won't remember the pain or the disgusting things she does to her, but… I imagine she'll be aware of the gap in her memory. For some people that large of a gap every day, until we are free, may be too heavy a price to pay. For most people even. Do you understand?" she said, looking at Saleece.

Saleece nodded as she implored. "Will you be able to repeat what you have done for me tonight? The idea of losing large pieces of my memory does not appeal to me, but with help like you gave me tonight, I can manage."

"Yes, whenever you need it, as long as we are careful not to get caught. And I've taken your body's pain, but I left the bruises and bites so no one will become curious as to how you healed. If anyone else needs the same just ask. It may give us a chance to escape later on if they think we are too beat up to run from them," she explained.

"Thank you, Ember," Kasik replied. As everyone settled down for the night it was obvious that something was still grating on Giddeon's mind. It was not long before it came to the surface.

"Perhaps you would like to explain now how you achieved such a thing while wearing a silencing collar?" Giddeon asked as he stared at Ember. Though Ember shrugged, it was Yrlissa who answered.

"She is Fae, Giddeon. We have no idea what they were... are capable of. We both know that she has no *cruus* to the earth like us, so who knows?"

Ember held up her hand to stop Giddeon's argument. "You don't need to argue with her," she said. "I don't understand any more than you do, but it feels like there is a wall inside my mind blocking off knowledge, or memories maybe, about me, my abilities, and my people. A small piece of that wall fell away when I saw what had been done to Saleece, and then the words for the spells were there, if that makes any sense to you?"

Giddeon, obviously at a loss for any explanations, rubbed his chin in thought.

Saleece answered instead, her voice weak and unsteady. "Sounds like the legendary Fae sense of injustice to me, Father. Do you not agree?"

Giddeon shrugged. "It's possible. Perhaps a discussion for another day, though. If no one has seen anything of value to help us escape then I suggest sleep would be the best option for now." He received only murmurs of consent as they all wrapped themselves in the single blanket they had each been given to sleep with and called the day done.

As Ember watched him closely, she could sense Giddeon struggle as he continued working on the Poghana around his neck. He frowned, shaking his head as if troubled by not being able to get past its magic.

She smiled at him and hoped he would figure it out, and soon.

Chapter Three

"To love someone who does not love you in return is the hardest feeling to understand. Kalmar told me to be patient, to let Kael heal. I will, even though everything about him makes my heart melt with happiness. To be with him now that we are free would the ultimate reward for so many years of suffering."

N'Ikyah, Dead Healer
Journal entry found on the shores of Siren's Bay, 5025 PC

SEA OF STORMS
THIRTY-SIX HOURS EARLIER

After being held captive and tortured for months, Kael, and Kyah—a young slave and exceptional healer—along with two wizards from Cethos, escaped the ancient Dwarven prison of Arkum Zul, where it was located deep below the surface of Tazammor Mountain. After being chased for two days through the catacombs below a long-forgotten Dwarven city by Orotaq guards and the subterranean creatures known as the Mahala, they finally managed to fight their way out of the mountain and across a small valley to Flatwater Bay where they stole a two-masted galleon and sailed to freedom. Though Kyah had been injured and suffered serious wounds in the fighting, Galen had healed her as best he could. Even so, after losing so much blood, an infection and a dangerously high fever quickly set in.

While the two wizards sailed the ship out into the infamous Sea of Storms, Kael laid Kyah on the captain's bed, stripped off her filthy, damp clothes, and did his best to bring down her fiery body temperature. A quick search of the cabin's storage chest produced a large blanket. Soaking it in cold water from the pitcher on the table, he covered her body with the blanket and used the corner to wipe the sweat from her forehead and cheeks. Still shivering himself from the cold mountain water and his saturated clothing, he removed his own damp rags and hung them on a chair to dry. Frozen and exhausted, he eased himself into the bed beside her and wrapped himself in dry blankets, hoping to catch up on some much needed rest. In seconds he was asleep.

Kael jerked awake unaware of how long he'd been asleep. Kyah's hand grazed his cheek and her fingers trailed through his thin beard. He smiled, feeling her forehead for signs of the raging fever. She was still warm, but her body had cooled considerably while they slept. As he opened his mouth to ask her how she felt, he found her lips pressed to his. He pulled back, knowing he couldn't possibly kiss her without thinking of Ember but one look in her strange silver eyes and his thoughts fled from his mind, vanished as if they'd never been. She slowly removed the still damp sheet from her bare body and let it fall to the floor as she slid under the dry covers with him. His thoughts returned for a moment and he tried to object, to stop what was happening between them, but for some reason, his mouth filled with cotton and his body went to work against him. The thrill of feelings and emotions that were not pain and suffering brought along a quickly building desire. It swallowed all of his urge to resist.

As Kyah snuggled closer and leaned in to kiss his lips, their noses bumped and a nervous laugh escaped her mouth. Being more careful this time, she tried again and he tilted his head as their lips brushed together, soft and gentle like the touch of a dove's wing. Moving even closer, she lifted his arm and slid his hand around the curve of her waist onto the small of her back as she kissed him harder. Her tongue darted out, teasing his own. Pressed together, her flesh ignited in him an intense need to feel anything that was not the insufferable agony of the past five months.

Kyah shifted her body and slid on top of him and her warm breath tickled his ear. "No more games, Kael. Be with me. Let me love you. We need this. I... need this, please." For reasons he could not fathom, he had no desire to resist. As his mind tried to object one last time, the spicy scent of her body smothered all conscious thought. His heart raced, the heat of arousal lit an urgent need and he no longer cared about whether it was right or wrong. Kyah moaned as he sat up with her nestled in his lap. Trailing his fingers up her smooth legs, he caressed her thighs softly. He smiled nervously and released the faintest amount of black electricity from his thumbs. Tracing along the inside of her thighs, the dark energy gently snapped and popped under his fingers as it reached the soft mound between her legs. A sharp gasp caught in her throat and her breath stuttered as she inhaled. Kael could see the pleasure dancing in her eyes and along her mischievous smile as he rolled the black energy under his thumbs, gently pushing it against every nerve-ending he could sense. Little bumps of bliss rose on the skin of her thighs and outwards to the rest of her body. Her response excited him further and he buried his face in her neck.

Kael continued to explore the tender rise and the moist creases of her flesh as more writhing sparks of magic crawled up and across the flat of her stomach to her chest. A smile crept across his lips when it was clear she was no longer able to stand the mystical teasing. Returning his crooked smile, her fingers traced down his chest and across the muscled wall of his stomach until she found him more than ready. She pushed herself up on her knees and slid onto him, slowly, as her lips pushed against his once more.

Kael felt a shudder roll through her body and he gasped as he slid into her warmth. The slow, gentle, movement forced Kael's hands out onto her hips as he laid back. She followed him down, nestled firmly in his lap. As their lips parted, he gazed into her eyes, and her mischievous smile returned, fuelling his desire further. As he reactivated his teasing currents of magic under all his fingers this time, his hands moved from her hips up the sides of her ribcage to under her breasts until his thumbs found the soft flesh of her nipples. Teasing, he tickled and tugged gently until the pink flesh swelled with need. With his hands and body sparking her passion to greater heights, she moaned, increasing the pace of her hips. Her enthusiasm spurred his own movements and his own need built quickly.

Kyah opened her eyes and pushed her lips harder to his, crushing his lips into his teeth, her tongue danced along his as her own ecstasy raced to finish. Abandoning her breasts and grabbing her waist, he pulled her closer, increasing the pace to match their mutual need. Kyah buried her face in his neck, crying out in ecstasy as they climaxed together. She collapsed onto his chest, panting, as waves of intense pleasure rolled through him.

Unable to speak, Kael sighed and held her. Neither moved for several minutes as they lay together, enjoying the glow of emotions and feelings that were something other than the torturous pain of so many months. Kyah raised her head and looked into Kael's eyes, a tear ran down her cheek. Gently, he wiped the tear away as his thumb rubbed her cheek. She cuddled into him and drifted back to sleep. Kael sighed, his mind a whirl of emotions. As if his own senses were returning, guilt slowly replaced the glow of intense feelings still humming through him. He stared up at the wood ceiling above the bed thinking of Ember as Kyah slept to the easy rhythm of the boat sailing across the ocean.

A loud crack and intense bright light jolted Kael and Kyah from sleep hours later. Seconds passed before Galen stormed into their cabin.

"You two need to get out of here. A storm's coming. It's just minutes away. Hurry, Kael, it's going to be bad." Another blast of lightening, followed immediately by the pounding concussion of thunder emphasized his words as Galen slammed the door shut. Kael and Kyah hurried to get dressed. Kael heard Kyah complain, but it did not affect the goofy smile plastered to her face.

"I knew it would not last," she said, shaking her head. "The Goddess of luck has given us all she will."

Revitalized by the rush of feelings and emotions from the previous night, but still plagued by guilt and confusion as to why it happened, Kael slid into his leather cloak, his new weapons snug in their sheaths sown to the back.

Slinging his backpack over his shoulder he shook his head and pushed the puzzling emotions aside as he chuckled, for her sake. "Lady Lykke doesn't care about us any more than the other gods do." The young healer merely smiled wider and wiggled her way into the white bodice, pulling the attached soft leather hood onto her head.

"These are beautiful, Kael," she added, stepping into the ankle-length, white, doeskin skirt.

"I found both pieces last night. They look brand new." He rushed to the cabin door, but stopped dead as he caught sight of her fully dressed. The corset clung to her body, pushing her small breasts together, yet it left her midriff bare. The velvet smooth skirt hugged her hips as if it were painted on, but flowed outwards down to her ankles. With her hair still tousled from their lovemaking, her casual outward beauty struck him for the first time in the months he had known her. Rushing too now, she slid her ratty leather slippers on and snatched her travel pack as well as her cloak before running to the door.

"Come on, handsome," she said, kissing him softly and caressing his cheek. "I wish we had more time for... everything." She smiled. "We have to go."

They joined the others on the quarterdeck where Journeyman Wizard, Galen Vihr, had taken over the helm from the older man, Master Wizard Kalmar Ibess.

"What do you need us to do, Galen?" Kael yelled, having to shout to be heard above the pounding fury of the incoming storm. With one arm around Kyah and the other hooked through the rear ballistae's winch bolt, he held on for both their lives as rain pelted his skin and the wind threatened to toss them overboard.

The Sea of Storms hit hard when in the mood to claim more victims, and Kael felt her fury, as if the ocean were alive and hungry for victims. He stared out into the storm to the south-east and as the waves dropped, a massive city with high towers faded in and out of his vision.

"What the hell? Kyah?" He nodded in the direction of the city. She looked, but her puzzled expression told him she did not see it. As the waves crested again, the city flickered and vanished.

"Pray, Kael," Galen shouted, catching his attention. His brow furrowed in concentration, the soon-to-be Master Wizard spun the ship's wheel hard to the right, turning the ship into the coming waves. "The sails are already down. Just hang on and pray for the best. Topside is the only place to be if we go down, not in the cabins," he barked back. With a crooked smile powered by the rush and excitement, Galen winked at the two new arrivals to the ship's top deck.

Twenty minutes passed as they rode out rolling waves, fifteen feet high and getting larger by the minute. The keel cracked and moaned from the stress as the ship shot down from a wave well over twenty feet in height. Kael stared in awe at the raw power of the ocean as waves even larger loomed ahead. Shivering at the oncoming danger and knowing there was nowhere to run, he held Kyah tighter to his side. As if it were a premonition, the boat slammed into the wave's far side and started up the thirty-foot rolling incline of the next monstrous wall of water. Like nothing more than a toy in the hands of a rampaging child, their ship crested the massive wave and jetted down its far side as rope, barrels, and all manner of other supplies fell to the ship's bow. Losing his footing, Kael hung on to the ballistae for dear life, clutching Kyah's waist in a death-grip as she screamed and grasped at his cloak.

The ship slammed into the ocean, plunging beneath the surface for several seconds. The keel twisted sideways and shattered from the stress as the next wave crashed over the top of the boat, knocking all four passengers to the deck. Full of water, the sturdy ship listed heavily to the port side. A second, larger wave followed seconds later, smashing into the ship and obliterating it. Kyah was ripped from his arms as the four friends were tossed into the water.

Kael surfaced first, with Kyah only feet away, floating face down in the cold ocean. With a strong kick, he was at her side. Rolling her over, he checked to make sure she was breathing. A large piece of the ship's hull banged his shoulder as it rode along the bottom swell with them. He grabbed it to help keep them afloat. With one arm around Kyah, Kael climbed onto the debris. Forcing it below the waterline, he managed to float the unconscious young woman up onto the top. Once she was up, he held her with both arms, but couldn't climb up to join her without sinking it.

As they crested the next wave, Kael looked out for miles across the ocean. His heart sunk; there were no other ships and no land in sight, even the mysterious city was nowhere to be seen. Passing the giant wave's apex, the debris-raft rushed down the wave's far side and ploughed into the ocean. Kael shook the water from his eyes and saw Galen and Kalmar using smaller pieces of the ship to stay afloat. They passed close enough for him to hear them shout, but he could not make out the words, and the storm-fed waves were too strong to try and swim closer. The movement of the ocean currents and the power of the storm soon had them too far away for Kael to keep them in sight. Things could not get much worse.

Full dark settled over the ocean early because of the storm, and Kael tried several times to climb onto the wreckage. Shivering and teeth chattering, his strength waned in the cold ocean water, but every time he tried to board the makeshift raft, it threatened to dump Kyah into the water with him. Little time passed before it was so dark he could not see her in front of him on the raft. He held on to her Orotaq cloak with one hand and clutched the wooden planks with his other, making sure she stayed on top for as long as he could. In the sheer black of the late night storm, it seemed every time they crested a wave, the ride down was taking longer and the impact at the bottom more violent.

As the make-shift raft rode the lazy side of a massive wave up into the air one more time, it reached the top just as lightning ripped across the dark sky, lighting up the night and the ocean for miles. Kael's eyes shot wide with terror as he stared down at the forty foot drop to the bottom. He grasped at Kyah with both hands, anchored his feet to the raft's bottom, and held on for dear life as the wave pushed him over the crest, rocketing the raft down the thundering swell. Again the storm's electricity high above the ocean lit up the darkness, returning Kael's sight just as the raft slammed back down onto the water's flat surface. The whiplash effect drove the wooden planks of the raft into his face. Stunned, his hands slipped from Kyah and his head scraped against the side of the wooden wreckage a second time. Kyah and the raft were wrenched from his grasp.

"No!" he screamed, his vision wavering.

Dazed, blood flowed into his eyes, mixing with ocean water and adding to the sting. Kael turned onto his back and relaxed his muscles in order to stay afloat. The salt water carried his weight like a buoy in a harbour until his body scraped something rough as it passed underneath him in the water. Panicking at the thought of some kind of unseen water monster or perhaps a school of sharks, he jerked upright. The sudden movement washed his mind in dizziness and disorientation. Without noticing, he sank below the surface. Confused, he choked on salt water as a pair of arms gently circled his chest, holding him while his body shot back to the surface. Kael gazed in concussed awe as the violent ocean settled to an unnatural calm for as far as he could see.

Trying to understand what was happening and desperate to stay conscious, Kael drifted in and out of awareness as his head eased back against something cool, but soft. A warm breath tickled his neck. Music drifted over the calm waves, far away at first, but it glided closer as if riding on the ocean's gentle air currents. He suddenly realized it was not actually music. His addled mind relaxed and he listened to the beautiful melody of several women singing as they swam in the ocean around him. Smiling, Kael drifted in the cold water of the Sea of Storms without a single care coming to mind. The angelic voices were unlike anything he had ever heard back on Earth. Stunning harmony was the closest description that came to mind, but it was not adequate. The warm breath returned, on his cheek this time, and as the black spots clouding his vision grew and his consciousness faded, he heard one of the melodies stop and a voice whispered in his ear.

"Sleep, dark wizard. My sisters and I will carry you safely home."

The words carried a softness, a peace, that calmed him further. Her hushed tone was sweet and added to the mellow harmony. Kael blacked out with the muddled understanding that such incredible beauty would never harm him and would forever keep him safe.

With the gentle movements of their long, finned tails, the women floated Kael into Siren's Bay, as the melody of their magical voices drifted out over the ocean.

WILDLANDS EASTERN SHORE PRESENT DAY

The pain of recalling the events of the past two days turned Kael's stomach and he suspected he had suffered a concussion.

"With my luck, probably smashed my head in," he muttered. Kael tried to focus his blurry vision. He felt the side of his skull where the makeshift raft smashed his head and found a five inch gash that felt bone deep. Unable to do anything about it, he made sure his travel pack was whole and wrapped a cloth rag around his head. His heavy cloak and bizarre looking blades were still on his back, and though the inside of his pack was soaked, the contents were still intact, including Jasala Vyshaan's book and letters he took from her abandoned tower.

He stood, trembling, as a bad case of vertigo assaulted his senses. Looking around, trying to figure out where he was made the dizziness worse. He stumbled and dropped to his knees in an attempt to stop his world from spinning out of control. After several minutes, Kael glanced up, making out a beach that ended after a hundred feet. At that point a large forest began, stretching in both directions as far as he could see.

Kael struggled up from the sandy beach and walked a little over half way to the forest when he chuckled about the huge mound of sand in his way.

"Where the hell did all this sand come from?" he said, cackling. His mind, so clouded from the impact with the raft, never felt himself fall face first into the sand. Exasperated, he turned over to look at the morning sky, when it dawned on him that he was trying to walk while lying down.

"Oh, my head. Can't think straight." Kael's thoughts kept drifting away, disrupting his sense of balance. For only a second, he thought about trying to heal himself, but it flashed through his mind and was gone. As his mind began to shut itself down, all he could think about was that he kept forgetting to heal himself. The throbbing and ringing inside his head continued to get worse until he was writhing in agony on the beach.

It lasted several minutes before he blacked out again.

Opening his eyes, several hours later according to the sun's position in the sky, Kael struggled to understand how he could still be alive. As Kyah's face leaned into his vision, he understood.

"You saved me," he said, almost accusing her.

"Yes, handsome. I figured it was only fair seeing as how it must have been you who put me onto that wreckage. Correct, am I not?" she asked, smiling.

"Yeah." His voice was a croak from swallowing too much salt water, and he coughed to clear his throat. "But I couldn't get up there with you without dumping us both into the ocean."

She bent over and gave him a quick kiss on the lips. "Thank you. Your selfless choice saved us both, it seems. Now, can you walk? It has been hours since I watched you fall into the sand." Still with some difficulty and disorientation, he stood.

Looking around, he asked, "Do you have any idea where Galen and Kalmar are? Or where we are? Did they make it?"

"I have not seen them. I came to shore a few miles north of you, but there was no sign of them. I am sorry, Kael. I know not if they live. It is a miracle from the gods that we made it alive ourselves. You, even more so. With that head injury, you should have drowned."

"I thought I had," Kael said, confused by the flashes of memory from the night before.

"How did you get here?"

"I'm not sure. I smashed my head on the raft and was having trouble staying awake, when..." He hesitated, afraid to tell her what he remembered. "If it's a memory and not some brain-addled hallucination."

"When what, Kael?" she prodded. "What happened?"

"You're gonna think I'm nuts..." When he stopped the second time, she moved closer and touched his chin, forcing him to look her in the eyes.

"Tell me. What do you remember?" she asked, and gave him another gentle kiss.

"All right, but I warned you." He smiled, uneasily. "I heard music, singing, but no words. It was strange. I was in and out of consciousness the whole time. I remember sinking below the surface, I think, and then something brought me back up. The ocean calmed at some point and I floated here. Someone was holding me above the water. I don't know, Kyah. My head's messed up. It still hurts." As he tried to explain, it became clear that he actually did sound like a mad man.

"The music, female?"

"I think so, yes, there were several different inflections, different voices, maybe, is a better way to explain it."

"Women singing without words in the Sea of Storms," she said, frowning and looking over shoulder out into the water. "We must have washed ashore on the Siren's Tails or in Siren's Bay. We must be in the Wildlands, Kael. For some reason, the sirens saved you, instead of killing you. I am not sure what is more terrifying, the fact those creatures saved your life or the fact that we are now stranded in the Wildlands."

"It can't be much worse than being stranded in the Forsaken Lands, can it?" Her look told him he should know better. "Don't look at me like that. I've only been here for five months, remember? The Wildlands might as well be on one of the moons for all I know about it!" he snapped, as he pointed skyward.

"I am sorry," Kyah said, smiling. "I apologize. I forget that sometimes. You deal with everything like someone who was raised here. But you need to learn these things and fast. When we stop to rest at night from now on, I will teach you the little that I know. For now, we must be very careful. The tribes of these lands care not for intruders. They are violent and their society is built on the blood of slaves. Some tribes are cannibalistic. We must not be found here, babe," she explained, in detail.

Kael flinched at her use of the last word. Ember had called him 'babe' from the time they were both twelve years old. With his dream of her and Max still fresh in his mind, he needed to figure out what to do. He was also confused about why he had allowed himself to be intimate with Kyah on the ship the night before. Before he came to a solution, she called his name and the thoughts left his mind for the time being.

"Come, Kael, this way," she said, heading into the forest. With no other choice, Kael looked to the north, the way Kyah said she had come.

"Good luck, Galen, Kalmar. May your gods see you guys home safely." He prayed for them, figuring it could not possibly hurt.

He turned and followed after Kyah, entering the forest and heading west. She recommended travelling into the forest for only a mile before turning north and trying to get out.

"Some of the tribes will use the ocean as a source of food. Travelling the beach could be dangerous, but we do not want to get too deep into the forest. They are like ghosts in here, Kael. We will never see them."

"We can't sense them?" he asked.

She glanced over and shook her head. "Not always. Arabella said once that the tribes in here use spirit magic and that it interferes with normal magic. You may find your senses unreliable, or you may not. You are... unique."

They were less than two miles in and heading north as mid-afternoon approached, when Kael grabbed her arm and pulled her to the side, down into the heavy brush.

"What is it?" she whispered, just above his sense of hearing.

"I can sense a group of people less than a mile ahead. There can't be more than twenty of them. We should check it out."

"Would such a thing be wise? Wait... Did you say a mile ahead? Gods, Kael. How far away can you sense someone?" she asked.

"I don't know, just over a mile maybe. I never tried to see how far, at least not since we escaped. I'd like to go see what's happening ahead. It could be Sythrnax's people. If not, then maybe it's someone we can get supplies from. We only have what we're carrying and it ain't much. I'm going. You can stay here if you like," he snapped, sharper than he intended. A slow resentment towards her was growing. Mixed with the confusing emotions from the strange dream, he could feel an irritation fuelling his ever-present anger. It was an uncomfortable feeling.

"Fair enough. I will follow you wherever you go, just be careful. This forest is full of dangers," she responded, her voice calmer.

Kael could sense the group ahead had two sentries posted away from the majority of the group. He made sure to pass between them using the cover of the forest. Concentrating, he successfully silenced both his and Kyah's footsteps as they used the heavy brush to sneak by the two guards undetected. A small rise covered in thick grass and heavy vegetation gave them an excellent vantage point of the small camp on the far side. The site was situated in a large bowl, located on the right-hand side of a small creek running through the gorge. It was obvious that a larger camp was normally set up in the valley floor. The current camp consisted of a dozen tents spaced evenly in the shape of a wide letter U. A small cook fire was in front of the tents at the deepest part of the curve, the farthest point from where they were hidden. A six foot rack at the opening of the camp was the dominate feature on the closest end to Kael and Kyah. Twenty tribesmen patrolled the interior camp.

"There's no reason for us to stay," Kael whispered, nudging Kyah's elbow. "Come on, let's get out of here." He turned to go, but she grasped his arm as he slid back.

"Kael, wait. Look," she said quietly, pointing down into the small valley. Kael looked back to the camp as two more men, clearly not tribesmen, came out of the biggest tent, dragging a long-haired man with a beard who'd been beaten to a semi-conscious state. A third man followed them. Kael recognized Grodin immediately and couldn't believe his luck. The two large, muscled men who worked for Sythrnax both had magic nullifying amulets hung around their necks, bouncing around their bare chests as they dragged the prisoner to the rack. Kael smiled, knowing the amulets wouldn't work against his magic as long as he used his connection to death in order to power it.

Kael smiled even as his blood boiled at the sight of Grodin, Sythrnax's stunted right-hand man. Memories from Arkum Zul returned, flooding his mind. He struggled to control the raging fury as Grodin ordered the two big men to string the prisoner up on the rack at the front of the encampment. After kicking him to his knees and securing him to the frame, one of the men grabbed the prisoner by the throat and wrenched his head back so that Grodin could talk to him face-to-face. Kael stared in disbelief, his anger forgotten the moment he saw their prisoner.

"Holy shit. I don't believe it," he gasped, cursing just loud enough for Kyah to hear.

"What is it, Kael?" Kyah whispered.

"That's Giddeon Zirakus," he said, as he exhaled on the ragged-edge of panic. "The prisoner they just tied to that rack. It's him," he panted, breathing hard, still stunned by the turn of events.

"The ArchWizard from Cethos? The one hunting you?"

Kael nodded and moved closer for a better look. Now positive beyond a shadow of a doubt that his dream had to be real, Kael's mind whirled with confusion about what to do.

"Ember's alive!" he whispered.

"Kael?" Kyah asked, as if not hearing him right.

"Never mind," he said, focusing on the people and terrain around the camp.

The only man who would know where Ember might have been taken was less than forty feet from where he was hiding. He twitched with excitement at the thought of her being alive, but his stomach did a cold flip at the impossibility of getting her free.

Creeping into heavy cover closer to the edge of the hill overlooking the camp, Kael pushed the grass aside for a closer look at Giddeon. Kyah crawled up beside him as what he saw sunk in. Grabbing at his throat, Kael cringed at more memories, as he lightly touched the lumps under the scars at the front of his neck. The puncture holes from the Gyhurra collar had closed, healed by Kyah's magic, but regenerating months-old scar tissue was beyond her abilities, even with magical strength boosted by the re-emergence of the Fae somewhere in Talohna.

At some time, and quite recently judging by Giddeon's physical condition and the weeping wounds in his throat, his captors had managed to snap a Gyhurra collar around his neck. Kael shook his head at the cascade of memories that tore through his mind. Heaving with the effort of suppressing the caustic images, he grasped at his head and dug his fingers into his tangled and matted hair. Something dragged his memory back to Arkum Zul as he struggled not to scream.

"Kael? Kael, are you all right? Your skin is white like mountain snow," Kyah murmured, touching the side of his face. Sweat soaked his face and dripped from his nose. His face flushed red. "Calm yourself, love. Here, let me help," she whispered.

She leaned in closer, chanting. *"Huggan Mein."* Clearly afraid to use her own healing spell, she recited the one Galen taught her instead. Resting her forehead against his, the words of her spell washed over him, easing his tormented mind. Kael felt the memories recede.

"I hate those god damned Gyhurra collars, it felt like I was back in Arkum Zul with one still around my own neck," he cursed, shaking, as he rubbed his nose. Scratching the prickling sensation at the sides of his neck, he tried to shake off the horrific memories. It took a few minutes, but with Kyah's spell and his own willpower, Kael reasserted control over his mind and pushed the flashbacks deep into his memories, where they belonged. "What the hell was that?" he mumbled.

"Not sure. Do DeathWizard's have eidetic memory? Maybe your magic did that? It matters not. Come on, Kael, leave that fool to his fate. If you free him, he will kill you the moment after. Let us go." Kael knew he should turn and run, leaving the ArchWizard to die. Kyah was right; Giddeon would continue hunting him, but the ArchWizard was in no condition to do it right now.

"I can't leave him to die; it'd be like killing him myself."

Kyah shook her head. "No, Kael. Leave him, he would not do the same for you."

He looked at her, slightly puzzled. "But I'm not him..."

"Fair enough. I understand," she said, frowning. "What do we do, love?"

Not wanting any more guilt eating away at his soul, Kael slid back amongst the thick branches and drooping green leaves surrounding Grodin's camp and tried to come up with a plan to free the man who had been trying to kill him since the day he had arrived. Part of Kael couldn't help but wonder how Talohna's most powerful wizard ended up captured, collared, and tied to a torture rack in the middle of the Wildlands.

Chapter Four

"This world is smaller than you think. That is a saying from my world, from Earth. As I sit here writing this so many years after the events following our arrival in Talohna, I realize how true those words really are. One can be within reach of the one they love and still be countless miles away – a problem easily solved by Fae magic. You cannot begin to imagine how badly I wish I had known that back then. Perhaps things would have been so very different..."

Ember Symes, Journal entry,
logged and preserved by the TimeKeepers, 5027 PC

TAKTALA/KORDANU NEUTRAL CAMP
TWENTY-FIVE DAYS EARLIER

The next five days were almost identical to the first. Ember healed who she could during the nights when they were locked back in their cage. The princess and her lady-in-waiting were also brought to the cage every night. That soon came to a stop once the threat of the new slaves escaping lessened. The princess and her lady-in-waiting were eventually sent to stay with the village's other slaves in order to help prepare for the move and long trek south. Their duties were to cook and serve the communal meals and clean up as well as other domestic tasks needed for the move. The sixth day was a hectic pace of tearing down huts and preparing the camp to disappear without a trace. Giddeon, Ember, and the others were granted no such freedoms. Watched closely from sun-up to sun-down, they were under close guard even when performing their duties for their owners.

With war on the horizon, the Taktala normally moved their camp every seven-to-ten days, making it harder for anyone to find them, but the need to move south had become more important after Giddeon and Ember's group were captured. The new slaves were not released to help break down the camp and were only allowed out when the camp began the two-day march south-east to the new site. Their cage was the very last thing taken down and the first to be built on arrival at a new camp.

The chances for their escape began to look worse and worse. The Taktala never wavered in their vigilance. They had been at the new camp site for only a day when Saleece asked Ember to perform the spell that would blank her mind whenever her owner began to hurt her. The abuse and degradation had become too much for her to bear and Ember performed the spell with tears in her eyes from frustration at not being able to do more. Saleece returned the following night beaten and abused several times over. Her lack of response had outraged the female warrior who had bought her, adding to her suffering, but Saleece remembered none of it. Ember took away her pain and Yrlissa put her to sleep with the same Elvehn technique she had used on Ember many months ago. The ancient skill was unaffected by the Pogahna collar. When Giddeon asked about it, she explained that it was more of a hypnotic effect than magic. He seemed satisfied by her explanation.

Their situation seemed to become dire as the days went on. Ember wondered where Kael was every minute of every day and if he even knew she was alive. Positive her last DreamWalk spell had been successful, she remembered bringing Kael to their camp and begging for his help, constantly trying to make him believe that she was real. Something distracted him at the end before she was finished and eventually it broke him free of her control. She sensed afterwards that he had been drowning and using the spell's failing power, she sparked his mind, hopefully waking him in time. Deep down she was afraid that it was merely another form of torture he was enduring. Water-boarding had been a popular method of interrogation and torture on Earth for decades before being outlawed. Such thoughts made her soul ache for what he might be going through.

The Taktala stayed at the same location for ten days before scouts brought word that the Kordanu Tribe further south had begun their march north. The next day was spent tearing down and moving once more. It was a welcome respite for Ember and Giddeon's group, knowing they would have the day to rest and recuperate. Tear-down meant no duties.

Full dark had just begun to settle over the forest after their first day of travel south when a rider approached the camp on horseback, using the tribes' native tongue to hail for entry. Smoke from the fires ghosted over the camp and prevented the group of prisoners from seeing whether the warrior was alone. Giddeon knew very little of the language used by most of the tribes, but Ember seemed almost obsessed with learning what she could and was picking up the different inflections fast. Like the Ancients' language back in Stillwater, she was picking it up at an amazing rate. It was common knowledge that the Fae had been able to speak every language of their time, adding to their repertoire of skills that had earned them the reputation as universal peacekeepers.

Ember hushed everyone as she tried to overhear what the commotion was all about. The rider was welcomed to the centre fire where Chief Vattis, accompanied by several warriors, soon joined him. Ember listened, her eyes shut tight with concentration. They were just within earshot.

"The rider seems to be from another tribe, the Koduuku, I think," she whispered, as she glanced at Giddeon.

"The Kordanu?" he corrected.

"Yes. I think you're right. He says the Taktala are invited to a war council and trade gathering with his tribe. Oh no, that can't be good. Saleece's owner is excited. Oh God, no. She wants to trade her. Four days... I think their camp is four days away and... and... Vattis accepted," she said, turning to Giddeon, fear dancing in her eyes. "What does this mean?"

Giddeon shook his head. "It means that in four days any tribesman who is not happy with their slaves can sell them to the Kordanu tribe at the gathering. There is a damn good chance we'll be separated once that happens. I'm sorry. I am so very sorry for what I have brought on you. I can't get around this collar. It's been altered by some kind of magic that I can't figure out."

"If we get separated, we'll need a plan," Kasik said.

"If possible, escape and head for Corynth. Don't try to free anyone, get home and warn the Elder and Wizards' Councils," Giddeon offered. The others nodded their agreement and then tried to get some rest. Ember laid down and stared at the ArchWizard. Like a stubborn old mule, he continued trying to crack the secret magic fused into their collars.

The next day, the camp was torn down and ready to leave by dawn. It seemed the entire tribe was excited to be moving and to gather with another of the Wildland tribes.

"Why all the excitement, Giddeon?" Max asked.

"This is not a regular occurrence. These tribes often fight amongst themselves. The Kordanu tribe and Vattis' are two of the few tribes who have many intermingled families. They're close because of it, even during the war they fought as one tribe. I would imagine this will be the first time in years some of them have seen family members married into the other tribe."

Max snorted at the ArchWizard's answer. "Half-civil savages, who'd a thought," he sneered, sarcasm riding heavy on every word.

It took four days to arrive at the Kordanu temporary camp. It was a long and boring walk for everyone. The Taktala set up a very basic and minimalist camp a quarter mile away from the Kordanu camp, for safety reasons. Though the two tribes were close, the possibility that problems arising from the slave sale could escalate into a full-blown tribal war was still there. It was a rare occurrence but it did happen. Both camps were nestled back in the heavy foliage of the forest even though they had to be torn down and the tribes on the move the day after the slave sales and war council had ended.

The slaves served the midday meal while the two chiefs and several elders from both tribes discussed the intrusion into their lands. Ember felt her stomach flip as she overheard the council's decision. It came after only thirty minutes of talk.

"They're sending small groups to notify all the tribes so that a gathering to vote on war can be set. The Kordanu chief and the few men with him are returning to their own camp. The slave sale is set for morning," she whispered. "Nothing was mentioned about who would be offered for trade."

Ember and the others were brought food and left under heavy guard. Never in her life had she ever felt more desperate. They had no idea who would be sold the next day or if any of them would. Chances were pretty good that they would be separated, making escape with the princess and then finding Kael almost impossible. If Kael knew she were in trouble, he would be there to help in an instant. It had been so long since she had seen him; it felt like a lifetime ago. Her heart and soul ached with the loss every single day, only getting worse with time. Still, she refused to surrender to despair, instead deciding to try and contact him through the dream spell one more time.

Closing her eyes, she tried to remember how she had done it last time and soon realized as she concentrated that it was not nearly as difficult. Within minutes she knew that he was alive, but something was definitely wrong. She could not get through to him.

Someone or something was blocking her. Knowing Kael had to be in serious trouble, her frustration took over and she instinctively pulled more magic into her dream. Her mind searched for the person or the magic blocking Kael from her, but every time she drifted closer to an answer she was pushed away. Powered by concern for him, Ember dragged more magic into her sleeping state, using it to clear the fog.

The forest around her materialized and for a moment she struggled with what was real and what was not. She could see a U-shaped camp in a small clearing by a slow-moving creek—it was clearly a tribal camp and Giddeon was tied to a rack just inside the camp's entrance. Her mind struggled to make sense of what she was seeing. In reality, Giddeon lay at her side resting in the sun and heat of the humid forest.

Panicking, she glanced around the forest, not recognizing where she was, until she saw Kael below her. Calming slightly, she realized he was awake, not dreaming, but was suffering incredible pain as he held his head in his hands. A small, dark haired woman was with him, her forehead resting gently against his. Ember could hear the woman's spell as she tried desperately to ease Kael's suffering.

Using her DreamWalk magic, Ember floated closer to them. Halfway there, the dream spell wavered and a crack of power tore the forest apart, leaving a pulsating dark rift where Kael and the woman had been. A giant demon stepped from the tear and grabbed her with its massive, clawed fist. Panicking, Ember released all the dream spell's magic into the demon. It roared with rage and tossed her aside, its claws ripping into her arm.

Ember woke with a scream, back in the cage at the Taktala camp, holding her arm. Everyone jumped and Yrlissa quickly slid to her side.

"Ember? What happened?" she asked, as Ember stared at her arm. It still throbbed. Yrlissa slowly lifted her friend's hand. It peeled away with a sticky squelch and blood poured down her arm.

"Jesus, Yrlissa," Ember snapped. "You said DreamWalks pose no physical danger in the real world."

"They don't, or shouldn't. What happened? Tell me." Yrlissa said, binding Ember's wounds. "They're not too deep. You're lucky," she quickly added. Giddeon settled in beside them on one side and Max rolled over, getting to his knees on the other.

"What is it?" Giddeon asked, as he rubbed his eyes in an attempt to banish the fugue of partial sleep induced by the warm sun. Ember explained in detail, what her DreamWalk showed her and how the demon attacked, but more importantly that she saw Giddeon tied to a rack in an unfamiliar location somewhere in the forest.

Yrlissa sighed, shaking her head. "The Dead Sisters must be using a demon and his magic to keep you out of Kael's mind. It must have distorted what you saw."

"Was it real?" Ember asked. "Giddeon's here with us."

"It might be," Yrlissa said frowning and shaking her head. "I'm not sure. The demon magic mixing with yours might have shifted your perception to the future, or perhaps the past..."

"Definitely not the past," Giddeon offered.

"Perhaps the future then," Yrlissa continued. "I'm sorry, Ember. I never thought the Dead Sisters would ever be capable of such impressive magic..."

"Impressive?" Ember barked. "That damn thing is keeping me from Kael and he's here in the forest, or he will be at some point. He could be closer than ever. No damn demon is going to stop me..."

"But we don't know when Kael will be here, or where," Max pointed out.

Ember shook her head, clearing the cobwebs from the dream state. "I'll find him, just give me some time."

Yrlissa shook her head and glanced over at Giddeon. "Max is right, and with time, Ember can get past that demon and we can find Kael. But regardless, Giddeon, your council or the Inari are going to have to do something with these witches. They're using power they shouldn't have access to, let alone be able to actually use. They're a serious threat, not taking into account *if* they get their hands-on Kael or another DeathWizard you missed or if another Black Sun happens."

"For once we agree," Giddeon said. "First chance I get, I'll tell the Wizards' Council. The Inari will have to hunt down the Dead Sisters, if enough of them can be called back. Most are hunting Braiga." It earned him a nod from Yrlissa.

The evening stretched on to just before midnight. As Talohna's three moons hit their apex, a shout pierced the air and echoed through the makeshift Taktala village.

"Someone has asked for permission to enter camp," Ember said, kneeling.

"Who?" Max wondered.

"Shh! Let me listen," Ember whispered.

The group watched as Chief Vattis verbally granted entrance to his camp. To Ember's and everyone else's surprise, Chief Karlag Kordanu strode into the camp just as he did earlier in the day, but this time he wasn't with his own men.

Ember listened closely, relaying the information to the others. Three men had arrived in the Kordanu camp two hours before. It was clear by their easy banter that Chief Karlag had been dealing with Sythrnax's men for many years. Grodin was likely responsible for buying slaves the Kordanu tribe no longer wanted or had uses for.

When Sythrnax's men were introduced to the Chief of the Taktala tribe, Vattis offered to show them his new acquisition of slaves.

"They're coming our way, Giddeon," Max pointed out.

Trapped in the cage with nowhere to hide, Grodin recognized Giddeon, Saleece, and Kasik right away. "Well, Chief," he sneered. "It looks like you have the prized slaves of tomorrow's auction." He bowed to both tribal chiefs. "We would be honoured to attend. I promise you, we'll pay for these. We'll pay whatever you want." Grodin laughed and then turned to walk away, howling with glee at the prospect of the next day's sale.

Ember recognized the little man as the one who was with the strange eyed creature who had taken Kael months earlier.

The only thing that kept her secret was the fact she said so first. "That's the little bastard who helped take Kael," she said in a normal voice. Both Kasik and Max looked at her when she spoke. Seconds after she said it, she exploded off the ground, cursing the whole way, but Kasik and Max were already moving.

"You god-damned son of a—" she screeched, just as Kasik wrapped his arms around her waist and pulled her back to the ground. She bit, kicked, and fought. She did not care what happened to her. Never had she wanted to hurt someone so badly. Max threw himself on top of her, clamping his hand over her mouth and whispering in her ear, his voice full of anger.

"Stop, Ember! You can't let them know you're Kael's wife. For fuck's sake, they will take you and use you against him."

"Think, girl, now. Is that you want?" Kasik breathed in her other ear as he held her close.

"You know full well that Kael would do whatever they want in order to keep you safe. Now, stop... Please." Max said the last word slowly and calmly, clearly hoping to get through to her. Closing her eyes, she nodded and he slowly removed his hand.

"All right," she snapped. "All right." They let her go as she rolled over, Yrlissa held her, offering her support, but Ember stared after Grodin. The little man and the tribe's chiefs had been too far away to notice.

Max looked at Giddeon. Both sighed with relief.

The tribesman returned just after dawn the next morning to collect them all for the sale. Ember and Yrlissa were escorted to Chief Vattis' daughter while the others were taken to a platform that had been built just for the occasion. Princess Corleya and Lady Alia were already there; the tribe must have decided to sell them as well. It was not a good sign. The bartering lasted four hours, with Princess Corleya and her lady being traded to a single warrior from the Kordanu tribe for the price of a single horse. From what Giddeon and Max had seen from the rest of the trades and the bartering, there was at least some hope for the two young women. A good horse normally seemed to purchase at least eight slaves their age. It weighed heavily on Giddeon that he could do nothing to change their situation. The night before, he had struggled for hours, but was still several days from being able to work around the Poghana collar that silenced his magic, if he could ever get past it.

Giddeon, Saleece, Kasik, and Max had all been held back until the end of the sale. They were brought up on the platform and forced to stand at the front, facing the crowd that consisted of people from both villages. The bartering itself was only a token gesture for interested parties from either tribe, as no one from the two tribes could afford to outbid Grodin. The little man had already made sure of his winning bids with the gifts he had offered both chiefs the night before. The crowd let out a roar of disapproval when the last tribesman backed out of the running, but no tempers were lost and no trouble came of it.

Grodin and his two men climbed the stairs of the auction platform, while the priestess removed the Pogahna collars from Giddeon and Saleece.

Grodin approached and gave them a dead serious warning. "The four tribesmen behind you have blowguns loaded with poison darts, not the sleep darts you must have felt when you were captured. If you or your daughter open your mouths to cast a single spell, they have orders to kill you all, do you understand?" he asked. Not willing to take any chances, Giddeon merely nodded.

"Very good, ArchWizard. You learn fast. You'll be coming with me right now. Master Sythrnax will have many questions for you all," he assured them.

Max was not afraid to speak, clearly figuring he was not a spell-casting risk.

Taking a step forward, he asked, "I recognize you, little man. Where's Kael, and what have you done with him? Answer me now!" he demanded. Grodin raised his hands to stop the guards who had moved forward to prevent Max from harming the man almost three feet shorter than him.

"You must be the fearsome warrior who came through the dimensional bridge with Kael. I've heard some things about you, big man. Your prowess in battle is getting around. As for your question, the last time I had the pleasure of watching your friend cough blood from his lungs was almost a month past. I can promise you, mighty warrior, that he wishes you were at his side, every minute of his very long suffering day. I'm sure of that." Max tried to get to Grodin, but with his hands and feet tied together, the guards quickly dropped him on his face.

Grodin bent over and whispered into his ear. "I can tell you, Max, with no doubt in my mind what so ever, that your friend's *mind* will have broken long ago. Even if they had not died off over ten thousand years ago, the Fae would be of little help to his scrambled brains by now." He laughed hard. Standing, he kicked Max in the face.

The distraction was exactly what Giddeon had been waiting for, knowing that the little man's overconfidence would cause him to make a mistake. Giddeon only had one offensive spell he could cast without speaking, an ancient gift passed down by other ArchWizards. The spell would drain his physical strength, but should give them a chance at escape. He pushed his hands to the side as frost began to form around them. Curling like white serpents, the frost spell grew and spread, seconds from release.

The others watched helpless as the spell sputtered and died. Giddeon fell to his knees as if his legs had vanished into thin air. Wincing as raw agony arced through his body, Giddeon's senses became overwhelmed by suffering. For what felt like hours, he shook before regaining part of his senses and the pain lessened. In less than an instant, he realized that his magic was not just silenced, or untouchable, but completely gone. Real fear passed through him like wind through the forest trees as he touched the device embedded in his throat.

Grodin howled in a fit of laughter as Giddeon realized he had been baited into using his power for the sole purpose of the demonstration he just received. He heard his daughter cry out and turned in time to see her fall, an identical collar wrapped around her neck. Four long spikes attached to the collar were buried deep in the flesh of her neck and he guessed that his was the same. Grodin stopped laughing long enough to give a brief explanation.

"Damn! I love those fucking collars, Giddeon. Like neutering a young steer. What do you think of it? Ah, don't worry, you can save your breath. I was told the first few hours are horrible for any being that can touch the power of the earth. I will tell you though, when I snapped one of those collars around Kael's neck, your son convulsed like a brained pig during slaughter, even though he refused to use any magic against us at the time. Instead he chose to stand toe-to-toe with Sythrnax, fighting with blades. Your son has more courage than you could muster in your whole pathetic life."

"What in Perdition's hells is this thing?" Giddeon struggled to ask.

Grodin laughed again. "It's called a Gyhhura collar, ArchWizard. Ancient magic. A type you never even knew existed, and while you wear it, you are as mortal and weak as the rest of us born without the gift from Inara."

"Impossible..." Giddeon coughed in agony.

"Tell that to the collar that has cut you off from your magic, fool," Grodin snorted, as spit sprayed in Giddeon's face.

"All right, boys," he said to his men. "Pack them up. The good Chief Vattis Taktala has offered twenty-two of his men to help escort our new prisoners out of this forest. You're lucky, Giddeon. Our ships were destroyed in the storm two nights ago. Now we'll return on horseback. It will save you all weeks of torture at the hands of the Dead Sisters, but you'll have to wait those weeks before you can see your son. I'll settle our payment to the chiefs. We leave in an hour. The sooner we have some answers for Sythrnax, the better."

He smiled, and walked away, leaving his men and the tribe's warriors to prepare the prisoners for departure.

The Taktala tribe left the area with their remaining warriors the moment the slave auction came to an end. Two of their elders were chosen as envoys and went with the Kordanu as part of the future war council. The small group of their fighters would escort Grodin and his prisoners to the forest edge and then return. Bala Takma was in charge of the warriors sent on the escort mission, his second in command would remain in charge of protecting the tribe. With the Kordanu moving south, there would be no immediate threat to the rest of the tribe. The Taktala's minimal camp set-up paid off. They disappeared into the forest within the hour.

The chief's daughter refused to put Ember and Yrlissa up for sale, but with the others being taken by the people who had captured Kael, every ounce of Ember's being wished she was with them. She was almost positive, though, that Kael had escaped, having felt his closeness in the forest during her dream spell the previous afternoon.

The tribe headed north and their horses covered a good distance in a short amount of time. The new mounts from the slave auction allowed for more of the heavy supplies to be carried and made for faster travel. The further they were separated from the rest of their companions, the bleaker Ember and Yrlissa's situation became. The Kordanu tribe left after the remaining debts owed to them had been paid. Princess Corleya and Lady Alia, with no choice in the matter, went with. Their future as much in question as the others'.

Grodin and the members of the Taktala tribe who joined him and his men were the last to leave the sight of the Kordanu camp. They travelled north heading for Dasal, where Grodin told them more of their group might be, and failing that, they could hire a ship to take them back to the hidden harbour at Arkum Zul. They were roughly ten days from Dasal by horseback. A ship from the small port city would have them at the hidden harbour a day and a half later. If they were forced to travel the rest of the way on foot it would add at least another ten days, likely more with the prisoners in tow.

Grodin called for the group to set up camp for the night in a small valley north of a fast-moving creek. The sun had not yet dropped below the tree line—farther south the days were longer. The Taktala escorts set up the tents in a U-shape within the curve of the steepest side of the valley wall for protection against enemies and the weather. The prisoners' tent was positioned at the forward part of the camp, close to where Grodin instructed his men to build a rack that would hold the prisoners for questioning. With two guards posted on an outer perimeter, the short, but powerful man told his men to secure Max to the rack first.

"Anything you would like to ask or volunteer before I begin my questions, big man?" Grodin asked.

"You're wasting your time, grub. I've been under the hot blades of our world's most radical, religious extremists. I won't tell you anything, but you can tell me where Kael is, little worm, so when we escape from you I know where to go," he demanded, and flashed a smile.

Sythrnax's right hand man chuckled as he shook his head. "You are persistent, I will give you that. If Kael is still alive, he's being tortured by the worst of the Dead Sisters, Max. I promise you'll see him when we arrive, or what's left of him anyway," Grodin shivered. "You cannot imagine what those psychotic bitches were doing to him the last time I saw him. Damn near shit myself just watching. I know you're as tough as they get, Max. We're not as dumb as the people you travel with."

"What the hell are you talking about?" Max demanded, as he tugged against his restraints.

Leaning in close, Grodin whispered into his ear. "Master Sythrnax has a theory about you, Max, perhaps we should test that theory. What do you say?"

"You can test whatever theory you so desire, ya little shit. You'll find that I bleed like anyone else," he said.

"Then let us begin."

Grodin spent the next hour interrogating Max about Kael. He asked about his childhood, his past, his family, and even the women he had loved or slept with. It was clear that he was trying to find something to use against his closest friend. If Kael was still being tortured, it meant he refused to give in to whatever it was they wanted. The very least Max could do for Kael was keep his secrets. There was only one thing on this plane that could be used against Kael—Ember.

When Max refused to answer a question, he was lashed with a braided leather bullwhip covered in sap from a plant called devilweed. The whip was then rolled in rock salt. It took an hour and twenty-two lashes before Max finally lost consciousness and Grodin's men dragged him to the tent. The welts raised by the whip quickly caused ugly fluid-filled blisters from the sap as it burned its way into Max's flesh.

After double-checking that Max was secured inside the tent with leather straps tied to stakes driven deep into the earth, Grodin had his men bring Giddeon out next.

The ArchWizard was already in bad shape from the effects of the Gyhhura collar, but Grodin smiled with glee as they dragged him from the tent and tied him to the rack.

Chapter Five

"How many people do you know have walked away from the scene of an accident without helping? Or turned a blind eye to a person in need? The world that I come from is a selfish world. More people on Earth will ignore a cry for help or pretend that they didn't see something bad happen than there are those who will answer that cry or see the bad that happened. I have seen it first hand, and worse I've been in the middle of it, needing someone's help only to watch them walk away, more concerned about their daily goings-on than helping their fellow man. I can't do that. I've never been able to. What hope does humanity have if callousness and selfish behaviour continue? It doesn't bode well for us as a species.

It matters little to me now, I guess, because I'm no longer there. I'm in Talohna, a realm in a dimension far different than ours, and yet, I still see the same behaviour here. I guess the problem isn't with the world or with the dimension. It's with us, the human race. Hopefully, someday, mankind will learn that our only salvation lies in the co-operative, open hands of each other, and not in the selfish, closed fist of our own needs."

Kael Symes' journal entry
Found on the northern shore of Salzara,
just west of Forja Vehlo, Date unknown

GRODIN'S CAMP, NORTHERN WILDLANDS

Kael knew from his own past experience that Giddeon would not last long before the pain would drop the blackness over his mind in order to protect his body. He needed the ArchWizard conscious so he would be in good enough condition to tell Kael where Ember and Max were. Kael's thoughts rolled around in his head while he tried to decide on the fastest and safest way to help Giddeon.

"Stay here, Kyah, and don't move. I'll deal with the sentries and be back," he finally said, turning to leave.

"Be careful," Kyah said. He glanced back and nodded.

The first sentry was just up the hill from where they were hiding, and in minutes Kael was only five feet behind him. The guard was vigilant, never letting his sight linger in any one direction long enough for Kael to close the last five feet. Giddeon's first scream of intense agony gave him the chance he needed as the tribal warrior turned away from him and looked down into the valley to watch.

With his feet silenced, not so much as a whisper escaped to warn the guard of Kael's approach as he quickly crept up behind the tribesman. Kael drew his right Vai'Karth, the scythe-like blade immediately dulled its surface so it did not reflect the sun's rays. He smiled—the weapons never ceased to amaze him. It was like they had a mind of their own at times. A quick step and the blade would crumple the guard like a rag doll leaving him unconscious, but a sudden urge to kill the man nearly overwhelmed him. Shaking his head, he sheathed the blade.

Approaching the man quietly, Kael grabbed the guard in a choke hold and pulled him backwards. The man fought, hard. Squeezing the artery in the warrior's neck harder, he realized the man was older and much stronger as they rolled into some heavy bushes. Pure instinct took over, pushing aside his fear, and Kael slapped his free hand to the man's face. A puff of black magic exploded from his hand, shooting up the tribesman's nose and into his mouth as he quickly succumbed to unconsciousness. Bending over to check and make sure he hadn't killed the man, Kael sighed a breath of relief feeling a strong pulse throb under his finger.

After checking to make sure that the other guard had not moved, Kael left the warrior hidden inside the bushes and rounded the top of the hill, coming at the second savage from his left side.

Lazier than the first, this one leaned against a large tree, blocking the view of Kael's approach from the guard's own left hand side. Creeping up from the blind side and around the tree, Kael stood and wrapped his left arm around the man's throat and pulled him backwards across his left knee. With his left hand locked inside his right elbow, the choke-hold was tight. The tribal warrior fought desperately to break free, igniting Kael's insane anger. He had to force himself to resist the urge to snap the man's neck. Instead, he opened his right hand and slid it down over the warrior's face. A burst of black smoke surrounded the man's face, just like the first. He was unconscious immediately.

"Tough bastard," he whispered. "My bad, Max. All those hours wrestling at the precinct's gym did come in handy. Sorry I ever doubted you."

Looking around a second time to be sure he had not been spotted, he dragged the unconscious body into deep cover, doing his best to ignore the flare of anger that was always so close to pushing past the surface. Kael stood from the brush and realized that his teeth were still clenched. The fury refused to subside. He breathed deeply. Feeling the tattoo-like vines of his death-flower curl through the skin of his hips and lower back let him know why his anger was so close to the surface. His shadowed feet must have caused the vines to begin growing under his skin, and as always, his pulsating hatred and anger seemed to fuel their progress. When the day came when there was no place left for the thorn-covered vines to go, he could not help but wonder what might happen.

It was a problem for another day.

Kael was back beside Kyah less than fifteen minutes after he left her, and as he glanced down at Giddeon, he could see it was just in time. The ArchWizard was bleeding from several whip marks on his chest and back that had welled up with massive blisters. Bloody saliva hung from his chin in long strings. He would not last much longer.

"You did not kill those guards. That gives us little time," Kyah pointed out.

"You were watching?"

She nodded.

Shaking his head, he added, "Why? Worried I couldn't handle it?"

"No," she said. "Worried you would leave them alive."

"I'm not going to kill them if I don't have to, Kyah. Hopefully none of them will have to die."

"I hope you are not going to walk down there and just shake their hands," she said, pointing to the camp. "There are still twenty men there. We are going to have to fight. I know what you did to Arabella and her Sisters bothers you, Kael, but if you can't do this, we should walk away," she warned him.

"Twenty-three men, to be exact, but don't worry. I'll give them the option to leave, and if they don't, then we'll fight. Except for Grodin. He's not going anywhere," Kael said, his eyes wide with animosity again.

"All right, Kael," she agreed. Pulling her shirt up, she winked at him and unwound the bladed kinrai chain from around her belly. The metal of the gods flashed silver, twinkling with purple and orange from the veins set within. "I know not of the others, but the tribesmen will likely fight as opposed to leaving. Be aware of that," she added.

"Then they'll die. Giddeon has information I need, and I'm not leaving without it," he said. Not used to hearing such cold callousness from him, the words caused a visible shiver to roll through her entire body.

Kael crept towards the creek so they could enter at the front of the camp. He saw the look Kyah gave him as he turned, but he no longer cared. If these warriors stood between him and Giddeon, then they stood in the way of finding Ember. Now that he was finally so close to getting her back, no one was going to stand in his way.

When they got to the bottom of the draw by the rushing brook unnoticed, both Kael and Kyah headed for the camp. They were within fifteen feet of the rack Giddeon was tied to before anyone knew they were there. The perimeter guards, unconscious in the heavy brush, were unable to notify them of the stranger's approach. The four tribesmen who did see them yelled a warning as they jumped onto the path from the high grass at the sides. Kyah ducked behind Kael as the four fired darts from their blowguns. Two darts stuck in his neck like hyperactive mosquitoes. Kael pulled them out, thinking the worst when he noticed the poison on the end dissolved on his skin as he touched the tip with his finger. Five more of the little darts struck to his neck and upper chest in less than a second.

"Immune?" Kyah asked, uneasily from behind him.

"It would seem so." He pulled the last dart from his neck. "Still stings like a..."

"Thank the gods," Kyah muttered, but Kael heard none of it. Anger and hatred fired in his mind a split second before black and purple sparks of lightning jumped from his left hand. He never even bothered to say the words of Gabriel's old spell. So wrapped up in hatred and storming fury, he never felt the black vines tear farther across his lower back and into the top of his hips. He smiled as the dark electricity pounded through the tribesmen with no resistance. The bodies dropped to the ground, smoking from the wounds created by the volatile magic.

Kyah's second mutter did not register either. "Holy, Mother Mylla. Kael, what the Nine Hells of Perdition are you doing?" No answer followed the rhetorical question.

Not a single person anywhere inside the camp dared to breathe, let alone move. The tribesmen seemed to be frozen in place, too stunned or scared to move a single muscle. Kael watched everyone carefully for a few seconds, prepared to unleash another onslaught. Instead, the tribesmen all dropped to their knees with their hands above their heads and began murmuring and whispering in voices trembling with pure terror.

"Oh no, you don't you, little bastard," Kael yelled, as he saw Grodin duck behind a tent. "Grodin! Don't go trying to sneak away now. You're the one we travelled so far to see." The little man turned and walked back out slowly, surrounded by two men. Both drew their swords.

"If you have any control over your men, Grodin, you might tell them to drop their weapons," Kael commented, as he drew both reaper-blades from the sheaths on his back. The sight of the strange blades sent the tribals' chattering into overdrive.

Grodin's voice quaked with fear as he looked at his two bodyguards. "I'd do as he says you two, the sooner the better. If he escaped from Sythrnax, he will be too much for all of us," he said, surprising Kael with the honest attempt to convince them.

"He's gonna kill us anyway, Grodin, why should we not—"

With nothing more than a thought, Kael covered the ten feet between them, flipping his blades upside down so they curved upwards. He plunged a blade through each of the little man's guards.

"Too late, stupid," Kael hissed, as he saw Grodin wince and turn away. The black vines tore into his thighs as he pulled the blades back with enough force to send the two men crashing to the ground.

"Your perimeter guards are unconscious, Grodin, and your savages don't look like they want to fight for you."

"Ah... Yes, they seem to be a little afraid of you, Kael. Not really surprised, are you?"

Now that things had quieted down a bit, Kael could hear the tribesmen clearer. The fact that the blood was no longer hammering inside his ears helped. The tribals seemed to be repeating the same two words over and over.

"Katak Sarak."

Looking down at Grodin with the blood-soaked blades of his Vai'Karth only inches from the little man's face, he asked, "What are they saying? Those two words... What do they mean? And don't lie to me," he threatened, lifting Grodin's chin with the gore-smeared blade of his right Vai'Karth.

"I think the first word means 'god', but the second means 'death'. They seem to think you are a death god. Not really that far off, are they?" He laughed, even as fear filled his eyes.

"Tell them to leave and return to their own tribe. The two perimeter scouts are up over that ridge. They should wake soon."

"You left them alive?" Grodin said, clearly shocked. When Kael offered nothing more than a shrug, Sythrnax's right hand man turned and spoke to the tribesmen in a language Kael did not understand. But when nothing happened, Grodin turned back to speak to Kael.

"They're not going to leave. Maybe when you leave, but not before. They probably think moving will be their death. They won't attack you. I'm not even sure if they will breathe," he said, trying to be funny.

Though Kael did not feel comfortable with that many possible enemies close by, he left them be, stepping back so he could keep an eye on them all.

"Kyah, if they try to move against us, let me know," he ordered.

"I will. You know that," she answered.

Grodin withered as Kael's attention turned back to him.

"Come here, Grodin, now," he commanded, sliding his left Vai'Karth back into its sheathe.

"Just stay calm," Grodin said, as he stepped closer, stumbling as he hurried.

Giddeon hung on the rack to Kael's left, but it looked like he was unconscious. Kael decided to deal with Grodin first. He leaned down on one knee so he could look the little man in the face when he asked the questions he needed answered.

"Tell me, Grodin. How did the good ArchWizard come to be with you?"

"You know what will happen to me if I tell you anything. You may be a DeathWizard, but you're a child. Your power is nowhere near what it should be, and Sythrnax is a lot stronger than you. You honestly can't expect me to betray him, do you?"

"You can save your poor me speech, Grodin. You were with Sythrnax when he put me in that machine, you saw it take both my crua. The connection to both sides of my power were gone, right?" he asked. Grodin nodded. "Then if he is so powerful, how do you explain the Gyhhura collar that is no longer around my neck, and the fact that I can do this." Kael pulled the cloak back so Grodin could see the scars left by the collar and then held up his left hand. Black lightning had already started to crawl across Kael's palm.

"I can't. I don't have magic, but when Sythrnax is done with what he needs to do, he'll grant me magic, something you can't ever do."

"You are a fool if you believe that," Kyah said. "You remember the wizards imprisoned in our cage?" She stepped forward so he could see her better.

He nodded. "Council wizards, both of them."

"Yes. Kael replaced their cruus. Both were casting magic when the storm hit our ship. People with power do not give it away, Grodin. When Sythrnax has what he wants, there will be no need for you. Besides, those without magic cannot be given it. Real magic comes from the goddess Inara; only she bestows it on people. Anything else is corrupt and evil. I know that better than any other living soul."

"Don't fool yourself about what Sythrnax knows or doesn't know, traitor. It's more than you might think. He has knowledge from ancient times, maybe even the power of the Ancients, themselves."

"Your master doesn't understand what I am, even I don't know what I am," Kael said, "but I can make you talk, I know that much. How about it, Grodin? Tell me, or suffer."

"Give it your best shot. I'd rather suffer at your hands than Sythrnax's." The man glared at him with conviction, but Kael could see the fear dancing in the back of Grodin's eyes.

"Don't be so sure." As if by design, Kael's weapon pulsed, changing back to the strange shiny blade marked with ancient writing.

"Where did you get those weapons?" Grodin asked. "You know what they are, don't you? The Vai'Karth are sentient. Sythrnax has been looking for them for several millennia."

"They are not alive, little man," Kyah said. "We checked; they respond to Kael's will, like the rest of his magic."

"You're a fool," Grodin said. "You will never control those weapons. You don't have the power, and you won't for a thousand years. Like it or not, those blades will twist you into the gods only know what."

"They work fine now," Kyah said. "Last chance—talk or Kael will make you." Grodin shook his head, refusing to cooperate.

"You like lightning, Grodin?" Kael asked, as his lips curled into a crooked smile. "It was the first spell I learned when I arrived here in Talohna. It's my favourite; it's easy to control, so easy, in fact, that I bet I could get it to crawl right up under your flesh," Kael said, as black lightning jumped and spit, crackling around his left hand.

When the frightened man shook his head, Kael continued. "No? How about ice then? Perhaps the cold will loosen your tongue, at least until it freezes solid." Dark purple frost formed on Kael's hand as the black electricity faded and disappeared. The intense cold caused wisps of frosted vapour to rise from his hands. A four-inch-long dagger of purple ice grew from his palm.

Again, the little man could only shake his head, though more adamantly this time. "Well if you don't like ice, you must like fire then," Kael said. "You'll like my fire, Grodin. It comes straight from the bile of the deepest corner of all your Nine Hells."

Kael sneered and his anger began to rise once more. A whoosh of magic swallowed his hand in black and purple flames, flickering with blades of dark green energy. Sparks spit and sputtered while long strings of colourful flame fell to the ground like thick oil. The gut-rot stench of death wafted from the magic as it was called forth from the underworld. Grodin raised his arms in order to protect his face from the intense heat.

The sight of him cowering only fanned the fires of Kael's rage. "What's the matter, Grodin? You've tortured more people than I can count, and yet you shy away like a fucking coward the moment it's done to you. Look at me!" he yelled, grabbing the little man's face as the flames in his hand vanished. The black vines began their tortuous journey again, making Kael wince as they always did, though it was slowly becoming a part of who he was.

Grodin's eyes bulged with raw terror as he gasped. "Gods, Kael, what did they do to you after I left? You refused to hurt anyone when I was there, even to save yourself. By the grace of the Ancients, you're just as much of a monster as all of us now."

Kael's smile darkened and flames jumped to life once more. The downy whiskers on Grodin's face curled from the heat and flames singed his long hair as he struggled to pull away, but Kael's strength was fuelled by his fury. Grodin managed to squirm, but little else.

It forced Kyah to act. She grabbed Kael by the shoulder. "Stop, Kael! Please." It seemed to work as the flames extinguished themselves for a second time as Kael took a deep breath.

"We have only been free for five days, Grodin. Do you know what that means?" she asked. Not understanding, Grodin shook his head, his eyes never leaving Kael's face. "One hundred and fourteen days Kael held out against the worst pain the Dead Sisters could give him," she explained. "He never gave in, and I healed him and brought him back from things that made me sick while trying. He watched Lycori and her grandfather die at the Sisters' hands and still he refused to give up. And you, you had a part in that, Grodin. For that, you can tell us what we want."

"No. When you live like we do, you pick a side. Don't whine because you chose wrong." Grodin chuckled, until Kael shook him hard enough to rattle his brain, leaving his eyes swimming in their sockets.

Leaning over, so that her face was only inches from his, she whispered, "I did choose right, Grodin. I chose Kael. I will always choose him. I am sorry. I tried to help you, I did, but this was your choice. If Kael breaks every bone in your body and leaves you here for the animals, you will deserve every second of your god's forsaken miserable death," she said and then gave him a sad smile. "Just kill him, Kael. He will not help us," she said with finality.

Grodin began to beg and plead, stammering over his words so fast he made no sense. "I have a better idea," Kael growled, punching the little man to shut him up. "Look at me, Grodin. Look... At... Me," he said as he concentrated on the knowledge hidden inside his head.

Without thinking, Kael slid the other reaper-blade back into the sheathe on his back and grabbed Grodin by the chin with his right hand, his thumb on one side and his four fingers on the other, spread out across his cheek. He knew what he wanted to do, but not how to go about it. Anger made the blood hammer in his ears, but when he tried to force magic into his captive, his weapons pulsed with power and a whisper echoed through his mind.

Easy, slowly.

Kael took another deep breath and refocused. Concentrating harder, he closed his eyes as black fluid seeped from his hand and wormed its way through the pores of Grodin's skin. The fluid crawled under his flesh like tendrils as it worked its way up his face and into his head. Grodin's eyes filled with it only moments before his terror-filled babbling stopped.

Kyah gagged, muttering, "Mother Mylla," but could manage nothing else. Kael was lost in the throes of ancient magic. A twisted mix of fury and euphoria coursed through his soul and he no longer cared about anything but answers.

"Tell me where Sythrnax is," he snarled, through clenched teeth, and forced the influence of his magic to strip away all Grodin's resistance until nothing was left but a puppet whose strings belonged to him.

With no free will, Sythrnax's right hand man had no choice but to talk. "He's in the ancient Dwarven mountains."

"Will he answer me, Kael?" Kyah asked, having regained control of herself. Kael nodded slowly, but his focus never wavered from the magic under his control. "Grodin?" Kyah asked. "What is he doing up there?"

"Research on both Kael and an ancient Dwarven weapon," he answered. His voice was even and carried no emotion.

Shocked, Kael's mind started to spin with the idea that knowledge of what he was existed somewhere. It pulled his thoughts away from Grodin and left Kyah free to question him further.

"Why, Grodin?" she asked. "What is up there? And where exactly?"

"I don't know why. There are millennia-old tablets there written by Kael's kind. They are filled with information about the DeathWizards as well as a hidden weapon even the Dwarves were too afraid to use." His words tore Kael from his thoughts.

"If he's up there doing research, then what does he want Giddeon for?" Kael asked.

"Sythrnax believes the power or the blood of the ArchWizard will allow him to open a seal to the greatest Dwarven weapon ever constructed. We bought Giddeon and the others from the savages when we saw him. We're on our way north now to wait for Sythrnax to return." He finished speaking in the same monotone voice.

Kael's energy was fading fast so he pulled his magic from Grodin's mind and face. The black tentacles retreated just as fast as they had entered. Physically and mentally exhausted, Kael dropped further onto his knees and Grodin fell to the ground unconscious. The puppet's strings vanished without Kael's power.

A moan from Giddeon at Kael's side made him glance over his shoulder. The ArchWizard glared back. "Your powers have grown greatly, son," he said. "You shadow-walk already and are capable of mind control. But I see that you've little compassion left, just like the prophecy predicted, and for that, I am sorry."

"Don't waste your pity, Giddeon," Kael snapped. "You and your group never gave me a chance to be anything other than what you think I should be."

Giddeon held Kael's stare as he continued. "I knew there was no way your heart could remain free of evil. Using dark magics to invade someone's mind and force knowledge from them leaves lasting damage no matter how careful you are. Grodin will never be the same. You've destroyed a man's mind just to get information. It proves what DeathWizards are capable of. Of course we'll hunt you down!"

Kael's rage surged with renewed vigour as an intense desire to destroy Giddeon washed over him. He grabbed the ArchWizard's face in the same manner as he had Grodin's, but stopped for a moment to take a good look at the man who was so determined to kill everyone like him. The thought of adding to the man's current misery was more than Kael could handle, and the ever-present, growing vines slowed and became idle as he forced himself to calm down.

"I'm not what you think I am, ArchWizard," Kael said. "I have seen true evil, and you cannot imagine what it's like until it destroys all that you care about."

Kael could see the beating Giddeon received at the hands of Grodin and his men. Both eyes were swollen shut and his nose was shattered. His fingers had all been dislocated and so had his right elbow—Kael winced at the odd angle and protruding joint. But it was the Gyhurra collar that was doing the most damage. Memories flooded Kael's mind as he remembered the suffering and intense pain the spikes from the collar caused when they pierced the large nerve clusters in his neck.

The rage storming through his body for so long finally cooled. The agony in Giddeon's eyes was all too familiar. Kael took a deep breath and shook his head and was swarmed by agony more intense than the last flash back. He screamed, grabbing his head and falling to the leaf-mold. Kyah grabbed him, holding him tight as again she began the spell to help him.

"What's wrong with him?" Giddeon asked as Kael's cry came to an end.

"The collar around your neck, Kael wore one like it for five months..."

"Merciful Mylla..." Giddeon began, but clearly could not finish.

"The collar has lasting effects, I think."

Struggling and using sheer willpower, Kael forced the memories from his mind and empathy crept back in. "Cut him down, Kyah. He can't hurt us with that collar on." Though exhausted from the flashback and the spell he had used on Grodin, Kael regained his feet and held onto Giddeon as Kyah cut him down, then helped drag him to the nearest tent where they laid him against one of the poles.

It did nothing to relieve Giddeon's suspicions. "What do want from me, Kael? You might as well kill us all now, or we will continue the hunt for you."

Kael knelt in front of Giddeon and lifted his head by placing a single finger under his chin. The ArchWizard grunted at the pain as the Gyhurra's four spikes dragged against the nerves inside his neck.

"You should be more careful of exactly what you ask for, Giddeon, especially when you're staring into the face of my kind. After all, I did come here looking for you as well," Kael said, as he let Giddeon's head fall to his chest.

It was long past time the ArchWizard provided him with some answers.

Chapter Six

"I have trained hundreds, if not thousands, of Broken Blade assassins. Long before there was a guild, I placed the first enchanted wooden blade in the hands of Yrlissa Blackmist. I have never trained nor seen an assassin of her equal since. Until now. If Desiree Star can manage to control her emotions and focus her instincts on anticipation, she will become a killer who may one day surpass the best assassin to ever live."

Ella Navasha
From a journal found inside a house in Argela, 5025 PC

ARGELA, ELLORYA

Desiree Star hit the stone and mortar wall hard, crumpling to the floor in a heap.

"Again, Miss Star," Ella said. No emotion crept into her voice, not even disappointment. Desiree stood slowly. Her body ached, every square inch of it. Bruises, scrapes, and contusions covered her skin. She even had bruises in areas she could not see. Weeks had passed as they tried to hunt down Kael, but news about him was extremely rare and progress had been slow. This meant more time Desiree had to spend training and sparring against a fighter centuries beyond her own skills. Desiree sighed.

After returning to Argela with the White witch, Ella Navasha, and meeting up with her apprentice, Katarina Desolla, the three rented a small house with an open basement for training and had been waiting for two weeks on information about Kael's whereabouts.

During those two weeks, Katarina and Desiree sparred every day, and every day Desiree got pounded on, tossed around, and beat to a living pulp by the tall, dark-haired woman. Desiree studied hard and paid close attention to her lessons, but Katarina had been Ella's apprentice for many years and had clearly learned her own lessons well. After spending hours each morning teaching Desiree skills she had yet to learn when still with the guild, Ella watched the two fight for hours every afternoon. The witch would offer guidance and advice to both fighters, but would not allow magic to be used until Desiree had advanced to a certain level. At that point, Desiree hoped Ella would fix her tattoo, which would restore her speed, strength, and reflexes.

The thoughts cost Desiree dearly as a spinning kick sent her twisting sideways through the air.

"Desiree!" Ella barked. "Stop your mind from wandering. Focus."

"Yes, Mistress," Desiree groaned, pulling herself to her feet.

"Again," Ella said, her voice returning to normal.

Desiree set her feet, knowing the powerful attack that would be coming could knock her back down. She was right. Katarina lunged, and Desiree put her arms together, blocking the front kick. It still slid her back a full foot as Katarina exploded with violence, punch after punch darting in at Desiree's head.

"Control, Katarina," Ella said with just an edge of warning.

As Katarina slowed the pace of punches, gaining more accuracy and control, Desiree focused harder, not wanting one of the strong blows to slide past her defence and knock her out. Blocking and deflecting every swing, Desiree knew the kick was coming. It always came, but she could never predict it quickly enough to stop herself from being launched into the wall.

Katarina's knee shot up. Desiree thrust her open palm down, slamming her attacker's knee hard enough to stagger her for a single second. Something clicked in Desiree's mind and she knew the spinning kick was coming. She ducked instantly, and swept her foot out as the kick whistled over her head. Knocking Katarina's foot out from under her, Desiree jumped to her feet as the dark-haired woman crashed to the floor, hard.

"Excellent, Desiree," Ella said, clapping slowly. "Perfect anticipation. So, you did learn something from Yrlissa after all. Enough for today. Both of you head over to Natalia's and soak in a hot mineral bath to soothe your aches. Return here before the evening meal. We have a special guest joining us tonight.

"Info on Kael's location, Mistress?" Katarina asked, pulling herself up with a wince.

"No. Something about a crazy alchemist capable of changing our world as we know it. I think our hunt has shifted. For the moment."

WILDLANDS NORTHERN FOREST

"I came here looking just for you, Giddeon," Kael said. "When I first arrived here, a bounty hunter captured me and tried to take me to a city called Corynth. Just before he died, he told me that my wife Ember and my friend Max died during the crossing that brought me here. Yet, last night, Ember came to me in a dream begging for my help."

"What? Why did you not tell me?" Kyah asked. He gave her a dirty look, warning her not to do it again, and continued.

"She told me she was with you, here in the forest, captives of the tribals and that you needed help. And here I find you, Giddeon. In the dream, I saw you in a cage with others. Max and Ember were with you. Where are they?"

The silence that followed lasted several minutes before the ArchWizard spoke. "I am truly sorry, Kael, but your magic dragged them into the bridge. My daughter, Saleece, almost lost her life by dragging them away from you in an attempt to save them, but when they arrived in my tower it was already too late, they were dead. A dimensional bridge can only support one life and most often that one life doesn't survive. We tried, Kael, I swear, we tried, but there was no way to save them. I'm sorry," he said. "I truly am. You have my condolences."

The little bit of hope Kael had vanished quicker than it had grown when seeing Ember in his dream. Kael's eyes glossed over and another onslaught of horrific memories set in, this time from the day he was pulled off the picnic table at Tinker's Bar and Grill and dragged into Talohna through a twisting dimensional vortex.

"It's not your fault, Giddeon," Kael whispered, as if in a daze. "It's mine. I reached to them for help... I didn't know..." Kael's voice faded at the images storming his mind. Kyah placed her hand on his shoulder.

"It's never too late. Stop running and come back with us. Show the kingdoms you're not a killer, and maybe all this will stop. Please, son. It's never too late," Giddeon begged, his voice filled with hope.

"I'm not your son, Giddeon. I'm a thing that's been condemned to death from the moment I first drew breath as a baby. You took me from my parents, who likely wanted me, and you left me in a world that was not mine with people who didn't want me. Ember and I have been on our own since we were both fifteen years old. Being pulled back here caused the death of the only two people important to me. It is long past too late for me, Giddeon, but I won't surrender to you until I know for sure there's no cure for what's happening to me. I wasn't always like this. Maybe I can get rid of it."

"It's not a disease, Kael. You can't get rid of it," Giddeon said in disbelief. "Any more than you could get rid of an arm or leg. This world doesn't work that way..."

Not in the mood to argue, Kael frowned. "Don't waste your breath, I'm not listening. Now, hold still unless you want to spend the rest of your life with that Gyhurra around your neck. I'm the only one who can remove one," he informed Giddeon.

"Please, Kael, listen," he said, quickly.

"Go ahead, but I won't discuss what we already have," he warned.

"Fair enough. Can you actually remove this collar? I've never felt the likes of it. My magic can't touch it..."

"Like your cruus is gone right?"

"Yes, exactly. My daughter, Saleece, she's in the tent over there. They put one on her as well. Please help her, too."

"I will. No one should live like that. Kyah, bring her here, and be gentle, she's probably terrified."

Her response was not what Kael expected. She shook her head. "Kael! They will heal each other and be hunting us in less than an hour. You cannot do this. They will kill you the first chance they get."

"Kael?" Giddeon asked, interrupting. "Get these things off of us and I promise, we'll not come after you. We're down here because the King's daughter was captured by the Taktala tribe and he tasked us with returning her. We must rescue her first. It will give you time to get away, likely a few weeks head start." Kael didn't believe him, but he nodded to Kyah to bring Saleece anyway.

"Thank you, Kael. I mean it," Giddeon said, sincerity filling his voice. Kael nodded as he prepared to remove another of the cursed magic suppressing collars.

"All right, don't move, or your head *will* come off with the collar. And don't attempt to heal yourselves until we're gone or all promises will be forgotten. I may have little magic left, but my blades don't require magic. Besides it'll be a couple of days before you can use magic without experiencing intense pain. Understand?"

The ArchWizard nodded and then sat perfectly still as Kael placed a single fingertip to the collar. A crack of power split the metal down the middle. Without hesitation, Kael's fingers shifted to each of the spikes driven into Giddeon's neck, and a black magical fluid coiled around the spikes like a snake on a branch. The spikes dissolved under the touch of underworld magic. Without having to sustain Giddeon's life force and create a new bond like he did with Galen and Kalmar, removing the Gyhurra was much easier. Kael grabbed the remains of the smoking collar and tossed it into the bushes, a streak of black lightning followed, destroying it. Giddeon's sigh of relief was loud enough to hear. Kyah returned with Saleece at the same moment.

"Father," Saleece cried out, rushing to his side and giving him a hug. "Are you all right?" Sitting back a moment she stared at his neck. "Your collar's gone... Who are these..." Her sentence cut off in mid-sentence when she noticed Kael. "I know you! Your name is Kael. Em.."

Giddeon interrupted before she could finish. "You're right, Saleece, Kael has been looking for us with the hope that he could find out what happened to his wife and friend. They're the ones you tried to save in the dimensional bridge the day Kael was brought here. I told him that they didn't make it despite your efforts, and I told him how sorry we are for his loss."

Saleece turned to her father, with her back to Kael and lowered her head, as if in shame. "I'm sorry, Kael, I tried to help them, but the gate exploded, there was too much power." Kael grabbed her arm and spun her around, her moist glossy eyes revealed the truth.

"It's not your fault. Thank you for trying." She nodded and wiped her eyes with her sleeve.

Giddeon shifted his position, coughing. "Kael has agreed to remove our collars in exchange for a two-week head start while we're trying to find Princess Corleya." Saleece nodded to her father and then stepped up to Kael.

"I'm sorry for what has happened to you. Please return with us so we can help you. I can see the conflict in your eyes. You're not the person you are turning into. Give us the chance to help you. Please," she begged.

"I may have little to live for, but I'm not handing my life to the people who have been trying to kill me for months. You might want to help, Saleece, but your King has made it clear my life is worth nothing. If I am going to die in this god-forsaken world, then I have someone to kill first. At least I can leave this world better than I found it. If I survive, I'll be waiting in the Dwarven Mountains for you to come get me."

"Kael, you cannot," Kyah snapped, as she grasped his cloak, but he raised his hand to quiet her.

"I'm not gonna spend my life always running. That's no life for anyone. Now enough. Saleece, sit back and don't move. I won't let you live your life with that collar on."

Saleece winced at the pain in his eyes. "You wore one, didn't you? After they took you?" Once more, Kael pulled his cloak aside to reveal the scars.

"Four or five months," he replied. He matched her stare as she spoke.

"Four... Five... months" she echoed, "Mother Inara, what in all Perdition are these things? How did you survive? I'd rather die. My connection to the earth mother is gone, and the pain..."

"Not gone, that feels even worse. If you ever see Galen Vihr or Kalmar Ibess again, ask them. They can tell you."

"They're alive?" Giddeon asked, nearly dumbfounded.

Kyah nodded. "Kael freed them from Arkum Zul when we escaped."

"You were inside the old Dwarven prison?" Saleece whispered. Kyah nodded.

"How did you escape?" Giddeon asked.

"We fought. Now be quiet. These collars are old, ancient even, their secrets are far beyond me..." As they talked, Kael watched Saleece's face and actions for signs of sincerity, but his eyes kept shifting to her strange hair. His voice faded as he focused on the distraction. Strange ripples of colour stood out as an emerald sheen undulated through her long, blonde, braid. Something tugged at his mind, a power hidden deep inside her, foreign compared to her cruus, but there none the less. Perplexed, he intensified his scrutiny, almost as if he was in a dream. Without conscious thought, he reached out and touched her braided ponytail. Her aura mushroomed out around her, making him gasp.

Dazzling lights of varied hues chased each other like little wisps, circling her body as they emanated with a restrained energy. Kael smiled at the beauty being created by the wisps, he had seen them before. It was the polar opposite of what he witnessed the odd time he had seen an aura produced by a Dead Sister.

"You're not Human," he whispered, still smiling with awe at the hidden magic. He shook his head and the trance was broken.

"What did you just say?" Giddeon asked, squinting, as he turned his head, trying to get a better look at what Kael was doing to his daughter. It was clear he had not heard Kael's statement. Saleece had, though. Her face paled and her eyes opened wide in confusion.

"Nothing, he told her she's gonna have to sit still," Kyah said to Giddeon, as she handed the ArchWizard a water-skin before returning to Kael's side.

"You need to be more careful, Kael," Kyah breathed into his ear. Not bothering to look her way, he nodded. No longer able to see the multitude of dancing colours, he focused on removing Saleece's Gyhurra collar instead.

"What did you see, Kael?" Saleece asked, nervousness making her voice climb in pitch. "Is something wrong with me? Please, if you can help..."

"Shh! Don't move," Kael hushed, as he struggled to maintain his concentration. She did as he asked and he let out a sigh of relief, placing his hands to the collar.

Kael repeated the same process that freed Giddeon from the sadistic collar and its effects. The collar cracked and the four spikes dissolved, leaving behind no permanent damage. Knowing that Saleece was more than she appeared to be, Kael pulled one of the blowgun darts from his Orotaq cloak and stuck it in her neck.

"You bastard, how could y..." she cursed, but slumped over out cold before she could finish her sentence.

In a desperate attempt to help her, Giddeon struggled to stand, yelling at Kael. "You son of a bitch, what did you do to her? You promised you..."

"Easy, Giddeon," Kael warned as he stood and used his right foot to push Giddeon back against the tent. Too weak to hold against the light thrust, the impact knocked the ArchWizard back to the ground. "I stuck her with a sleep dart, nothing more. I don't trust you to keep your word. You might feel that you're defending your kingdom, but you'll find my life not so easy to take. I'll make sure the Taktala watch over you and allow you to leave when you wake. I'm afraid I'm going to have put you to sleep as well," Kael explained, as he jabbed the dart into Giddeon's neck and watched him slide into sleep, joining his daughter.

"Anyone else inside that prisoner tent you were in?" Kael asked Kyah, as he stood and cast his eyes over the camp.

"Yes, two others, but they have no collars. I guess they have no magic, warriors probably. One is awake, but the other was whipped and beaten senseless." Kael checked his

Orotaq cloak and found several darts still stuck in the fur and cured leather so he handed her two and nodded towards the tent.

"Be a sweetheart and stick them with these darts while I talk to the Taktala, if I can."

She smiled and left, calling back over her shoulder. "Anything for you, my love, you know that."

Kael approached the still murmuring tribesmen, examining every last warrior for signs of aggression. When he saw nothing but fear, he clapped his hands together to get their attention.

"Listen to me. Do any of you speak the common tongue?"

One warrior stood, slowly. Once waved forward, he stepped up to Kael, still trembling with fear or awe. "I, Bala Takma," the tribal warrior said. "I have little common speak."

"Can you understand our tongue?" Kael questioned.

The warrior nodded. "Understand, have little," he said.

"We are leaving this place, Bala Takma, but these people," Kael said, as he pointed to Giddeon and Saleece, "must be allowed to leave when they wake. You will not harm them and you will not take them as slaves, do you understand?" Again, the forest native only nodded, but seemed to understand. To be sure, Kael pulled both reaper-blades from the sheaths on his back; they rasped with a dull whisper as they slid against the scaled dragon skin. Bala Takma's eyes tripled in size as he began to shake even more. "If anything should happen to them, Bala, I will return and bring Sarak to all the Taktala, you understand?" He crossed the large blades over his chest and bowed. Bala bowed back, as low as he could get before looking up at Kael for permission to resume standing.

Once Kael nodded, the scout leader stood. "Friends safe, Bala be safe, Taktala be safe, yes." Now positive he understood, Kael nodded as he felt Kyah's presence return to his side.

"What now, handsome? North to the Dwarven Mountains? That is weeks of travel, months on foot." He nodded. With so many miles ahead of them, he watched as she began to scavenge for supplies, starting with Grodin's two hired killers.

Kael joined her. "If there's some tablet up there with knowledge about my kind, then yes. North, I guess. Hopefully we can find horses somewhere. Long ways on foot, I imagine," he pointed out. She huffed as she dug through the travel packs, adding what she found to their own meagre supplies.

"Check Grodin. See if he has any gold on him. Horses are expensive even if tribals decide to sell to a death god," she added. Kael spun on his heel and headed towards the rack where he had left Grodin a crumpled pile of twitching pain, but stopped dead when he noticed the little man was gone.

"That might be a problem, Kyah. Grodin's gone." Puzzled, his eyes scanned the camp, the bushes, and the forest around them, but Grodin was nowhere to be seen. Kael closed his eyes and focused his esoteric sight, but he couldn't sense Grodin either.

"He wandered off?" Kyah asked.

"Yes," Kael replied, frowning. "He's headed south, deeper into the forest. Leave him be."

"No. If he gets back to Sythrnax, he will tell him everything. Sythrnax and his forces will know exactly where we are going. They will try to capture us again." Kael listened to her words as he chewed his bottom lip and stared south into the forest.

"How bad are the tribes further south?"

"I would guess they would respond to you the same way these men did. Grodin cannot have gone far, Kael..."

"No," he said turning back to her. "We need every bit of head start we can get. Too many things could go wrong. If Giddeon wakes earlier than we expect from the sleep darts or if we come across other tribals and they're not afraid... We'll have to hope Grodin gets lost or the forest finishes him—I can't sense him and I'm not a tracker. We have to go. Giddeon will come after us the moment his people are able."

Kyah nodded and put her arm around his waist. He didn't object. Ember was gone and everything inside him was numb. The smallest part of him wanted to believe the dream was real, that she was alive. In his heart, he knew he'd been grasping at the threads of desperation. He shook his head. All he wanted to do was keep moving to the north and hopefully to some answers.

Chapter Seven

"The Fae and the Dyrannai Elvehn have been the closest of allies for thousands of years. So close, in fact, some of the Elvehn eventually learned how to use magic known only to the Fae. These select individuals are capable of casting both types of magic and have a deep understanding of their own emotions – the place from where the Fae draw their magical power. Now that the Fae are extinct, there will be less and less Elvehn born every year who are able to use this incredible gift. Even so, I still hope these skills survive far into the future."

Author unknown From pages found
in the Ancient Library of the Arcane, 5015 PC
Original work dated at over ten thousand years.

WILDLANDS NORTHERN FOREST

After leaving the Taktala camp, Kael and Kyah pushed hard, running off and on for close to six hours in an attempt to leave Giddeon and his group far behind. Always moving north, Kael was nearly asleep on his feet when they came across a ten-foot-wide creek formed by a waterfall spilling from a wide crack in the ridge above them, some twenty feet up. The falling water created a pond at the base of the small rise before it flowed lazily downhill. Kael stumbled to the edge, dropping to his knees. Scooping up the water in both hands, he splashed his face, washing away the blood, sweat, and grime.

The moment the water touched his face he spit, shaking his head. "The water's warm. Is it safe?"

"I know not," Kyah said, joining him at the edge. "You should be able to tell. Use your senses, feel the water flow through your fingers, and let your magic tell you if it's safe."

Even exhausted, Kael could sense something different about the water. He released his mind and let it enter the running stream. As his head tipped sideways and his body slumped onto the damp grass, his mind was already far away, chasing the creek upstream to the pond below the small waterfall. From there, he raced against the flow of the cascading water up the rock into the wide rent that allowed the warm current to rush forth. Drawn deep into the earth, his consciousness unexpectedly slammed into the raw force of a thundering underground river; locked into the sensitivity of his magic, he panicked at the devastating power and felt his control slip.

Desperation clawed at his mind as the river's raw fury pulled and pushed at his consciousness, trying to sweep him away. Panic overruled common sense, and he inhaled. Water flooded his lungs. Flashes of heat and molten rock fuelled his frenzied state further as he screamed, but instead, his head was snapped around, twisting his neck. The pain pushed the fear back and Kyah's voice filtered through only seconds before his tortured lungs drew in the sweetest air he had ever tasted.

Choking on the mix of fresh air and warm water, his presence snapped back into his body with a violent jolt, just as Kyah slapped him. Eyes still wild with fear and panic, Kael heaved and coughed, expelling water from his lungs. Warm water and strings of bloody saliva sprayed from his mouth, soaking Kyah from chin to belly.

"Sorry," Kael said. He groaned, coughing a second time and hacking more water from his lungs. "God in heaven, why does this shit keep happening to me?" He moaned and rolled to his hands and knees, expelling more water from the underground river.

Fighting her own fear, Kyah thumped his back, stuttering. "I... I am sorry, Kael. I was not thinking. I knew you were tired, but I did not know such a thing could happen. Has it before?"

Sitting back up, he nodded and cleared his throat, trying his best to suppress the urge to cough the dull burn from his throat and lungs. The memory of the last time he physically left his body was fresh in his mind.

"Yes, when Lycori and I were in the northern mountain pass between Cethos and Yusat, this happened. I left my body and drifted through the pass, miles away. It's how we discovered Giddeon was chasing us. I could hear them speak, but I couldn't talk to them and there was no physical connection like this." He wheezed, his lungs still burned from the invasion of water. "What would cause this? I almost drowned. I thought it was real. Why?" He gasped, still trying to catch his breath.

"I know not. Projecting your spirit away from your body like that is far beyond my knowledge. Spirit magic is only practiced by necromancers and the tribal witch doctors from this forest. It is very dangerous, Kael. You must be careful from now on. If I were not here, you *would* have drowned. Somehow, you are able to leave your body behind and walk in the physical world with your spirit... or perhaps your soul, depending on your beliefs. But the physical connection to your body must mean it can still suffer the effects of your spirit's surroundings." He could see she was still distressed and shaking from the close call. He stared at her hopelessly, but said nothing.

"Come," she offered, helping him up. "Let's get cleaned up. We haven't had warm water in months. It is safe, is it not?"

Gaining his feet, Kael stumbled, but caught himself before falling without too much effort. "The water comes from deep in the earth. I could see molten rock, so it might not taste the best, but should be safe to bathe in." He took Kyah's hand and she headed upstream to the deeper water of the pool. "Maybe I can do something with this rat's nest on my head," Kael mumbled, referring to the knotted, tangled mess of hair that hadn't seen a brush or shampoo in almost half a year.

"I agree," Kyah said, adding her support. "We cannot show up in Dasal looking like we do, or we will be turned away. One of the kinrai blades from my waist whip will work for you to shave and cut your hair." Arriving at the pool below the waterfall, Kael and Kyah shed their clothes before sliding into the warm water. Far beyond exhausted from the day's events, it was all Kael could do to stay awake, at times failing to do that as he floated on his back in the chest deep water. The magma-heated spring, high in mineral content, eased the pains from the shipwreck and the lingering effects from the months of torture he suffered prior to their escape.

He woke with a start as the caress of something soft slid across his chest. Kyah smiled as his eyes found her in the water beside him. With a fist-sized ball of purple moss in her hand, she washed away months of sweat and grime. It tingled his skin, easing away even more of the agony and stress that always seemed to be weighing on him.

"Turrin moss," she said softly, seeing his confusion. "It will ease some of your pain and allow you to relax." Too exhausted to speak, he nodded as she slid under him, placing his head on her shoulder as she continued to rub the ball of moss over the rest of his sore muscles. A faint purple residue remained on his skin for several seconds before his body absorbed it. The magical properties calmed his mind and eased away his worries, just as she said they would. Once she finished, he returned the favour. Clean and relaxed, they floated in the pond for an hour before swimming to the waterfall where they stood underneath it, letting the water wash away any leftover grime and turrin moss. Kael couldn't believe the dark streaks of filth than ran downstream from where ever they stood. Then they gathered their ragged clothes and washed them as well, before heading into the cave system behind the waterfall.

The ten-foot-high ceiling in the unoccupied cave gave them excellent shelter from the elements and allowed a small fire to burn, the smoke dissipating as it rose through the crashing water of the falls. The long nights of the Wildland Forest could get cool enough to be uncomfortable. After a quick bite of food stolen from the Taktala tribe, Kyah offered to cut Kael's hair. Exhausted from using magic that was well beyond his ability, he didn't object, sitting cross-legged in front of her. She ran her fingers through his hair, untangling the mess as best she could.

"We have not a lot of options here, love," she said, smiling. "Your hair has grown a lot since I met you. Even knotted like this, it is still well past your shoulders. You want me to shave it all off or spin it into Salzaran braids?"

"Sal...what?" he asked. Half asleep, he wasn't sure he heard her right.

"I will never get the tangles and knots out, Kael. I can spin thin strands of your hair into tiny dreadlocks and then braid them if you like? Or we can shave your head. The braids will allow you to fit in better; a shaved head may make you stand out. A lot of male wizards shave their heads. It may draw attention to us."

"Do the braids then, I guess. Though people are more likely to notice these barbed vines everywhere on my skin long before they notice a shaved head."

Kyah frowned, as she removed one of the small blades from the whip she wore around her waist. "At a glance, your markings look like tattoos, nothing more, and many Northmen wear their hair like this. You are a bit small after losing so much weight, but you could pass for a Northman, especially if we shave the sides of your head. It will keep people from staring and will stop curious questions when we arrive in towns or cities. People are afraid of the Northmen and go out of their way to leave them alone. It will be good, Kael."

"All right, whatever makes people look anywhere but us." The kinrai blade gently scraped across the skin above his ear and a chunk of ratty hair fell in his lap. He shivered and pulled his cloak tighter as Kyah worked to make his appearance somewhat civil. The last hair from the shaved sides of his head fell, and he felt her hands begin to spin the rest of the frazzled mess into thin strands that she could braid.

With only his Orotaq cloak and a single blanket, nights were going to be cold and miserable in the forest. He no longer even had a shirt; the one he wore when he arrived had been destroyed long ago. The leather pants he found in Jasala's tower were torn in a few places and still damp, but were no longer caked in salt from their time in the ocean. The soft leather boots, also from Jasala's hidden room deep inside her ruined tower, were still in perfect condition, but he knew it was the enchantments. No matter how much weight his travel pack was loaded down with, his feet never ached because of the strange footwear.

They both had planned on taking the clothes found on board the stolen vessel, but the shipwreck happened so fast, he never had time to grab anything. Kyah still wore the white bodice and skirt he found in the captain's cabin, and though it was stained everywhere, the supple white leather still looked like it was brand new. He was beginning to think there might be more to it than might meet the eye, as well. Oddly enough, the curve-hugging outfit often seemed to catch his eyes, even though he wished it wouldn't. There was so much about Talohna that he did not understand and his knowledge of it didn't seem to grow fast enough in relation to what he was discovering.

The lack of understanding tripping around his thoughts jogged his memory, and he remembered the letter and potion bottles he found in Jasala's hidden suite, deep below her tower so long ago. Realizing months had passed since he'd had the chance to read her letter, he sat by the fire with his travel pack between his legs and dug around inside until he found them. Kyah continued to work on his hair as he set the small potion bottles aside. Kael sensed that they caught Kyah's eye, but he was focused on the letter in the hope that rereading the first page would enlighten him, at least a little, to the secrets of his magical lineage.

The moment he put the paper to his heart, he knew it was a waste of time. He had yet to acquire the power needed to read it. Desperate, he opened the second letter anyway, and stared at it, his frustration rising. Like before, it was written in gibberish he didn't understand. Refolding it he put it back in his travel pack. Kyah was still staring at the three bottles when she started to braid the spun lengths of his hair. He picked them up and held them tight while he closed his eyes. With his outer sight much stronger than it had ever been, he focused in an attempt to see what was inside, but the glass bottles prevented his magic from penetrating, leaving him as clueless and as frustrated as before.

"What are those?" Kyah asked, the gentle tugs from her braid-work moving his head back and forth as he tried to concentrate on the bottles.

"Some things I found when I first arrived, why?"

"Those bottles, what do they say?"

"The first says B.B. Purge, and the second two both say Fae's Dreamwalk. Why? Have you heard of either?" he asked, turning to look at her. A frown of concern washed across her face, and Kael thought a flush of red coloured her cheeks, but the campfire also danced across her features and he couldn't be sure.

Her voice confirmed his suspicions though. "Where did you find those?" she asked, almost snapping at him. A genuine anger accompanied her words.

“In... Jasala Vyshaan's tower, why?” As he watched her reaction to his response, Kael wasn't sure if she was going to faint or run into the dark forest, screaming with disbelief.

When she managed to stop gasping, she put her hand to her forehead. “Gods, Kael.” She paused long enough to shake her head. “Why in all the Nine Hells would you ever take something from that place? By Mylla's holy grace, that festering hole of dark magic has never had anything good come from it, do you not know that? Those bottles are probably full of some putrid death poison, or the gods only know what else, Fae's Dreamwalk is a very powerful Fae spell that can be made in no bottle, I assure you. The other, I have never heard of before, but the word purge has a pretty clear meaning,” she said. Each of the words, she spoke slowly so he would understand. “She was the worst of all the DeathWizards to ever walk this world. The most vile monster we were ever taught about in our lessons. The Dead Sisters worship her like a god, like some twisted dark hero, for what she did. That should tell you all you need to know,” she finished, abruptly. Shocked by her outburst, he wasn't sure what to say.

“I...” he began, but she cut him off before he got started, so he turned away. The tugging on his hair began again as she spoke.

“I am sorry... I did not mean... Just...” She took a deep breath, cleared her throat and tried again. “You must see, Kael, that you are not like most of your kind. People fear you—wizards like you, I mean—for very good reasons. By the blessed Mother Mylla, you even scare the Nine Hells out of me sometimes. I...”

Taking another second to steady herself, she continued. “I love you, Kael. I really do, but your kind are capable of things you shouldn't be. You move unlike anyone I have ever seen and when you surrender to your anger, the compassion in your heart, and even your very soul, is gone, like the flame blown from a candle. During our training, my sisters and I were taught all that the Dead Sisters know about the DeathWizards from the past. You are not at all like the ones we were taught about, but I see them in you. Jasala was one of, if not the worst, of all them. The common people of Talohna call your kind what they do, because of the death your kind usually bring in their wake."

"I know, but I can't change that, and no one would listen to me, even if I tried." Her hand slid around his chin and cheek, turning his face back to hers. She kissed him softly.

"I know this, Kael, but you must remember these things when you are some place where one of these monsters from the past has walked. The smallest thing could awaken such a creature inside you. I could not bear it if that happened," she said. Standing, she stepped around and knelt before him by the fire. "Do you understand that?"

Kael nodded, as she leaned against him and cuddled closer. He opened his cloak and she turned, nestling in against his chest. Telling her about the other things he found would only upset her more, so he sat back against the cave wall and said nothing as they shared their warmth.

She looked up at him and smiled. "Your hair is done. It will be more manageable now. You can shave in the morning. Both grow fast, so it will not take long for your hair to grow out straight and you can get rid of the Northman style if you want."

Kael grabbed one of the spun braids and stared at it. "Definitely grows faster here than on my world."

Kyah smiled up at him. "Magic has that effect on things."

Kael nodded. Kissing her forehead, he leaned back against the cave wall and tried to sleep. Kyah stayed inside the cloak with him for a few minutes before she returned to the cave's entrance to watch for threats. Twenty minutes of silence passed and still the calm of the dreamworld refused to grant him entry.

"Kyah?"

"Yes, Kael," she answered, still at the cave's entrance.

"Where's the closest city from here that's on our way to the Dwarven Mountains?" He yawned, but still couldn't sleep.

"Dasal, our destination is the closest. It is a port city beyond Yusat in the Free Lands. There are some smaller towns, but out of our way. If I remember right," she explained.

"If you remember, right? I thought I was the one with a concussion," he baited.

"You were the one with the concussion, before I healed you. You were trying to walk face first into a sand dune, remember?" She chuckled, making him smile. "I have never been here, Kael. The Sisters made us study maps of both the Bloods and the Southern Kingdoms for when we were to leave with them, but I remember not all the towns of this area," she pointed out.

"I figured as much," he mumbled, and yawned a second time, fatigue starting to settle in.

A couple minutes passed and still Kael couldn't sleep. "Kyah, is there any chance we could get decent supplies in Dasal?"

"Yes, if we had anything of value to barter or trade."

"Well, I guess we'll be walking and freezing all the way then," he scoffed.

"We are still three weeks away by foot. Worry not about it now, handsome."

"Fair enough. Good night," he yawned, closing his eyes.

"Kael?"

"Yes, Kyah?" he smiled. He found the reverse in questioning quite amusing. Proof he needed sleep, badly.

"Your magic is getting stronger, is it not?" she asked, politely.

"Yeah, it is. Yours?" Several minutes passed and still she hadn't answered the question. "I can sense it. You know that, right? Your aura is brighter."

"The fact you can sense auras is disturbing enough, but yes, my magic is stronger. So was Galen's. He should not have healed me so well back in the cave."

"You almost died. I wouldn't call that well."

"Galen is not a trained healer. Besides stabilizing a patient, he has no further skill in healing. Closing my open wound so you could move me was incredible."

"I know," Kael said. "He told me as much after he finished. What does it mean?" he asked, not sure if he wanted to know the real answer.

"Your magic will continue to grow stronger the more you use it or the more you understand it. This is normal. But other magic is getting stronger too. I know not why, unless Kalmar was right, and the Fae have returned to Talohna. We must be careful. When magic changes, it can change many things." She smiled, but he could tell she was guessing.

"All right, careful it is."

"Kyah?" He chuckled as the back and forth carried on.

She smiled and turned from keeping watch. "Yes, Kael?"

With a more serious expression, he asked, "What is a shadow-walk?" He didn't need to see her face to know it darkened with concern.

"The shadow-walk spell is magic that was very rare in its time and was lost many thousands of years before the Cataclysm, or so we were taught. It is among many others that have been lost from that era. Because DeathWizards used the spell as well, I know only what the Dead Sisters told us."

"Which is?"

"It is supposed to be a mix of Fae and Demon magic, used mostly by assassins during ancient times. The Sisters claim that your kind, the Kai'Sar, mastered this magic and that, when strong enough, you can fade from view and reappear short distances away, often trailing black smoke or shadows. When a DeathWizard uses this magic, people cannot see them because they move too fast," she stated.

Shrugging her shoulders, she added, "When you killed that Mahala in the cave after he cut my stomach, I saw you... You were fifteen feet away. I blinked when he cut me, and you were behind him. I did not see you move." Kael shook his head as he searched her eyes for the truth in what she said. There was pity there, but no signs of exaggeration.

"How is that possible? I didn't realize... Is it instinct, you think?" he asked, the idea starting to unnerve him.

"I know not. The same happened today when you killed Grodin's men. You moved so fast that all I saw were black shadows as I felt you pass by. It is terrifying to see. Your enemy can stand no chance when you do such a thing. They cannot even see you move. I saw nothing and have been watching for it since it happened in the cavern under Tazammor Mountain. It must be what Giddeon meant by you shadow-walking, though it is clearly not the same spell used by ancient assassins. These are terrifying powers, Kael. Your mind control of Grodin is another of these ghastly magics your kind are feared for. There is a very good reason for this fear, and I am sorry for that, because you are not the DeathWizard from legends." He could see her watching closely from across the fire and knew his face was a mask of dark thoughts and fears, but he had nothing to offer her. Finally, her eyes shifted back out into the night as a sound echoed from somewhere in the forest.

"It hardly matters what people think of me now, I guess," he whispered, curling his right hand around the engraved handle from one of the strange weapons they found far below Arkum Zul, should the noise in the forest become a threat.

When Kyah clucked her tongue and shook her head, he relaxed. "Maybe we'll find some answers in the mountains. Ones that don't involve the twisted beliefs based on the Dead Sisters' reverence of my kind or the paranoid solution of death sentences handed out by everyone else."

Kyah smiled as she glanced back over her shoulder. "Perhaps. I certainly hope so. But for now, sleep well. I will wake you in four hours."

Kael was finally able to sleep, his dreams plagued with images of shadow-walking assassins. Of killing and tearing innocent people limb from limb. Deep within the dreamworld, it warmed his soul with a morbid excitement. The terror of it shook him from sleep kicking and screaming. Kyah was at his side before he understood he just woke from a dream.

"Calm, Kael. Breathe, listen to me all right."

"Aw, Christ," he sighed.

"Nightmares again?" He nodded as she held him tight.

"They won't stop. I'm afraid to sleep, but I'm so tired all the time."

"I know, love. Relax. Breathe and close your eyes." He did as she asked, forcing himself to calm down and relax. Minutes passed and he felt himself slipping back into the realm of nightmares. His heart jumped, beating faster as adrenaline flooded his body once more. He heard Kyah's voice as if it were a mile away.

"Easy, my love. Relax. Just breathe." His body calmed as her voice finally reached him. A soft musical hum followed her gentle words, and it took several seconds before he realized it was her. His body relaxed further, and he felt sleep edge closer. Words slowly mixed with the gentle hum as he felt her stroke his hair.

"*Kaisaney Savanomin,*" she whispered within her humming as her eyes flared with power, lighting the cave in a silver glow.

Kael eased into a restful sleep for the first time since he woke in Talohna almost six months ago.

Chapter Eight

"For several thousand years now, when I have found the time, I have searched for the mythical blades forged for the strongest of DeathWizards to wield. Few of the Guardian Pact remain, and though I was present during the creation of our kind, my DeathWizard was not strong enough to handle the mighty weapons. None of them were, and they were granted to those who helped create them. They were tasked with hiding them from the world until a true Kai'Sar was born and the weapons accepted him or her as their owner.

Forged in the fire's of Pantheon Island, the double-bladed scythes can only be mastered by the strongest wizards with two crua. The depth of the weapon's powers is not known, and although only a true Kai'Sar can unlock their full potential, this will likely never happen. The DeathWizard's true magic has always been broken. It will remain broken forever. Lost long before the Battle of Six, the Vai'Karth haven't been seen in many millennia. My new DeathWizard has tasked me with finding them in the hopes they can be used to grant her the full power of her birthright."

Author and date unknown From pages found in the Library of the Arcane, in DormaSai in 5006pc

WILDLANDS NORTHERN FOREST

The main tribe of the Taktala headed just west of due north, travelling by horseback for two days before stopping and setting up their full main camp. Ember and Yrlissa had become fully integrated into the tribe's daily routine. They were both helping the other slaves now when the chief's daughter, Nyrta, had no real need for them. The novelty of something new had worn off. Yrlissa had been sent to help with washing clothes in the small river that ran past the camp, less than a hundred yards downstream from the main camp. Ember was with the younger slaves, who did the majority of the communal meal preparation. Both women were still being watched at all times.

With Takma away escorting friends of the tribe, his second, Nohkta, was the acting Bala. Ember had come to learn that a Bala was a type of war leader, and in times of peace, a lead hunter and tracker. Her understanding of the language was getting more complete every day.

Around camp, Takma always had a smile or a nod for any slave he crossed paths with, but Nohkta was a very different man. He never took his eyes off Ember or Yrlissa when he was in camp and always had a guard watching over them both. When the tribe had been threatened by a large pack of hungry Wildland wolves the night before their arrival at the new camp sight, the guards used sleep darts on both women instead of risking their escape in the confusion. Nyrta told Ember those orders came from Nohkta, and until Bala Takma returned, any risk of their flight would be handled the same way. It made for a long day suffering the side effect of a day-long headache that always followed being darted.

The second morning after arriving at the Taktala's new site, Ember could see that Bala Nohkta was in an extremely irritated mood. It didn't take her long to understand that one of his scouts had not reported in yet, and a second scout told him about sighting a young northern couple in the forest, whom he could not follow or keep track of, only getting a glimpse here and there. Nohkta was livid that a scout had lost track of two people in their own forest.

As far as Ember could tell, it was unheard of and the backhand to the mouth the scout received let the whole camp know it was unacceptable.

As the acting Bala, the camp's safety was Nohkta's sole responsibility. Ember smiled as he accused his scouts of getting into the ta-sor. The fermented alcohol often made men see things when they had drunk too much of it. Ember knew that with Takma away, the scout who had not checked in yet would wish he had stayed out in the forest to sleep off its effects, especially after Nohkta got his hands on him.

The sun had been up for an hour, the night's fast had been broken, and still the second scout had not shown up for the morning report. The other slaves warned Ember that Nohkta was on the verge of losing his dangerous temper. The scout's actions made the scout leader look like a fool in front of the whole tribe. With Chief Vattis and his two guards out hunting, the acting Bala couldn't afford to look weak in front of the tribe. Ember saw him cursing to himself as she walked his way so she put her head down, and covered by a hood, she could not see him that well. Her arms were full of pots from the meal. She never saw him coming.

Clearly in the mood to vent his anger, he gave her a good shove as she walked by. Her feet tangled together and on instinct alone, she threw her hands out to catch herself. The top pot, used to cook the porridge based meal landed upside down on his head. Slaves and tribe members alike burst out laughing as Nohkta pulled the pot from his head and swung it full force at Ember's face. Knowing it would bust her skull like a melon, she ducked, and Nohkta's follow-through tumbled him into the large central fire. Reflexes born of a lifelong warrior saved him from serious burns as he rolled through the flames and out the other side.

Ember knew it would not save her, though. Peeking out from under her hood, she swallowed hard when she saw the rage in his eyes.

It took mere seconds for Nohkta to cross back over the fire, his agile frame cleared the spit cage over the fire at the same time as Ember dropped to the ground and curled up in the foetal position with her arms around her head and face. Lost in his anger and embarrassment, he pummelled her with his fists and feet, finally stomping on her head.

Losing consciousness was not good enough, as he grabbed the metal rod for the fire's roasting spit and struck her across the back and chest with the hot metal. Ember's torn clothes smoked with each impact, flaring up and starting on fire. Four Taktala warriors jumped to restrain the scout leader, but not before several solid blows bounced off the back of her head. If she died, the elders would remove both his hands, the punishment for murdering a slave. For a warrior of Nohkta's ability, it would also be a death sentence as the tribe would carry no one. Several of the other slave girls smothered the fire and quickly dragged Ember to the tribe healer's tent in the middle of the very southern edge of the oblong circle-shaped camp used by the Taktala.

Yrlissa had been granted permission to return to the camp to see if she could help with the meal clean-up, when one of the slave girls ran to inform her of what happened. Though her magic was still restricted by the Poghana, and the tribe would not let her use it anyway, they had come to respect her knowledge of healing plants and poultices, so under heavy guard she was walked back to camp in the hopes that she could help.

"The inability to communicate has started more wars than any other misunderstanding in history. But when handled by skilled diplomats, the same can form the foundation for the strongest peace."

Dyrannai Elvehn proverb
Author and date unknown

Yrlissa entered the north end of the camp on her way to help Ember when she saw a young couple walk into the camp from the south end. From Ember's description and their many talks, she recognized the young man immediately. It was Kael. The young woman with him wore a white hood so Yrlissa couldn't see her face, but her aura was a confusing, throbbing mess of red and white. White was usually seen in a healer, but the swirling waves of red caused by hatred were never seen in any healer. With the exception of the strange throbbing pulse she'd never seen before, Yrlissa knew instantly what the colours meant. The girl was a slave, even if she was now free, the marks of hatred had eaten into her aura and marked her soul.

She quickly forgot about the strange young woman, realizing that after all this time their luck had finally turned for the better. Raising her hands, she opened her mouth to yell at Kael for help. Two feathered darts struck her throat. The immediate disorientation darkened her mind for a few seconds and she came to face first in the dirt, clawing the grass and desperately trying to scream. Her voice was paralysed by the poison's effects; only a harsh croak escaped her lips. Her legs refused to push her from the ground, so Yrlissa used her arms to push herself up against one of the tents. With every ounce of will power she possessed, she focused, slowing her heart to a dozen beats per minute in the hope she could delay the effects of the sleeping poison. Calming herself further, her pounding heart slowed to a half dozen beats. Any further and she would lose consciousness. Hopefully, it would help her remain awake long enough to see what would transpire on the camp's far side. Helplessness ate at her heart as she thought about Ember, injured inside one of the tents, only a dozen feet from where Kael stood.

Yrlissa sat back and watched as the warriors from the tribe moved to confront Kael and the young woman he was with, but she could not understand how they had just walked into the camp without the tribe being warned. It finally dawned on her fuzzy mind why the missing scout had not checked in with a report. Her lips curled into the smallest grin even though she beamed inside. The effects of the poison were spreading. Yrlissa had a clear view of Bala Nohkta as he challenged Kael. The tribal scout was over twenty feet away from the two intruders and backed by the remaining Taktala scouts and warriors.

Already clearly furious, Kael yelled at the Taktala scout leader. "We watched you beat that slave half to death. Free them all or we'll do it for you, you god damn coward!"

Yrlissa assumed he was talking about Ember, but for some reason he had not recognized her. As of late though, Ember had always been wearing her hood, her eyes had taken on a subtle glow to their bright green colouring that was getting brighter in very slow increments. It was something they all hoped was caused by her Fae magic as it increased in strength. Giddeon recommended the hood in the hopes it would hide the increased brilliance in her eyes from the Taktala. Their paranoia of northern magic could mean her life if the tribals noticed.

Nohkta, not understanding the common tongue, barked the command for his furthest men to shoot their sleep darts. The woman dodged behind Kael to shield herself from the half dozen darts that struck his neck and throat. Nohkta smiled at the successful attack. Even though the paralysis from the sleep poison was almost complete, Yrlissa still twitched with surprise when Bala Nohkta died before completing his smile. Kael had vanished, leaving behind a shadowy black haze, before reappearing twenty feet away in the blink of an eye, where he lifted Nohkta off the ground, impaled on both of his blades.

As he pulled them free from the scout leader's body, Yrlissa blinked in wonder as she recognized the weapons. The Vai'Karth reaper-blades were in Kael's hands. Her mind whirled at the revelation. The potent weapons had already begun augmenting his powers. They were weapons Yrlissa knew well. Most scholars who studied the DeathWizard's history believed them to be a pure mythical fabrication, but she knew better.

Losing her focus, Yrlissa nearly passed out. The struggle to stay awake was becoming more difficult as the poison continued its slowed migration through her blood stream. Control of her meditative state wavered. Yrlissa refocused with more determination and witnessed the outcome of the fight between the remaining twelve warriors and Kael.

She was surprised as the first to act was the woman with him. While Kael let Nokta fall to the dirt, he pulled the last few darts from his throat. It was obvious they left him with no ill effects. The woman emerged from behind Kael with a spinning, bright silver chain Yrlissa strongly suspected was made from kinrai. The small blades attached to the chain flashed, reflecting in the sunlight shining through the thick leaves of the trees. One of the tribe's scouts jumped forward to attack, and in two quick seconds, both of his arms were flayed wide open, confirming her suspicions about the metal. Yrlissa had seen such weapons before. Like most scholars who had studied the bladed chains, she believed they were Fae weapons. The long chain was full of circular, razor-sharp blades with three inch daggers at both ends and at the middle.

They were devastating and the young woman was a sight to watch as the chain spun and darted out, striking so fast the attacks were difficult to see. Another spin of the chain and one of the circular blades sliced through a warrior's throat. Blood sprayed as he crashed into the bushes to bleed out.

Though the woman fought extremely well, Yrlissa could see that the real threat to the tribesman was Kael. Black lightning from his left hand tore through two men at once while two others charged him from the opposite side. Both died at the exact same time, cut down by the scythed blade in his right hand. Refusing to stand still, three more tribesmen fell from a single swipe of the reaper-like blades as again Kael shadow-walked twice in as many seconds.

With seven of their fellow fighters dead in almost as many seconds, the other five dropped to their stomachs begging for mercy, chanting the word 'katak' and 'sarak' while on their knees prostrating. Yrlissa tried to smile as the tribe chanted the words "god of death" over and over.

Losing the fight to control the poison ravaging her senses as it forced her closer to sleep, Yrlissa continued to observe the situation at the camp's far end.

Kael pointed to one of the warriors, shouting. "If you move, you will die." Looking to his female companion, he added, "Watch them, let me know if they attack."

She nodded as he started to walk through the camp. Yrlissa could see Kael's eyes searching the camp. She hoped it was for a slave who might be capable of speaking the common language of the land. As he crossed into the north half of the Taktala camp, he saw her lying half against the tent and partly sprawled on the ground. He raced over and sat her back up against the tent's wall. Checking her for injuries, he found the two darts and yanked them out, even though it wouldn't help.

She was still conscious, though likely not for long. She ached to speak, but nothing came out, not even a gasp.

He held her face with his hands. "Do you speak the common tongue?" Yrlissa tried with all her heart, again, trying to will her voice to work, but all that came out was a small squeak followed by the slightest of nods as she tried desperately to spit the word *Ember* from her numb throat and tongue, knowing it would get his instant attention and stop him from leaving the camp.

"I'm sorry that you can't speak," Kael said. "The darts have no effect on me, but I don't know how to clear it from your system. Please, listen instead. First, this poor excuse for a Gyhhura collar must go. Be grateful. A real one is pure hell," he said, and with gentle fingers, removed the collar, tossing it far into the forest.

"If these tribesmen are like the ones we came across days ago, then you will wake long before they stop prostrating themselves against the ground. I recognize you from my dream, you were with Giddeon. We freed him and the others a couple days back, and now you are free as well. These savages call me Katak Sarak, I think that it means Death God. Should they try to stop you from leaving, then you tell them I will return. Any of the slaves who would freely go with you are welcome to. It is the best I can do for you now. We must go to the Dwarven Mountains and we have very little time to spare. I'm sorry I can't help more, but I will get Kyah to heal the woman that bastard beat. I'm sorry."

Yrlissa screamed with internal rage at her inability to do more, but the words Dwarven Mountains caused her eyes to open wider for just a second, she felt them, and Kael stared at her, as if looking for any sign that she would speak. Finally, Yrlissa could see the hope dim in his eyes, he got up and left, waving at Kyah to join him.

"Kyah, the slave that piece of sh... Check her and see if you can help her. I'll watch these animals, but at least do what you can for her." She nodded and jogged to the tent where she'd been taken.

No! Yrlissa screamed inside her head. *Go yourself! It's Ember! She's in there. You must.* A tear of frustration ran from the corner of her right eye when he refused to move, standing guard over the prostrate tribals. With a sigh, she said a silent prayer and hoped it would be enough to keep Ember alive. Kyah returned several minutes later.

Kael glared at her but said nothing. "She will live. I healed her broken ribs and stopped the bleeding inside her head and that in her lungs. Without the increase granted by... I couldn't have saved her without it..." Kyah stopped herself and glanced at the semi-conscious Yrlissa. "That poor girl would have died had we not shown up here. The rest of these tribesmen should not be allowed to live. They are slavers, just like the Dead Sisters."

"You're sure the girl we saw beaten will live?" he half asked, receiving a nod in return.

"She could use more healing over the next few days, a week even..."

"Then we've done enough," he interrupted. "It's not my place to fix everything in this world or to pass judgement on the way these people live. The useless gods from this screwed up world can do that, if they care to bother. Let's go."

Yrlissa stared after the two as both wasted no time leaving the camp. They grabbed some of the dried meat from the rack along with some bread from a nearby table and faded from her peripheral vision as they exited the camp's north end. She was heart-broken at the missed opportunity and knew Ember would be crushed. No matter what they seemed to do, they were unable to catch themselves a break.

Kael, Yrlissa was happy to see, looked more than capable of doing whatever he needed to get by, somehow even managing to find the Vai'Karth, weapons forged for his kind by unknown hands during a lost era. Not surprisingly, it seemed the Vai'Karth were created for Kael's hands alone. The time was fast approaching for her to tell Ember and Max everything she knew, yet she feared it and welcomed it with equal abandon.

The reaper-blades would continue to enhance Kael's abilities as time went on, but Yrlissa had also sensed the growing darkness within him. It would be getting stronger just as quickly as his skills were. His time in captivity had been explained in great detail by Ember when she had seen him months ago while dream-casting. It was a miracle from the gods above that the darkness hadn't taken him over completely. Few DeathWizards had ever held out against the corruption for as long as Kael had, especially under torture.

They needed to go after him as soon as it was possible for Ember to travel once more. With luck, the Taktala would no longer be a problem. Free of the Pogahna collar though, Yrlissa no longer cared if they were. There was nothing else to see and no longer any reason to fight the sleep poison's effects, so she let go of the meditative state that was keeping her somewhat lucid and slid into the dark dreamworld brought on by the sleep darts.

Kael and Kyah left the Taktala camp by the north end, passing the Taktala's horse corral. Stopping, Kael turned back to the corral.

"Are you sick of walking yet?"

"Yes, why?"

Kael pointed to the horses. "Can you ride without a saddle?"

"If it means walking no longer, I can," she smiled. As she hopped the fence into the horse pen, Kael joined her and approached a sleek, but strong looking white and brown Pinto. After sliding a set of reins over its head, he picked up another set and secured a second dark brown mare. Kyah also grabbed a second Pinto after finishing with the reins on her first. Both horses were a bit smaller than the ones he chose, but looked like good, fast mounts.

Opening the gate, they walked the horses out of the pen, jumped up and were gone from sight in a matter of seconds, with spare horses for trade when they reached Dasal.

Chapter Nine

"The prejudices in this world never cease to disgust me. Wildland Tribals beat their slaves and keep them in abhorrent living conditions. To give them credit, though, killing a slave is at least punished by removing the murderer's hands. Yet in Dasal slaves live better, but are treated horribly. They don't even have real names, just a label. I guess it's not surprising, seeing as how Talohna's last ancient slave market is located there. I hated Dasal, but the two wizards and a certain artist who live there will always have a friend in me should I survive this world for any length of time."

Kael Symes From journal pages found on the shore of the Sea of Storms during the Days of Light, 5025 PC

FREE LANDS

Thanks to the horses, it only took six days for Kael and Kyah to be within sight of the small city of Dasal. Kael could just make out the towering Dwarven Mountain Range to their left. The mountains' outline was just visible as the last rays of Talohna's third moon cast some light on the dark world before finishing its decent. With no light radiation like there was back home on Earth, Kael found the utter darkness around them unnerving, even six months after being in Talohna.

Kyah's voice jarred him back to the present as she explained that the city lay many miles into the unclaimed Free Lands of what had once been the Dwarven Kingdom countless millennia ago, and that Dasal was a small, but tough city controlled by even tougher people.

Too restless to sleep, Kael had pushed hard for Dasal. As always, Kyah gave no complaint, and they hoped to arrive by dawn. It was only an hour before sunrise, and they were still thirty minutes from Dasal's northern gate when Kael first sensed a small group of riders leave the city and head in their direction. The fact they rode straight for them in the pitch dark, suggested the group from Dasal had a wizard accompanying them.

Fifteen minutes later, the small group were close enough to make out. They called out immediately.

"Hail, riders! You approach the free city of Dasal. Please identify yourselves." Adorned in wizard's robes, the speaker held an aura of confidence that bothered Kael.

"Fair enough, riders from Dasal. Though I find it disturbing should this be the normal way you greet visitors to your fair city," Kael replied.

Again, the wizard spoke for the five riders. "I assure you that this is not a customary welcome from our city, but I must ask you to identify yourselves one more time. If you refuse, you will not be allowed entry. Our circumstances require such safety measures for the time being," he said, his tone brooking no argument.

"Fair enough, wizard. My name is Kael. This is my wife, Kyah, and we do seek entrance to your city for a day's worth of trade and rest."

The two had decided earlier fewer problems would arise if everyone in Dasal thought Kyah was Kael's wife. She had warned him Dasal paid tribute to no king. The city was located outside of the Blood Kingdoms' borders and home to the last of Talohna's old slave markets. As his wife, if someone tried to take either of them for the weekly auction, Kael and Kyah would be within their full rights to retrieve the other by any means necessary. It was rare, but such things could happen. Desperate people would often do desperate things.

None of the other riders from Dasal said a single word, but the wizard looked both Kael and Kyah up and down, immediately interested in their rugged appearance.

"If you don't mind my saying so, it looks like you and your wife have fallen on hard times; you don't look like you have much to trade, and with the problems the city is having, you will have little to benefit us."

Puzzled, Kael wasn't sure what he was getting at. "I'm sure I don't have to tell a wizard about making the mistake of judging someone by how they look do I?" Kael asked. "I've no issue with telling you the truth of our circumstances, wizard, if you would do the same," he offered.

"Forgive me, but for some reason I cannot sense anything about either of you, and that worries me. Also, I am not a novice wizard, so I would appreciate it if you quit implying that I am. Your condescending attitude does little to make me want to invite you into my city."

Vaguely remembering that Lycori had once told him that those just beginning their training were referred to simply as wizards, Kael realized he'd insulted the likely high-ranking wizard several times.

"My apologies. I meant no offence. We've been away from civilization for too long it seems."

"I understand, Kael, I do. How about we start over, and both of us be more courteous? I am Master Wizard Seifer Locke."

"It is good to meet you, Master Locke, and though I'm afraid I can do nothing that will help you sense me, as a show of faith you should be able to sense my wife now." Kael said, remembering Lycori's instructions on addressing high ranking wizards. "As for our tale," he continued, "we were shipwrecked during the storm eleven or twelve nights ago.

We lost everything but our travel packs, weapons, and a small amount of food. Trying to get out of the Wildlands was not an easy task. We had a few encounters with the tribals, but the last scuffle earned us a couple horses each. So, you see, we do have a little to trade, though not much."

"Fair enough," Seifer said. "We've had many like yourself brought to us by the wrath of the Sea of Storms over the years. It's amazing that I can now sense the magic your wife controls. How do you mask yourselves like that, young man? It is truly remarkable. A family gift?"

Kael shook his head. "No mystic reveals their closest secrets, Master Locke. You should know that by now."

"Forgive my curiosity. I meant no offence. Your wife's magic, it is mostly healing, no? That could be of help to us."

"You will be hard pressed to find a better healer."

"Good, then I will offer you the only deal I can. If you will permit us to escort you to the city watch barracks and allow a search of your person and other belongings, should we not find what we are looking for, I promise to welcome you both to our city and to offer an explanation for the added security."

Kael sighed, but had no other options. "That sounds fair. We are agreed."

Seifer held up a hand as his horse pawed at the ground and stepped sideways, sensing his rider's nervousness. "I... would also ask that you both surrender your weapons until after the search," he asked, his other hand eased onto the staff secured to the saddle.

Kael glanced over at Kyah, surprised to see her shaking her head in a persistent manner. She spoke before Kael could decide what to say. "You understand our concern. You are the last city to maintain a slave market," she pointed out.

"I do, Mistress Kyah, but I give you my word as an official member of the Eye and as one of Inara's chosen that the slave market is the furthest thing from our minds right now."

Kyah bowed. "Very well, Inari, but I promise you, there is very good reason you cannot sense my husband's power, and once unleashed, you will pay a heavy price for treachery."

"I don't take kindly to threats, young lady," Seifer warned, as the men with him reached for their weapons.

Kael smiled, raising his voice. "If your intentions are noble, then her words are not a threat, merely a friendly warning. In which case neither of us has to worry, am I right?"

The Master Wizard agreed, nodding. "Very well. Surrender your weapons and follow us. Our little city seems to be getting more interesting by the day," he chuckled, as he led the way back to Dasal.

After handing their weapons to the guards that accompanied Seifer, they all turned their mounts and headed towards the city. Kyah's new clothes from the ship no longer allowed for her to hide her kinrai chains, so they were forced to surrender them as well. As they followed the six riders, Kael glanced at Kyah and mumbled, so only she could hear.

"We need to find you something to go around your belly so those chains can be kept hidden next time, yeah?"

"I agree. You better hope he tells the truth. Most people would betray us for the amount of gold my kinrai chains would bring, let alone your blades and our flesh-weight to a slave market," she said, her tone worried. Kael nodded as they arrived at the city. The portcullis gate was already rising.

Walking their horses under the heavy gate, both were immediately surrounded by soldiers with bladed pikes. Kyah's cry of warning was seconds too late.

Kael looked at Seifer and smiled, doing his best to appear calm and in control. "I warned you about this," he said to the Master Wizard, as he tried to decide how to best push the pike-men backwards with his magic.

"Please," Locke said, "do nothing foolish. It is merely a precaution, I promise you. If you will dismount and follow me, I assure you, all of your property will be returned when we are finished, including your weapons and the four horses."

Kael glared at the Master Wizard, trying to decide if his words were true or if they should fight their way back out of the city. Again, with no other feasible options—they were severely outnumbered and no longer had their weapons—Kael smiled at Kyah, then bowed to Seifer before dismounting and following the Master Wizard on foot.

Seifer led them away from the gate, heading right and into the building used by the gate's watchmen. As he walked, he explained how twenty guards patrolled the area in and around the heavy iron gate during all hours of the day and night. Still in the barracks, they passed through the mess area where three dozen men had gathered to break the night's fast, served by men and women dressed in grey from clay bowls heaped with spiced, scrambled eggs and fried root mash. Kael's stomach did a back flip at the smell of real food, growling loud enough for Seifer to hear.

The Master Wizard smiled, almost laughing. "Fallen on hard times for some while, young man?"

"Yeah, stale bread and dried meat gets old pretty fast," Kael replied. Kyah's stomach rumbled at his words as if to agree.

"I understand all too well. Once we're done, if everything goes well, we'll see about getting you both some decent food."

"Our thanks," Kyah said, as Seifer led them into his private office. The Master Wizard worked side by side with the guard captain when it came to the city's defences, and both of the large offices were located at the barrack's far end. The five guards that followed them through the building entered the office, closed the door and spread out behind Kael and Kyah. With hands wrapped around their sword handles, all were ready for trouble.

Seifer stared at Kael uneasily and raised his hands. "I do apologize for the search of your belongings and that of your person, but we are looking for something very distinct. If you could both please remove your clothes, we can begin. If you are wearing underclothes, you do not have to remove them."

"I'll go first," Kael offered, in the hopes his scarred and adorned skin would take some of the prying eyes from Kyah. As he was still shirtless, the moment he removed his Orotaq cloak, Seifer and the five guards with him gasped at the myriad of healed scar tissue and the tattoo-like ornate vines and wicked thorns that had magically grown across Kael's skin in the past months. Not hesitating and with little sense of pride remaining after his tenure in Arkum Zul's prison, he quickly removed his leather pants as well and covered his privates as best he could, seeing as his underwear had also fallen apart long ago.

"Heavens of Paradise, you have seen some battles, young man and where did you have that tattooing done?" Seifer asked, as he moved closer for a better look. The death-flower over his heart hadn't changed since it appeared so many months ago, but the twisting black vines and cruel-looking thorns continued to spread out over his body. "I thought only people far to the south, in Salzara, had such intricate work like that. It's amazing. If I were to touch your skin, I'd almost expect to feel the vines underneath your flesh," he added, clearly impressed.

"You'd never believe me if I told you," Kael stated.

Seifer stared into his eyes. "Somehow, I believe you."

"Do you see what you're looking for?" Kael asked, shaking his head.

"No, and your wife doesn't have to remove her clothes. Neither of you are pirates, that's quite clear. We were looking for the Suns of Blood pirate tattoo. I apologize again for having to be sure," he said, as Kael finished dressing.

"Please, both of you have a seat, and I'll explain *our* predicament." He chuckled, as he used the term Kael had used earlier when explaining where he and Kyah came from. "We've been under threat of a pirate attack for three days now. The Suns of Blood have demanded entry to our city so they can look for people whom they have an interest in, but we don't allow known pirates within the city walls. If we haven't granted them permission to enter the city and search for those they're looking for by dusk this day, they say they'll enter the city using force," Seifer explained.

"Do you think they will actually attack if the deadline passes?" Kael enquired.

"I fully expect the attack to come by noon today. Their captain has a reputation, and he'll try to surprise us, I'm sure."

Kael stopped to think for a minute, giving Kyah the chance to speak. "Master Seifer, do you know the name of this captain and his reputation?"

"Yes, Mistress, as far as we know, Captain BlackSpawn isn't here. It's his second, Captain Dominique Havarrow. He's a Salzaran-based pirate, and most say even more savage than Blackspawn. Rumour has it, he's a Northman, but he doesn't have the patience of one."

"Since when do pirate ships have two captains?" Kael interrupted, confused and naive as always.

Seifer stared at Kael as if he'd spent all twenty years of his life on one of the moons. "The Suns of Blood are a pirate armada. They have at least thirty ships, probably more, a lot more. Bauro BlackSpawn united most of the pirate factions in both kingdoms under his flag many years ago. Every ship has its own captain, but they all follow and do as he says, making him an admiral, though he's yet to claim that title."

Rolling his eyes and shaking his head, Kael struggled to understand how any criminal would ever be allowed to gain such power, in any world. The he remembered the mess Sam's Bay was in when he and Ember had first arrived so many years ago. Biker gangs topped the criminal tier with several mafia families controlling the middle of the ladder, but it was the street gangs who ruled every day life in Sam's

Bay. Until Max's Sheriff's Department with help from a cross-state multi-agency task force brought it all down—bikers, mafia, and street gangs.

Kael shook his head a second time, returning to reality. "How many ships and men are in your harbour now?" he asked.

"He thinks to fool us, I believe, because there are only two ships in the harbour, but five more are only ten minutes north, hidden in a small cove."

"Is there any chance he would talk with me, do you think?" Kael asked, a plan starting to grow in his mind.

Seifer shrugged. "He has a rowboat waiting for a city representative to be brought out with an answer. If you have any ideas, there is still time for us to speak with the city leaders; they may let you go in their man's stead."

Kael nodded at the information, his idea growing further. "Master Locke, I'll make you an offer. My wife and I will talk to this pirate and see exactly what he wants, if you allow my wife and I some time with your local tailor and a hot bath at the inn. Even a greasy pirate would take us for beggars right now." Kael chuckled even as he wondered if getting involved in a city siege was perhaps not the smartest thing to do.

"Why would you risk your life for us like that? What would you hope to gain?" he asked.

Kyah was the one to answer. "We are here now, Master Seifer. You allowed us entry when most would have not. We are sore and tired, and you cannot begin to imagine the road we have travelled. If we can help, we would only ask to be allowed to stay in Dasal while we recover from our journey, along with that hot bath and a change of clothes." She smiled, making Seifer smile in return. She added, "A city under siege is not a good place to rest, so let us help prevent it."

"It's worth a try. I'll send my apprentice to the tailor and then on to the inn. I would recommend seeing the tailor first, in case he needs to alter what you purchase. All the charges will be forwarded to myself for now. We can settle up after we know how things turn out. Worst case scenario, I can always use a new horse," he added still smiling. "Should we all not die under a pirate's blade that is."

True to his word, Seifer had the guards return Kael and Kyah's weapons before he took them to their horses and offered the use of the city guard stables. They left their mounts in good hands and headed for the local tailor. The sun had just risen when they arrived, but the seamstress and several apprentices were already hard at work. The tailor himself arrived right after, having been held up at home by Seifer's apprentice.

Kyah bought a second outfit, a woollen shirt with a hood and a pair of light brown, soft leather pants that would be warmer than what she currently wore. A pair of knee-length boots finished her purchases. Kael managed to find a pair of black, soft leather pants that the seamstress altered while they waited. He added a full-length cloth shirt, as well as a heavier one made from wool that was similar to the one Kyah chose.

The tailor offered to have the Orotaq cloaks cleaned, a part of his business that his teenage daughters took care of.

Knowing they'd be heading into the mountains before long, Kael nodded at the tailor. "Could you add a heavy, lined hood to each of the cloaks?" he asked.

"Yes, master," the tailor agreed. "I will also repair the lengths of leather that I assume you've been using for masks?"

"Yes, thank you," Kael said, and smiled at the older man. His personality was a refreshing change from psychotic witches and arrogant wizards. The tailor promised the repairs and alterations would be done later in the day, so Kyah asked for them to be sent to the inn. The old man nodded as they left, already busy giving orders to several apprentices to make the changes before handing the cloaks off to the seamstress and her helpers.

Kael and Kyah arrived at the two-storey inn to find that a room had been set aside for them already, thanks to

Master Locke's young apprentice. They were shown to their room on the second floor by a young girl no older than twelve.

"You may call me, Sani, Master, Mistress. Should you need anything during your stay, please ask for me, the hour is not important."

"Sani?" Kyah said, with a strange look on her face. "You are a slave then?"

"Yes, mistress. You are correct." Kael glanced at Kyah, unsure of how she knew.

"Sani is an old Dwarven word for slave. I have never heard it used before."

"It is used here often, Mistress," the young girl offered, bowing. "I hope it does not offend. If so, you may call me whatever..."

Kyah shook her head. "No, dear, it is fine. Do not worry. I promise you, no trouble will come from us, especially for you."

The young girl bowed again. "Thank you, Mistress. Please, let me show you the room that was reserved for you." Kyah smiled and gestured for her to lead the way, but her eyes bored into Kael's. He hoped the city's policy on slavery wouldn't get them into trouble. Kyah's temper towards slavers had become worse of late, something he contributed to her own first tastes of freedom.

Their room was one of the three largest suites in what was clearly the city's most prestigious inn. Their room, situated along the inn's front-facing side, also had a balcony large enough to hold a round table and two chairs. The view of the harbour was incredible. Since the sun had been up for less than an hour, an abundance of rays and colours glistened off the rippling waters of Fang Bay, even though the glare blinded them to the rest of the shore and docks.

After the long, cool night, entering the room with a large stone fireplace blazing, Kael almost succumbed to the warmth and the sight of a real queen sized bed that sat to the left of the door. The balcony doors beyond the bed allowed for the spectacular view of the harbour down the hill and beyond the city even when laying in the bed. The bath however, quickly caught his eye and overruled the need for sleep. A permanent part of the room, it was built into the wall on his right. Made from stone tiles the size of his hand, it was three feet deep and close to six feet in length. Over four feet wide, one could stretch out easily and relax, and there would still be room for another in the bath. Kael noticed a single lever on the tub's ledge, but could see no taps or spout to fill the large tub.

Noticing his confusion, the young slave approached and turned the handle. "The water comes from a deep well of hot springs, Master, far below the surface. All you do is let it fill," she said, bending over and placing a heavy yellow sponge in the drain hole at the tub's far end. Kael smiled with awe as air gurgled from inside six small holes spaced along the tub's outer edge on the wall opposite of where he stood. After a few seconds, water poured from the holes and began to fill the tub with water.

"It's warm." Running his fingers through the steaming water, he laughed. "God in heaven. It's almost hot. Hot running water." He sighed as steam rose from the bath.

"Yes, Master," the girl said. "We try to offer only the best to travellers here." It only took fifteen minutes to have the bath nearly full. Sani showed them where the towels were stored—in a cupboard to the left of the tub, and then showed them how to operate the dumb-waiter chute used to bring firewood up to their suite without actually having to leave the room. Once finished, the young girl stood by the door and waited. Kael rummaged through his travel pack until he found the small pouch of coins and gems from Jasala's tower.

Removing a small nugget of raw gold, he handed it to Sani. "You may go, if we need anything we'll let you know. Thank you, Sani, for everything." The girl beamed a bright smile, turned and dashed from the room, excitement overruling proper etiquette.

Chuckling, Kael closed the door and turned back into the room. "You can have the bath first, if you like."

Kyah declined. "Go ahead. I want to brush out my hair. Seifer's apprentice made sure we have a brush and a comb. A straight razor is on the nightstand as well. We should both clean up in case the city wants us to try speaking with the pirates anchored in the bay."

It was a good thing. He had not shaved since arriving in Talohna, and though his hair was more manageable since Kyah rolled and braided it, it still hung past his shoulders, much longer than he had ever worn it back home. Kael debated shaving and cutting his hair but shook his head and headed for the bath. Five months without a real bath was just too long.

Once undressed, the cloying stench of his own body nearly knocked him over. Gagging, he coughed. "Ah, damn, I can't believe I smell that bad. It's only been a week or so since the hot spring," he said, more to himself than to Kyah. She smiled in the mirror as she brushed out her hair, which was now well past the length of her own shoulders.

"You are always complaining about how bad you smell," she chuckled. "You act like people bathed every day where you come from."

"Yeah, that's because we do, or did... You know what I mean," he replied, shaking his head again before throwing his clothes as far away as he could get them. Kyah laughed harder and returned to brushing her hair, though he noticed her eyes never left his reflection in the mirror.

It was something Kael still found hard to deal with, the first few weeks inside the cells as a prisoner of the Dead Sisters, the stench nearly drove him insane on its own. Over the months that changed, until his senses were deadened by the overpowering odours from the cells, but free again, his nose was slowly returning to normal.

"I think you mentioned before that people bathe daily where you are from, but I still find it hard to believe," she added, combing through her hair.

Kael finally climbed into the hot water, the first real bath he had been able to have in over five gruelling long months—it was like sliding through the front doors of heaven, ambrosia for his body.

"I didn't think anything could feel this good," he mumbled and closed his eyes, asleep before he could take a full breath. A splash and movement woke him and he opened his eyes to find a naked, smiling woman sitting comfortably in his lap.

"What exactly do you think you are doing?" he asked, though he already knew.

Kyah's slight smile grew even wider. "I thought maybe it would save time if I joined you," she lied, trying to be sly.

"Oh, you did, did you?" Kael asked, as he stifled a yawn, still exhausted from another night of no sleep.

"I was hoping you would wash my back for me," she suggested, as she turned around in the large tub and lay back against his chest. She took his hand, and placed a square of soap in his palm before she slowly placed both on her belly.

"That's, ah, not your back," Kael stammered. Sliding her hand on top of his, she used it to guide the soap up the delicate skin of her stomach to between her breasts.

"Mhm. I do not mind. Do you?" Kael felt his face flush red.

That familiar feeling of helplessness he had felt on the boat before the storm, hit him again, and he knew there was no way he'd be able to resist her.

"Why do I have a hard time saying no to you?" he asked, as his heart raced with desire. She turned around and slid up his chest until she was face-to-face with him. An all too familiar feeling rose to the surface between them.

She caressed his cheek, kissing him. "Maybe somewhere in there," she said, trailing her finger over the death-flower markings above his heart, "you love me the littlest bit. You must be lonely, and I am falling in love with you more every day. I am here, now, right now, and I will never leave you. We were both so tired on the ship, I remember very little. Be with me now, love me now, so we both remember." She climbed back onto his lap as the last of his willpower faded away.

Kael knew part of what she said was right. Though racked with guilt, he didn't want her to stop. He wanted to feel something. Feel anything that was not guilt, regret or pain. The feelings he had for her had begun months ago, though he tried hard to ignore them. The dream with Ember had silenced them for a while, but they had started to return again only days before arriving in Dasal.

Kael gasped as he felt their bodies come together, and his thoughts scattered, replaced by need and desire. He wrapped his arms around her and pulled her close as he eased into her warmth. Kyah leaned forward and kissed him softly as she rocked back and forth in his lap. It was different this time, not urgent and needful like on the ship sailing across the Sea of Storms.

Their pace remained slow and his hands roamed across her body exploring, until his right settled on her hip and he used it to slow her movements further. The fingers of his left hand teased its way to her breasts. Soft like a feather, he tickled, squeezed and pulled gently as she sighed. Time seemed to stand still as Kael lost himself in feelings and emotions that brought no pain and carried no suffering.

Kyah pulled him closer, nuzzling into his neck. Her own moans of pleasure brought him to the brink of ecstasy and then over as they held each other tight and finished as one. Kyah relaxed into his body and he could feel her muscles trembling. He wrapped his arms around her and realized he was shaking as well. Neither said anything, instead enjoyed the glow as they relaxed in the warm water.

Someone banged on the door to their room and entered without their consent. Kyah jumped from the bath, her chains already in hand, as she prepared for an attack.

Instead, a young woman blushed bright red and apologized. "Oh, Blessed Inara, I am so, so sorry. I didn't realize you were back yet. I'm so humiliated, please forgive my rudeness," she begged. Kyah grabbed a towel from the table and tossed it to Kael, but stood there stark naked, inducing even more embarrassment in the young girl as she finally spun on her heel. Turning her back, she looked out the balcony doors.

Refusing to even look over her shoulder as she spoke, the young woman shook her head. "Please forgive me, Mistress, my name is Kittrix Dawn, or Kit if you please. I am Master Seifer's apprentice. He asked that I wait for you in your room so that I may bring you to the city leaders the moment you both returned. The city council wishes to speak with you now."

"Very well, Kit," Kyah acknowledged. "Let us dress and then we will follow you."

Turning back around, a new shade of red brightened her cheeks as Kit stuttered. "T...Thank-you... Mistre..." She stopped in mid-sentence. Kael had only managed to get his new pants on and the young apprentice was unable to take her eyes from the black vine and barbed thorn markings that covered his back, chest, arms, and neck.

Realizing that she was staring, she bowed to a knee. "Please forgive me, Master. I was told of your markings, but I didn't understand. I apologize for my poor manners once more, please forgive me."

Kael walked over and took her gently by the arm. "Get up. They're just tattoos. You have nothing to be sorry for. Now take us to the meeting." He grabbed his new shirt before walking out the door.

Kyah, after giving Kael a wink, took Kit's arm and smiled at her.

"Worry not, Kit, most young women look at him that way, the first time. They cannot decide whether to run or whether to chase." She snickered and soon both young women were laughing as they started down the stairs.

Chapter Ten

"Illusion magic is one of the few practices of magic rarely studied. Those who have sought to perfect their skills in this discipline quickly learn that the greatest illusionists can fool even the most alert minds, whether or not they actually use magic."

Kamen Astrick, Cethosian Wizard's Council Representative
4918 PC

DASAL, FREE LANDS

It took only minutes to cross the market square and arrive at the city guard barracks, where they were to meet the city leaders in the dining hall. Seifer and Jarvis Kern, the city watch Captain, were already present. As were the city council members.

Kit started the introductions with a well-muscled, bronze-skinned man with long, braided black hair.

"Kael, Kyah, this is Salisar Pollondo, a Salzaran merchant who controls most of Dasal's import and export businesses. He is a businessman, who, until the last few years, spent most of his life on the ocean with his ships."

Kael nodded and shook the man's hand when he offered it, remembering that Southern Kingdom citizens did not shake arms at the elbow. Wealth dripped off the man like a physical attribute. Gemstone earrings, several in each ear, and numerous chains hung around his neck, one with veins of orange and purple blazed with brilliance. Kael recognized the metal immediately. It was kinrai, the steel of the gods. The chain stood out above all the others as an excessive showcase of wealth. The fingers on both of the man's hands were adorned with gold and silver rings, all embedded with large gems. Kael was shocked the man could even walk under all the weight and chuckled to himself, thinking the weight contributed to the merchant's impressive physique. As it seemed to be the custom, Kael bowed to Pollondo after shaking hands, and Kyah quickly did the same, getting a nod in return as Kit approached a smaller built man dressed in flowing, exotic robes.

"Kael, Kyah," she began. "Please meet Lircang Yorcali. Before moving here many years ago, he lived in the Southern Kingdom country of Kariya. He is owner of the local gentleman's clubs and the inn you're staying at, as well as being the co-owner of Dasal's slave market and auction."

Kael took an instant dislike to the overweight little bald man. He had sleaze ball written all over him, from his expensive silk robes to his lecherous smile and fancy carved bone pipe. The heavy, rancid smoke that curled up from the bowl was the worst smelling weed Kael ever had the displeasure of having to endure, but the noxious stench of cheesy, fat ass that swarmed the man deadened the pipe's odour as he approached and shook Kael's hand. A prominent Adam's apple jiggled in his throat even though the man didn't speak. Kael realized that on Earth, Lircang would be from Asian descent, but on Talohna, his people were from Kariya.

He remembered Lycori telling him the country was the home of mercenaries who were trained from birth, and when ready, were always auctioned off to the highest bidder. These men and women were loyal to the point of death once the sale was contracted, whether the death was their own or their employer's. For all intents and purposes, Kael believed it was just another form of slavery. Kariya had no king or emperor. Instead, a council made up of representatives from the one hundred training schools ruled the country by committee. Kariyan parents literally bred children to sell to the school for a living. Mercenaries were Kariya's only real natural resource Lycori had joked once. He shook his head in disgust that such people could even exist.

Kit introduced an older woman last and Kael wrangled his wandering mind.

"This is Nessedra Vantaur, our Elvehn mystic and scholar. She is originally from the city of Kyll'Darhen in the Elvehn country of TaCeryss, but now she owns the financial institution here in Dasal. She has a reputation throughout the Free Lands as a fair woman."

Kael nodded. "Mistress Vantaur." His respectful reply earned him a generous bow from the powerful woman. Nessedra reminded him of a strong businesswoman from back on Earth. Considering she owned the bank in Dasal, it made sense. He found himself admiring her even more as he noticed the woman's strong dislike of Lircang Yorcali. It hung in the air between the two like the rancid stench of fat ass permeating the chubby man, and it solidified Kael's own first impression of the man.

Kit introduced them last. "Everyone, this is Kael and Kyah. They arrived this morning and have offered to help with our pirate situation."

Kit took a seat beside Seifer when he stood to speak. "Now that you have met the city leaders, we would all like to know what you think might be gained by sending you to speak with Captain Havarrow?" Though Kael hadn't been in Talohna for very long, he was starting to understand how things worked, and felt it was only fair to warn them.

"If you send someone from the city, my guess would be that you get that person back in pieces, unless you plan to give Havarrow what he wants?" he asked.

Salisar spoke first, and Kael wasn't surprised by the boast. "We plan to do no such thing, young man. The Suns of Blood will pay heavily for even trying to enter this city."

Kael smiled and nodded as if agreeing with his assessment. "Then it harms no one for us to go see *why* he wants into the city. There has to be a reason. These pirates don't normally threaten cities, do they?" Kael asked, hoping to gain some practical knowledge of the pirates.

"You are correct in your assumption," Lircang Yorcali offered. "But you will likely be killed should you wish to speak with him on his ship. I believe it is a bad idea. He most likely bluffs. Only a fool would enter this city by force. I vote we wait, no more, no less. It would be a waste of such delicacy and beauty if your wife was harmed while on that ship. Why not let the guards deal with the ocean scum, and you and your wife come enjoy the pleasures of my establishments instead?" A violent desire to choke the sweating, funk-ridden fool surged through Kael, but he didn't need Kyah's hand squeezing his own to know that he was being tested.

"Perhaps we will take you up on your offer later, Master Yorcali, but for now we should discuss whether you would like our help," Kael said, as politely as he could muster, swallowing the urge to do bodily harm to the slave master.

Yorcali's lecherous smile returned. "If that is the case," he said, licking his swollen, greasy lips and eyeing Kyah up and down, "then you have my vote to put an end to these threats as soon as possible so that you may join me at my club."

Again, thanks to his extreme lack of knowledge, Kael had no idea what had just occurred, but soon figured it out when Seifer gave Lircang a strict warning. "These people are our guests, Lircang. I expect you treat them as such."

"Oh, fear not, wizard. We have our hands full with the postponement of the auction yesterday. I was only having some amusement at the young couple's expense," Lircang said, smiling as he waved his heavy pipe around in the air, spreading more of the vile stink through the room, both his own and the pipe's.

Nessedra Vantaur clearly heard all she was willing to listen to, bringing everyone back to the topic at hand. "Would it not make more sense to decide whether this young couple will speak on our behalf as opposed to listening to Yorcali's disgusting deprivations?" she advised. Lircang snickered, blowing her a kiss as he rubbed his crotch. Kael checked their dislike away for later when it might come in handy.

Nessedra shook her head as she frowned at Kael. "One must learn to ignore the stench and sounds a pig makes if one wishes to keep them around for their few benefits, and then remember such things when the butcher's hammer falls. I'm afraid the same applies to Mister Yorcali, Kael. Now, to the matter at hand, do you believe the pirate may talk to you? I would hate to send you and your wife to your deaths on our behalf, though you may convince the pirate you're a Northman long enough to get him to talk."

"I assure you, Mistress Vantaur, my wife and I can handle ourselves if need be. I don't think they want to attack your city or they would have already. Maybe we can at the least get a couple extra days for you to prepare for the fighting, and with luck, maybe even find out exactly who or what he wants, preventing an attack all together," Kael offered.

Jarvis Kern, the city watch guard captain spoke for the first time. "I believe it may be worth the try," he said, more to the city leaders, before turning his attention to Kael. "If you succeed, though, you must return to us here with the names of the men he wants. We cannot allow you to grab them and turn them over to Havarrow if they are respected members of the city, you understand."

"Of course," Kael agreed. "If you like, and he doesn't try to kill us, we'll return here first with what information we gather," he agreed.

The others deferred to Seifer Locke.

Nodding, the Master Wizard agreed as well. "Kael, you have our permission to try. At least it may save the life of the representative who was chosen to go at noon. Come, I'll walk you out and show you where Havarrow's rowboat and man are waiting."

As they left the dining hall and entered the front of the barracks, Seifer looked around. When it was clear no one was close by, he touched Kael's arm to get his attention. "I wanted to walk you out, to make you aware of what Lircang Yorcali was up to in there. You were informed that he is the proprietor of both the local entertainment dens and co-owner of the slave market?" he asked, still looking around for prying eyes.

"I'm well aware. Why?" Kael asked, the hairs on the back of his neck tingling.

"Be careful, both of you. Lircang seems to have an unhealthy interest in Kyah. I've never been able to prove it, but it would not be the first time a young couple disappeared in this city after Lircang Yorcali expressed an infatuation in someone. I can warn you both, but proof is something Yorcali hides too well," he explained.

"Thank you for the warning," Kael whispered. "My wife and I are often unaware of the intentions of others; having both been raised in seclusion, we sometimes miss the subtle hints others are aware of. I do promise you, Master Wizard, that we can defend ourselves, much better than most."

He hoped his explanation would cover some of the suspicions he knew Seifer was having. Most of those questions likely rose from their lack of knowledge about Talohna and their shallow etiquette when dealing with city officials.

They followed Seifer through one of the city's smaller markets closer to the docks. An artist on the end of one of the aisles was opening for the day, giving Kael an idea. "Master Locke," he said. "I've an idea that may help us. Do you have a couple of silver or gold coins on you?"

"Yes, why?"

"Follow me. Kyah, this way," he whispered, as he headed for the artist's tented market stall. Seifer said nothing as he followed, a frown of confusion on his face.

The artist had no customers at such an early hour, but was cleaning brushes and preparing for the day when they arrived.

"Excuse me, sir," Kael said, addressing the young man. "Do you speak the common tongue?"

"I do, Master," he said, bowing. "How may I be of assistance? A portrait for your beautiful lady, or perhaps a sculpture instead?"

Kael smiled at the sales pitch. "No, but I do have an offer for you," he began. "I want to borrow your finest brush, some black paint and the privacy of your closed tent. I'll pay you two gold pieces," he said, looking at Seifer. "Is that fair?"

The Master Wizard rolled his eyes and leaned into Kael's side, whispering, "Ridiculously fair, unless you're planning to kill him afterwards."

"God, no," Kael sputtered. "What the hell is wrong with you? Ugh... Never mind." He turned back to the artist. "Two gold, and we'll be done and gone in thirty minutes. Deal?"

"For two gold pieces, Master, you can use my belongings all day, thank you. Thank you so much more than you know," he replied, overly excited. He was already collecting the things Kael asked for when Kyah finally figured out what he was up to.

"You are going to try and bluff the pirates. Are you not? It is a good idea," she said, smiling. "I will describe to you the symbols used by many witches. They will not harm us if they believe your wife is a witch. So long as they do not kill us the moment we step aboard. Very clever, my dear." She chuckled.

Seifer didn't agree. "You two are crazy. You walk on to Havarrow's vessel with a witch, Kael, even a fake one, and he'll kill you both. Slowly."

Kael shook his head. "I don't think so, Seifer... Sorry, Master Locke. He wants something or someone in this town bad enough to threaten invasion. If we offer to bring him what he wants and have the capability to actually do it, it'll save the lives of his men. He might not be happy about it, but he won't kill us."

"That's a big gamble."

"I don't think so. If I'm wrong, we'll have to fight our way out, and the city will be dealing with the invasion anyway," Kael said.

The artist introduced himself as Tavin as he entered the tent and closed the flaps, handing Kael the paint and brushes he had asked for. He bowed as Seifer gave him his two gold, and left the tent with a second bow and numerous thank-yous.

Seifer shook his head and rubbed his neck. "You know that artist probably makes less than that in several years worth of legitimate work."

"If it stops a pirate invasion, it'll be worth it," Kael mumbled. He shrugged as Kyah sat down on a chair and told him what demonic markings to paint on her face.

The most important design was one he had seen many times before. Tattooed on the throat of nearly every Dead Sister he had ever met, he replicated the symbol for a KiPara demon, the four-horned, monstrous guardians of the ninth and deepest level of hell. Most witches worshipped at least one demon and some were even granted their magic, as Arabella had been, in order to use it on Kael during his internment inside Arkum Zul.

He began by painting a solid black pentagram on her throat, followed by what looked like a double-ended, three-pronged pitchfork that ran through the pentagram from top to bottom. Then, through the centre from left to right and right to left, he painted two hanging capitol letter 'T's. Back on Earth it was called a Gothic cross.

Next, he painted her face, from the centre of her forehead down over her right eye and all the way around to her cheekbone to the corner of her mouth. The design itself resembled the vertebrae and ribs of a snake, the ribs flaring out from the corner of her eye. On the left side of her forehead and face, Kyah had him paint several demonic symbols representing creatures witches would often summon from the underworld, familiars or bottom-dwelling demons. When magically tattooed on a real witch's face, Kael knew the actual summoning was completed simply by touching the symbol and calling the creature's name. The more symbols a witch had tattooed on her face and body meant the more creatures she could summon at one time or the more demon favours or power she had procured. The average witch had two. They agreed to put three on Kyah; any more might be unbelievable.

It took a half hour for Kael to complete the designs and for them to finish drying. Tavin's finest brush allowed for an amazing amount of detail, so it took a little longer than Kael had hoped. Once the paint dried, Kyah pulled her hood up, covering her face. They thanked Tavin and followed Seifer to the docks. After he pointed out where the boat was docked, Seifer returned to the barracks so he was not seen with them.

"What's the best way to handle this, do you think?" Kael asked, taking a last check of Kyah's painted face.

"You must do most of the talking. I will keep my hood up and my head down until needed. Please, love, show them no fear. These are hard men and fooling them will not be easy. Tell them the truth of what you are. They respect power, even if it is magical, and nothing else. I know not what else to offer for advice. For most of my life, I have been out in the world very little, and what I know is from books and lessons the Sisters gave us." Feeling her touch on his arm, he turned to face her and she kissed his cheek. Kael smiled, nodding as she took his arm and they walked down the docks where one of Captain Havarrow's personal body guards would row them out to his ship, the Twilight Reave.

Chapter Eleven

"The gift of magic still holds many secrets. Perhaps more so since the Cataclysm triggered by Jasala Vyshaan's death. Granted, the world no longer looks as it did, and magic has suffered greatly because of it, but there are still many secrets to discover for those who know where to look."

Kalmar Ibess
4818PC

WILDLANDS FOREST

Giddeon regained consciousness just before dawn the day after Kael and Kyah freed them from the Taktala. Saleece had woken up an hour earlier and had been at his side from the moment she could stand. Kasik was also up and moving around, trying to quickly remove the after effects of the sleep dart's poison. Max had been awake for hours, having not been given a dart by Kyah because he was already unconscious from the beating he had received from Grodin and his men. Grodin himself was nowhere to be found. Even after Kael left, the little man had not returned, lending support to Giddeon's theory that Kael had fried his mind.

Bala Takma waited patiently just inside the tent he had given the former slaves. He had dragged both Giddeon and Saleece into the tent after Kael's departure the night before. The rest of the Taktala fled in the middle of the night, taking all the horses and most of the supplies.

Giddeon sat up, groaning as pain spiked in his neck. "How long have I been out?" he asked, eyeing Saleece.

"It's morning, Father. Kael has been gone for well over twelve, maybe thirteen hours now." Though clearly still in considerable pain, Max knelt in front of Giddeon. His bloodshot eyes bored into the ArchWizard with an intensity he had not seen in the big man since the fight in Stillwater.

"You do realize," Max began, pausing as if to collect his thoughts for a second, "that I should break your scrawny wizard neck right now? He was here, you asshole. My name. Three little letters are all it would have taken to calm Kael down and keep him here." Kasik stepped closer to the two men in preparation of yet more violence.

Max ignored him as he continued. "You have a shit-load of explaining to do about that, Giddeon. Right now. You'd better convince me that you have a goddamned good reason for letting him walk away without telling him that I was here and that Ember is still alive. His coming across us like he did was a one in a million chance opportunity."

Giddeon could sense Max's desire to do him bodily harm. "I do, Max, though I don't have to answer or explain myself to you..."

Max snatched Giddeon's robes and jerked him up off his feet, purposely applying pressure so that the collar pressed into the weeping wounds made by the Gyhurra collar, eliciting a moan.

"You fucking do now! I'm sick of your snide comments and your sanctimonious attitude.' Either you answer me, or we will see if Kasik is good enough to keep you alive, because I don't give a shit anymore. Got it, wizard?" He shook Giddeon.

"Fine!" Giddeon relented as he struggled against Max's grip. "You and Ember both need to understand that the young man you knew is gone. Last night, I watched him use dark magic to force knowledge from Grodin's mind. Kael physically forced an insidious black magic into Grodin's face until the tentacles spread through his eyes and deep into his brain. When Kael had what he wanted, he tore the magic back out, likely leaving the poor man with permanent brain damage. Grodin is probably stumbling around the forest like a simple-minded fool even now. So yes, I did tell him you both died during the crossing, Max. You will come to learn, and very soon I suspect, exactly what your friend has become. The sooner you accept it, the easier it will be for both you and Ember, if we ever manage to find them again."

Max slowly released the ArchWizard to stand on shaking legs. Max turned to leave the tent, but glanced back over his shoulder as he stepped out through the tent's flap.

"I know what my friend has become, Giddeon. He has become harder than he was, of that, I'm sure. But he has also become the only person in all of Talohna capable of removing the collars from you and your daughter's necks." Max turned back as he carried on. "The ones that drove three-inch spikes into your neck and that you and Saleece both swore you would rather be dead than spend the rest of your life wearing, remember? Oh, and so you don't conveniently forget—we are no longer slaves because of Kael. So, you're right," Max added, his voice riddled with sarcasm. "He's become a wanton destructive force for evil and doesn't deserve to live another minute."

Giddeon felt himself blush as he shied away from Max's intent stare.

"You're a fucking fool, Giddeon, if ever I have seen one. You can learn to accept that," Max said, shaking his head as he spun on his heel and the tent-flap closed.

"You need to find better arguments, Father, if you plan to convince them of what Kael has become," Saleece pointed out after Max left.

"Don't you dare start as well. How are we supposed to convince them, if you don't believe it yourself?" he scolded.

"I do believe; you know that. But you cannot deny that he is acting very differently than a DeathWizard would normally. The one we missed on Kael's day of birth was the perfect example of how they act. You remember what she did, and she was only ten. There is a reason we have kept the others secret from the common people, but they did not act as Kael has. He has harmed no one yet—besides Grodin, a man any of us would've killed given the chance," she reminded him.

"It matters little, now," Kasik added. "We know what we have to do, if we can acquire Ember and Max's help, then it would be better, yes. But for now, what do we do? Go after Princess Corleya or Kael?"

Giddeon sighed, knowing the repercussions and the affect his choice would have on both Princess Corleya and on King Bale's reign. "The princess is on her own and the Pillars will have to keep King Bale on the throne," he said. "I hate turning my back on them, but we don't have the numbers or the skills to free the princess. Even if we could find her now, the Kordanu will be heading deep into the forest south of here where more tribes will be gathering. It would take an army to free her. We might as well go after my son."

"Seeing as how we are no longer slaves, perhaps the tribesman who has been watching over us will give us horses to go after Kael," Saleece suggested.

Giddeon stood and stepped over to Takma. "You are Bala Takma right? I remember you from the peace talks years ago. You were the youngest war leader your people had. That scar on your cheek, the wound was made by my king's blade, right?" he asked as he ran his finger down his own cheek.

"Yes, Spirit-talker. Mighty warrior, your king." Bala Takma shook his head as if it were irrelevant. "Matter no. The Katak Sarak makes you free. I take to village, get your women. We walk. Others flee with high moons," he explained, and left the tent.

"Great," Giddeon said, looking at Kasik and Saleece. "I guess we're walking after all then."

It took four days for Takma to escort Giddeon's group to the new campsite the Taktala had agreed upon at the auction. Originally, Takma had been ordered to escort and provide protection for Grodin, so he was aware of both possible sites planned. They arrived the morning after Kael and Kyah had passed through the camp. A camp that was on the verge of civil war.

Chief Vattis Taktala returned from his hunting trip only a half hour before Giddeon and Takma arrived. He was not taking the idea of freed slaves very well, and he was taking the fact that his men thought it was a good idea even worse. The moment he understood what was happening, Takma left Giddeon's side and went to explain to his chief what had happened while he was gone.

Saleece noticed Yrlissa near the doorway of Nyrta's tent. The assassin looked ready to fight her way out if she had to. "Father, there's Yrlissa. Come on."

Giddeon and the others joined Yrlissa by the tent as the fighting between the chief and his men heated up even more. Bala Takma weighed his voice into the fray and the situation quickly got worse.

Yrlissa smiled as she saw the others approach. "I am very glad to see you all, but I hope you are ready to fight. Our freedom may not be earned so easily," she said, nodding towards the dispute in the middle of the camp.

Looking around Max asked, "Yrlissa... Where's Ember? What the hell happened?"

She shook her head in disgust. "The man Takma left in his place beat her close to death yesterday morning. Literally just moments before Kael and a young woman nearly destroyed what was left of the warriors guarding the camp, including the coward who almost killed Ember," she said, retelling the events of the day before.

"Is she... is..."

"She's alive, Max, but only because the young woman with Kael healed her with powerful healing magic, the likes of which I have never seen."

Giddeon's concern caught Yrlissa's attention, but Max spoke first.

"Kael's here then? God dammit, where is he? With Ember? Come on, tell me where he is... Finally, after all this time," he said, his excitement getting the better of him.

Giddeon, Saleece, and Kasik stepped back slightly and looked around the camp.

"He's not here," Yrlissa started, but held up her hand when Max tried to interrupt. "Let me explain. Takma's second gave standing orders for Ember and I to be darted with sleep poison if there was any chance of our escape, whether during an attack or even a significant distraction. I was hit the moment they saw Kael and the young woman. Ember was barely alive and she'd been put in a tent with their healers. He wasn't even aware that she was here," she explained.

"Well, of course he didn't know," Max snapped, and turned to stare at Giddeon. "It's not like Kael would be looking for her, or me, for that matter." Max finished, clearly still fuming from his argument with Giddeon four days earlier.

Yrlissa frowned, giving him a strange look. "Why not? What's happened?"

"Kael came through our camp as well, Yrlissa. Giddeon had himself a nice conversation with him in, fact," he said, his voice dripping with sarcasm.

"Would that not be a good thing?" Yrlissa enquired, looking over at Giddeon.

"It'd be fucking perfect, had he not told Kael that Ember and I died during the crossing in the portal."

Yrlissa never had the chance to reply as the disagreement escalated between the chief and his personal guards. Unable to convince his chief that freed slaves were a good idea, Bala Takma and those who had seen what Kael was capable of found themselves under attack by their own tribesmen.

The warriors who had fled from Grodin's encampment had not arrived at the main camp yet, so the fight was almost even in numbers.

Aware that things may not turn out as they needed, Giddeon nodded to Yrlissa. "We need to get out of here."

She pointed to the trail at the rear of the tent. "That fight will give us the chance we need, but everyone in here first," she said, ducking inside the tent. "Max, take Ember, but please be careful. She shouldn't be moved yet, but we have no choice. The rest of you grab your weapons and travel packs. Nyrta brought them back to me this morning filled with food and water bottles. She wants no more trouble from Kael... If only her father would listen," Yrlissa said.

Max lifted Ember off the bone and fur bed as gently as he could while Yrlissa and Kasik watched at the opening of the tent for a safe chance to run.

"Now," they both hissed in unison. Yrlissa lead the way behind the tents as Kasik held open the door flap so everyone could follow. She headed north through the backside of the camp, ducking close to the tents when the fighting came close enough to reveal their escape. It soon appeared that escape was exactly what they were doing, as Giddeon noticed the Chief and his warriors gain the upper hand over Takma and those terrified of Kael.

Racing on, Yrlissa led the group to the Taktala horse corral. Their best chance to stay free and to catch up with Kael would be on horseback.

"Make sure to grab extra mounts," Kasik shouted, slipping a halter over the horse nuzzling his hand. Hopping up on the chestnut coloured mare, he rode over to Max as he entered the corral. "Give Ember to me," he offered, "and grab a couple of horses. We may need to outrun the tribesmen."

Yrlissa obviously had a better idea. She hung back on her horse and the red roan mare she chose as a spare. Yelling at the others to head north and to use the left of the three trails, she used her mount to chase the remaining horses out of the pen and up the trail after the others. At the very least, it would limit the pursuit ability of the Taktala. All the horses followed after Giddeon and the others, only breaking away into the forest an hour later.

Giddeon and his group rode until the early afternoon with no signs of pursuit. Ember rested easily in Max's arms as his mount skilfully picked its way amongst the sodden terrain, but out of nowhere, sudden, explosive and violent seizures racked her body and knocked both of them from his mount. Twisting in mid-air after being thrown from the horse, he landed on his back in the bushes, cushioning Ember's convulsing body with his own.

Grunting as he landed, he still managed to shout for help. "Yrlissa! Jesus, what the hell is wrong with her?" He gently laid her shaking body on the grass, rolling her onto her side.

Yrlissa arrived in seconds and closed her eyes. Placing her left hand on Ember's forehead, she examined Ember's shaking body.

"I knew it was too soon to move her. That bastard broke half the bones in her body and several of her organs were damaged," she explained swiftly as her magic searched for what could have started the convulsions. "Her heart is still weak from that jump to Corynth. Few people would have survived the beating she received. Thank Mylla for that woman with Kael. Giddeon, we need a place to stay, somewhere dry and safe for a couple of days, at least. It will have to be some place we can keep warm. If we keep riding, she'll die. Please hurry, Giddeon," she pleaded.

The ArchWizard nodded. "Kasik, you and Max come help me. We'll see what we can find. There are plenty of caves around. We'll return the moment we have a place that will meet her needs," he promised, and the three left, moving through the forest as fast their feet would take them.

"Saleece, hurry and give me a hand please. We have to stop these seizures. Kneel behind her," she instructed, while rolling Ember over, "and hold her gently by the shoulders. That's it, now place her head on your knees." Saleece did as she was asked without saying a word. "Good," Yrlissa added. "Keep her from moving too much, but be very careful not to hurt her," Yrlissa explained.

"What else, Yrlissa? Tell me what I can do," Saleece asked, quietly.

"Nothing, the rest is up to me," she smiled, already beginning her spell. "*Anavah Vallanomin.*" The words were soft, yet her voice strong, as green and blue magical light enveloped and then slowly permeated Ember's body.

Saleece gasped at the display of magic. "What in the name of the gods did you just do? Those words, they're not VosHain. They're not Inara's language. I've never seen or heard of magic like that before," she asked, her voice crawling with suspicion.

"I told your father..." Yrlissa shook her head. "Considering your father would not even tell Kael that Ember and Max are alive, I'll not trust any secrets with you. I'm sorry," she apologized with a smile.

Taking a quick glance around, Saleece seemed to understand. "I might not mind, but my father will. He may have let your different magic go without an explanation the first time back in the Forest of Whispers, but he would push if he were to see this. My own sense of morality demands I warn you, Yrlissa, but no more."

"I understand, but if he pushes me, he won't like the results. Especially with Max here," Yrlissa said, as Ember's thrashing spasms subsided and finally stopped.

"I know, that's what worries me," Saleece added.

Yrlissa watched Ember for the next hour, never leaving her side. Max returned, alone, shortly after.

"We found a cave," he said. "It has fissures in the back that have cold water trickling from them, but the front is dry. It's small enough to heat with a fire if need be as well," he said, as he carefully lifted Ember once more. "Come on, it's a fair walk," he added, and headed back the way he had come with Ember cradled in his arms.

Once at the cave, Max placed Ember on the makeshift bedding that Yrlissa had put together, and then went outside to help the others with setting up a secure site. Staying put for days at a time in the Wildlands meant extra precautions would have to be made for security, food, and even a backup escape route should they come under heavy attack.

With the exception of Yrlissa and Ember, they all worked late into the night before Kasik and Max were both satisfied they had secured the entire area with traps and early warning alarms. Saleece had also managed to find a path up the right side of the cave that would allow for an easy getaway down into the valley behind them.

WILDLANDS FOREST

Luthian Bathory had been on a relentless search for Giddeon and Ember's group for almost two months. As one of DormaSai's best spies and a close, personal friend of King Nekrosa Kohl, he had been asked to track down the location of the young Fae woman who had been seen with the Cethosian ArchWizard. Luthian had been staying in a small town just south of Corynth while waiting for his next assignment, which he hadn't expected to start for at least a month. It was a surprise when Nekrosa's shadow raptor found him that morning in Breth. Cethos executed necromancers on the spot if discovered, so blending in was a must for Luthian; it was something he was very good at, especially in a town of several hundred people.

Never believing that Nekrosa would find solid proof that the Fae had once again walked in the world of mortals, Luthian was stunned when he received the new orders. Being a necromancer, he never used his powers to heal; there were other, more efficient ways for a necromancer to heal his or her wounds and sicknesses, so he hadn't noticed an increase in his own abilities.

Healers and other mystics sensitive to helping the sick and wounded had seen a difference though, something Nekrosa and Sephi had been watching for since their coronation. The necromancer King and Queen would have left within two weeks of contacting him to join him in the hunt.

Though it had not been easy, Luthian finally tracked the ArchWizard's group to the Wildlands. Hours later, the injured young woman they had been carrying went into a convulsive fit. Now, the entire party had fortified their position in a cave they had sought refuge in.

Luthian had no ideas as to the identity of the young Fae. His suspicion lay with the young woman with brilliant red hair, hair that blazed like a beacon through the forest as he followed. Dug in like they were, he would not get a better look until they left the area. Luthian's abilities could help get him past the traps and alarms with ease, but not into the cave. Deciding to stay back and keep an eye on them as best he could, the necromancer went about preparing a hidden camp.

His ancient Dwarven-made charm would keep his presence hidden from the ArchWizard's magical senses. It had cost him dearly, but the engraved kinrai charm was well worth the price he paid, especially seeing as how the charm didn't offset magic like some rumours claimed. Artefacts like his always seemed to find their way to DormaSai, where every trader and nobleman paid well above fair value for any magical trinket, book, or artefact. The country was known far and wide for such practices. Mystics of every discipline would travel from across the Southern Kingdoms in search of antiquities that were found nowhere else.

Even magic users from the Bloods, as everyone in the Southern Kingdom called its northern neighbour, would often risk the dangerous journey to DormaSai when searching for rare or much-needed magical artefacts. With the only land route crossing through the Wildlands, and the ocean route often controlled by pirates, travelling to DormaSai from the north was an incredible risk to take during the last two decades.

To some however, the risk was worth the reward, so some would cross using the Eastern Gulf's ancient trade route from the city of Dasal on the Yusat border to Forja Vehlo in Salzara. It was an extremely dangerous route because of the volatile condition of the Sea of Storms south of Dasal. The strange sea constantly pounded the Gulf with storms that showed no mercy. Only the most experienced sailors or pirates would sail the gulf, and ships still went down in the storms.

Luthian choose to make camp at the edge of a small clearing about a mile from the ArchWizard's cave. The heavy brush and small stream coursing by made the decision that much easier. The moisture-laden earth had caused the branches of several massive sycamore trees to curl downward, and the twisting, python-like limbs of wood added to his privacy. The falcon nest at the top of a tree across the clearing was the deciding factor. His innate ability to take over the minds of animals would increase his security further and make it easy for him to spy on the other camp, simply by using the falcons nesting forty feet away.

Luthian remembered Drexa Bakar's lessons well. The crippled old necromancer treated the four orphans like they were her own children. She took in Nekrosa and Luthian when both were seven years old, a year after she found Sephi and her sister Dekayna wandering lost on the southern edge of the Midnight Canopy. The enchanted forest hadn't harmed the two girls even though they were only five and six years of age. She raised all four and taught them how to bond with the magic called upon when tapping into the Void's power. Including its most sinister power—mind control.

The takeover of another creature's mind or body was not just a prejudicial rumour when it came to necromancers. It had taken Luthian decades to learn the advanced ability. When capable, a necromancer tapped into the power of the Void—the massive, dark dimension between life and death—and used its magic to suppress the spirit of a living creature in order to take control of the mind and body. It was why the most powerful necromancers were so feared.

Though Luthian only used the skill on animals, taking control of people—though difficult—could be done. By using the power from the Void, a necromancer suppressed the human soul in the same manner, temporarily making it dormant. The body was then easily controlled for whatever purpose was needed. Luthian shook his head as he remembered his mentor's warnings only to use such magic in life or death situations and never for personal gain. Such abilities were the primary reason necromancers were executed in every country of Talohna except in DormaSai.

Though DormaSai had more than a hundred practising necromancers that he knew of, only two besides him, the king, and the queen were capable of controlling a living person. Realizing he momentarily forgot about the Necroeeyse, he sighed. He and Nekrosa's fight against the insidious cult never seemed to end.

Controlling the living was a mess from start to finish, and he shook his head to dispel the thoughts.

Building a small fire, Luthian used the last of his jerky, some root vegetables he found the day before and the two bulbs of wild garlic he crushed while kneeling behind a rotted log watching Giddeon's group, to make a somewhat hearty stew. Though he could survive in the woods with ease, the DormaSain spy was much better when around people or in towns and cities getting information for his King.

He finished eating and was putting away his clean pot when a shadow raptor appeared on the tripod over his fire and screeched into his face, making him jump. His pot clattered to the ground.

"Silence, you shadow-stuffed pigeon," he snapped clenching his teeth. The command forced the summoned bird to quiet. "I swear to every god known, you do that on purpose," he mumbled. "Wings of death's shadow, words of the faithful, speak." The chant activated the undead bird's magic, allowing whomever was on the other end to speak.

"Luthian, my friend, has Lady Lykke blessed you with a location on our young Fae?" Nekrosa asked, as his voice crossed through the Void and out of the vulture-like raptor.

"I found them this morning, my lord," Luthian replied. "They'll not move from this location for a day or two I suspect. One of their party is injured quite severely."

"Keep an eye on them then. We will arrive in Dasal in three more days. Sephi and I left aboard the Twilight's Reave two days ago out of Forja Vehlo in Salzara. We will contact you then, old friend. Be safe," Nekrosa said.

"You as well, my lord," Luthian replied. "Wings of death's shadow, words of the faithful, be gone." The shadow raptor dissolved into wisps of black shadows as the words of the release spell returned the summoned bird to the underworld from where it came.

With Giddeon's group staying put, Luthian prepared his camp so he could sleep. Using the eyes of the mother falcon from the nest above him, he scoured the forest until finding exactly what he was looking for. The Wildlands forest was a very dangerous place to spend the night alone. Through the falcon's eyes he located a dead woodlands bear only a half hour walk from camp. Two Orotaq obsidian arrows were still lodged in the decaying bear's stomach, but Luthian was not alarmed. The bear likely wandered ten miles before finally succumbing to the grievous wounds.

An hour later, he was sleeping soundly as the two thousand pound monstrous bear circled his camp, the rotting stench of death and decay keeping any dangers at bay while the reanimated bear kept away those the stench did not.

Chapter Twelve

"I have studied every document and piece of knowledge I could find when it comes to the mystics most of Talohna call a DeathWizard. I have tracked down every lead, every person who has had a relative who encountered one, and every small village story or rumour. Still, we know so little about them, and the Arcane Library in DormaSai has more written texts about them than anywhere else. The DeathWizard and their multitude of abilities are still an enigma wrapped in a mystery. A very dangerous one."

King Nekrosa Kohl's personal journal
DormaSai
5020 PC

DASAL, FREE LANDS

The Twilight Reave was a monstrous galleon with three masts and what looked to be a crew of at least twenty men and women. Captain Havarrow's boatman brought Kael and Kyah to the ship where they climbed a wood and rope ladder to get aboard. Havarrow's second mate, Anton Pere, introduced himself and ordered them to follow. Kael tried his best not to stare, but still managed to catch a glance at the men aboard the ship. Kyah had been right. Havarrow's crew were hard, cruel men. Every pirate they passed on the way to the captain's cabin was scarred from old wounds and all looked capable of incredible violence, the second mate even more so. Kael was shocked to see almost as many women, all cut from the same violent mould as the men. Most of the pirates carried several different bladed weapons and many had an assortment of blunt wooden and metal maces, or morning-star type weapons as well.

Yet, even so, common to every single sailor were two axes carried through a belt at the back of their waist. Two long spikes arched back off the head, forming a double hook opposite the blade. A memory flashed in Kael's mind of pick and ice hammers that mountain climbers used back home on Earth. Seifer told them the boarding axes allowed Havarrow's Reavers to scale the wooden plank walls when attacking bigger merchant ships and that the axes were rumoured to be magically enhanced. The Master Wizard's instincts had been dead on. Kael smirked as the axes blazed a myriad of colours within his magical sight.

Men bred on violence, the pirates sent a ripple of fear down Kael's spine. Even so, their own fear of what had been allowed on board the Twilight Reave was clearly visible and numerous whispers of 'crone', 'hag', and even 'witch'' drifted to Kael's ears, making him smirk for a second time, even as some pirates spit on the deck and used strange hand signs to ward off evil. He found it funny how people of violence often only respected people capable of violence on a greater capacity than their own.

The two guests were asked to wait outside the captain's cabin while Anton stepped inside. A few moments later, the door opened and he reappeared. "The Captain is ready for you," he said. "Come."

As they stepped inside the door, they passed a woman the same size as Kael, she grabbed the swinging door to close it, but shouted first.

"SM Pere! Make sure those orders are prepped for the other ships. I'll hand you the last when we're finished here."

"Yas, ma'am. I be on it," the second mate replied. Kael sensed a slight undertone of disrespect in his voice, but the cabin door slammed shut before he could discern more. The woman stood in front of the door with her hands on the daggers strapped to her waist. She frightened Kael almost as much as Havarrow did.

The Captain's quarters were larger than the one Kael and Kyah had while on board the vessel they had stolen in order to escape from Arkum Zul. With walls fifteen feet square, the cabin had room for the bed and a small table with two chairs neatly tucked underneath, still with some space to spare. The plank flooring was spotless and must have been stained or sealed at one time with something that gave it a deep golden lustre. Velvet and silk curtains hung from the ceiling around the bed, both matched the dark blue blankets.

Kael stood with his thumbs hooked through the new wizard's belt he had acquired at the tailor as he got his first look at the pirate captain feared by so many. A monster of a man, Captain Havarrow towered over Kael by at least eight inches and outweighed him by a hundred pounds. Dominique Havarrow had the appearance of a thirty year old man, but Kael knew that the Northmen did not age like normal humans from back home. Piercing blue eyes that never missed a beat stared at Kael with heavy suspicion, and he knew the pirate was seldom fooled or bluffed. His stomach flipped, turning cold at the prospect of trying to do just that.

Four kreeda braids hung within the pirate captain's long, dirty blonde hair. When Kyah had done his own hair in the cave, she explained that the kreeda were clan loyalty braids. Loyal to a fault, only the Northman wore the braids as a symbol to show which clans or faction that they were personally loyal to. They would never betray that loyalty, even if it meant staying neutral during a dispute between two of their loyal parties. Most clan braids were given to people from their own clan or village. It was extremely rare for someone outside Kastelborg Island to earn a Northman's loyalty to the point of being handed a lock of their hair. Kael smirked at the memory of the conversation. Who would have ever figured... A pirate with a code of honour.

The two grizzled young men and one heavily-tattooed woman accompanying the captain each had their weapons drawn and looked more than ready to use them. Whether they were being careful or paranoid, Kael couldn't begin to guess. Havarrow's rough, raspy, voice was indicative of a long life of violence. The deep hangman's scar wrapped around his neck was offset by an old knife wound that had at one time opened his throat from below his left ear to his Adam's apple and then down to his chest.

For several minutes, the pirate stared at the two new arrivals, eyeing them like a wolf unsure of whether he had come across a helpless cub or a grizzled, battle-scarred bear.

Finally, he spoke, shifting his focus back to Kael. "It's been many years since I've met anyone and was not sure what to say. Why in the Nine Hells would you bring a gods-cursed hag on board my ship, young man? Answer me that, truthfully, and I may not kill you both," he barked.

"My name is Kael, Captain, and this lovely woman beside me is my wife. I assure you, threatening either of us is in no one's best interest. She is what others have made her, beyond that, it matters little to you what she is. We arrived in the city this morning, and offered to speak with you on the city's behalf," Kael explained, doing his best to keep his voice firm in an attempt to display no weakness. He did not want to jump start the fighting, but knew men like Havarrow thrived on fear.

"When you are on my ship, pup, everything matters to me, and your life is at the bottom of a very long list of those matters. Bringing a witch on board my ship is punishable by death. It is trouble I don't need right now. So, if you have something you wish to say, you might want to get on with it... Boy." Kael could tell the man's next words would be followed by violence, so he offered him the truth.

"Fair enough. I offered to come out and speak with you. I believe you'll attack the city in order to look for whatever it is you are after. Let my wife and I find it instead. We'll bring it to you and it'll cost you nothing, especially lives. It's a good deal, Captain, and we won't fail," Kael promised.

"You must be joking. Or maybe trying to buy the city more time to prepare is more like it, pup. Perhaps you think I'm stupid, is that it?" he said, hatred dripping from the words.

At a loss, and starting to lose his temper, Kael struggled to keep his own voice from rising. "Our offer to help is real, Havarrow. I promise you, that help is not something you want to turn away."

Captain Havarrow smirked, grunting as Kael finished. "Exactly how is a young, inexperienced, whelp and an old hag gonna help when you could not even begin to imagine what is happening here? Answer me that. And your last answer it may well be. My patience is at an end, boy" he growled.

Kyah touched Kael's arm so he stopped arguing and let her take over. "I warn you, Captain," she said. "I am not a common bush hag, or an *old* hag for that matter." She raised her head and pulled back her hood. Havarrow's men whispered back and forth, their tone layered in fear as Kael heard the words 'mountain witch' and 'demon sister' over and over.

He could see none of it affected Kyah, as she continued, unabated. "I also promise you that my husband is no mere boy, any more than you are a mere pirate, Dominique MyrkrVatn." She smiled as the pirate's cheek twitched at the use of his real name. His right hand crept towards the blade on his waist while Kyah turned to Kael. "Perhaps they need a small display, my love," she prompted. Kael nodded as he called forth a small ball of black and purple fire, doing his best to keep the dancing flames and sticky plasma from falling onto the captain's polished wood floor.

"You see, Captain, there is a reason why my husband travels with a witch. If you know your folklore and ancient history or even your myths and legends, you will understand that most DeathWizards did. Now, I believe he was offering our help. Is your patience still at an end?" she asked, the question full of sarcasm.

Kael recalled the dark flames from his hand as Havarrow stared at Kyah, his voice escalating with his anger. "You have my attention, lass. Now, let me grab yours. The next time you or your freak husband utter a whisper that threatens my crew or my ship, all the dark powers of Hell will not walk you from my ship alive. Are we clear, witch?"

Seizing the opportunity to calm the situation without losing the pirate's respect, Kyah replied, "We are here to offer our help, Captain, not to threaten you. My husband and I need to leave this city... by walking free from it before that idiot wizard discovers what my husband really is. Our deal with Dasal is to help you, which in turn helps us. Believe me, we are not doing this out of kindness to you or the city. This arrangement will give us both what we want. See it for what it is."

Havarrow stood in silence for several minutes as if pondering his decision. "We're not here looking for people who have crossed the Suns of Blood—I assume that's what you were told? If we were and they were important enough, Captain BlackSpawn would've come himself with our full fleet—" he began.

Still trying to control his irritation, Kael interrupted. "It was. Why are you here then?" he asked.

"I'm sure you are well aware," Havarrow began again. "That this city is home to the last of the northern slave auctions."

Kael nodded, but Kyah was the one to answer. "We had the pleasure of meeting one of the owners."

"Lircang Yorcali, I would imagine. Putrid little fat blob of shit," Dominique cursed as he nodded. "My ship is crewed by mostly Salzaran men and women, and currently the Twilight Reave has no bounty on it, so we have been docking at the Salzaran port of Forja Vehlo where my family lives. My eighteen-year-old son lived there and took care of my daughter—she's fourteen. Two Kariyan mercs whose lifetime contracts I held guarded them both. The last time we came to harbour, I found my son dead, their guards dead, and slavers had taken my girl. Forja Vehlo is my port, so it took less than a day to discover most of what happened. The slavers left Vehlo on the dusk tide the same day we arrived. We tracked them here; they arrived a couple days ago," he explained.

"Of course," Kael said, shaking his head. "They were gonna sell her in yesterday's auction."

Havarrow stepped towards Kael, growling with a savage ferocity that nearly made Kael drop the entire façade. "What do mean they 'were'?" the pirate snapped. Defensive instinct kicked in and Kael's hands flared with dark power, forcing the pirate to back up a step. When no attack pursued, both men relaxed the smallest bit.

Kael tried to explain one more time as the magic faded from his hands. "The auction was cancelled because of your presence in Fang Bay. Yorcali told us as much." His mind a whirl of thoughts, Kael added, "Do you think he knows you're here for your daughter?"

"No," Havarrow snapped, still seething with anger. "But whoever his partner is likely does. Yorcali handles the auction, not the incoming slaves. It matters not. I came here to kill Yorcali and his partner. I'll find my daughter's buyer in their records." With a slow nod, Kael smiled as a plan began to grow in his mind. It would need a lot of work and a lot more planning before they could pull it off.

"Let us take care of it, Captain. We'll get her out of there. Just give us a couple days. It will save the blood shed," Kael suggested, as he watched Havarrow pace back and forth across the cabin floor as if struggling to decide what to do.

Stopping abruptly, he turned and approached Kael. "I'll give you 'til noon tomorrow, then my ships enter the harbour and we come get her. If I think for even a second that you or this sleaze-ridden city is up to something, my Reavers will hit that shore and the beaches will run red," he said as they came face to face. The beads on his kreeda clacked together as the pirate bristled with anger. "Are we clear, DeathWizard?"

"It will be close," Kael agreed, "but it should work. How will we know your daughter? We'll also need the names of two other people the Suns are after to give the town leaders. I can't tell them we're after your daughter. If Yorcali is aware of her, it'll be over before we start."

"You make sense, pup," Havarrow said, finally seeming to calm a bit. "My daughter has blond hair. It was very long, but likely the slaver's will have cut it, maybe even coloured it by now. She carries Tyr's kiss behind her left ear."

Once more, Kael was at a complete loss. "What the hell is a tire's kiss?" he asked as he looked back and forth at everyone in the captain's room.

A woman with over a dozen tattoos and short, dark hair, answered his question. "Northmen children blessed by the wargod, Tyr, are born with his mark. Shaped like a battle sword, you cannot miss it. It's identical to mine." Pulling her hair away from her neck, she revealed a mark on her throat shaped exactly like a great-sword. Kael nodded his thanks to the woman.

Captain Havarrow introduced her. "This is my first mate, Shasta Trey. She will have eyes and ears on you both most of the time, and she will report straight to me if you do anything stupid." Kael shrugged as if it mattered little, but he noticed the lone kreeda sewn into the woman's hair, giving away her Northman descent. No one had to tell him the dirty-blonde kreeda belonged to Havarrow.

"What about the names of two men we need?" Kyah asked, breaking the uneasy silence.

"The two men most wanted by the Suns are formal rivals, Hamus Stark and Keldon Ross. Both are captains, but they could be anywhere, even here, so be ready for that."

Almost as an afterthought Havarrow added, "If I find out that you tell anyone about my girl, Kael. I promise you, witch, DeathWizard or God. I. Do. Not. Care. I will find you, and you will suffer."

Kael smiled at the idle threat and turned to leave. Havarrow might have believed it, but he knew better. Still, making enemies in Talohna just ensured you died before your time, painfully.

Looking back over his shoulder, Kael smiled. "We have no interest in betraying anyone, Captain. Let alone the Suns of Blood or your Reavers. We just want to leave this city, supplied and alive, before someone realizes what I am."

Havarrow nodded to Shasta to show them out.

It was mid-day by the time Kael and Kyah left the Twilight Reave, so they headed straight to see Tavin for some things Kael would need for his plan. He also asked the artist if he knew the men the Suns were looking for. Tavin gave them what Kael asked for and told them both that he had never heard of Hamus or Keldon. Kyah tried to remove the markings put on her face using a paint scrub Tavin had, but to no avail. The paint had a dye in it that would have to be scrubbed off later or maybe eventually wear off. Tavin noticed her difficulty and asked them to return tomorrow and he would have a salve to remove the marks with ease. Kael smiled at her indignant frown. All things considered, she took it quite well and simply pulled her hood back up over her head.

Heading back to meet with the city council and their Master Wizard, Kyah and Kael crossed the market square. It was swollen with customers out shopping for the day. A young couple smiled as they strolled past, arm in arm making him smile. Covered in dark tattoos depicting skeletons and zombies, the couple reminded him of the teenagers and young adults back home who followed the goth and death metal lifestyles.

Kael's smile quickly faded as he felt a quick bit of pressure inside his head. Frowning, he glanced at the pair and pushed back with his magic in anger. The man's knees buckled as if they had vanished under him and he pitched forward, unconscious, his face scraping the dirt at the exact moment Kael and Kyah passed by them.

Kyah stopped to help, but Kael grabbed her arm, pulling her along. "Come on," he whispered. "We don't have the time, Kyah. If my plan is going to work, it must be completed before dawn, let's go."

"But, Kael, he's hurt, I have to..."

He tugged her arm, gently, keeping her moving. "No, dammit," he snapped, brooking no argument. Kyah nodded as she stared back over her shoulder. He knew she longed to help, but their priority had to be Havarrow's daughter. Besides, had the man not pushed at him with magic, he would have been fine. Kael was sure he still would be. The nosey couple would not be using magic to discover who and what Kael was.

The couple slipped from his mind as they returned to the town leaders waiting at the city barracks.

The names and descriptions Havarrow supplied caused no warning bells to go off among the city's leaders, so Kael and Kyah were given free rein to search the city—for men who were likely far from Dasal. Kael certainly hoped they were because they would have to make a token show of asking and looking for the men as part of their cover.

To top off a long list of growing problems, Nessedra Vantaur saw Kyah's painted face. Kael winced as a vein throbbed in her forehead.

"What in the blazing fires of all Nine Hells are you two playing at? She could pass for a mountain witch, even fooling Ella the White if she were standing right here!"

"That was kind of the idea and it deterred any problems when we were on the pirate ship... Well, mostly." Kael smiled sheepishly, earning a frown and a quiet prayer from the Elvehn woman.

"For the present time," Nessedra added, "keeping her hood up should hide most of her face and the demonic markings. You don't need to be scaring the city's citizens. Please. We do not need to incite another lynching, do we, Lircang?"

The fat slaver shrugged. "Nothing to worry about, I assure you, Mistress Vantaur. Ah, Kael. Please, wait for me before you leave, if you will?"

"Lynching? At least we can agree there's no need for that," Kael muttered, shaking his head as they readied to leave the barracks.

Lircang Yorcali refused to let them leave without talking to him first. "Thank you for waiting, young man," he said, addressing Kael, but made a blatant point of staring at Kyah. Or more correctly, at very specific locations of her body. Kael gently lifted Lircang's chin with his finger, tilting the slaver's head towards himself. The threat was clear, and Lircang's quivering bottom lip let Kael know he had accomplished his goal.

"My pardon, young man," Lircang said. Finally regaining control over himself, he cleared his throat and continued. "I was hoping you would still consider my offer to spend your evening at my establishment, to unwind and relax, of course. A gesture of my hospitality and gratitude, for helping with the pirates, you understand." His nasal-heavy voice grated on Kael's nerves, but as the slaver spoke, more of Kael's plan came together. He smiled at Lircang as if the fat man was their new best friend.

"I think we just might do that, Master Yorcali. We were thinking, that if things go well here in the next day or so, my wife and I may be interested in..." Kael hesitated and looked around. Seeing no one, he carried on. "Shall we just say... Acquiring some additional help to accompany us when we leave," he said, adding a copious amount of sleaze to his voice. Again, he looked over his shoulder, and then Yorcali's, to see if anybody might be eavesdropping.

Lircang sneered like Kael had just granted him the keys to Paradise after a thousand year wait. "I shall inform my employees that your beautiful wife and you be permitted to see and go anywhere in my establishment that you require. Because of the postponement, the selection is rather extensive right now. Please, have an enjoyable evening at my expense. I will make sure your food and drink... And any other needs you may have will be provided free of charge, of course." He smiled ear-to-ear. Kael's spine twitched with disgust.

Kyah belayed any suspicions the slaver might have had by sidling up to him and trailing her fingers across his cheek. "Our thanks, Master Yorcali. I must admit, we are both looking forward to enjoying what your establishment may have to offer this night." Lircang shivered with delight as she touched her tongue to her lips and then pecked his cheek leaving behind a trace of damp. After his eyes rolled back down from his skull, he used both trembling hands to straighten his robe, then he returned her bow and hurried away. Kael smiled at the awkward, duck-like scurrying caused from a suddenly uncomfortable fitting tunic.

Once he was out of earshot, Kyah shook her head. "I know not whether you are the smartest person I have ever known, or the dumbest. You are playing a very dangerous game with that man."

"Lycori used to say the same thing to me all the time," he replied.

"Only you could walk us into a trap in the exact place we need to be, on the one night we need to be there." Kael bowed as he took her hand and started walking towards the inn and their room.

"Yorcali won't try anything at his place, not directly," he said. "Though, I fully expect something to happen, eventually," he replied, as they walked the rest of the way in silence. Kael kept running his plan through his head, hoping he hadn't overlooked anything.

Upon returning to their room, both were surprised to find their Orotaq cloaks folded neatly on the bed and a large platter of breads, cheeses, and meats, along with several bowls of fruit and nuts placed on the table. A note of thanks from Seifer Locke accompanied the food. With no time to grab a meal all day and with dusk fast approaching, Kael and Kyah carried the trays out onto the balcony and sat down to eat. Kael could not remember the last time he had eaten real food. He couldn't stuff his mouth fast enough.

"Slow down," Kyah said, reaching out to touch his hand. "Your plan might just work, but it will not if you are sick to your stomach all night. I know it is hard, but small pieces at a time and only one small piece of fruit."

"I'm starving, Kyah, I haven't had real food like this since I got here," Kael mumbled, through a mouthful of meats, grabbing another handful from the platter.

"Stop!" she snapped, snatching his hand and offering him a small cloth. "Here, wrap some cheese and meat up in this and bring it along. Take small pieces to eat throughout the night. It will help your hunger, but you need to stop eating now. We have been on dried meat and water for weeks, and gruel for months before that. You will make yourself physically ill if you do not stop eating."

Frowning, Kael surrendered the argument, wrapping up some sliced meat he didn't recognize for later. "Okay, you're right. I hate this place, too much crap happening to even eat properly the one chance in months that I actually can."

"I know," she said, sliding her hand up his arm and over his shoulder to the back of his neck. "But things could go very wrong before you move at dawn to finish the last of your plan, and we need to focus on that, not you heaving from stomach cramps or worse." He could see the worry in her eyes, and not just about possible stomach problems.

"I know, but I can't see anything else that will work to save Havarrow's daughter, can you?" he whispered, hoping she had come up with a better idea.

She sighed, shaking her head. "Without killing many people, no. What we have will work. It *is* very risky, though."

"I know."

She smiled and kissed his cheek. "It is time to leave."

They left the room a couple hours before midnight and walked down the street to Lircang Yorcali's more prominent place of business. The slaver owned several whorehouses in Dasal, the gritty reality of a city beholden to no king or country and essentially no law. Only one of his many places of business was a club-like establishment that catered to wealthy customers.

Leaving the lobby of the inn, Kyah pulled the hood of her Orotaq cloak up onto her head and shivered in the cooler night air that blew in off the bay. Noticing, Kael wrapped his arm around her and smiled. Lircang's business was located in a fancy two-storey building, easily twice the size of the inn, but a ten minute walk to Dasal's business district. A sign hung from an iron arch above the door. The symbol of a nude dancing girl had been burnt into the wood below the name, The Far Exotic. One of the two guards at the door asked for their names and then asked them to follow him inside.

The door guard led them through the main floor and around an island bar in the centre that was busy with customers. Round, heavy, wooden tables were spaced evenly about the remaining section of the lower main level. All of the tables were occupied, and several had young women dancing on top with little to no clothing left on. Kael stared in disgust as every so often, the women would leave with someone at their table and head upstairs to where he assumed Lircang supplied private rooms. Coming from a world and existence where such a thing was illegal in most western countries, it was hard for Kael to stomach. Breathing slow and easy, he tried to strengthen himself for what had to be done.

The main floor of The Far Exotic was circled by a raised, second tier six feet higher than the main floor. The guard escorted Kael and Kyah to a private booth on this raised level that allowed them to overlook the entirety of the main floor. Once seated, a young girl of no more than sixteen, dressed in a delicate, chained waist-belt with three foot lengths of cloth hanging from the front and back, approached their table. Adjusting her white velvet top to reveal more cleavage, she bowed before making introductions.

"Evening Master, Mistress. Welcome to the Far Exotic, if you require anything, please let me know. Would you like something to drink tonight? We have the best wine Dasal has to offer, a local red from the Yusatan river valley, or we have a red and a white from the western mountain steppes of DormaSai, in the Southern Kingdom. It is very expensive, but I've been told it's superb. Or perhaps something else?"

Kyah smiled at the enthusiastic young waitress. "The red from DormaSai will be fine," she answered.

The young girl left, leaving them alone. "We probably shouldn't drink that wine," Kael suggested, "I would bet nearly every dollar we have it will be drugged." Nodding her agreement, he saw Kyah was busy surveying the building from their vantage point.

"Well," she said. "I doubt it will harm you, seeing as how a dozen tribal sleep darts gave you not so much as a single yawn, but yes, better safe than not. Lircang Yorcali is a very dangerous man. It will not be sleep poison in the wine," she said, still taking in the details of the large building. Staring intently at the far side of the room, she continued speaking. "Where do you think they keep the slaves that will be up for auction? We need to find out where they are kept."

Kael followed her eyes around the main floor, taking into account the raised level where they sat, when it dawned on him.

"Holy crap," he whispered. "Kyah, this is the auction house, I'd bet money on it."

Turning back to give him a look, as if to ask he felt all right, Kyah shook her head. He ignored her and continued. "When I was ten years old, my father... The man who raised me, took me to several cattle sales at the local auction mart near our farm. The auction floor was always lower than where the buyers sat, just like in here. We're sitting on the buyer's level."

"If that is so, then the slaves might well be in this building, or one nearby."

"Then maybe we should just ask, Lircang did say we had full access..." He winked, garnering a nod.

The waitress returned with their wine, placing it on the table. Kael touched her hand. "Miss?"

"Yes, Master," she replied, bowing.

"I know Master Yorcali is not here tonight, but do you have a boss we can speak with for a moment," he inquired, not realizing what he had done.

"Of course, Master. I am sorry if I have done anything to offend you or if I took too long getting your wine, please..."

"Whoa, slow down," he said, interrupting her. "You've done nothing wrong. That's not why I want to talk to your boss. We're just wondering if we could discuss some permanent companionship for when we leave the city." He smiled a deviant's grin as best he could.

Still way over his head, Kael turned a shade of red when the waitress pouted, staring at him with big brown eyes. "Do you and your wife not find me pleasing, Master?" she asked, on the verge of tears.

"Jesus, son of god," he muttered. "How did I get myself into this... Give me strength." Exasperated, he looked to Kyah for help.

Shaking her head, she took the waitress by the hand. "My dear, you are very pleasing to both of us, and we would love to have you with us for the evening, but right now we are looking for someone like you, whom we can bring with us when we leave tomorrow, understand?" Kyah explained. "Now, please go get your boss, so we can discuss our business. I promise you will receive no trouble," Kyah continued, sliding a gold nugget into the girl's palm.

"Yes Mistress, right away." The waitress' smile returned as she bowed and left.

"What kind of a screwed up place is this that would cause that young girl to act like that?" Kael asked, more of himself than anyone else. "She can't be more than sixteen.

Kyah shook her head, but answered anyway. "This is slavery. Many slaves pay a heavy price for failure in this world so they do whatever it takes to avoid it. This is a city where slaves are not permitted names, remember?"

"Yeah, I know. I'm sorry for saying that without thinking." His words could only remind Kyah of the loss of her family for failing the Dead Sisters when she was younger than their waitress.

The waitress returned with an older woman, who was wearing a tight fitting red dress and a lot of make-up, something Kael had not seen before arriving in Dasal.

"Shareese tells me you wish to speak with me, young man. My name is Dahlea, and the daily operation of Master Yorcali's business is my responsibility. I assure you I am a very busy woman, so what may I do for you?"

"My name is Kael, Miss Dahlea. My wife and I would like a tour of the contents of yesterday's auction. We'll be looking to leave with a purchase or two within the next day," he said, doing his best to imitate what would be her more exclusive, but sleazy clients.

"You'll be able to see the contents the morning before the auction like everyone else, I assure you, Master Kael. Until the pirates in the harbour are dealt with, the auction's contents are off limits, I promise you," she argued.

Kael's anger flared at her arrogance when speaking to, what was to her, a preferred guest of Lircang Yorcali.

"I can promise you, Miss Dahlea," Kael said, in threatening voice, as he stood up from the table and met her face to face. "That I have already discussed our requirements with my friend, Lircang, and he has promised me that you will show my wife and I whatever we want to see, as well as sample any contents we wish to before the auction. Do I make myself clear? Or do I have to walk to Lircang's mansion and bring him down here to give you an order I know for a fact he has already given you?"

Not realizing that his anger was getting out of hand, Kael swallowed a powerful urge to choke the madame. The vines of his death-flower bored through his flesh, and the two that had been working their way up the front of his throat crested on the point of his chin and wormed their way to his bottom lip before sprouting the barbed thorns that always followed.

The look of sheer terror on Dahlea's face as she watched the vines calmed his anger enough for the foreign magic to stop and for him to regain control of himself.

Kyah's hand slid down Kael's arm as she whispered by his ear. "Easy, love, she just wants to be sure who we are, right, Miss Dahlea?"

Still shaking from fear, the madame did her best to smile. "Yes, absolutely, there's no need for violence or threats. I'm aware of Master Yorcali's orders. I was just very busy when he was here and I did not catch the name he gave. I apologize, Master Kael. If you would come with me, I will be happy to show you what was originally up for auction yesterday. Please," she offered gesturing them to follow.

Miss Dahlea led them downstairs, along with one of her guards who followed from a distance. The basement level of the building was just as large as the main floor, but was lined by corridors with rooms side-by-side like a prison from Kael's own world. The doors were made from solid iron with only a slit at waist level, probably used to pass food to the hungry slaves.

The small string that Kael had desperately been holding on to in order to retain his humanity began to jerk and pull away from him, knowing there was nothing he could do to help these poor people. Thoughts of blood and violence flashed inside his head, followed by the strong urge to kill every perverted and sadistic patron and guard in the building. Kyah grasped his hand as he shook his head in order to clear the insane images from his mind. It seemed that killing was often becoming an easier way to deal with problems, and it scared him that such a thing was bothering him less and less.

"How many were up to be auctioned? What sexes and races?" Kyah asked, with a firm voice, in an attempt to ground Kael to the here and now.

"There were twenty-three, Mistress. Seven female, and sixteen males. All the young girls are elf, except for two—both are Human, though one is horribly ugly and weak. I doubt she'd last long on the road with you. Four of the males are elf as well; the other twelve are Human. Forgive me, Mistress Kyah, but are you not warm with that heavy hood up?"

Kyah slowly pulled the hood back, revealing the facial markings they had placed there earlier. Dahlea's gasp of fear and surprise made Kael smile.

"It's a long story," he offered, "but you understand why she prefers to keep the hood up, even indoors. Less panic, and no riots or lynchings that I hear the Dasalan people are so fond of. For my wife and I, killing large groups of people can be... distasteful, when there's no profit in it. You understand if the hood stays up. I'm in the mood for pleasure tonight, not pain," Kael said.

Dahlea shook as she tried to nod at the obvious threat. "Of course, Master Kael," she answered, still shaking as she bowed. Kyah returned the hood to her head to avoid striking further panic.

"Show us the Elvehn girls first," Kael requested, purposely to avoid any suspicions later when questions were asked, but only got a funny stare from Dahlia.

"No need to be so civilized," Kyah said, quickly. "This is Dasal, after all. The proper term of elf will suffice." Kyah's response nearly turned his stomach, but he was glad she caught it in time to avoid ruining the charade. Lycori's face flashed inside his mind, the memory of when he arrived in Talohna almost six months before and how she told him that elf was a derogatory term used by slavers. It also reminded him of what she told him of DormaSai.

"You're right, of course. I forget that our magic status permits us a different insight toward slavery."

"Oh, you are from DormaSai then?" Dahlia asked.

"Originally, yes," Kael said, smiling in an effort not to choke on his own words. "And it has been a long time since we've been to a city where purchasing an elf for pleasure is not frowned upon."

"Hmm, it has been some time, since we have been able to find one to enjoy," Kyah purred, wrapping her left arm around his waist and sliding closer.

"Too long," he replied, keeping the charade up while forcing the sour taste in his mouth back down.

Dahlia nodded and handed them a ring of keys. "I understand. Please, help yourself to whichever cell you please, and what's inside, naturally. I will remain here with the guards to ensure the rooms are secure once you leave. Take your time."

They spent a couple of minutes in each of the Elvehn girl's cells, Kyah passed each a small bundle of food she had prepared and hidden in her cloak. Some of them were very young, only ten or twelve years old. Kael stood in front of the door blocking the food slot and any view from outside. He smiled at her gentleness as she talked to them and tried to offer hope, knowing in reality there would be none. Helplessness swarmed over Kael, knowing that trying to save the slaves would only get him and Kyah killed. Chances were trying to save just one would get them killed.

Once they exited the last cell and returned the keyring, Dahlea took them to the far end of the basement to the cells occupied by the Human girls. The madame opened the door to the first cell just as they were interrupted by another guard.

"Miss Dahlea, you have a visitor," the guard said. "The man you have been waiting for is here."

"I must see to this, Master Kael. I will give my guard the key to the other cell as well. Please take as much time as you would like with either, or both of these two girls. I promise you, it will be worth it, especially if you don't actually look at the ugly one."

"Thank you, Miss Dahlea," Kael said, as he glanced back down the long hall. A guard waited for her along with a man who looked vaguely familiar. Kael and Kyah entered the cell, but he left the door open a crack in the hopes of getting a better look at the familiar man Dahlea was talking to. He couldn't help but feel that there was more going on than what they were aware of.

Dahlea stopped to talk with the man and dismissed both guards. It told Kael the madame must be quite comfortable with him. With the guard by the cell and Dahlia standing in front of her guest, Kael could not see well enough to recognize who he was, but he had definitely seen him, and recently. Suppressing a snort at the thought of only meeting a few dozen people during his entire time on Talohna, which meant the man had to be from Dasal. Kael shook his head, wondering if anyone was who they appeared to be in this world.

Kyah talked quietly with the slave girl behind him, so Kael closed his eyes and tried to walk his mind to where the madame and the man were talking, similar to what he had done when with Lycori in the Northern Mountain Pass almost half a year ago.

Somehow, Kael had sent his consciousness across the pass where he could see and hear Giddeon's party as clearly as if he had been standing right there with them. The magic would be perfect right now, but try as he might, he had no idea what to do. He had no idea how long had passed before Kyah tugged at his arm.

Snapping back from his thoughts, her voice entered his head. "Kael... Dammit, Kael, what the hell are you doing? We found her. She has the mark Havarrow's first mate told us about." The second Kyah said the words, it clicked home and Kael realized why the man in the hall was so familiar.

"It's Havarrow's *second* mate. The man who escorted us to the captain and then left to attend to other duties." The disrespect in the mate's voice, the hatred in his eyes and the harsh words from the female first mate. It all hit Kael at once.

"Ah shit, Kyah. We are in a crap load of trouble here. Havarrow's second mate is the one talking to Dahlea at the end of the hall. We're gonna have to fight our way out of here. Shit," he cursed a second time, keeping a close eye on the two at the far end of the corridor.

Always the optimist, Kyah peeked out the crack beside him. "Hold on, think about this for a minute. Maybe Dahlea will say nothing of us. If she believes we are only interested in buying..." she whispered. Looking down the hall, Kael held his breath and prayed for a miracle as the pirate nodded to the madame and disappeared back up the stairs. Dahlia spun on her heel, and headed back towards the cells.

Kael eased the door shut and turned to Kyah.

"You might be right," he said, letting his breath out. "He went up the stairs out of sight. Quickly tell Dominique's daughter our plan and make sure she understands what to do when we act. We're beginning to run out of time." With six hours until dawn, they needed to move precisely at the right time or the whole plan would backfire and Havarrow's pirates would attack the city of Dasal based on what Kael now suspected was a kidnapping arranged by one of the pirate captain's own crew.

Chapter Thirteen

"Walking in the Void between life and death takes skill and power few necromancers have ever achieved. Even for those who have, the Void is a dangerous place to roam with your mind. The living are not meant to be there."

Feydon Azmerack
Necromancer and King of DormaSai, 4918 PC

DASAL, FREE LANDS

It took Sephi Kohl almost half an hour to carry Nekrosa back to the inn after he blacked out in the dirt for no apparent reason. It was late evening and still Nekrosa had yet to regain consciousness. She tried what she could to bring him around, but as a necromancer, she had little ability in healing. Besides, there did not seem to be anything actually wrong with him, except for not waking. Though her abilities with the dead were not nearly as sophisticated as Nekrosa's, she was sure something had happened in relation to their gifts. Many, many thousands of years had passed since a necromancer of Nekrosa's natural skill had been born. A prodigy, their master had called him when they were five and living in the mountains of DormaSai.

Nekrosa had told her moments before he lost consciousness that he had felt something strange in the small city of Dasal. She knew he had been tapping the Void all morning, trying to learn what inside the city was out of place with the natural order of life and death. Not being nearly as sensitive, Sephi had felt nothing out of the ordinary.

Necromancers were not like normal wizards. All mystics drew their power from somewhere, like wizards from their bond with the earth. Elemental sorcerers pulled their power from the elements or from raw nature, amplifying the smallest of nature's wonders into devastating forces of destruction. Witches were often granted their powers from the different demons they worshipped, and very few from the angels of Paradise.

Those with the power to control the dead, on the other hand, called accessing their power "tapping the Void". The dark void between life and death was a dimension filled with wild and powerful energies, energies all necromancers could touch and manipulate. It allowed them to reanimate the dead, assume control of an unconscious or weak mind, and if strong enough, even speak to the spirit of a person recently dead.

Nekrosa had all these abilities as well as numerous others. The DormaSain King was the only necromancer to ever drag a spirit back to its dead body. Doing so saved Sephi's life during their desperate fight to ascend the DormaSain throne. For all his skills and experience walking the fine line between life and death, he still hadn't come back from whatever had happened, and it terrified Sephi to no end. Placing a cold cloth on her husband's forehead, she sighed and crawled into bed with Nekrosa to wait for him to wake or to die.

Sephi dozed and another hour passed before Nekrosa jolted awake, shouting, "Let me go!" Sephi shivered; she could feel a primal fear within his voice. Biting his lower lip in an obvious attempt to silence himself, blood ran down Nekrosa's chin as he stared into space. "He's here, by the darkest gods, he's actually here in Dasal." Nekrosa stumbled on his words as they spewed forth almost too fast for Sephi to understand.

Still by his side, she sat and cuddled closer. "Who are you talking about?" she asked, holding his hands. He turned to look at her, his swollen eyes bloodshot and seemingly unaware of his surroundings.

"I am back?" he asked her, still confused.

"Yes, my love," Sephi whispered as she took his face in her hands, touching her forehead to his own. "You are here, with me in our room. We are in Dasal, do you not remember?" she asked, her voice filled with worry.

Nekrosa gasped, laid back in the bed and took a deep breath. "We need to find the young Fae, Sephi. This DeathWizard is well beyond our ability. She will be the only one who can temper him if we can't find a living Guardian."

Now just as confused, Sephi frowned, but laid her head on his chest. "What do you mean? What happened?"

"The DeathWizard is close. Here in Dasal, Seph, I'm sure. I could feel him when we were in the market. I tapped the Void when we walked by that young couple to see if I could locate him..." He stopped talking and a shiver rippled through his body.

"Then what?" she prompted.

"I found him... The young couple, I'm positive it was... They were right beside us, but... I only touched my power for a moment, enough to know if it was him. The Void, it just... swallowed my mind. It was like walking the Void to talk to a newly passed spirit, but infinitely larger and there was no way out. It took a long time to figure out how to get back. I don't understand even now how I did it," he explained.

"Why would that happen? I don't understand."

"I do. It's a defence against those who would try to control him or his power. It's to ensure we cannot take over a DeathWizard the same way Azmerack took over the

Cethosian Queen during the rebellions. Any necromancer who tries to tap their power while in his presence will trigger the defence," he finished, pushing both of his tattooed hands through his long, shiny black hair. Sephi could see that his silver eyes were lined with dark from the stress of his ordeal.

"Come. You need some rest. We can do little until we hear from Luthian about the Fae girl, anyway." She shifted her weight and moved into the crook of his arm, where she felt his fingers trail through her hair.

"True," Nekrosa agreed. "We can't risk an attempt on the DeathWizard, not yet, it would only end in our deaths," he confessed, his fears always safe with her.

"Then we shall wait. Luthian will tell us when they come our way." She did her best to reassure him as she lay curled in his arms. With full dark settling outside and her left arm resting across Nekrosa's chest, she was soon asleep.

DASAL, FREE LANDS

"Yes, Dahlea," Kael said, as they stood outside the cell that held Captain Havarrow's daughter. "We'll inform Lircang of the three we wish to buy. If we can't reach an agreement with him privately, we will bid for them at the auction, after the pirates have left."

"That will be fine. I would imagine the auction will be rescheduled the moment the pirate threat is over, should you be unable to strike a deal with Master Yorcali," the madame said. Kael nodded to her to show he understood.

After their quick conversation, Dahlea left to go tend the brothel while Kael and Kyah managed to sneak by Havarrow's second mate without being seen. Should Dahlea mention them when she and the pirate continued their talk, Kael's plan would still work. Knowing the exact location of Havarrow's daughter, and with no further reason to stay, they exited the Far Exotic in search of a secluded spot from where they could watch the second mate when he departed the brothel.

Anton Pere, the Twilight Reave's second mate, left the Far Exotic a half hour later with a bag of gold in hand. Kael watched from the darkened entry lobby of the warehouse down the street as the pirate strolled through the district and past the open air markets, heading in the opposite direction of the harbour docks. Kyah stayed behind Kael, watching their backs as he followed the pirate from a safe distance. The darkness and lack of street lights made trailing the second mate an easy task. He continued in a south-easterly direction until arriving at the spot where the Dasal city walls met the ocean.

Anton disappeared into some thick brush and short trees as Kael hung back and waited. The pirate stumbled from the heavy cover dragging a rowboat identical to the one that had taken them to and from Havarrow's ship earlier in the day. Kael stared out from cover as Anton rowed back to the Twilight Reave in the darkness. With light cloud cover hiding both moons and the third yet to rise, no one would ever know he had left the ship.

Moving back up the street to get Kyah, they headed back to the main docks, but skirted the water's edge by staying inside the last row of buildings to avoid being seen from Havarrow's ship. In less than a half hour, they were at the ship. The captain was waiting on the deck.

He was more than a little upset to see them back aboard his ship so soon. "You'd better have a damn good reason for being here, DeathWizard. You're wasting valuable time my daughter does not have." The corner of his eye twitched as he approached them both the second they stepped onto his deck.

"Your daughter is fine, I promise, but you need to trust that we're here to help," Kael tried to explain, yet kept his voice low. "You have a traitor on board, and you need your men to bring him to your cabin before he sees us here again."

"My men are all loyal, Kael..."

"They're not, god dammit!" Kael barked, but was quick to calm himself, knowing the danger. "Trust me, Havarrow. I can prove it."

"So, explain yourself, now," the pirate captain ordered. Kael could see he was still on the verge of losing control of his temper.

Kael glanced across the ship, but couldn't see the second mate, so he explained what they saw. "We have just come from the Far Exotic where we both saw your second mate talking to Lircang's madame, Dahlia. The one who escorted us to your cabin, remember? He's not a Northman, is he? I don't think his loyalty is as solid as you think it is." Kael could see Havarrow start to piece some things together, maybe things the pirate captain had been thinking on his own long before Kael's arrival.

The big Northman turned to his first mate and growled, "Bring him to my cabin, and do not let him know why."

"Right away, Captain," Shasta Trey said. The first mate grabbed two others and went to find the traitor.

The rest, including Kael and Kyah, followed Havarrow to his cabin, where only minutes passed before Anton Pere knocked on the cabin door.

"Cappin? Ya wanted to see me?" he shouted through the door.

"Come in, Anton. Tell Shasta to come in as well." Captain Havarrow got up from his chair and pulled his cutlass several inches out of its sheath before gently letting it slide back. Kael had seen others do such a thing if they were expecting a fight. A sword stuck inside the sheath could easily mean death. He shook his head at the memory of when it happened to him after he first arrived.

The second mate entered the cabin and stood to the left of the door. Shasta entered last and closed the door behind her, once again standing right in front of it. It was clear by the look on her face that anyone who tried to get out would have to go through her. In the short time she was in the room, Kael could not help but notice that she carried at least twenty knives, all of which had balanced handles for throwing. Anton looked completely at ease; there were no signs of nervousness at all, and Kael wondered briefly if his assumption about the man had been wrong.

"Cappin? There sumin ya wan me ta do?" he asked, his poor grammar by far the worst Kael had heard since being in Talohna.

"Yes, Anton, there is. I would like you to tell me why you were in the city tonight at the Far Exotic whorehouse. You did not have permission to go off ship," Havarrow said. He crossed his massive, tattooed arms as he looked down on Anton's much smaller stature.

Anton never blinked and never missed a beat. "I wuddnt cappn, nevr luft da ship all day or night."

"You were seen earlier tonight talking to the madame of Lircang's fleshpit, and not so long ago, you were also interested in where I spend my time when we are docked in Forja Vehlo, the city where my children live. Explain your actions, Anton. Did you arrange the death of my son and the kidnapping of my daughter?" Havarrow barked at Anton as he uncrossed his arms, putting his left hand on his sword.

Anton merely chuckled at the accusation. "Who saw me dere, Cappin?"

"I saw you there, Anton, you cleaned yourself up a bit and had on clean clothes, but it was you," Kael claimed, as Kyah nodded her head.

"Cappin, deeze witches lie, wud neyer betray ya, Dom. I ne'er met yer gurl, ya know dat, only know her whatcha tell me," he said, calm and cool. "Der no proof, Dom. Me sail wit ya fer ten n two. Me word true, yer know dat, Cappin." Kael could see the twenty years of loyalty start to sway Havarrow, as the big man began to relax his anger towards his second mate. The charade had gone on long enough. Kael now knew the pirate would never confess and time was running out.

"You know, Anton, it's too bad the captain's daughter couldn't tell us who took her or who arranged it," Kael wondered, as he turned towards the man.

"She tell ya da same, spook, dat I never met 'er," he snarled, trying to spit on Kael's boots.

"Oh, I know you never met her, Anton. You were paid twenty-five gold for your part in arranging her sale to slavers," Kael said, finally triggering a reaction. Anton never tried for the door, but instead pulled his sword from his thick leather belt while reaching for Kael with his other hand. He was not fast enough though, as he found Shasta's dagger filled right hand pressed firmly to his throat and Kael's left Vai'Karth pressed against his chin.

Even with a dagger and strange looking reaper-blade to his throat, Anton refused to stop speaking, somehow maintaining his cool. "I never ranged nuttin, yung Neria tell ya herzelf, wuz she here. I swear, Cappin," he said, yet again.

A young, soft, but very shaken voice came from under Kyah's hood, but it wasn't Kyah who spoke.

"I am here and you may have not met me, but I have seen you," Neria said, as she pulled back the hood on Kyah's heavy Orotaq cloak and stared at Anton. Gasps of shock rolled through the cabin. No one had any idea Havarrow's daughter was in the room the whole time. The witch markings painted on her face told the story of how Kael had smuggled her out of the slave cells.

Havarrow's daughter carried on speaking, never missing a beat. "And I will tell my father that you arranged it all. You and your slavers talked too much when you thought I was still out cold when you got the first part of your gold," she said, trembling, as tears ran down her face.

The terrified and traumatized fourteen year old could hold her strength no longer as she began crying. "Father" the only word she could get out as she threw herself into his arms and collapsed just as he managed to catch her. Knowing what was coming, Kael lowered his blade and stared at the doomed man.

Anton was clearly stunned. "Huh? Das nut rite, I juz saw er n da cell...I saw ya an yer witch sneak outa Dahlea's. I cheked, she wuz dere..." At a nod from Havarrow, Shasta stuck her blade in the back of Anton's thigh, severing the hamstring. A second dagger followed the first, but cut deep into the second mate's other leg.

Captain Havarrow consoled his daughter, making sure her face was buried in his big arms while Anton paid part of the price for his betrayal. Shasta wiped her blood-soaked hand on Anton's cloth shirt and kicked the cabin door. It opened and she tossed Anton out to two waiting pirates.

"Prep him," Shasta growled. "We'll keelhaul his ass the moment we clear the bay." She closed the door and approached Kael with a curious look on her face.

"Where was my niece, and how did you get her out?" she asked.

He took her arm and led her to the other side of the room. "It doesn't matter right now. Half of our plan is complete with her safety, but I still have to pull the rest off on my own," he said.

"Fair 'nuff, Kael, but others were involved. Blood price must be paid to those who cross the Suns. If not, BlackSpawn will collect it himself," Shasta said, as she sheathed her blades.

"I will make sure I find out all who were involved, but you need to stay here, anchored in the harbour. It will make the next step easier for me. Oh, and keep Anton here, don't dump him overboard or something stupid. There are still more partners of Dahlea's I haven't identified yet. I don't know if Lircang Yorcali was involved, but if the wrong person were to talk to Anton or find his body, it would really screw things up, all right?"

Not realizing Havarrow had been listening, Kael turned with surprise when he heard the Northman's voice. "We can stay in the harbour once the rowboat is done taking you to shore, but I need to know what the chances of retaliation are once the slavers find out she is missing—if they don't already know. I must protect my crew."

"I promise you, Captain, that for now, they don't know she's gone. Anton just said so. I have to go now. Time is short and I have to get back. I can't be seen leaving your ship. I'm sorry to have to ask, Captain, but I need Kyah's cloak back."

"Of course, and I will send a runner for the other ships, they can be here before dawn. It will give us added protection if the slavers come after us, and it will also look like you have not found the men you were after, or my daughter."

"Perfect," Kael agreed. "That should work even better."

Careful not to wake her, Havarrow stepped over to the bed where his daughter had fallen into a restless sleep and removed the Orotaq cloak, covering her with blankets instead.

He handed Kael the heavy cloak and offered his arm to shake.

"My daughter is alive and safe because of you and your wife, Kael. A very large debt stands between us, my friend. I must do this, though my actions seem strange to myself," Havarrow said. With a puzzled expression, he drew a hooked dagger from a sheathe under his arm. Kael panicked and dark mist began to curl around his hands as he stepped back, preparing to fight.

Shasta stepped forward, touching his shoulder. "Easy, brother, you are not in danger." Kael stood his ground as Dominique grabbed a thick length of his blonde hair. Slicing it off with the hooked blade he handed the braid to Shasta.

As she turned back to Kael, she held it in front of him. "May I?"

Still not sure what was happening, he nodded, but didn't release his magic. Shasta pulled the length of rawhide holding Kael's own braids back and let his hair fall loose.

Taking a thin length of dried sinew from around her neck, she weaved Dominique's hair into a braid above Kael's left ear. In seconds, she released the length of Dominique's blonde hair, spun it into dread strings and re-braided it to match Kael's hairstyle. Finally tying his hair back up, she left the lone braid of the pirate's hanging loose beside one of his own. Holding out her hand, Havarrow dropped two carved bone beads into her palm.

Kael let go of his magic as the Northman woman smiled and slid the beads up the blonde braid. "The first bead marks you as an ally to the MyrkrVatn clan. The second shows that you have saved the life a MyrkrVatn clan member and that the Kreeda Oath lies to your favour. You are now a member of our clan and will always be welcome on Kastalborg Island. You are our brother, in name and in blood spilled. We wear the left side kreeda as an oath of loyalty to our family. You are the only person not of Northman descent that I have ever known to be granted one – the life of my niece demands it be so. All Northmen and women live or die by this bond of loyalty, do you understand that?"

"I... I do," Kael stammered, as Shasta cut free a loose braid of his own. The pirate captain dropped to a knee and she weaved Kael's braid into Dominique's hair, also on the left side. It was only the pirate's second kreeda to hang by his left ear, though six others hung from the right side.

Dominique stood and approached Kael, clasping his arm. "If ever you need to find me, you wear this," he said, handing him a blood-red sun pendant carved from what Kael guessed was whale bone. "Then make your way to the Suns of Blood port of call. It's an island far off the western coast of DormaSai in the Southern Kingdom. Any pirate will take you there if you show them this. The pendant will grant you access to the port, but do not lose it, my friend, it carries my mark on the back," he warned, with his last words.

"You owe me nothing, Captain–" Kael started to say, when Havarrow held up a hand.

"My first name is Dominique. Feel free to call me by it. You may want nothing in return for what you have done, but you have earned my friendship. It is not something a Northman gives easily. Whether or not you ever call for it, the oath will remain until your dying breath flies free to Tyr's hall."

Kael shook his arm and wished him well. "Take care of your daughter, Dominique, and your crew." He nodded to both Havarrow and Shasta and left.

Dominique's boatman took Kael back to shore. Not knowing whether the docks would have spies, he put Kyah's cloak underneath his own so no one would see him carrying it. It was past the middle of the night and just a few hours until dawn. Kael planned to enact the last part of his plan about an hour before dawn so he headed to the room at the inn to lay low for a couple of hours. With only three hours of sleep in the last two days, he was barely able to keep his eyes open any longer, but knew sleeping now would have disastrous effects for the remainder of his plans.

Chapter Fourteen

"Illusion magic is used to trick the eye into seeing things that are not real, or into seeing something different from what is there entirely. But true masters of illusion often have no access to real magic. Using people's beliefs or arrogance against them in order to trick their eyes and their mind is the art of a true illusionist. It is amazing to witness those with such power. Kael Symes is one such master illusionist. I've seen what he can do first hand when using no magic. The thought still chills my blood."

Master Wizard Seifer Locke
Dasal Wizard Journals, 5025 PC

DASAL, FREE LANDS

Since arriving in Talohna so many months ago, Kael had learned that not paying attention and letting your guard down often led to fatal consequences. It was a lesson he had learned all too well in the basement of Jasala Vyshaan's tower, the Black Arc. The price paid that time was a sword through the belly. He still had no idea how he had survived.

After leaving Dominique Havarrow's pirate ship, try as he might, Kael could no longer keep the fog caused by nearly three days of no sleep from clouding his mind. He climbed the stairs to the room he shared with Kyah, unable to stop yawning.

Kael opened the door and stepped into their room, wondering how he was going to stay awake for a couple more hours. A bright multi-coloured explosion rocked his foggy mind. His body hit the floor and he slid to the far side of the room. Pain bloomed inside his skull and neck. Running his hand from the base of his skull upwards, Kael pulled back fingers coated in blood and hair and what he desperately hoped were not small pieces of bone. More pain seared the nerves behind his eyes and dizziness overwhelmed his faltering senses as he rolled himself onto his back. Though conscious, he could not stop his legs from twitching like a brained animal.

Several wavering sets of three rugged men stood by the door. The first set closed the door while the other two sets advanced in his direction. Blinking with frantic desperation, Kael's muddled brain slowly informed him that he was seeing triple. He fought to understand that the three identical men carrying matching heavy black clubs were in reality the lone man who hit him as he entered the room. Even dazed, Kael could tell the man's enormous size accounted for the damage to his skull. How he missed sensing them was the only mystery. Kael knew he was in mortal danger, but his body refused to co-operate with his mind even though his legs quit jerking.

"Well look at that, Grunt, the big scary wizard is so stupid he didn't even have a shield up," the large man with the club said.

"Yeah, boss. Lircang's doodad musta worked. The dummy had no clue we were here." Grunt laughed, as he fondled a carved bone charm that hung from a hide strap around his neck. Just by looking at it Kael could tell the charm was dulling his esoteric senses and his magic. He couldn't sense the three thugs and he couldn't tell how much damage the club had done to his head, but he knew the wound was life threatening.

Grunt leaned down over him, still chuckling about the effectiveness of the charm. "Where might that weird little wife of yours be, wizard?" he asked, as he put his hand out for the big man's black club. The words entered Kael's head through a red haze of pounding torment, but he could not get his mouth to work. A throbbing pulse had started thumping in his chest and shifting voices from far away washed at his consciousness.

"Gods, Jaz, I think ya kilt him. How we supposed ta find out where the girl is now?" Grunt slammed the club into Kael's ribs, snapping at least two. It was pain he knew intimately, having felt it many times before. Not so much as a gasp escaped his lips as he smiled. The man asked again.

"Where is she, boy. Huh? Lircang has tried to track you two down all night. Ya refused to drink the wine we sent to your table. You left the Exotic but didn't come here and we couldn't find you anywhere in the city. Then, when you do finally come to your room, the sweet little thing ain't with ya. Last chance, little wizard. The boss wants a new toy and we're gonna kill you anyway, just like all the others. Where is she? I promise, you'll die fast. What ya say?" he asked, raising the club above his head.

Between the splitting pain in his head, the thumping inside his chest cavity and the shrill voices that kept getting louder, it was all Kael could do to keep conscious, or alive for that matter. Answering his attacker in any way was out of the question. Completely helpless, Kael saw Grunt shrug and bring the club down, powering it towards his head with every ounce of strength the man had.

All he could do was flinch as he felt the impact. Kael screamed as more anguish exploded from his arms and hands. Biting his lower lip, he opened his eyes to see that he had somehow managed to raise his arms in defence. Mangled and broken, they had stopped the blow from killing him. Though happy to be alive, Kael's mind was overwhelmed by the torment racing through his body. With no magic, unable to move, and his mind trying hard to shut down, he knew his life was running out fast.

"Son of a bitch, you see that?" the big man named Jaz said, clearly shocked that Kael had defended himself. "Stubborn fucking wizard, ain't he?" he said with a laugh.

"Only once," Grunt smiled, as he lifted the club for a second swing. Kael closed his eyes, expecting death, but instead the wish-wash sound of voices and shrill cries echoing inside his head suddenly cleared. Short phrases and sharp words jumped around his mind. Trying to focus, he reached for them.

'*Call us.*' echoed through his pounding head.

'*Let us help you.*'

'*We're here, listen.*' And one voice louder than all the others was so clear it hurt his head. As if two voices had been melded into one. A gruff male voice reverberated around inside his skull, but calm overtones of a relaxing female voice mixed with it.

'*Let me save you, Kael.*'

Kael knew he had to be dying and his scrambled mind was hallucinating, grasping at the straws of hope. He looked up just in time to see Grunt start his second swing when the door to his room slammed open and a woman entered. Kyah glanced his way, but she quickly disappeared as waves of confusion swamped his mind. She was locked inside a slave cell blocks away. Blinking, he stared at the woman. Though she looked familiar, he realized he did not know who she was.

The same height as he was, the woman was lighter, fit, and ten years older than he. She had unnaturally bright blue eyes and an even stranger hairstyle of looping braids that circled her entire head. She was covered in tattoos—the skulls and zombies flared with power, moving on her flesh as if alive. Kael blinked repeatedly, wondering how much of what he was seeing was real.

As best he could tell, she was wearing nothing more than the gown she had been sleeping in. A strange dagger appeared in each hand as if by magic, both blades glowed with ethereal blue light. The first dagger immediately sprouted from the big man's neck. Her throw was so fast, Kael never even saw it. Jaz fell to floor opposite Kael, bleeding out, his pumping blood crackled on the dagger's blade as if warming the cold metal.

Stepping further into the room as Grunt turned to face her, the woman merely smiled, though outweighed by over two hundred pounds. Kael flinched as the light blue dagger punched through the back of Grunt's neck. The black club clattered to the floor, followed by his body.

The woman looked at Kael and he could see the concern in her eyes, but she did not see the third man behind the door. He approached her silently, his sword already drawn as she bent down to pull her dagger from the big man's throat. The voices in his head renewed with a savage vigour, screaming to be released, promising only to help. Kael tried to warn her, but only managed a croak that drew her attention and distracted her further. The thug pulled back his sword to drive it through her back when Kael screamed inside his head with every ounce of energy he had left.

"Help her, yes, whatever it takes, save her... Please!"

Thinking it was only his busted head hallucinating anyway, Kael opened his tear-filled eyes to watch the death of the woman who had tried so valiantly to save his life, knowing he could do nothing to return the life she had given him.

Instead of watching her die, a strange tearing noise ripped through his room. A black rift appeared in the air behind the man who was about to stab his saviour. The woman spun around in time to see what Kael was witnessing. Several sets of black, demonic hands reached through the dark tear in reality and grabbed the thug by both arms. Another set of hands grabbed his legs. Yet another arm emerged and slid around the man's neck with such gentle ease it reminded Kael of a lover's embrace. Terrified, the woman stepped backwards, tripped on Grunt's body and fell on her butt. She scooted closer to Kael, tearing her nightdress as the head and one cloven foot of the creature stepped through the tear, almost fully into Talohna's reality.

A face born of pure demonic nightmare glared down at Kael and his rescuer. Two horns grew from the side of its head above the temples, but split into long spiralling forks that stretched out into the air. From the same location, two more horns grew along its jaw line, protruding out from its chin like a set of spiralled tusks. Chains and carved bone adorned the horns, clicking against each other. The demon's blood red eyes and solid black pupils bored into Kael as he watched the creature snort through its wide, flat snout. The demon held the would-be killer in an iron-like grip as the man struggled in a futile attempt to escape.

Shocking Kael even further, the demon spoke, flashing four long fangs inside its mouth.

"Your magic called, dark wizard, and we have answered," it growled. The deep, rumbling voice reminded Kael of heavy boulders grinding together in the quarry outside his city back home. "As payment for helping you, we claim this body and soul for our own." It lifted the thug off the ground with ease. "Are we in agreement, wizard?" he asked, looking right at Kael as if daring him to say no.

"Say yes, Kael. Now!" his saviour whispered. Unable to speak, Kael nodded his head as best he could.

"Perhaps next time you will not wait so long before granting us the permission required to help you." It smirked. Kael could see the demon's joy over the fact he did not have a clue what was happening. When he could not verbally answer, it accepted his nod of agreement and bowed.

"Until you call again, child of Death, be well." The demon stepped back into the tear. The extra sets of claws followed as both dragged Kael's third attacker with them. The would-be murderer kicked and fought, cursing the whole way. A second tearing sound ripped through the room and closed the rent in the air as if it were never there.

Exhausted, Kael collapsed back on the floor, causing more pain to pound through his head. The woman who saved him looked down at him when he opened his eyes.

"I don't know how you did that, but I'm glad you did. Even if it did nearly scare the shit right out of me and that's not something easily done to my kind. You saved my life, thank you. I had no way of knowing how many were in here when I entered. My husband can't be in the same room as you, so he couldn't help us either, even if he were in the condition to do so," she explained. It made absolutely no sense to him.

Who the hell was she and how did she know his name? And why couldn't her husband be in the same room as him? In no particular order, questions and thoughts kept revolving through his head, but he was unable to hold even one of them for more than a second.

Kael tried again to talk, but his mouth gasped, opening and closing as he tried to force the words out.

"It'll be all right," she said. "Stop trying to talk and just lay still. My name is Sephi. I'll do my best to help you, but I'm not a healer and these two are dead. I can't use magic to leech their life and heal you."

Still trying to speak in order to get her to destroy Grunt's pendant in the hopes that he could heal himself, he grabbed her arm as once more words failed to find their way free. Sephi moved her hands over his body, looking for wounds. She came to the back of his head and her face went pale.

"Curse the Void," she gasped. Locked onto his eyes, she placed her hand on his chest. "Our room is right beside yours, all right? I have something there that will help. I don't think it will save your life, but it may give you some time, a few hours, perhaps. We'll find you a healer… I promise. Be right back." With that she got up and left. He hoped she was true to her word, he felt himself fading, and fast.

Kael suddenly jerked awake, realizing he'd lost consciousness. Sephi was trying her best to force something down his throat.

"Come on, Kael. Stop fighting me and drink. It's the last we have. It'll help you get back on your feet. Try, dammit," she cursed, finally getting his mouth open. A thick, putrid, sludge slid down his throat and into his belly, burning like the fires of Hell the whole way. Once it hit his stomach the fire spread to his limbs and then up to his chest and head as if molten lava flowed through his blood veins.

The smouldering heat enveloped his head. Suffering and intense agony overruled all conscious thought, becoming his only concern. The bones of his skull shifted and ground together, turning his stomach with nausea as some kind of obscene magic began to meld the bone. He shut his eyes as unending waves of torment rolled through his head and he felt tears run down into his ears. Pain so severe it rivalled the corruption of the Dead Sisters' demonic magic forced his eyes wide and his whole body shook with tremors and seizures.

Sephi slid on top of his stomach and sat, using her weight and elbows to hold him down at the shoulders as her hands firmly held the back of his head. Her blazing blue eyes and the hot breath of her exertion were the only things he recognized through the blur of agony. Focusing on her blue eyes with every ounce of willpower he had, Kael rode out the agony as it increased further. Blood and fluid drained from his eyes and ears as broken ribs flexed, clicking back together. The shattered bones in his arms and hands crunched, popping as they reformed to the way they were before being smashed by Grunt's club.

Finally, after what seemed like days, blackness numbed the excruciating experience and Kael passed out from the stress of the accelerated healing potion.

Chapter Fifteen

"The true measure of any person will always be taken when they are cornered and out of options. The calmest, kindest, and quietest people can become aggressive and vindictive when pushed too far. I've seen it first hand and it always seems to leave everyone involved with scars, even those who are merely witnesses."

Entry from Master Wizard Seifer Locke
City of Dasal's joint-commander journal, 5025 PC

DASAL, FREE LANDS

"Wake up, Kael. Come on now." The female voice was slow to permeate Kael's concussed mind, but he used the words as an anchor to pull himself back to consciousness. A loud crack echoed in his ears as the verbal lifeline filtered through once more.

"Dammit. Come on. Wake up. We don't have much time to find you a healer. Now get up," the woman barked. It was the same woman who saved him earlier. Kael opened his eyes and grasped her hand in time to stop the second incoming slap, but instead realized she was not slapping him, but clapping her hands in an attempt to bring him around.

"Oh, thank the Void, you're awake. Come on, can you stand now? Or talk?" she asked.

He sputtered, his mouth felt full of cotton. "H... How. Ugh," he gagged, as his tongue caught the back of his mouth, forcing him to cough. "Long. How... long was I out?" he asked, flooded with worry that time had run out on Kyah.

"Only about a half hour. It's incredible, your body is trying to heal you. You must heal five times faster than a normal human," she said, much to Kael's relief.

"Who are you? And what did you give me?" It was the only thing he could think of to ask. His head still blazed like an inferno, and it was taking him longer to collect his thoughts than he would have liked.

"My name is Sephitro... Sephi Kohl. I gave you the last potion of accelerated healing that we have in the entire country of DormaSai. It's a mystical elixir that was made during the reign of the Ancients. It speeds up your body's natural healing ability. In your case, it fixed your caved-in skull and removed the blood and fluid in your head by draining it through your eyes and ears. We still need to find you a healer. The swelling in your brain will kill you before the day's done. The potion's not a miracle cure for fatal wounds," she explained.

"That explains this god damn sadistic headache then," he winced, grabbing his head. He sat up with little trouble, but fell over when he tried to stand. Settling for leaning his back against the bed, he moaned.

"Come on, let me help," Sephi offered, trying to get him to his feet, but pain washed over his mind in pounding waves.

"Stop, stop. Christ, stop. Please..." he begged, holding his head. The pressure inside his skull pushed against his eyes to the point where he was sure they'd burst from his head.

Sephi helped him back down. She had a softness about her that reminded him of Ember. "We have to go, Kael. I don't believe there is a healer in this city skilled enough to help you, if one even exists. We must leave Dasal to find you one. You will die otherwise."

Still holding both his aching head in his hands, Kael whispered, "How about you find that cursed charm that greasy bastard was wearing, so I can heal myself, instead." She looked at him like he was from another world.

"Can you do that? I never knew a DeathWiz... Ah... That, ah, wizards could heal themselves," she stuttered, as she slid across the floor on her knees to the two bodies that had been left behind.

"Yeah, nice try," he whispered. Even though speaking just caused more pain, he added, "I caught that in case you were hoping I didn't."

"No wonder I had no idea how many were in here," she said, lifting the charm from around Grunt's neck. "This is Dwarven-carved whalebone. It must shut down a mystic's senses," she suggested, changing the subject, or trying to at least.

"I'm painfully aware of that," Kael groaned. "And not just senses, most magic. Smash it, please," he begged. She put it on the floor and slammed the butt of one of her blue daggers down onto the bone. It took several blows before it shattered. Kael's extra senses rushed back to him. Feeling his inner sight instantly relieved some of the pounding agony in his head, he sighed with relief.

"It's done," she said, glancing over her shoulder. "Can you heal yourself now?"

"Give me some time. How about you tell me why you helped me, and more importantly, how you know what and who I am," he insisted, as he closed his eyes to concentrate on lowering his inner sight into his body.

"My husband and I are here looking for a young woman. She's Fae. Magical healing is getting stronger again here in Talohna. Not like it was in ancient times, but it is definitely increasing. We believe this means the Fae have returned to our plane, but maybe only a few of them. She's nearby, so we've been waiting for news from the rest of our group. If possible, we'd like to offer her our protection, if she needs it. I know who you are because your presence almost killed my husband this afternoon in the marketplace..."

"I remember you," Kael said, without opening his eyes or breaking his concentration. "Your husband passed out right beside us. I wouldn't let Kyah help. I'm sorry about that... There were other lives on the line."

"He is sensitive to your underworld magic. As necromancers, we draw most of our magical power from the Void and you draw your underworld magic *through* the Void. Your magic instinctively protected itself from my husband. Your friend couldn't have helped him anyway. It wasn't your fault. Neither of us would hold a grudge against you for it."

"That would be a first, and you should. I can't control the magic I have, that's why it hurt him."

"Nekrosa was trying to find you. Our magic and yours doesn't mix, yes, but we didn't know that before. It was our fault. We're experienced magic users, and it was our responsibility to be careful. We come from the country of DormaSai. Have you heard of it?"

"I think a friend told me about it once. Southern Kingdom, right?" Kael asked as memories of Lycori came back to him.

"Yes. It is a country where all magic and its practitioners are welcomed. Even a DeathWizard. If you ever need asylum or even just a place to learn about your gifts, go to the castle in the capitol city of Drae'Kahn. The library there is incredible. Thousands of shelves in the library are lined with books and grimoires. Some are over ten thousand years old. There are written documents there about your kind as well, you know. I've seen them, read some of them," she explained.

"They would just allow someone like me to walk around or study whatever I like? That's absurd," he scoffed. "I have been hunted since the very first moment I arrived here. Everyone fears me or wants me to do terrible shit for them. I don't believe you. Even the ArchWizard is trying to kill me."

"DormaSai is in the Southern Kingdom. Our country is devoted to the preservation, understanding, and practice of all magic. My King and Queen are necromancers, and because of that, no magic is prejudiced against there. I promise, you will be welcomed there just by telling them who and what you are. My husband and I work at the castle there. We may even be there should you get there some day. His name is Nekrosa Kohl..." she said hesitating. "Our last names are known here, Kael. Death warrants exist for our lives just because of our magic and our King's. Please keep our secret as we have kept yours."

With his eyes still closed, Kael noticed the pause when she spoke about them working at the castle. He assumed they were both royal mystics of some sort, or spies maybe. It explained the warrants for their deaths, but it mattered little to him.

"Your secret is safe with me, and thank you for your help. I don't know if this will help you or not, but my friend, Kyah, has said the same thing about the Fae, and she is a *very* powerful healer. You might be right that they are in this world again. It's no business of mine, but I do hope you find what you are looking for."

Kael opened his eyes, and dizziness washed over him. "Right now, though, I need you to help me get my friend back because I can't heal myself."

"I thought you said that you could? Have you not done it before?"

"I have, but not using magic from my earth-bond cruus. I haven't figured out how to make it work, and my connection to the underworld healed me with disastrous side effects last time. I'm not really sure how I did it, or if it was even me that did. I had just pulled a six-foot-long sword from my stomach at the time. But it doesn't matter, I can't get it to work right now anyway."

"You're not a very good wizard are you, Kael?" She smiled, and he knew she was not being rude.

"No, not a very lucky one either, as you can tell," he said, touching his sore head.

"I'm sorry. I truly wish I could help you with that, but my magic doesn't come from a bond with the earth. We use... more efficient magic to heal ourselves."

"I got that, when you said something about leeching their life... It's all right, maybe one day. Perhaps in DormaSai, you can explain to me about the Void and how your magic works, but for now I need to find Kyah."

"I will hold you to that talk someday, Kael," she said. Her voice held an eerie edge that made Kael shiver. "Now let's go find your friend, all right? Come, I'll help you walk, where do we go?"

Waves of nauseous agony rippled through Kael's head as Sephi helped him to his feet. He fought through the pain as best he could, but still could not walk on his own. The vertigo and dizziness became too much and he fell to his knees. With strength that belied her frame, Sephi helped him back to his feet and steadied him as he recovered before leading him down the inn's back stairs.

"We have to get to the city barracks," Kael said softly. "I know the Master Wizard stationed here, his name is Seifer Locke." He panted in agony, cursing. "Christ, my head hurts. You have to get us to the barracks with no one seeing me. The city's slavers are after me and my friend, Kyah. We told everyone she was my wife, hoping to avoid problems, but it didn't work. Those men we killed belong to Lircang Yorcali," he explained, as Sephi checked the darkness for signs of trouble.

"It's still full dark. Don't worry. The shadows will come to our aid and protect us. It'll keep us out of sight."

He heard her whisper and frowned, not recognizing the language.

"*Na gravasay, shadus mal.*" A calm, eerie quiet settled around them. The shadows cast by the inn and surrounding buildings lengthened, swallowing them along with all the light.

Once clear of the inn's back door, Kael did what he could to help.

"*Hush,*" he whispered, passing his hands over both their feet, silencing them with black smoke. "No one will hear us now. Just keep us out of sight."

"With the magic I have seen you use tonight, it truly is a loss that you cannot heal. You should keep working at it. You have abilities that are unheard of, especially for your kind," she complemented.

"Yeah, all but the important ones," he grumbled.

"Give it time, it will come. Nekrosa and I have been studying magic since we were old enough to read, nearly twenty-seven years it has been now, and we are still considered children, even though Nekrosa is a prodigy in his discipline. Learning magic does take time, my friend," she said, leading the way to the barracks. The elongated shadows of buildings and warehouses shifted and stretched, but constantly kept them covered and away from prying eyes.

"I know it takes time," he said. "But it's *time* that I never seem to have enough of."

They came around the corner of the last building before the barracks and saw no one. A quick shuffle across the lit yard to the barrack's front door and they arrived without drawing attention. Once inside, they found Seifer sleeping on the bed in his office. The door whipped open and cracked against the wall as Kael stumbled, tripping Sephi as the two of them crashed into the master wizard's partially open door. With both hands filled with fire, Seifer bounced from his bed in less than a second.

"Kael? What in Inara's name are you doing here?" he shouted. "Mistress Sephi, good to see you again." As he got a better look, he asked, "What the Nine Hells happened to you?" Offering Kael a hand, Seifer helped Sephi guide him to the bed. Six guards stormed into the room with weapons drawn as Kael sat with his back against the wall. The wizard barked at his guards to stand down before anyone got hurt. As he took in the situation, it was clear Seifer didn't know what to say. Kael coughed, wincing at the stab of pain from his previously broken ribs. They were still far from being healed.

Gasping for breath, Kael tried to explain. "You told me yesterday... That you knew what Lircang... was doing, remember? You said kidnapping and murder?"

Seifer knelt down beside the bed and looked Kael face to face. "I remember," he said. "I warned you... Where's your wife? Why is she not with you?" He placed his hand on Kael's chest and muttered the words to an unfamiliar spell. A small amount of strength returned to Kael's broken body and the pain subsided, even his head cleared enough to think. "I cannot do more, Kael. I'm sorry, but I never trained in healing. Besides, you are far beyond what magic can heal. Tell me what happened and I promise your death won't go unanswered."

Kael drew in a rattling breath before he continued. "I promise you, Seifer. I'll tell you everything, but for now... You have to trust me. Lircang's goons were waiting in my room when I got back. They had a charm that prevented me from sensing them. Sephi heard the commotion and came to help. There are two bodies in my room."

"Holy Mother Inara. I knew he might try something, but not while the pirates were still here," Seifer said, shaking his head in utter disbelief.

In too much pain to nod, Kael smiled. "If you want to catch Lircang with all the proof you need, then get as many men together as you can and head straight to the slave cells in the Far Exotic's basement. Dahlea, is just as guilty, maybe more so. I promise to explain later. Kyah is in one of those cells, and his men tried to kill me so he would get away with it. That's how he's been doing it right under your nose. No husband or boyfriend to complain, and no proof of what he's doing."

Seifer nodded and stepped outside. Kael winced as he yelled for the guards to send out a call to meet at the Far Exotic, but gave orders to stay back, out of sight until he arrived. Sephi helped Kael back up and Seifer slid under his arm on the other side, with both their help it took less time to return to Lircang's establishment.

The Master Wizard immediately sent his most trusted men to watch the back exits, so there was no chance of escape. The rest entered through the front. It should have been no surprise to see Lircang sitting in the upper section of the main floor surrounded by would be witnesses able to clear him of any wrong doing in Kael's death.

Lircang's bottom lip quivered like a young boy caught playing with himself when Kael walked into the Far Exotic still alive. He smiled at the sweat-covered fat man, applying a subtle, but ever increasing pressure to the situation.

It took only a handful of seconds before the city guard were positioned throughout the building. Lircang composed himself and met his new arrivals just before they reached the stairs to the basement slave cells.

"Master Locke. Captain Kern. Might I assist you with something tonight?" the slave master asked.

"You look a little nervous, Yorcali," Kael pointed out, his words slurring the slightest bit from the crushing force building inside his head. "Disappointed to see me alive?" he wheezed, as fluid and blood trickled from his ears again.

"I can assure you, Master Kael, that I have no reason to want you dead, so why would I be disappointed that you are not?" Kael knew he was trying to sound sincere as he put his fingers together in front of his chest, but the slaver's voice quivered just a touch. "Might I say, however, that you don't look like you're feeling so well? Is that why you and your alluring wife left early tonight?" The corner of his mouth twitched, forming the start of a sly smile, as if to tell Kael there was no way to prove anything he might accuse Lircang of.

"We're wasting time, Seifer," Kael snapped, inducing a coughing fit. More blood trickled from his left ear. Sephi used her sleeve to wipe it away as he continued. "She... He has to have her... In the slave cells downstairs," he managed after the throbbing in his head subsided. Kael struggled to concentrate and focusing was becoming more difficult.

Polite, as always, and quickly regaining control of his confidence, Yorcali pasted a fake smile on his fat face. "Perhaps if you were willing to tell me who you were looking for, Captain Kern, I would be able to help you achieve your goal. Without wasting more of everyone's time. Especially my own. I'd hate to have to send a bill to the city for the unnecessary occupation of my valuable time."

"Master Yorcali," Captain Kern replied, his voice stern. "This young man has accused you of trying to have him killed and of kidnapping his wife. Would you like to respond to these charges?"

Kael could see the relief flood Lircang's very being as he thought, again, there would be no proof. It confirmed that Kael's elaborate plan had been a success and Seifer was going to get his justice against Lircang Yorcali, after so many years.

"I have taken no one, Captain, and I have been here most of the night with family and friends who can all attest to..."

"Then we will continue our search, Master Yorcali, but we would appreciate it if you would accompany us," Seifer said. Kael smiled at Seifer's tone of voice, he clearly was not asking.

Lircang bowed his agreement. "Absolutely, Master Seifer, anything to help you search for the young man's wife. The sooner you see that she is not here the quicker you will find her elsewhere," he offered. Kael's smile widened at how totally oblivious the slaver was to what was actually happening.

The group walked down the stairs and Kael did his best to make sure the search quickly worked its way to the cells in the back corner, the ones containing the human females. The beaming, arrogant smile, Yorcali kept flashing his way finally wore into Kael's last nerve and he could no longer help himself from saying something.

"You know, Lircang, you really should make sure you know what kind of person you have running your businesses. That shit-eating grin of yours is about to disappear."

Lircang's confused look was priceless, but it was short lived. The bravado returned. "Whenever you are ready, young man," he said, smiling wide. "It takes more than a powerful wizard to make things... appear where they have never been," he laughed, waving his arms in front of Kael's face. The fat man assumed his men had Kyah stashed somewhere far away from the brothel, his statement a veiled joke only the two understood, but Kael knew better.

"Funny thing, Lircang," he said, smirking, as they approached the female cells. "A friend of mine, a real wizard he was, not long ago told me that the best kind of magic is illusion magic." Lircang snorted in disbelief, but it didn't stop Kael from continuing. "But... the most powerful illusion magic uses no real magic at all. To make something appear or vanish in front of your eyes is the secret to true illusion, magic or not. Shall I show you? It seems I may just have a knack for it." Kael trembled from the effort of speaking, but his smile never wavered.

Lircang scoffed, and bowed to Kael. "By all means, Master Illusionist. Let's see which of us is better. I've forgotten more about illusion and deceit than you will ever know, Kael."

"I warned you Lircang..." Kael barked, and stood a little straighter, yelling as loud as his pounding skull would allow. "Kyah? Are you down here? Kyah? N'Ikyah!" He shouted even louder, staggering jolts of pain stormed his swollen head and blood sprayed from his nose. Lircang Yorcali snickered, thinking he had won, but his mirth was short lived.

"Kael? Kael, is that you?" Kyah screamed, terror riding every word. "Kael, help me please, in here," she shrieked, and began banging on the door in a fit of hysterics.

Kael turned to the slave master and sneered. "Real illusion is designed to make you see what's not there, Lircang. You should have left us alone, you would have been perfectly fine."

Lircang was overwhelmed with confusion. "What... How... What the hell is going on? How did she get in there?" he said, beginning to panic. One of Captain Kern's men pushed Lircang into the wall face first and secured his hands with leather straps. Other guards came down the stairs escorting Dahlea, already bound. Lircang looked at Kael and then to Dahlea. Kael chuckled as he watched Lircang make part of the connection as to what was going on.

"This is your fault you, stupid bitch. By the dark halls of Perdition, you screwed us both," he swore, lunging at his madame.

The madame merely grunted. "I learned from the best, Lircang. Stolen slaves bring more profit than bought ones, did you not tell me?" she laughed, as her words buried them both.

Lircang exploded with violence. Kicking out at her, he lost his balance, and if not for Captain Kern's guards, the slaver would have fallen on his backside. "I should have left you rutting on your back, making me money, you ugly bitch. Instead you manage to ruin us both. How could you be so stupid, even knowing who my partner is?" Dahlea blanched white with fear at his words, her quivering lips even looked pale through the thick rouge. Kael was shocked when the woman lost control of her bladder, a puddle forming around her feet. He was glad to be done with them both at last.

After tearing the keys from Dahlia's waist belt, Seifer opened Kyah's cell and she stepped out looking for Kael, she ran to hug him but stopped short when she noticed he was being held up by others.

"What happened?" she asked. Concerned, she placed her hand on his chest, the other cupped his cheek. "Kael! You are dying," she cried, tears starting to well in her eyes. "What happened to you?"

"Lircang tried to have me killed. There were men waiting in our room. They had some Dwarven charm thing. I never sensed them," he explained. Coughing again, he grabbed at his head before he could finish the tale. Sephi introduced herself and finished filling her in, telling her about the attack, his broken skull, and her potion that had kept Kael alive this long.

Kyah placed her hand on Kael's head. "Thank you for helping him, Mistress Sephi, but we must get him to our room so I can try..." Her hand dropped and a vacant stare swallowed her features. "So I can spend the time he has left with him."

Sephi frowned. "You can't heal him, can you?"

"My magic will not be strong enough to save his life. I cannot heal him fast enough to get ahead of the swelling inside his head. I am sorry love," she said, touching Kael's face.

He could see the depth of her pain and it took all Kael had to concentrate enough to answer. "We... were bound to... run out of luck eventually," he said.

"But not this day, my friend," Seifer said, gently placing his hand on Kael's shoulder. "Come, let us take you to your room and I will help her heal you."

Kyah smiled. "You have healing magic too? Together we can..."

Seifer held up his hand to stop her. "I have something better... Augmentation magic."

Sephi laughed, her relief obvious. "You have Elderblood magic."

The Master Wizard nodded. "If I can boost Kyah's natural healing ability, she should be able to stay ahead of the swelling in Kael's head."

"Thank you," Kyah said. "But we must hurry."

The guards took Lircang and Dahlea off to the barracks, while Captain Kern, Seifer, and several guards escorted the trio back to the inn. Once there, the guards took the bodies of the men Sephi had killed earlier.

Kyah and Seifer went to work on healing Kael's wounds. He managed to thank Sephi before he slipped into unconsciousness, the lack of sleep and injuries finally catching up.

Chapter Sixteen

"The countries of Talohna are all known for creating unique individuals. DormaSai is known for magic and the people who use it. Cethos and the people who live there are known for their willingness to help others, even if it means defending them during conflict. Though these are never universal truths, they are more common than not. The Northman, however, are uniquely different. Each and every Northman, whether male or female, value loyalty above all else. The men and women from Kastalborg Island would rather die than betray one of their Kreeda Oaths. It is impressive in a world that is often so easily corrupted."

ArchWizard Giddeon Zirakus' speech to the 2024 PC University graduating class.

DASAL, FREE LANDS

It was near dark when a loud argument woke Kael, he managed to catch the tail end of Kyah's sentence.

"...will not wake him up, Captain. He barely survived the healing process! He needs to rest!" she yelled. As Kael sat up, a wave of dizziness swamped his mind and he fought with his equilibrium to remain upright.

"It's fine, I'm awake. What's... happening?" he asked, struggling to sit on the bed.

Kyah looked at the Captain and scowled. "If I had the ability, Captain, I swear I would roast your backside for waking him," she huffed, as she stormed away and sat beside him, careful not bounce the bed. Placing her hands on him and closing her eyes, he knew she was checking to see how well her and Seifer's healing had worked.

"Captain Kern, how can I help you?" Kael asked.

"I'm sorry to bother you, Master Kael, but there are now seven pirate ships in the harbour, and they will speak with no one from the city. Havarrow's boatman says he is there to take only you. People are starting to panic. Some citizens are even arming themselves. We were hoping you would go speak with him and ease the tension before open fighting breaks out," he requested. His voice trembled with fear, either from the pirates or from Kyah's threats, Kael wasn't sure.

"Shit, forgot about him. All right, let me get dressed and we'll go talk to Dominique. Okay, Captain?"

"Thank you. We'll wait for you in the barracks."

Kael nodded and started to get dressed as Kyah snorted her disapproval.

"You need to rest," she said, glaring at him.

He did his best to ignore her. "Let's just get this done. I can rest tonight and then we can leave this place in the morning. I've had enough of it. I don't think the disgusting filth of this city will ever wear off."

Captain Havarrow met them on the deck of the Twilight Reave the moment Kael and Kyah stepped aboard.

"It is good to see you well, brother," he said, smiling. "My daughter still rests, so you will not leave this ship until you tell me how you freed her and what happened upon your return. Yes?"

"Fair enough," Kael chuckled, wincing as a jolt of pain spiked in his head.

They followed the pirate back to his cabin and sat at the table as he opened a bottle of wine and the ship's cook brought in a plate of bread, with meats and cheeses layered to the side.

Still starving, Kael grabbed a slice of smoked meat and took a bite before he explained how they achieved sneaking his daughter out of the slave cells.

"I knew breaking Neria out by force would only get us hung, so when we left your ship the first time, we stopped and borrowed some paint from a local artist. Kyah painted Neria's face to match her own demonic markings while we were in your daughter's cell 'shopping' for slaves to take with us when we left. They switched clothes, and Kyah's Orotaq cloak and hood made sure no one even noticed that Neria left with me, while it was actually Kyah who stayed behind."

The Northman pirate rubbed his jaw as he listened, but never interrupted, speaking only after Kael had finished. "Risky, Kael, had someone noticed..."

"True, but when was the last time *you* looked a witch directly in the eyes? Even now, your men won't make eye contact with my wife. It was a risk, but the best chance we had. Your second mate almost ruined our plan when he came in looking to settle-up the money he was owed for arranging Neria's kidnapping and sale. I never considered that one of your own might be involved."

Havarrow nodded and shifted in his chair. "Then what? You had trouble upon returning. I can see it in your eyes."

"We did. Luckily my magic attracts the most exotic of help," Kael smirked, before he carried on. "Kyah spent most of her time in the cell under the lone blanket all the slaves are given. The slavers who took Neria actually helped us when they cut her long blond hair and tried to colour it with ash and charcoal. It was close enough in colour to Kyah's dark hair that when Anton looked in on her after we left, it fooled him. After bringing Neria to you, I had planned to go back to our room for a couple hours' rest before going to the city's Master Wizard and telling him that Dahlia had taken Kyah. With no proof, I couldn't frame Lircang Yorcali, as much as I'd have liked to. His thugs actually worked to our advantage, or would have if they hadn't nearly killed me by caving in my head. A young couple were staying in the room next door; she heard the commotion and saved my life. Afterwards, we went to see Seifer and the city guard. Finding Kyah in the slave's cells was all the proof he needed after years of trying to prove Lircang was kidnapping young women. You should have seen the fat bastard's face, Dominique, and his Madame! She pissed herself when she realized your daughter was gone and they were caught." Kael's sadistic laugh echoed through the room and was soon joined by the pirates and their captain. Though it was all an act, he saw Kyah shiver at the brutal cruelty in his words.

Dominique, clearly impressed that the plan had worked as well as it did, added, "Had Lircang not moved against you, the fool would still be a free man. A stupid mistake. Thank you once again, Kael, for all your help, but we must haul anchor and drop the mainsail. I will keep my word. We will leave Fang Bay the moment you step upon dry land and my boatman returns to the Reave. We are overdue for a meeting with a very dangerous and unstable man," he chuckled.

With a deep frown, Shasta raised an eyebrow towards the pirate commander. "How many ships we taking south, Captain?"

"All of them. Just the Reave will enter the Lover's Embrace once we arrive at the twin cities. It stays our private business, First Mate, until you're ordered otherwise. Signal the other ships to prepare for the journey." With a nod, Shasta left Havarrow's quarters and the Northman turned to escort Kael off the ship.

"Heading south, Captain?" Kael asked as he followed the pirate to the rowboat.

"Yes. Should our trip go well and we meet again someday, this ship and all Suns of Blood vessels will be a floating fortress of armament. Until then, brother, be safe, and raise all the hell you can," he said, laughing.

Kael smiled. "We will meet again, Captain, of that I am sure. Until then, may the waves carry you safely." The Northman thanked them as they left his ship.

True to his word, Captain Havarrow led his other six ships from the harbour as Kael and Kyah watched. The sunset at their backs danced on the bay's waters and wooden planks of the pirate vessels.

Back at the barracks, they informed Captain Kern and Seifer Locke of the pirates' departure. Seifer promised to meet them at dawn when they were ready to leave Dasal.

It was not soon enough for Kael. All he could think about was closing his eyes and having a good night's sleep in a real bed, but not before having something substantial to eat.

Not quite remembering how he got there, Kael woke the next morning to find it still dark in their room and Kyah gone. Getting dressed, he remembered his saviour in the room next door and wanted to do something to thank her for her help.

Sitting cross-legged on the floor, he closed his eyes and tried to figure out how to use his magic to find the young Fae woman Sephi and her husband were looking for. Concentrating hurt his head and he realized his skull was far from healed, but ignoring the pain was easy thanks to the months of torture he received at the hands of the Dead Sisters. Taking a deep breath, he refocused and sent his esoteric senses out into the world around Dasal. A subdued blaze of white magic flashed inside his mind, but it was far beyond where his senses could reach.

Instinct took over and his mind expelled a pulse of magic that raced for the white light. He followed it in his mind until his magic hit the failing light, making it blaze with renewed energy and return to him, twice as fast. It slowed and entered his mind, telling him that the light was indeed a young Fae woman.

He smiled. "That's cool." Laughing as the rush of magic subsided, he knew immediately that she was to the south-west, the same direction he and Kyah had come from.

"What the hell is going on out there?" he mumbled, opening his eyes. "The ArchWizard's down there, we were down there, and now a Fae is down there. God in Heaven, what's next?" Kael shook his head gently and stood. It mattered little to him in the long run, it really was not any of his business. He walked next door to thank Sephi for her help and to tell her what he had discovered.

She stepped outside seconds after he knocked. Closing the door, she gave him a hug. "You two take care of yourselves, all right?"

"We will, and thank you. For everything. And your Fae? The one you're looking for?"

"What about her?"

"She's to the south-west, moving in this direction," he offered.

"How do you know that?" He shrugged and smiled, making her chuckle. "Thank you, Kael." He nodded and returned to his room to finish packing his few belongings.

When Kyah had not returned by sunrise, Kael gathered his things and headed downstairs, finding her outside with Master Locke and their horses.

Seifer walked with them to the city gate. Their horses and both spare mounts had been loaded with supplies and gear. He handed each of them a small fist-sized bag of gold and silver coin.

"You have our thanks, both of you," Seifer said. "You are welcome in Dasal at any time you may need or like."

"Take care, Master Wizard," Kael said, smiling. Seifer grasped his arm and shook it.

"First names are for friends, Kael, regardless of rank," he said

"Good bye, Seifer." Kael smiled again, mounted his horse and galloped away with Kyah right behind him.

Seifer turned on his heel and headed to the barracks. A very long day awaited him.

Chapter Seventeen

"There are many people in Talohna who play the game of power and money. Yet very few seem willing to pay the price when the time comes to pay the toll for losing. Families like the Talos never lose and so they never pay. But I have always found those who play the game best continue to win even after they have paid the price for losing. Very few people have the foresight to plan that far into the game. Planning beyond my death has given me a distinct advantage."

Lircang Yorcali,
Private journal entry, 5021 PC

BARRACKS PRISON, DASAL

Cold and dark ruled the dungeon. The funk of human waste lingered in the air, rising from the filthy buckets in each prison cell. Water or some foul liquid fell from the ceiling with an incessant tap as it struck the stone floor. The subtle noise added to the convicts' misery. With only two long candles lighting the room inside each barred cell, tall shadows danced on the walls and added to the oppressive weight of doom that soon ate into all prisoners. The Dasal Barracks Prison was one of the few true dungeons left that had survived the Cataclysm five thousand years before.

Master Wizard Seifer Locke stood in the heart of the dungeon, having heard enough excuses. "You know, Lircang, you're already a dead man walking. The city and guard Councils voted for you to hang, unanimously, so what would it hurt?"

Dasal's ex-slave master scoffed. "Hurt? What does it gain me? I'm not telling you where she is, Seifer. You can go fuck your own arse, you..." The wizard's backhand fist flashed with blue light seconds before it struck Lircang with enough force to knock the chair he was tied to backwards. Both crashed to the floor. The slaver groaned and twitched as minute currents of electricity danced across his jaw and over his bald head.

"Fucking wizards," Lircang griped, rubbing his face against the dirty stone floor in an attempt to ground out the last of Seifer's electricity. "Can't just fucking hit someone, gotta use magic, too."

"Pick him up," Seifer snapped. Captain Kern and one of his guards, a freshly-trained recruit, grabbed the chair, picked it up and slammed it back down, eliciting another moan from Lircang. "I gave my promise to her dying father that I'd find her and free her. You have nothing to lose except a shit load of pain, Lircang. Tell me where she is!" Seifer's voice instantly calmed as he placed his hands on the arms of the wooden chair and bent over so he was eye to eye with the man he hated more than anything. "Tell me and you can spend the rest of the time you have left eating and drinking yourself into a stupor before the hangman's noose snaps your fat neck."

Without breaking eye contact, Lircang exhaled his rotten breath into Seifer's face. "There's a winning argument, you... Fuck. Commute my sentence instead and you have a deal. I'll tell you exactly where she is... wizard," Lircang said, using the University term for a first year mystic on purpose.

"I don't have that authority and you know it. You sat on the Council in judgement for how many years yourself? How many times did you sentence people? Only those who sentenced you can commute it, and they won't. I can offer you one final option. I can't give you your life, but as Master Wizard, I can make sure that your businesses and financial earnings pass to your son unimpeded when he returns from where ever he disappeared to."

The slaver snorted with amusement. "That will happen anyway, Locke. Right of Succession—the Legacy assures it. Looks like we're back to you fucking yourself, all mighty wizard," Lircang mocked. Another flash of power lit up the darkness, red instead of blue. Chair and slaver spun, crashing to the floor. Both slid almost six feet before slamming into the closest set of prison bars. Lircang screamed in agony, but his voice quickly climbed to a shriek as the oily flames licking at his face refused to die out.

Panicking, and without thinking, the inexperienced guardsman grabbed the waste bucket from inside the cell and tossed the contents into Lircang's face, dousing the magical fire.

"Mother-screwing piece of dog shit," Lircang sputtered, spraying urine and slimy faeces from his mouth.

"I'm sorry, sir, I..." the guardsman stuttered, as he apologized. The wizard could see the guilt written all over the young guard's face.

Seifer chuckled as he bent over the fallen slaver. "Well, now... Funny, don't you think? I always thought you were a slimy, shit-ridden piece of garbage. Guess the Gods agree." He shook his head, laughing. The slaver returned the smirk and spit at Seifer. More human waste misted from his lips, but inches from Seifer's face, a pale yellow glow flared to life as Lircang's expulsion hit a magical shield and stuck before oozing to the floor. It never touched Seifer's flesh or clothes.

"Ah! Fucking wizards," Lircang moaned, as he lay back.

"Just tell me, Lircang. Get it over with. You know you'll give it up eventually. I'll make sure your Legacy passes to Kyro. You have my word. Because of your conviction, the council and city guard are already talking about severing your Right to Succession. Kyro would get nothing. Your Legacy, everything you own, would be siezed and sold. Kyro could possibly even be convicted if it can be proved he knew what you and Dahlea were up to. You won't get a better deal," Seifer said, as he tried again.

"It's true, Yorcali," Captain Kern said, speaking for the first time. "And to be honest, they'd have my vote. Especially to charge that animal son of yours. I'm tired of handing your money to scarred young women, for his transgressions, just because you held a third of the city's power."

Still laying on his side, Lircang burst out laughing, a full, hearty honest laugh, but after several seconds it died down to a chuckle and his eyes shifted from the guard captain back to Seifer. "I was wondering how long it would take you to stop playing kiddie games. Always knew you had it in you, wizard. You want to make a deal? Then listen. That sweet soul you're so worried about? Ah, what was her name, again?" Lircang paused, being dramatic.

Seifer, unable to help himself, fell for it. "Katarina Desolla. You know exactly who she is, you piece of..."

"Yes, yes. I remember who bought her too. You really should stop talking, Seifer. Listen instead and we might actually make some progress," Lircang said, continuing to chuckle.

"Spit it out," Seifer barked, as flames flickered to life in his right hand. "Or there won't be a piss and shit filled bucked to douse you with this time. I'll make sure of it."

Lircang swallowed hard, his prominent Adam's apple quivering in his throat. "Fair enough, Seifer. First, my deal, and I don't want to hear you can't. You do it or I will die with your beautiful bride-to-be's location buried deep in my mind, clear?" As much as he'd rather choke the slaver, Seifer nodded instead. He'd just have to persuade the councils to deal if he ever wanted to find his fiancée.

"My sentence commuted, either banishment or life inside this cell. I don't care which, but if I hang, you won't find her. Second, all my Legacy passes to Kyro. No exceptions. Once I have a contract in hand, I'll tell you where Katarina is, and how to get her back. That won't be as easy as you think, Master Wizard, but what do you say?" Lircang flashed an enigmatic smile, but covered in human waste, it didn't have the desired effect.

Seifer sneered with contempt, instead. "I'll have to call the city and guard councils back to session, Lircang. They won't agree, not to reducing your sentence."

"You better try." Lircang moaned as Kern and the rookie guardsman lifted his chair back into a sitting position and then cut him free. "You have plenty of goodwill coming your way, especially after letting young Kael deal with your pirate problem. Never thought I'd live to see a DeathWizard walk free in Talohna," he chuckled.

Seifer knew his stunned and puzzled expression told Lircang everything he needed. "Oh, you didn't know. Tell you what, I'll throw in a little DeathWizard historical knowledge for free as part of our deal. I'm sure when the ArchWizard gets here, you'll want to have a respectable excuse ready for why you let such a creature walk away free as a bird!" Lircang's chuckle shifted to a cackle as Seifer stormed from the basement prison, the hysterical laughter followed him.

Seifer's apprentice, Kittrix Dawn, had just finished her own interrogation of Lircang's madame. Washing the grime and blood from her hands in the wash basin inside Seifer's office, she scrubbed her skin relentlessly as she struggled to hold back the tears brought on by her own actions. Splashing her face with water, she took a deep breath, just as Seifer entered the office. Grabbing a towel from the rack beside the basin she dried her face and stepped aside, giving her mentor the chance to freshen up.

With his own hands turning the water red and then black, he sighed. "It never gets easier, Kit. Even after two hundred years, interrogation wears a body out faster than most magic."

"Torture is hard work, Master, for those who inflict it, as well as for those who receive it. Yet it must be done. Did you find her? Did he tell you?" she asked, handing him the towel as he turned.

"No, not without lessening his sentence. Dahlea?" He raised his eyebrow in the hopes the Madame knew where the love of his life was located.

"I'm sorry, Master," Kit said, shaking her head. "She knows nothing about Katarina. I do know where the money from the stolen slaves is hidden, as well as the list of illegal buyers who purchased them. We'll have to petition the Eye for help, Master Seifer. It's too much for us alone. It'll take months to track down and the free people they took. Dasal would be defenceless against magic in our absence."

"Fair enough. I suspect the ArchWizard will be here within a matter of days anyway. We'll pass it to him. There are Cethosian citizens on that list?" he asked.

"Yes, Master, dozens, but why would Master Giddeon come here?"

"Unless I cracked Lircang's brain, it seems that Kael may be a DeathWizard. It'll fall under Giddeon's jurisdiction, just like the names from Lircang's illegal slaving." Kit frowned, and Seifer could see she ached to say something. "Something you'd like to add, apprentice?"

"No, Master. I apologize." She bowed out of respect for over-stepping her bounds.

Seifer sat at the chair behind his desk and stared at his young apprentice. The talented sixteen-year-old could go far, especially under his tutelage, but he worried her former Master had been a hard man. "Why did you volunteer to come to Dasal? You had a Master Wizard, a good one, too. You were the only volunteer. The other three apprentices were put up as part of a punishment detail. Why does a twelve year old girl volunteer to apprentice with a Master Wizard in the Free Lands? You may speak freely, Kit, with no concerns."

"I had hoped things would be different here, Master."

"And are they?" he asked, judging her actions and facial expressions.

"Yes, Master, they are. I love being here. I've never been happier."

"Good, I'm glad. Now stow the University etiquette bullshit and speak your mind. That's what the Gods gave it to you for, didn't they?"

"Yes, Master," she replied, shock settling over her features, but her eyes lit up with excitement.

"I assume you'd like to remain here under my tutelage?" he asked, getting an emphatic nod. "Then if you have something to say, speak. The Eye has no power here and they hold no sway in the Free Lands. Why do you think *I* came here?" he asked with a smile.

"Yes, Master," Kit said beaming with delight. "I just wanted to ask you... If... If Kael is a DeathWizard, shouldn't we be dead?"

Siefer laughed, an honest, hearty laugh. It felt good. "Your first lesson on your first real day as a Free Land's apprentice... What is *actually* true and what the officials of Talohna tell its citizens is true, can often be two very different things—though, I have always believed the same when it came to DeathWizards. I helped Giddeon subdue the last two—my magic kept Giddeon alive after he was attacked. And I've read countless documented accounts of a DeathWizard's brutality. That being said, it probably means Lircang is spinning a lie. We'll know if the ArchWizard shows up, because he'll be doing everything in his power to catch and kill Kael." The conflict of emotion was written all over his face.

"Are the rumours true, Master Locke?"

"Which?"

Kit hesitated, but only for a second. "At the Eye, before you came to get me, I heard that you originally left for Dasal because you and the ArchWizard hated each other. That he was jealous of your power and refused to let you Trial for ArchWizard. That you're more powerful than he is." Her eyes darted to the side, as an embarrassed smile crept onto her face.

Seifer sighed, chuckling. "Apprentices and their rumours. No, the ArchWizard and I have been very close friends since we were children together at the Eye. Oripar Lightfoot, Giddeon, and I were known as the Prodigal Trinity. We were brothers in every sense of the word. You know the story about the night Professor Lightfoot died?" Kit nodded without interrupting. "I was there, as well. My magic extended the portal long enough for Giddeon to return from the other dimension. Oripar was one of three Elvehn mystics who anchored the portal. He died with the others but not before he held the gateway open on his own for several seconds. The ArchWizard and I will always be close friends, at least I would hope. I came to Dasal because I don't like politics and I was being seriously looked at as a successor for the Third Pillar. I have no interest in becoming the King's Wizard. The Pillars of Rule even creep the shit out of me; I sure as Nine Hells don't want to be one. Also, I have no interest in being ArchWizard. I've been to the Forsaken lands several times and have run the ArchWizard Trials many times while overseeing those who have died trying to pass them. If I wanted the title, Kit, I'd have it. As for who is more powerful, it doesn't really matter, does it?"

His apprentice lifted her eyes and stared at him. Seifer knew what was coming before she even opened her mouth, but he let her ask any way. "It might matter, Master, if he asks you to help him hunt down Kael. He saved this city, from pirates and from a rot within our own walls. You can't help him, Master. It's not right!" Realizing she was yelling at her Master Wizard, Kit dropped to her knees, slapping her hands over mouth. "I'm so sorry, Master, forgive me. I shouldn't..." she mumbled through her hands.

Rising to his feet, and stepping around his desk, Seifer grabbed her arm and gently lifted her back up. "I asked you to speak your mind. I'm not going to punish you for obeying my commands. If Giddeon shows up here, he won't receive our help to hunt down Kael. Who could I send? No one would go." He laughed. "But we have more important things to worry about now. Come, we have two councils to convince that it would be a good idea to let Lircang Yorcali live. Waking them in the middle of the night is going to be a poor start."

AVELERA CITY, ELLORYA.
SOUTHERN KINGDOM
TARTS OF KALLI WHOREHOUSE

The door to Kyro Yorcali's room swung open with a loud crash. Secure in his own little world, he merely lifted his head from the soft satin pillow to see who had caused the ruckus. Not surprised in the least, he shook his head.

"What is it, Niko? Care to join us this fine morning?" he asked, slapping the bare ass of the woman lying face down to his right. "I'm sure we can make room for you." He smirked, pushing over the young woman on his left.

"Nope," Niko smirked. "You know the answer to that before you asked. Drinking and whoring are your vice."

"Damn, woman, you need to learn how to enjoy life a little." Exasperated, he lay back, closing his eyes.

"You enjoy it enough for both of us, boss. I'll stick to keeping you alive. Speakin' of which, you might wanna drag that ass of yours outta bed. Emperor Mero's messenger is downstairs. Any chance of earning an audience with his Holy

Righteous Asshole will walk out the door along with his man in about... Oh, sixty seconds." Kyro bolted up, tossing a pillow at his most trusted companion and the highest ranking captain in his organization, but succeeded only in knocking one of the women in the bed to the floor.

Niko Sattori chuckled, tossing her long black hair as she strolled out the door, laughing even harder as Kyro's words chased after her.

"You evil bitch. Don't you think you should have started with that informat..." His words were cut short to the sound of crashing furniture and more swearing drifted out into the hall.

"Serves me damned right for making that cursed woman my right hand," Kyro mumbled, as he tried to untangle his right leg from the left arm sleeve of his long jacket, having mistook it for his trousers in the hurried attempt to not miss the emperor's messenger. The alcohol-induced, pounding in his head was not helping matters either. For days, he had waited for a reply to come from the emperor, but with the yearly gladiator tournament being held during the last week, it had taken until the tourney's last day to finally get a reply. Kyro couldn't afford to let the chance slip by. Forcing his thick head to co-operate, he was dressed and out the door in under thirty seconds.

"Ha!" he barked at Niko, slapping her ass as he passed. Hurrying down the stairs, she followed after him without saying a word, a smile still dancing on her lips.

As Kyro rounded the corner at the bottom of the stairs, his eyes immediately shifted to the Emperor's messenger, or more importantly, to the six-man guard of crossbow-armed Elites who accompanied him. Straightening his clothes, he approached with caution, but was addressed before he could welcome them to his establishment.

"Kyro Yorcali?" the messenger asked, his voice tainted with disgust.

"I am. You've brought good news, I assume?"

"Good news? Well, perhaps." One of the guards, dressed in white bone armour with the blazing red sash worn by all the emperor's men, held out a rolled and sealed document also wrapped in red as the messenger continued. "This writ is signed by Emperor Mero. Show it to the guards stationed at the Nobles' Gate on the Arena's west side. They will escort you to the Gods' Balcony where Emperor Mero has agreed to watch the noon executions and afternoon matches with you and one guest. This is an incredible honour, Kyro Yorcali. Arrive by the high sun today or not at all."

"Fair enough. We shall be there," Kyro said, smiling at the good news.

"The Emperor has cleared the balcony, insulting several of Ellorya's noble families. He wants you to know that the debt he owes your father is now flush. If you are not at the arena by the high sun, you will not leave Ellorya alive. Are we in clear understanding, Kyro Yorcali?"

"We are. Tell Emperor Mero, I'll be there."

"Excellent," the messenger replied, offering a fake smile. "Then I suggest you find proper attire for yourself and your guest of choice. You will be seen in public with the Emperor after all." Kyro nodded, as the man and his guard left the Tarts of Kalli.

Niko scoffed as the door closed behind the emperor's men. "You had better know what you're doing, Kyro, or we'll both end up in that gods-forsaken arena."

"You worry too much, Niko. You're far too pretty to be thrown into the arena. I'm sure the Emperor's harem is a far more likely destination," he chuckled, and then ducked, but still was not quite fast enough as the woman's fist crashed into his shoulder instead of his jaw. His left arm went numb as he raised his right hand in surrender, then bowed and returned to his room. The first part of his plan was completed.

He hoped his father had been just as successful on his end of the plan back in Dasal.

DASAL, FREE LANDS

All assassins did extensive research and recon when they were on the hunt. It was safer that way, even for members of the infamous mystical guild known only as the Broken Blades. Frightening magical killers from Talohna's oldest and darkest myths, Broken Blade assassins never failed. Upon agreement, one Broken Blade contract equalled one patron, one killer, and one corpse. Targets were never discussed. Targets could be missed or could escape. With the Broken Blades this could not happen. A Blade never gave up the hunt until they had their corpse. If they become a corpse themselves, more Blades were sent.

Broken Blade senior councillor member, Merethyl Bellas, watched from the far side of the street as two wizards departed the Dasal city barracks. Even though she had never met either personally, Seifer Locke and Kittrix Dawn were well known to Merethyl because of her research, and she did not care to cross paths with either, let alone both. She knew that Seifer Locke's magic ran heavy with the Elderblood that enabled him to enhance any magic near him, including his own. She frowned at the idea of fighting the pair once Seifer enhanced their magic.

As Seifer and Kit turned the corner and disappeared from view, a coy grin and a simple nod from the Broken Blade Queen spurred her two hiding killers to action. Sliding through the shadows, both soundlessly entered the barracks as Merethyl kept watch outside. Sixty seconds passed before the door re-opened and two puffs of magical flame lit up the darkened doorway, prompting her to move. Sliding through the shadows unseen, she reached the barracks as Pok waved from the far stairwell entrance.

"Here, Merethyl," he whispered. "Yorcali's on this side, the whore on the other."

"Good work," she nodded. "Send your rat to watch the door, we'll go down." Pok nodded at his apprentice, a young girl of fifteen years named Lany. She frowned, but did as she was asked. Merethyl noticed the girl's objection. It merely added to her dislike of Pok's orphan. Leading the way down into the dungeon, Pok said nothing. The two women and their hatred of each other was common knowledge, yet it never interfered with guild business. The guild always came first.

Merethyl stepped onto the stone floor of the dungeon and wrinkled her nose at the evasive odour, the stench tripled in strength from the top of the stairs. Ignoring it, her eyes settled on the first cell and its occupant.

"Lircang Yorcali," she mocked, laughing in a little girl's voice as she approached the barred cell. "Such a fine mess you've gotten yourself into, love. I don't like cleaning messes, you fat Kariyan bastard. Especially other fool's messes."

Free from the chair he had spent the last eighteen hours tied to, Lircang looked up through swollen eyes. "Merethyl? What are you doing here?"

"You're sitting in one of the most vile dungeons in Talohna when you have an agreement with myself and Sythrnax. What else would I be doing here? Taking a lovely late winter vacation in Talohna's beautiful city of Dasal?" Her calm and cool demeanour sent undulating shivers of fear through Lircang. His reaction brought a quiet smile of pleasure to Merethyl's lips.

"No. Mer... I... I didn't say anything, Merethyl. You know that. I wouldn't—" The assassin held up her hand to silence him.

"Then why would the town wizard and his lapdog bitch be heading towards the mansion district of Dasal at three o'clock in the morning? Perhaps the remaining council members are ready for their pre-dawn magical massage? Is that it?"

"No! I—" But again, Merethyl didn't let him finish.

"Where's your son, Yorcali?"

"Merethyl?" Lircang asked innocently, but his quivering tongue gave away his nervousness.

"Your son, you fat fool. Where in this gods-forsaken world is your bastard son?" For the first time in years, true anger crept into her normally stoic voice.

"On trade business, Merethyl. Meeting with slave contacts."

Merethyl lunged through the bars and grasped Lircang by the neck, pulling him towards her until the fat of his face enveloped the bars. "You're lying, you sack of shit. I can't find him anywhere," she growled. "Tell me what he's up to. Now! And I'll have Sythrnax make all this crap you've brought on us go away."

To her surprise, Lircang scoffed. "Now who's lying, Merethyl? I always knew I'd end up dead on your wooden blade. It's a price I've always been willing to pay. You'll never find Kyro; he's beyond even your reach, and when he returns, your mysterious benefactor won't be able to hurt him or ruin what we've done."

Full of confidence, the slaver smirked at the assassin queen, but it soon turned to a frown as Merethyl smiled back. "Ah, but I will. You just told me where your son is, which puts him well within my reach."

The blood drained from Lircang's face as he realized his mistake, but he was unable to speak.

"What's the matter, slaver?" she teased. "Snowcat got your tongue? Out of my reach? You're slipping, Yorcali. Ellorya is the only country without a Blade sanctuary. Sent your boy to collect on an old debt from Emperor Mero, did you? Perfect. I can kill both of them with one trip south."

With a shove, she released the man's throat and sent him crashing to the floor.

"Pok?" she asked. The newly-elected Broken Blade Commander turned towards her from the other cells, his wooden blade dripped blood, but it was intact. "Kill this weasel so we can go, please. And don't use a Broken Blade. Sythrnax doesn't want any more attention headed our way." Pok nodded but said nothing as he used a key from the wall upstairs to unlock Lircang's cell. The Kariyan slave trader whimpered, begging for his life as he shuffled to the back of his cell. Pok cornered Lircang at the rear wall.

Bending down, he locked eyes with the slaver and smiled. "*Asalm,*" he whispered. Unable to break free from the hypnotic gaze passed to Pok through a very long line of Elderblood, Lircang smiled an idiotic grin as drool slid over his quivering lip. "Open your mouth, dead man," the assassin added, his voice vacant of emotion. Though Lircang trembled with the effort of trying to fight the hypnotic command, his bottom jaw slowly fell. Pok pulled a thin, six inch bamboo tube from inside his dark coat and slid the razor-sharp point under the slave master's tongue. As a single fear-filled tear wept its way down Lircang Yorcali's cheek, Pok gently pushed the poison-tipped weapon to a depth of one inch into the slaver's flesh. The untraceable venom, drawn from the stinger of the rare Salt Flats GrandScorpion, raced through Lircang's blood until it stopped his heart—five seconds later.

As Merethyl watched Lircang die, she could not help but wonder the repercussions of Sythrnax's death warrant against Yorcali. The slaver was old and had mellowed considerably with age. His son, Kyro, however, was young and a very dangerous man. The real power behind Yorcali's operations for many years had been Kyro. Lircang's Legacy—all he owned—money, men, power. All would pass to the youth upon his return to Dasal. It made the dangerous young man even more powerful.

Merethyl's extensive contacts had not been able to locate the young man or learn what he had been up to, but an overconfident egomaniac seldom kept secrets. She shrugged it off; it was now a minor inconvenience for a group of her assassins already hunting a traitor in the Elloryan Forest. Once turned to a new focus, they would kill the younger Yorcali long before he left the Southern Kingdoms.

Sending others to do what should be done by oneself was considered breaking one of the Broken Blade Assassins' most sacred decrees. Sending other assassins after Kyro Yorcali could turn out to be a mistake.

But Merethyl shrugged it off. She never made mistakes.

Chapter Eighteen

"To be forced to raise a child marked by the most sinister of evil is a burden that should not be wished on anyone. I will curse my dead brother every day until I finally see him for myself in the fires of Perdition, and then I will curse the bastard in person. My family have been under the threat of death for eleven years now, thanks to his putrid little spawn. He even had the balls to give her our mother's name. Cassandra. I hope Mother curses him daily as they both suffer in the fires of all Nine Hells."

Crissa Daniels,
Personal journal entry, 5025 PC

CAIRN'S WOODS, FREE LANDS

The forest flashed by under the young girl's feet as she leapt from branch to branch and tree-to-tree. She moved with the skill and grace of a hunting predator. Her toes barely touched the wood of each limb she landed on. Her hands never slipped and her feet never stumbled as she moved through the trees high above the ground; only a true hunter would have detected the subtlest of movements overhead.

Cairn's Woods was her own personal refuge. She knew every tree, every branch, and almost every single leaf for miles around the town, and she spent every second she could in what she considered to be her forest. The animals knew her well and had stopped running from her years ago. Even the mother bear that lived in the caves up the mountain trail would no longer growl at her presence. Though try as she might, Cassandra still could get no closer to her cubs than ten feet before the mother snorted and lead them away. But they never ran, and she never gave chase.

Cassandra lived in the village of Cairnwood, about five days' ride north of Dasal. It was a respectably-sized town for the area, and like Dasal, it belonged to no king or country. The town was one of the last that still existed in the remains of the old Dwarven Kingdom. The area surrounding it was forest and mountain; with the town situated in the foothills of the Dwarven Mountains. The town's economy was dependant on the timber provided by the massive forest and the mining that was done in the hills and mountains.

The Greystone River that ran through Cairn's Woods from the mountains to the west of town moved the timber to the city of Samitor in Yusat in a matter of only five days. The strongest and bravest of the town's people worked the lumber trade. The river runners who escorted all the lumber to Samitor for sale were responsible for defending the lumber and themselves during the journey.

Mining was the town's only other resource. Iron, coal, and a few veins of gemstone were mined in enough quantity to keep Cairnwood's economy stable and the town itself growing in size, even if at a turtle's pace.

The main reason most of the miners stayed in Cairnwood, however, was for the slim chance that they would once again come across more of the volcanic glass that would sell for triple its weight in gold. Only Orotaq blacksmiths had the knowledge that could turn the glass into obsidian weapons; shiny, black blades that never needed sharpening and powerful bows that never broke. Bows no normal man could even string, let alone draw. They shot twice as far as the best Elvehn longbows and could penetrate plate armour to a depth of twelve inches.

Obsidian weapons were almost unheard of south of the Black Hollow Peninsula where the Orotaq made their home. Most black glass that was found made its way to Black Hollow by way of Talohna's black market. Two of Cairnwood's most elite traders were permitted dealings with the Orotaq directly. They were the only exception. Anyone else who entered the Black Hollow peninsula never returned.

Cassandra, or Cassie as most of the townsfolk liked to call her, had lived in Cairnwood since she was almost two years old, brought there when her mother and father died. She lived with her uncle and aunt in a small house in town. A miner, her uncle was the last to find a vein of the precious black glass. Two years ago, he had found it down a deadhead shaft, and the proceeds from the sale to the Orotaq had given him the money to build his own house, a luxury few in Cairnwood had. However, he was now on the coal crew, working in the dirtiest and most dangerous of the mines. For almost two years after his discovery, he had the easiest of jobs trying to locate new veins of glass, but eventually everyone was forced to earn their pay for the town, and the town was paid by what came out of the mines, not by looking for what might be there.

Cassie's aunt was one of the town's herbalists, the best, in fact. With no wizards living in Cairnwood, natural and herbal healing as well as minor surgical knowledge was all the town had. Herbs, roots, and other remedies helped all ailments, from cuts and infections to easing the miners' lungrot after years in the deep earth. Cassie would sometimes tell her aunt about the rarer plants she would see when out in the forest, but it was a place her aunt and uncle did not like her to be.

They fed her and gave her a bed in the corner of the kitchen at night, but they had two of their own children and mining with the coal crew paid very little, healers made even less. Both boys were younger than her. Ben was eight and Bastion six. They were good boys, Cassie often thought, but they were boys nonetheless. They liked to tease her or pull her long, strawberry-blonde hair, and they constantly tried to follow her around, but they were never mean and they never hurt her.

Cassie always had food, but she often noticed her cousin's plates were usually heavier than hers, even though they were younger, and Cassie was required to do all of the house chores to pay for her keep. If she was seen sneaking off to Cairn's Woods, she was given more work to do. The boys would try to pitch in and help, knowing she longed to go to the forest if she finished early. She loved them for it.

This day, Cassie had managed to sneak off after lunch. She knew when she got back her aunt would take the switch to her backside, but it would be worth it. For now, the wind and fresh air filled her with energy as tree limb after tree limb passed under her feet with ease. Burning with the need for oxygen, her arms and legs ached, but as she breathed faster, her lungs supplied the need to her agile young body and the discomfort disappeared. It caused an increase in her speed and the ground flashed by twenty feet below her. The thought of slowing or falling was never a concern.

Cassie lived for these moments, like she was meant for more than being a miner's wife or a town herbalist. Though her father had been raised in Cairnwood, no one would talk about him or her mother. Even her aunt and uncle refused to speak of them, saying only that she was better off where she was. She knew only that her father and her aunt had been very close as kids growing up together. Her aunt had said so one night when she though Cassie was asleep. Her aunt got angry whenever she asked about either of her parents, but it was something Cassie desperately wanted to know.

No matter what her aunt said, Cassie refused to believe the rest of the world was not worth seeing and experiencing. She felt in the core of her soul that her mother and father would have wanted more for her. She sometimes imagined that she had a great destiny to fulfill, as she dreamt of someday helping people in need or fighting dangerous monsters and evil people. As she raced through the trees, changing heights and speeds, she imagined she was an Elvehn scout, gliding through the trees defending her forest from creatures of darkness. It would not be long before she would have to return home so she laughed out loud and pushed herself to greater speeds, her spirit singing with the smell of the forest and the thrill of her movement.

Many times, Cassie spent the whole night out in the forest, but winter refused to relinquish its grasp on the lower elevations of the Dwarven Mountains, so the nights remained too cold to stay away from home. With chores that still needed to be done back home, she started to head back, travelling through the trees the entire way. Over two miles passed before she noticed the heavy smoke coming from her village, and still Cassie had not touched a single toe to the earth. Had she done so or had she been travelling on the ground, she would already be dead.

Cassie headed to the west, still in the trees, knowing she could get into town by staying hidden up in the trees. Heavy movement on the ground reached her ears, coming from the edge of town, but the setting sun and the village walls prevented her from seeing who they were. The smoke and screams coming from her village told her the movement she was hearing belonged to people who were far from friendly.

Her final jump over the wall and into the massive oak tree on the north-western edge of town by the village square confirmed her fears. Everywhere she looked, people were running and dying, chased and dragged down by massive black hounds. People she knew and talked to everyday screamed and died as she watched. When bright purple and red lights flared on the southern edge of town, she knew she had just seen magic used for the first time in her life. More magic sizzled, lighting up the south by the front gates with pale blue. Cassie snuggled down into the big oak tree for comfort, hoping she would not be seen as the noise of baying hounds reached her ears.

She could see the majority of the town from her hiding place up in the oak tree. The attackers were giant men, some close to eight feet tall, but most were well over seven. Their skin had a pale blue sheen. Cassie whimpered lightly as she realized they must be the Orotaq. Living just south of the Dwarven Mountains, the Orotaq were the town's boogeymen. Growing up as children, her and her cousins were told if they didn't behave, the Orotaq would come and eat them. BlackHollow Peninsula was north and west of Cairnwood, beyond the Dwarven Mountains, but as far as Cassie knew, no one from Cairnwood had ever actually seen even a single Orotaq except for the village traders. Tonight, the whole town was seeing a lot of them. They were everywhere. She had never been so terrified in her entire life.

Staying hidden in the tree, mere minutes passed before she saw her aunt and uncle with both her young cousins running across the square in front of her. She yelled to get their attention, and when they stopped, she quickly climbed down the oak tree to join them. Landing on the ground for the first time in hours was a mistake. Cassie looked up just as a speeding arrow pierced her uncle's throat. A scream of horror escaped her lips as he stumbled and fell to his knees. Blood sprayed from the front of his neck only five feet from where she stood. The boys sobbed, realizing their father was dead. Her aunt cried as she knelt by the body, desperately trying to hold her husband as the last of his life fled.

Too terrified to move, Cassie flinched as a hail of arrows whistled by, cutting people down whether they stood or ran.

Even though in a daze of shock, she heard her aunt scream at her. "This is your fault, Cassandra. If you hadn't yelled for us to stop he would still be alive..."

Her aunt's scream turned to sobbing and Cassie mumbled. “I... I'm... sorry,” she managed.

The apology only seemed to enrage her aunt further. “Just like your cursed mother, never caring for anyone but yourself,” she screamed even louder. “There is not a single shred of your father's blood in you, all of it from that vile bitch...” Her scream was suddenly cut short.

Cassie winced as warmth and wet slapped her face. She opened her eyes in time to see three feet of blood-dripping black sword as it was pulled back through her aunt's chest. Her dead body fell to the side as her aunt's blood ran into Cassie's eyes.

Cassie blinked through the gore in an attempt to clear her sight, before she grabbed the boys and ran. The laughter of the giant, blue-skinned man who killed her aunt followed after her. With the boys screaming hysterically, Cassie pulled them both along with her. Doing her best to avoid more of the giant men, as well as dodging the black phantom-like hounds that hunted the town's residents, she raced to the north-side gate. It was broken, shattered in the initial assault, but it lay wide open and her heart pounded at the prospect of freedom. With a jolt to both her arms, the boys yanked their hands from hers and she realized they were no longer crying.

She spun around as both of her cousins fell to the ground, their small backs littered with black-feathered arrows sunk to the flights. The monstrous Orotaq male covered in branded flesh who had killed her aunt, stood only feet away. The shiny black bow fell to the dirt with a clatter as he drew the black sword once more. Tears coursed down Cassie's blood stained face and she fell to her knees knowing she was going to die.

She bowed her head in defeat, not wanting to see it coming, and sobbed, realizing for the first time that she'd been born to die in the blood-soaked streets of Cairnwood and not for something far greater like she had always dreamed.

DASAL

Seifer Locke stormed out of Salisar Pollondo's sprawling estate located on the northern end of the mansion district in Dasal. Kit was right on his heels. It had been their second stop at a city councillor's home in the last hour. The first visit had gone much better. Having spent an hour convincing the City Guard council to stay Lircang Yorcali's death sentence, Seifer and Kit moved on to the City Council. Nessedra Vantaur's residence was closer, so they had stopped there first. It took little time to convince her that overruling the execution order so that Lircang would reveal the location of Seifer's fiancée, Katarina Desolla, was a fair deal. The Desolla family name was well respected throughout Talohna. Salisar, however, disagreed, adamantly. Without a unanimous vote from both councils, the execution decree stood.

"What now, Master?" Kit asked, as her shorter legs struggled to keep up.

"If Yorcali is going to die anyway, then I'll beat Katarina's location out of him. Sooner or later, he'll break." Fifteen minutes later, the two wizards were back at the barracks. Kit opened the heavy, metal-crossed door and stepped inside. The familiar tang of blood and magic hung in the air.

"Master?" Silence drifted on the dead air and both noticed that the three guards were nowhere to be seen.

"Shit," Seifer snapped, as he dashed for the far dungeon door. "Kit! Check on Dahlea." Seifer raced down the stairs, not bothering to check if his apprentice had listened. Jumping the last few stone steps into the dungeon, Seifer's hands lit up with a flash of bright blue electricity. It snapped and popped, darting out and dancing on the moist air permeating the cells. Already positive of what he'd find, he crept around the corner of Lircang's open cell and spotted the still body. With his senses pushed as far as he could and nerves drawn tight, Seifer turned his back to the dead man and eased past the slaver's cell to check the others, looking for the killer. The cells past Lircang's held another stilled body, the criminal's throat had been cut, but the empty cells hid no assassin.

Quieting the magic in his left hand, Seifer returned to Lircang's cell and pushed the iron door the rest of the way open. The squeal of the hinges grated on his rattled nerves. He knelt at Lircang's side, but could see very little in the dark. Closing his eyes, he let his esoteric senses float from his body. His eyes snapped open as he felt a flicker of life.

"*Skipta Bal.*" Barely more than a whisper, Seifer's spell transformed the lightening in his right hand, changing it into a ball of bright fire. The flames illuminated the cell as if the sun shone overhead. With his left hand, Seifer rolled Lircang's body onto its back with a wet smack. His senses told him the spark was gone.

"Come on, you bastard. Wake up!" He slapped the slaver, twice, but the body remained still. "You fucking bastard. Leave it to you to get killed with your secrets. Damn your sorry soul all the way to the gates of Perdition." The heavy door at the top of the stairs opened, and though he couldn't see her, Seifer felt Kit descend into the dungeon. Light from her lamp moved across the floor outside the cell.

With nothing more he could do, Seifer stood to join her. A shallow nod from his apprentice told him that Lircang's Madame, Miss Dahlea, was also dead. He shook his head and cursed. A clawed hand dug into his calf with enough strength to make him swear a second time. He spun and looked down. Lircang Yorcali was holding on to him as if the DeathGod's reapers were trying to drag him to the deepest pits of Hell. Seifer bent back down and grabbed Lircang's crud-covered shirt, pulling him closer, wrinkling his nose at the stench.

"What happened? You were dead, Lircang. I sensed it. Your body's riddled with poison."

The slaver struggled to drag a breath into his lungs, a wet gurgle followed by a hollow rattle told Seifer that the man's lungs were more mush than lung. "Shut up and li...

listen." The four words launched the slaver into a coughing fit. Blood and mist sprayed from his mouth and nose.

"Tell me where she is" Seifer barked, shaking Lircang. "Before you die, do something right."

"Right? We've been trying Seifer. My son..."

"I don't care about your damn son. Where's Katarina? Tell me!" Another coughing fit racked Lircang's body as the poison raced to end his life.

"Listen," the slaver rasped. "She... she's with..." With no warning, Lircang's eyes rolled back in his head and his stomach and lungs turned themselves inside out, splashing Seifer with blood. The GrandScorpion's venom doing what it did best. The Master Wizard didn't notice and shook Lircang again. Finally, he wheezed his way back to consciousness. "Help my son, Seifer," he coughed.

"Not unless you tell me where she is. I promise..."

"Stop!" Lircang barked, and grasped Seifer's arm, his nails dug in. "Kat... she's with... Ella," Lircang spit as he struggled to speak.

Seifer's world crashed around him as he slumped to the floor with Lircang on his knees. "No... That's not possible. No one has seen her in decades. Yorcali, why?"

"Her... Elderblood. The God's... Favoured. She..." Lircang heaved again and more blood rushed from his mouth. "My... son..."

"Elderblood? What the Nine Hells are you talking about? Kat has no magic!"

"Exactly. Her... Her... Elder bloodline..."

"Yorcali! Where is she? Where do I look? Dammit!" Seifer yelled as he watched the last signs of life flee the slaver's body. He stared in disbelief and let Lircang fall to the floor dead. Furious, he lashed out, kicking Lircang's still body and tearing the filthy remains of his shirt. Disbelief flooded every ounce of Seifer's being as he glimpsed a mark on the lower part of Lircang's right rib. Kit stepped closer with a lamp, focusing the light on the intricate design.

"No wonder he didn't die sooner, Master," Kit said as she knelt beside the body. Eyeing the symbol, she moved the light even closer, showing Seifer.

"You've seen it before?"

"Not this exact mark, Master, but I know what it is." Seifer glanced at her, raising his eyebrow. "It is a symbol of the White, I think."

"You're right. It's the mark of rebirth for a cleansed soul. It makes you immune to most poisons, resistant to others. Lircang knew he'd end up this way and tried to protect himself. His killer used GrandScorpion poison. The mark slowed its progress, but it couldn't save him."

"GrandScorpion? Is that possible? Who would even attempt to acquire it?" Seifer shrugged his shoulders. His apprentice was right. The race of beings known as the Salt Flats GrandScorpion were survivors from another time. The humanoid scorpion-like creatures were armoured in living chitin-like bone. Ferocious and extremely anti-social even amongst their own kind, they attacked on sight. Most people would live their entire lives never even hearing news of them. There had never been confirmation of one being killed, let alone one hunted and harvested for the extremely lethal poison located inside the tail stinger and the quills that lined their massive claws.

"Questions I can't begin to answer, Kit. Focus on the mark instead. What do you know?"

"Back in Corynth, Master Tahn said only those who practise the White can lay the blessings of the Higher Brethren. He called them the Mark of Angels."

Seifer nodded his agreement, his mind a whirl of thoughts. "The fact that Tahn researched such a thing is disturbing, but it's trouble for the Wizard's Council, and on another day. We have our hands full enough for today. Did Tahn ever mention Elderblood, Kit?"

"No, Master. I know what the heritage bloodline is: families with special magic, but I've never heard much of Elderblood. Just rumours."

"I have. Elderblood runs through my veins. Heritage bloodlines and their magical gifts is common knowledge like you said. But it began with six wizards blessed by the gods personally, or so my family taught me. These wizards held the six Elder powers. Invisibility. Rapid healing and immortality. Mind control or hypnosis. Time and dimension magic. Levitation. And..."

"And augmentation, your bloodline power," Kit said, interrupting.

"Yes. Most are lost now. As far as I know, only Giddeon and myself still have Elderblood, and Giddeon's has never quickened. We don't even know what family Giddeon's descended from."

"Master? Does that mean Kael will have Elderblood as well?"

"Holy Mother Inara!" Seifer cursed, realizing he had never even thought about it. He shook his head. "Tomorrow's problem, Kit."

"Of course," she said, bowing.

"Lircang said that Ella had Katarina. Perdition's fiery gates, what's going on here?"

"I know not, Master. But he must have meant Ella Navasha. The White witch. She gave him the mark." Seifer stared at his young apprentice as uneasiness raced through his body. He hadn't heard the name of Ella the White in decades. It was a name he dearly hoped to never hear again, let alone have to see her again. A White witch handled angelic power granted by an angel, a power very few had. Angels only granted their power to their most devout mortal servants, or when they were tricked into turning it over. Even fewer stole an angel's power by killing one.

Seifer shook his head at the rush of memory. He was the only single person alive who knew how Ella Navasha had gained the magic of the White.

Even fewer people could predict how she would use it on any given day.

ARGELA, ELLORYA

Katarina and Desiree had been gone for twenty minutes when Ella heard a soft knock at the door to the house she rented. Opening the weathered plank door, she smiled.

"Cormack WhiteFrost, Court Wizard to the Duchess Fiera Starl." Ella said, offering a mock bow. "It is so nice to see you again, especially seeing as how far you've stepped up in the world."

Cormack dipped his head. "Ella. This my apprentice, Selia." The sixteen year old bowed to show her respect. Ella disliked the young girl immediately, after bowing her chin returned to its original position—high and full-on arrogant. Hubris in the young was a fatal flaw, and it irked Ella every time she witnessed it.

"Nice to meet you, dear. My, my. Two runecasters in one room, and we're not even on Kastalborg Isle. Lucky me," she said, sarcasm dripping from her voice. "Come in, then. Don't be shy, especially when you have information for me."

The wizard shook his head as he entered. Ella noticed both his hands were closed, his fingers moving slightly. A quick look to the young apprentice showed her the same. "Be careful, Cormack. Rub those runes any harder and they might break. We wouldn't want that, would we?"

"I don't know, Ella. Last time I saw you, you threatened to 'turn my black ass inside out' I believe is what you said."

"Well, you broke a promise. You and that fucking Giddeon... Both of you should have died that day..."

"Easy, Ella, I had nothing to do with what the ArchWizard did. I was on a Reaver ship, you know that. We couldn't come back for you. Bale's troops had us outnumbered by—"

"Leaving me stranded in the Wildlands, you shit!" she hissed, memories swarming her mind.

"Ella? You asked me here, remember? I didn't come to fight you, for Freyla's sake." Ella nodded her head, trying to regain her composure.

"You're right," she sighed. "Tell me about this alchemist. Is it true the Broken Blade never got close?"

"No. Not even to the stream, from what I was told. You'll never make it that way, Ella. If you believe the reports, the traps and magic he uses are unlike anything we've seen."

"So I'm told. It seems that Giddeon made a mess of his dimensional bridge twenty years ago."

"That would explain this man's knowledge; he's not from our dimension. No wonder he's so dangerous," Cormack said. Ella bowed, smiling at the foresight of the runecaster. Cormack had always been smarter than most wizards.

"Is there an entrance to the Deep Earth nearby this madman?" she asked.

"Yes," Selia answered. "Between the Elloryan Forest and the mountain range. But it's full of Mahala. Only a fool would go that way."

Ella glared at the arrogant young woman. "Hush, child, while the adults talk."

"But, Mistress, I know the area well, The Deep is lousy with Mahala. It would take an army to get past them—"

Ella frowned at Cormack as the brazen youth's voice grated on her nerves.

"Selia," Cormack whispered. "Enough."

"Your apprentice needs to learn her place," Ella said. "Back up a few paces, girl, and be silent. I don't give second warnings often and never a third."

"*Bitch,*" Selia muttered under her breath. But not quite low enough.

Ella stared at her. "You should have explained the concept of respect to your apprentice, Cormack. She will live longer."

"I did, Ella. She's young and hot-headed, like all Northmen pups. She meant no offence, right, Selia?" The apprentice nodded, but said nothing as, a small smirk curled on her lips.

Ella smiled, still staring at Selia. "It's all right, Cormack, I'm not offended." With an outward twist of her hand, Ella activated her White magic. Selia's neck glowed white as her head snapped to the side, her neck broken. "Not any more, I'm not," Ella said, turning back to Cormack.

"No!" Cormack yelled as he grabbed Selia's body before it crumpled to the floor. "Ah! You're a bitch, Ella," he said, rubbing the runes in his hand faster. "A murderous bitch to boot." Ella lifted her hand for another spell just as both broken runes tumbled to her feet. A blaze of white light blinded her. Her hand shot out as more angelic magic lit the room in dazzling white as pops and sizzles echoed off the wooden walls.

She heard Cormack snap his third rune, but could not see it surround him in a shield as her explosive blast of air slammed into him, launching him through the door and out into the alley. By the time Ella's vision cleared, he was gone along with Selia's body.

Ella screamed. "Elderblood! Next time it won't be your ass. It'll be your whole fucking body I turn inside out, Cormack!"

She sat staring out the broken door and into the street until both her prodigies returned home almost an hour later.

Chapter Nineteen

"To fight for the glory of the gods and our patrons is what it means to be a gladiator. Victory in battle is all that matters."

Saiis Doran, Osok champion
4134 PC

AVALERA CITY, ELLORYA.
SOUTHERN KINGDOM
THE OSOK ARENA

Alec Terraine had been patiently waiting to die for weeks. As another body was dragged down the ramp of the great arena, trailing all manner of gore and fluids he didn't have a name for, the young thief wondered if he would soon look the same. He prayed to the gods his own death would be cleaner and far quicker. Shaking his head at the fairy-tale thoughts that reminded him of the stories his wife used to tell their daughter and son, he sighed. They were fables that always came to a close with a happy ending. He watched with eyes of the condemned as a second body followed the first, trailing evidence of more violence. A crack in the stone floor snagged a piece of exposed flesh and the poor bastard's leg tore free, remaining behind. Alec laughed out loud as he stared at his own happy ending—death and severed limbs and then to be dragged away by hooks through his ankles. All because of a jealous, wealthy merchant married to nobility. He sighed. At least he would be with his wife and children again soon.

"Welcome to Ellorya," he muttered.

Preoccupied by the thoughts that kept invading his mind, Alec missed the first call from the arena's DayMaster, the large, scarred former champion in charge of the daytime arena fights.

"Terraine? Brethren curse your stinking hide. Terraine! Yer next, coward. Time to pay your debt to Elloryan society." The big man howled with laughter at his own words as two others released Alec from his shackles and pulled him to his feet.

"Yer a lucky coward as well as a thief. Emperor Mero himself is in the Gods Balcony today, along with some Blood Kingdom guru. Yer gonna shit yerself into the afterlife in the presence of royalty and the rich, boy." More abrasive laughter bounced off the walls as the two men, stinking of death and gods only knew what else, led Alec up the ramp to the weapon room of the arena's south side entrance.

"One blade and one shield, shitter," barked the first man, shoving Alec into the middle weapons rack. Not knowing any better, Alec grabbed a chipped, rust-covered Salzaran scimitar and a large, beat up round shield. The shield was too heavy; his arm ached from holding it for only a few seconds. The next two he tried were the same, leaving him with only one real option.

He picked the only shield left on the middle rack, a small metal buckler. The inside handle was equipped with a skeletal metal glove for added support, but he knew it wouldn't save his life. Taking too long at the weapon stand earned him a punch to the head as the men wrestled him to the large steel gate and stood guard behind him as they waited for it to rise. A horn blared, coming from somewhere out in the arena. Even though he knew it was the signal for the next fight—his fight—to begin, it felt so surreal that he stood there, transfixed, and lost all control of his own muscles, completely unaware that the gate had started to rise.

Alec's calves and thighs quivered like the strings of a bard's banjo during a dark tale of death. Breath shot from his mouth in explosive gasps and sweat poured into his eyes, burning, before it mixed with fear-induced tears, both falling from his nose as he shook. A lumberjack by trade, he had never swung a sword in his life, let alone had reason to lift a shield. With a loud ping of ringing metal, Alec noticed the bottom of the giant steel gate passed his face and the arena stood before him. As the fear overtaking his body reached a climax, the sensation of warm urine running down his left leg brought him back to the realization that he was going to die. Too terrified to feel the shame of soiling himself, he took an uneasy step into the massive granite arena.

The Osok, filled to capacity, roared with the voices of thousands as the Emperor's announcer gave an exaggerated account of Alec's crimes.

"Stealing the lock boxes of two Elloryan vendors," the voice boomed. "Guilty. Failing to submit to demands issued by city guard: guilty. Assault on several members of the Elloryan city guard: guilty." The voice, amplified by magic, echoed out across the arena, reaching the ears of all in attendance. "Alec Terraine, your sentence, issued and signed by his holiness, High Emperor Colias Mero, is to fight, one on one, with Osok Champion, Lavik Natairis. As it is the final showing of the Day of Elites, the noon-sitting, this fight will be to the death. Pardon can be offered by his Holiness only."

At the revelation that this would be the final execution match, the crowd noise escalated to a frenzy pitch. Alec froze in panic as the sound reached a deafening state, booming off the arena's walls on all sides. The two men quickly entered the arena and shoved him forward, until he stared up into the emperor's private balcony.

Scared beyond reason, Alec dropped to his knees and prayed to the gods for a quick death.

DEEP EARTH, TALOHNA

A cloaked figure stood with his hands out to the side, pulling power from the earth. A dark energy so black, it seemed to draw in and absorb all the light around him. The stone and dirt began to shake with a hollow rumble from deep inside the underground cavern where he cast his frenzied magic. The surface cracked open with a roar as flames erupted and more dark energy poured forth. The wizard, if one could call the figure such, manipulated the black forces with ease, pushing it back into the earth at five distinct and evenly spaced locations, all marked by unknown glyphs. Purple and black ripples of ore shot from the five points of power, spiralling skyward and bursting through the surface above him.

The five spiral towers of the unknown ore ceased their heavenly push at a height of over four hundred feet. Months passed as the cloaked figure oversaw the completion of the powerful towers. Once completed, he stood at the top, looking out at the foundations of eight more towers positioned at all four points of the compass and the four shared points between them. Standing at the top of the central tower, the ninth, he knew the kingdoms of man would finally be subjugated beneath his people's feet.

Every option and every road travelled through the future always led to this point. Zaddyk watched it all from inside his fevered mind. With a wretched twist inside his stomach, the prophet jolted back to the present as he jerked upright in his bed... Again. He jumped from his bed in fear as the nightmare ended, but once again, realized it wasn't a horror-induced dream but a possible premonition of things to come. The young prophet had once again fallen asleep and somehow managed to grasp the pendant hanging around his neck. Its power sent his mind to the future at the faintest touch, and mixed with his dream-state, left him confused and terrified as yet again he saw only darkness and a world headed for destruction.

It had been roughly a month since the goddess Cortina had touched Zaddyk with her power, and still he was no closer to solving the mystery of what the Goddess had called 'Giddeon's mistake'. He had heard those very words from his Goddess the night she had gifted him her power and every night since, but didn't know what she meant. Now, a month later, she still refused to tell him.

"Please, Goddess, help me. I don't understand. I can't see Giddeon's mistake." He prayed again, asking for the hundredth time. Her voice rolled through his head as it had so many times before.

I cannot, my child. I can interfere no further or the results will be worse than any future you have seen.

"I know," Zaddyk said, sighing. "I will keep trying, My Lady."

I know you will find the answers if you persist. He felt her presence rush from his mind. It left an aching emptiness that would last for hours.

Everyone else was positive the future Zaddyk often saw was one where the DeathWizard Giddeon currently hunted was allowed to live. He did not agree, but had to admit that it was starting to look like the cloaked and hooded wizard from his visions was using the dark power of the underworld to build massive magical towers just like Jasala Vyshaan had once done. It made his knees weak; Jasala's tower had produced frightening power, but the nine he saw were capable of immense destruction.

Deciding to tell Brother Donis that he could see no other coming paths that would avoid the apocalyptic future was the hardest thing the young man ever had to do. The power of a DeathWizard was a threat to the entire world of

Talohna. His death may just save the horrific destruction of both the Blood and Southern Kingdoms that Zaddyk kept seeing. Or it may lead Talohna head first into its apocalypse. Giddeon needed to know the choices and the triggers for both paths.

Brother Donis agreed and advised King Bale to send missives to every city and town that they could.

King Bale asked Brother Donis to write the missive himself. Zaddyk insisted a private letter for the ArchWizard be sealed and sent with every missive. He wanted Giddeon to know that though he agreed with the action against the DeathWizard, some decision Giddeon made twenty years ago was wrong and that he needed to use caution moving ahead. Stamped with the Pantheon Priest's seal of privacy, the letters would be opened by no one but Giddeon; anyone else opening the letters would unleash a deadly magic that could only be countered by Giddeon. It was likely a death sentence. Orders for the letters to be destroyed if the ArchWizard had not collected them in one year's time were included. It should ensure all the extra copies would be seen by no one besides the ArchWizard.

The couriers left the next morning, all with their own list of cities and towns where they would stop to deliver the King's word and Giddeon's letter.

The Kai'Sar, the DeathWizard, was to be killed or captured at any cost. The King's reward of two thousand gold pieces would be paid upon confirmation of death or capture. It was only a matter of time before Kael was killed or captured; two thousand gold pieces was almost enough to buy anyone their own small kingdom. It would draw Talohna's best bounty, magic, and monster hunters to the chase.

AVELERA CITY, ELLORYA

Walking arm in arm beside Southern Kingdom nobles, Kyro and his lieutenant, Niko, arrived at the heavily guarded entrance to the Gods Balcony of the Osok arena as the sun approached its highest point in the sky. As they stood and waited for the Guard Captain to turn away a young couple from an Elloryan noble family, Kyro admired Niko's extremely expensive new gown.

Made from the softest leather, it hung loose from her waist in the customary style worn by most Southern Kingdom noblewomen. The top half fit much tighter, moulded to Niko's flesh as if painted on. Only the sleeves were loose, with puffed out material at the wrists. Pushing her ample breasts together, the corset underneath the dress had been a nightmare for her to figure out. Finally forced to ask one the Tart's women of pleasure for help, Niko was still cursing at him as they left the establishment for the five minute walk to the Osok. He smirked at the memory of her trying to slide her dagger under the corset, along her spine. She succeeded, but only by nestling the handle under the dress between her ass cheeks. Weapons weren't allowed in the Emperor's presence, but the hand-written invitation should deter any thorough searches. Niko Sattori never went anywhere unarmed. Kyro chuckled at the lengths the woman would go to in order to keep him alive. Naturally, Niko thought his mind was elsewhere.

"Put yer sleazeball eyes back in yer cross-eyed head, Kyro, or I'll be wearing them as earrings by the time we're seated," she hissed, as she caught his lingering gaze.

"You're supposed to be acting like a noblewoman, not a damned pirate," he quipped quietly.

"Then quit staring at my tits. Act like a nobleman, not a deviant—" An argument ahead prevented her from finishing.

"What do you mean the Gods Balcony is closed to nobility this afternoon?" The young noble gentleman asked.

The Guard-Captain raised his hand to stop the man from pushing his way past. "The balcony is closed by personal order of Emperor Mero. You and your guest will have to sit in the balcony below or else in the Nobility Terrace across the arena."

"Come, dear," the woman said, raising her nose with an air of arrogance. "We will notify my father of the Emperor's insulting behaviour and this pompous guard's attitude after the rest of the events."

"I'm sorry, Mistress Vi," the captain added. "I'm only following orders."

"I'm sure you are, Captain. My husband and I will miss the noon execution fights now. That is completely unacceptable." She huffed, and walked away. The other nobles, followed, complaining.

Making sure they were out of earshot, Kyro turned to Niko and whispered. "Arrogant bastards." He smiled. "They have a twenty minute walk to the far side of the arena. I hope there's a line up at the gate when they get there."

Niko snickered. Restraining himself, Kyro chuckled as he approached the captain and handed the monstrous man his hand-written invitation.

Opening it, he shook his head. "You're the reason two dukes, a high priestess, and a Master Wizard are all going to be chewing on my ass by morning. You better know what you're doing, Kyro Yorcali. There are a lot of pissed off people who are going to eventually look your way."

"Are you going to let us in? Or do we anger the Emperor further because you're concerned about the welfare of your ass?" Niko asked. "Captain," she added as a respectful afterthought. Grunting, the captain waved to the other guards. Two of them moved their crossed pikes from the door. A third opened the stairwell door leading to the Gods Balcony and ushered them up the solid wood stairs. Taking the last step through the heavy metal doors into the emperor's private balcony, Kyro grabbed Niko's hand, tucking it through his arm.

The guard escorting them cleared his throat, opened the scroll and read. "Emperor Mero. May I present your viewing companions for the afternoon matches?" Getting a nod and a wave, the guard continued. "First, Mistress Niko Sattori from Kariya. She is the invited companion of your registered guest, Kyro Yorcali, also from Kariya. Mistress Sattori, Mister Yorcali, I proudly introduce, his Holiness, High Emperor Colias Mero. Ruler of Ellorya." Kyro and Niko both took a knee, bowing their heads and waiting for Emperor Mero to acknowledge their entrance. Seated in a round golden throne covered in green satin pillows, the emperor seemed in no hurry for the couple to stand.

"Your expectation of a meeting during our most celebrated week borders on arrogance, Yorcali-younger. Many of my nobles are insulted."

Kyro felt his ears turn red, anger flaring up at the pompousness of the fat fool. "Permission to speak freely, Your Holiness?" he asked. Getting a nod, he said, "I asked for a simple meeting, Emperor. Not an afternoon in the Gods Balcony that will get me killed long before I leave Ellorya."

Emperor Mero burst out laughing. "Bravo. You handled that much better than your father did many years ago. Don't worry about my nobles; they won't act against my special guests. Stand up, Yorcali-younger. I apologize for the test of humility. I needed to know your visit was legitimate. You are as welcome here as your father is and ever was. That is why you are sitting with me in the arena today. Your family holds a place of honour here. Now come." He waved the guard away as Kyro and Niko rose. "Take a seat, my friend. Eat, drink. We can discuss our business after the noon execution. I'm told a thief is due in the Osok any time now."

"Thank you, Emperor," Niko said, smiling as she sat to the emperor's right. Kyro took the seat on his left, grabbing a goblet of wine from the food-heavy table laid out before them. As a rule, Kyro never worried about the dangers around him; it was what Niko excelled in. Even now, he could see her examining every square inch of the Gods Balcony for danger. Her eyes suddenly fixated on the emperor's four guards. One stood motionless in each corner of the balcony. Even while under her scrutinizing glare, they never moved.

Kyro wondered, briefly, if they were even breathing. The knights discipline was so impeccable that even dressed in Ellorya's ceremonial white armour, they never moved. Only their eyes were visible through the horned helmets, constantly moving and on the alert for any and all threats. As Niko grabbed a goblet of wine, Kyro knew they were safe. Her nod confirmed that she saw no danger and no threats.

"You have my thanks, Emperor Mero, for agreeing to see me. I thought perhaps I would be forced to leave without being granted an audience. Such a thing would be detrimental to my father's and my plans." Clearing his dry throat, Kyro swallowed a large mouthful of wine from his goblet as he closely eyed the emperor's response.

"The Festival of Revail is a busy two weeks, my friend. This last week during the Osok Tourney is the worst. My responsibilities prevented an earlier meeting. Besides, I find that the best business decisions are made while on this balcony, as if the Gods themselves bless the deals made here."

"I understand, Emperor," Kyro said, bowing slightly. "Shall we begin?" Frowning, the emperor stood.

"Not yet. A thief must pay for his crimes first." Waving across the arena to the announcement booth, the emperor smiled from ear-to-ear and clapped his hands twice. A horn blared, rolling out across the Osok as a heavy steel gate to the left of the balcony thundered open. Kyro stared uneasily as the thief was escorted into the arena, coming to a stop on the packed sand floor below the Gods Balcony.

The Osok, packed with nobles, artisans, wizards, and commoners, cheered as the list of crimes were read. Glancing at Niko, disgusted, Kyro shook his head. Closing her eyes, she mimicked her agreement. Kyro cleared his throat as the thief, whose name he now knew was Alec Terraine, dropped to his knees and prayed.

"Get up and fight," Kyro muttered, more to himself than anyone else. "Stop praying. The gods aren't going to help you." Niko slapped her palm to her forehead and shook her head at his brazen words.

"Something you wish to say before the fight commences, Yorcali-Younger? Emperor Mero asked.

"No, emperor. Let the fight begin." His stomach went cold. Having seen it plenty of times in his life, Kyro never understood the spectacle others made of death.

It was a necessary part of business, yes, but he firmly believed inciting crowds to elevated states of euphoria by using bloodshed rarely ended well.

"I have nothing to give and even less to leave behind. This country has taken everything from me and now it wants my life. I'm a lumberjack, not a thief. But a rich man's word is law, and a labourer's is a crime."

Alec Terraine
Last will and testament.
Recorded by TimeKeeper Volaire
As required by Elloryan Law

AVELERA CITY, ELLORYA
THE OSOK ARENA

"Fight!" The words thundered through the loudspeaker, booming off of the granite walls encircling the arena as Alec Terraine rose from his knees, shaking, to face death. The Osok Champion, Lavik Natairis, entered the arena through the opposite door. Lavik had reigned as champion for four years. It was an exceptionally long time for the Osok, and Alec remembered the very day the scarred man was crowned. The taverns surrounding the Osok took all the wood he could bring them, and the celebration dedicated to the new champion lasted days. Alec had bought two silver lock boxes to hide the extra gold coin he had earned, stashing it safely in the root cellar below their home. Every victory

Lavik achieved, meant more gold that fed his family, repaired their home after the sand storms brought by the year-long winter winds, and eventually, just two months prior, afforded him a third lock box to hide in the cellar. Alec was only months away from having enough money to move his family from the corrupt, vile world of Ellorya, to the sought after dreams of a truly free life in the Blood Kingdoms' prosperous country of Cethos.

He scoffed at the delirious fantasy. Never being a fan of the arena, Alec caught his first close-up look at the man who'd nearly made his dream a reality. Eight inches taller than his own five foot ten, and heavier by almost a hundred pounds, Lavik's two hundred and fifty pound body was covered in scars. Deep cuts, healed several inches in width showed Alec the terrifying depth of the fresh wound many months ago. A sickening depression on the lower right side of the man's ribcage revealed the location of a wound that forced royal wizards to remove the champion's two bottom ribs after the punishing impact of a Reaver's hooked axe a year past. Lavik survived, as he always seemed to. Alec trembled harder as his opponent's introduction boomed through the speakers, the rest of the words were lost behind the throbbing pulse of his hammering heart as it thundered in his ears. All but three words.

"... The Unkillable Champion..."

Drawing both of his wide-bladed Salzaran scimitars, Lavik approached. Unable to move forward and too scared to run, Alec instinctively lifted his shield, his fingers snug in the metal glove as he held his ground.

Lavik's blade rushed in from the left, forcing Alec to drop his shield. Catching the full blow mid-shield, the powerful impact twisted his elbow, torquing his shoulder. Alec stepped back as the champion's other blade descended. Too slow, the tip of the razor sharp blade separated the flesh of Alec's stomach. Dread overwhelmed him and he look down, stumbling. Blood trickled from the shallow wound. Alec sighed with relief.

Looking back up, the champion's sword handle smashed his mouth, knocking him to the ground as the ringing vibration of the crowd echoed inside his head. Scrambling to his feet as an urgent panic lit a wildfire deep inside his belly, Alec raised his shield again. Lavik's curved blade hit at a strange angle and bounced off. Pure instinct drove Alec to swing his sword. The waist-level swipe was easily batted aside by Lavik's second sword; the big man's foot followed immediately, hammering Alec in the stomach. He dropped to a knee, winded. Defenceless, Alec grunted as Lavik's knee slammed into his mouth. A sense of weightlessness enveloped Alec and seconds later, he crashed to the ground, dazed. Rolling to his back, a quiet calm settled the icy claws of fear ripping at his guts as he realized the end was close.

Alec felt the arena champion straddle his waist and grasp his throat, understanding what so many fans meant when they retold stories of Lavik's reputation for killing opponents in a personal fashion. Dropping his sword, Alec grabbed Lavik's wrist, but couldn't tear it from his throat; the man's grip was immense. Struggling for breath, Alec pushed his shield against Lavik's ribs where the old wound was with every ounce of his faltering strength, to no avail.

The cartilage inside his throat crackled and popped, shutting off his air completely. Panicking, Alec pushed harder against his shield as black spots appeared within his vision. He dug his nails into Lavik's wrist with his right hand and kicked his legs as a red pulse flashed over his eyes. Knowing he was about to die, Alec screamed soundlessly within his throat and instinctively squeezed his left fist inside the shield's metal glove. A loud click snapped inside his head.

GODS BALCONY, OSOK ARENA

Kyro Yorcali watched the noon execution match with bated breath. Try as he might, he could not keep his disgust from bleeding through his much-practised emotionless appearance. The minute he saw Alec Terraine's fight stance, he knew the young man was what the Kariyans called the 'fighting dead'. Having clearly never fought with a shield and sword—or even any weapon—all his weight was on his forward foot, the same side as his sword. The shield was up, but protecting little. The first strike the thief caught with his shield was a given-blow. Lavik was playing with Alec, and Kyro knew it. It sickened him all the more. Grimacing as the champion's sword nearly gutted Alec from chest to waist, Niko frowned a warning, but she was too late.

"I would have thought a man of your pedigree would be thrilled at the chance for such a view of the Osok Arena, Yorcali-younger," Emperor Mero said, sweeping his arm out across the massive granite structure.

Kyro scoffed at the snide remark. "I have killed hundreds of men and women. Even children, Emperor. I have never seen the desire to make a spectacle of it. When you are wronged, you kill that person or someone they care about. Even my father knows that, regardless of whatever angle he is working at the time."

"I agree, partially," the Emperor said. "However, this arena has stood since the time of the Ancients. It is a part of our history, our heritage, and it gives the people a reason to celebrate."

Kyro bowed in deference. All it really did, in his opinion, was give Mero's military more money for a war with DormaSai that everyone knew was coming.

"Emperor Mero?"

"Yes, my lovely Niko," he answered, his eyes never leaving her chest.

"Your champion is about to win." Emperor Mero jumped to his feet, cheering, as Alec tumbled through the air after being kneed in the face by Lavik. Plopping back down on his throne, the emperor snatched a full goblet of wine, draining it as his champion mounted the thief, choking him.

"It seems so, my lovely." Emperor Mero grabbed her hand, gently, and Niko smiled, but Kyro could see her repulsion. Turning back to the arena, Kyro watched as Alec pushed his shield against the stronger man's chest, kicking and scratching his way towards the afterlife. A dull snap reached Kyro's ears as Alec went limp and Lavik's tense body relaxed. Kyro smiled. He had heard that snap before. It was some time ago, but it was a sound he had been hoping to hear and one he had never forgotten. The arena roared with excitement at Lavik breaking the thief's neck.

"Well, Yorcali-younger, it seems our thief has paid for his crimes..."

"I wouldn't be so sure, your Holiness." Kyro laughed as Lavik tried to stand, and failed, falling to the dirt at Alec's side. The thief struggled to rise, pulling a twelve inch blade attached to his shield from the champion's side.

The emperor leapt to his feet. "What sorcery is this?" he barked. "Guards! Get my healers down there. Make sure Lavik survives and bring me that sorcerous thief!"

"Isn't the Osok warded against magic? By the Ancients' magic, Emperor?" Kyro asked.

Emperor Mero frowned, furious as Kyro added, "It was just a spring-loaded blade inside the shield. Terrible luck for your champion."

Emperor Mero spit with uncontrolled rage. "Not as terrible as for that damned thief." With a wave of the emperor's hand, guards flooded the arena fight-floor. Unlike the ceremonial armoured men in the balcony, they were armed and protected by well-worn and battle-scarred equipment. Beating Alec into the dirt, they stripped his shield from his arm and dragged him to the Gods Balcony. The crowd went crazy, shouting, "Judgment! Judgement! Judgement!" Forced to his knees, Alec stared up into the balcony with blood-shot eyes and a broken nose.

Kyro joined the emperor on his feet, and whispered in his ear. "Emperor Mero. Let us talk before you pass sentence."

"Why? He's a thief. He avoided his punishment. It'll be done now, by the guards."

"Give me two minutes. It has to do with why I'm here."

"You have thirty seconds, Yorcali-younger. Starting now." Emperor Mero raised his hands to quiet the crowd. Knowing what was coming, it only succeeded in exciting the masses further. As the crowd slowly began to settle, Kyro spoke fast, desperately trying to save the thief's life.

"Spare his life, Emperor. Please. I'll consider it a personal favour in the negotiations to come."

"We'll be negotiating, will we?" Emperor Mero said, his interest clearly piqued. "Owing me a favour will put you at a distinct disadvantage, Yorcali-younger. Not a sound business tactic. Are you sure?"

"I am, Emperor. I agree." As Kyro finished speaking, Emperor Mero, with his hand still raised, prompted the crowd with a thumbs down. Hundreds cheered, but a rousing echo of boos joined them, slowly drowning out those cheering for a man's death. As Kyro stared at the emperor, a smile crept onto the old man's lips. Turning his thumb back up, he raised his thumb on his opposite hand and the arena exploded with a chorus of screaming cheers. Emperor Mero's smile widened as he turned to Kyro.

"Looks like the crowd agrees with you, Kyro Yorcali. Your thief lives, though I promise you, he'll wish he had died the moment he steps into his first Ludus, the training homes will be ruthless to him, especially if Lavik dies." Kyro nodded as the Emperor addressed the Osok.

"Lords, ladies, men and women, you have spoken. The thief, Alec Terraine, shall live. He is hereby remanded to the Bloodrooms below the Osok until chosen by a Ludus. Please enjoy your short break as the sun passes through its crest and the afternoon's Champion Fights begin." Sitting back down, he nodded to the guard standing to the left of the door. Opening the locked, solid gate, the guard nodded to someone outside. The man who escorted Kyro and Niko to the balcony entered.

"Your Holiness?" He bowed.

"Get me some information about Lavik. Now!" The man bowed a second time and exited. The guard closed the gates, locking them.

"Well, Yorcali-younger? We have some time. Why did you come all this way and call in your father's favour with me?"

"I'm sure you've heard some of the rumours from up north?"

"If you refer to strange beings and their powers of influence, then yes. Personally, I think King Bale is losing his mind. It seems to be the rulers of Cethos suffer from that curse all too often, considering his father and grandfather died from the same."

"Well, my father and I can't count on the respected borders of an insane king or an influenced one, if he's not insane. You know Yusat is just a puppet kingdom."

Emperor Mero poured himself some more wine. Offering to fill Kyro's cup, he said, "True. I cannot blame you. Living within reach of an insane monarch is a burden I know all too well. Had your ArchWizard and the rebels not dealt with DormaSai's last insane king, we would have had to invade and put an end to that vile Azmerack bastard." Kyro nodded, but snorted inside. The damned coward had been too afraid to march on DormaSai and fight the King of the Dead during the necromancer rebellions. Now that the current king and winner of those same rebellions wanted peace, Mero blustered and threatened him with war.

"You understand, then," Kyro said, "how we cannot sit by and allow the Free Lands to remain unprotected, or protected by the grace of good neighbours."

Swallowing another glass of wine, Emperor Mero sighed. "So, you come here looking for what? Yorcali-younger, you know my own borders are not safe at the moment. Even if they were, were I to support you and your father, officially, I'd break at least a dozen treaties by putting soldiers on Blood Kingdom soil. I cannot do that. I'm sorry." Kyro nodded his agreement as Niko cleared her throat. It caught the emperor's attention.

"Something you'd like to add, my lovely?" Emperor Mero asked, as his wine-heavy eyes drifted down to the waist-high kick-slit on her extravagant new dress.

Niko smiled, shifting in her seat to cover her legs. "We were thinking something a little less official, Your Holiness."

Without taking his eyes from where they had relocated to settle on Niko's chest, Emperor Mero asked, "Care to explain, Kyro? I really don't want to insult the Bloods. Not with all the trouble up there. Missing princesses, DeathWizards, witch cults, and now I'm hearing stories about broken treaties with the Wildlands. I would just as soon not talk about this any further." He smiled at Niko. Lifting her hand, once again, he kissed it this time. Staring into her eyes as if trying to seduce her with nothing but his pungent charm, he added, "I would rather have much more satisfying conversations. Would you not agree, my lovely creature?" Kyro recognized the emperor's desire for Niko the moment they were led into the balcony. Never one to 'sell' or 'bargain' his people in any situation, Kyro still couldn't help but smirk at Niko as she swallowed hard, as if trying to stop her rebelling stomach. Her eyes pleaded for help. He decided to end her torture the only way he knew how.

"I want your gladiators, Emperor Mero. All of them." The Elloryan emperor gently placed Niko Sattori's hand on the armrest of her own chair and turned to Kyro.

"Well, Yorcali-younger, that is indeed unexpected. Perhaps we do have something to discuss."

Chapter Twenty

"My father, the King of Cethos, always told me that the Bale family bloodline never had magic and likely never will. Why would a Goddess we so fervently worship not grant her gift to us? Inara's University of Magic, The Eye, as everyone calls it, stands in the capital city of our country. As a nation, we offer free scholarships to our neighbouring country's gifted and free education to all of our own who show any real affinity to mystical power. All graduates are employed wherever they will help the most or where they most desire, but still She doesn't bless our family. My father says that the Bales have a strength that goes beyond magic, but it doesn't quicken until we taste battle. If I continue to be coddled by my father, by my King, then how will I ever find my true strength? If finding it means I will be a better Queen, then I will find it on my own. I'm sorry, Father, but I must."

Journal entry Written by Princess Corleya Bale
On the night of her disappearance

WILDLANDS MIDDLE FOREST

Princess Corleya Bale opened her eyes with a start, her heart pounding from suddenly being woken from the clutches of yet another frightening dream. A sharp pain, similar to a bug bite, stung her back. After only four hours sleep, she rubbed the uncomfortable blur from her eyes, stretching to feel what caused the agony to her back. As she turned, she saw the flashing white teeth from a smile and another stab of pain lit up her ribcage.

"Bastard!" she growled, turning quietly. A sharpened stick slid through one of the many openings in the slave cage, poking her above her left breast. After piercing her flesh, the stick was quickly withdrawn. Corleya slid further from the side of the cage as the stick darted in again. Moving out of the deep shadows cast by total darkness, Alia Ryanez, Corleya's lady-in-waiting snatched the stick from the young man and threw it into the heavy brush behind the slave pen. The young tribal warrior flashed another smile and disappeared into the dark.

"Are you all right, my... Lady?" Alia asked. The hesitation in trying to keep the princess' identity a secret was a subtle slip, but still a slip.

"I'm fine," Corleya mumbled, biting her lip. "Just stings." Alia crawled closer, inspecting the shallow puncture wounds caused by the same man who'd been tormenting the slaves ever since they arrived—the tribal chief's son.

For two weeks, she'd been a slave to the Kordanu tribe who lived deep in the Wildlands Forest. The memories of how she and her lady-in-waiting had first been captured by the Taktala tribe, further north, a month and a half ago, came flooding back on the tail of her nightmare. A month had passed after their capture before they were sold to their current owners. Compared to the Taktala, the Kordanu were a vicious and ruthless tribe of Wildlands natives. Any failure or misstep resulted in several lashes with a soaked leather whip. Nowhere near as lenient as the Taktala, Corleya and Alia worked from before the sun rose until late at night, at which time they were locked in a cage with almost a dozen other captive slaves.

Corleya's heart calmed as the dream receded, and she realized that a loud argument outside the slave pen was becoming heated, the escalating voices what woke her seconds before the pain. Though unable to understand the tribe's language, she crept across the enclosed slave pen for a closer look. The tribe's leader, Chief Karlag Kordanu, was in a serious dispute with one of the high priestesses, but the princess was not sure which. Chewing her lip with frustration at not being able to understand what was being said, she never heard another slave approach.

"They're fighting about where to go next," a soft voice said, coming from her right. Corleya turned to see Damien Krass crouched in the deep shadows. The newest addition to the Kordanu slave pen had said nothing in the two days since he had been purchased from another of the gathering tribes.

"You understand their language?" she answered, whispering as well.

"Aye, been in this forest a long time. You'll save yourself a lot of anguish by learning it," he said, nodding towards the healing whip scars on her back that peeked out from under her stained and tattered shirt. Corleya pulled her shirt over the wounds as the argument grew louder.

"What are they saying?" Corleya asked.

"They're going to war, and the tribes are coming together in preparation. The priestess wants the Kordanu to head into the mountains, to ask the... I don't know the word. It's not one they normally use, but to go and ask for their help."

"She wants the chief to ask the Bruja to come to war with them," another woman rasped. "That priestess has been pushing the chief since I arrived with the Asazai tribe." The young blonde woman coughed. Though Corleya was well aware that age and youth meant little to those with magic, the woman appeared no older than twenty and was also a new addition to the Kordanu slave population. Washed out and weak, often struggling to breathe, Corleya could see the woman's blood veins through her skin, especially in her neck and throughout her face. They had a silver tinge to them during the daytime sun and an ugly scar marked her neck under her chin. She could not help but wonder what the woman had been through.

"How do you know what they're saying?" she asked, instead.

"How old are you, little girl?" the woman rasped, her voice as weak as her body.

"Sixteen, why?"

"Because I have several hundred years on you. I've been able to speak most Wildlands dialects for half my life, and those I don't speak I will pick up fast. You do after a few centuries of living." The woman sighed and lay back against the woven wooden cage that made up the slave pen.

"Why doesn't the chief want to go to the... Bruja?"

"Bruja is just their word for evil magic users. The rest of the civilized world calls them witch doctors. The Wildlands tribal people don't use magic like we do," the woman said, still lying back. "Their priestesses access a power that Humans and the Elvehn don't understand. It's some kind of nature magic. They use it to hide their camps or cover their trails by making vines and the forest trees grow quickly or to find water in times of drought. It's the same magic they used to create these slave cages. Overall, pretty mild magic compared to ours up north. But the Bruja? That's a different story. They use some strange kind of spirit magic that doesn't exist in the rest of Talohna. When these tribal children are born with this magic, it's considered a curse and they're ostracised. Removed from the camp and left to die."

Damien turned from the argument and sat, his eyes on the knowledgeable woman. "They don't die do they, though? I've heard stories in the time I've been here," he said, shivering. Corleya wasn't sure whether it was the cold night air or talk of the Bruja that made him shake.

The woman struggled to sit up, another slave helped steady her, receiving a nod of thanks. "I would imagine some do, but it seems like most find their way to the Sartaq tribe. Being born with these powers happens often enough that the outcasts formed their own tribe. It's where the priestess wants to go, but the chief disagrees."

"What does that mean for us?" Corleya asked.

"That will depend on how much the Sartaq demand as payment to fight a war they have no interest in," the woman answered, as she groaned.

Damien shook his head at her words. "Well, it's not like things can get any worse," he complained. From outside the cage, Chief Karlag Kordanu roared with anger and barked at the priestess in their guttural language.

The woman chuckled and laid back once more. "This is Talohna. Things can always get worse. I told a friend that a long time ago, but he wasn't born here. You were. You should know better," she laughed, holding her sides in agony.

"How?" Damien blurted out. "How could it possibly get any worse?" He held his hands up and looked around, emphasizing the slave cage and their situation.

The woman stared at him for several seconds and then leaned forward. "Because," she said, her eyes glaring at the priestess thirty feet away. With a nod towards her, she continued. "The chief just agreed with the priestess. We're going to the Sartaq."

"You look like you are only twenty years old. Are you a wizard then?" Corleya asked, and then slapped her hand to her mouth when she realized what she let slip, even looking back over her shoulder to see if any of their captors had heard. Lowering her voice to a whisper, she added, "You don't have a Poghana collar. They don't make mistakes like that..."

"I'm not a wizard, girl," the woman replied. Confused, Corleya glanced over at Damien, not knowing what to say.

"She's a vampyr," he hissed, in a hushed tone. "One that has silver running through her veins by the look of it. Not quite enough to kill her would be my guess. Never seen that before, it normally doesn't take much. You should be dead." The woman snorted, but said nothing.

Corleya stepped back, instinct taking over. "Why would they let her live? They're supposed to be eradicated when they're captured."

Laughing lightly, the woman scoffed, but it was Damien who answered her. "If they knew, they would have, even though these tribes follow no laws but their own. Talohna's universal laws don't exist here. Still, it's a mistake we can use to get out of here." Turning to address the woman, he smiled. "My name is Damien, this is Cora. What do you say? Care to work together to get out of here?" he asked, as he scooted forward with his arm out, in an offer to shake the vampyr's arm.

A weak arm grasped his, but then unearthly power ripped him from his feet. In less than second, he was staring into silver-fevered eyes, his nose touching hers. "Why would I help a pirate who will stab us all in the back as he runs to freedom over our recaptured bodies? You think I don't recognize a Sun of Blood when I see one?"

"Doesn't really matter what any of us are right now, does it... vampyr? A slave is a slave, but together, perhaps we can escape. Right?" The woman pushed Damien hard enough to knock him over backwards.

"Don't make me regret this, pirate," she snapped, through clenched teeth.

"You won't," Corleya said, crawling forward, as Alia joined her from the shadows. It was clear she stepped forward to protect her friend should the vampyr attack. "You have my word and that of my friend. This is Alia. How about telling us your name?"

The woman stared at the odd group of slaves: a pirate, a Salzaran mercenary, and a Cesthosian noblewoman. She shook her head as she answered. "What do I keep getting myself into...? All right. My name is Lycori. Lycori Alatar."

Corleya gasped. "Alatar? I knew a wizard from Corynth with the last name of Alatar, Gabriel. He sat with the ArchWizard when my... when the King held court. Are you related?" she asked.

"He was my grandfather," Lycori offered, emotionless. "He's dead." She put her hands on her knees, placing her head on her hands to rest and said no more.

"I'm sorry, Lycori, for what it's worth. He was well liked and respected in Corynth, I know that much."

With such a dour mood hanging over the slave pen, Corleya sat down between Alia and Damien, her mind a whirl of thoughts. Escape would be their only real hope of freedom. She knew Giddeon would not try another rescue without going back to Corynth for more troops, maybe even for the whole army. That would only happen if he considered her more important than stopping the DeathWizard, which she doubted. The corrupted wizard would destroy all Talohna held dear, so he would be Giddeon's primary concern now that her rescue attempt had failed. Her foolishness and childish behaviour had put her in this mess. She and Alia would have to fend for themselves, with a little help from a pirate and a vampyr.

Their best bet would be if the tribe moved far enough south to be within eyesight of the Ghyreni Salt Desert. The warriors from the tribe wouldn't chase them into the desert and risk encountering the mysterious race of scorpion-people living there. Alia told her she had crossed it before when she lived in Salzara. If the Kordanu tribe kept the same pace and direction they were going, the salt desert would be visible in a week or so, but if they headed into the mountains, the desert would remain out of reach.

Only time would tell.

ELLORYA/SALZARA BORDER
DOCK OF ONE, TWIN CITIES

Dominique Havarrow leaned against a stack of crates as he waited for the Dock of One's harbour master to finish reviewing his ship's log. Known to sailors as the D'One, the shared border-port was the Twin Cities of Alegra and Argela's most distinguished feature. With Alegra situated on Salzara's side of the border and Argela in Ellorya, the Southern Kingdom's largest seaport was a constant swarm of activity. It was also extremely difficult for criminals and nefarious individuals to enter from the seaward side. All ship logs and documentation had to be provided, while sailors and ship names were checked for wants and warrants before any ship's crew were granted access to the bustling two cities.

After sailing the treacherous waters of the Ghyreni Desert's SaltRock River, Dominique and his crew were more than ready for some time ashore. After the unforeseen delay that took him and six Suns of Blood ships to Dasal, finally they were back to Suns of Blood business. To make up time, his first mate, Shasta Trey, suggested using the SaltRock River in order shave ten days travel from their sails. Most crews, pirate, merchant, or military would have mutinied at the mere thought.

The crews of the Twilight Reave and the six ships following Havarrow voiced two words on the subject. "Aye, sir." And nothing more. Even though the Salt's unpredictable currents tossed both The Squealing Merchant and The Demon's Bride into the dreaded DeadMan's Silt located on the river's right delta, all hands were rescued safely. Unable to free the two galleons, Dominique ordered them to be scuttled and burnt where they sat buried in the thick quagmire of the salt sands. If a ship was not salvageable for any reason, it was destroyed to avoid it being taken by others. The ships would be easily replaced upon leaving the Twin Cities, *if* the D'One's harbour master ever granted them permission to dock.

"Come on, Sai," Dominique barked. "You know full bloody well there's no wants on my Reave and no warrants on my crew. Get the fuck on with it."

"Your log says you came from Dasal. That's a slaver port, Dom. You know I have to check your ship. I'm not losing my job because you like to skirt the law." Coughing as he wiped sweat from his forehead, Sai Yomo, one of the many Dock of One harbour masters, added, "Once you're clear, signal your other ships to stay within Lover's Bay and their crews can come ashore by rowboat with only a customs check, fair enough?"

"My ships sitting docked within the points of the Lover's Embrace better not be an issue with Queen Bitch and King Perv," he said, mentioning the Twin Cities' defences. The flat, level terrain of the east and west cliffs held countless hundreds of massive ballistae and catapult engines, and the jaws of the bay were piled hundreds of feet high with massive boulders that could be dropped into the mouth of the bay in a moment's notice, cutting off any ship's escape from the Twin Cities.

Shaking the thoughts from his head and stepping closer, Dominique's hands came to rest on his sheathed blades. "I don't have all damned day to sit here while your fucknards screw around and then have to convince the Twin Royal rejects that my six ships do not constitute an invasion force!"

"Easy, Captain," Shasta said, walking off the gang-plank from the Twilight Reave.

Losing his patience, the harbour master's voice rose considerably. "Listen, asshole, the last time the Reave docked here, one of your men murdered a dockworker over losing a card game. You're damn lucky your permit wasn't given a lifetime revocation. It's the best I can do, Captain. If it's not good enough, take your ships and harbour them elsewhere. My dock, my rules."

"Just get on with it," Dominique barked with frustration as the older man turned away. "Sai?" he added. The aged harbour master glanced back over his shoulder. "Fuck you." Storming off, Dominique headed for the customs office as Sai's officers returned from below decks on the Reave. They nodded to Sai.

"You're welcome, asshole. You and the Reave's crew are cleared to enter customs," Sai hollered after him. Ignoring, the harbour master, Dominique entered the customs building and slammed the door. Shasta touched the harbour master's shoulder as Sai boarded the Reave. He stopped when he heard her voice.

"It's been a rough haul, Sai. His son is dead and we barely got his daughter back from slavers," she said, in a clear attempt to explain Dominique's uneasy behaviour.

"I understand. But keep an eye on him, please. Two years have passed since your last dock here, but Sonny was well-liked; he had three children and was always the first to help those in need."

"We know. Dom strung Cornwall from the crow's nest for his crime and gives Sonny's widow Cornwall's share, and will continue to do so as long he draws breath. It would have been easier to sail away. The Twin Cities authority ends at this plank. We didn't have to consider the city watch and their demands at all."

"I know that, too. But people have long memories here, especially when it comes to rumoured pirates. Keep your men clear of trouble, Shasta. There will be no leniency if something happens this time, authority or not. If the King or Queen drop the Lover's Embrace, you will all die, either drowned in the bay or hung from the Crow's Walk." She nodded and followed after Dominique.

It took an hour for all the Reave's crew to clear through customs. Satisfied the men and women had no warrants outstanding in the Southern Kingdoms, Customs Major, Arest Naru, escorted Dominique and his crew down the tunnel separating the customs warehouses at the docks and the massive bronze, side by side gates to Alegra and Argela. A serious man, Dominique never knew the major to smile.

"Captain Havarrow?"

"Yes, Major?"

"You know the laws vary in the Twin Cities, but please make sure new crew members understand the differences. Also, a new law has been passed for the Dock of

One. All departures must be approved twenty-four hours before you ship out. If not, the Embrace will close and Royal Court Wizards will scuttle your ships. That being said, the Queen of Alegra and the King of Argela have granted immediate departures to those they've deemed worthy, should you need to leave urgently."

Dominique nodded, but Shasta answered. "Thank you, Major Naru. I'll be sure to notify you of our departure date and time." With a frown, the major disappeared back into the tunnel as Shasta released the crew to shore leave. The majority passed through the gates of Alegra, the Salzaran city being a better fit for sailors looking to have some fun. Taverns and brothels were numerous and alcoholic beverages were cheap. Its Elloryan sister-city attracted two of the Reave's paired couples. Quieter and more formal, Argela was known for its shops, markets, and open-aired dining establishments, along with its sanctioned gladiator arena. Shasta watched them go, making a note of who went to each city. It left her alone with Dominique.

"You want to do this alone, or you want me to watch your back?" she asked.

"Better come. I've dealt with lots of crazy fools over the years, but never one who can make things explode. What do we know?" He entered the small door, set to the side of the heavy bronze gate, stepping onto Elloryan soil.

"Merethyl's killer said that the rumours point to a grove several miles outside of Argela. Northwest of the main road to Avelera City."

"She give you a name? Any truth to the rumours?" he asked.

She smiled. "His name is Eamon O'Leary."

"What kinda name is that? Tyr's bloody blade, as if I haven't dealt with enough fucknards lately."

Scratching her eyebrow in a desperate attempt to avoid laughing, Shasta shook her head. "I don't know, Captain. I spent all three days we were in Forja Vehlo at the castle with King Vhorez's Coat of Arms Herald and his Gene

Chronicler. No person, Human or Elvehn, has ever been born in Talohna with a family name of O'Leary, not since the Cataclysm anyway. The given name Eamon has never been used either. If there weren't so many witness accounts of this crazy bastard, I would doubt he existed."

"This no name fucknard supposedly killed a Broken Blade assassin and Queen Killer herself won't retaliate against him. What does that tell you?"

"That we should tread lightly. All the merchant gold riding Ageaus' waves couldn't convince me to cross those magical, murdering freaks of hers. If she won't avenge one of her own something is really wrong here, Captain."

"I agree. All right. Horses and supplies for a week. Meet me at the southern gate in a couple hours," he said, tossing her a bag of gold. "One of the royal court wizards here owes me a favour. Hopefully a big enough one to save our asses from being blown back to Dasal by some crazy alchemist mixing the wrong chemicals."

Shaking her head, Shasta caught the coin and disappeared into the crowd.

SOUTHERN WILDLANDS' FOREST

The Kordanu tribe set up camp at the foot of a massive mountain range called the Cauldron's Teeth. Bordered on the west by the Black Cauldron Ocean, the Gyhrehni Salt Desert and the Deadman's Silt to the south, the Wildlands' southern forest was a festering domain of dense, green wet. For twelve days, the Kordanu tribe marched through the forest to the mountain range where all the tribe's magical outcasts had made their home centuries ago. The

Kordanu tribe's chief, Karlag Kordanu, grew more aggressive and short-tempered the closer they got. The tribe's slave community suffered the worst of his outbursts, catching a foot or a fist whenever they were close by.

Corleya was the most recent recipient of his latest burst of rage. She nursed the hours-old contusion on her left arm and ribcage the only way she could: by painfully stretching it to prevent it from stiffening. With the camp set-up complete and the morning meal finished, she was led back, under guard, to the cage with the other slaves. It was a sure sign something was different from their normal day. Corleya settled down for some much needed rest.

Removing her worn-out leather boots, she wiggled her pruned toes, hoping they would dry out before she was forced back to work. The forest humidity and sodden leaf-mold had almost rotted the boots beyond use. Incredibly invasive, the damp soaked into everything. In a matter of weeks, she would be barefoot like everyone else, which presented a whole new level of discomfort. The last time her feet were dry for more than ten minutes at a time was a lost memory.

She sighed as Alia sat down beside her. "I wonder what happens now?" she asked. Alia shook her head, saying nothing like always.

Damien, however, rarely had nothing to say. "We'll likely sit here until the spooks come down from the mountain. Or worse, when Karlag decides to go up. If so, he'll have to offer them a sacrifice for trespassing."

"One of us, you mean," Lycori added from the rear of the cage. With a moan, she shifted forward. The silver-coloured, swollen blood veins had receded back into her flesh only the slightest bit, the marks were still visible after the two weeks of travel south. She remained weak, but slowly healed with each day that passed. She had also begun to age, suffering from hunger.

The pirate spit at her feet. "I can guarantee you a tribe member won't pay it, so who does that leave? I thought vampyrs were smart?" he mocked, earning a fanged sneer from Lycori. As the past two weeks had crept by, Damien and Lycori's hatred for each other had grown by leaps and bounds. She refused to participate in any escape attempt he proposed, saying that without her strength and speed, the plan was doomed to failure. Corleya often wondered if the pirate's intent *was* to escape at the expense of Lycori's life, or her own even. Every time they argued, Damien's temper and patience grew shorter.

"Do not start, you two. Not now," Alia barked. Being one of the rare occasions she spoke, both quieted. "Rest."

Corleya, sliding sideways, leaned against the slave cage and watched the bustling tribals as they prepared for the possible arrival of the outcasts living higher up the mountain range.

"I've heard stories about these people," Corleya said, absent-mindedly.

"About who?" Damien asked. "The tribals?"

She shook her head. "No. The outcasts. I remembered when you said witch doctors. The wizards back home in Corynth also call them that."

Lycori scoffed, her words loaded with hatred. "Witch doctor. The word witch in front of any word just means evil."

"I agree." Corleya smiled. "I've only met one good witch in my life. She's nothing but a vague memory, and it's still terrifying." Alia took her friend's hand, offering a small bit of comfort.

"So, what kind of stories do arrogant wizards tell their apprentices in Corynth as an excuse to keep them in line?" Damien laughed, his voice riddled with disrespect. Lycori smacked him in the back of the head, hard. The blow pushed his face into the dirt.

"Bitch!" he snapped, as he looked up. She punched him in the mouth, harder. Dazed, he collapsed, one hand holding his jaw, the other up as a gesture of surrender.

"My grandfather lost his life because he was a Cethosian wizard. You cannot begin to imagine what men and women like him sacrifice so that shit-piles like you can enjoy freedom in the Blood Kingdoms. If you ever show such disrespect again, I'll kill you without warning... even if it means exposing myself as a vampyr. Understand?" He nodded, leaning back against the cage opposite her.

Sighing, Corleya rubbed her swollen eyes and tried to rest.

Hours passed by quietly. The camp settled into an eerie silence as if no one knew what to expect. Corleya, along with several of the other slaves, managed to get a couple of hours' sleep as the humid afternoon approached. As the sun appeared over the towering mountains west of the camp and its rays began to peek through the leaves, Chief Karlag, his daughters, Kasna and Nvesa Lotti—both priestesses—were accompanied by several warriors as they approached the slave pen. Lycori, one of the few slaves who spoke the tribals' language, translated as Nvesa caressed the living plants that made up their cage. The plants retreated, slithering like snakes as the cage opened. The Chief barked at the slaves, clearly not happy about something.

"Everyone on your feet," Lycori translated as Corleya helped her to stand. Lycori nodded her thanks, and Corleya moved on to assist others weakened by the hard work, little sleep, and the two week walk south.

"He wants us to follow, but only the four of us," Lycori added, as one of the tribal warriors muscled her from the cage, securing her hands behind her back. As the chief snapped in his guttural language, Lycori continued to convert his demands to the common tongue.

"Cora, he wants you and Alia. Damien, too." Stepping out of the cage, their hands were bound behind their backs. Linking the four prisoners together with the same hemp-like, braided rope used to bind their wrists, the priestess, Kasna, strung the rope from their hands to between their legs and looped the rope through the next person's wrist bindings until all four were secured and uncomfortable. Keeping the line snug and with only three feet between each of them, Corleya realized that any escape attempt would immediately turn into a clustered tangle of limbs and sore crotches.

"This is perfect," Damien whispered, looking to Lycori at the front. "It's just the four of us. We can escape."

Tossing a warning frown over shoulder, Lycori whispered, "Shut the hell up. We're not going anywhere trussed up like this." The pirate glared, returning her dark stare. Kasna yanked the rope between Damien's legs hard enough to make him wince his way to the tips of his toes before she finished securing it to his hand bindings. Grabbing his beard, the priestess gently turned his head to meet her eyes.

"No escape," she said, using the common tongue. Her soft breath washed over him. "Only obey." Pulling him even closer, her tongue slid from her mouth. Licking his lips, she nibbled and nipped, biting, as Corleya stared, horrified, yet fascinated. The pirate's breathing slowed and his eyes glazed over with a wet shine as if they were full of tears. The priestess smiled and walked away.

"Fucking witch," Lycori cursed under her breath. Corleya, next in line, overheard and glanced at her, hoping for an explanation. The vampyr shook her head, murmuring, "Glamour poison. Tribal witches..." Chief Karlag punched her in the mouth, cutting off the rest of her sentence. Clearly having had enough, he barked more orders. Wiping a thin thread of blood from her mouth, Lycori turned to the others. "Follow and be silent, or you'll be praying for a kiss from that witch." Slipping a noose around Lycori's neck, Karlag tightened it, cutting off her breath. Once he was sure she understood trying to escape meant strangling to death, he slipped his fingers under the rope and loosened the knot so she could breathe easier. Taking a quick look to make sure the other slaves were secure, he jerked on the rope, almost pulling Lycori from her feet. Dragging the daisy-chain of prisoners from the camp, he led the way up into the mountains.

Somewhere above them lived Talohna's most vile magic users. Corleya shivered as she realized they were being taken to the people considered too evil to be part of the various tribes.

Even as cruel and sadistic as they themselves were, every tribe feared the Sartaq outcasts.

Chapter Twenty-One

"Magic and alchemy from other dimensions can have devastating effects in our own world. They are also extremely hard to defend against. It is why a witch's demonic magic is so terrifying and why alchemists long for alchemical supplies from the Nine Hells or the Paradise realms.

"A different dimension doesn't mean a completely different reality from ours. There are dimensions within dimensions. For Talohna, that means the Paradise and Perdition realms of the afterlife."

Excerpt from ArchWizard Giddeon Zirakus' speech to the Wizard's Council on the emerging threat of demonic witchcraft, 5025 PC

WILDLANDS FOREST

It took three long, but uneventful days before Ember recovered enough to travel. It had taxed Yrlissa's healing abilities to the maximum, leaving them both exhausted. Refusing to let anyone tell Ember about Kael and how he had passed through their camps, Yrlissa waited until she felt Ember could handle the physical and emotional stress. The night before they left the refuge of the cave, Yrlissa sat down with Ember and told her everything, from Kael talking to her while she was unable to talk or move because of the sleep poison, to Giddeon's lies about her and Max's arrival through the dimensional portal. Ember stormed out of the cave to confront Giddeon the moment Yrlissa finished telling her what had happened. She found him sitting at the fire with everyone else, except Max, who was on patrol out in the forest.

"I want you to answer something for me, Giddeon. Do think you can actually be truthful?" she asked, standing over him, her anger still under control.

"I can try."

"What gives you the right to force your beliefs onto me or Max?"

Giddeon sighed, easing himself back against a log by the fire. "What makes you think I am?"

"You've been telling us since we arrived here that the man I love and have known for my entire life is evil, that he is corrupted by power we can't possibly understand. That is your opinion, is it not?"

"You know it is. I've never hid it from you."

Staring down at him, Ember resisted the urge to smack his smug face. "You are so afraid that a DeathWizard is going to force his beliefs and desires onto this world. Yet you've done the same thing to us from the time we arrived here. You honestly expect us to believe you are the good guys?"

"We are, Ember. We always have been. I think you know that by now."

Ember bent down, glaring into his eyes. "When it comes to some things, yes, but when it comes to Kael, your own flesh and blood, you're forcing the issue because you're afraid you've been wrong all these years. So much so that you'll try to kill him just to save your precious ego and from having to admit you might be wrong."

Giddeon's eyes flared with anger and Ember knew she'd hit a nerve. It was satisfying, so she pushed harder. "If you can't face the fact that you're not perfect, then do not, under any circumstances, make us or Kael pay the price for it. You will be the one to suffer for it in the future, I promise you." Ember stood and turned to walk away, but stopped. "Oh, and Giddeon?" she added, while turning her head to look him in the face once more. "If you ever stop me from finding Kael, or stop him from finding us again, I promise you, I will jump all three of you to the Dragon Isles and leave your asses there in the Forest of Whispers without any of their precious binding stones. Even if it kills me to do it. Do you understand me?" she asked quietly, her voice held an edge of finality.

"I understand," he said, leaning forward, "but you understand that before we are done and long before we catch Kael, you will see exactly what I already know. It won't be long before he loses complete control, and when he does, many innocent people are going to pay the price. With their lives." He stared at her hard. Ember shook her head as she walked away, knowing beyond all doubt that she, Max, and Yrlissa were going to have to fight Giddeon and the others in order to save Kael. It was something that no longer bothered her.

They packed their belongings before settling in for the night so that they could leave first thing the next morning. The plan was to get to Dasal to see if Kael and his female companion had stopped there to resupply before heading north to the Dwarven Mountains. Giddeon had made it clear to everyone that he believed Kael had no reason to lie about his destination so that was were they planned to start looking.

DASAL, FREE LANDS

Dasal's high city walls were in view five days later. The group reached the gates just after dawn and were granted access by Master Wizard Seifer Locke, one of Giddeon's oldest friends.

"ArchWizard Zirakus, I hope you've been well," Seifer asked, giving Giddeon an official greeting as he shook his arm. The welcome quickly transformed into a hug that only friends, brothers, could share. "Kasik, Saleece, it's good to see you also," Seifer added as he let go of Giddeon. "All has been well, I hope?" They both smiled as Saleece handed the reins of her horse to Kasik and stepped over to Seifer, hugging him.

"It is so good to see you again, Uncle," she said, her smile turning to a laugh as he lifted her off the ground and spun her around as if she were twelve.

"Gods, I missed you. How is my favourite niece?"

"I'm all right, Uncle," she said, sincerely, but her voice had a hollow echo to it. "I'm just glad to see you again."

"You don't sound all right," he said, lifting her chin and forcing her to look in his eyes. "Don't tell me you're fine, girl. I can see the pain in your eyes. Giddeon, what's been happening?"

"Is there somewhere else we can go to talk, Seifer? There's much to discuss, but not out here," Giddeon said, glancing around, clearly looking for prying eyes.

Putting his hand forward, Seifer offered, "Of course. Follow me. We can speak in my office." Pointing to two guards on the left, he nodded towards the group's mounts. "The guards will take your horses to the stables. Come."

They spoke very little as they walked to the city guard barracks and Seifer's office. Saleece introduced Ember, Yrlissa, and Max, but offered nothing else. Not in public. Arriving at his office, Seifer closed and locked the door, putting up a warding spell to stop prying eyes and ears, a common practice whenever high ranking wizards spoke.

"So, Giddeon, what happened? I can see the shadow of agony and the essence of powerful magic in Saleece's eyes."

"We just came from the Wildlands," Giddeon answered, as Kasik put his arm around Saleece. "We spent almost a month as captives to the Taktala tribe. Saleece suffered the most."

Seifer put his arm on her shoulder. "I'm sorry..."

"I'll be fine, Uncle. Thanks to Ember," Saleece said offering her friend a smile.

"In time, I have no doubts. Stay strong and lean on those who will help you," Seifer said, getting a nod in return. He hesitated for several seconds, as if checking to make sure Saleece would be all right before he continued. He turned to Giddeon. "I guess you should know that a courier was here yesterday with a sealed letter for you. He also delivered a public missive from King Bale stating that a mature DeathWizard is alive and to be killed or captured at all costs, by anyone with the ability to do so. We were given the first name of Kael. How is your son back? After all we... All those lives lost... It wasn't supposed to be possible. After everything we went through to get him to a magicless dimension alive. Now there's a kill or capture order? Why?"

After months of hearing such things, Ember's anger had tempered, but she still rose from her chair in protest. "I promise you, Master Wizard, no one is going to be killing Kael. Not if I can help it. You may also want to reconsider sending any soldiers after him as well." The implied threat was obvious.

To her surprise, Seifer agreed. "I happen to be in total agreement with you, Miss Ember. No soldiers or bounty hunters—or anyone else for that matter—will leave from this city to hunt for Kael. You have my word." Ember laughed in disbelief at the unexpected reaction, but it turned into a slight smile as she caught a glance of Giddeon's angry expression.

"What in the Nine Hells of Perdition do you mean you'll send no one after him? He can't be more than five days from the city!" Giddeon said, shouting as he stood up from his chair. It crashed to the floor behind him.

"Oh, I happen to know he's only two days from here—exactly two days, in fact, but I won't tell you the direction. You heard me right the first time. I will *not* send anyone after them. Though if you plan to follow your king's orders, Giddeon, I just might send some of *my* soldiers to help defend him," Seifer stated.

A strange, relief-filled laugh rushed from Ember's mouth as she eased back into her chair. "Thank you," she gasped. "Finally." Taking a deep breath, she looked up at Yrlissa and Max, laughing. She could see Giddeon was incensed as his face turned red with anger.

"What is wrong with you, Seifer! You know what he is. It's our duty, your duty. We are brothers, you know what we were taught, what we experienced ourselves. The last DeathWizard nearly killed me... You were there!"

"I remember," Seifer said. "My magic kept you alive and then saved your life by boosting that healer's power, but he is different. Kael is different. This city would be a smoking pile of death and rubble right now and a multiple murderer would still be on the loose if it wasn't for him. The Suns of Blood had seven ships in our harbour because illegal slavers, Lircang's men, kidnapped Captain Havarrow's daughter. Kael and Kyah rescued her and gave us the proof we needed to arrest Lircang Yorcali. They saved this city from open war with the Suns. The creature we faced before is not what he is. The markings on his skin, his demeanour, his mental stability, all of it is different." Seifer explained in great detail, clearly hoping Giddeon would see the truth.

Giddeon shook his head, his disbelief obvious. "We have our orders from our King. You know the treachery a DeathWizard is capable of. We have our orders, brother," he repeated.

"Your orders!" Seifer snapped, losing the struggle to stay calm. "I live here, in Dasal. Joran Bale is not my king. We have no king here. We don't even have a country, and the last forty years that I've been stationed here have opened my eyes to some things, things I should have seen long ago. Not everything is as we were taught. Kael is your son, Giddeon. I was there, right beside you when you walked through the portal to take him across. Oripar, our brother, gave his life for that crossing. Something happened to Kael while he was over there. I stood by his side in this very office three mornings ago as he suffered from injuries so severe that we had to help him walk, and still, his only concern was for the safety of others. He is not made of evil. He is not evil, and you saying he is over and over does not make it the truth! Neither does it make it right. I will not help you murder Kael, and you have no authority over the men here. Even if you did, they wouldn't follow you, not to hunt down Kael. Every soldier and knight here knows that they're not burying loved ones and friends today because of him. I'm sorry, brother, but get what you need from the merchants here and get out of my city."

"Then we'll do it on our own, and I am sorry to see a brother fall to the wiles of a DeathWizard so easily. Give me my letter. We'll see to our supplies and be gone from your city in a matter of hours, you have my word," Giddeon promised, as he took his letter and left. Ember, Max, and Yrlissa stayed behind.

Seifer looked at the three who stayed behind, carefully, before speaking. "I assume that you three are not in agreement with Master Giddeon?"

"No, we are definitely not in agreement with that goddamn fool," Ember said. "I have known Kael my whole life..."

"Wait, what? What do you mean your whole life, that's not even possible. Is it?"

"I can assure you it is," she said, continuing. "Max and I crossed over with Kael from our world. We were with him when the vortex formed and pulled him in, and he in turn somehow pulled us in. Saleece managed to bring us through alive to Giddeon's tower."

"Of course, because Giddeon would have been watching for anyone to try bringing him back. Kael must have tapped his power out of desperation and pulled you two in with him. Amazing. You're actually from another dimension?" Ember nodded at Seifer's deduction. "You're both very lucky to be alive."

"That is what they tell us," Max said. "So, we plan to use the chance we were given to help Kael. Jesus, he must be completely lost in this goddamned place. With only one arm, I have no idea how he's made it this far."

"I think you underestimate your friend, Max. He's doing all right and I promise you he has the full use of both his arms, though he hasn't had an easy journey. He was very thin and he's scarred horrifically, both physically and emotionally."

Ember and Max both stared at Yrlissa. The assassin shrugged. "Talohna's magic must have healed the damage from when he was injured. I never even thought of that. In the Taktala camp, he was fighting with both blades, no disability."

"Of course," Seifer offered. "Upon his return this world would've restored his body to the condition it was in. When he left as a babe, there was no damage. It's amazing. I spent a fair bit of time with both Kael and his wife when they were here. I didn't notice any disability at all."

Ember's face turned white as she faltered and moved uncomfortably in her chair, Kael's injury completely forgotten. "What? Wife? I'm his wife. We were married four years ago..." she said. The dead quiet that followed carried an aura of unease. Everyone could only look back and forth at each other, not knowing what to say.

"I... I..." Ember tried, her voice suffering a complete failure.

Max finally asked, "Did they act like a married couple, Master Seifer? I don't understand why he would say that another woman was his wife."

Yrlissa answered part of his question before Seifer could begin. "You mean you cannot understand why someone in his situation would look for comfort from another person, Max... Ember," she said, her voice full of kindness.

She carried on, as if carefully choosing each word with Ember's feelings in mind. "It has been nearly a half year since you died, to his belief. He is here alone and was tortured for months, *mai nahlla*, and by Dead Sisters, women who breathe pain and exhale suffering. You cannot begin to imagine the horror or the desperation..." She stopped to take a breath as if steadying herself. "I'm sorry," Yrlissa apologized, breathing slowly. "Suffering like that will break anyone and everyone. Perhaps she was just there to help when he needed it, nothing more. I know in your heart it is hard to hear. He loved you and still loves you, but he believes you are dead. You have Max and you have me, but he had no one, *nahlla*, no one at all."

"Yrlissa is right, Em. Kael loves you, but remember who he is. We almost lost him when he killed that punk back home. A piece of garbage that was going to kill you, and he did it to save you, I know, but the guilt over the life he took tore him apart, you know that? God, you were the only thing that got him through it. Now he's here, and everything he has gone through, and even worse now, he thinks we are dead and that he was the cause of it," he finished.

Ember looked at him as she felt tears well up in her eyes, but she quickly choked them back, refusing to give in to despair. "Max, what's going to be left of him?" she asked, feeling hopelessness creep into her soul.

Max coughed and turned around to leave. "I really don't know, Ember. I'll... ah... go look into getting our own supplies," he sniffed and wiped at his eyes. "In case you decide we should go our own way from now on." Stepping out of the Seifer's office, he closed the door behind him.

"God, Lissa," Ember sighed. "Why did Giddeon do that? Why would he tell Kael that we died in the crossover? Why? How could any human being be so cruel, especially to their own son?" she asked, more to herself than anyone else.

Seifer suddenly spoke up, as if not knowing what to say before. "I don't know if this will help you or not Ember, but maybe it'll tell you something. I thought it was strange at the time."

With her arm around Ember for support, Yrlissa said, "Go on, Master Locke."

"Please, both of you, just call me Seifer, there's no need for more. The slavers in this city took a pirate captain's daughter captive, remember I told you?" Ember and Yrlissa both nodded, not wanting to interrupt. "Kael and Kyah—the woman Kael claims is his wife—got Captain Havarrow's daughter out of the slave cells by switching her with Kyah. Kyah then spent hours inside the cell while Kael took the girl back to the pirate ship and then waited 'til dawn to report her missing, knowing that when we searched the cells we would find her and I would have the proof against Lircang Yorcali I have been trying to gather for some time. It didn't quite go that smoothly, but close enough. Something else happened to solidify Lircang's guilt, but I found it odd that any man would leave his wife in the hands of slavers in that situation. So many things could have gone wrong. Do you understand?"

"Yes, Seifer, I do," Ember replied, "and thank you, it does help. Kael would never have risked my safety like that... ever. Any more than I would his." Looking at Yrlissa with some hope, she carried on. "You must be right, Lissa, some comfort maybe... He's lonely, you think?"

"I do, I really do. He doesn't love her, he cannot, because he loves you," she smiled, as Ember grasped her in a hug. Yrlissa mouthed the words 'thank you' to Seifer and he gave her a slight bow.

"She is very lucky to have a friend like you here, Mistress Yrlissa... I know it might not be as important now, but I feel should tell you anyway. Giddeon Zirakus is a good man, but years and years of always being right, of always being the smartest and most importantly, of being the only ArchWizard, a title that nobody will argue or speak out against you, have all contributed to the arrogance you both know is there. It will take a devastating event to convince him to change his beliefs, so please keep that in mind. I absolutely do not believe that Kael is evil, and I have always suspected there is more to the prophecy about him that we don't know or understand. Please, do your best to help him, and to keep in mind that Giddeon only does what he thinks is the right thing." he said.

"Thinking it doesn't make it right, Seifer," Ember replied. "Our world was nearly destroyed three times by men and women who firmly believed that they were doing the right thing. The first two times, the world came together to stop it. The third time was just before Kael and I were born, and it divided our world. A division that still stood the day we were brought here. I know he's your friend, and I'm sorry, but men like Giddeon are dangerous. Only a fool thinks he can do no wrong."

"I agree, Ember. Change his mind if you can, but if you can't... You will have to kill Giddeon to stop him. I truly do wish you all the best."

"Thank you again. For everything." Ember said, expressing her gratitude with a bow.

The wizard bowed in return, holding out his hand.

"Now, come," he said. "Let's go help your friend with those supplies."

SOUTHERN GATES OF ARGELA, ELLORYA

Shasta Trey waited outside the southern gates of Argela for Dominique to meet her. After buying supplies and three horses, she had stopped at the bathhouse and enjoyed an hour-long soak in the company of two beautiful women, followed by another hour of muscle massage. It was no secret among the crew that Natalia's Rest was the best place to relax for those with no interest in drinking or whoring away their shore leave. The legitimate establishment offered baths, deep muscle massages, clean rooms, and fabulous food. The fact that is was *not* a brothel was the sole reason Shasta never stayed anywhere else. The crew sometimes harassed her that she was spoiled for a Northman woman. She never cared.

A smile crept onto her lips as she sat against a warm boulder and waited for her captain to arrive. Flexing her shoulder muscles and stretching her back, she sighed. The massage had loosened every knot, cramp, and twinge that plagued her muscles after so many months at sea. She closed her eyes as the supply-heavy horses grazed on the patchy grass to her right. It was short lived, however, as squealing wheels from the sliding gates disturbed her rest, but still, she did not open her eyes. Both cities were well aware by now that Havarrow's crew were docked for shore leave, and no one would dare bother his first mate, not in broad daylight anyway. No one, that is, except for the man himself.

"Come on, Shasta, get your lazy ass up. It's time to go," Dominique barked. "You stopped at Natalia's, didn't ya?" Shasta nodded, easily jumping to her feet.

"Of course. I don't mind waiting for you, Captain, but I knew you'd be a while. And you brought company, I see," she said, noticing the tall man with dark skin accompanying Dominique.

"Shasta, this is Cormak WhiteFrost. He's Duchess Feira's court wizard. Cormak sailed with me many years before you were born."

"You're... You're a Northman?" Shasta said, taking his hand in greeting, as was customary in the Southern Kingdoms. The shock of meeting a Northman wizard made her smile. His long black hair, plaited into Salzaran dreadlocks, was just as dark as his skin and showed no signs of grey. Shasta guessed he was well under two hundred years old, but couldn't be sure. Magic and Northman blood was an oddity.

"Miss Shasta Trey. It is a pleasure to meet you. I have heard much." He released her hand and bowed. "I am a Northman and a wizard, yes. Rare as we may be, we do exist."

"Incredible," she replied, still in awe. "I thought the Ama Taugr were a legend, a myth even." Dominique scoffed, but Cormak answered.

"You need to return home more, young one. It is saddening to see so many of our youth not return after their Bloodborne years have passed. Once your Trail of Blood has ended, you should consider going home," he said, referring to the Northman tradition where youths leave Kastalborg Island and travel the world, living by their sword. After twenty years, most returned home to their clan, but it was becoming more common for Northmen, male or female, to not return home.

"If you two are done...?" Dominique asked, his patience clearly wearing thin. Getting a nod from both Shasta and Cormak, he said, "Cormak can answer any questions you have about home as we travel. You'll have plenty of time."

"Three days' worth," Cormak said, smiling. "Or so I'm told."

"Three days to the grove where this mad alchemist lives?" Shasta clarified, climbing into the saddle of her mount, a strong white horse flecked with black spots.

Cormak nodded. "The reports I've seen from those who've encountered this man seem to say the same. And we should hurry. I told Dominique earlier, we're not the only ones after him. I had a rather violent meeting with a certain White witch a couple days ago."

"Ella the White is here?" Shasta said, her voice riding high.

"She is," Cormack said, frowning. "My apprentice could have testified to the fact her demeanour hasn't changed in the last twenty-five years, if she weren't *dead*." Shasta could see the fury radiating in the runecaster's eyes as he continued. "It doesn't matter, we have time. Ella's going through the Deep to get to this man."

"Good. Let's go then," Dominique snapped, holding his hands up.

Cormack nodded. "Right. A small grove three days' ride to the south and west is our destination, as long as we don't run into any of the emperor's Centari. Many people have lost their lives during these run-ins with this man so Emperor Mero has dispatched small groups of cavalry to patrol the roads between here and Avalera City. I've researched this Eamon O'Leary as well, Shasta. He is a ghost in our records too. A very dangerous ghost who may not be from Talohna." Shasta felt her bottom jaw drop and shook her head at the possibility.

Pulling himself onto his horse, Dominique snorted. "He's a man, Cormak. One who has managed to stay out of the Southern Kingdom registry, that is all. He has something Bauro wants, something I want. Let's go get it." Giving his horse a light heel, Dominique, riding bareback, galloped away.

Shasta smiled at Cormack as they raced after him heading for a three-day ride into the jaws of madness.

The journey south and west passed quickly and easily. As the sun set on the second day, a snake spooked Cormack's horse, tossing him from the saddle. He was unharmed, except for his pride, so Dominique called a stop for the night. They shared a camp with two of Emperor Mero's Centari. The horse-mounted cavalry soldiers were normally abrasive brutes, but the young and untested soldiers in camp were excellent company who lightened the load for night watch.

The morning of their fourth day out from Argela saw them arrive at the grove where the mad alchemist was rumoured to live. Dense with heavy brush and tall trees of varying species, the grove grew for miles, reaching to the mountain range an hour's walk to the west. It took half an hour to settle the horses and make camp. As Shasta finished brushing her white stallion, she approached Dominique and

Cormak. Both stared into the heavy foliage and trees that grew within the grove, but neither said a single word.

"Problems?" she asked.

"Death weighs heavily on this place," Cormak muttered. The wind shifted direction and Shasta caught the pungent scent of rotting flesh, rotting human flesh. Once it fouled your nose, you never forgot it.

"The stench riding the wind tells me that, Cormak," she said.

"People die every day," Dominique scoffed. "It just means they were greedy or stupid. Let's go, we're already way behind schedule. Bauro will nearly be at Rejtett Island by now. We don't have time to waste." He stepped forward, but Cormak grasped his shoulder.

"Greedy and stupid created the stench here, brother. We do not want to add to it." Releasing the pirate and bending over, Cormak pulled four fist-sized rocks from the dirt at his feet, piling them one on top of the other in his left hand. Taking a small square sapphire and a coin-shaped pearl from the pouch at his waist, he winked at Shasta and placed both between his front teeth. Grasping a dirt-covered stone from his left hand, he tossed it a foot into the air and caught it as he surveyed the grove before him.

"Something inside there killed the last to walk this way," Cormack said, his voice muffled by the runes held in his teeth. He tossed the rock into the grove to the right of centre, about fifteen feet into the trees.

Nothing happened. Without another word, he took the pearl from his teeth and snapped it between his fingers, palmed the pieces and placed his hand over the remaining stones, freezing them. Grabbing a second and third stone, he stared into the heavy foliage again, throwing the stones twenty feet upwards and another twenty feet into the grove. The stones landed, shattering from the cold as pieces of rock rolled in every direction. A second of eerie silence hung in the air before a piercing snap echoed through the trees. A high-pitched mechanical whirl whistled out immediately after.

"What the..." Shasta whispered, as two more mechanical whirls whistled out of the trees on the heels of the first. Shasta and Dominique both drew their blades as Cormak spit the sapphire into his right hand. Snapping the gem, he pulled the magical essence seeping from the two halves and expanded it into a shimmering blue shield that covered him and his companions. A large 'ping' echoed out of the trees and long blades exploded from the ground inside the grove, shredding everything within thirty feet. Five seconds turned to ten and finally the mechanical blades slowed as they lost whatever had powered them to begin with. Cormack let his hands fall and the magical shield dissipated on the light breeze.

"Amazing," Shasta mumbled. "Never seen Ama Taugr magic before." Cormack smiled, offering a low bow.

"It has its benefits," Dominique growled. "Also has one serious weakness." Shasta titled her head as she stared at Cormack.

The wizard shook his head, staring back. "No runestones, no magic. It's not like we can carry thirty pounds of runestones around."

"Come on," Dominique cursed. "Let's see what this Gods-crazy, fucknard bastard's done in here." He and Cormack slowly entered the dense grove to examine the mechanical devices as the court wizard rolled another sapphire runestone through his fingers. "What are these things, Cormak?"

"By Lady Freyla's grace, I have no idea," he said, crouching to examine the open-flower design of the five-foot-long blades. Spread like the petals of a flower, the three devices, side-by-side, each covered ten feet in diameter. The wind shifted again, blowing through the grove.

"Ugh," Shasta gagged, standing behind Dominique and Cormak. The entire area, cleared by the spinning traps, smelled and looked worse than any battle Shasta had ever seen. Chunks of rotting body parts hung from trees, flies swarmed over putrescent pieces of gore she had no name for, and maggots swarmed over and inside unrecognizable Human and Elvehn flesh that had been scattered everywhere by the power of the whirling blades. "That's just... wrong..."

"Yeah," Dominique agreed. A veteran of hundreds of battles, it was clear he struggled to control a revolting stomach as well.

"That's funny," Cormak added laughing. "I can't smell a thing." Shasta gave him a strange look, so he trailed his finger through the air in front of himself, triggering sparkling waves of reverberation from his new shield.

"Damned wizards," Dominique griped, kicking a disemboweled torso out of his way. Cormak flashed a frown at his disrespect, eliciting a grunt. "Come on. These idiots smell too bad to care about a boot to the ribs, but that crazy bastard hiding in there can still feel it."

"Easy, brother," Cormak snapped. "Perhaps it'd be better if you two stayed behind me? Let my shield take whatever this fool has to send our way. These blades are genius. Something you might find deep within a Dwarven ruin. We need to be careful."

Dominique chuckled. "Lead the way, brave man." Turning to Shasta, and bumping her shoulder, he added, "Enjoy this, First Mate. It's not very often you see a wizard lead the way anywhere." Getting another dirty look from Cormak, Dominique howled with laughter. A clang from behind them cut his laughter short as the blades lifted, closing like a pre-bloom flower.

"Run!" Cormack yelled, as the blades slowly recessed, lowering into the ground. "Now! Before we trigger them again."

Rushing deeper into the wooded grove with Cormak leading the way, the group encountered no more traps and the scent of death faded, staying behind them. The mechanical blades stayed quiet, hidden below ground as if in wait for the next group of unsuspecting fools to stumble onto them.

A half-hour walk led them to a shallow, fast moving stream a stone's-throw wide. A clearing on the far side of the stream held a large two story wood cabin nestled against the first of many sheer cliff-faces heading into the mountains, light smoke trailed lazily from the clay brick chimney. Shasta crouched inside the treeline behind Cormak.

"That cabin is something else," she muttered.

"So crazy people are good with wood, who cares," Dominique snapped.

Shasta shrugged, agreeing. "What now?" she asked as Cormak sat in the grass. Crossing his legs and closing his eyes, he thumbed a blue stone in his right hand. The stone flared with magical energy, making his shield pulse visibly. With a solid snap, the stone broke and the wizard's shield rolled out across the stream and into the meadow, across the clearing to the little cabin. Nothing happened. He opened his eyes, but stayed sitting in the tall grass.

"Whoa," Shasta whispered. "I've never seen magic move like that. What was it?"

"I hoped that the pressure from my shield would trigger any traps hidden in the clearing out from the cabin. The blades behind us triggered by pressure, like the stones I threw in. That meadow is completely undisturbed. I suspect there are traps there, but they're not pressure-sensitive."

"Great," Dominique muttered, staring into the cleared meadow. "Any chance you can expand that shield of yours around all three us without weakening it?"

"Yes," he answered, as Shasta sighed with relief. "I think I have a couple sapphire runes left. And this." Cormack took a black runestone from a small pouch hanging around his neck. "This is my last onyx stone, Dominique. I can use it now, or wait..."

"Use it." Getting a strange look from Shasta, Dominique turned her way. "Black onyx stones are rare and highly sought after. Kastalborg Island has almost been mined clean. It's augmentation magic, powerful too. Elderblood powerful. Strengthens or reinforces magic, in this case, his shield."

"Think bigger and stronger," Cormack added. Smiling, he held out his hand. "Give me a length of hair, both of you." Taking the single hairs the two pirates handed over, Cormack wrapped them around the two gemstones. Rubbing them together between his thumb and first finger, he grasped both, squeezing hard. A sharp snap rolled through the trees as the stones cracked. Blue magic swirled from his hand, mixing with a soft black essence from the onyx stone. Cormack manipulated the blue magic, pulling and pushing it up and around himself, Dominique, and Shasta. Holding the blue shield in place with his left hand, the wizard coaxed the black essence with his right, layering it against the blue, once, twice, and finally a third time before slapping his hands together. The shield shimmered and a second later cleared. Double-checking, Cormack slowly swung his arm out around his body, triggering a response. The shield reverberated, shimmering a dark blue as shadows of black swirled through it.

Shasta did the same, chuckling as the shield in front of her became visible for a few seconds. "That is incredible," she whispered, more to herself than the others.

Cormack smiled. "It'll cover us all, but we won't be able to fight under it," he said as the shield cleared once more. "Both of you stay within five feet of each other or you'll weaken it. It's tied to you through your hair so you can't walk away from it. The further away you wander the more it stretches and the weaker it gets." Both pirates nodded. "Good. Let's go."

Cormak rose from the grass, untying a pouch from his waist. Shaking the contents into his left hand, a dozen stones and gems tumbled out, all the size and shape of a man's thumb or round and shaped like coins. All were raw, uncut gemstones, some clouded from not being polished, while others, though uncut, shone with clarity, including the bright blue sapphire he took from the pile. He quickly grabbed a shiny, round, red-fire opal, and a cloudy moonstone rectangle. Inscribed with a magical script-like lettering only the Ama Taugr understood, the stones were a deadly weapon in the hands of the very few who could use them.

"Dominique?" Cormak asked, turning his head. "Across or around the side of the meadow?"

The pirate captain frowned. "If this fucknard has traps here, they'll likely be in the middle and to the sides of the meadow. Take us along the very edge of the mountain face to the left." Cormak nodded and started out to the west, crossing the river and making his way to the rock face of the mountain cliffs on the meadow's south side. Shasta and Dominique followed close, keeping the umbrella of Cormak's magical shield strong. Reaching the meadow, Cormak crouched in the shade cast by the looming mountain and waited. Watching for movement within the cabin and the outbuildings, they saw nothing.

"Maybe the bastard's already dead," Dominique offered.

"I doubt it," Cormak said, shaking his head as he pointed to the smoke still drifting from the chimney. "Someone lit the cook fire inside the cabin. He's gotta be here." Shasta could see Cormack eyeing the rock face carefully and her eyes followed his as he checked for any signs that might suggest a trap or trip-lines. Seeing nothing, she guessed he sensed even less as he waved for Shasta and Dominique to follow. He crept against the mountain face, edging his way closer to the cabin. They were still a hundred feet from the cabin when the door crashed open and an older man stepped out onto the porch. Without the slowed ageing gifted by magic or Northman and Elvehn blood, Shasta put the man's age in his fifties, a long scraggly beard hung from his chin and his hair was a mess of knotted lengths.

"Crazy hermit if ever there was one," she whispered, getting a nod from the others.

The man stared at the three intruders, finally yelling in a strange accent. "Go back! Get off my land, or die like everyone else."

"Cormack?" Dominique asked quietly. "Care to reason with a madman?"

"I'll try." He sighed, standing slowly with his hands held above his head, the fire opal between his thumb and forefinger. "We mean you no harm, Sir," he said, raising his voice. "We came here looking for you. We're hoping you could answer some questions for us."

Clearly not fooled, the old man shook his head. "I have no answers for anyone, and there is nothing I can help you with. Leave, now!"

"Make something up, Cormack. Calm him down and get us closer," Dominique whispered into his hand, so the hermit didn't see.

"Sir? Please?" Cormak tried again. "We've heard that you're a skilled alchemist. We've travelled from the city to find you and lost most of our companions to the bladed traps a mile or so behind us. Please, just a moment of your time, we've come for help, looking for healing medicines."

"You ain't after meds, gobshite. How dense ya think I am? You're after what they're all after. This," he said calmly, pulling a sword handle with no blade from his belt. A gem on the pommel flashed in the sunlight. Cormack squinted, trying to see what the man held.

The old man yelled again. "Last chance, Holy Joes. Go back and leave me be."

"Fuck this shit and this old man," Dominque snarled, standing. "Distract him, Cormack. Shasta, put a bolt in his foot." His first mate obeyed immediately, reaching for the small crossbow slung across her back.

Cormack dug through his pouch of runestones, muttering. "Bad, bad idea, Dom. Something's not right..." He looked up as the old man's words reached his ears. Reaching blindly for both Dominique and Shasta as she followed her captain's command, Cormack stared helplessly. The old man smiled, waving as he spun the sword pommel in his hand and pressed the red gem.

"Get down!" Cormak yelled. Shasta stared at her section of shield. It flared with strength as the runecaster did what he could to rebalance the magic. In an instant, Shasta realized he pushed his share to her and Dominique.

The meadow heaved, exhaling fire and thunder. Cormack's shield flared to life, but quickly winked out after absorbing a massive amount of concussive pressure. A second blast erupted under Shasta's feet, swarming her, Dominique, and the wizard in fire and tossing them through the air as rocks and dirt swirled in their vision. Pain swallowed all conscious thought as Shasta struck the ground.

Cormack cursed. "Dammit, Dominique," he slurred, and lost consciousness.

Screeching birds flew from the trees and animals bolted into hiding as the shockwave rolled over the mountain range. Minutes passed before the dust settled and a calm quiet returned to the grove. Shasta could hear giddy laughter, like a young girl, or a crazy old man. Her vision wavered as she tried to remain conscious.

Eamon O'Leary's cackling laughter echoed across the meadow as he sat down on his porch. "Effing gougers never learn." Shasta heard him snort as the darkness closed-down her mind. His last words barely reached her in time. "Magic never stands up to good old fashioned Irish boom."

Chapter Twenty-Two

"News from DormaSai has been quiet. According to our wizards and several fleets, the rebellion was successful. The castle in Drae'Kahn succumbed to the siege, thanks to an infiltration group led by the rebel's military strategist, Nekrosa Kohl. He now sits as king of DormaSai, and for all the reports we get, it appears most claim he is rebuilding two hundred years of damage caused by the Azmerack family during their reign of necromantic terror. Few reports state that this man is also a prodigal necromancer. I certainly hope not; DormaSai has suffered enough under the cold hands of death callers."

Excerpt from ArchWizard Zirakus' report to Talohna's Elder and Wizard Councils on the post-rebellion status of DormaSai, 5015 PC

DASAL

Ember, Yrlissa, and Seifer walked to the lower open air square where most of the city markets and vendor stalls who dealt in food and travel supplies were located. Max was talking to a merchant at a stall selling dried goods like meat and fruit. The vendor also had some dried vegetables that would travel well and allow for healthier, warm meals. With a full three weeks of journeying ahead of them, he was buying as much as he could, but the three of them on their own had very little money compared to Giddeon and the others, so he was trying to haggle a better price from the merchant; Ember could see it was not going well.

"Problems, Max?" Yrlissa asked in a sarcastic, but sweet voice.

"You could say that," he grumbled. "This merchant doesn't want to deal on his goods. He wants my bow in exchange for the amount of food we need. Asshole." He swore at the merchant, who only smiled in return.

"That's because he knows what your bow is worth more than you do. Orotaq bows are priceless and you are the only person besides an Orotaq Arkas to have one. You can't blame him for trying." she said, smiling. Then turning to the merchant, she said, "The bow is not for sale or trade, peddler. Do you want our business or not?"

Smiling, the merchant nodded. "Always, child of TaCeryss, but the price is seven gold for what the big man wants. Or the bow."

"We don't have seven gold, Yrlissa, not even close. Fucking little crook," Max snapped.

Seifer stepped up beside Yrlissa, placing a hand on Max's shoulder. "Morning, Malikai, business going well?"

"It's all right, Master Locke, steady as always." Ember smiled; the merchant was lying in order to protect his argument.

"These good people are my friends, Malikai," Seifer said. "And they are Kael's friends. This is Ember, Kael's real wife. This is Max. He and Kael are like brothers. Did your son, Tavin, get the medicine your granddaughter needed, Malikai?" Seifer asked.

The merchant's face turned bright red as he looked to the ground and mumbled, "You know he bought it, Master Locke He told me you were there when he paid your captain's sister."

"Little Namara is feeling better, I hope?"

Still too embarrassed to look up, the merchant nodded. "She is, Master Locke. She was just here helping me open and getting some fresh air for the first time in months. Thank you for asking about her, and please thank Mistress Dara for the elixir when you see her."

"I will, Malikai, and I'm sorry... very sorry to have to remind you where your son got the money to pay for her medicine, but Kael paid your son two gold coins for a couple coppers' worth of paint, did he not? And Mistress Dara only asked your son to pay for the fleshleaf needed to enhance the strength of the elixir so it would help Namara, did she not?"

"She did, Master Locke, and I'm sorry, it's just times are hard, she has been sick for so long, and not everyone was truthful or helpful like Mistress Dara was. We have no money left, and she still is going to die... You know that. But at least we will have some time with her now." Ember's heart dropped to her stomach as the merchant's eyes turned red and glossed over with moisture.

"I understand, Malikai, I do, but charging unfair prices for your goods is not right and can get you tossed from the Merchant's Guild, should they find out. Myself and Dara consider your family our friends. I don't want to see you lose your livelihood over a few gold, right?" The merchant nodded as he finally looked up, his face red with embarrassment.

Ember said nothing as the conversation played back and forth, her thoughts kept drifting to the news about Kael travelling with another woman. Though she had not been listening that closely, the merchants last few words seemed to snap her back, as if her mind had heard him without her consciously being aware of it it.

"Excuse me?" she asked "If you don't mind my asking, what is wrong with your granddaughter?"

"We don't know, Mistress, but she is very ill. It is known only as the wasting sickness. She feels better now and she can walk a bit after Mistress Dara helped, but she cannot cure her. No one knows what is wrong," he said.

"Can you tell me how it started, and everything that happened afterwards?" Ember asked, a frown creeping onto her face. The merchant nodded and sat on a wooden stool to the side of his stall.

"She was three when it started," he began, looking up at Ember. She nodded for him to keep going. "It was nothing bad at first," he continued. "She would bump into things or drop the spoon when she was eating, but from there it got much worse. She was tired all the time and she would get muscle spasms and cramps that wouldn't go way. Her little muscles seemed to be vanishing even though she was still eating, and she would just fall over sometimes when sitting. It got worse as the years went on, and then about six months ago she could no longer walk. She was even beginning to have trouble breathing. It was terrifying. My son's wife died birthing her, so she is all he has left. We knew it wouldn't be long before she passed, but the fleshleaf we needed is so expensive. It doesn't grow here, so it must be imported. Kael gave my son the gold to get it by purchasing some cheap ink. My son tried to tell him it was worth much less, but..." he finished, trailing off.

Ember felt her eyes mist with moisture as Malikai looked down at his feet not wanting to say any more. It sounded exactly like the Kael she knew and loved.

Reasserting self-control over her emotions, she cleared her throat. "I... I'm sorry, Malikai, for everything. But how about we make a deal? You give my friend here a fair deal on the supplies we need and I will come see your granddaughter. Maybe I can help her. Sound fair?" she asked.

He nodded. "Two gold is a fair price, Mistress, but you need not come see her. You will not be able to help Namara anyway. The Blessed Fae wouldn't be able to help her were they not so many millennia gone from our world."

Putting her hand on his shoulder, Ember let a trickle of magic flow into the old man, her only intention to give him hope. "The Fae are not as far away as you think, Malikai, and it won't hurt Namara any for me to see her, will it?" she asked, whispering. He gave her a smile and nodded his agreement.

"Malikai," Seifer said, just as they were about to leave. "I'll go let Tavin know that Namara is having some special visitors, all right?"

"Thank you, Master Locke," Malikai said, as he waved to the wizard.

Most of what Malikai had for sale, Max took. Paying the old man the two gold Yrlissa had given him, he began packing it up for the horses as the merchant closed up his stall.

"Meet you at the stables when you're done?" Max asked, getting a nod from Yrlissa.

Malikai led Ember and Yrlissa on the long walk back to his house. He told them eight-year-old Namara would be resting.

Ember noticed Yrlissa staring at her as they walked back to Malikai's. "What is it?" she asked.

"You know what is wrong with the girl, do you not?" she answered.

"I might."

"Can you help her?"

Ember glanced at Yrlissa and smiled. "If I am right about what is wrong, then I hope so. She will die before too much longer if my suspicions are correct."

"What is it?" Yrlissa asked, as they started up the massive stone steps leading from the market square.

"On Earth we have a disease called muscular dystrophy. Well, it's not really a disease, I guess, though it is usually called so. It's a genetic disorder, where the body cannot make what our muscles need to grow and work properly." She tried to explain while keeping in mind Talohna's drastically different approach to medicine.

Yrlissa frowned, looking around as if to make sure no one was within earshot and to make sure Malikai was still well ahead of them.

"The Fae could heal most things. Not usually mortal wounds and some poisons, Ember, but diseases, yes. What you are could... will change this world. You have already started to change it, I believe. But we must be careful. Many would seek to take you for their own selfish reasons. You must remember that you cannot help everyone. You are only one, you are the last, and you are important," she warned.

"Maybe, but someone gave birth to me and someone took me to Earth, which means there are other Fae somewhere. And I'm starting to learn what people are like in this world. A little too quickly in fact, but one little girl is not everyone, is she? Besides, I'm not helpless, especially with you and Max to help keep me safe, right?"

Yrlissa smiled. "Always, and your heart is true to the Fae. They would never have turned away from someone in need, even if it meant their life. But please be careful. I've read stories from ancient times when countries fought wars over Fae-trained healers, let alone a real Fae like you."

Ember smiled, nodding in agreement as they saw Malikai wave that they had arrived.

Ember and Yrlissa entered the small stone and mortar, single story house. With only three rooms, it was warm and cozy. Malikai led Ember to the back bedroom where a young girl was resting on a small bed. She was awake and sat up when her grandfather entered the room. Ember noticed she almost fell face forward when her body was unable to stop her forward momentum from sitting up.

"Papa!" The little girl smiled from ear-to-ear. "You are home early today. I am so happy to see you!"

"As am I to see you, my little princess," he said, giving her a hug. "I have brought a friend to see you. Her name is Ember, and she would like to see if maybe she can help you feel better, all right?"

"All right, Papa, but I feel good for now, and we can worry about later when it comes, right?" she said, bravely.

"That is right, my brave girl, but you tell Mistress Ember what she wants to know and be a good girl, like always."

Namara smiled. "Yes, Papa."

Ember sat on the side of the bed and placed her hand on Namara's knee, careful to be gentle. The contact would allow her to feel what was wrong as they talked.

"Hi, Namara, my name is Ember. I hear you haven't been feeling well for quite some time, huh?"

"Yes, Mistress. I know it cannot last but I have been feeling a little better, and I can walk again now, most of the time. And I only fall a few times a day now. The last two days, anyway," she rambled, nervously.

"I see," Ember commented, smiling, though a part of her mind was far away concentrating on the little girl's sickness.

"Namara?" Ember asked. "Would you like to feel better all the time, and never fall or bump yourself again, and be able to run all day and play with your friends outside?"

Namara's eyes took on a haunted look as her voice lowered to a whisper. "Yes, Mistress, but Father and Papa told me that only the Blessed Fae could help me, and they have gone from this world thousands of years ago," she sniffed, and wiped her nose before continuing in a whisper that Ember could just make out. "It's all right, Mistress. I only wish my Father and Mama and Papa would stop crying all the time. It makes me sad."

Ember took Namara's hands in hers, and leaned forward. "Would you like to know a secret about the Fae, Namara?"

Namara's uneasy smile nearly broke Ember's heart. "Papa says the Fae will never return to our world because they have all died, and Father says that they will never come back because people have become too mean and bad so the Fae don't want to be here any more."

"Oh, baby girl," Ember chuckled. "There is so much more to it than that. I don't know why we left this world,"

Ember winked, offering a mischievous smile as the green of her eyes flared bright with power. "But I promise you, sweetie, that we have returned. Well, one of us has," Ember said, waiting for Namara to catch what she said. It took only moments before her eyes popped open and Ember was afraid they might burst if they grew any bigger.

"Yes, sweetie, I'm not Human," Ember whispered. "Though we look mostly like you do. I'm the only Fae in this world right now, Namara, and nobody else knows. Do you think you can keep that secret for me?" Though she said it to Namara, Ember was staring at Malikai. His eyes were as large as his granddaughter's.

"Does... Do... Can you really help her then? C-cure her?" he stuttered. Ember smiled, the reason for her love of most people becoming clear. Back home, she had begun her studies to be a doctor, Kael's injury being the initial incident that drove her to try and help, and then later, the social injustices of Extended Life Medicine, or ELA as it was called, drove her on further. It was all so clear to her now.

Another piece of the wall inside her mind crumbled away, bigger this time, spilling forth more knowledge and memories that were not hers.

"Yes, Malikai. I think I can help her," she answered. Turning to the little girl, she asked, "Would you like for me to help you, Namara? Make all this go away and make sure it never comes back?"

Namara sobbed. "Please, Mistress... Ye-yes... Pl-please."

"Then lay back and close your eyes. When you wake up, perhaps what is wrong with you will be gone," she said.

As soon as she was laying on her back and comfortable, Ember caressed her cheek, putting Namara into a deep sleep. Tavin, Namara's father, burst through the front door and into the bedroom at the same moment his daughter slumped unconscious.

"What did you do to her?" he screamed. Stepping forward, he snatched Ember's arm, jerking her from the bed.

"Get away from her," he growled. Before he could finish speaking, a metal blade slipped around his neck and pressed on his throat drawing blood.

"Let go her, now, or your daughter will be an orphan," Yrlissa hissed, and pressed her blade harder against the artery on the left side of his neck. Tavin released his grip, and Ember spun back to the bed to check on Namara.

"Wait! Mother Inara, stop!" Seifer yelled, as he burst through the door of the small house. "Everyone please, just calm down. Tavin, they're here to help. Why didn't you listen? You just took off." Even with the partial explanation, Yrlissa wouldn't release the girl's father.

"I overheard the ArchWizard talking about an assassin here in the city, when they came to the far market. I assumed that after I helped Kael, someone hired her to get back at us. Lircang might be dead, Master Locke, but his associates aren't."

"Assani's blood, are you stupid?" Yrlissa snapped. "Is the girl all right, Ember? Had you started yet?"

"No," Ember said, leaning over the little girl. "Thank God, I hadn't. Two more seconds and I would have."

Yrlissa released her blade from Davin's neck and spun him around, twisting the man's shirt. "You stupid little man, you realize that had she started to heal your daughter, you grabbing her like that would have killed both her and Namara? The only damn Fae in the world, and you could have killed her. When a wizard tells you something, fool, you damn well listen!"

"I'm sorry. Master Locke said Namara was getting special visitors, with what the ArchWizard said, I just...panicked..."

Yrlissa shoved him out of the bedroom. "Go sit down, and let her heal your little girl." The reality of the situation came crashing down on Tavin all at once, and he stumbled before finally sitting on one of the kitchen chairs.

"She's gonna heal her," he laughed. "Da, you hear that?" Malikai wiped his own eyes and grabbed his son in a hug, joined by his wife.

"Yes, son, I know. She is in good hands. That's Kael's real wife in there. She'll take good care of her."

Lost in emotions, it was clear Tavin no longer cared who was who, only that his daughter would be all right.

Working from the lost memories deep inside her mind, Ember was not sure whether the little girl would feel any pain as she healed her, but something told her if the girl was asleep, it would work much better. Knowing the problem in the girl was as deep inside her as was possible, Ember let her feelings take over while her genetic memory guided her magic.

A pale blue and green light emanated from her hands and easily slid through the little girl's body the moment Ember spoke the words that drifted around inside her head.

"Amaeh aidora, shalaness – Anavah vallanomin," she said, softly. Ember repeated herself, her eyes closed and her face wrinkled in concentration. A small whine escaped the lips of the sleeping girl as she squirmed with discomfort, but Ember pressed on until the genes that were not working properly in the little girl's body were whole and complete, the damaged and missing qualities repaired. The colourful magic faded as she brought the spells to an end.

Exhausted from the use of magic required to repair a deadly genetic defect, Ember again thanked the hidden knowledge in her mind and her years of schooling towards being a doctor. Both saved Namara's life.

Yrlissa managed to catch Ember before she fell, overcome by exhaustion – the price called for by the laws of magic.

Malikai, quickly came to her aid as well. "Is she all right, Mistress?" he asked, worry showing all over his face.

Looking up at him, Yrlissa nodded. "She will be. Healing someone as deathly ill as your granddaughter requires magic beyond even my understanding, Malikai. It has drawn a portion of her own life force, but she'll recover, with time," Yrlissa insisted, massaging Ember's forehead and temples. "She's just exhausted from the magic. I must take her to our friends where she can rest and recover." Ember woke with a start and grasped Malikai's arm.

"Let her sleep until she wakes on her own, even if it is days. It will take time for her strength to return, but she is... better... I... I promise." She closed her eyes and laid back against Yrlissa, slipping from consciousness.

"Malikai, please go find the big man who was trying to buy all your supplies when we arrived earlier. I'll need his help to get her to our camp outside of town," Yrlissa said as she continued to hold Ember.

"Right away, Mistress." He nodded before turning and leaving the small house.

After Max returned to the merchant's house to help Yrlissa with Ember, they collected their horses and supplies. None of them wished to spend the night inside the city. It would mean losing a half day's travel time and with Kael only two days ahead, everyone was eager to try and catch up to him. Seifer provided a ramshackle cart for them to use in helping Ember. Physically drained, she had yet to regain consciousness. For such a young Fae, she was quickly coming into staggering abilities when it came to helping people. They left the city to find Giddeon, Kasik, and Saleece waiting for them.

"Max," Giddeon said, greeting them. "So, do we still travel together or do you wish to go your own way?" Max stared at Giddeon for several minutes, trying to decide the likelihood of a fight when they caught up with Kael.

"I guess that's up to you," he tested. "Kael is only two days ahead now. Are you going to try and talk with him or just straight up try to kill him?"

Giddeon merely shook his head. "I told you both right from the beginning that I would give him the chance to talk to all of us. I haven't changed my mind."

"Yet your actions show otherwise," Yrlissa snapped.

"From your point of view, perhaps," Saleece said, as she rose from the side of the campfire and poured a pot of water over the flames. "You need to understand that Kael might not want to talk when we catch up, even if it's what we want."

"Travelling together is safer," Kasik added.

Too tired to argue further, Max looked at Yrlissa, who nodded. "Then I guess we might as well travel together. From what I understand, we're heading into some dangerous country."

"We are," Kasik said. "It's not too bad before Cairnwood, but after that, the mountains are full of all matter of problems."

"After everything we've been through, how bad can it be?" Max asked, as he smirked. "A couple giants and a few ogres, maybe? No problem."

"It scares me that I can't tell whether or not you're joking," Yrlissa said.

"What? I wasn't being serious, but I figured the way things have been going we're due for about that much shit."

Giddeon grunted. "You tell him, Yrlissa. I cannot believe that after everything he has seen and been through, that he could still be that gods-forsaken ignorant." He tugged his horses reins to turn his mount and cantered away.

"What?" Max repeated.

Yrlissa glared at him as if he were a ten year old in big trouble. "Do I really have to answer you? Only a donkey's ass would laugh and joke about giants and ogres. Even your strength pales in comparison to either of them. Hopefully, they're both still scarce." She smiled, winked, and then rode away, leaving him to bring up the rear with the squeaking, bouncing old wagon.

He looked back over his shoulder into the wagon to make sure Ember was secure and as safe as she could get. He stared towards the city gates of Dasal before taking a quick glance back down the road in the direction of Corynth. Try as he might, he could no longer sense someone following them, not since they escaped from the Taktala. He was concerned that if his group was no longer being followed, where did their followers go? With Kael meeting up with Giddeon and then passing them, were they actually after Kael instead?

Maybe they *were* following Kael. He hoped whoever it was meant no harm. Kael had been through enough already.

"Ha," he barked, out loud, thinking again about giants and ogres. "Ah, Kael. I wish ya were here, buddy. It'd be a blast fighting an ogre together," he joked to himself. "I can't believe it's come to this, sis," he said, checking on Ember in the back of the wagon yet again. "Ah well, some day very soon we'll be back together. I promise."

DASAL

Queen Sephitrotha Kohl woke from her sleep by a repeated banging on the inn door that belonged to her and her husband. Without even bothering to dress, she sprang from the bed with little effort, landing only feet from the door. She swung the door open, having recognized the uniformly coded knocks. Luthian quickly entered the room without being seen, she hoped. He turned to offer his Queen a bow, as well as a reason for his urgent intrusion, when he realized she had yet to dress.

Staring from surprise, he quickly averted his eyes. "My queen, I apologize for staring. I just assumed you would be awake. Forgive me, Your Highness, please," he begged.

Walking over to a tall closet, she removed a long silk cloak and covered herself.

"It's fine, Luthian. Why are you here?" The second she finished speaking, the door opened a second time and Nekrosa walked in backwards, a platter of food filling his arms.

He turned. Surprised to see his spymaster, he asked, "What are you doing here?"

Luthian began to bow. "My king, I..."

"Get your ass up," Nekrosa snapped, taking a half-hearted kick towards him with his bad leg. "None of that at the best of times, let alone in a kingdom where it could get us killed, understand? I really don't want to say it again," he said, with a stern voice, and then started to laugh as if he could no longer keep up the serious tone.

"Come on, old friend, have a bite to eat and tell us why you're here. It's well after the noon meal. You must be hungry, and Sephi was on watch most of the night. She needs to eat too. Here." He sat the platter down on the table and retrieved his walking stick from his belt. Not bothering to waste time with the food, Luthian explained his unexpected visit.

"She's here, My King... Sorry, Nekrosa, Sephi. Here in Dasal. They arrived this morning and spoke with the Master Wizard here, then left to gather supplies. I know which one she is. A merchant, his granddaughter is, or was, dying. I asked around and it sounds like she has the wasting sickness... or had, Gods. The redheaded one, Nekrosa. She healed the little girl. I waited three hours before coming here. I saw the little girl, the mark of the Void is gone. All signs of death are gone from her body. This young woman healed a deadly illness. I still can scarcely believe it and I saw it all through the eyes of the wing. As sure as I am standing here... She is a real Fae," he described.

Nekrosa paused for only a moment before taking several candied dates from the platter of food. He tossed one in his mouth and looked over at Sephi, she smiled from ear-to-ear.

"Well, my dear, this has been a most enlightening trip has it not?" he asked. With a gentle glide across the floor, almost as if she were floating, Sephi stopped in front of him, and nodded. She opened her mouth as he placed a date on top of her tongue, kissing her mouth before she closed it and swallowed. "Mhm. Except for using up our only vial of enhanced healing. All we have left is the spelled Brethren blood. But a DeathWizard in debt to us for his life, the only living Fae right in front of us, things couldn't have gone better even if we had planned it, could it?"

"No, it couldn't, my husband. Things seem to be going exactly as we had hoped they would. Before long, the only living DeathWizard and the last Fae will be returning with us to DormaSai."

"All right then, Luthian," Nekrosa said, limping across the room to retrieve their travel packs. "Supplies, horses, everything we need, I want to be after them in an hour's time." He tossed Luthian a bag of gold nuggets, DormaSain gold coins would only get then in trouble.

Luthian started to bow but saw the look Nekrosa gave him. Standing with his back straight, he nodded instead and left.

Chapter Twenty-Three

"Hollow Dogs. What can I say about these creatures? I myself have never seen one, though I have talked to a northern trader who has. Corbin Sayde, an Elvehn caravan trader, has survived several far north expeditions into the Black Hollow peninsula in order to barter with the Orotaq. This is what he told me:

'Trading with freakishly strong blue monsters is merely a matter of having barter materials they want, a lot of said materials, and having them often. The Orotaq can be quite civil, though I wouldn't recommend breaking any fast with them – in fact, avoid them completely during meals. As for the hollow dogs, the wild ones are rarely the real concern. They live in the gas swamps, a place no sane person would ever go. Most of the Orotaq-tamed dogs are very well trained; they usually only kill when ordered to do so. They have every nasty attribute of their wild counterparts, only they're trained to obey extremely complex commands. They're dangerous and damn smart.'

"Corbin never said as much, but avoid Black Hollow during your travels across Talohna. There's nothing up there but death for any race other than the Orotaq."

Garren Sallus, Myths and Creatures of Talohna. Vol. 1

ROAD TO CAIRNWOOD

Kyah and Kael pushed themselves and their horses as hard as they dared while still leaving themselves in fighting condition and the horses with enough energy to flee if they encountered trouble. Never believing for a single second that Giddeon had gone after the Cethosian princess, Kael was positive it had been a ploy to slow them down and allow for the ArchWizard and his group to catch up. The fast pace of travel left both tired, though still able to defend themselves should they need to. Even so, Kael made sure to always switch watch with Kyah throughout the night. Seifer had warned them of the serious dangers of the high country.

The first four days were uneventful; no creatures or threats surfaced. Knowing they were getting closer to a serious battle with Sythrnax or his forces, Kael had been trying to teach offensive magic to Kyah. Considering his own limited abilities with underworld magic and no abilities with earth-bond magic, it was actually going quite well. Kyah was a bonded wizardess, so once he had taught her the words to Gabriel's lightening spell, she found it easy to cast, and was soon capable of staggering power. She explained to him that as far as she had been taught, power was power, which was why Dead Healers were forbidden to learn offensive spells.

As the time drew near for the evening meal, they debated pushing on for Cairnwood in order to spend the night at an inn. The hours of darkness brought temperatures close to freezing in the mountain foothills. Only a few miles away from the town, they walked their horses as they talked back and forth trying to decide whether or not to push on.

Kael stopped dead in his tracks as if running into a brick wall. He gasped, putting his hand on his forehead. Crouching on one knee, he closed his eyes to concentrate.

Several minutes passed before Kyah broke the silence. “What is it? Do not go drifting off on me again.” Kael shivered, all his muscles twitched and hummed as his eyes popped open.

"There's heavy movement in the forest several miles to the north. It feels familiar but I don't understand it. I can smell smoke as well, but it's faint," he said, then closed his eyes again, but for only a second this time. "Magic. I can sense magic. It's different, strange." Kael stood, chewing his bottom lip, deep in thought. "Come on, something is not right."

Climbing onto his horse, he took off at a gallop as Kyah shouted for him to wait. Realizing he did not hear her, she jumped up on her mount and followed, racing to catch up.

Galloping flat-out at breakneck speed, Kael pushed his mount for all it had when it suddenly hit him. He pulled back on the reins, forcing the horse to stop, and he closed his eyes and concentrated once more. Kyah had never seen him like this before, and he knew it was starting to worry her. She was right to be worried.

He opened his eyes. "Oh, Jesus. Kyah, the village is under attack," he said, looking at her. "There are so many. Too many to count."

"Who? Who are they?" Sensing his distress, Kael's horse pawed the ground and spun to the right, eager to be off.

"I don't know!" he yelled. "But there are dozens dead already. Come on. We have to hurry before it's too late to help." The words had just left his mouth when his mount spun to the north and jumped into a gallop. Letting it have its head, the horse's hooves tore up the dirt trail as it raced for Cairnwood. Only a little over a mile out from the town, they arrived in minutes.

With Kael in the lead, the two horses burst from the trees into the clearing before the town of Cairnwood. At a full gallop and their mounts heavy with sweat from the mile-long dash, the first thing they saw was smouldering ash—all that was left of the town's front gates. Screams of horror and cries of pain echoed through the smoky air as they entered the town.

Kael slid from his horse, landing in a full run with both his Vai'Karth reaper-blades already in his hands, but stopped, staggering after only ten feet. The south end of the town was engulfed by flames, the buildings on the ground and those built into the cliffs were all on fire. Smoke hung thick in the air, darkening the sky, and the entire section of the town was overrun by large black dogs, all three hundred pounds and four feet high. No wonder he couldn't count them all with his magical sight.

The hounds reminded him of the darga he'd fought while in the Forsaken Lands, until he got a good look at one. These creatures had no horns and were covered in shiny black fur that blurred their exact outline. The jaws were huge, powerful, but they only had half the amount of teeth compared to the twisted creations he had fought up north. What they lacked in horns and teeth, they more than made up with their large feet and retractable claws. There were more than twenty of the black hounds within sight. Some were dragging helpless people towards the centre of town. Others had stopped to feed on smoking bodies, their powerful back legs and vicious claws tore the dead apart.

"By the blessed Fae," Kyah prayed. "Those are hollow dogs from Black Hollow. No," she cried. "That is why they seemed familiar, Kael. The Orotaq are here!"

A booming voice echoed from across the street. A seven foot tall Orotaq mystic, covered in thick, runic scars exited the front door of a burning house and tossed a young woman's body to the black dogs.

"Right ya are, little girl, and ya arrived just in time to die," he snarled, as he put a whistle to his mouth and blew it for two seconds. Every hollow dog in the vicinity stopped what they were doing and started towards Kael and Kyah.

Both unleashed hellstorms of blistering lightening and dozens of dogs were fried by Kyah and sliced to pieces when hit with Kael's writhing black current. Even with only a couple dogs still standing, the Orotaq mystic laughed as if it didn't matter.

Kael barked the words of his spell again, focusing every ounce of power he could bring forth. "*Kveysa drepa.*"

The words tore from his mouth as euphoria from the magic flooded his veins. The black and purple electricity shot across the street, enveloping the shaman. The big man laughed again and pulled a massive battle axe from a sling on his back. Slamming the butt of the axe into the earth, Kael's sizzling and crackling magic quickly dissipated and died out. The remaining dogs bolted, disappearing down the street. Without hesitating, Kyah followed his attack with one of her own, her lightening slammed into an invisible wall in front of the Orotaq mystic and ricocheted up towards the sky as he lifted his axe above his head.

"Never fought a fellow brother of the arcane, have you, little girl? And you, simpleton," the shaman barked, as he turned his attention to Kael. "Such a useless waste. You need to start thinking like a DeathWizard, boy, not like a Human. Your death magic cannot help you if you do not understand your enemy. Orotaq shamans are immune to all magic. You've been fighting warriors, newborn." The shaman howled with laughter as he held his black battle axe ready for attack. The single word bounced around inside Kael's head. *Newborn.* Just like Sythrnax had called him.

It was all Kael needed to act. His anger flared to life, more at his own incompetence and lack of knowledge than anything else. As always, the deathflower's vines jumped to life all across his body, continuing their obscene journey through his flesh, but this time an instinctual solution to their problem came along for the ride. Kael stepped forward as his rage peaked and vanished in a haze of black smoke. The Orotaq mystic quit laughing.

"What the..." the shaman began, as two shiny blades burst from his chest, curving upwards towards his face like two bizarre silver tusks. Using strength he never knew he possessed, Kael held the huge Orotaq up on his toes.

"I don't need magic to kill your kind" Kael growled, grinding his teeth. "Your shields can't stop my blades, and you can't stop what you can't see."

The Orotaq mystic coughed as blood gurgled in his throat. He smiled, and pulled himself free of Kael's weapons.

Turning towards Kael, the shaman wheezed. "You are a fool, Kael. We all know who you are, what you are, but more importantly..." Dropping to a knee, he reached for Kael. Stepping forward, Kael plunged both blades into the shaman's stomach, pulling him closer as the shaman continued speaking. "I may have been easy to defeat, but I'm a young Shaman. My elders are stronger, Kael. I will die, but you will follow me, if not today, then very soon."

He coughed once more and Kael twisted his blades, ripping them out of the shaman's body. One tore its way out the top of the shaman's left shoulder and the second through the right hip. With the weapons no longer holding the body up, it fell to the ground with a wet thud.

"Yeah, I've heard that before too. 'Very soon' never seems to get here," Kael muttered. The Orotaq Shaman was well beyond hearing it.

From his peripheral vision, Kael caught a glimpse of Kyah as she ducked under the leaping attack of the last savage black dog that had been lurking behind a burning wall. It sailed over her head. The little blades on her kinrai chain held tight between her knuckles gored the beast's stomach. The hound's momentum increased the severity of the razor-sharp blades. It hit the ground in a smear of blood and entrails and twitched in the throes of death.

"What now?" Kyah asked, wiping blood from her face as she crossed the street to Kael.

"They know who we are. That means they work for Sythrnax and the Dead Sisters. What do you think we're gonna do?" Fired by up by anger and a surprising bloodlust, Kael realized his harsh response took her by surprise, but it was short lived.

"I think we should kill them all," she said.

Kael smiled, her reply was exactly what he wanted to hear. "Let's go."

"Do not forget, even Orotaq warriors are resistant to magic."

"I won't," he growled, spinning the Vai'Karth in both hands.

Lost in the coursing waves of fury that boiled through his blood, Kael led the way further into the village of Cairnwood. They entered a narrow alley between two single-story homes and crouched as they watched the remainder of the hollow dogs drag people to the centre of town. Keeping to the eastern edge of the village to avoid the bulk of the Orotaq invading forces, Kael and Kyah were quickly forced to make their way back to the north, killing two more capable warriors they encountered along the way. Young and inexperienced, even by Kael's standards, they still put up an impressive fight. Blood dripped steadily off his fingertips from the wound in his shoulder—proof of the young warrior's skills.

As they reached the northern edge of the village, Kyah grabbed Kael by the arm. "Kael!" she cried, "help her, quick."

Glancing to where she pointed, he saw a little girl on her knees, her head bowed before a mountain-sized Orotaq warrior about to end her life with an oversized obsidian greatsword.

"Shit," Kael swore. His words echoed as he vanished within a cloud of black smoke.

Cassie held her breath and waited for the blow that would end her short life. When splashed with wet warmth, the taste of iron and salt filled her mouth, but there was no spark of pain accompanying it. Something heavy landed beside her and she opened her eyes, clearly surprised she wasn't in the afterlife. The Orotaq who tried to kill her was dead at her side. A man ten years older than she stood in front of her.

Kael reached his hand out to help her, the heat of battle still rushed through him. Staring at her, he could see fear and regret filled her eyes, as if wishing she had died. Realizing his tattooed face and dark eyes along with the wisps of black smoke rising from his arms made him more terrifying than any Orotaq, he smiled to ease her fear.

"Never die on your knees, little one," he said. "Begging won't save you. If you have to die, do it kicking, screaming, and fighting the whole way, and drag as many of these overgrown bastards with you as you can. Understand?" he said, offering his hand again.

She looked up and nodded, but her face suddenly paled in horror as the vines on his face continued to grow, tearing through the skin of his cheeks and around his eyes before they finally stopped just above his eyebrows. He suppressed a grunt of agony. Still trembling, she slowly took his hand and he helped her up just as Kyah joined them.

"Are... are you... here to help us? Please, you have to help us," Cassie asked, her voice hollow of emotion. Kael frowned as the little girl stared, transfixed, at the dead bodies of two young boys less than five feet away. A quick shake of Kyah's head told Kael there was nothing she could do for them.

As Cassie let go of his hand and knelt beside the bloody, arrow-filled bodies of the little boys and cried, Kael answered her. "Yes. We'll try and help, now come. If we win, there will be time to bury and honour the fallen, even if I have to help you myself. Now come," he said again. "It's not safe here, and we can do nothing to help the dead." Cassie nodded, still in shock, as Kyah pulled her close and held her tight.

"We need to move. Now," Kael said, whispering. Scooping Cassie up in his arms, he dodged behind a house, just missing a four-man Orotaq patrol. Kael set the girl down and knelt at her side as Kyah grabbed a cloth from her travel pack and wet it with water from her water skin.

"What is your name, little one?" Kyah asked as she tried to wipe some of the gore from the little girl's face.

"Cassandra, Mistress, people call me Cassie." Kael stood and kept a close watch around the corner of the house while Kyah tried to learn what she could from the girl.

"You can call me Kyah, and this is Kael. Can you tell us what happened here?"

"I don't know what happened. I was in the forest and I returned to see this," she said, waving a hand around the destroyed village. "I think they are the Orotaq. I have heard stories of them, but..." she answered. Her whole body shook with fear and Kael glanced her way as the little girl's teeth chattered.

Kyah smiled to reassure her. "It is all right. You are correct, they are Orotaq. Do you know how many are here?"

Shaking her head, it was clear she was trying hard not to cry. "No, they killed my aunt and uncle and my cousins. We were trying to run." Unable to hold it in, she started to cry as Kyah pulled her close again.

She stared past Kyah's shoulder as Kael shook his head. "I can just make out the town square from here. The situation doesn't look good," he said. "Two Orotaq Shamans and at least ten warriors are in the square. Each are handling one or two dogs. They're keeping watch over the prisoners who survived the initial attack. Without help, this town is doomed."

"I know," Kyah whispered.

"Dammit," Kael cursed. "We need to get closer, so we can hear what they are saying." Cassie pulled back from Kyah and stared up at Kael.

"I can help," she said. "There is a big tree on the edge of where they are gathering the people. They can't see you up there if you are quiet and the town square is right there."

"Tell me how to get there. Kyah, keep her close," he ordered, and shrugged an apology as she gave him a dirty look for telling her to do the obvious.

Under Cassie's whispered directions, they arrived at the big oak tree on the north-western edge of the town without being seen. She showed both Kyah and Kael how to climb the tree swiftly, using the backside so none of the Orotaq would spot them. Once in the higher branches, they climbed out onto the limbs that were closer to where the Orotaq had assembled the town's inhabitants. It looked like most if not all the invaders had returned there as well.

The moans of scared people and the sharp report of a slap or the thud of a punch given to whomever made too much noise drifted up to Kael's ears. The odd snarl or bark from the black dogs kept the rest of the townsfolk in line. Kael could see most of the town square through the branches of his hiding spot. The Orotaq were waiting for something. Kyah was on the branch to his immediate right.

"What do we do?" she asked. "If they decide to massacre everyone, we cannot fight that many. Without effective magic, the advantage is with them."

"I know," he replied, concerned. "Maybe they don't want to kill everyone."

While they were discussing what might happen, Cassie pointed out a guard and his dog heading their way. She tugged Kael's leg and pointed a second time as Kael missed the first. As the Orotaq and his dog drew near, he could see panic light up in the little girl's eyes. He smiled to reassure her. With his innate ability to hide himself and others from magical detection, he was not worried, at first. When he whispered that it would be all right, Cassie pointed at the dog while tugging her nose.

"Shit," Kael swore, under his breath as he realized what she meant. The terrified look on her face returned. Kyah held both her hands up and shook her head to let him know that she had no ideas, either. Cassie panicked and started down the tree. Kael gently grabbed her arm as he tried to think of something to help. The hollow dog and his handler continued to approach.

With no other choice, Kael tried covering their smell in a similar manner to how he silenced his feet. Putting his hands up and closing his eyes, he concentrated on smothering their smell.

A quiet gasp escaped Kyah's lips. Kael opened his eyes to see long, dark, swirling wisps of smoke curl around all three of them. The long, snake-like shadows chased each other around their bodies like three dark comets. The shadows circled several times, then dissipated. Taking a deep breath, Kael choked on the stench and Cassie covered her mouth to smother her nervous giggle. Kyah frowned and shook her head.

Somehow, he had managed to increase the smell of their bodies instead. Less than twenty feet away, the hollow dog and its handler were joined by two others and headed for the tree. They had less than a minute.

At a loss for what to do, Kael shook his head and stared at Kyah.

Chapter Twenty-Four

"Spirit and soul magics draw the heaviest price from magic users. Using the soul or forcing spirits to gain magical power is immoral and highly illegal. Resist this temptation at all costs, or you will see me much sooner than you'd expect."

Excerpt from Giddeon Zirakus' speech to newly bonded students on the dangers of dark magic.

CAULDRON'S TEETH MOUNTAIN RANGE

Chief Karlag Kordanu followed his scout up into the mountains for over an hour before the man slowed to an easier pace. Corleya watched the forest closely. The birds stopped chirping, but had not taken flight, and no insect buzzed or clicked from the underbrush.

"Is it just me..." she whispered, hoping Lycori could hear her, but not the priestess.

"No," Lycori said, softly. "It's not. We're being watched. The chief and the scout both know, so do the priestesses."

Kasna spun, hissing lightly for the two women to be quiet as the scout called the chief forward. Tugging hard on the noose around Lycori's neck, Karlag's stone features threatened violence if they did not remain silent. Lycori turned to Corleya, her finger pressed to her lips. Understanding the situation, Corleya bowed her head in deference to the Kordanu chief. Karlag's scout carefully picked his way forward, following a small game trail that headed deeper into Sartaq territory, and higher into the heavily-forested mountain range.

In a matter of minutes, the scout pushed his way past the thick leaves of a tall plant to discover the trail ended at a steep cliff. Whistling back to Chief Karlag, he stepped sideways a dozen feet, making room along the edge for the others. As Lycori and Corleya stepped out from the brush, the princess gasped at the yawning chasm between the mountains. Looking to her left further up the range, she saw smoke from a cook fire drifting through the treetops. A gentle breeze carried the scent of woodsmoke and cooking meat as well as the sweet smell of citrus fruit. Her stomach growled at the tantalizing odours as she realized they had not been fed in over twenty-four hours.

The scout clicked his tongue. Catching Karlag's attention, he pointed towards the smoke. The chief nodded. Tugging at Lycori's noose, he once again followed his scout up the mountain.

An hour passed, then two, as the sun began to drop behind the mountain skyline and the scout led the way to what Corleya hoped would be the Sartaq camp. Tired and sore, sweat ran down her back and dripped off her nose. The forest's oppressive humidity never ceased. The scent of cooking game grew stronger until her rumbling stomach became a physical ache. She glanced ahead and could see the smoke through the trees less than a hundred feet ahead.

Smiling, she poked Lycori gently and pointed. The vampyr's eyes were wide with what could only be fear. Corleya opened her mouth to ask what was wrong, but the blonde woman shook her head fiercely, making a circular motion with her finger. Before Corleya could comprehend the woman's meaning, the scout and Chief Karlag stumbled into a clearing occupied by the Sartaq main camp. Hearing a light rustle behind her, Corleya turned to see they were completely surrounded on all sides except for forward. An old woman stood in front of them, twenty feet into the plateau mountain clearing. A quick look told Corleya all she needed to know: the Sartaq had been waiting for them. Her body reacted out of instinctive fear and she clenched her legs to avoid wetting herself.

The old woman leaned heavily on a staff as tall as she was. Decorated with charms, bits of poorly forged metal, and bleached humanoid finger bones, the staff was gnarled and twisted, as if an extension of the old woman holding it. A purple flower topped the staff. Its thick meaty petals, the size of a human head, trailed thorn-covered vines that coiled around the staff like a living entity. Corleya recognized them as the same vines used to create the slave pen back at the Kordanu camp, only much smaller in width. Chief Karlag bowed to the old woman and spoke in the tribe's guttural tongue. Corleya looked to Lycori, hoping she would translate.

"We bring tribute for trespassing on Sartaq land," Lycori whispered to the captives, translating straight across. It was wasted on Damien. His eyes still rolled in their sockets like over-boiled eggs. The effects of the priestesses' poison was still in full effect. Ever calm and quiet, Alia said nothing, listening as she always did. Corleya shivered as the old woman lifted her dark red dress clear of the dirt and shuffled closer, her dark eyes studying the princess and the other captives. Lycori continued translating, her voice low, as the chief and the old woman spoke.

"Her name is Vexa. She wants to know why traitors walk on their lands."

"Traitors?" Corleya mouthed, but Lycori held up a finger to quiet her and strained to hear more. Corleya stared, unable to tear her eyes away from the old woman's strange appearance. Even taking magic into account, the woman was ancient, her face weathered and wrinkled, yet her breasts were perky and her body firm and lean, her legs smooth like a young woman's. Gold strands of some exotic wild plant had been threaded into the knotted mess of her long, black and silver, ratty hair. The old woman slammed her staff into the ground, breaking Corleya's concentration.

"Vexa is the Sartaq matriarch. She says that all the tribes are traitors for abandoning them. She wants him to leave," Lycori said, her pale face turning even whiter. "The offerings stay." Corleya could see Chief Karlag struggle to remain calm, clearly unaccustomed to such disrespect. Lycori returned to translating.

Swallowing his anger, Karlag took a deep breath and bowed. "Mistress, listen to what I have to say. If you want me to leave after, we will go and you may keep our offerings. Agreed?"

Vexa frowned, staring into Karlag's eyes, as if looking for signs of treachery. "Say your piece, traitor, and then begone."

"The northern defilers have trespassed on our lands. All the tribes are in danger. The Kordanu have been chosen to ask for your help. We go to war."

Vexa tilted her head, nodding. "You are welcome here. For now. We will share of the flesh—our hunters were blessed with a kill this morn, and we will consult the spirits. If the vile goddess agrees, the Sartaq will fight your war."

Shifting on feet far too agile for a woman her age, the Sartaq matriarch slowly approached Lycori, Corleya, and the others. Crouching between the two young women, princess and vampyr, Vexa grabbed a handful of Corleya's black hair, pulling her close. Raw fear tore at her stomach. The coppery scent of blood and the rancid stench of death permeated the hag's body, overwhelming Corleya's sense of smell, making her dizzy and short of breath. Rotting breath washed over her face as the old woman smiled.

"Your offerings are acceptable," Lycori explained, by way of translation. "They will not be returned, even if the goddess refuses your request." Karlag nodded his agreement.

Vexa pulled Corleya closer, until their noses touched. On the verge of turning her stomach inside out, Corleya turned her head. The witch whispered in her ear so only she could hear, using the common tongue.

"Welcome to your new home, sweet child." Trembling and trying desperately not to gag, Corleya sighed with relief as the women rose and walked away. "Come, eat," the old woman said, as Lycori translated once more. "We must fill our bellies before we fill our minds. *All* the offerings and slaves may eat."

Karlag tugged the rope attached to the noose around Lycori's neck. Pulling her up from the ground, he followed after Vexa as she shuffled towards the massive cook fire. Out of immediate danger, Corleya's empty stomach groaned with a renewed desire as the scent of cooking meat from the fire hit her once more. Two of the Sartaq children turned the spit as a large chunk of unrecognisable game slowly roasted over the fire.

The closer they walked, Corleya could see Lycori's nose turn at the smell of the roasting meat. Not wanting the Kordanu tribe to realize that she was a vampyr, Lycori had not fed in weeks. Corleya had watched helplessly as Lycori nibbled on the food fed to the slaves to keep up appearances, but continued to grow weaker as the days passed. She'd even begun to age. A stiff breeze blew through the camp and Lycori gagged, nearly overwhelmed by the smell of cooking meat. Corleya wiped the drool from her mouth, shaking with hunger.

Forced to stop and sit on the ground twenty feet from the fire, Corleya was positive Lycori was turning a shade of green. "You all right?"

"No," she said, clearly fighting a battle with her stomach.

"How long can you go without eating?" Corleya asked, worried.

"It's not that, it's..." The clang of metal on metal interrupted her and Corleya turned to where two tribal teenagers were helping the young boys remove the heavy spit from the fire. As the boys dropped the spit-handle closest to the captives in the dirt, the spit spun, revealing the bounty of the successful morning hunt. Corleya gagged, instantly dry heaving in her mouth as she recognized the top half of Chano Kordanu's cooked body hanging from the spit. Alia turned sideways, tossing her meagre stomach contents as well. Lycori groaned for the third time.

Karlag and his scout jumped to their feet, weapons drawn, but they were seconds too slow, finding themselves surrounded by spear-wielding Sartaq warriors. Karlag's daughter and the other priestess never moved, as if somehow not surprised at what transpired.

Vexa turned and tilted her head. "No one hungry?" she said in the common tongue.

CAIRNWOOD

Frozen by panic and indecision, Kael realized he had to do something, even if it meant using himself as a distraction. As the first hollow dog reached the bottom of the oak tree, he eased Cassie back up into the tree and prepared to act. A series of whines and snuffling grunts drifted up from below as the Orotaq handler led his black dog around the tree. About to drop from his hiding spot onto the two below, Kael reached for his blade just as Kyah snatched at his wrist.

Joined by two more dogs, the first finally caught their scent, barking and snarling, the others added their sharp cadence as well. Desperate and short for time, Kyah clawed at Kael's travel pack. Opening the flap, he turned to give her better access, hoping she had an idea. When he felt something pull free from his pack, he turned to see a pack of their leather-wrapped dried meat and the cloth bag of spices that Seifer had given them before leaving Dasal.

Working as fast as possible, Kyah grabbed a piece of jerked beef and dropped it down the side of the tree the dogs had not gotten to yet while she grabbed a handful of spices and sprinkled it down through the leaves and around the tree, finishing above the agitated black dogs. In seconds, the barking stopped and silence ensued, but it did not last as the dogs began to sneeze and whine. Kael watched through the leaves as one of the dogs jumped to the far side of the tree and snatched the jerky. It let out a quick growl, and it was all the other dogs needed to race in for their share. The three powerful, black hounds fought over the single piece of dried meat and the Orotaq handlers yelled, beating them with leather whips. Never known to cower, the hollow dogs immediately turned and attacked their masters. Kael, Kyah, and Cassie, heard what was going on below, but could not make out much through the heavy leaf cover. Snarling dogs and cursing Orotaq told them that the three on three battle had no sure winner. Finally, a loud, solid crack and several simultaneous yelps rolled up into the branches, followed by whining from the two cowered dogs; the fight between hollow dog and Orotaq handler over, one dead dog was a clear loser.

"Swamp-cursed hound bit me," the Orotaq handler cursed, as they heard a body drop to the dirt.

"Stop crying, newbie, serves ya right for being so damn slow," a second handler barked. "These stupid things are tame. Wait 'til ya have to get yer own from the Hollow."

Quiet up until that point, but clearly amused, the third handler snorted. "You wanted to be a Handler, Scrot. You don't get faster and learn how they work, yer ass will feed the wild ones out in the Hollow's bog. Come on, wasted 'nough time, nuthin' here." The handlers and two remaining dogs circled the tree and headed back to the town square as Kael and the others watched through the leaves.

"Crap. That was close," Kael sighed, leaning back against a branch. "What the hell was all that about?" he asked in a quiet voice, not really expecting an answer.

Like always, Kyah surprised him. "That one handler must be a new recruit. He's still learning to understand the temperament of the hollow dogs. From what we learned about the Orotaq from the Dead Sisters, once a handler is experienced enough, he ventures out into the swamps of Black Hollow to capture one of the wild hollow dogs that live there. If he survives, the creature is his."

"It sounds like those dogs are called wild ones," Kael added.

"So it does," Kyah replied. Cassie shivered. Kyah slid her arm around the young girl and held her tight.

"That was quick thinking, Kyah. Smart."

"More like luck. It is something that seems to follow you around at times. I did not expect that to fool them."

"Glad you see it that way," he snorted softly. She shook her head and shrugged to let him know that either were irrelevant. He agreed. It worked, that was all that mattered.

To their right, about thirty feet away, the door to the town lodge slammed open and three more Orotaq joined those already watching the citizens.

Kael was positive the leader of the raiding party was the monster in the middle of the three. Towering over the two with him, Kael guessed his weight at close to four hundred pounds. His entire head was bald, except for the fist size patch of jet black hair at the back of his skull. Braided, it hung like a thick, black viper to just below his waist line. The man was massive, with tight corded muscles everywhere, and Kael could see a glint of sharp teeth past the man's scarred, crooked smile. With no shirt and dirty, bloodstained, doeskin pants, he was a fearsome sight. Branding scars covered his pale blue flesh, but he was covered in so many battle scars that Kael could not tell where the brands began and the scarring ended. The left side of his neck, shoulder, arm, and ribs were a mess of burnt scar tissue. There was very little flesh that did not have a scar of some sort present. Several stab and arrow-wound scars added to the big man's tally. Kael shook his head. The monster looked unkillable.

"God in heaven, that big bastard must be hard to kill," he whispered, in awe. Remembering what Lycori had told him after meeting the Orotaq for the first time after being captured by Sythrnax brought back a plague of memories. Just like back in the Wildlands Forest, Kael felt his mind slipping and his body began to shake.

"Fight it, Kael," Kyah whispered, leaning forward. "Focus. Control it. Do not lose control here, we will be caught." She shifted position again in order to move closer. Grabbing his face, she stared into his eyes. "Fight it!" Her voice grounded him to reality and he pushed the caustic memories away.

"Is this ever gonna stop?" He sighed, wiping sweat from his face and forehead. He realized the flashback also left behind Lycori's knowledge about the Orotaq.

Remembering that she told him the Orotaq considered almost everything below them on the food chain good to eat did not help to do much but make him sick. Though they looked relatively human, they were bigger, meaner, and a hell of a lot stronger. They were not cannibalistic towards their own kind, but anything smaller than them was fair game when it came to the cook fire.

Some of the raid leader's wounds and scars were likely the result of mere hunting trips, though Kael recognized most were from war, pillaging, and killing. He focused on the big man, knowing that as tough as it might be, he would have to find a way to kill him. The Orotaq leader walked out to the square and took a careful account of all the people from the town. Feeling helpless was all Kael could do as they watched what unfolded before them. As much as he wanted to help, sacrificing their lives wouldn't help the townspeople.

Without looking directly at anyone, the Orotaq leader seemed to be staring at all the townspeople at the same time. Kael felt the branches below his feet shake and knew it was coming from Cassie without even having to look. A booming voice reached his ears and he parted the leaves in front of his face in order to get a better look.

"My name is General Wairekk Blackborn and your town now belongs to me. Those of you here will work the mines starting on the morrow at the rise of day's light. Some of you will be chosen to cook and feed the others who work the mines. During this day's darkness you will all rest. The morn will bring mining, cooking, or dying. That choice will be for each one of you to make for yourselves. It will be your last act of free will," he explained. "Your people had a leader. If he lives, come forward. Now."

Cornelius Redding had been the mayor of Cairnwood for as long as most people could remember. With a fair and honest reputation, not a single person in Cairnwood would wish him harm. When he stood up as ordered, to help his people through the current crisis, no one expected him to survive the encounter with Wairekk Blackborn. He went anyway.

"I am the mayor here," he said, standing with his hand in the air. His wife, Anise, grabbed his leg and pleaded with him to sit back down, but with a gentle touch only a loved one can give, he placed his hand on her cheek and kissed her forehead. Leaving her sobbing in the arms of friends and family, he walked to the front of the crowd to speak with Wairekk.

The Orotaq leader was almost three feet taller than Carinwood's mayor, but still, Cornelius looked up at the towering warrior even though visible tremors of fear quaked all the way into his leather boots.

"I am Cairnwood's mayor," he repeated. "I can speak for the village. What can I do for you?" he asked, his voice like his body, trembled with despair.

"You reek of fear, little man, and yet you come forth to represent these... people," Wairekk said, the last word layered in disgust.

"I do," he said. "It is my responsibility to the village."

"Your settlement has chosen a wise leader. Even terrified and facing death, you stand up to commitment. The Orotaq respect bravery. You have earned my respect, surprising as that is. You will help my warriors and give them what they ask. Any questions?"

"Yes, two. Questions, I mean," Cornelius replied. Nervous and still shaking, it was clear to everyone, including Kael and the others up in the tree, that he was pushing his luck.

Wairekk, however, laughed at the mayor's persistence. "Your bravery knows no bounds. It has earned you the right to receive two answers, little man. Ask."

"Why did you attack us? Why kill every child you could find? Why? We have never threatened you. Your lands are far to the north. Why would you do this?" he yelled, no longer able to control himself.

Wairekk's hand grasped Cornelius's neck so fast no one but Kael and Kyah saw the big man move. "First answer—because we can. Second answer—human grubs are too small to work enough in the mines to be worth feeding, and though I said two answers, I will answer your third. The Orotaq prepare for war, and your mines have black glass. I have been patient waiting for you stupid humans to find it. I will wait no longer. My shamans will show you how to find it," he snarled. Cornelius struggled to draw a breath, finally succeeding in pulling some air into his lungs as Wairekk continued speaking. "We use black glass to make all our weapons. Your town is claimed by no king or country, so I claim it on behalf of the Orotaq. This town now belongs to Black Hollow. You will work, you will eat, you will shit, and you will die until we have what we need. Any resistance will be met with death. There will be no exceptions. Am I clear?" The big man yelled, his voice carrying out over the crowd.

The murmurs that rose from the gathered townspeople were ones of submission, but Kael detected a few mutters of dissent. His stare found and locked on the few with hatred emanating from their voices. They were the ones he needed to get to.

Having made his point, Wairekk dropped Cornelius to the ground without harming him.

Addressing the town once more, his voice rose in volume. "My second is Commander Varrush Dawn. He will command this work camp in my absence. Any concerns you have, we do not care. Mine, cook, or die. Breeding will result in death the moment the grub draws breath. We will not waste food on those who cannot work. Rest until the morn, but you will remain in this area. Attempting to leave will result in your death and as punishment for not stopping you, food rations for everyone else will be halved. Is that understood?" Though his voice reached everyone gathered, Wairekk's eyes were locked to Cornelius'.

The mayor nodded.

CAULDRON'S TEETH MOUNTAIN RANGE

Corleya and Lycori could both see the struggle Chief Karlag fought with himself, as every ounce of warrior blood demanded vengeance for the death of his son, while the chief's mentality knew such action would only lead to his immediate death. With no other choice, he dropped his weapons and ordered his scout to do the same. The Sartaq warriors took the weapons and forced the two men to sit, where they remained under heavy guard. As Chano's body was pulled from the campfire spit, still steaming, and carried to a wooden table, Vexa shuffled closer. Stopping in front of Karlag and slowly sitting, she crossed her legs and faced him. The tribe's youngest children added more wood to the fire, lighting the clearing as full dark settled in.

"All speak from this point will be in the common tongue, understood?" Vexa asked, getting a nod from Karlag.

"The blood-price for trespassing has been paid, Chief of the Kordanu," she continued. "Now we may speak of agreements and war."

"You killed my son. The future chief of our tribe..." A wave of Vexa's hand cut him off.

"Your son violated our pact, the one we have with every tribe of this forest. You and your kind are not welcome here, Karlag Kordanu. Choose carefully your words or you will join your son." Karlag struggled to control himself, Corleya could see his muscles flexing with the desire to attack.

Instead, he bowed. "My apologies. We came at the request of the other tribes, we felt the slave offerings would suffice for payment of blood-price."

"Slaves work or breed, Chief. They don't fight and they don't die to pay the price of your crimes. Your tribe has forgotten this. I will speak no further on this matter. Make your request of me so your daughter and I can take it to the vile goddess."

"But..."

Karlag's objection was cut short again, this time from the words spit from Vexa's mouth. *"Hugr stiltr."* The old woman raised her right hand and smoke-coloured magic swirled through her fingers as it slowly drifted up Karlag's nose and into his ears. His body stiffened, every muscle went rigid and his eyes turned a dark grey.

"This conversation about your son is over, Chief of the Kordanu. Do I make myself clear *now*?" Vexa said, venomously. Karlag nodded as his body began to tremble. "Say it, Chief."

"The conversation about my son is over." Corleya felt an obscene chill crawl up her spine at the chief's monotonous tone. Every ounce of the proud warrior's will had vanished as if swallowed by the witch's magic.

"For the last time, what is your request to my tribe?" Vexa repeated, and closed her fist on the smoky magic. Karlag's muscle tremors eased even though several grey strands continued drifting up his nose.

"To join us in war against the northern defilers," he gasped. As Karlag struggled to catch his breath, Vexa opened her hand, pulling the last strands of magic from his mind. Finally free of her magical influence, but barely conscious, he added, "They... They have violated the peace treaty. Two of the slaves we... we brought are proof that our lands have been trespassed on." The chief collapsed, unconscious, as Vexa wiped at the blood dripping from her nose and eyes. She turned, catching Corleya as she stared with horrid fascination.

The witch doctor smiled. "Exerting your magic over another person's mental power in such a manner carries a price. All magic does, northerner. It is merely a matter of what price you are willing to pay. I have paid it willingly for thirty years." She rose and walked away, the two Kordanu priestesses followed without saying a single word.

Unable to tear her eyes from the old woman, Corleya couldn't stop herself from shaking. "I'm not an expert on magic, but that's not normal, especially for only thirty years. Is it, Lycori?"

"No," Lycori said, slowly shaking her head. "That was Sartaq spirit magic, it demands a heavier price from the user than any other magic that exists, except for a DeathWizard's maybe. From what my grandfather told me, tribal spirit magic gets worse. Much worse."

Chapter Twenty-Five

"ArchWizard Giddeon Zirakus asked to me write this for those of you who enquired. Due to increased raids on Kastelborg Island by the Orotaq, Northmen have engaged them in open and sea combat with more and more frequency. Orotaq strategy is simple. When they cannot overpower you with brute strength, they try with sheer numbers. Between their hundreds of black dogs and archers with obsidian bows that will puncture plate armour, or warriors strong enough to tip a catapult, they are not easy to defeat. You Humans and Elvehn are not Northmen. Should you end up facing the Orotaq in battle, my only tactical advice is to run."

Kasik Blodhjorr
Written tactical assessment of the Orotaq, 5018 PC

CAIRNWOOD

Kael watched from between the leaves as Wairekk and his two guards returned to the lodge. For nearly an hour, the handful of the Orotaq warriors, now guards, began setting up a shelter over the town square.

With a lost look in her eyes, Kyah stared at Kael. "What now? Please tell me you have an idea." she whispered.

Kael shook his head. "I have no idea what to do." Guilt over not being able to help ate at him. Cassie glanced at them both, back and forth several times, before focusing on Kael.

"You have to help us... Please, Kael. Please help us," she begged, in a whisper.

"Let's just wait until after dark and see what happens. I don't suppose there are any wizards down there?"

"No, why?" she asked.

"I was hoping there would be a wizard here who could at least help, maybe teach me a few words that would help us. My one lightning spell won't do enough damage, neither will fire or ice, and I can't kill that many Orotaq by shadow-walking all of them. I'd be exhausted long before I got even half of them."

They sat back against the tree to rest as best they could. Kael tried to relax, but his mind whirled with ideas and options, all turned out to be useless. Closing his eyes, he forced his mind to calm, as he waited for full dark to arrive, so he could do what little he was able in order to start trying to put a plan together.

Managing a few hours of broken and uncomfortable sleep, Kael woke close to midnight and decided to explore Cairnwood while he had the cover of darkness to move around.

Wairekk had left the town while they rested, and as of yet, had not returned. Four Orotaq warriors walked a patrol around the newly-constructed slave tent in the town square. Each pair of guards walked in opposite directions. The rest had retired to the lodge for what Kael assumed would be food and sleep. The continuous patrol made any plan hazardous at best, especially considering Kael's desire to talk to the town's people and its mayor.

Sitting up, he poked Cassie's foot with his toe. "Is there anyone down there still alive who I could talk to about the townspeople helping to fight back?" Several minutes passed in silence as Kael watched her decide about who would be best.

"Your best chance is Mayor Redding. He's honest and fair, and I think he can get the others to help. There are some who would tell on you if they thought it would help them. Some people have children, and there are no kids down there. They might help," she said.

"All right then. You two stay here while I go snoop around. I mean it, though. Any chance we have will only be with all of us fighting. If you two leave and something goes wrong, I cannot help your people. Cassie? Do you understand?"

She nodded. "I'll stay here with Kyah. I promise. Kael?"

"Yes, kiddo?"

"Thank you for helping." He could see tears glistening in her eyes as the moonlight shone through the leaves of the tree.

"Don't thank me yet, sweetheart. I haven't done anything. But I promise we'll do what we can," he said, and slid down the back of the tree.

Kael's esoteric sight allowed him to locate and keep track of every Orotaq in the town now that he knew what they felt like. Using his extra senses to move to the side of the lodge undetected, he noticed a side window open. As he approached, the voices of several Orotaq drifted out the window. With muffled feet, he crept closer and listened.

"...no way all the grubs were caught, Shaman. At dawn, the two of you and six warriors can scour the top levels of the mine and find them. It's why Wairekk brought you two with us. Your magic will save time with such things. Now rest, and at dawn, find the rest of the little buggers. I want fresh meat while we are here. It will keep us strong." As Kael peered inside the window, he recognized Varrush Dawn as the speaker, and his stomach did a flip at the topic of their discussion.

"So shall it be, Commander," the shaman said, as he bowed. Unlike the Orotaq mystic Kael had killed earlier, the shaman inside the lodge was heavily adorned with archaic scarification designs. Swirling symbols and strange writing that Kael didn't understand covered the shaman's entire body, even disappearing into his black leather pants. There was no room left anywhere on the pale blue flesh for more branding.

Kael knew he was seriously outmatched against the shaman. The power radiating off the Orotaq mystic was intense, far beyond what he himself could wield. There was no way he could fight the shaman head on and win. It was one more thing to worry about as he turned from the lodge and headed towards the main square.

Thanks to the Orotaq patrol that followed a set direction, Kael easily weaved his way through the town without being seen. But when he got to the tented square, four more Orotaq guards were on guard at the tent's entrance. They were alert and watching every direction carefully. The only thing that would get Kael inside the tent, unnoticed, would be to shadow-walk his way in, but he had only done it during battle.

In order to avoid the chance of an accident, he kept his weapons sheathed on his back, pulled his hood up on his head and acted instead of thinking about it. With a quick step forward, a swirl of black smoke appeared, and he vanished. Reappearing inside the tent, he stumbled as a wave of dizziness washed over his mind. It was something he never felt before. Crouched beside some crates the Orotaq had moved into the tents, he looked around. He smiled as the last of the disorientation dissipated. No one had seen him appear, and no guards raised an alarm from outside.

Kael wasted no time looking for the mayor, and asked a young woman his own age if she knew where he was.

"You are not from our village," she whispered, looking over her shoulder towards the tent's entrance.

"I know," he said. "I'm here to try and help, but I need to speak with Cornelius Redding and quickly. I don't know how often they do inside checks... Please."

"All right, I'm sorry. Just... How did you get in here? Unless... You must be a wizard." Kael nodded. "Please. Come with me. Mayor Redding's over here." Keeping his eyes on the door, Kael followed the young woman as she made her way through the mass of prisoners to the far side of the tent, where a group of people were surrounding a woman lying on the ground. Kael recognized her as the woman the mayor had kissed before facing Wairekk.

The woman leading Kael placed a gentle hand on the mayor's shoulder, grabbing his attention. "Cornelius, I'm sorry to bother you, but there's a young wizard here to see you. He came from outside."

Cornelius turned to look at Kael, relief washing over his face. "Oh, thank the Ancients. Please, young wizard, you have to heal my wife," he begged, tears flooded his face. "She was brutalized by those monsters because of my defiance. Please, you must help her." Kael looked down on the woman, seeing that she'd been beaten severely. He bent over and let his magical sight drop into the woman's body. Four broken ribs, a bruised sternum, and a broken arm stared back at him. There was nothing he could do.

"I'm sorry, Cornelius, but that defiance saved all of your lives. I can't heal your wife, I don't have the ability to do so," Kael apologized.

Confused, Cornelius asked, "What kind of a wizard are you then? How could *I* possibly help *you*?"

"My name is Kael. I'm not a healer, but a very good healer is hidden in the village waiting for me. But she can only heal your wife if you can help me get rid of the Orotaq. There are too many for us to fight alone. Your wife won't die in the mean time, I promise you,"

"I am sorry, Kael, but no one has any fight left. All the children have been murdered. Nobody will fight, there is nothing to gain but death."

Kael could not believe what he was hearing. "You don't know, do you?"

"Know what?" Cornelius asked, as others began gathering around him.

"Some of the children are still alive. They're hiding in the mine. The Orotaq shamans are going to do a sweep with six warriors at sun-up to find them. If we're going to save them, we have to act tonight," Kael said. He could see Cornelius was unsure what to say as he looked around at the faces of those he had known for his whole life. Kael knew these were people who trusted in his leadership and his ability to keep them safe, and he marvelled at how none of them showed any sign of distrust in the man, even after what had happened. Six men, clearly miners, stood behind him and several others whispered their support.

Finally turning back to Kael, Cornelius nodded. "All right, young man. What do you have in mind?"

"I have to take care of those two shamans, first," Kael said, wincing at the thought. "The older one is a lot stronger than I am. If I can't do it quietly, all hell is going to break loose and your people will get the worst of it. Where in town can I get weapons for those willing to fight?"

"We use the old ranger quarters by the north gate for our armoury. The rangers pulled out decades ago, after the last Wildlands War. The weapon armoury is in the base of the north-west watchtower. Most of the fighting men are already dead, and none of the town guardsmen survived the initial attack."

Kael nodded. "I understand, but the most dangerous people are the ones fighting for their children and their families. The Orotaq suspect *most* of the children escaped into the mines. Make sure everyone knows this, and you'll find enough fighters, I'm sure of it," he said, then left.

The shadow-walk out of the tented area was even easier the second time, and he was positive he'd begun to understand how it worked. Again, it took a couple seconds for the dizziness to pass, letting him know he had only a handful of times left before he would be too tired to use the spell. The words of the novice shaman came back to him.

You need to start thinking like a wizard, boy, not like a Human. Kael shook his head, it *was* good advice.

Already on the north-west end of the village, it took only minutes for Kael to reach the barracks. Hiding within the late night darkness, he watched both towers, noticing that there was an Orotaq warrior at the top of each watchtower. With silenced feet, he crept into the small building at the bottom of the west-side tower. Swords, pikes, and bows lined the walls all the way around the inside, and stacks of filled quivers were arranged neatly against the wall by the door. A pile of dusty woollen sacks had been tossed into a corner, along with plenty of rope. Seeing this gave him an idea for getting the weapons into the prisoner tent.

Kael filled three bags with weapons, two with swords of varying types and one with bows and quivers of arrows, having first strung six longbows. He stuffed all the bags with extra sacks to help muffle the clanging blades, then picked up a length of rope he guessed was a hundred feet long. As an afterthought, he grabbed two bladed pikes and left the armoury. On the way back to the prison tent, he stopped at a large congealing pool of blood, soaked the rope in it before rolling it in the dirt to ensure it was dark as night. The Orotaq guards would never see it, even if they stepped on it.

Returning to where he'd shadow-walked out of the captive's tent, Kael felt and saw no guards, so he dropped the rope and made sure it was free of tangles. With one end of the rope in his right hand and the two bags of swords hung on the two pikes in his left, he dashed across the open area and under the tent, unseen. Cornelius and a battle-scarred older man were waiting for him.

"You made it. I was starting to worry you wouldn't return," Cornelius whispered, with a sigh of relief.

"There were guards at the watchtowers. They slowed me down. Now listen," he said, as he dropped the first bag of swords and the pikes. "I'm going back for the rest of the weapons, so when you feel a tug on this rope, you start pulling it in while someone else watches for the guards. I have two more bags of weapons ready but I couldn't carry it all. When I get back, I'll tie them to the rope. Pull them back after the patrol has passed by, okay?" he explained.

"I understand. And thanks," the older man said. Kael nodded and was gone again, back into the shadows outside the tent, without actually having to shadow-walk.

Kyah and Cassie never heard Kael until he landed on the branch between them. He startled them both so badly they nearly jumped out of the tree.

"Blessed Fae, Kael. Do not do that," Kyah whispered. "You scared me."

"And me," Cassie added, still holding one hand to her mouth and the other to her chest.

"Sorry," he said, by way of an apology. "I forgot I silenced my feet."

"Do we have a plan yet?" Kyah asked.

"I think so," he said as he sat on his heels. "I smuggled some weapons to the people in the tent, so when all hell breaks loose, they'll be ready to fight. Both shamans need to be dealt with first, so we won't have to deal with their magic. But if I fail or the other Orotaq notice, it will get ugly and fast. Cassie, you stay up here until one of us comes for you, okay?"

"I will. I promise," she said, her voice quiet. She grabbed his arm and quickly added, "Can I come with you and Kyah when you leave? I have no one else... Please?" she asked, her big eyes wet with moisture.

Kyah answered when Kael hesitated.

"I am sorry, sweetie," she said, as she gently cupped Cassie's chin. "But Kael and I will likely not survive where we are going. We cannot take you into that situation. Someone here will take care of you. We will make sure before we leave."

Cassie's face fell as a deep sadness washed over her, but she nodded nonetheless. Kyah had spoken the truth. Kael no longer cared that it was possible they could die in the Dwarven Mountains, as long he dragged Sythrnax to Hell with him. The attack on Cairnwood had to have been instigated by the strange creature as the Orotaq prepared for whatever war Sythrnax and the Dead Sisters planned on fighting.

"For years, the Elder and Wizard Councils from the Blood Kingdoms have studied interrogation techniques, both magical and mundane, in the hopes of finding the quickest way to the truth in urgent situations like the one we face now. I, myself, have spent years searching through forgotten dusty scrolls in the Ageless Library of the Arcane in DormaSai's capitol city of Drae'Kahn. Ancient writings claim that the effects of pain vary from dimension to dimension. It appears that the Fae would have been the most effective torturers and information extractors, if only their overwhelming empathetic nature would have allowed it. Because of this, we've come to believe that the most effective method of torture or interrogation is using magic from another dimension. Such magic is extremely rare now that the Fae are extinct, but it does exist. If only we had access to a dimensional traveller, we could get the answers we so desperately need. At this point, both councils would sanction the most extreme methods of torture possible if it produced any usable information."

Excerpt from Agravar Desolla's personal journal
DarkWinter, 618 PC

EAMON O'LEARY'S GROVE

Dominique Havarrow woke with start, cold water dripped from his long blonde beard and multi-coloured kreeda. Shaking his head, the clan-loyalty braids clacked as the attached glass beads struck the decorative bone rings Shasta had attached to Kael's kreeda during their sail south.

"Fucker," Dominique swore, spitting bloody water onto the wooden floor of what could only be the crazy alchemist's large cabin. Looking up, his vision cleared, and his eyes settled onto his captor's face, inches away. The older man smiled, his white teeth in perfect condition, but there was no humour or mirth in his expression.

"Your magic user is strong. You should be dead," the old man said, slapping Cormak upside the head, hard. Dominique realized Cormak was tied up beside him. Instinctively, he looked to his left and saw Shasta tied as well. Unconscious, a deep cut under her hair still bled, and blood dripped from her right ear. The same side of her face was blistered and burned all the way down her neck and onto her chest. Dominique grunted as she groaned, fighting her way back to consciousness. She'd live. Cormak slowly came around to his right. The runecaster coughed and winced from the pain caused by the singed flesh on his face, arms, and side. The wizard's cloak had burned clean away in places, leaving melted cloth stuck to his blistered skin on almost half his left side. Dominique understood, without question, that the wizard paid the price for saving Shasta and himself, likely weakening his section of shield to strengthen theirs.

"Not as strong as you apparently," Dominique said, flashing a smile in return.

"Ya think I use magic?" the old man asked, scoffing.

"That... That fireball destroyed my shield," Cormak added. Still woozy, he struggled to speak. "It threw us, far... Too far. Who are you?"

"Most fellas call me Eamon O'Leary. Don't be troublin' yerselves about the rest. I ain't no filthy magic user."

"That was magic if ever I've seen it. If not, what was that fireball that almost killed us?" Dominique asked, staring at the old man as if he were crazy.

"Magic? You short a few shillings, boyo? Piss-poor Irishman I be if I couldn't cook explosives here." Raising his left hand, the old man pointed to the rear of his cabin in a westerly direction. "Mountains are lousy with shite that goes boom, let alone what be in the halls full of tech under the mountain. Boom-storm heaven for an Irish engineer like me." He laughed, slapping Dominique's cheek like an affectionate father.

Cormak sighed, struggling to hold his head upright. "Explosives? Like alcohol in a bottle explodes if you throw it against something?" The old man snorted, as if to ask whether Cormak was really that stupid.

"Alcohol burns, wizard. Did ya not feel my shite shaking the earth below your feet? Before your feet went sky-walking that is." The old man cackled.

"You're not from here, are you?" The old man slowly clapped his hands, mocking Cormack and stepping sideways towards the wizard, yet he remained crouched at eye level.

"Aye. Give the magic man a pint."

"How long?" Cormak asked, wincing.

"Twenty effing years. One of you Holy Joe's must have brought me here. Purple effing tornado and all, like Alice in effing wonderland, dumped me arse at the gates of the city north of here. Seems that magic can't hurt someone who just arrived in your world after di-men-shy-nal travel. Your dwarfs call it *arrival ascension.* Another year or less and I can leave this shitehole because of them, though. Smart little tech-monger bastards."

"Eamon," Cormak said, perking up. "Are there ruins under these mountains? Dwarven ruins? You think you can get home using something you found? Maybe I can help you. The Dwarves were masters of technology in this world, before they became extinct. I've studied them for almost a hundred years, let me help you." Eamon smacked Cormack upside the head, the sharp crack echoed through the confines of the large wood cabin.

"I don't need your help, boyo. I need to be left alone. Seeing as you won't, and I'm not a cold-blood killer, ya dense gobshites'll just have to enjoy me lovely Irish hospitapality. How's bout I wet the tea and we get to know each other? Oh yeah, that fine thing over there ain't foolin' no one," he said, sliding over and lifting Shasta's chin. "You been awake the whole time, sweet, don't be a tease. Say hi." Shasta opened her eyes, squinting in the brightly lit cabin.

"Hi? Good to meet you too much of a mouthful, Ir, Irish... Irishman?"

"Easy, Shasta." Dominique whispered.

Eamon bowed. "Good to meet ya, Shasta. I hope you're having a great effing day," he mocked, his speech stilted. "Feel better? Kinda whiny for a pirate, ain't ya, lass?" He chuckled, and stood. Stretching his back, Eamon stepped over to a brick and wood cubby-stove and poured water into a kettle, his back to the captives.

Shasta leaned forward as Eamon started whistling a strange tune. She caught Cormak's attention. The wizard gave her a funny look as she lightly tapped her tied hands on the floor, making a dull clunk. Frowning, Cormak took a closer look, seeing the rectangle sapphire rune he had been holding when the explosion hit them in the clearing. Some how she had managed to grab it. He smiled as she raised her eyebrows and slid the rune across the wood floor to his tied hands. Fumbling with partially numb fingers, Cormak grasped the rune and warmed it between his first finger and thumb. Pressing down, it snapped, and a bright blue essence escaped. Closing his eyes in concentration, Cormak forced the shield magic to start small, positioning it between the ropes that secured him and the others to the cabin's support posts. He held the magic between the bindings, letting it build power until he could no longer hold it. The bright blue shield exploded outward, snapping the ropes and slamming Eamon into the stove. The old man crumpled to the floor and Cormack winced at the distinct report of bones breaking. Shasta's scream told him who the recipient was.

"Fuck," he whispered, instantly ashamed of his mistake, but quickly ignored it, helping the others stand.

Struggling back to his feet, Eamon turned to see his captives free from their bindings less than ten feet away.

He laughed as the empty tea pot rolled into his boot. "Magic man! Well done, though I really wish ya hadn't done that. I have better luck finding hen's teeth than the plants for that tea. You wasted the whole pot. Damn. And ya broke the sheila's wrists, boyo."

Pulling a hidden blade from inside his belt at his back, Dominique sneered. "You got more worries than spilled tea and broken wrists, old man." The small dagger gleamed in the light as Eamon glanced around.

"Really, gouger?" he asked, peering into all corners of his cabin as if looking for said worries. Finally looking back at Dominique, he pulled a round ball from his jacket and held it up for them to see. "All I see are three gobshites who're lucky to be alive. Leave me home and tell everyone ya meet I don't exist, and ya can go now. Alive, even. Sore, but alive."

"You have got to be the dumbest, or the craziest, son of a bitch alive, O'Leary. We're not going anywhere until you tell us how to make that explosive."

"Aye, was afraid you'd say that, boyo. Very well. I agree. The recipe's inside here, catch!" Pressing the top of the round ball, Eamon tossed it to Dominique. Cormak grabbed at it but missed. The second Dominique's hands wrapped around the ball, it popped. A blazing bright light lit up the house and a thundering crack of noise shook the cabin to its foundation. Dust fell from the roof as both pirates and the wizard dropped unconscious to the floor like stones down a well.

Pulling green moss from his ears and blinking open his eyes, Eamon laughed like a madman.

"I haven't had this much fun since Ireland last qualified for the World Cup. You pirates are just as stupid here as you are in me own world."

Chapter Twenty-Six

"Orotaq magic. For fifteen years, I have studied every text and document I could find on the subject. I have even ventured forth to the Black Hollow peninsula with an Elvehn trader in the hopes of seeing or learning how such powerful magic came to exist. Having witnessed Orotaq magic myself on the shores of Kastalborg Island while fighting these monsters beside the Northmen, the origin of their magic has always puzzled me. They don't use Lady Inara's language to release magic, and Orotaq Shamans cast much faster than a bonded wizard. The first time I faced it was nearly my last. I was lucky in so many ways. I got to witness Orotaq magic first hand, and I survived to write this thesis for my Master Wizard trials. Orotaq magic is similar to ours from what I have seen. But where the Orotaq are so much stronger than us physically, their magic seems to be as well. The raw power behind what they cast is more than capable of cracking the bones inside a mortal man's body. It was truly frightening to see for a wizard of my lesser experience and abilities."

Journeyman Wizard Galen Vihr
Thesis introduction, 2025 PC

CAIRNWOOD

Kael silently moved through the dark, avoiding the burning torches by sticking to the shadows cast by the buildings and trees as he made his way back to Cairnwood's north watchtowers. Without making a sound, he slid two spears through the handles of the watchtower doors to hold against the Orotaq's superior strength if the guards above him left the towers.

Hurrying, Kael grabbed the two bags of weapons he had hidden earlier and ran back to the rope laid out from the prisoner tent. Tying both bags to the rope, he gave them a good tug, and saw Cornelius and another man look out between the flaps of animal hide covering the wood-framed tent. With no patrols in sight, they pulled the weapons back. Once again Kael was on the move, this time towards the lodge, with the hope that he could sneak inside and kill both Orotaq shamans before anyone noticed what was going on.

For the second time in less than two hours, Kael crept up to the open window on the far side of the lodge. Thanks to his esoteric sight, he knew the room with the window was clear of the Orotaq that occupied it earlier. Sure to be careful, he peered over the window sill, just in case his inherent, extra sense of sight missed someone.

Kael glanced around, taking in the lay of the room. There was a bar to the left along with a few tables and chairs scattered throughout the rest of the room. A hallway that led past the bar suggested the rooms were towards the back, just past the hallway with a set of stairs that led up. Closing his eyes to concentrate, he sensed one shaman upstairs while the second one was on the main floor at the back of the lodge. Without making a sound, he crawled through the window and headed for the room at the back of the main floor where he had felt the powerful shaman's presence.

Not able to see in the pitch dark of the hallway, Kael focused on his magical sight, sensing all the rooms but one were empty. As he crept to the closed door, a rumbling snore came from beyond. He tried to adapt the silence spell swirling around his feet to hopefully quiet the hinges of the door before opening it. His hand passed over the hinges, top and bottom, and a trace of black essence remained behind. The door opened without a sound for the first half foot and Kael assumed the magic worked, just as the door let out a short, high pitched squeal. He froze, ready to attack if the shaman woke. A quiet sigh of relief passed his lips as the snoring mystic rolled onto his back, but didn't wake up.

Shaking his head, Kael wondered if he would ever figure out his magic. Trying again, the door opened another foot and Kael managed to slide into the room sideways and sneak to the side of the Orotaq shaman's bed.

The reaper-blade from Kael's shoulder sheathe came free with nothing more than a whisper as his right hand wrapped around the carved bone handle. Staring down at the sleeping Orotaq shaman, he tried to control his breathing as he struggled with killing the defenceless man.

Killing someone who was trying to kill you in battle was one thing and it still ate at Kael's soul, but the shaman was sound asleep. Kael's conscience screamed at him to stop as he stood there contemplating his first cold-blooded murder since he had arrived in Talohna. Come dawn, this man would lead a group of Orotaq warriors in hunting down the village's children for the Orotaq cook fire.

Firming his resolve, Kael forced the blade to descend just as all hell broke loose outside in the town square. The shaman's eyes popped open just as the honed magical blade slipped into his throat. Panicking, Kael shoved the blade harder, right to the hilt of the dragon-bone handle and into the floor under the bed. It brought him face to face with the Orotaq shaman and he used his weight to hold the blade and the large man down on the bed. The struggle almost decapitated the shaman as he fought for every last second of his remaining life. Still face to face, Kael tried his best to keep the big man from kicking out and making noise. He was forced to watch as the last of the shaman's life dissipated through his bulging pale-green eyes. Kael's first murder was a success; his body shook with the stress of what he'd done. Taking a deep breath, he pushed the feelings aside, for now.

Slowly, he pulled the reaper-blade from the shaman's throat and wiped it on the blankets before leaving the room. The fighting outside increased in tempo and Kael picked up his pace as he rushed to help the other villagers. Running down the hall, he turned the corner to the lodge's common room and hurled himself behind the bar as the second shaman launched a ball of fire from the doorway across the room.

The spell detonated immediately and the pressure slammed Kael's airborne body into the wall behind the bar. Believing he still had the bar counter for cover, he took a breath and shook the stars from his vision in an attempt to gather his wits. As he tried to regain his feet, he noticed the bar's island had been obliterated and the shaman had another fireball already formed between his massive hands. The fire hissed and crackled as it grew to double the size of a human head. The shaman smiled and released the spell. Kael ducked, pulling his heavy Orotaq cloak around him for protection.

His entire body compressed as the explosive shock wave blasted him through the wall into the back-storage room of the lodge. With barely time to realize he was still alive, another fireball slammed into his chest and blew him through a second wooden wall, out of the storage room and into the courtyard. With a jarring stop, Kael came to rest against a large tree on the far side of the rear courtyard. The smouldering back wall of the Cairnwood lodge wavered in his hazed vision. He stung everywhere, his exposed flesh seared by burns. Try as he might, he could not concentrate through the pounding disorientation, even though the fire coating his cloak quickly died away, leaving the material unharmed. The heavy magic-resistant Orotaq cloak was the only thing that saved him from burning alive, but it had not protected his exposed flesh and body from the concussive force of the explosive fireballs.

Taking a deep breath on pure instinctive need, an all too familiar pain raced through his chest as he recognized the savage agony of shattered ribs for the umpteenth time since arriving in Talohna. Delirious from lack of oxygen and overwhelmed by blistered burns, shooting spasms of agony from grinding rib bones racked Kael's body, adding to the misery. Knowing the shaman would come to check on the success of his magical barrage, Kael frantically tried to stand and defend himself. Shaking from muscle tremors, he managed to get to his feet in time to see three Orotaq shamans as they swirled through his vision.

All three stepped through the destroyed wall of the lodge and walked out to the middle of the open area some ten feet from where he struggled to stay on his feet. He knew if he could not tell which shaman was the real one, the fight would be over in a matter of seconds.

One of the shaman chuckled. "You are stubborn, little Human. You fight hard to live. Like a Hollow-Bred, but your little revolt is already crushed. It is a shame my master is not here to see me slaughter you. How the mighty DeathWizards spread such fear among Humans and the Elvehn is a mystery to us. Your weaknesses are astounding." The shaman smirked as he taunted Kael.

Exhausted and delirious, he gasped for more air. "Do you Orotaq ever kill anyone without having to brag about it first?" It earned him a crooked smile but no words. "Oh, by the way," Kael added, panting and still out of breath. "If your master is the other shaman, he's not here because I killed him." The returned taunt caught the shaman's attention as Kael lifted the reaper-blade in his right hand. "With this. I pushed it right through his fat, snoring mouth."

The Orotaq shaman roared with fury and renewed fire-spells swirled in each hand. "Coward," he snarled. "To slay a sleeping enemy."

"Braver than killing little children," Kael snapped, through clenched teeth. "Guess you know exactly what a true coward is."

As the shaman roared a second time, Kael knew his time was up, and he was still seeing wavering, alternating sets of the big shaman. Not knowing which of the swirling, throbbing enemy was real, he did not bother replying to the challenge, instead he vanished in a cloud of black smoke and shadow-walked into the middle of the three dizzying mystics. Reappearing from a second cloud of black smoke, Kael swung both his Vai-Karth blades at waist height, crossing the blades as they passed each other slicing air and nothing more.

When the blades missed, Kael's scrambled mind filled with the familiar voices promising to help. Allowing himself to be distracted by the whispers and the reality that he had actually missed the shaman quickly turned into a mistake. The shaman recovered from his own surprise as Kael turned towards what he hoped was the real enemy. Granting permission to the voices mattered for not. A large pale blue fist crashed into his jaw.

Kael never had time to curse before a violent darkness shut down his demon-portal spell and his consciousness.

DWARVEN RUINS, EAMON'S GLADE

Dominique Havarrow returned to the waking world, riding undulating waves of nauseous pain, again. His brain felt scrambled, and it was difficult to hold a single thought for more than a second. The ringing in his ears was so intense he couldn't tell if it was making his eyes burn and water or if his vision problems had their own agonizing issue.

"Crazy fucking bastard," he moaned.

"Maybe. But you are one stubborn fecking gouger, pirate," Eamon said, as he crouched, smacking Dominique on the side of his head. "Clear the cobwebs, boyo. You'd think ya got the fear from being ossified or something." As the insane cackling reached his throbbing ears, Dominique's mind cleared enough to remember what happened.

"Fucking O'Leary. You crazy bastard, what in the Nine Hells was that?"

"Flashbang, boyo. Maybe used a bit too much of the red shite though. Put a bit less in next time, I think. Even fecked me own head a bit. I told ya to leave, big man. Now you're desperately effed."

Dominique blinked his eyes, repeatedly, finally forcing his vision to clear enough to realize they were no longer in the old man's cabin. The heady scent of earth hung in the air and the coldness of the Deep seeped into his bones. "We're in the Dwarven ruins you mentioned."

"Aye, give the gouger a pint. Ya ain't short a few shillings after all. Take a closer look while you wait for your magic man and the sweet to come round."

Dominique eyed his immediate surroundings. Along with Shasta and Cormak, he was laying in a stone cell, the only opening was forward and heavy brass bars could be slid across to lock the cell at any time. Eamon tossed a bucket of cold water on Shasta and Cormak. The water splashed against Dominique as his two companions sputtered their way back to consciousness. Shasta shook the water from her face and hair, cursing. Dominique winced. The movement would only make her broken wrists throb with agony.

"Prick!" she snapped, lashing out with her left foot. Eamon smiled, safely outside her reach. "I'm going to enjoy killing you slowly, old man."

Eamon laughed. "Spirited lass, she be. Quite the bunch ya bring to me door, pirate. Ya should be thanking me that you all still be breathing. But seeing as ya won't leave me property..." Standing, Eamon grabbed the bronze bars and stepped through the door, sliding the bars shut. The heavy thud echoed through the ruins. "Enjoy the stay," he added. "I got work to do." Rattling metal swallowed Eamon's last words as Dominique pulled his tied hands, not realizing a bronze ring had been slid through the ropes and attached to a chain anchored in the wall.

Taking a closer look, he could see the ropes on his wrist had been coated in a kind of resin. Testing it with his teeth, he bit the rope hard and gagged. Leaning over, he spat on the floor and wiped his mouth on his sleeve. The crazy old man had covered the ropes in resin from the prickle trees covering his property. Besides tasting like rotten mint-flavoured ass, Eamon had clearly heated it first, turning it into a super adhesive. Pirates and sailors used it to patch everything from sails to leaks in their wooden hulls below the water's surface. Dominique sighed. He would wear out his jaw before chewing through it. Turning to his left and right, he could see Shasta and Cormak were identically secured.

The old man laughed even harder. "Lookit that, boyo. Let's see your magic man get out of that one. I'll bring ya gougers something ta eat later. Enjoy your day."

"Eamon?" Cormak shouted, wincing from the effort. "Have you checked all these ruins? They are creatures here in the Deep..."

"Been here twenty years, magic man. Only creatures that wander this way are gobshites like yous. Now hush it. Ya make too much noise, then I can't concentrate. I want to get home not spread me ass all over the multiverse. Later, creatures." Cackling with madness, the old man disappeared down the stone hallway.

"Crazy bastard," Dominique sighed. As the hour passed, he became more bored than he ever thought possible.

Clearly, just as bored, Shasta continued the hour old conversation.

"Crazy bastard who knows shit we couldn't dream of, Captain. Exploding gods-know-what, and blazing bright clay balls? Who is this guy?" Shasta asked, snorting in an obvious attempt to clear her head. Dominique noticed both her wrists had been set, bound, splinted, and wrapped tight, giving her broken wrists some support. The pain did not stop her from speaking though. "That exploding ball of bright light could change the outcome of every ship we take, let alone whatever that was that exploded in the glade. We could sink armoured Royal ships with that stuff easy."

Cormak groaned and shuffled into a sitting position. "We need to get out of here before we worry about any of that," he said. "We're bleeding and both Shasta and myself reek of broiled flesh. If this ruin is far enough under ground and exposed to the caverns of the Deep Earth, this abandoned ruin won't be abandoned for long."

"I'm open to any suggestions, Cormak." Dominique grunted, pulling on the ropes once more to emphasize his point. "Got any runes left?"

"No. Crazy fool took my belt-pouch."

"Great," Shasta mumbled. "Guess we'll have to catch him off guard the next time he's in here." Dominique grunted his agreement as a ringing crash of metal echoed from down the hallway.

"I got a funny feeling we're going to have figure out something else," Cormak said. "And soon." Another crash rolled down the hall as a metal dinner plate spun sideways towards the cell, scraping along the stone floor.

As if in reply to the wizard's statement, an answering *nook, nook, nook,* reverberated off the walls, bouncing its way to the three prisoners.

"I know that sound, Captain," Shasta whispered, panic raising her voice.

Dominique nodded as the blood drained from his face. "Yeah, me too. The Mahala are here." The words were barely out of his mouth when the stone floor beneath them heaved, lifting them a full foot, as an all too familiar explosion rocked the ruins. As the dust began to settle, Eamon's voice drifted down the hallway towards them.

"Hooya, little bastards. Get the feck out my goddamn ruins!" Several more smaller thumps shook the floor under Dominique and the others. The shrill cries of fleeing Mahala bounced off the stone walls all the way back to their cell.

"Damn that crazy fool's smart," Cormack muttered. "The Mahala use echo location. They'll never come back here after those bangs. The ones who survived will have fried senses for a week, some permanently even."

"Do you really think our half-cooked asses brought them here?" Shasta asked.

"It's possible, though you'd think they would have found him some time ago. He has been here for twenty years. Strange..."

Eamon strolled out of the dark hallway, a huge smile pasted to his face. "Bracing," he said. "Skittery little feckers can bloody move. Too bad for them they're stupid and can't see tripwires." He laughed. "Now why would they come here, after twenty goddamn years? Don't suppose you gobshites know anything about that, do ya?"

"Of course we do, you decrepit old fuck," Shasta shrieked. "You roasted us half to death and put us in a cell, in a ruin open to the air currents of the Deep Earth. What the fuck did you think was gonna happen? The Mahala eat people, you half-wit!"

Eamon cackled, clearly finding her outburst hilarious. "And here I thought you'd be a little grateful I set and wrapped your wrists instead of leaving you to become a cripple." Folding his hands at the wrists, he curled his arms across his chest, mocking her. "Don't think you'd make much of a pirate when you can't hold a sword, shiela. Don't matter, the skittery little fecks are dead, or long gone. Fast as they move, they're likely half way to holy-roller town."

"They won't be back, Eamon," Cormack offered. "They move like that because they're senses are stronger than ours—"

"You don't say, magic-man. Echo-location, dumbass, like bats back home on Earth," Eamon interrupted. Speaking slowly, as if talking to to a simpleton, he added, "That's why they left so fast. The pressure from the big bangs were too much for their senses. Of course I know that, you eejit! Now maybe now I can get some work done today. Especially with you stupid pirates asleep."

"We're the idiots?" Shasta said, as she snorted. "We're not going to go to sleep, dumbass."

Eamon smirked. "Night, folks." Tossing a small tube into their cell, he turned and disappeared down the hallway once more.

"What the fuck now?" Dominique said, kicking the tube away from himself.

"No! Don't— " Cormack yelled. Dominique's boot hit the cylinder with a loud pop, breaking the tube in half. Purple smoke hissed out, filling the cell.

"Crazy fucking bastard," Dominique sighed, as he lost consciousness, but not before he watched Shasta and Cormack slump over out cold.

CAIRNWOOD, FREE LANDS

From high in the oak tree beside the lodge, Cassie muffled a cry as she watched Kael fall beneath the powerful fist of the Orotaq Shaman. Breaking the promise she made to him, she hopped across the branches and slid down the tree in less than a second. She vanished into the throngs of fighting throughout the town square. Despair swallowed her common sense as she raced to find Kyah; she had joined the fighting the moment it broke loose. Cassie stared out into the throng of fighting, but couldn't see her. No one else had magic that could save Kael from the shaman. Something with his plan had gone very wrong.

Everything would have gone exactly as planned had Kael not made one mistake, though it was ultimately a mistake that allowed the people of Cairnwood to gain the upper hand. When he locked the doors to the north watchtowers, he did not know that a shift change was due. As Kael was sneaking through the lodge, the watchtower relief arrived and discovered the spear-locked doors. Instead of returning in silence, the four Orotaq guards sounded the lookout alarms instead. It kept the four of them out of the initial fight, and gave a big advantage to the town.

When Wairekk left earlier in the evening to return to Black Hollow, he took his blood-mate with him. Very few Orotaq warriors had one. Orotaq magic was a mystery in Talohna, even to those it affected. When two Orotaq warriors stand side by side facing imminent death on a battlefield and blood has mixed with the enemy and with each other, should both survive, a magical bond forms and the blood-mates are connected to each other, protecting the other in any situation. They fight together, live together, and eventually die together. It was a rare and powerful form of Orotaq magic. The two warriors gain the strength, speed, and stamina of the other. Orotaq blood-mates were almost impossible to kill and had two of the oldest still been in Cairnwood, the outcome would have been very different.

Wairekk's departure left eleven Orotaq warriors and the two shamans in the village. The four at the watchtower meant the Cairnwood citizens only had to deal with seven as Kael dealt with the wizards. Kael's weapons smuggling had armed close to fifty men and women, but the two pikes turned the advantage heavily for the town's people, allowing them to stay out of the range of the Orotaq's powerful physical attacks.

Kyah had been darting through the mass of people using the lightning spell Kael taught her to distract the Orotaq fighters while the townsfolk cut them down. Her kinrai chain hummed and whistled as it darted out, left and right, though both chain and magic did little harm because of the Orotaq's thick hide and natural resistance to magic.

The last Orotaq warrior was chopped down while the men with pikes buried in its flesh did their best to hold the monstrous fighter still.

As he fell, Kyah approached Cornelius Redding. "Mayor! There were still at least two of the enemy at the watchtowers," She glanced around and took a quick count of the Orotaq dead. "Probably four."

"Who are you? You're not from our town," Cornelius asked, as she got closer.

"I am a friend of Kael's. We travel together. We must go after the last four Orotaq. You have yet to lose a single person from Cairnwood. Should you hope to keep it that way, we must hurry." He nodded and yelled for others to help. They were just leaving to go to the watchtowers when Kyah heard Cassie scream for her, she turned around as the young girl rushed into her arms.

Sobbing, Cassie let go and began pulling Kyah with her while trying to explain what happened. "You have to come, Kyah. Now. He needs you. Please hurry! I think he's dead!" she screamed, tugging on Kyah's arm with all her strength.

Cornelius overheard and yelled at Kyah. "Go with her. If Kael needs help, we'll handle the last four. Go quickly! If he dies then we will have won but a token victory. He gave us the chance to fight. Go." He nodded and turned toward the watchtowers, waving for his fighters to join him.

Kyah nodded. "Where is he, Cassie?"

"Behind the lodge, the last shaman beat him, Kyah. Please hurry," Cassie begged, as she began crying once again.

"I will, but you stay here with the people who are not going to the watchtowers, yes? Promise me?"

"I want to help him, Kyah," she persisted.

Kyah touched her cheek. "I cannot help him if you are there, sweetheart. I will be too worried for you. Battle magic is unpredictable. If you were to die, then we will have saved nothing. Please stay here." She smiled and took off for the lodge, and for Kael. "Gods, keep him safe," she mumbled to herself.

Kyah rushed the short distance to the lodge, her toes seldom making full contact with the dirt below her feet. With her heart in her throat, she burst through the front door and stared in awe at the gaping holes in the rear of the lodge.

Picking her way past burning wood and straw mattresses that danced with growing flames, she jumped through the opening into the spacious courtyard. The Orotaq shaman had a massive fist wrapped around Kael's throat and shook his unconscious body like a rabid dog with a rat. A full three feet from the ground, Kael's feet swayed back and forth, matching the movements of his upper body. Kyah's stomach lurched into her throat at the sight, positive the man she cared so much for was already dead.

She screamed at the top of her voice. "Stop, you goddamn animal!"

The shaman turned at her words, a suspicious frown on his face. After a quick look, he instead offered a sly smile. "Ah, Wairekk was right. This purge has brought forth many profits. Even this offal's healer has come to play magic," he said. His deep voice was full of amusement as he tossed Kael's body to the ground and turned his full attention to Kyah. It made her heart hammer with rage.

The shaman continued talking as he moved closer, and it forced Kyah to circle away. She glanced left and right to see if anyone would come to her aid.

"I thought you came to play magic, healer. You must know no one will come to help you. This town's people are not that stupid. You risk your life to save them, but they would let you die to save themselves. It is something far beyond your ken."

"You know nothing of what I understand, you disgusting freak of magic."

The shaman laughed. "You know, little one, we've heard many tales of this DeathWizard and his healer," he sneered, as he pointed at Kael. "When I am done showing you real magic, you'll heal for us. Warriors returning to battle only minutes after serious injury will impress Wairekk to no end."

"Healing magic does not work that way, you ugly bastard. You are as big a fool as you are ugly, Orotaq," Kyah said, still looking back and forth in all directions. "I am not Fae. I cannot heal like them." Looking down as she came to

Kael's broken body, grief and despair threatened to overwhelm her. "Oh gods, what did you do to him, you animal? Wake up, love, please. You have to help me. Kael, wake up!" she screamed as loudly as she could, then bent down and shook him, careful not to injure him further, but not so much as a twitching muscle moved.

The shaman clucked his tongue and chuckled. "He's broken, little girl. Might you last longer? Perhaps your not-Fae healing magic can stop me better than his pathetic death magic did?" he mocked.

The Orotaq shaman's maniacal laughter, as well as the thought of Kael lying close to death, ignited Kyah's anger. Once it spiked, her true nature tore free from her control. One last look around the courtyard and through the destroyed lodge showed her that no one was coming and Kael was well beyond helping and hearing.

Her voice strengthened and she rose from Kael's side. "The only fool I see is you, dog! Your commander needs to supply you witless fools with better information," Kyah sneered. As hatred dripped from her words, she stepped over Kael's unconscious body and stood her ground against the shaman, using her own body to shield Kael.

"You shall see who the real fool is, little one, after you are broken and lying in the dirt beside your lover." The shaman frowned as fire formed in one hand and swirling ice in the other. The two magics reacted violently as he brought his hands together and compressed the two spells, releasing the twisting mess straight toward Kyah and Kael.

Kyah refused to move as the hissing wall of steam roared towards her. The shaman's wide grin showed the confidence of his attack. Moments before the magical storm slammed into them both, Kyah lifted her right hand, and with the palm facing out, barked words that had not left her mouth in almost a year. A solid green shield materialized over her body and Kael's. The raging storm of vaporized water coated her shield, but with a simple twist of her wrist, the shield snuffed out the Orotaq's magic.

"You witch!" the shaman snarled. Clearly intending to say more, Kyah was quick to interrupt.

"You have no idea, you goddamned dog. Your filth has knelt before my kind since the dawn of time," she cursed. The venom of hatred coated every word.

The shaman stood completely still, as if unsure of what to do. Only one group of people would ever speak to an Orotaq shaman with words like that, and if he used violence against a Dead Sister, it was punishable by a lot worse than death. Kyah smiled, yet still seethed with anger as she watched the shaman try to figure what had just happened.

"I... I..."

She cut him off, again, before he could say anything else. "Enough," Kyah barked. Her right hand shot up, putrid green magic frosting her fingers. "Your lesson is learned too late, dog." She sneered and walked towards him, long strands of green mist trailed from her fingers and hissed as they hit the ground, fusing rock, grass and dirt alike. The shaman dropped to his knees in obedience. Too late to save himself, his selfless act of reverence might help his brothers down the road. Kyah's smile widened. Almost immune to normal magics, the Orotaq were extremely susceptible to demonic energy of a witch's magic.

Standing almost face-to-face, Kyah grasped the shaman by the throat. "Foolish. What a waste," she hissed. "You will die in as much pain as I can give you. I was not to reveal myself for many years, if ever. You will pay for that, animal," she scowled, as acidic green magic wormed its way from her fingers and into his pale blue flesh. From her hand on his throat, the vile green magic spread, darkening the shaman's veins as it entered his bloodstream on its way to his heart. His eyes bulged from the pain and his teeth ground together as he tried to suppress the intense agony rushing through his veins. To the Orotaq, to cry out during death is the same as begging for mercy. There was no greater shame or disgrace.

Knowing this, Kyah poured more magic and suffering into his body with every ounce of power she had hidden for almost a year, hoping to see the disgrace in the shaman's eyes. Realizing he would not scream, and not wanting to risk discovery, she slipped her left hand to the back of the shaman's head.

"*Auka orka.*" The two words of demonic power suffused her body with immense strength and she snapped his neck like a dry twig. The shaman fell without a wound on his body. The shaman's neck, thicker than a five-year-old bull's, was broken and twisted like a rotted twig.

"Shit," she whispered. "Fucking bastard Orotaq." With no way to explain what happened, she dragged the shaman's body past Kael to the nearest tree and sat him back against the base. Wrapping her kinrai chain around the shaman's thick neck, she tossed both lengths behind the tree. Standing at the rear of the tree, Kyah picked up both lengths and used the tree as a brace while she sawed the chain across the shaman's neck. It took a handful of seconds before she felt the head fall from his neck and her chain dig into the tree. Freeing her chain, she admired her handiwork.

"Good enough. *Haeger bal,*" she mumbled. Passing her right hand over her face and down her left side, a gentle fire scorched her flesh. The heat popped and split her skin, leaving blackened scorched marks, crackled flesh, and raw blisters across her left arm and ribcage. After a lifetime of suffering, her face merely twitched at the grievous pain, but to others it would look like she had fought the shaman to near death before winning. It would also give her a reason to force Kael to try and heal her. His lack of earth-bond magic had been disappointing at best, yet his death magic was frightening, even if it was unpredictable. Satisfied her story would be believable, she dropped to Kael's side to make sure he was alive.

"Oh, thank god," she whispered, relieved, once she realized Kael was still breathing. Burns covered most of his exposed flesh, along with numerous cuts and a few splinters the size of her finger that had punctured the flesh on his arms. She began healing him right away, and fifteen minutes passed before some of the town's people, led by Cassie and Cornelius began filtering through the lodge to the courtyard while others fought to contain the blazing fire.

"Kyah!" Cassie shouted and then stopped suddenly as she spotted Kael on the ground. "Is.. is he..?"

"He is alive, sweetheart. Come, you can help me," Kyah offered.

Hesitant at first, the little girl finally knelt beside Kael. Kyah took her trembling hand and placed it on his ribs. "His ribs are broken on this side," she said. "I need you to help me. I am too weak to heal him without you." Cassie's eyebrows drooped and her face wrinkled up in a frown.

"I don't have any magic. I can't help him. You have to do it."

"Cassie, I would never lie to you. Now, come and listen, but most important, believe. I can feel magic in you. Why can you not?"

"I don't know..."

"Your bond..." Kyah hesitated, casting her healing spell again. "You have not taken the Bonding yet."

Kyah shook her head at the oversight. Placing her hands on top of Cassie's, she began healing Kael's broken side, at the same time teaching the young girl the simple words to activate her limited magic. When she had the pronunciation correct, Kyah waited for only a minute before removing her hand, but the magic continued to slowly flow into Kael. Even though it was much weaker than Kyah's, the magic came from Cassie.

"Am I doing it? For real?" she asked, looking from Kael to Kyah and then back.

"Yes, you are," Kyah said, her voice quiet. "We believe that the Fae are back in our realm once more. Teaching to heal is much easier than it used to be, especially to one as gifted as you are."

With a big smile of excitement, Cassie asked, "How do you know that?"

Kyah pointed at the magic flowing from the twelve-year-old girl who was not even aware she had magic and had yet to complete the Bonding ritual. It was all the proof she needed. It was disturbing.

"The proof is in what you are doing right now, and Kael is very lucky for it. Now come, we must get him to a bed where we can finish healing him. We are not done, not by far."

The freed townsfolk were happy to carry Kael to Cassie's aunt and uncle's house, it was one of the few still standing. Kyah worked through the night to heal him.

Cassie helped as much as she could, but without a true connection to the earth she tired quickly and soon fell asleep in the corner.

DWARVEN RUINS, EAMON'S GLADE

"Crazy fucking bastard," Dominique sighed, regaining consciousness.

"That crazy bastard really, really, knows too much," Shasta moaned.

"Uh, my head," Cormack whispered. "Talk about being here before. Didn't we already have this conversation?"

"Yesterday? I think."

"Were we out that long, Shasta?" Dominique asked. Pushing his stiff body up off the cold floor, he leaned his back against the cell wall.

Rubbing his eyes, Cormack agreed with the pirate captain's first mate. "She's right, feels like a full day. I'm damn hungry. Where is that insane old fart?"

As if the universe were answering, a crash down the hall cut Cormack's words short. A bright flash cast a shadow identical in shape to Eamon two hundred feet down the darkened stone hall. A fiery explosion similar to the one out in the glade days earlier quickly followed as again the floor of the ruins sighed, lifting the captives by a foot before they crashed back to the floor. Cracks in the walls and out in the hall rocketed into the cell as the ceiling beyond Eamon's shadow collapsed and dust rolled their way like a living being. Dominique rolled to his right, dragging his ropes with him, as several foot long slivers of stone jutted from the cracks racing into the cell. A long, low howl echoed down the hallway.

"What the fuck is going on out there?" Dominique asked, quietly. Eamon walked out of the heavy smoke and dark gloom with a large pack slung over his shoulder. A second, muffled howl bounced off the walls behind him.

"Well, boyos, that was refreshingly terrifying. Seems you gobshites brought all kinds of fecking weird with ya." Falling stones rumbled down the hall, and Eamon turned back, clearly uneasy. It was the first time any of them had seen him startled.

"What's coming?" Shasta asked. The old man trembled the slightest bit. It was alarming to see the normally stoic, but crazy fool in such a state. "We heard the Mahala yesterday. What's here now?"

"Bloody fecking werewolves!" he exclaimed.

"Werewolves?" Cormack said, shaking his head in disbelief.

"Ya, werewolves. And not the cuddly fuzzy ones that keep you warm and smell like wet dog. Big, fecking, walk-on-their-back-legs-with-bloody-big-fecking-teeth-and-claws-to-scare-the-shit-out-of-you-type of werewolves. Mary, Mother of God, what the goddamn hell is wrong with this screwball world of yours? I blew one of its arms off and the bloody thing didn't even slow down." Turning away from the cell, Eamon used the lantern on the table outside the cell to light another short tube he pulled from the pack on his back. It sparked, hissing as he stood there watching for trouble.

"This is our fault, Dominique," Shasta whispered. "The northern forest clans must've got word we were here. It's the only thing that makes sense. Torgo and Shae have been after us for years."

"No," Cormack said, frowning. "They came from deep inside the ruin. They're Ella's forward scouts..."

"That's why the Mahala were here yesterday. The wolves pushed them ahead. Probably hoped to flush the crazy fart out of the ruins," Shasta said.

"Doesn't matter," Dominique said. "Eamon won't hold them off and this cell won't keep them or Ella out."

"Ask him if there's another way to leave these ruins. Paranoid bastard has to have an escape plan," Cormack said, sliding over, his ropes slithering across the stone floor. Another howl and the sound of more falling stones came from down the hall. "They're digging their way through, we don't have much time. Dominique, Ella still wants to kill us, even more so now... We need to get out of here."

The Northman shook his head. "It doesn't matter. We can't trust him and he sure in the Nine Hells won't trust us." Eamon tossed the sparking tube down the hall. It detonated, shaking the ruins and adding more dust to the already chokingly-thick air. The old man coughed, spun around, jogging back to the cell.

"You a Northman, ain't ya?" Eamon asked, staring at Dominique.

"I am."

"I heard a rumour once, about ten years ago," Eamon continued. "That a Northman never broke his word once he offered it on an oath of his blood. True?"

Dominique frowned. "It is."

Eamon smiled. "I'll make you a deal, Northman. I ain't dying in this effed up world. I'll give ya everything ya came for and more, but we leave here together and you protect me until I can leave this crappy world of yours. Your wizard says there's more Dwarf ruins, which means there's more machines to take me home. Deal?"

Dominique shook his head. "I can't trust you, you crazy bastard. You'll blow the shit out of us the moment we're free of here."

"I'm an Irishman, arsehole. My word's worth more than all the gold stashed on your ship."

"We're running out of time here, Dominique," Cormack muttered, leaning in so Eamon didn't hear. "There's at least a dozen weres on the other side of that collapse and something—someone—I've never felt before. Not Ella. My esoteric senses aren't that strong, but trust me, we do *not* want to be here when they break through. We need to leave."

"How do I know I can trust you, Eamon? For all I know, every Irishman could be a crazy fucker, just like you."

"Oh, now you're effing asking to get punched in the fecking mouth. Well, we are all crazy feckers. Don't mean our word ain't worth nothin'. Tell you what, pirate, we'll grab your gear before we bail into the mountains. The traps and mines I've put there will slow these overgrown hellhounds, and then if it makes you not so scared, baby-boy, you keep me prisoner until I rig your ship with cannons and barrels of black powder. You'll be an effing seagod in half a year."

"What the fuck is a cannon?" Dominique asked.

Eamon frowned. "Of course there's no gunpowder in this ass-backwards world. That explosion that lit up under your ass two days ago? Imagine being able to aim that anywhere you want. What I'm offering will change warfare in this world forever, and it'll all be yers for as long as you can hold it. What do you say? Ready to be a god?!" he yelled, as more stones tumbled off the collapse down the hall. Eamon pulled a small blade from inside his boot and sliced open the top of his forearm before sliding his hand, blade, and a key through the bars of the cell. "Northman's oath, bound by blood. Deal?" Eamon repeated.

Dominique stood and stared at the crazy old man. Taking the blade, he slowly cut his own arm on the opposite side. "The blood oath isn't just a word of honour or a deal, old man. If you betray this oath, my kin will spend their entire lives and fortunes tracking you down. They *will* kill you slowly."

Eamon shook his head. "My word has always been *my* oath, pirate. I won't break it. And I am not dying in this effed up shitehole."

Dominique grasped the old man's hand and pressed his arm to the old man's, surprised by the strength he found there. Eamon nodded and released his grip, pushing the cell door aside.

"Let's leg it, pirate, unless ya want to become overgrown-dog shite." Turning, Eamon barrelled down a side hall away from the collapse.

With no other choice and the deal struck, Dominique and the others followed.

Chapter Twenty-Seven

"After so many years of fighting the Wildlands' Tribes, I have come to one conclusion. You can never predict what they will do in any given situation. The Sartaq Tribe are even worse. Somewhere in those twisted minds, corrupted by the spirit magic that ages them so fervently, there is a vile, sinister plot to advance only their own kind, even at the cost of the other tribes, let alone the rest of the world."

Calladia Veht, ArchWizardess
Personal journal entry, Darkwinter, 4952 PC

AVELERA CITY, ELLORYA
THE OSOK ARENA

"Yorcali-younger, you can't possibly expect me to force my Lanistae to sell all their gladiators, not even to you and your father."

"Ellorya owns a lot of gladiators, Emperor Mero, surely..."

"The state—*I*—own over half of the Ludi, yes, but there are arenas in every city and most major villages. Even a few of the smaller towns have arenas. The amount of fighters you would require... I understand the desire to defend your borders, Yorcali-younger, but the cost would be beyond your ability to pay."

"The cost beyond our ability to pay? Sounds like the opening of negotiations, Emperor, not a refusal," Niko added, smiling.

"Perhaps it is, my beautiful flower. Does your boss have the means to negotiate at this table, Miss Sattori?"

"I promise you he does, Emperor Mero. We have something you will definitely want."

"Well then, I guess we had better invite the Senate's gladiatorial accountant into these proceedings. He will have an accurate set of numbers of available gladiators for you to look at." Niko nodded, bowing her head slightly as Kyro smiled at her skilful manipulation of the Elloryan ruler. Emperor Mero waved at one of the ceremonial guards and the big man unlocked and opened the door. The young steward entered once again, bowing to his emperor.

"Find me Senator Illius," the Emperor said. "Tell him his services are needed here. Now." The steward bowed a second time, retreating from the Gods Balcony as fast as he could. "Now, Yorcali-younger, it's clear you have something in mind to trade for my gladiators. Care to share?"

"Sorry, Emperor Mero. Starting a negotiation with your strongest negotiating tool is rarely the best strategy. You understand, of course?"

The emperor laughed. "I do understand, all too well. We shall wait for Senator Illius." A knock at the balcony's door heralded the steward's return.

"Enter," Emperor Mero barked.

Stepping onto the balcony after the guards opened the door once again, the steward bowed. "Emperor Mero, guests, may I present Senator Marcus Illius, head of the Senate's empirical gladiator finance houses." The newcomer bowed and took the seat offered by Emperor Mero. Seated with Emperor Mero to his right and Kyro to his left, the senator grabbed a cup of wine.

"Emperor Mero, Kyro Yorcali, Mistress Sattori, thank you for the invitation. How may I be of assistance?" With the steward gone from the balcony, the guards closed and secured the door, remaining at their posts.

Raising his glass of wine, Emperor Mero smiled. "It seems that the Yorcali family have something we desire, greatly. They wish to trade this information and a large weight of gold for as many of our gladiators as we can spare. How many can we spare, Senator?"

"And still keep all of Ellorya's arenas operating?" Senator Illius asked, disbelief riding every word.

"Of course. We can't deprive our citizens of their national pastime now can we?"

Wincing and hesitant, the senator replied, "I'm... not sure, Emperor. Maybe a hundred."

Kyro frowned. "You must be able to do better than that," he said. "I need at least fifty times that many."

"How many active gladiators do we have in Ellorya, Senator?" Emperor Mero asked.

Closing his eyes, deep in thought, Senator Illius finally answered. "Ten, maybe twelve thousand. Perhaps a couple thousand more, but they're bloodless—no arena experience."

"I think we can do better than a hundred men then, can we not? Say... Two hundred?" Emperor Mero sighed, and the two men began talking faster back and forth. Without a number and no reason to further his argument, Kyro winked at Nikko and sat back listening to the banter.

The emperor and his senator's voice soon faded, transforming into a whisper humming monotonously in Kyro's ears. His eyes grew heavy as he relaxed in his velvet padded chair. The heat, wine, and the emperor's rich food all added to his exhaustion.

Without even realizing it, Kyro nodded off, succumbing to the after-effects of the previous night's partying and too many glasses of wine in the last hour. As if being injected in the heart with ice, he gasped and jerked awake. His surroundings had changed ever so slightly. The droning voices were still present, but the entire balcony and the people in it were surrounded by a muted, hazy glow. Sitting up, he frowned, his body moved slowly, as if weighted down by the confusion of a dream. It was happening again – his mind had shifted in time, showing him some distorted vision of the future. It was a rare occurrence, but one that had happened six times since he had turned sixteen. Kyro glanced around the emperor's personal balcony, noticing everyone was still seated where they had been when he drifted off. Even the newly arrived senator sat to his right.

"Kyro? What is it?" Niko asked. Her voice had slowed, garbled by the distortion of what he was seeing, or by the vision itself. It got worse as the arena horn blared on, almost endlessly, and the announcer's enhanced voice added to the ear-splitting combination of sounds and dizzying sights.

The voices faded and movement from his peripheral vision beyond the senator caught his attention, pulling his focus to the moving guard. Turning slightly in his chair, Kyro was too slow to stop the guard from pulling a strange blade from within his armoured white gauntlet and stabbing the senator in the back of his neck, right at the base of the skull. Realizing the other two guards were already moving, Kyro could only stare in horror as a guard stabbed Emperor Mero in the exact same place with an identical weapon while the third guard did the same to Niko. Grinding his teeth in anger, Kyro felt a blade pierce the back of his neck at the base of his own skull, understanding he'd forgotten about the fourth guard. A sharp explosion of pain shot through his entire body and he watched, helplessly, as the guard who stabbed Niko jerked the handle of his dagger downwards, snapping the blade off inside her neck. The identity of the killers dawned on him as the blade poked out of his throat before the click of it snapping off inside his own neck echoed in his ears. Kyro cursed as the last of the trademark kills were completed.

"Fuck!" Kyro coughed, jerking awake. Pulling a shuddering breath into his lungs, he grasped at his own throat, as if the memory and agony of his vision were real. Emperor Mero and Senator Illius stared at him.

"Kyro?" Niko asked, sliding forward in her chair. Like in his vision, everything seemed to be moving at a crawl. "What is it?" The arena horn blared just like in his vision and he glanced to the right. The guard to her rear had already moved to attack, the wooden blade sliding free from his gauntlet.

"Assassins!" he shouted, his eyes leading her to the direction of the attacks. With no time to explain, Kyro grabbed the senator by the collar and pushed him to the ground. Niko drew her hidden blade and twirled out of her chair. Tossing it to Kyro, another dagger appeared in her hand as if by magic, making him wonder for a brief second where she could have possibly hidden it. Caught off guard, her attacker moved in for the kill, but clearly unaccustomed to the restrictions of the heavy armour he wore, he was too slow. Niko struck first, sliding her dagger past a gap in his armour and into the assassin's armpit.

As Kyro's fingers closed around the tossed dagger's hilt, the world seemed to catch up, returning to normal speed. Spinning out of his own chair, and knowing he had no time to hesitate, he grabbed the descending wooden blade and pulled the assassin forward, stabbing the phony guard in the throat. The assassin's wooden blade clattered to the balcony floor as the third guard grabbed Emperor Mero in a choke hold, pulling the Elloryan ruler backwards off his chair. The assassin tore his dagger free from his heavy gauntlet as Kyro kicked his own chair forward. It crashed into the assassin, shifting his arm at the last second. The blade sliced the side of Emperor Mero's face and neck, missing the base of his skull by inches.

Niko spun towards the fourth assassin in time to see him or her vault over the balcony's railing into the arena. The two guards who had been holding Alec Terraine on the arena floor earlier moved to intercept the killer. Both died seconds later, no match for the Broken Blade assassin. The armoured figure disappeared through the open door to the fighter pits. With the immediate threat gone, Kyro released the balcony door's lock-bar, allowing the emperor's real knights to enter.

Niko crouched down to help the senator to his feet. "Shit," she muttered, touching his neck. Looking up at Kyro she shook her head. "He's dead. I'm sorry, Emperor. The fourth assassin must have gotten to him in the commotion."

Easing his bulk back into the throne, the emperor cursed as he held his face together with both hands. "May the blessed Fae guide him to Paradise," he mumbled, his speech garbled from the ghastly wound. "We're lucky, it could be all of us lying dead. Damn assassins. Why in the Nine Hells of Perdition would someone try to kill us? Who was the primary target? Kyro?"

"There's no reason to target Niko or myself that I'm aware of. My father assured me our plans travel well away from any factions who would do this. The contract has to be you, Emperor, or Senator Illius. He was the only one killed."

"Kyro?" Niko asked, as she bent over, looking closely at the senator's neck. "We have a big problem." Sliding her blade into the wound, she hooked the wooden blade and pried it free from the man's body. "That's a wooden blade!" she gasped.

Kyro grabbed his throat absent-mindedly as he remembered his vision.

"You're right," he said. "Wait, didn't one of them drop their blade?" Niko joined him in a quick search, but they found no dagger and no further evidence from the Broken Blades' Guild. "The one who fled through the arena must have taken their blades."

"No surprise there," Niko huffed.

"Well, that's a comforting thought, isn't it?" Emperor Mero asked. "I suppose it was only a matter of time before they decided getting rid of me would be the easiest way to set up a presence here in Ellorya. Captain?" he said turning to the tallest of his knights. "Triple the personal guard for myself and all our senators. And send for a healer to fix my damn face." The tall man bowed and left the Gods Balcony as Emperor Mero stared across the table. "I thank you, Yorcali-younger. Your warning saved our lives. I can't give you the five thousand gladiators, not for any price or information. If I did, my own people would be cheering these killers on. I will, however, give you one thousand men. Your choice, all blooded, and the ships to take them home with you. For a city the size of Dasal, a thousand men will guarantee your defences. Even Cethos only has a standing army of two thousand men. You owe me no gold—I'll settle for the information you offered, if it is as valuable as you claim."

Kyro nodded, smiling at the sudden change of respect towards him. "Make it two thousand and we have a deal."

"If your information is as good as you claim, then perhaps fifteen hundred men, but no more. But you will be unable to choose any of the ludi's champions."

"I accept, Emperor." Sighing into his chair, he wondered if Mero really was the assassin's target. "What a day," he added. Shaking his head, he plunged his borrowed bloody dagger into the wine table. Niko frowned as she pulled the blade from the table and started cleaning it with a cloth.

A young wizard with long blonde hair entered the balcony to examine the emperor's face. Healing the wound with magic as much as possible, the wizard still had to stitch the bone-deep wound closed. Two knights carried the senator's body from the balcony, leaving three battle-hardened knights for protection as the wizard worked.

Gingerly prodding at his face, Emperor Mero winced. "And I thought healing magic was getting better." Clearing his throat, he glared at Kyro. "It seems you owe me some information, Yorcali-younger. Tell me and you can hand pick your new gladiators."

"You mentioned that healing magic was getting better?" Kyro asked. The emperor nodded, but said nothing.

"Not better," the wizard mumbled.

"Speak up," Mero growled between clenched teeth as the wizard used a needle and thread layered in sparkling magic to stitch the emperor's face.

"Yes, Emperor," the wizard replied. "Not better. Magic seems to be getting stronger. The same spells heal more efficiently, and there's less strain on our connection to the earth power. If it keeps up, we'll soon be able to heal cuts like this without permanent scarring by using just magic, instead of enchanted needles and thread. Maybe even heal internal bleeding or diseases."

"Are you sure?" Niko asked, shocked, as she watched the wizard's stitching closely.

Laughing, the wizard shook his head. "Probably not, but as a healer, I can hope. Can we all not?" He winked, a deft smile curling his lips replaced the laugh.

"That... That makes sense. A lot actually," Kyro muttered.

"Care to elaborate?"

"Absolutely, Emperor. The information we have to trade for your gladiators explains it. If the myths of old are to be taken as fact."

"How so?"

"Rumours have been running rampant in the Blood Kingdoms that the Fae have returned. Magical healing is greatly heightened, as your wizard said, and Niko and I have personally spoken with two people who witnessed what sounded an awful lot like realm-jump magic. If you can find these Fae, your people—"

"Will have a living embodiment of our gods." Emperor Mero gently pushed the wizard from his side, the needle and enchanted thread dropped, hanging from the last stitch before sticking to the sweat beaded on his neck. "It would mean everything to my people. Citizens from all over Talohna would pilgrimage here to worship. It would—"

"Make Ellorya the most powerful country in existence." Kyro finished for him. "Is that information sufficient for our trade, Emperor?"

"Yes, Yorcali-younger. More than sufficient, and so I will be fair. Two thousand gladiators."

CAULDRON'S TEETH, WILDLANDS

The Sartaq feast lasted for an hour. Corleya, Lycori, and Alia suffered horribly as they tried their hardest not to watch the cannibalistic meal of Chano Kordanu. As the feast wrapped up, Vexa returned to where the new slaves and Chief Karlag remained under guard. She carried a bowl and a tall glass made from horn that steamed lightly in the cool evening air; Lycori could smell the blood from the horn cup, it was Human and fresh. Kasna and two other priestesses followed Vexa, carrying several bowls as well.

Vexa sat down cross-legged in front of Corleya and offered her a bowl of the gruel-like grain mush the tribes ate during their morning meal.

"Eat. There is no meat within." Corleya took the bowl, and Kasna handed out the bowls she carried to the others.

Offering one to Chief Karlag and his scout, Kasna tried to give one to Damien, but he was still incoherent from the poison she had given him earlier in the day. Sitting the bowl of gruel aside, she pulled a short, but extremely thin bamboo tube and a glass vial from the pouch at her waist. Removing the ball of cotton from the razor sharp point, she dipped the bamboo needle in the vial and titled Damien's head to the side. He offered no resistance as she eased the point into his neck behind the artery. Rolling the bamboo between her fingers for several seconds, she stopped and removed it from Damien's neck. She put everything away as

Corleya, Alia, and Lycori stared in horrid fascination. Kasna smiled at them and turned back to the pirate, slapping him hard on the cheek. He blinked quickly, as if something were burning his poached-egg eyeballs. Seconds later, he opened his eyes and looked around, once again somewhat coherent.

"W... Where? W... What the h-hell is going on?" he asked as Kasna pushed the bowl of grain mush into his hands.

Lycori shook her head. "Eat and be quiet Damien, or they'll just put you back out." He nodded. As if half-starved, he shovelled his food into his mouth.

Vexa stared at her. "You are a blood-feeder?" she asked.

Lycori nodded. "Yes."

"You are ageing. You have not feed in weeks, a month..." Vexa reached for Lycori, making her flinch. "You suffer," Vexa added, as her hand gently caressed Lycori's cheek. "Silver?"

"Yes."

"Closer," Vexa said, motioning with her crooked, bony hand. She offered Lycori the steaming cup. "My priestesses give it willing. Drink." Unable to control herself, Lycori snatched the cup and tipped it back, drinking the fresh blood as quickly as she could. Her stomach rebelled instantly. She swallowed repeatedly to avoid throwing it all back up. As her stomach settled and strength surged back into her body, Lycori breathed easy for a few seconds before her blood-flow and metabolism increased. Wrinkles and grey hair slowly receded, and the agony of burning silver in her blood returned. Sweat broke out on her brow and she grunted with the effort of controlling the pain.

"Here," Vexa said, sliding closer, until her knees touched Lycori's. "Let me remove the toxin from your blood. It will hurt, but you can recover afterwards."

"I don't think you want a full strength vampyr in your camp, do you?"

Vexa scoffed. "We both know you are more than that, silver kills the vampyr, but not a vampire. Matters not. You will be watched and darted if needed. Instead, if you open your eyes and look around, you will see no desire to flee in the eyes of Sartaq slaves." Lycori had already noticed the slaves had no desire at all to do anything other than what they were told, certainly not escape. More Sartaq spirit magic.

"That doesn't make me feel any better," Lycori said.

Vexa smiled. "We have given you food to your preference and offer to heal your suffering. The treatment you have received at the hands of the other tribes will not be repeated here. I promise you."

"All right," Lycori said, knowing she had little choice. She was still not sure if Vexa would let her refuse anyway. "What do I do?"

Vexa drew a long thin blade from within the folds of her clothes as two more priestesses joined them. "Sit cross-legged. Try not move," she said, offering Lycori a crooked smile as she did what the witch doctor asked. "This will hurt."

As Kasna stood by and watched, the first priestess took one of Lycori's arms and lay it on top of her own, from wrist to elbow. With long lengths of cured leather, the priestess wrapped their arms together repeatedly until secured. Once finished she sat cross-legged beside her and rested their bound arms on her knees. The second priestess immediately did the same and Vexa handed her blade to Kasna.

"Points of power, Kasna," Vexa said as a second blade appeared in her hands. The hooked, sacrificial knife made the hairs on Lycori's neck stand on end.

"Lycori?" Corleya asked, breaking her silence as concern overwhelmed common sense. Kasna quickly stepped past Lycori and slapped Corleya to the dirt. Alia jumped to her defence and caught a backhand from Kasna that spun her into the dirt beside Corleya.

"Silence," Vexa hissed, holding up the hooked dagger. The threat was clear. "Do not open your mouths after I begin, or you will beg for death."

"Do as they ask, Corleya," Lycori said. "Both of you. If they wanted us dead, we would be already. Just sit and watch."

"Wise choice of words," Vexa said, her smirk returning. "Kasna. Begin please."

Kasna eased between Vexa and the priestess tied to Lycori's left. Grasping Lycori's secured arm, she pushed the blade into her elbow. She felt the point hit the bone of her elbow joint as she ground her teeth together, but her fangs dropped, slicing her cheek and gums. Blood dripped from her mouth.

Kasna never hesitated and spun the blade several times. The point dug into the bone before the priestess stopped and tilted the dagger to the left and right and then up and down, cutting a cross into Lycori's arm without removing the point from the bone. The priestesses tied to Lycori held her still as she trembled from the pain. Kasna stepped to the other side and repeated the process to the top of Lycori's right elbow.

"Here, my dear," Vexa said, offering her a smooth piece of wood. Lycori nodded as sweat dripped from her nose, and Vexa slid the wood between her teeth, making room for the six fangs that had dropped. Wiping the blood from Lycori's chin, Vexa nodded. "Only seven more and we can begin."

The next ten minutes passed in a blur of agony as Lycori shook and bled. Kasna quickly moved to her knees after finishing at her right elbow, boring a hole and cutting a cross into each. As Kasna's blade eased into Lycori's throat, she struggled not to move, realizing the priestess was coring a hole through the nerve core in the front of her neck. With the fourth hole in her neck completed, Lycori understood for the first time how Kael must have felt wearing the Gyhurra Torque for so many months. With a hole cored into all four nerve centres, every tremble and twitch of her body was amplified by intense nerve pain shooting in every direction possible.

"One more, dear." Vexa smiled. Using the hooked dagger, she cut Lycori's ragged shirt until it fell away exposing her chest. Kasna stepped over Vexa and sat gently in Lycori's lap as the priestesses carefully made room. Kasna pushed the thin dagger into her breastbone, dead centre of Lycori's chest. It stopped against the bone and one last time Kasna spun the dagger to embed the tip in bone and then cut the cross, withdrawing the blade as Lycori bled slowly from all nine wounds.

"We are ready to begin. No one must speak from this moment. Do not even open your mouth," Vexa said and turned to Lycori. "The real agony begins now blood-feeder, prepare yourself." Taking the hooked dagger, Vexa cut deep into the flesh on the back of her left wrist. Using her finger, she used her own blood to transcribe a strange script-lettered writing over the bleeding points of power across Lycori's body.

Closing her eyes, Vexa chanted. *"K'Veoja Nattura Audoefi. K'Veoja Nattura Audoefi."* The ground shook and the torches placed earlier by the young teens fluttered crazily as a gust of wind blew through the Sartaq camp. Three ethereal spirits appeared behind Lycori and immediately jostled and fought each other. Several seconds passed before a single spirit broke from the confusion and rushed into Lycori's partially opened mouth, invading her body. Corleya and Alia gasped as Lycori went rigid and her head jerked back. Staring up into the sky, her eyes clouded and the spirit took full control of her mind and body.

"What the..." Damien muttered.

One of the two remaining spirits rushed into his mouth, and Vexa quickly barked, *"Flytja Foss."* The remaining spirit vanished as her banishment spell completed. Vexa pointed as the spirit inside Damien forced him to his feet as it tried to run. Several hunters darted it with sleep arrows and Damien's body crashed back to the dirt unconscious. Corleya instinctively pressed her hand to her mouth as Alia closed her own and bit her lower lip.

The spirit possessing Lycori dropped its head and glanced around for a single second before it tried to run as well, but tied to the priestesses and with their knees locked under Lycori's, it could not even unlock her crossed legs. The priestesses held the spirit firm and it quickly stopped struggling.

"Free us, witch," the spirit demanded. Its voice sounded nothing like Lycori's. It had a deep rasp, heavy with strange reverberations.

Vexa nodded. "I will do you this favour. If you help me first."

"One granted, one received. It is the way of the spirit world. Ask your boon."

"The body you possess," Vexa said, cocking her head. "Force the metal inside her out through the points of power marked on her body. And I will free you from your captivity."

"Agreed. Give me the words."

Vexa nodded. "*Foss silrf Innan.*"

Lycori's body remained rigid, and every muscle in every limb stretched to the breaking point as the spirit forced the silver running through her blood and organs to come together. Blood veins stretched and bulged as the spirit rushed to expel the burning metal. A crazy silver road map emerged under Lycori's flesh, just like the moment she'd been stabbed by Arabella months before, only this time the liquid silver had somewhere to go. It wept from the holes at her elbows and knees and dripped from the wounds in her neck. More silver trickled down her stomach from the point of power over her breastbone. The priestesses wiped the silver with soft cloths as it burned into Lycori's flesh after exiting her body.

The spirit grinned, turning Lycori's mouth into a twisted mockery of her true smile. "It is done. Your turn. Free me."

"As you wish, spirit." Vexa closed her eyes, casting the spell to excise the spirit from Lycori's body. "*Flytja Nattura.*" The spirit's ghostly essence spilled from Lycori's mouth, forming into a humanoid shape between them as Lycori slumped forward.

Vexa was not finished. Her right hand shot out. "*Halda!*" The single word spell immobilized the spirit as if held by magical strings attached to Vexa's hand. More words quickly followed the first. "*Husl Svala.*" Vexa jerked her right hand back to her shoulder and the spirit hit her body, disappearing into her.

The spirit struggled to take over Vexa's body, but weak from the massive amount of energy required to clear the silver from Lycori, it quickly lost its fight.

Vexa smiled as she wiped the blood dripping from her nose and eyes. "Lock them up. It's time to wake the vile goddess."

Chapter Twenty-Eight

"This man we hunt – I have seen the world he comes from. Alchemy is a powerful force in Talohna, but in the dimension called Earth, men mastered the art of mixing chemicals long ago. Taking into account that magic and alchemy from other dimensions feeds off the energy of this world, then Eamon O'Leary will some day be capable of destroying Talohna. Some day soon."

Ella the White Personal journal entry found on the shores of Lover's Bay, 5025 PC

CAIRNWOOD

Kael slowly and painfully regained consciousness. His body felt broken; there was no other way to explain it. Groaning in agony, he gasped. It triggered a fit of explosive wheezing and brought Cassie running to his bedside.

"Kael, what's wrong? Tell me, so I can help you." Her voice was full of concern.

"Get Kyah..." he moaned, she gently pushed him back down. To his surprise, his extra senses noticed her release magic that he had failed to sense in all the commotion. It raced through her body like a wild fire and bloomed like a new flower as it exited her hands. Relief quickly replaced the pain as the young girl directed the energy into his aching body.

"Kyah told you I would wake up in pain?"

"Yes. She said that when healing someone, unless they were conscious, there was no way to tell if the pain was gone. Damage can be repaired, she said, but the pain can also remain after magical healing."

Catching his breath, he smiled at the words he had heard too many times before. "Well, look at what you learned. It seems like your village has a real healer now. You're almost a young woman and this village is going to look to you for help."

Cassie's cheeks flushed red as she tried to hide an embarrassed smile. "I guess so. I promise I won't let you down. I would still rather come with you and Kyah. Maybe? Please?" she asked. He could see the hope in her eyes.

Shaking his head slightly, Kael closed his own as he winced. "We can't take you, Cassie, you know that. What happened here in Cairnwood is minor compared to what we're heading into. Even if we weren't, you could never come with us. There are people hunting us because of what I am. You would be killed just for being with me."

"What are you, Kael? You did things last night and used magic no one has ever seen or heard about. The whole town is talking about it. They say you're not a normal wizard."

Because he did not see Kyah and Cornelius enter, the mayor's response took Kael by surprise.

"He's not a normal wizard, Cassie. Kael is a DeathWizard. That is why they cannot take you and why they cannot stay here," he said, but no hatred or malice tainted his voice.

Knowing where the conversation would go, Kael quickly shook his head and sat up. "We're going, Cornelius, now. I promise you no trouble will come to you if we leave before the ArchWizard gets here and you tell him which way we went."

Nodding his head as if in thought, the mayor suddenly smiled. "No. You misunderstand, I'm not here to ask you to leave. And you won't until you're ready to do so. This town will forever welcome you as a friend, Kael, wherever we eventually end up settling. We're not asking you to leave, but you should know that a rider from Dasal arrived this morning with a message from your friend, Master Seifer Locke. He wants you to know that Giddeon arrived in Dasal a few days after you left. Seifer sent the courier the moment Giddeon got there. The letter also said to tell you that King Bale has sent official notices to every major city and town all across Talohna, calling for your capture or death."

"It was only a matter of time," Kyah offered. "Too many months have passed without any sightings of you." She gave Kael her arm and helped him stand.

"Yeah, five months in the Dead Sister's Dwarven prison will do that," Kael muttered. She nodded her agreement.

"I would imagine," Cornelius said, politely interrupting. "We are leaving as well. The Orotaq believe there is black glass here now. They'll return for the mines and in larger numbers. We cannot defeat another force without help. The cost in lives would be devastating for the town. So, the blue bastards can have the mines, but they'll not have us to work them. We should be leaving the town in a few hours. I wish you well, both of you, and thank you from the whole town for your help. Know that you are always welcome with us."

Kael stood on shaky legs, extremely stiff joints ached in a dozen different places. "Where will you go, Mayor?" he asked.

"South first, and then we plan to cross the river at the western ford. From there, we'll go farther west along the mountain ridge to see if we can find another good location for a town. We like living up here. We are beholden to no country. If you ever need to, look for us out that way. Understand that your secrecy is knowledge this town will never betray. We owe you our lives and those of the town's children. Most were found in the mines this morning, though several of the youngest children died during the attack, like Cassie's cousins. The rest survived only because of your selfless actions. My wife and I have asked Cassie to come live with us. Our daughter died of the wasting sickness a few years ago and we would love to have her. I promise you, I'll keep her from the hands of the ArchWizard and his country. We have no love for them here, and they have no right to take magically-gifted children from the Free Lands."

Kael nodded. "That's good to know, Mayor."

"Now that Cassie has formed her bond, her magic will not be dangerous," Kyah added. "But once you settle in a new location, I highly recommend you try to find some books for her, especially healing grimoires, so she may learn stronger healing magic."

Kael snorted. "Some offensive spells to help your village wouldn't hurt either."

"We will," Cornelius said, smiling.

"Good," Kael said, and shook Cornelius' arm. "Books about VosHain, the magical language, would be extremely helpful to her. It'll help expand her knowledge." He raised his eyebrows and glanced at Kyah. "You helped her with the Bonding? No complications?"

"I did," Kyah said. "I helped younger healers with their Bonding all the time for the Dead Sisters. Besides a nose bleed, Cassie did amazingly well. I have never seen someone so young with so much potential. You're very lucky to have her, Cornelius, so is your town. She will be an exceptional healer within a few years."

"We definitely are." The mayor smiled. "Our debt can never be repaid, to either of you. Know that we will be there if you ever need us to be. But there is much to do my friend, so I must go. Please take care of yourselves and may we one day meet again," he said, as he turned to leave.

He stopped and looked back for a moment. "The town merchants have more than we could ever carry, Kael. See them before you leave. They have all pitched in and bundled some supplies for you and your mounts to take along when you go. Good luck, my friend. You're heading into dangerous country. I sincerely hope you find what you're looking for," he said, and walked out the door.

Slowly, Kael dressed with some help from Cassie and then they left as well.

Kyah and Kael went to gather what they needed from the town's merchants and Cassie left to go help Cornelius and her new family for the weeks ahead spent on the road.

DWARVEN RUINS, EAMON'S GLADE

Torgo's werewolves dug with a frenzy for almost an hour before breaking through the collapse in the old Dwarven ruin. The alpha male scrambled through the moment there was room.

"Clear larger way for Mistress. Desiree, come," he growled, his voice gravely and distorted as it exited a canine throat not designed for speaking. The young assassin followed Torgo through the collapse and out into the hallway beyond. In moments, they were several hundred feet down the hall at the cell where Eamon had held Dominique and the others.

"Gone," Desiree mumbled.

Torgo growled as he shifted into Human form. In seconds, the seven-foot-tall monster was replaced by an average-sized man as naked as a newborn.

Desiree scoffed. "Not everyone wants to see you naked. Cover up for Assani's sake." She tossed him the blanket slung between the straps of her travel pack. It was not the first time Shae's young husband shed his fur in front of her and it was still just as disturbing as the first time. The last thing she needed was a jealous female alpha werewolf on her ass about a man she had absolutely no interest in.

Tying the blanket around his waist, the young man sniffed the air. "They were here. An hour past, maybe less. I smell blood, cooked flesh, and, and... Lotus, but not the flower or powder... *or* resin. It smells like when we found you covered in your mentor's... everything. 'Vaporized' is the word Mistress used." Torgo turned his head to the side and inhaled deeply, stopping as he began snorting and sneezing. After several seconds, it ceased. "Strange. Vaporized lotus, I smell. It's weak—tickles deep in my nose. A day old."

"Crazy alchemist, my ass. Vaporized lotus. Dominique Havarrow, Shasta Trey, and a court wizard from Argela. All captured by one man? I've met Havarrow, briefly anyway. No way some old fart took him, especially alive."

"You think too much, dear," Ella Navasha said from behind her. Desiree spun to see both the white witch and Torgo's nude wife behind her and she felt her cheeks turn red at the sight of the woman's naked body. "But you're right," Ella continued. "He's not a simple alchemist, crazy or otherwise. Torgo, Shae, track the path they took to leave the ruins. Come, Desiree. I'll explain." The werewolf couple took off down the side hallway, both in Human-form. Desiree knew that inside the tight halls of the ruins, the added senses of wolf-form were no longer needed.

"I've never seen magic do some of the things he's done, Mistress Ella," Desiree said, walking beside the older woman.

"He doesn't use magic. What he does use *is* closer to alchemy than magic—chemical mixtures, dear, that's all. I told you when we found you that we'd be hunting a DeathWizard, remember?" Desiree nodded, but did not dare interrupt. "Twenty years ago, Talohna experienced a Black Sun event. I assume you've heard the tale?" Desiree nodded a second time, holding her tongue, even though questions bombarded her mind. "Good. At the time, there was a child born, and our illustrious ArchWizard had this wonderful idea to banish the child to another dimension – one with no magic. Your fellow assassin, Yrlissa Blackmist, tried desperately to get to the child first in order to stop it, but failed." Ella bowed at Desiree, letting her know she was free to ask a single question.

"The 'last light' prophecy. That's why he banished the child, instead of killing it like the law demands?"

Ella smiled, clearly proud that the question was more a statement, and a correct statement at that. "One of the reasons, yes. The other was because the child was his son." Desiree stared at Ella, positive her eyes were full of shock. Ella laughed. "It's not a secret, dear, but it's not common knowledge either. Anyway, dimensional gateways are fickle entities. When Giddeon opened his gate-bridge, he used three anchors when he should have only used two, or four; simple magic dictates balance, but Giddeon's ego rivals that of a god. Power anchors for dimensional travel must also balance, but in the fool's defence, only the Fae ever really knew such things. It's why his gate killed everyone. And the third anchor opened a wild gate on the other side of the world he sent his child to. This wild gateway dragged back a man into our world, the man we seek here today. A man who was raised in a world of technology and chemicals is a man who has the knowledge to tip the balance of power in our world. And right this moment, he is on the run with our world's second most powerful pirate." Ella bowed, freeing Desiree to speak.

"Is this why we came here first, to try and save him like we are Kael?"

"No, my dear. We are going to do all we can to help Kael, yes, but this man? This man, we're going to do all we can to kill. Hopefully before his knowledge changes our world forever. Understand?"

"Yes, mistress." Desiree smiled.

Even at only fourteen years of age, killing had never been a problem for a Broken Blade assassin.

TWIN CITIES, ELLORYA

"All right, O'Leary," Dominique barked. Tired, dirty, and weary, he was in a miserable mood. "We're almost back to Argela, you're alive, and contrary to our agreement, you're not a captive. So, what do we need to make these cannons and black powder of yours?"

After a week or so of working their way back to Argela on foot and fighting or avoiding werewolves constantly, all four were exhausted, but Eamon was by far in the worst shape. Exhausted and bruised, the old man walked slower and got crankier every day.

"That depends, pirate," Eamon said. "You gonna share what I tell you with that bastard, Bauro Blackspawn, or is it time for Dominique Havarrow to stand up and take the Suns of the Blood for himself?" Dominique frowned. The thought of betrayal wasn't an easy one.

"Can't say you haven't thought of it, Captain," Shasta replied.

"You got my vote," Cormack added. "He's the reason I left your crew in the first place."

"You'd never leave that comfy life of being a court wizard behind," Shasta teased.

"If Dominique made a play for the Suns? In a heartbeat. I'd be casting runes from the bow of the Reave, just like old times." He laughed.

"Why does it matter, Eamon?" Dominique asked, ignoring the original question.

"The retrofits to your Reaver ships will take months, you'll have to decide. Either you give Bauro the knowledge or keep it for yourself and find a place to hide long enough to complete the retrofits to a couple ships. Seeing as Bauro's bastard reputation is well known, my vote is with you to keep it. I'll have a better chance of getting home if you keep it. I don't trust Bauro to keep his word." Dominique grunted by way of a reply, so Eamon carried on. "You'll need trustworthy blacksmiths – good ones. Damn good ones with experience in sand cast moulding. Black powder also takes time to make – we'll need grinders and mixers. The charcoal's easy, and finding sulphur should be easy too, there's plenty in the mountains by my glade..."

"You talking about a yellow powder, stinks like hell?" Cormack asked.

"Yes."

"No problem then. He's talking about wound-flash, Dominique." Turning back to Eamon, Cormack added, "Alchemists use it to burn deep or festering wounds clean and to clot bleeders. Healing magic isn't effective for serious wounds."

"Good," Eamon nodded, panting as he struggled to keep up. "Saltpeter's gonna be the tricky part."

"What the hell is that?" Dominique asked.

"I'm an engineer, not a chemist, so our best chance in finding it in this world will be from the earth itself. Cool, damp areas, preferably where sewer run-off goes underground. I ain't digging through age-old piss and shit to find a few saltpeter crystals, but it forms underground nearby such areas."

"What does it look like?" Shasta asked.

"White fluffy brushes, or short fuzzy hairs," he said, holding his fingers a couple inches apart. "We call it efflorescence." Dominique stared at Cormack, smiling.

"It can't be that easy," Shasta breathed, as if suddenly short of air.

Cormack stopped walking and rubbed his forehead. "I never thought keeping that weird little shit on your good side would ever pay off."

Eamon snorted, sitting down in the grass by the side of the road, taking the opportunity to rest. "Clearly you gobshites know something I don't. Care to share?"

Dominique laughed. “Your efflorescence. It grows everywhere in the Deep, and we don't have to risk our own lives or crew members fighting the Mahala to get it. A sawed off little freak who lives in the mountains by Sorai will pull anything you need from the Deep for next to nothing. Alchemists commission him all the time.”

“Ya can't be serious. Natural-forming saltpeter in our world is somewhat rare and the quantity you do find is light. And you got someone who'll get it for you?” Eamon said, his mouth open in shock.

“He's serious,” Cormack muttered. “Everyone calls him the Old Raven. He's more interested in trinkets than real wealth, just like a raven or a crow.”

Shasta turned from further up the road. “We're here,” she said. “The west gate's in sight. And they're telling you the truth, Eamon,” she said, rejoining them. “If it's the same stuff you mean... This saltpeter? Then the Deep has it growing everywhere. We've been down there. Though we haven't seen much of Talohna's underground in comparison to its size, this fuzzy stuff you're talking about is everywhere we have been. Now come on, the crew’s going to be wondering what happened. We shoulda been back days ago.”

Eamon moaned, getting back to his feet. “Good, the more saltpeter we have the better,” he said. “It'll make the black powder more powerful.”

“We'll worry about it later,” Dominique said. “Our first stop is for a bath and food at Natalia's.”

The four entered the city a half hour later, easily passing the security check because of Cormack's position in the Duchess' court. The short walk to Natalia's was quiet and uneventful. Dominique and Shasta went straight for the baths the moment they stepped inside Natalia's Rest. Eamon stayed with Cormack as the wizard made sure the charges went to him.

“Fancy-pants bunch of pansies spend time in a place like this,” Eamon complained.

"I rather enjoy it here. Give it a chance." The old man frowned, shaking his head in disagreement as Cormack continued. "You might like it, besides, if I could smell anything beyond my own horrid stench, I'm sure your smell would knock me over. We can't order food or drink like this and I need a damn stiff drink."

"Drink, ya say?" Eamon smiled, the frown vanishing as he licked his lips.

"Yes. I'm thinking a bottle of Northman whiskey, from Yrstak preferably, or perhaps a bottle of High Mountain Ice Wine from Stillwater..."

"Whiskey, ya say, huh?"

"Yes..."

"Haven't had real whiskey in... Where be the bloody baths then, boyo? If there's whiskey to be drinking 'ere, I need to fine meself up." Cormack pointed up the stairs and the old man took off.

"Third floor!" Cormack yelled after him. "Third fl... Damn, that man must love his whiskey." The wizard chuckled, following at a more leisurely pace. A hand grabbed his shoulder before he reached the stairs. Cormack whirled, a small dagger whispering free from the sheath under his cloak.

"Easy, Ama Taugr. I mean you no harm." Cormack tried his best to take in the features of the person in front of him, but his mind failed miserably. The black robe, hood, and mask hid every feature used to identify someone. In seconds, Cormack's eyes caught the man's own and found himself transfixed as red slitted pupils and throbbing purple, star-burst feathery irises swimming in a sea of black sclera stared back at him.

"You were with Captain Havarrow when you came in. Correct?" the stranger asked.

"Yes," Cormack answered, almost as if he had no choice.

"I'm interested in booking passage with him. Please, join me at my table when you and your party are ready to eat.

I have a private booth on the second floor, just tell your hostess that Sythrnax is waiting for you."

"All right," Cormack answered, swallowing hard. A hollow sense of fear hung in the air, affecting him more the longer he talked to the strange man. With a slight nod, Sythrnax whirled and walked away, but not before Cormack caught the strangest sight. Several appendages hung under the stranger's hood, but he was not able to see their full length. He did notice they were covered in silver scales.

"What in the Nine Hells... Never mind. I need a bath."

Too tired, sore and dirty to figure it out, Cormack climbed the stairs to the third floor baths.

CAULDRON'S TEETH
SARTAQ TRIBAL CAMP

Vexa, her two priestesses, and Kasna Kordanu entered the Sartaq ritual tent and quickly made the preparations needed to summon the vile goddess, the only deity the Sartaq had ever worshipped. With the weakened spirit inside of her, Vexa knelt before a towering altar. Made from the twisting green vines of living plants, the huge effigy was an incredibly accurate representation of Reetha, the demon queen of suffering. A large stone offering bowl sat between the effigy's feet.

Not having the power or magic to summon the demon queen to Talohna, Vexa focused the power she could access, barking the words to her spell.

"Lauss, Likami Andi." The spell sparked to life instantly. Combined with the weakened spirit inhabiting her body, the witch doctor used her magic to shift her body and souls from the mortal coil of Talohna. She opened her eyes and found herself in the Spiritlands. The ritual tent around her shifted fluidly, as the stolen soul fought for control of her

mind. The sickening sensation made the distorted reality waver in her vision.

The vile goddess woke from her slumber and the vine effigy came to life.

"Why do you disturb my rest, witch of the Sartaq?"

"The other tribes have asked us to go to war against the northern defilers. The Sartaq seek your counsel, mistress, as always."

"What benefit would this war bring to me?"

Vexa frowned as the spirit within her tried again to exert itself and take over her mind. She pushed the mild inconvenience away, knowing the attempts would only get stronger and more frequent.

"The arrangement my mother's mother had with you for the war seventy-five years ago? Would it suffice?"

"No. Your young ones were too slow tagging the bodies; most of the souls had already fled the flesh by the time they were marked into my possession. However, your tribal warriors use a cutlass-type blade during close fighting, do they not?"

"They do, Goddess."

"Then offer the Sartaq's help only if the other tribes promise to forge my mark into the guards and butts of their swords, and then use the weapons to mark their kills."

"It will be done. As you declare it. Is there anything I can do for you personally, my Goddess?"

"There is." The effigy held out a large key-like amulet. "You need to take this relic to a... man named Sythrnax. He will meet you on the northern side of the Wedge, on the mountain's far side. Arrive prepared and do not trust this man, but honour or agree to any deal or offer made. Do not refuse him. Understand?"

"Yes."

"Be sure you do. This man is not to be crossed. Your tribe's magic will not help you against him. Your warriors even less so."

Vexa nodded her agreement and bowed. The demon queen faded from view as her priestesses tore the spirit from her body and sent it back to where it came from. The witch doctor's body and mind returned fully to Talohna as the relic dropped from the effigy and clattered in the offering bowl.

She gasped and turned to Kasna. "You, your father, and his scout may leave. His offerings stay. Tell him we'll help fight his war if all the gathered tribes agree to our terms. Make him aware the Sartaq will be at the tribal war council."

"Yes, mistress," Kasna said. She bowed and left.

"Prepare a full travel party," Vexa said, and turned to the other priestesses. "We travel to the Wedge. Be sure all the new slaves are ready to travel with us. They must begin learning our ways."

Chapter Twenty-Nine

"Ember continues to amaze me. She studies the charcoal rubbings from the ruins in Stillwater with an eagerness that makes me envious. I watch her edge closer and closer to unravelling the secrets of a language very few could speak fluently even when there were thousands of people speaking it. It pains me that I'm unable to help her when she's so close to translating several phrases properly. When she does, the effect on Talohna will have far reaching effects. I will not sabotage her progress. I will wait and watch until she figures it out. Only then will I decide how much of the truth she can accept."

Yrlissa Blackmist's personal journal
Found within the remains of Kazzador City, 5026 PC

THE FREE LANDS

The first night out from Dasal, Giddeon and Max found a campsite overlooking a large valley that stretched down to the ocean called the Sea of Storms. The breathtaking view left little chance of any attack from the steep hillside. Yrlissa helped Ember from the wagon. She had woken a few hours earlier and was relieved to be feeling better. Max and

Kasik left the camp to secure the area and to try hunting. They had plenty of dried goods, but fresh meat would become a lot scarcer the higher into the Dwarven Mountains they went.

Still tired, Ember sat on a log by the fire and rubbed her head.

"You all right?" Yrlissa asked.

Ember sighed, massaging her temples with her fingertips. "Just a headache. It's from that smell."

"What smell?" Yrlissa asked as she glanced around the camp.

"I don't know. Can't explain it. Like rotten cinnamon. You have cinnamon in Talohna?"

"Shit," Yrlissa said, looking across the camp again, more intently this time.

Giddeon perked up at her words. "Did she say...?"

"Your mask, Father," Saleece snapped as she pulled the soft leather cowl sewn inside her robe up over her mouth and nose.

"We need to find it, and now," Yrlissa said, her own mask already in place.

Neither noticed Ember walk away until she spoke. "It's over here," she said, from the far side of the camp and twenty feet down the embankment.

"Stop!" Yrlissa yelled, rushing across the camp to her side. "Back up, Ember, now."

"No," she said frowning. Yrlissa's voice was irritating, but it quickly passed as a calm settled over her. "The flowers are pretty, they look like your tattoo." An incessant need to touch the petals overwhelmed her. "I want them." Yrlissa grabbed her and quickly pulled her back up the rise.

Ember shook her head, and it felt like a powerful dark fog receded from her mind. "What happened? I remember rotten cinnamon and then nothing." Looking back down the hill, she smiled. "Look, Yrlissa. That flower's gorgeous."

"And deadly too," Giddeon said approaching. "It's a death-flower. That's why it looks like Yrlissa's tattoo."

"Someone care to explain?" Ember asked.

"Can anyone make out the colour of the bloom?" Saleece asked as she approached.

"Light blue, but some were red." Ember answered.

"It's not black, at least," Giddeon said, chewing his bottom lip.

"I swear to God," Ember snapped. "Someone explain. Today preferably."

Yrlissa nodded. "Sorry, *nahlla*. It's a death-flower, like Giddeon said. They grow where ever a powerful wizard dies and his or her body decomposes naturally. It's why wizards are cremated. Two colours on the blooms means a second wizard fell victim to the plant's effects, like you almost did."

"Lovely thought," Ember muttered. She knew the sarcasm gave her voice an edge.

"Extremely," Saleece said, staring down the mountainside. "The scent of the blooms clouds your judgement, and when you get close enough to smell one of the flowers, it's lights out."

"I'll destroy them," Yrlissa offered. Giddeon nodded and lead Ember back to the fire and to sit down.

Yrlissa slid down the hill and out of sight of their camp. Pulling her mask down, she inhaled deeply before lifting the mask back up over nose as a precaution, even though she was immune to its effects. Sliding a dagger from behind her waist, she bent her knees. Glancing back over her shoulder to make sure no one was watching, she used the point of her blade to pierce the very bottom of the blooming bulb where it met the stem. The plant twitched and lengths of vines snaked from the grass, coiling around her legs.

Yrlissa reached inside her leather armour and pulled a small pouch from the pocket hidden inside. She rarely used the small collection of poisons and antidotes, but had still brought it with her when she left the Blades' sanctuary after talking to Falcon Yorsair. Opening the flap, she withdrew a small glass vial and carefully removed her blade from the bulb. A noxious liquid oozed out and filled the vial a quarter of the way. Repeating the process with several other blooms until the vial was full, she replaced the cork stopper and put the poisoner's kit away.

The thorny vines continued to crawl up her legs slowly, as if caressing their way up her body. She smiled as one curled around her hand like a gentle and curious snake.

"Sorry," she said, easing the sentient vines to the ground. "*Frosehnee Ashan.*" The ancient Dyrannai spell activated immediately, jumping from Yrlissa's hands, the magic flash froze the plants and all their vines. A second spell followed on the heel's of the first. "*Foss Hrinda Ashan.*"

Another tight, compacted spell hammered the plants as compressed air shattered the frozen flowers into millions of pieces. Yrlissa smiled, satisfied the plants wouldn't take root and regrow, putting travellers at risk. She returned to the fire and nodded towards Giddeon to let him know it was done.

As Giddeon sat at the fire while Saleece readied the tripod for a pot of water, he sighed. Digging through his travel pack, he took the letter that was sent to him by Zaddyk at the same time as King Bale's extermination missive. Ember frowned, she was pretty sure he hadn't read it yet.

"Saleece?" Giddeon asked.

She turned from the fire. "Yes, Father?"

"My dear, come sit and read this letter from Zaddyk to those of us here. Perhaps explain who he is to Yrlissa and Ember first. I'm growing weary of the secrets and the conflict they're causing amongst the group. Read it aloud, if you please," he requested.

"Are you sure, father?" Saleece asked. A look of incredulity marked her features.

"I am. No more secrets. Go ahead," he urged.

"All right," Saleece said. Turning towards Ember and Yrlissa, she sat down by the fire before beginning. "Zaddyk Lauren is a young prophet a few years older than you, Ember. He was raised in the goddess Cortina's chapel. Just before leaving, we were asked to go see him. Remember, Yrlissa?"

Yrlissa nodded. "I do." Looking at Ember, she added, "You were sleeping when the courier arrived. Max and I stayed to watch over you. We were afraid that Captain BlackSpawn would attempt to kidnap you again."

"Yes, exactly," Saleece said before continuing. "Well, when we got to the monastery, Zaddyk's mind was trapped on the temporal winds of the future. It happens when a prophet's power becomes active."

"Or when they mature into adulthood if they are born that way," Yrlissa added.

"Yes, exactly," Saleece said. "We had to confer the goddess' power to an amulet. It's a ritual performed by an ArchWizard or a member of the Inari. It allows a prophet to control their powers and use it to some beneficial end." She stopped to take a breath, as if gathering her thoughts.

Giddeon nodded to her and she continued. "All right then. This letter is from Zaddyk, I guess. He's the only prophet we know of currently, the first in over four hundred years. Now, keep in mind that what ever he says about the future is only one possible outcome of many. The temporal lines of the future are fluid, shifting and changing, dependant on the actions of mortals... and perhaps even the gods, as of late," she said shyly.

Giddeon nodded a second time, Saleece opened the letter and read.

Giddeon,

I have tried as many times as my aching body will allow to see what lies ahead in order to help you. You were always like a father to me, and I want you to know that I have always considered you such. I want you to know this while my sanity still controls my mind. It slowly slips away, Giddeon, into the horrors I have seen ahead of us all. I know what's in store for me, but perhaps I can help before things get too bad. I will continue to try, though I fear insanity will take me for good long before you return to Corynth.

Because of this you must know that a prophet's words cannot be interpreted with any certainty. Please, understand this. I have read many prophecies here in the monastery and though I understand what they mean, I promise you, every assessment of ours here has been false. Even Brother Donis', so please heed this warning; if you do not, the worst may come to pass. Prophecies are handed down by the gods, to be understood by the broken mind of a prophet, not the stable mind of a mortal man. Another warning I must make you aware of is that all of the prophecies about Kael are gone, stolen from Cortina's vault before I could read them. Brother Donis will try to find them, but I suspect it was done to stop me from reading them and giving you the proper meaning of the warnings written within the prophecy's words.

Last of all, and most importantly, is what I myself have seen ahead. Please remember that the night I was granted Cortina's blessing, I heard very clearly in her words that when she and her sister took you back to Jasala's tower, the Black Arc, all those years ago, she said it was a wasted warning and that you did not understand what you were supposed to. She also said that you are failing in your guardianship of the realm, though exactly what she means I do not know. I am sorry. I will keep trying to find you answers, that much I promise.

The future holds many paths forward, and I have seen many of them, yet not one would I want to live in. I have watched Corynth burn as friends dear to me fought and failed to protect this city we both love. I have seen the southern cities of Drae'Kahn and Avelera crushed beneath creatures whose names I know not. I witnessed a lone wizard pulling dark power and strange ores from inside the very deepest earth to use in order to build soaring dark towers of death and destruction – more frightening even than the Black Arc. All of this as one being looked down on the rest of us like we were mere insects beneath its feet. The darkness comes, a darkness unlike any other. It is anchored within the earth below us and this being, whatever it may be, will pull it free with the sole purpose of using it to subjugate and destroy us all.

I've yet to see another path open to us. As it stands today, this will happen. I am as sure of that as I am terrified for us all. Please, listen to me. I have seen the critical split in our future and I believe it lies when you meet your son in an underground ruin. He will tell you this, I quote: "You need to listen to me, Giddeon. You don't understand what is happening here. Please, you need to leave. Now!" His life or his death will bring what I have written above, but I do not know which. Please, for the future of all our souls, please be sure before you act. I can only tell you that Saleece, Kasik, and a woman I do not know are the ones I saw with you when you meet him. You are all in a ruin that looked Dwarven. While the others from Kael's world are with you, this pivotal event cannot happen. I do not know what Cortina means about your mistake, but please, for all our sakes, do your best to figure it out. You have protected Talohna for so many years and saved us from all types of peril. We believe in you; we always have and we always will. I have faith that you will know what is right.

Goodbye, my friend, and may the gods bless your travels.

Cortina's Prophet, Zaddyk Lauren
Written by Brother Donis Kincaid
End-Winter, 5025pc

Ember let the words from a prophet who had seen the worst of where Talohna could be headed sink in.

Saleece sat staring at the letter. "Holy Mother Inara," she whispered. "Father, what in the Nine Hells are we going to do?" Giddeon shook his head. For the first time that Ember could remember, the ArchWizard was obviously at a loss for something to say.

"Giddeon?" she said.

"Yes, Ember," he sighed.

"Do you think maybe now you can sit back and think about what I know you are planning to do when you see Kael?" she asked, determined to make him see.

He stared at her with a look of total confusion. "I don't know, Ember. If I misinterpreted what I saw in the past when I was there, and we had the meaning of Kael's prophecy wrong then... I honestly don't know what to do. I... I..." he said, trailing off, as if more lost than when he began. Saleece wrapped her arms around him as she sat at the fire. Taking a breath, he struggled to focus. "Zaddyk spoke of a dark energy being pulled from the earth. That threat has to be from Kael."

"No, it doesn't," Ember snapped. "All it means is that there is a threat to this world that might come from within the planet. You need to stop blaming Kael for every thing that goes wrong in this world. There are other mystics who use dark magic. You've told me so yourself."

"She is right, Father," Saleece said. "We have never heard of any mystic *pulling* magic from the Deep Earth. That could be a new threat decades, even centuries, from now. Kael's life or death could simply be the active-effect that makes it so."

Giddeon shook his head and winced, Ember could see the stress and weight of future decisions weighed heavily on him. "I'll grant you both that much, but regardless, something beyond our current understanding is taking place, and a mistake now could have lasting consequences. Think on that, all of you."

Utter silence ruled the small clearing with an iron fist and would permit no one to offer so much as a thought out loud. Kasik and Max returned with a pig-sized keske. The goat-like creature was slung over Max's shoulder. They both stopped the instant they saw the look on everyone's faces.

"What the hell now?" Max complained.

"It's not that," Saleece interrupted, as she handed him the letter from Zaddyk.

Shaking his head, he gave it to Kasik. "I can speak it because it's the same as our English, but you know I can't read it. Your written words are different," he said, referring to the common tongue. Kasik read the letter out loud for him, and the words were somehow even more dire the second time.

"What the hell are we going to to do about that?" Max asked, nearly shouting as he dropped the keske and tossed a length of rope over a tree limb as a prelude to dressing the goat. "You think maybe you jumped the gun a bit on the kill the DeathWizard band wagon?"

"What in the Nine Hells did you just ask me?" Giddeon barked, clearly confused. "You make no sense at all. Gun, band wagon? From what you explained about guns, how do you jump one, and what is a band wagon?" he asked, of phrases from a world so very different from where they were.

"Never mind. It would take too long to explain and you wouldn't get it anyway. Besides, you know what I mean. You could have told Kael a couple times that you were here to help him, or that Ember and I are alive. Perhaps with him here, we could find some answers, but you didn't talk to him. You understand *that*?" Max said, the last three words dripped with disgust.

Already riled up from the tone of Max's voice, Giddeon leapt at the chance for an argument. "Just because we have a bit more information does not mean I have completely changed my mind. It only means that I will not act against Kael until I talk to him, or until I know more about what is going on. We have to start agreeing on these matters. This is your world now too, and from what Zaddyk has seen, it might well get very bad here. We may encounter the things he saw, regardless of what happens to Kael. Sometimes the future is difficult to avoid. We know that all too well. We have been trying to avoid this very situation for more than twenty years. What we desperately tried to stop, what good people have given their lives to stop, has still come to pass. Kael is here, and he is a threat, but I'm starting to understand that acting without knowing all the facts is a mistake. Does that make sense to you?"

Max nodded. "Yes, Giddeon, it does. It's the first thing you've said in a long time that *does* make sense," he said, and plunged his dagger into the goat. He remained quiet as he prepped their supper for the cook fire. It helped quell the group argument.

Everyone agreed with what Giddeon had said, and for the first time in many months, they all enjoyed the fresh meat off the roasted keske that Max shot with his bow. As they ate, Kasik told the tale of how Max had shot the goat before the Northman had even seen it. Finishing the meal, they all got ready for the cold night ahead. With six of them, and in an area where more dangers were common, they took double watches. Ember and Yrlissa agreed to take the first, Saleece and Kasik volunteered for the second, while Max and Giddeon agreed to keep the last watch until dawn—the span of night when attack was most likely.

Ember and Yrlissa sat by the fire before going a little farther from the camp to keep watch. The rest were already sleeping.

"Yrlissa?"

"Yes, *nahlla?*"

"Giddeon said Kael was on his way to... to... Kazza..."

"Kazzadar Mountain, yes. It's north of here, one of the highest peaks in this mountain range," Yrlissa answered.

"Why would Kael go there?" she asked.

Yrlissa flinched, Ember ignored it and stared into the fire.

"I do not know why he would go there, *nahlla,*" the assassin said. "Giddeon said he was going there to kill someone."

"That doesn't sound like Kael," Ember said, a little testy.

"If he is after the ones who tortured him for months and believes you have passed on, then maybe he goes there to kill them, or just to die. I do not know, *mai nahlla*. I am sorry."

"You don't have to apologize. I should know better," Ember whispered sadly.

"I know you miss him, but stay strong. It won't be long now," Yrlissa smiled, as she took Ember's hand and gave it a squeeze. Ember slid her travel pack to her feet and opened the flap, removing the charcoal rubbings from Stillwater.

"Lissa?"

"Yes, Ember."

"All your years and travels... You're sure you've never seen this language," she said. Opening the rubbing and laying it across her knees, Ember grabbed the other two charcoal transfers and did the same.

"I don't know it. You must remember that the Ancients were a race of several different beings and they ruled for many millennia. Languages change."

"That's true, but look here," Ember said, pointing to a line on each rubbing. "This word that Giddeon says means bug-like? It's pronounced 'dosa'. But I think it's a noun, not an adjective." Yrlissa stared at the strange word and Ember could see old memories haunting her.

"You may be right, *nahlla*."

"You really think so?" Ember asked, getting a nod. "I think the word means 'pest', not bug-like. I don't think they're talking about demons at all, Yrlissa, I think they're talking about a race they consider lower beings than them."

"Perhaps. Keep studying. You'll find the evidence within the writings to prove it if you're right," Yrlissa suggested. Ember smiled and turned back to the rubbings. Still not interested in leaving the warmth of the fire, she looked up and asked another question.

"What's up past the mountains? Max and I know nothing of these lands."

"The Orotaq and the Black Hollow Peninsula are north of here. The Black Kasym is as far north as one can go. That is about all. Beyond the Kasym should be the old lands of the Ancients, if the lands survived the Cataclysm and still exist. No one knows for sure. Even as far as I know, no one has ever been beyond the Kasym since it formed."

"Where are those lands from here? Where is Orotaq from where we are right now?" she asked curiously.

"The Orotaq are not a land, *nahlla*. They are a race of Humanoid beings. Very large and very strong. They are nearly immune to most magic. You can't miss them, they have faint blue skin and are very dangerous to... Well, everything. They live in the swamps of Black Hollow north-west of those mountains out there." Yrlissa pointed to the north, over her left shoulder. "The swamps produce a heavy blue gas. It's poison to the Elvehn, Humans, and even the DragonKin. Most scholars believe this gas is what makes the Orotaq resistant to magic and tints their skin a faint blue. All you really need to know about them is that they eat anything smaller than they are, including us."

"Lovely. This place doesn't get any better does it?"

"You've seen the beauty here. These mountains are scarcely populated for a reason. Since the Cataclysm, some of Talohna's more rare species have migrated here, especially creatures."

"Well, hopefully we don't run into these Orotaq then. What about the Black Kasym? What is it? I've seen it on Giddeon's maps. It's huge."

Shaking her head, Yrlissa said, "You really don't want to leave this fire do you?"

Ember laughed. Refolding the charcoal transfers, she put them back in her travel pack. "No. It's warm here."

"All right. I can sense no danger for at least a mile. We'll be safe for a while yet. Now, the Black Kasym... The Black Kasym is a deep tear in the earth between this kingdom," Yrlissa said, raising her hands and turning them in all directions, "and the kingdom the Ancients used to live in. Jasala Vyshaan's dying magic created the Kasym somehow. It is a dark and very wide canyon that reaches far into the Deep Earth. No one knows why her death caused the Cataclysm or the devastation that created it, but the Ancient Kingdom has been cut off from the rest of Talohna since that time."

"Is there no other way to get there?" Ember asked, suddenly interested.

"No, the ocean passage is impossible to navigate. There are jagged spines of rock and ice hidden just below the water line. The northern most part of the WhiteWyrm Ocean and Orotaq Bay have been called Agaeus' Claws for thousands of years. As far as I know, no one has returned after trying to enter the Ancient Kingdom by using the ocean. The ruins of hundreds of ships can be seen in the northern waters of Orotaq Bay, and those I have seen. There are also a few people, mostly the Elvehn, who believe the Dyrannai Forest is in the Ancient Kingdom, so I tried to get there. Two of my fellow Blades and I failed and then spent almost a month running from Orotaq hunters and their dogs," Yrlissa explained with a mischievous wink, as Ember listened closely to every word.

"Creepy, very creepy. I remember hearing about Jasala. Giddeon said she was the DeathWizard who tried to take over the world, and all the countries went to war against her. Finally, three heroes killed her."

A dark mood settled over Yrlissa's features, it was unlike anything Ember had ever seen from her friend. "I know what Giddeon says. I also know what he says about Kael. Remember that, whenever he references their kind, for all our sakes. Sometimes things may not be as they appear," she said absently, as if her thoughts were many miles and many years away.

"You really don't believe that the Kai'Sar are evil do you, Lissa?" Ember asked once more, hoping for more answers.

"Council wizards and nobles use that term. For no other reason than to make themselves look intelligent by using the Ancient's dead language. I doubt they even have the translation right."

Ember scoffed. "You don't have to convince me. I'm positive that Giddeon's translations are missing an inflection on one of his prepositions. There's a big difference between the words 'from' and 'with'."

Yrlissa frowned. "How so?"

"Think about it for a minute. In English... sorry, the common tongue. To 'travel with' or 'to travel from'. Combined that with an adjective actually being a noun and Giddeon's translations could be a mile off. Every translation could."

"The bug-like word we discussed earlier?" Ember nodded but said nothing. "You're probably right. The Fae spoke every language ever used. If anyone will figure it out, it will be you. And to answer your question, no. I don't believe Kael's kind are evil, but they are susceptible to some kind of corruption. That part of their history is true, I've read some of the journals from long ago. I also know that some of them fought hard against that corruption. Now come, let us do our watch, so we can rest."

The night passed uneventfully and the six rode at dawn, headed towards Cairnwood, the only small centre of civilization left before entering the upper reaches of the Dwarven Mountain Range.

NATALIA'S REST
ARGELA, ELLORYA

"What the feck kinda spook you supposed to be?" Eamon said, as Dominique's group approached the private booth of the stranger Cormack met when they arrived.

"My name is Sythrnax, Mr. O'Leary. Please have a seat. I took the leisure of ordering the best bottle of Northman whiskey the house had." Eamon slid into the booth on the opposite of Sythrnax without hesitating.

"Trust me, Mr. Spook, the pleasure'll be all mine." Grabbing the tall-neck bottle, Eamon pulled the cork and tilted the bottle back.

"Easy," Cormack said, jumping forward in a futile attempt to warn the old man. "Northman whiskey can knock out a giant."

Lowering the bottle with almost a quarter of it gone, Eamon belched. "Mighty piss-poor giants ya got here then, boyo, but the swill be good." The words were barely out of his mouth before the bottle went back in.

"You'll have to pardon our associate," Cormack said, offering his hand in greeting to Sythrnax. The stranger ignored him.

"Every man's allowed a drink when he's been hiding out for twenty years. He's fine."

"Cormack tells me you might want to book passage on the Reave?" Dominique said, skipping any small talk.

"I do, Captain."

"Just yourself or others? And to where?" Dominique asked, clearly not in the mood for talk.

"That's a difficult question to answer, Captain. I wish for you to take me to the Cauldron's Teeth. First. I have a quick pick up to make there. After that, if you would be gracious enough, I would like to sail to FlatWater Bay, beyond Dasal, in the Free Lands. Once we arrive, I would be willing to lease you the hidden docks under Tazammor Mountain. For the retrofits Mr. O'Leary has planned. Everything you need is there. You merely must hire the men you require." Dominique glared across the table at Eamon, but was too far away to do anything.

"Big-mouth," Shasta snapped, smacking Eamon in the back of the head, making him choke on the half-empty bottle of whiskey.

"Manky wenchling sprat!" he spat. "I ain't say nothing. You think I want every Tom's Harry Dick hunting me for my bang? Use your head, woman-to-be. Spook here can probably read your empty minds." Without another word, he returned to his bottle, eyeing Shasta every few sips, as if watching for another smack that might spill his whiskey.

Sythrnax lifted his right hand. "Mr. O'Leary told me nothing, I assure you. But it's not a stretch to understand why he's with you. Just consider it. If ever you need a hidden, secure dock with everything you will ever need—including Dwarven forges—the offer stands, but the offer is good only for you Captain."

"Dwarven forges, ya say?" Eamon asked, perking up. Even though the bottle was three quarters gone, his words were as clear as a ringing bell.

"Yes. There are three of them, all dockside, all vented. There is also a large furnace for melting and mixing metals or for making sand casts. I can have whatever source heat you prefer ready."

"Sounds perfect, pirate," Eamon said, staring at Dominique. "Three forges will shorten the retrofit time. By a lot. Two months to be done, maybe less, depending how many ships we do and their sizes. The Reave and her sister ships will be floating fortresses of destruction."

"There are five Reaver ships docked in and around Lover's Bay. Six, counting the Reave," Shasta reminded Dominique as she leaned in closer.

Ignoring both men and Shasta, Dominique frowned. "All Reaver ships leave on the morrow's early tide. Shasta, get us clearance, Cormack can help with the less than twenty-four-hour notice. As for you," he said, staring at Sythrnax. "Be aboard the Twilight Reave an hour before sun-up or you don't board. You will clear customs on your own. My crew and ships are presently clear of wants and warrants, and I don't need your past or current problems fucking that up. Agreed?"

"Absolutely, Captain. We have a deal," Sythrnax said, his smile tugging at the sides of his mask.

Chapter Thirty

"The Eyes of the Wing. This spell has many names. Soul suppression, the living dead, and even mind control, though that is quite inaccurate. It is magic only the strongest necromancers can use. It is outlawed everywhere in Talohna except for the country I live in—DormaSai. It is illegal for a good reason. A powerful-enough necromancer can use the spell in order to suppress a Human or Elvehn soul and take over another person's body. King Azmerack has used this magic to take control of the Cethosian Queen. It is the first attack of the necromancer rebellions that are sweeping across Talohna. My mentor, the only mother we ever knew, would want us to fight this madman, and so we will. This necromancer rebellion will be stopped by rebels within its own ranks, and by those who follow us and fight from the outside."

Nekrosa Kohl, Necromancer and general of the DormaSain resistance, 5007 PC

LOWER DWARVEN MOUNTAIN RANGE

Nekrosa and Sephi ordered Luthian to watch Giddeon's group closely, and by doing so, managed to stay a couple hours behind them, as they followed the group into the mountains. All three necromancers had Eyes of the Wing spells active inside Giddeon and Ember's camp when Saleece read the letter out loud and during the conversation between Ember and Yrlissa. Nekrosa was not alarmed by news they were already well aware of. It was why they were in the Blood Kingdoms. As for what the two young women said, it merely confirmed what he already suspected. If given an opportunity, they planned to grab the three they needed and then high tail it home to the Southern Kingdoms.

Nekrosa knew what was coming, but he had no ideas on how to stop it. DormaSai had been collecting magical artifacts and documents as well as written history and personal accounts since before Jasala had torn the lands asunder with her death spell. He did not know everything, but he knew a lot more than the ArchWizard ahead of them did. Nekrosa couldn't tell Giddeon though, because the fool would try to kill anyone who had tapped the Void's power the moment he sensed it, not to mention what he would do to someone like Nekrosa.

It no longer mattered to him whether Giddeon knew anything though. Nekrosa had tried to send an emissary to Giddeon just before the DeathWizard had been returned to this world. Though he was not positive, Nekrosa strongly suspected the emissary—his younger brother, Tallin—was now dead, executed by King Bale. Tallin had not been a necromancer, but bringing advice and knowledge from one had likely cost him his life. At the time, Nekrosa had been unaware of the extent of Cethos' hatred for necromancers; after all, the country was a long way from DormaSai, and they had helped overthrow King Azmerack during the rebellions.

He sent his brother to Corynth with the information because Tallin was not gifted at all. Nekrosa had received his brother's arrival letter, just like they had agreed, but there had been nothing further, and neither Luthian or Dekayna could find out what happened to him after he stepped foot inside the Cascade Citadel in Corynth. Considering he was nearly the equal fighter to Sephi, Nekrosa was sure his brother had died at the hands of Giddeon or Joran Bale.

As hard as it was to ignore, it was a score he would settle at a later time. Now, more important things mattered.

ROAD TO CAIRNWOOD

Three days of travel passed slowly as Giddeon and his group continued to close the distance to Cairnwood. Just before noon on the third day, Giddeon, Saleece, and Yrlissa all sensed a large body of people coming their way from the north. Not knowing whether they were hostile or not, Max and Kasik entered the forest to the side of the trail and headed out to try and track the large group. Max found them first and he was appalled at what he saw. Men, women, and children were all fleeing at the best speed they could and the few armed guards were too close to the group to save anybody during an attack. He approached them with his bow across his back and his hands in the air.

As soon as the armed guards saw him, they all ran to make sure he was secured, leaving the entire group completely exposed at their rear and sides.

"I mean you no harm," he said, raising his voice. "I am with others and we are after a friend, you may have met him. We should only be a couple days behind."

A short man emerged from the crowd and walked up to Max.

"We know who you are. You're hunting Kael. He left our village days ago, headed west. My name is Cornelius Redding. I am the mayor of Cairnwood. We've had to flee our town because of an Orotaq raid on our village."

Max knew Cornelius was lying the moment he spoke. Years as a Ranger sniper, sheriff's deputy, and eventually a sheriff had taught him how to spot liars long ago.

"Why would you lie about where Kael went? Unless you don't want us to find him, or more correctly, you don't want Giddeon to find him, do you?" Max asked.

"I do not know what you mean," Cornelius said, clearly trying to keep the charade going.

Looking around and still not seeing any sign of Kasik or the others, Max tried again. "I know why you are trying to protect Kael, but if you really want to protect him, then tell the ArchWizard when he gets here how Kael helped you. Not all of us are chasing him to kill him. I promise you," Max pleaded.

Before either could say any more, Giddeon and the others came around the bend and Kasik exited the forest on the far side of the travelling townsfolk. Cornelius went to speak with Giddeon. Max followed.

Cornelius stood before Giddeon and offered a quick bow.

"We know why you are here, ArchWizard. Kael headed north from our town two days ago after liberating us from Orotaq control. Kael and Kyah helped free us and asked for nothing in return, so please keep that in mind. Also, if you please, a young girl from our town, she was my ward. She disappeared our first day out here away from the village. Her name is Cassie. Please keep her safe if you find her. You should only be a day or so behind her. Maybe two behind Kael," he replied.

"Thank you," Max said. "And Cornelius?"

"Yes," he replied.

"Keep your guards further out so they can return with enough warning for you to prepare a defence. And tell them to work in pairs and never leave their position like they did with me. Had we meant you harm, there was nobody behind you to protect your people from the back or sides. You'll be safer like that, all right?"

He nodded. "Thank you, young man, for the advice, and good luck," Cornelius said as he looked at Giddeon. "We're both going to need it."

Deciding to walk their horses for a bit, Ember came up to walk beside Giddeon.

"Another group of people Kael helped. You didn't want to question them?"

"There's no sense," Giddeon replied, smiling. "They'd only tell us how he helped them."

Ember scoffed. "That's what everyone who has encountered him have said. Every single one. Are you starting to see now? You can't deny his behaviour. It's not what you thought it would be, right?"

"I will give you that much. But you do not understand how his power works. I cannot even begin to guess how it works, and I have studied magic for almost two hundred years. The last thirty of those years I have studied everything I could find about Kael's kind. All I do know is that bonded wizards have a connection to the earth and to their power. It..." He stopped talking for a minute while tapping his lips with his thumb, as if thinking about how to explain his point.

Smiling as if it finally came to him, he continued. "It is like being connected to all the power, grace, and peace that is the soul of the earth and nature. It fills us with its power and makes us feel younger, even extending our lives well beyond people from your plane of existence, even with your advanced technology. It is a bond that we create with magic when we are strong enough. If it is broken, then we die. Kael has this connection as well, but he was born with it, like you or I are born with an arm or a leg. It is a part of his very being. But Kael was also born with the exact same kind of bond to the underworld, to death. If my earth-bond fills me with everything I told you—the peace and grace of nature and this earth—what is Kael's death-bond filling him with?" he asked. He stopped walking and turned to her.

"I don't know," Ember said, "but it's clearly not affecting him the way you thought, or if it is, then he's obviously controlling it. Surely even you can't deny that now?" she asked, wondering if he would actually try.

"I don't, and perhaps you're right. My worry is how long it will last? And what will happen then?"

"I don't know, but if anyone in all of this multiverse can control this so-called corruption, Kael can. I know he can. I know his strength of will," Ember said firmly.

"I understand that you believe that, Ember, but I'm afraid for the people who will suffer or die if you are wrong. I was wrong about many things it seems. So, here is some free advice from an ArchWizard to the last of the Fae in our world. Being wrong carries a very heavy price for people who wield magic. It can create and destroy with equal ease. We are told in the university growing up to do no harm, even if it means doing nothing at all. That inaction is better than action that causes hurt. It is our most sacred covenant. But how do you do no harm when it is impossible to know everything that is happening around you and things may not be as they seem?"

"I don't know. You have to try and remember that Kael and I led a simple life. We worked, we danced, we enjoyed spending time with friends like Max, and we enjoyed that life. Concerns like these never entered our minds. We moved to the city from a rural town to get away from families who never wanted us. Kael, Max, and I have been here, what? Six months almost? I bet neither my family nor Kael's even know we are missing," she said, choking back tears. "And now... We are here. I am not even human, and Kael is a prophesied force of death. Can you even fathom how that is for us? If you actually think about that for moment, can you at least grasp a little bit of understanding?"

"Yes, but all any of us can do is the best with what we have at *this* moment. You have adjusted well, and you have saved our lives time and again. I promise you that when we catch up with Kael, I will tell him who he is, and we'll talk. As it stands now, we have to try to talk to him and hopefully avert this trigger event that Zaddyk has seen. As long as you are with us, Zaddyk says the critical turning point in Talohna's future cannot happen. Will that work for you?"

"It will have to," she said and walked faster in order to rejoin Yrlissa and Max. Giddeon nodded to her and then called for them to get on their mounts and carry on riding. They were in Cairnwood an hour before sundown the next evening.

CAIRNWOOD

Though the last couple of days hadn't been overly hot, Giddeon and Ember's group could smell Cairnwood long before they got there. Giddeon recommended they leave their mounts tied to the horse rail by the southern gate's watchtower. It was clear dozens of lives had been lost during the fighting. The putrid stench of rot permeated the entire town. Ember could only stare as they walked into the part of town where Kael had killed the novice shaman and Kyah the dogs.

Ember's eyes watered as she realized they were wide open and she had not blinked in several minutes. Pointing at the remains of what could be black dogs, she took in the devastation around them caused by fire and death.

"What in heaven's name are those?" she asked, her hand trembling.

"Bastard hollow dogs," Kasik said, spitting towards the carcasses. "Wild dogs from Black Hollow that the Orotaq have tamed, if you could even call it that."

Saleece nodded in agreement. "And lots of them, too. Look," she said, jogging over to a large humanoid body. She quickly covered her nose with her cowl and turned the body onto its back. A sickening squelch drifted up as the rotting body peeled from the cobblestone street.

"Dammit," Giddeon cursed as he shook his head and covered his nose. "I was hoping those townspeople were wrong."

Ember walked up and stared down at the dead Orotaq man. Glancing over at Yrlissa and holding her nose from the stench, she asked, "Orotaq, I presume?"

"Yes, *nahlla*," she answered. Bending over, the assassin ran her hand over the brands on its arm. "And a shaman as well. Right, Giddeon?"

"Good call," he praised, and then pointed to where she had touched. "You can tell by the scarification on the chest, neck, and arms. He was a novice, roughly, or maybe our equivalent to an apprentice. The branding done on his arms is an easy way to identify him as a lesser mystic. As he gets stronger, more brands will be added. Right, Kasik?"

"Yes," the Northman replied. "We saw a grand shaman during one of the attacks on Kastalborg Island. My clan were one of several defending Ikstad during the necromancer rebellions." Curious, Ember looked up at him. "Two dozen Northman ships sailed south to help the Blood Kingdoms during the rebellions. It left Kastalborg weakened so the Orotaq tried to invade—"

"Kasik's people have been fighting the Orotaq for centuries," Giddeon added.

"True," the Northman nodded. "As for the grand shaman, every inch of his flesh was covered in brands like these. They represent a chronicle, a tale of their power, rank, and even their battlefield achievements. Their warriors have them too, but to a lesser degree and with none of the mystical designs."

"This must have been a large scale attack," Giddeon said, returning everyone's focus to the matter at hand. "At least for the Orotaq, anyway. Probably twenty or so warriors, three or four shamans. I imagine they were after the mines. I'm pretty sure that some obsidian glass was found in the mines here a few years ago. The Orotaq must have felt there was more to be found. Come on. Let's see what else we can find."

They kept walking until they entered the town square at the north end of the village where the largest battle between the townsfolk and the Orotaq had taken place. Ember was horrified by what she saw.

"Oh god, the smell," she complained, gagging. Looking around, sheepishly, she apologized. "I'm sorry, but the smell is so bad. How can you handle it, Max?"

"I was an overwatch sniper during the march on Baghdad, remember? This is nothing. Try breathing through your mouth, but only open it enough to breathe. No more or you might be tasting it as well. In Iraq, there were so many flies from the dead bodies even that didn't help. Breathe through your nose and smell the filth or breathe through your mouth and suck in filth-covered flies. Yeah, this is nothing," he said, frowning. Ember turned a shade of green at his story, desperately fighting the urge to throw up.

"Asshole," she muttered.

Saleece had been walking the outside perimeter of the battle, a habit taught to young wizards so they could observe and learn how a battle played out. She found two scorch marks on the ground.

"Father, over here," she called. He waved as he and the others came to see what she found.

"What did you find?" he asked.

Pointing at the scorch marks on the ground she asked, "Look. Are those what I think they are?"

Bending over, he touched the ash with his fingers and then lifting it to his nose, he inhaled and caught a distinct smell.

"They are. It smells like deep brimstone. Something materialized here from one of the lower planes of Hell. Look, there's another one," he pointed at the second mark close enough to the first that their outer rings of ash overlapped.

"Well, that is disturbing," Kasik said dryly. "I've never fought a lower denizen. Haven't even heard of anyone trying to summon a demon, not since that necromancer attempted to pull Rajazeye out. What was it, fifteen years ago, Giddeon? You were there, if I remember the tale right."

"It was sixteen years ago, just before Princess Corleya was born," he said, turning to Ember. "Rajazeye is the demon overlord of the first dimension of the Nine Hells, and it was hard enough stopping Azmerack from completing the spell. The demon never came fully across into our world. I would really rather not have to do such a thing again."

Ember had been listening, uneasy about what she was hearing, "'Again'? You mean you didn't kill it the first time?" she asked, clearly flabbergasted.

"You can't kill a demon overlord, *nahlla*," Yrlissa explained. "You can only send them back, or if you have a Fae high priest with you, you can banish them back without having to fight it," she smiled.

Ember laughed at the ever-increasing absurdity of her situation. "All right then, Brain. We need a banish demon spell, quickly please. If I can jump people across the continent, then banishing a demon back to Hell should be a walk in the park, right?"

"Afraid not," Giddeon called over his shoulder.

"Father's right, Ember. Based on the few texts we've read, only Fae males were high priests. I do not think women could cast the banishment spell. Sorry," Saleece said, shrugging her shoulders.

"Great, just great," Ember murmured as she sat down against a big oak tree on the north-western side of the square. She pulled her knees up and put her head on her arms, exhausted beyond words from nearly six months of stress, injuries, and worry. She dozed off in seconds. Yrlissa sat down beside her and rubbed her shoulders as Ember slowly woke up.

"I'm so tired," she said. "So much has happened, and I just can't seem to get a hold of it. I'm tired, worried, and even sick about the idea of what might happen. I don't like this place. It seems everyone is lying about this or that, and now there's demons? Real fire and brimstone, hell-walking demons? Jesus Christ almighty. I sometimes have to wonder if I am back home lying in a hospital bed with a broken mind, and that is what brought me here. If Kael were here, I could deal with it, but... I can't lose him, Lissa," she said, putting her head on her friend's shoulder.

"I know you are scared, *nahlla,*" Yrlissa said, putting her arm around Ember. "So am I, but we are nearly there. You must remain as strong as you have been. I have seen what you are capable of, and you are strong enough to deal with this. I am proud to call you my friend. Now, come on. Let's find a place to sleep for the night, and you can dream of having Kael in your arms in a matter of days. Maybe tonight he will allow you in when you dreamcast," she said, attempting to cheer Ember up.

"I doubt it. He thinks I'm those witches trying to get into his mind. The last time he shut me out, it hurt."

"I know, but years from now no one will be able to shut you out. It takes time, like everything else."

Giddeon called after them as Max and Kasik found a house in good condition with room for them all. They burned the bodies and got some rest. On the road early, Ember hoped they were closing the distance.

ARGELA/ALEGRA NORTHERN GATES

Ella the White and Desiree Star returned to Argela two full days behind Dominique and his crew. She sent Desiree to Alegra and immediately went to the house she had rented weeks ago. The run-down house was relatively inconspicuous, even if its tenants weren't. Katarina was waiting for her.

"Mistress," she said, opening the door and stepping aside. "The last treatment worked shortly after you left. He's awake and he's coherent. He can even walk, but barely." Ella stopped dead in her tracks. For eleven years, they'd been trying to help Cassel Morenax, Yrlissa Blackmist's husband and the father of her dead child.

"Of course, it did. Now I have to tell him his daughter died eleven years ago and Yrlissa almost six months ago. And that we're hunting his old captain, Dominique Havarrow. Can this day get any worse?" A crash from the back bedroom rolled out into the main room of the house. Both women dashed to the room where Cassel had been unconscious until a week prior. Ella rushed to the smashed window and stared out, but Cassel was no where to be seen.

"I thought you said he could barely walk?" Ella snapped.

"He must have been faking, but even so, after eleven years he can't have gone far." Glancing behind her, Katarina gasped. "He took our journals. I'll go after him, mistress. I..."

"You don't know Reavers very well, do you, dear? He'll be long gone, vanished among hundreds of sailors who all look alike. We have more important things to worry about. When did Havarrow and his ships sail out?"

"At dawn, yesterday. Five ships left, but two more joined him once they cleared the Lover's Embrace."

"Seven ships," Ella said, shaking her head. "Come. Hopefully Desiree has tracked down one of BlackSpawn's men."

The two women left the working class neighbourhood and headed for the north-eastern gate that linked Argela to its sister city, Alegra. Passage into the Salzaran city was relatively simple. With the northern gates next to the entrance for the Dock of One, travel between the cities was much easier. The entry requirements from the docks kept most serious trouble out of the twin cities.

Stepping foot into the Salzaran city was a far different experience. It was where the toughest sailors and pirates came for shore leave. Ella and Kat hadn't walked twenty feet when the catcalls began. Hoots, whistles, and offers of night-long trips of pleasure drifted their way. Kat glanced at Ella and smiled, nodding to their left. A sailor, grabbing his crotch and thrusting his hips, stuck his tongue out at the White witch. Ella laughed and closed her right hand, making a fist to activate her magic.

The sailor pissed himself and his crotch-grabbing became crotch-splashing as he splattered a bald man beside him. Ella laughed even harder. The bald man turned and swung, rocking the crotch-grabber and inciting a brawl. Ella and Kat carried on, entering The Stone's Throw tavern a couple blocks down from the fast-growing fight.

Ella stepped into the tavern and immediately saw Desiree in the far corner, her head down talking with a pirate. She waited until the pirate shook Desiree's hand and got up to leave the tavern. He nodded as he passed Ella and Kat.

Taking a seat at Desiree's table, Ella raised her eyebrows. Desiree answered the unasked question.

"That was Hack. He's captain of the Bled Trader. We can sail with him on the evening tide in about four hours. He'll take us to BlackSpawn. The man himself can't dock here, but Hack says he's only a day's sail from here. A small port called Fathom's Deep."

"I know it," Ella said, nodding her head. "It's just west of the Embrace's western tip, along the Cauldron's side of the Elloryan Forest and the mountains."

"What about Shae and Torgo?" Desiree asked.

Ella chewed her bottom lip. "Tell them to clean up and come to the house. We may need them with us, but send the rest of the pack home. Kat and I will go pack up the house and settle with the landlord."

"Yes, Mistress," Desiree said, bowing.

"And please make sure they're clean, Desiree, even if you have to drown them at Natalie's for an hour. The idea is to not attract attention."

"I will, Mistress." Desiree left the tavern, leaving Ella and Kat alone.

"What now, Mistress?' Kat asked.

"Now we go see if Bauro BlackSpawn still has any balls or if he's gone soft sitting on all that gold."

BLACK CAULDRON OCEAN
FATHOM'S DEEP

"Pull! You sons of bitches," Hack Orion shouted, as his men struggled to pull the massive caravel into the Fathom's Deep wooden dock. Finally, the scrape of wood on wood ground out the rasp of rope sliding around the pinion cleats as the big ship came to a stop.

Ella stepped up beside Hack and offered her hand. "You have my thanks, Captain Orion."

"Anything for you, Mistress of the White," he said, shaking hands. "You'll find Bauro in the dock tavern. It's called The Drink."

"How quaint," Ella replied, as the Bled Trader's boarding plank crashed to the docks. She turned to make sure Desiree and Kat, along with Shae and Torgo, were following and then left the ship, walking the short distance to the tavern.

Bauro BlackSpawn was easy to find. Sitting with his back to the tavern's outer wall, the pirate was surrounded by women, and bodyguards stood to each side of him.

"Ella, dear!" he shouted. "What brings you here? Or perhaps I should ask *who* brought you here. Ya don't usually slum in the gutter with us... vermin, I believe the word is you used."

"Only when referring to you, Bauro," Ella replied, her voice riddled with disgust. The pirate and his men burst out laughing, and Bauro bowed without getting out of his creaky wooden chair. The four women with him left quickly.

"Come now, Ella. You scared my ladies away. I guess you'll have to replace them. Have a seat if your pretty little ass don't mind some stains on that white dress. Come. Have a drink. Have several. It'll numb the pain."

She frowned and remained standing. "What pain?"

"The pain you're gonna feel after my men wear you and your pretty friends out." The laughter died away as two dozen men drew their swords and several loading crossbow clicks echoed over head.

Ella sighed. "Are we really going to do this again, Bauro? I have already kept *my* promise. I haven't killed you yet, and you've been in my presence for nearly five whole minutes. I'm not in the mood to fight. To be quite honest, I came here to warn you and to ask a favour."

Desiree chuckled as she fingered the handles of her wooden daggers. "It *would* be better to be owed a favour by Talohna's only White witch, than to die," she said.

"Boy, those Broken Bastards breed you nasty bitches really young, and nah," he said, shaking his head. "Think I'd rather just commence with the pain."

"Fair enough, Bauro." Ella smiled and raised both hands, turning her palms out as Bauro stood from his chair. But nothing happened. For the first time in more millennia than she could count her magic failed. "Desiree?"

"Nothing, Mistress. No magic." Instead, the assassin drew her blades.

"Clever boy, Bauro. But your Dwarven charm won't hold me long enough to save you..."

"Ah, but it will," he said, pulling the charm from inside his shirt as he approached. "This one has been altered. In fact, I bet you'd recognize the glyphs." He held it up for her to see.

"Ancient magic," she spat. "Very clever boy."

"I thought so." He smiled and blew her a kiss.

"But you made a mistake, Bauro. That's not so clever."

He laughed again. "I don't think so, witch. You travel with magic users and you can't use magic. I fail to see any mistake..."

Ella smirked. "I don't need magic. Like always, you're one step behind, Bauro. Your charm won't work on my companions back there," she said, tilting her head toward

Shae and Torgo. "Have you ever seen what an alpha werewolf couple can do inside a closed building like this?" As if to emphasize her point, Torgo dropped the locking bar into the front door's latch with a bang. "Don't imagine your blades are made of silver? Are they, Bauro? No?" The pirate shook his head. "Give me the charm," Ella demanded. "Now!" He shook his head again. "Shae?" Ella said, calmly smiling. Both werewolves transformed in seconds. Well over seven feet tall on their back legs, both howled as they shook the remnants of cloth from their fur.

Bauro pulled the bone charm from his shirt immediately. "Curse you, witch," he snapped.

Ella snatched it from his hand, snapping the strip of leather around his neck. She placed the bone carving on the counter of the bar. Kat slammed the butt of her dagger onto the charm, shattering it. Bauro flashed his teeth in anger or regret, Ella was not sure.

Power rushed back to her, flushing her face as she sighed. "Much better. Sit, so we can discuss why I came all this way to see you." The pirate dropped into his chair, clearly surprised to be alive.

Ella sat across from him and smiled. "I was telling you the truth. I came here to help you. Now, when we've concluded our business, I'll have to kill you, slowly, and painfully. But not now. We speak business now."

"What business do we have?" he asked, exasperated.

"The betrayal of your right hand man, to begin with."

"Bullshit. Havarrow hasn't got a disloyal ounce of Northman blood in him..."

"Yet he sailed away from the twin cities, heading north when he was supposed to come your way. He also had an old man on board I would very much like to kill. Preferably before he turns the seven ships Havarrow has with him into floating alchemical fortresses."

"You're serious."

"Very serious, Bauro. This man will change alchemy and warfare in Talohna, and not for the better."

"All right, Ella. I have twenty-two ships in range of my call. Where are we going?"

"Dasal, first. We need to take Kat home and find out exactly where Havarrow is headed. I need Seifer Locke to do that."

"Well then," Bauro said, smiling. "Assumin' ya ain't lying to me, let's go hunt a traitor. Settle-up between us afterwards? Deal?"

Ella nodded. "I look forward to turning you inside out, Captain BlackSpawn." Spinning on her heel, she turned to leave.

She didn't see Bauro smile as he mimicked cutting her throat.

Chapter Thirty-One

"Betrayal is often the cause of true suffering and the most devastating way to shatter one's heart and soul. People who betray those closest to them contain within them an evil so dark they are rarely bothered by the colossal agony and destruction they inflict. They simply betray someone and walk away, never looking back. These people will pay for what they do to others someday, even if it's at the moment of their death. When they are judged for their lives lived, the circle of life will always ensure judgement – the Ancients used to call it karma. Those who have betrayed me will pay for it much sooner than they expect. I am not a patient person."

Yrlissa Blackmist, From journal pages found in the catacombs below the Arcane Library in DormaSai
Date and location unknown

SOUTH OF CAIRNWOOD

It took Cassie all day to work her way to the back of the caravan as the people from Cairnwood headed south to the ford on the Greystone River. She played the dutiful new daughter to the mayor's wife and then asked to go play with her friends. The mayor's wife seemed relieved that she had not asked to wander the forest, but Cassie's ultimate goal was to get to that forest unnoticed. Kael and Kyah would have close to a half day on her by the time she left, but travelling through the trees like she was able to, she hoped to find them in less than three hours.

Cassie was smart for her age and knew she might have to spend days in the forest alone. It did not scare her, but it meant she had to get some things before leaving. Her first stop was the water wagon, where she managed to sneak away with two full water skins. Refilling them in the forest was easy for someone who knew where to look.

Next, Cassie got the town's young boys to tease the seamstress, bribing them with the bag of homemade sweets her aunt had kept hidden on the top of the kitchen cupboard. She took them just before the caravan had left the town. The seamstress was making new cloaks for the outriders, and Cassie knew the first one was done. It was folded neatly, tied securely at the back of her wagon. The young boys continued teasing and bothering the seamstress long after Cassie had taken the cloak and hidden it inside her own winter coat on the mayor's wagon.

She knew the caravan would stop for the evening meal about two hours before dark, so an hour and a half before they stopped, Cassie grabbed her water bottles and her new, heavy cloak and quietly made her way to the back end of the caravan, where the covered wagon with the dried goods was bringing up the rear. Again no one saw Cassie grab enough food for a couple of days and vanish from under the tarp and into the forest. Within moments, she had the cloak on, the water bottles crossed over her back, and the dried food tied to the back of her waist as the ground flashed by below her. She had to hurry. Kael would need her help. She just hoped she would be there in time.

Cassie could not stop thinking about what she saw in the courtyard behind the lodge the night before. Kyah told her to stay behind with the others, but she was worried about them both. She managed to sneak in beside the lodge hoping to see if Kael was all right. Cassie had never seen magic of any kind before the Orotaq attacked the town, but she knew that what happened behind the lodge was not normal magic. She was positive that Kyah was a witch or maybe something worse. Why else would an Orotaq shaman drop to his knees in subservience and allow her to kill him? She saw everything that had happened and knew that Kael had no idea what Kyah really was.

Cassie was determined to do her best to help him, as long as she got there in time. The thought made her push herself harder, and the ground flew by below as her speed increased even more.

NORTH OF CAIRNWOOD

Kyah and Kael made good time considering he was still suffering from aches and pains caused from being shook like a rat. Even so, they rode until just before sunset and made a small camp a hundred feet into the forest, off the trail they were using to travel north into the mountains. With no rain on the way, Kael chose a small depression in the earth that gave them some shelter from the cold wind that blew at night. Summer had yet to arrive, and Kyah guessed that the year-long winter was trying hard not to let go.

With very little energy left, Kael sat down to eat. "Kyah? I'm just gonna have some dried jerky and fruit for supper. I can barely keep my eyes open any more."

"Do you want me to take first watch? I mind not, if you need the rest," she offered.

"Yeah, sure. Wake me for my turn," he said, as he chewed his way through the dried meat and fruit they had brought from Cairnwood. Kyah sat beside him and he enjoyed her warmth. He offered her a piece of jerky.

Tearing off a small piece, she gave him a nudge with her shoulder. "Kael, wake up," she said, softly, taking the jerky from his hand and placing it aside. "Come on. You need sleep. You can keep your eyes open no longer." She unrolled his blanket and covered him up. Sleep found him within seconds.

Kael woke later and looked up to see the two moons were still high in the sky. It meant he had time for a couple more hours of sleep before his watch shift began. Kyah was at the edge of the camp, but his eyes were blurry and he was still so tired that he rolled over and went back to sleep. For some strange reason, he wondered how Cassie was getting on with her new family many miles to the south.

Just before drifting off again, Kael felt that pull on his mind that he had felt so many times since being free. It was always the same, a haunting illusion of Ember. He was convinced it was being sent by the Dead Sisters as they had done so many times when he was captured.

The first couple of times the illusion or dream was always the same: Ember begging him to listen to her as she tried over and over to convince him she was real. It was gut-wrenching torture, and far worse than anything physical the Sisters had done during the time he'd been held captive.

It took a while, but he learned how to shut them out of his dreams. The last time they tried, Kael let them in, hoping when he severed the dream it would hurt like hell to whomever had done it. In no mood to deal with them tonight, he pushed the feeling away and went back to sleep.

When Kael opened his eyes again, it was morning and Kyah was sitting on his lap with her bodice unlaced as she smiled down into his eyes. Her mischievous intent was clear. The sun was just starting to rise through the trees, but the air was still cold enough for Kael to see his own breath, and more than cool enough to make the soft flesh of Kyah's nipples harden and catch his full attention. He sat up as she gently straddled his waist.

"Morning," she sighed softly. "I was beginning to think you would never wake up." She leaned forward and kissed him, her tongue darted past his lips and tickled his own. Still with no resistance to her advances, he slid his arms around her waist and pulled her close, at the same time noticing her proper use of the negative word in her sentence. He smiled, thinking she had finally learned what he had been trying to teach her.

He eased her back to congratulate her when he felt the slightest familiar presence behind him, Kyah dropped her hands on top of his and pinned them to her waist. She was stronger than she looked. He couldn't pull his hands free. Panic made his stomach flip and the all-too-familiar click of a Gyhurra collar snapped shut around his neck. The spikes bit deep as they pierced the month-old scars.

He had just enough time to realize his mistake and the seriousness of it before pain blasted through his senses. A scream tore from his throat and pierced the calm forest as if a banshee had been let loose from the Ninth Hell. Every muscle in his body locked tight. His jaw slammed shut with enough force to sever the tip of his tongue, and his head cracked against the log he spent most of the night leaning against.

Kyah had enough foresight to release his hands or the force of constricting muscles would have broken her wrists. Flat on his back and unable to move anything but his eyes, Kael could not grasp what was happening. Kyah leaned over and gently kissed his forehead.

"Sorry, but after what happened in Cairnwood, we couldn't risk that someone had seen what I did to that stupid shaman. We had to speed things up a bit. I hope you don't mind," she purred. "You should be used to the Gyhurra by now." She waited, as if expecting him to answer. When he was unable to illicit so much as a grunt, she continued. "It doesn't really matter, I guess. As long as we get you to Sythrnax, it is *not* important whether you cooperate." She stressed the 'not important' part of her proper grammar. Even through the fog of pain, it suddenly occurred to him that she had been faking everything, including her poor grammar. Kyah was a Dead Sister. Likely the ones who specialized in spying or sabotage.

She smiled at Kael, as if she knew what he was thinking. "I am, my dear love. I have always been. I am a real Dead Healer, not what some muddle-headed old wizard thinks I am," she mocked coyly. With his body refusing to obey his commands, Kael had the use of his eyes, and nothing more. Movement at his peripheral vision showed him three more women as they stepped out from behind him. Two women and one girl.

It finally dawned on him that the familiar presence he had felt behind him was Ashea.

"Kael!" the young girl said. He could see she was excited. "Are you not happy to see me? I survived your cowardly attack back at Arkum Zul. Never believe someone is dead unless you see it with your own eyes." She smirked and walked around the campfire to stand over top of him. Kael cursed his own stupidity, he felt Ashea behind him, but had been distracted by Kyah. Believing the novice witch had died also fooled his mind and he failed to recognize the threat in time to stop her from clasping another Gyhurra collar around his neck.

Ashea knelt beside Kyah as she straddled Kael's prone, rigid body. "Please release him, Mistress N'Ikyah," she said. "The Cardessa promised the new Gyhhura will hold him this time."

Ashea stood back up as Kyah leaned forward and placed her hands on the collar. Magic misted from her fingers with a light hiss, sliding into the collar and along the spikes until disappearing inside Kael's neck. The Gyhurra's powerful effects calmed and the force that had seized his body was released. Even so, cramped and twisted muscles continued to tighten at the base of his neck, lower back, and in his left arm and shoulder where he had been shot four years ago.

"Hold on, Sisters," Kyah said. "While I help him with the cramps."

"Oh, look," Ashea said, giggling. "He bit off the end of his tongue."

"My, my, lover. We cannot have that, can we? Let me fix it for you. We must be moving soon. The Cardessa will be waiting for us farther north." Kael felt the remarkably gentle touch of her right hand as she caressed his chin. Healing magic flowed into his mouth, sealing the tip of his tongue. Her left hand glided over his neck, shoulder, and left arm, loosening the muscle cramps still reacting to the collar's magic.

As the initial ferocity of the modified Gyhhura collar faded, it still took every ounce of willpower Kael had to deal with the throbbing waves of savage agony ripping through his entire body. With the cramps easing away, he could at last move. He forced himself to his feet, if for no other reason than as a show of defiance.

His stomach flipped as he understood the women were Kyah's ternion. Desperate to maintain control of his rapidly rising fear and panic, Kael tried to steady his breathing as the seriousness of his situation set in. It had taken months to conserve enough power to break through the last Gyhhura, and Ashea was right. He could feel the differences in the one embedded in his neck.

Kael watched as Kyah and Ashea turned their backs and began packing up the campsite, giving him a few minutes alone. Having a better understanding of his magic than he did six months ago, Kael wasted no time in testing the collar's strength. Probing at it with the trace amount of magic he still had access to made him smile when nothing happened. At first. Concentrating harder, he released a second trickle of magic against the collar. Carefully, he guided the soft, black essence against where the spikes had been forged to the collar. Unable to see the symbols engraved on the collar's inner rim, his magic danced lightly over the runic script, triggering the collar's offensive magic. Every nerve in Kael's body lit up like a Fourth of July fireworks display back home. Sparks of torment raced along every nerve, exploding outwards from his neck and tearing down every limb. Unable to form a coherent thought, Kael couldn't pull back the trace amounts of magic. The agony rolled onward unabated, driving him to his knees. Kyah turned at the commotion and frowned, but Ashea burst into hysterical laughter. Though he had no idea which, one of the other witches planted her foot on Kael's back and shoved him into the dirt, cursing.

"Gods cursed whiny coward. Suffer like a true DeathWizard," the witch barked.

He sighed as the contact broke his connection to the magic he trickled onto the collar. The explosions of nerve pain lessened to a steady, familiar tingling.

For reasons Kael could not understand, Kyah refused to allow his torment to continue. "Quit wasting time, all of you. Get him on his horse, unless you would like to explain to the Cardessa why we're late!" she ordered. The two witches and their novice jumped to do as she asked and put Kael up on his horse. Though much reduced, misery continued to wash through him, matching the cadence of his palpitating heart. Desperation pushed at his soul as he focused on trying to fight against the steady affliction caused by the Gyhhura, to no effect.

During his rehabilitation program for gunshot wounds four years ago, Kael was taught methods of controlling and mastering pain. Grasping at these last straws of hope, he concentrated on his breathing. It was a futile attempt to bring the anxiety and fear under control.

Noticing his struggle, Kyah mounted her horse and moved closer. Shoulder-to-shoulder, she stared at him with narrowed eyes. "Forgotten how to deal with the Gyhurra's pain, my love?"

"Worse this time..." he began. His breath caught in his throat before expelling forcefully through clenched teeth.

"Worse?" Kyah snatched the collar, pulling him closer. The pain renewed ten-fold for a few seconds, but soon began to fade as Kael recognized the magic Kyah fed into the collar. His frazzled nerves returned to near normal as the collar's torture began to diminish. "A gift, love. I'd hate to see you in so much pain. We do have a ways to go."

Kael took a deep breath to calm himself further. The sweetness in her voice made his stomach lurch. With a crooked smile, her fingers slid from the collar and Kael heeled his horse in an attempt to be away from her. He followed the other women as they took their mounts and left the overnight campsite.

Less than twenty minutes had passed when Ashea rode up beside Kael. She said nothing, but eyed him up and down, closely. He turned, immediately regretting the pain it caused as the four spikes gouged the nerves in his neck. Even so, he still smiled, wondering whether the young novice had the courage to poke at him like a collared beast, especially after what had happened in Arkum Zul.

"Are you surprised to see me, Master?" she asked. Kael thought better about shaking his head, knowing from past experience the pain it would cause.

"Just disappointed," he replied.

Not phased by the remark, she continued, "May I speak freely with you, Master?" she enquired, as she touched his arm. He was surprised at her gentleness.

"I can't stop you," he stated.

"Why do you fight so hard against what you are? I see the spirit of dark magic radiating off you, and yet, you continue to try to help people instead of ruling over them like you were born to do. It is your right, Master," she said, her voice heavy with conviction.

Kael looked at her long and hard before answering. "Birth does not convey the right to rule any more than by force, fear, or intimidation. Do you understand what that means, Ashea?"

"I do. But that is wrong. Your kind were created by the gods to rule all of Talohna, by force if necessary. Jasala Vyshaan knew this, only she failed because the Dead Sisters of her time could not get to her to help her fight. She was hidden from us by the same type of people who want to kill you even now. Had we been there, there would have been no Cataclysm, no loss of innocent lives, and the world would be a prosperous place for everyone. Not just the rich, noble, and royal."

Kael could tell she was looking for his approval, as if a few words from him could validate everything she'd been taught. It was so ridiculous coming from the mouth of a twelve or thirteen year old that he almost laughed. The pain from the collar would have been worth it. He decided to try a different path instead. "I can promise you, Ashea, that my kind were not created or born to rule anything. We are either a freak of nature, a mutation, or else we're the spawn of Hell."

"I believe you are wrong, Master."

"How do you know what you believe? You were raised by a group of radical extremists. We have them in our world, too, and just like them, you believe what they tell you is true. You follow blindly, and you don't have the courage to seek out the truth for yourself." It wasn't a question, but the smile on Ashea's face sent a shiver up his spine.

"I don't need to look for the truth. I already know what it is." He realized he had said exactly what she had wanted him to. She carried on smiling as they rode north along the trail.

"We are taught from a very young age about our history and yours. The Sisters teach from written scrolls ten thousand years old. Our library in the DemonBone Valley is extensive. I spend as much time there as I am allowed. But the truth, the real truth, lies in the carvings of our monolith." Kael's breath froze in his lungs as the word crossed over her lips. Ashea noticed, and her smile widened. "Yes, Master. We have one too. There are several monoliths. It's why we travel north as well. With a second one, the Dead Sisters will have even more of the truth about you. You'll see, Master. You're best chance is with us. Perhaps Master Sythrnax will help open your eyes some day."

Doubt clawed at his mind. As a person who always believed the root of most evil resided in the lies created to justify the atrocities people committed, Kael paled at the idea that such lies could be the truth. It meant that he and those like him were created for the sole purpose of serving evil. It was something he refused to believe.

Contradiction is the greatest weapon against the lies put forth by evil, whether in Talohna or on Earth. Lies were seldom consistent. Kael had not been able to read much of the book he found in Jasala's tower, but he knew beyond a doubt that some DeathWizards predated the Dead Sisters by at least two thousand years, maybe more. A history of lies created to justify their evil gave him his contradiction.

"Ashea? Have you ever been to Jasala's tower?" he asked.

"No, Master. We can no longer enter without raising the alarm of the ArchWizard, the Third Pillar and certain members of the Inari. We haven't been able to enter the lands of the Forsaken since the Cataclysm caused by Jasala's death."

Kael smiled. "Were you aware that I came through your dimensional bridge just outside of her eastern bell tower?" Her eyes grew wide and for a split second she reminded him of Cassie, a young girl fascinated by something new.

"No, Master. We suspected, but we were not sure where you came through. Did you enter her tower? Oh, how I wish we could go there. To see where she fought the blasphemers... It is my dream." She responded with the eagerness of the excited child she still was.

“I read part of Jasala's grimoire while I was there...”

“What did it say, Master?” Ashea asked. She was almost giddy with excitement.

“I read that DeathWizards predate the Dead Sisters by two thousand years. Did you know that?” He watched Ashea process the information. She shook her head, vehemently.

“No. That's... Can't be true. You're lying.”

“Why would I lie?”

“Where is this book then? With your belongings?” Kael swallowed, painfully, as he realized what he just did.

“No, the room was warded, I couldn't remove the grimoire.”

“Oh,” Ashea said, disappointed. Kael sighed a breath of relief and hoped Kyah would forget the grimoire and potions from Jasala's tower were in his bag, especially with everything that was going on.

Kael knew that telling Ashea any more truth would cause nothing but more trouble, and as fanatical as the Dead Sisters were, it would only cause him more grief. The seed of doubt was planted, and he had have to wait to see if it grew further.

"There is nothing else there to see, Ashea. The tower is in ruins and the battlefield is littered with bones. That is all," he lied.

"Still, to see it..." she trailed off.

"Ashea, how about you tell your leader to come talk to me? Unless she is too afraid," he taunted, knowing it would get Kyah to talk.

"Mistress Kyah fears nothing, Master. I will pass her your request." She rode ahead until she was beside Kyah, who turned her head to glare. Nodding to Ashea, she gestured for the young novice to ride ahead. Kyah's horse slowed and Ashea rode further out front.

"You wished to see me, love? I assume Ashea's conversation and glowing worship of you is becoming a bore?" She chuckled.

Kael scoffed. "You finally found that sense of humour you were looking for, did you?" Not expecting an answer, he carried on. "Don't bother with the love crap. It demeans us both."

"I will not," she said. "My feelings for you have not changed. In fact, I love you more now than when I first met you, but we must do something about your insistent desire to ignore what you are. We will meet with the Cardessa, and she will tell us how to carry on with what must be done. You have hung on to the memory of your dead wife for far too long. I have tried repeatedly to make you love me, knowing it would be easier when this day came, but you have an unnatural resistance to my charms, and a mystical resistance to glamours and seduction spells. You have used every opportunity to avoid being with me physically, with only two exceptions. Tonight, however, you will have to resist the magic of all the Sisters who will be joining us, and even you can't do that. By morning, you will love me in return, even if it is by the grace of magic. Your wife's memory will be but a lost shadow wandering the furthest and darkest corners of your mind."

She smiled and ran her fingers along his cheek.

In for a long night and with no way around the path he was on, Kael turned away from Kyah and focused his resolve. He knew full well the only reason he was still breathing after so many months in Talohna was that others, mainly Lycori and Kyah, had been there to keep him alive. There would be no Lycori coming to his rescue like in Jasala's bell tower or in the mountain pass west of Ipea. No Galen to carry his unconscious body into the depths of the earth to hide from Orotaq hunters. No quick switch or tricks of illusion to pull and deceive his way out like back in Dasal, and no necromancer warrior staying in the room next door. This time he was on his own. It scared the hell out of him.

With no magic and his reaper-blades hung over a Dead Sister's saddle, spelled with shimmering magic that would probably kill him if he touched them, he was at a total loss for what to do, or for a way out. There was nothing he *could* do and that terrified him even more. The last time such a thing happened, people died. Deaths that fell squarely on his shoulders.

The thought of doing it again made him sick, even if it might mean his freedom.

HOURS EARLIER

Hours passed as Cassie raced through the trees in a frantic attempt to reach Kael in time to offer him the help he would soon need. Having been forced to slow down twice, however, her stomach was cold with the fear she might be too late. The first delay came at dark. Though she could see in the dead of night better than most animals—a secret Cassie had shared with no one—she still had to slow her break-neck speed as full darkness descended. Then at close to midnight with both moons high in the sky, just as she had enough moonlight to travel through the trees with greater speed once again, movement from below her forced her to stop. Only the Elvehn trackers of legends and myth could move through the tree-tops without making a sound.

Easing her way lower through the branches, Cassie watched as a group of twelve women travelled on the trail heading north. Since Kyah had helped her with the bonding and shown her how to use the magic hidden deep inside her, Cassie had discovered some things she had never noticed before. The first was the aura of energy around every single person she could see. If she focused on an individual hard enough, a living, pulsating aura of colour lit up around them. Every person's was unique, but some had startling similarities. The women below her all had a similar aura to Kyah, which meant they had to be on their way to help her.

Dressed in flowing white robes made them look like divine phantoms highlighted by the moonlight as they rode through the dark forest, but their auras showed something else entirely. Strands of darkness within the auras melted into the blackness of the forest's shadows as if they were one. It made her shiver with fear; the chill in her stomach increased further as the riders raced away.

Using their shimmering movements, Cassie followed, hoping they would lead her all the way to Kael. Running high up through the trees, she saw the campsite and angled directly for it, arriving several minutes before the robed women. When Kyah walked out of the darkness and met the riders, Cassie knew she'd been right. Kyah talked to the women about fifty feet from the camp. Frowning, Cassie left them and went to look for Kael, unsure as to why he hadn't woken at the pounding feet of the speeding horses. Kyah's laugh drifted to her ears, along with the fear-inducing boast about Kael not waking for some time.

Cassie's aunt had used different plants and roots to do such things for the injured and sick back in Cairnwood, and her throat caught at the reminder of what happened to her town only a few days ago. The loss suffered was quickly forced from her mind as she looked down at Kael from the tree. He was sound asleep, propped against a log. Struggling with how to help him, she dropped to the ground and crawled up behind the log Kael had chosen to spend the night against.

Peeking over the top and seeing no one, Cassie gently placed both her hands on Kael's shoulders and shook him, before quickly ducking back down as Kyah glanced back over her shoulder. Cassie hurried and shook him harder, but he merely groaned, mumbling something about embers. She did not know why he would be dreaming about a fire, but she shook him a third time nonetheless. Finally, he opened his eyes, but was looking at the far side of the camp, so she followed his line of sight just in time to see Kyah re-enter the camp. Cassie ducked again and scooted backwards to her tree, climbing up the far side and into the dense cover higher up.

Situated on a heavy limb, protected by foliage, she looked down in time to see Kael smile and roll over. He was back asleep in seconds. Knowing there would be no way to wake him with Kyah so close, Cassie watched the female riders disappear back down the mountain trail. Three stayed behind and entered the camp.

Losing her one chance to warn Kael, Cassie tried hard not to cry and instead found a double 'Y' branch in her tree and secured herself to get some sleep. Accepting she'd have to wait for another chance to help Kael, she closed her eyes but struggled to sleep.

Dawn came six hours later, and Cassie woke to movement below her. She climbed part-way down the tree for a closer look. Her cheeks flushed with heat as she saw Kyah straddle Kael, her unlaced top wide open, her breasts exposed. Her embarrassment quickly turned to horror as she saw a young girl her own age slowly approach Kael from the exact same direction she had the night before. The collar in her hand was radiant with magic, a putrid green mist coated the metal, dripping like diseased fog onto the ground. The sight of the cruel device and its magic turned Cassie's stomach. Cassie quickly covered her mouth with her hands, suppressing a scream of warning to Kael. Distracted by Kyah, he never saw or felt the young girl's approach.

Knowing she could not help, Cassie closed her eyes as tears poured down her cheeks. The collar snapped shut like a hunter's bear trap. She turned away and climbed higher up when she heard Kael's reaction to the collar. His cry of agony carried an essence of terror and pain unlike anything she had ever heard. It lasted a few seconds before it stopped as if silenced by the still of death. She hurried back down the tree, afraid the collar had killed him. Kael's rigid, muscle-locked body brought a sigh of relief to her lips, though she easily recognized the depth of suffering in his eyes.

Lost and confused as to how to help the man who had so selflessly saved her life and so many others in Cairnwood, Cassie forced herself to stop crying. Kael had called her a healer and a young woman. She had to act like one now and get ready to follow after him until she could help. No matter how long it took.

When the women in white left the camp, with Kyah dressed to match, they had a shadow following them in the trees high above.

Chapter Thirty-Two

"We have tried repeatedly to bring this DeathWizard, Jasala Vyshaan, to justice. Two of Talohna's four ArchWizards joined the raid on her new stronghold. We had her trapped alone. After a short fight, we finally managed to overpower her and lock her into the magical bindings given to us by Warden Karr from the EdgeCliff Gulag. The gulag's guard-wizards use the devices to secure their prisoners. One has never broken.

"But a DeathWizard is not a normal wizard. Once bound, Jasala changed over the course of only minutes. Black smoke wept from her eyes but drifted upwards. Her voice grew deeper and garbled, almost as if it had several other individual voices mixed in. The security devices cuffed to her wrists shattered as if they were made from straw when she flexed her wrists. Her physical strength was incredible. Dark magic unlike anything I have ever seen obeyed her commands, even though she spoke no words. I did what I could to boost the power of both of my ArchWizards' magics. I even dropped my own shield to give them even more power, but nothing harmed the creature we had woken. Nothing helped. She turned her magic my way, and I can remember nothing after that. Next time, I recommend we take no chances and send every resource we can muster."

Master Wizard Sebastian Locke's deposition statement
Provided to the Cethosian Wizards' Tribunal investigating
the deaths of two ArchWizards killed by Jasala Vyshaan
5001 ARE

CAULDRON'S TEETH MOUNTAIN RANGE THE WEDGE

The Sartaq had been waiting at the break in the Cauldron's Teeth Mountains for two days when a Reaver flag appeared on the ocean's horizon. A couple hours later, the Twilight Reave was anchored in the deep water offshore, and a rowboat brought several people to dry land during low tide. Vexa had two dozen blow-dart warriors hidden throughout the area in case the meeting went badly. As the rowboat crunched into the sandy beach, Dominique Havarrow and Cormack WhiteFrost escorted Sythrnax to where Vexa waited with her priestesses. Corleya and Alia, as well as Lyrocri and Damien, waited behind then. All four sat down and rested, still tired from carrying the camp's supplies on the way down the mountain and by taking care of the slave duties for the past two days that twice their number normally did.

Lycori watched with intense interest. Groaning when she saw Sythrnax, she quickly pulled her hood up and put her head down.

"What is it?" Corleya asked.

"That creature, the masked one..."

"Yes?"

"Do not attract its attention, no matter what you do. Keep your heads down and be quiet..."

"Hey, Havarrow!" Damien yelled. "Dominique! Over here. Fuck man, get me out of this gods-damned jungle." Lycori turned, her eye instantly catching Sythrnax. She ducked away before he could see her. "No, Damien. Shit," she hissed. She lunged for him, but missed. Corleya and Alia also missed as Damien side-stepped both and slowly walked towards the meeting with his hands up.

"Damien Krass? Tyr's bloody blade, what are you doing here?" Dominique shouted.

"The Bastard's Curse went down on the Storms' volatile waters two years ago. Been stuck with these animals ever since..."

"Silence," Vexa barked. "Return to the others or be darted. We have the Goddess' work to complete."

"That's all right, Vexa," Sythrnax said, softly, still staring at Lycori. "You have already enlightened my day. Let's finish here, so we can discuss the sale of a few of your slaves."

"Your relic," Vexa said, holding out the strange shaped key the vile goddess gave her. "My slaves are not for sale. These least of all."

Sythrnax gently took the relic from her hand. "But my dear, I think they are. The pirate, the two young women, and that enchanting creature under the hood. Anything you want, Vexa. Anything."

"Anything?"

"Of course."

"The black stone inside your glove," Vexa said, smiling. The mask covering Sythrnax's face twitched as if he were furious, but it quickly disappeared.

"Fair enough, Miss Vexa of the Sartaq. Tell the vile goddess I expect her to replace my stone if she's going to be telling mortals about it. We have a deal then? The stone for those four slaves?"

Vexa nodded, bowing low. "A deal is struck."

"Bring these four with us," Sythrnax said. "Your man may remain free, Havarrow, but keep the other three in chains." Passing Corleya and Alia, he arrived at Lycori. Lifting her chin, he slowly pulled back her hood. "Well, that is very interesting." He crouched, staring her in the face. "Nice to see you alive, Lycori Alatar. So very nice. I look forward to your explanation as to how you still live and how my DeathWizard escaped a Dwarven gulag designed to hold magic users. All while surrounded by Dead Sisters, Orotaq warriors, and a mountain swarming with Mahala."

Remembering what Kael had told her so many months ago, she looked up and blew Sythrnax a kiss. His mask twitched with irritation, making her smile. "I have no idea how Kael escaped. Your hags left me for dead, covered in rotting corpses at the bottom of a pit, remember? I'm not as easy to kill as you think, Sythrnax. Go back and follow the trail of rotting Mahala. And Kael? He's clearly a lot stronger than you think he is. I sincerely hope I'm there the day he tracks you down."

Sythrnax's fist smacked into her mouth. "I merely underestimated you both, my dear," he said. "It won't happen twice. Captain Havarrow?"

"Yeah?"

"You ever transport vampyrs or werwolves in that ship of yours?"

"At times. We do work for bounty hunters on occasion."

"Good," Sythrnax said. He turned towards the pirate but pointed at Lycori. "Make sure this one is chained and collared with silver. Hands, feet, and neck. Lengths of silver chain between her feet, to her hands, between her hands, and to her neck. If you please. You see, Miss Lycori, I rarely make mistakes, and never twice."

DWARVEN MOUNTAIN RANGE

It was an hour or so before dark when Kyah led the group off the trail and into the trees. Two hundred yards in, at a cleared cliff edge, a dozen Dead Sisters had already made camp. Exhausted from desperately trying to maintain his focus while riding all day and still keep the collar's pain at bay, Kael was having a hard time counting how many more Dead Sisters began arriving in the camp within thirty minutes of their own arrival. Positive there were at least five ternions including Kyah's, it took Kael minutes to realize the number was much higher than fifteen. Every ternion of three had at least one novice or apprentice, some had two, which meant he was outnumbered by better than twenty to one. It did not include how many travelled with the Cardessa whenever she showed up in the clearing. He suspected she wouldn't be far behind.

Once in the camp, Kyah's second and third, Kyrce and Avara, dragged Kael from his horse, tied his hands behind his back, and escorted him to the tent positioned at the cliff's edge. Once inside, he was forced to kneel in front of the tent's centre pole. Avara turned and left right away, but Kyrce bent down and knelt beside him.

"Sit," she snapped, pushing his forehead hard enough for him to land on his butt with his back against the pole. She smiled, whispering. "*Kykr nadr.*"

Kael stared in panic as the heavy braided rope in Kyrce's hands stirred to life. Like an unleashed serpent, it curled around her arm, rising off her wrist like a cobra preparing to strike. It swayed back and forth as the young witch smiled wider, her shiny white teeth showing her true age; the corruption of demonic magic had yet to set in and twist her features. Then as if quickly becoming bored, the smile dropped away, replaced by a sneer.

"*Oruggr,*" she hissed, and the rope struck. Too fast to follow, Kael winced, expecting a magical bite, but felt nothing until the rope slid around his already-bound wrists and yanked them tight to the tent-pole. Pulling a hooked dagger from her waist, Kyrce stood and stepped behind his back. Kael felt his initial bonds loosen and pull free seconds before the witch murmured the spell a second time. Kael gasped as the ropes tightened further. He felt them continue to move, assuming they were wrapping around the centre-pole.

She barked again, keeping the spell active. "*Oruggr.*" The single word commanded the ropes to tighten further, and Kael grunted from the pain.

Kael opened his eyes to find Kyrce nose to nose with him. "My sister loves you, DeathWizard. Our mother died so Kyah could have the chance to be the one trained to help you once you got here."

In no mood to argue, he shook his head. "Yeah? Kyah told me about you. That your mother was a snack for hungry Orotaq soldiers. That your cruelty knew no limits. So, make whatever point you're trying and leave me alone."

"I know what the Cardessa has planned, little wizard. When Kyah cannot follow through, I will kill her for disobeying orders and her ternion will become mine. That is what I wanted you to know." She sneered and then elbowed him in the mouth, splitting both lips. As blood streamed down his chin and onto his chest, she stood to leave.

Kael yelled after her. "Let me know when you plan to do that. The best part of my year will be watching you two kill each other." When she turned with a puzzled look on her face, he laughed. As the look on her face turned to anger, he laughed harder. Kyrce screamed in utter annoyance. Turning back, she kicked him under the chin and stormed out. Even with the added agony, several minutes passed before Kael could stop laughing.

DWARVEN MOUNTAIN RANGE

A few hours after dark, the Dead Sisters came for Kael, dragging him out to a roaring bonfire at the centre of their camp. The Cardessa was waiting for him.

"Master Kael," she smiled, but sarcasm filled her voice. "So good to see you once more. Did you enjoy your time with our beautiful N'Ikyah? She tells me you have been able to resist her... special qualities, to some extent." She chuckled.

"Well, you know me, Ugly," he responded. "I try to disappoint when I can."

The Cardessa looked at him and he wondered if she was debating killing him on the spot. "I see you have gotten no wiser, with your brain or your big mouth. But we are not here for that. I think, this time you may even enjoy our visit, dear boy."

"Don't think just for my benefit, please. I'd hate for you strain something at your age." Kael smiled as the Cardessa's cheek began to twitch. He recognized the tell from his days imprisoned at Arkum Zul. It meant she was already losing her normally stoic cool. Having that affect on her, he waited for the retaliation, laughing as the old hag backhanded him.

"I am tired of your mouth and your insistent disregard for what you are. Mistress N'Ikyah was given to you because your kind are born very rarely, naturally. However, a DeathWizard will always produce offspring born to the Black Sun. Her job was to make sure your Legacy does not end with you. You somehow managed to resist her, with only two exceptions. Those have not produced within her a child, yet, as far as we can tell. Though we cannot detect the early stages of pregnancy. My Sisters will make sure the next thirteen nights while you travel with them to Kazzador City, you will produce a child. Fifteen seduction spells will strip your resistance and Kyah's new glamour trinket will ensure it. And if not, my new second, Voranna Talavyr, will use her seventh hell magic to strip every ounce of what you are until only the tattered shell of your soul remains. Then, the same will continue until she is with child. Afterward, you will be handed to Sythrnax for whatever he needs you for. Beyond his use, we will take you home to the DemonBone Swamps where you will either become a stud horse for as many Black Sun births as we can get from you, or you will die. Do you understand? Is that thinking hard enough for you?" she growled viciously. Grabbing his chin, she squeezed hard until her dirty fingernails drew blood.

Kael closed his eyes as if to think about it for a while. The Cardessa's slap opened them. "Sorry about that. I was trying to remember everything you were babbling on about. You're worse than an Orotaq shaman, blah, blah..." A second slap rocked the other side of his face. It made him smile, his ever-tenuous hold on sanity slipped a little further and a hunger inside him stirred. The same as it had while in their captivity before. "I can't stop you, witch, so do your worst. Interesting things seem to happen when you do. Or haven't you learned that by now? You like to pretend you know what I am, just like Sythrnax does. But in reality, you have no more knowledge of what is inside me than I do. The last time you monsters pushed too hard, Arabella's entire group died, or at least they should have," he said, staring at Ashea as she stood at Kyrce's side. "How about we try again, see if a real monster shows up this time, shall we?" Kael laughed. Unable to help himself, and completely out of control, his laughter climbed to a cackle of hysterics, but he didn't care.

"We shall indeed see. You should know by now that Dead Sisters do not fear death of any kind. Not even one you can provide." Kael's laughter stopped short, like a switch clicking somewhere his brain.

He looked down at her and lowered his voice. "You might want to be careful, Ugly. I've learned a few new tricks since last time. There are some things far worse than death."

"I am well aware. But if you could ever overpower the effects of this new Gyhurra collar around your neck," she said tapping the metal collar with a hooked yellow fingernail, "any demon you pull into this world would simply answer to us. It is where our magic comes from, remember? Being blessed with demonic magic does have a few benefits. You forget too easily, boy. N'Ikyah?"

"Yes, Cardessa?" she said, stepping forward.

"Take him to the tent. It has been prepared. If you need help, it is here. My novices and I will return to the Bone. You have your orders." Kyah didn't move, so Kael stood and watched as the Cardessa raised her voice and addressed the entire coven. "No one is allowed to use demonic magic from this moment on, even in the face of death. The ArchWizard can't be more than a couple of days behind you. Should he overtake you, your cover story won't hold up if there are markers of the Lower Brethren all over this clearing and the essence of demonic magic on your bodies. You will all answer to Voranna; her ternion has the lead once I am gone. Understand?" Getting no objections, she added, "Do not fail."

Voranna stepped forward. "We won't, Mistress."

Kyah nodded and bowed, followed by the remaining Sisters. Several Sisters helped the Cardessa into the small carriage at the edge of the clearing. Three of the young girls joined her inside and the carriage left. Kael couldn't make out who or what the driver was. The hunched figure, dressed in a hooded, heavy black woollen robe never moved the entire time Kael had been questioned.

Voranna's voice grabbed his attention. "Kyah, take as many Sisters you need and get yourself cleaned up. Kyrce, return Kael to his tent, and then begin your preparations for the ritual we discussed. Make sure every Sister understands that no matter what happens over the next few weeks, no demonic magic is to be used, as per the Cardessa's orders. I don't care if a giant stumbles into this camp. Modern magic only. Anyone who violates the Cardessa's orders will be executed as a traitor."

"Yes, Ma'am," Kyah replied and turned away from Kael as several of the younger witches joined her, giggling and laughing. It made his stomach turn.

Taking Kael by the arm, Kyrce dragged him back to the tent. Pushing him inside, she tied his hands behind his back. Lighting several free-standing candle sconces, she smiled as he looked around, his eyes settling on the tent's new addition.

"I almost wish it were me joining you shortly," she said, pointing her chin towards the collection of fuzzy blankets laid out on a large soft sleeping mat. Surrounded by dozens of velvet pillows of varying sizes, along with an array of fruits and bottles of wine, Kael couldn't help but think of some crazy sultan's harem room from old movies back home. The tent was nice and warm, even cozy and inviting. His travel pack sat to the side. It and the soft bed would have been the best sight he had seen in weeks, if not for the camp full of crazy witches that went along with it.

"You won't be missing much," he said.

"I beg to differ. You underestimate what my Sisters can do, my dear. You have never experienced the combined power of a real coven once they have joined their power." Her voice suddenly shifted to a calm, almost soothing tone. "Six Sisters will shred your resistance, twelve will make it vanish completely, but eighteen or twenty-four will destroy all of what makes you… well, you." She laughed and stepped out of the tent, leaving him alone. Utterly exhausted, Kael lay down in the bed and quickly fell asleep, even with the painful collar and his hands tied behind his back.

Kyah entered quietly, but still he woke with a start, his nerves vibrating. He sat up, facing her, even though her mere presence made him uncomfortable. Looking up, he noticed she had changed her clothing. The long white dress was gone, replaced by a mid-calf length, tight, sheer black dress that looked more like a painted-on night dress. He scoffed. The dress had obviously been designed to entice. Her hair was shiny and clean, curled and pulled up at the sides. A light coating of make-up had been applied to her face and her eyes darkened with liner. For a split second, he realized the shy, plain-looking young woman he first saw in the prison cell below Arkum Zul was breathtakingly beautiful... or she would have been on any other night.

Now, just looking at her made him sick. The underlying hatred he had for these women burned so much hotter because of her betrayal. For some reason, she carried both his spelled reaper-blades, one in each hand. Slowly and calmly, she sat down in his lap, her face inches from his own. His blades slid a full foot into the earth as she pushed down on the handles and left them standing on their own as she slid her right arm around his neck and let it rest on his shoulders.

"All these years, my love, we Sisters have feared what these weapons would do should they come to someone like you," she whispered. The fingertips of her left hand delicately traced the razor sharp blade of the reaper-blade stuck in the dirt at her left side. A thin trail of blood smeared the metal as it gently separated the flesh of her fingers. In his peripheral vision, Kael watched in amazement as the blade absorbed her blood like a thirsty being.

"Mmnn," she moaned, putting her fingers to her mouth and sucking the blood from the fresh wounds. Her tongue slid along the gash, sealing it as she whispered the healing spell he knew so well. She failed to see the blood disappear inside the Vai'Karth's blade, and he quickly smothered a smile as the strange lettering flared with life.

"So sharp and so, so deadly, but nothing more. They are heavily enchanted, aren't they? Your powers are so much stronger when they are in your hands. You never even realized how much faster, how much better you were. Your fighting instincts are sharper than a Northman's, and your physical strength surpassed that of the fabled DemonKind. Do you feel their loss now? You must. You're much weaker without them."

Kael understood what she meant, her words were true. Without the Vai'Karth in his hands or on his back, he felt like part of him was missing. He shook his head. All this time, she had been studying him, evaluating what he was capable of. Never once had he suspected what she was. The reality of it weighed heavily on his mind. Try as he might, adapting to this new world was something he struggled with. There was no simple, straight-forward good or evil in Talohna. Trust was something that got you killed, or worse. He was at a loss to understand it.

"Why?" he asked. "Why the fake accent and poor grammar? The stories, the lies I should say. All of it, how could you?"

Wiggling down onto his lap as if for more comfort, Kyah cocked her head. "You were born wrong, Kael. The things the Dead Sisters do and the goals we have should be yours, yet you do not see that? Why?"

"You're asking the wrong person, you know that."

"I know. I think it is because Giddeon sent you across that damned bridge to stop you from becoming what you were meant to be. Your morality fights with your urge to kill and it's winning. The god-damned fool is too stupid to realize he actually succeeded in what he was trying to do, and so he tries to kill you. We tried to turn you into what you should be, and I believe that was the wrong thing to do, but I don't lead this coven. I believe we should have told you the truth and let the actions of Giddeon and his kind show you that we are who you belong with. But I had to follow orders, and I think your love for your wife has kept a small part of your heart pure enough to withstand our influence. Perhaps enough to withstand even your own magic's dark influence. That is my loss, Kael, because I *do* love you. We were meant to be together. To rule Talohna together."

Kael scoffed again, even though her twisted words did seem sincere. "You and your Sisters are what people in my world call psychopaths, Kyah. It is impossible for you to feel real love. You are right about one thing though, Ember has never left my mind. I will take everything she meant to me to my grave when your Cowardessa works up the nerve to finally kill me."

She laughed lightly, lifting her head back a bit. "Ah, Kael. This is a world where magic is the source of all things. Just because you call us psychotic does not mean I cannot love you. Anything is possible here. Talohna is not Earth, and you should have figured that out by now. It sounds like you have given up, lover, so let me ask you something."

"Go ahead. I'd rather talk than the alternative," he said, flashing her a quick smile.

"Don't be mean. We both know that's not true, besides, it's not really you." Returning his smirk, she continued. "Now. When Arabella dragged your sorry ass back home to us, did you and Ember leave any children back home? Any little Kaels or Kaelettes running around on Earth?"

"We didn't have any kids. You know that too, Kyah."

"You asked me how I could do this, remember?" He nodded but offered nothing further. "You need to remember who I am. The girl you have been with for months is a Dead Sister. You seem to forget that. It was my responsibility to bring you back into our family, your family."

"I won't forget again, I promise, and when your real sister plays for your spot at the top of your ternion, I hope I'm around to see it." He grinned, hoping the only piece of knowledge he had might bother her. He was wrong.

"Ah, poor Kael. You are hurt by what I did to you." She pouted, gently bumping his nose with hers.

With little else he could do, he chose to try one more time. "This isn't you Kyah, no one can act that well. You enjoyed being with me and I saw the look you got from helping people. Like when you healed Cornelius's wife. Help me Kyah. You're better than this, I've seen it. Let's leave this place, just the two of us." he pleaded.

"You know, you might be right," she whispered, as she leaned in closer, her nose nearly touching his again. "If only you loved me and not some dead, red-headed whore." She smiled, her eyes full of a wicked hatred he'd never seen there before. It was enough for his smouldering temper to flare to life. The Gyhhura responded in kind, forcing Kael to bite his lip in a desperate attempt to control the increased suffering. She growled lightly and grabbed the side of his lower lip with her teeth and pulled just enough to draw blood.

"I'm tired of taking second place to a dead woman. So right now, my sister Kyrce, with some help from Voranna, are working a very special ritual for us. Many of my Sisters are necromancers, you see. When the ritual is complete, the soul of your beloved Ember is going to be yanked from whatever level of Paradise the afterlife has given her and she will be dragged back here..." Having heard enough, Kael twisted his body before she could finish speaking, trying to throw her off even as the collar's new abilities scorched every nerve-ending in his body. Overwhelmed by pain, he stopped.

"Do not touch her!" he growled, torn by emotional and physical agony.

"Oh, I'm not done telling you about our plans. Kyrce is going to drag her chained spirit into this world, into this very tent so that your precious Ember can watch you make love to me unlike you ever did to her. My other Sister's seduction spells will make sure of it. And when I see her soul shatter at the hurt, Kyrce will send her to the deepest, darkest pit of the ninth hell where she will be ravaged day and night by the most vile demons our lord Garz'x can find. The only rest she will have will come at night as she watches us, linked to both of our minds so she can feel your love for me." She laughed as Kael tried to fight the power of the collar. "And you," she mocked, "will only be able to think about how you can please me." She smiled, and pressed her lips to Kael's mouth as his world finished crashing down around him, after so many months of trying to hold it up.

Despair and torment twisted inside him, eating at his soul and waking a dark, primitive desire for revenge. Born of pure seething hatred, it grew rapidly from deep inside his chest. Black vines and barbed thorns burst to life across his flesh as if the Gyhurra collar did not exist. Ripping through his skin, black vines tore down his legs, into his head and underneath his hair moving faster than ever before. Concussive waves of power from the Gyhhura scoured Kael's nerves with abrasive torture, but still the fury inside him escalated, climbing rapidly to staggering heights. A blackness so dark that it seemed to draw the light from the interior of the tent, narrowed the sides of his vision.

Kael could see Kyah's troubled face through the black mist that seemed to hover over his eyes, and he knew that something horrifically obscene had started. Faster than he could keep track of, his senses heightened and very familiar, yet far off voices flooded his ears. Darkness closed across his vision.

In seconds, a crazed frenzy to slaughter and destroy was born, fuelled by an intense state of sadistic madness that screamed through Kael's blood and soul. Ropes snapped and a hand shot out, grasping one of the Vai'Karth. The spelled magic protecting them evaporated as if never there. What had been Kael Symes only seconds before vanished into the ether of mystery surrounding the true power of all DeathWizards. Only the smallest awareness remained.

Something laughed at Kyah to run, in a voice that was no longer his own. The warning was the last act under his conscious control. As he felt his remaining bonds snap, he reached for the second Vai'Karth, its protective spells vanishing as easily as the first. A pure darkness from the deepest bowels of an abyss far darker than Talohna's Nine Hells flashed across Kael's eyes, swallowing him whole and giving rise to a whole new creature.

A being created solely to destroy anything in its path.

It had been easy for Cassie to follow the women in white after they had taken Kael. She stayed behind them, out of sight, all day as Kyah lead them to the north. As it neared dark, they turned from the road and entered the forest. She followed until they came to a clearing at the edge of a steep cliff. Just into the incline of the Dwarven Mountains, there were still a lot of trees for her to use and to hide in. It was a concern though, in a couple days the trees would be much more scarce. Should the women continue north with Kael, it would be harder for her to follow.

Cassie easily located a tree with heavy leaf cover from where she could see the entire camp. It also gave her a good angle on the front of Kael's tent. Knowing she could do nothing to help him yet, she got comfortable in her tree and ate some of the jerky she had brought with her. A few pieces of fresh fruit she had found earlier followed.

Cassie watched closely as the Sisters dragged Kael from the tent and forced him to stand before an old women who should have died from old age hundreds of years ago.

Every horrifying word the old woman said to Kael reached her ears, sending a shiver down her spine all the way to her toes.

After hearing Kael's fate, she watched with tear-filled eyes and trembling lips as he was taken back to the tent by the cliff. An hour passed as Cassie crouched in the tree debating what to do and watching the moon begin to rise behind the towering mountains to the east. Before the sun set, one of the witches began drawing complicated symbols in the dirt. Unable to recognize the designs, she could only guess it was some kind of complex magic spell.

After completing the strange characters, the witch created a five pointed star by pouring blood from the star's top point, to the bottom left point, to the upper right, then to the upper left, down to the bottom right and finally back to the top. She never once stopped the process; the star was drawn to completion by the constant, unimpeded pouring of the blood. The star and symbols burned bright red upon the completion of the pentagram, and the witch stepped into the middle, casting bones and other pieces of flesh, all of which Cassie did not want to identify.

Hours after the witch began her ritual, Cassie noticed Kyah enter the tent where Kael was being held. Her hiding spot high in the tree prevented her from hearing what was going on inside, but she knew it was not going to be good. It didn't take long before she heard Kael's muffled, but rage-filled voice yell.

"Do not touch her!"

Kyah's laughter followed, and Cassie heard nothing but empty silence for several moments. The quiet was broken by a guttural laugh and three words.

"You should run!"

Cassie was sure she heard Kael's voice mixed in the words somewhere, along with something terrifyingly inhuman. She quickly realized something awful was happening as the other witches ran to the tent.

She hung around long enough to see Kael walk from the tent with both of his weapons, one in his right hand and the other hanging in its sheathe under his backpack. The fingers of his left hand were spread wide and slightly curled, pulsating with black power. Emanating from his palm, the power had somehow wrapped itself around Kyah's throat. She struggled feebly, already weak from oxygen loss, as she hung suspended at the end of his magic, two feet away from his hand and four feet off the ground. Cassie cocked her head, confused as Kael plunged his blade into Kyah's side under her ribs. With a sickening twist, he pulled the Vai'Karth free and tossed her to the dirt. The Gyhurra collar around his neck was nowhere to be seen.

In need of a better position if she were to help him, Cassie moved from her tree as all hell broke loose below her.

Chapter Thirty-Three

"The true measure of a person's soul can only be seen when they experience true adversity. Those who fight for loved ones and refuse to surrender to the easy or corrupt path will be the ones who find true happiness."

Dyrannai Elvehn Proverb, Date Unknown

DWARVEN MOUNTAINS

Splashes of red, white, and green seared Kael's eyes, clouding his vision with imprints of horrific images. Like the flash of a camera, they were there one moment and gone the next. Screams of horror rang in his ears. Unlike the nightmare images, the agonizing shrieks came in waves, cresting and receding, adding to the confusion that swamped his mind. The hammering of his heart let him know he was alive, but he struggled to regain consciousness. The coppery tang of blood filled his mouth, mixing with the gritty, bitter taste of dirt and grass. Pain scoured every part of his body. Voices joined the ringing screams and he knew someone was yelling at him, but he couldn't make out what. Darkness slowly began to push back the flashes of vivid colour, and the voice evolved into that of a young girl's. Blinking rapidly, he tried to regain control of his dazed mind. It didn't work, so he shook his head, falling face first into the dirt and leaves of the forest floor.

"Kael!" the young girl cried, desperately, as he felt her tug at his arm. "Please, you have to help me. I'm not strong enough to carry you," she pleaded.

The disorientation cleared and he recognized the voice. "Cassie? What... What are you doing here?" More confusion drifted into his mind as he remembered leaving the girl days to the south. Panic settled in. "Cassie. You have to run. Kyah's a Dead Sister. Run, Cassie, please." He groaned, knowing Kyah and her Sisters would be close behind.

"Please. Get up," she said, pulling on his arm a second time. "I got you away from that nightmare. I won't leave you now. Come on. Get up. Please," she begged, as he tried to stand. Once back on his feet, Cassie slid under his arm and took as much of his weight as she could, forcing him to keep walking.

"You have to leave, Cassie. The Dead Sisters will kill you if they catch you helping me. Go."

"It's all right. They're not chasing us. I promise. Please keep walking."

"Of... Of course they'll be after us. W-Why wouldn't they?" Turning to look back over his shoulder, Kael tripped on his own feet and crashed to the leaf mould, dragging Cassie with him.

"Kael," she sobbed. She quickly knelt in front of him and took his face in her hands. "You don't remember do you? Gods, please help me..." She trailed off. Kael could see memories of what she witnessed ghost across her eyes, but he hurt everywhere and couldn't offer her support even though he wanted to. His head pounded worse that anything he had ever felt, and he had no memory of how he got out into the forest with her. Staring at her, half dazed, he wiped the tears from her cheeks as she gathered the strength to tell him what happened.

She took a deep breath, as if steeling herself. "They won't follow us... Because they're dead. All of them... You... You killed every single person... Even the little girls..." she stuttered. Putting her hand to her mouth, she cried, choking on the horrific recollection.

"Kyah?" he asked.

"I don't know if she got away or not. You stabbed her..."

"I... I don't remember..." Kael tried to explain.

"I know. I know you don't. It... It wasn't you," she cried, as tears dripped from the tip of her nose and chin. "But we have to go. We need to find you help. I healed what I could, but the rest of your wounds are too bad. I don't know how to fix them. They hit you over and over with magic but you wouldn't fall. They cut and stabbed you with knives. The deep wounds on your back and sides are bleeding so badly. I crushed some turrin moss into a paste from the creek behind us and pushed it into some of the deeper holes, it's slowing the blood, but... We have to find help. I don't know what else to do. I'm scared. I've never been so scared."

"Okay... All right," he said, pulling her close as she continued to cry, mumbling into his chest. "Shhh...it's all right, we'll find help." He groaned, the agonizing pain in his head and body continuing unabated. Kael tried to remember what had happened back at the camp, but it only made his head hurt more. Just as terrified as Cassie about what had happened, he was at a loss for where they would ever find help in the desolate Dwarven Mountain Range.

With no other choice, Cassie helped Kael stand and the two stumbled through the forest, moving as quickly as they could. An hour passed, and then two, without any sign of another person. Kael was getting weaker and weaker as his strength drained away through blood loss and whatever damage had been done by the Dead Sister's magic. With still over an hour until the false dawn, Kael fell for what seemed like the hundredth time. Cassie helped him roll over and lean against the stump of an old tree. She had been carrying all the supplies she managed to grab from the Dead Sister's campsite along with his backpack that she grabbed after a Dead Sister's magic had severed its straps.

Kael could see the exhaustion all over her face. Carrying only his cloak and both of his Vai'Karth, he was beyond exhausted himself. Grabbing a water skin from her back, Cassie tried to get him to drink. The water splashed against the back of his throat, gagging him. He coughed, spraying most of it back in her face.

"Sorry," he panted, "things aren't working right."

"It's all right. Here try again, you need water. You haven't had any since I dragged you out of there. Again," she insisted. Nodding, he swallowed a small mouthful before coughing and choking on the rest. The look of fear on her face almost broke his heart and more regret settled onto his soul. He knew she felt overwhelmed as a couple of tears ran from the corner of her eyes.

"I'm really scared," she whispered, shaking. "I don't know what to do for you. I can't make you better, I tried. My magic won't heal you, and you're getting worse.

Kael suppressed the urge to cough and tried to smile. "It's all right. It's just inexperience, Cassie. Even Kyah would've had trouble healing these wounds..."

"What do I do?" she asked, breathing deep and wiping the tears from her cheeks.

"You need to listen to me, okay?" he asked, still trying to catch his breath. She nodded, but said nothing, listening instead. "Leave me here and go find help. All right?"

"If I leave you, then I can't defend you if something comes. There are things up here. Scary things. You're burnt and bleeding, that's like ringing the dinner bell." She glanced over her shoulder as if expecting one of those things to come storming out of the darkness. Kael grabbed her hand and stopped her.

"If you don't leave to find help, I'll die anyway. Please, just go. You can move faster and cover more ground without me and you can use the quiet to try to sense someone who might help. Go, now."

"All right, but I'll be back for you. I promise. Goodbye," she whispered softly, and kissed his cheek. He watched as she scampered up the tree across from where he sat. Into its higher branches in only seconds, she was off and running from tree limb to tree limb twenty feet above the ground. As she disappeared into the dark, Kael shook his head, wondering if he had begun to hallucinate. Trying to calm his aching body, he laid back and closed his eyes in hope that Cassie would be back before his body gave out.

In less than a minute, he was out cold.

Unaware of how much time had passed, Kael woke to find the forest floor passing by. He was being dragged along by Cassie on one side and an older woman on the other. "Cassie?" he croaked. "Wh-What's..."

"It's all right. Save your strength. We are almost back to Aravae's camp. She's Elvehn, and she thinks she might be able to heal you. Save your strength," she ordered as again his consciousness faded.

"Come on, young one. He's in far worse trouble than I had hoped," Aravae Valyndir said, as they carried Kael through the forested lower range of the Dwarven Mountains.

"Hurry, little one," Aravae said. "We're running out of time."

"I will, mistress," Cassie answered. Pushing herself harder, their pace picked up as Kael's feet dragged in the dirt behind them. The drag marks quickly disappeared as snakelike green vines following the three erased any tracks they made. Aravae's Elvehn nature magic made sure they would not be found because of Cassie's honesty in telling her what happened. The Elvehn mother would never turn away the injured, but because the young girl had mentioned witches, covering the direction in which they were going was a priority.

Another half hour passed by the time they arrived at Aravae's camp. They laid Kael down on her bedroll on his side and she asked Cassie to get her some water. Cassie handed Aravae a water skin and knelt down at Kael's side, opposite the Elvehn woman.

"All right young one, tell me what happened in more detail this time. Remove his cloak and shirt while you talk." Knowing better than to explain exactly what she had seen, Cassie gave a shorter version, not all of it true.

"We are from Cairnwood, for the most part, mistress. We were forced to abandon the village because of an Orotaq raid. We were all afraid they would come back, so we fled the village, but he was caught by witches and they brought him north. He saved my life the night of the attack at home, so I followed them from up in the trees, like I was doing when you found me. I was hoping to help him, and when the chance came, I managed to sneak him out of their camp, but he was already badly hurt, and then we had to fight off a small group that caught up to us," she gasped, taking a deep breath. Having thought about what to say the whole way back, she hoped Aravae would believe her.

Aravae stared at her without suspicion. "Were they mountain witches?" she asked, as she examined the wounds on Kael's back and side.

"I don't know, but they were wearing long white dresses with hoods, if that helps," she replied.

"Very well, little one. The mountain girls usually dress in white, but I see no marks of the Higher Brethren," Aravae explained.

Confused, Cassie asked, "What are Higher Brethren, mistress?"

"Oh, I'm sorry, sweetheart. I assumed because of your gift you would know."

"I only found out two days ago that I could use magic."

Aravae looked at her intently. "That's amazing. I have never seen anyone heal even a scratch after only two days of being aware of their gift. Never, in the two hundred years that I have practised magic, have I even heard of such a thing. You are very blessed." During the praise, she never stopped her examination of Kael.

"Thank you, mistress." Cassie smiled and helped roll Kael over more so the Elvehn woman could take a closer look at the wounds on his back.

"Well, little one, here is your first lesson. At least an Elvehn lesson anyway. Every type of magic leaves a mark behind, if you know what to look for. And we Elvehn do. Few humans ever manage this. Mountain witches gain their power from the Higher Brethren, from angels. The planes of the underworld are all guarded by a race of being called the Brethren. The planes of Paradise are guarded by the Higher Brethren, angels, and the planes of Perdition by the Lower Brethren, or demons," she explained.

Cassie shivered as goosebumps crawled up the flesh of her arms. Images of earlier in the evening haunted her. She was well aware exactly what kind of demons walked the planes of Hell; she had seen Kael call forth several of them before turning them loose on the Dead Sisters.

"I see, mistress," she answered quietly.

Aravae gently touched Cassie's cheek. "I know, sweetheart. The world of magic can be very scary when you first discover it, but you must learn all you can in order to protect yourself and others. It is why the gods granted us the gift of magic and why the Ancients helped us to learn to use it properly, you understand?" Cassie nodded, not knowing what else to say.

"You are very brave. Your friend would have died out there without you. Now I want you to listen closely so you understand, all right?" Again, Cassie nodded, but said nothing. "As I told you before, most witches are granted their powers from the Brethren, but Kael has no signs of this magic on him anywhere, and I can sense no vile magic in him. His wounds are from normal magic and mortal weapons. We can heal him together. Will you help me, little one?"

"Yes, mistress," Cassie nodded.

Cassie and Aravae worked hard over the next hour as they fought to keep Kael alive. Aravae used her Elvehn magic to show Cassie how to heal residual magic harming a living body, and then the two healed the cuts and stab wounds he was suffering from. Two hours after dawn, they were done, and Cassie curled up beside Kael and fell asleep as Aravae watched over them both. Nightmares filled with hell-spawned demons chased Cassie through her dreams. It made for a restless sleep.

Kael woke an hour after mid-day. Confused and still disoriented, he was obviously surprised to be alive.

"Easy, young man," Aravae said, kneeling to check him. "We have done all we can for now, but you are far from healed."

Kael laid back and breathed slowly until the dizziness passed. "Thank you for your help," he whispered, noticing that Cassie was curled up against him sleeping.

"You are most welcome. My name is Aravae Valyndir. Your little companion found me not long after she left you. We brought you back here."

"Thank you, Aravae. My name is Kael." Aravae smiled, as if far away memories were flooding back to her.

"My son's name was Kael. It is a strong Elvehn name, and it is good to see others still believe so as well."

"*Was*? What happened?" Her look said he was being too forward. "I apologize. I certainly don't mean to pry."

"He has been gone for many years. He was just a baby. I... I am sorry, but it is hard to talk about."

"I understand. You don't need to apologize. I'm sorry I upset you. May I ask how you came to be here? It was lucky for me that you were," Kael said.

"The Elvehn live for many centuries, as I am sure you are aware. When a parent loses a child, and has no more offspring, we often spend many years in Commune. I believe

Humans call something similar a sabbatical or a retreat. It is a time of grieving while being alone to deal with your thoughts and feelings. When I lost my son, I waited for a couple years before I decided to spend some time with nature. I had an adopted daughter who was only twelve when my son... died. She needed me, so I stayed until she turned sixteen. Then I left for my Commune, to try to silence the screaming pain my soul had for my son. I have been out here in this forest for two years. Before that, I have been to many forests and even spent some time on the Dragon Isles in the enchanted Forest of Whispers. It is customary to Commune for eighteen years, one year of mourning for every year my son would have been a child. My soul will mend someday, and when it does, I will return to civilization," she explained.

"That's amazing. Your son lost as much as you did. Your devotion is incredible. My wife and I have been gone from our home for almost six months, I doubt either of our parents have even noticed we are gone."

"Where is your wife, Kael? She was not with you?" she asked. Not wanting to go into detail because the last thing Kael needed was to be hunted by the Elvehn, he told Aravae only the bare minimum.

"She passed away several months ago, shortly after we were taken from our home. We grew up together as children. She is all I ever knew. I will miss her until the day I die and rejoin her," Kael said solemnly.

"I am sorry for your loss. This world we live in can be a terrible place. I am also sorry that you are not closer to your parents. It is sad when things like that happen among family."

"It is, but we move on I guess, don't we?" She nodded, but did not speak because Cassie woke, and seeing that Kael looked a bit better, she smiled.

"Kael! You're all right," she shouted, hugging him tight.

He groaned from the tight hug, but still managed to smile. "I feel much better, thanks to you, I'm told."

"I'm so happy," she said still hugging him. "I was so scared when I left you. I thought I would never see you again." She laughed as tears rolled down her cheeks.

"Thank you," he said as he held her. "But you shouldn't have come after me..."

"I would never have left you with those witches, I had to try."

"I know, and you did good getting me out of there," he praised.

"She did very well helping to heal you, as well," Aravae added as Cassie blushed under all the attention. "You best take good care of her. She is a very gifted young lady."

Kael smiled. "I knew that all along, right kiddo?" He smiled, ruffling her hair and making her giggle.

Kael spent the afternoon resting, and Cassie helped Aravae prepare some herbs that would help Kael regain his strength. After the evening meal, with a little help from Cassie, Aravae gave Kael another round of healing magic. When finished, she told him she had done all she could with magic and he thanked her yet again. Feeling much better, he informed her that they would be leaving in the morning, for her safety he tried to explain. Though he didn't tell her, Kael was worried about the threat from Giddeon and didn't want her to get caught in the middle or end up getting hurt trying to get involved.

Aravae warned him to take it easy for a few more days. Overexertion could cause a major setback to the damage her healing magic had repaired.

DWARVEN MOUNTAINS

Savis Ephemeral had spent his entire life hunting Humans, the Elvehn, and even the occasional Orotaq. His first contracted kill was at the age of nine. Killing things turned out to be incredibly easy when most people could not see you coming. His inherent ability to bend light, making himself nearly invisible, had passed down his family line from thousands of years ago. It was one of the original Elderblood powers. How many other Elderblood abilities were left in the world, Savis had no idea. Documents about Elderblood magic were extremely rare, and his power allowed him to be very good at making people dead. Little else mattered to him.

He always succeeded where other guild assassins had failed. Only Yrlissa Blackmist had been better, and he had immensely enjoyed every part of becoming better than her. He smiled to himself as he thought about how she would never be better than him again, her body likely rotting in the river, somewhere on its way to the ocean. He only wished he could have dumped her body in the river himself. Instead, he had to pay two lowlifes who had helped him dispose of bodies before. Nobody looked twice at the local gravediggers when they hauled bodies around. Even Savis could never get away with that, so as he had done before, he paid them a few coins to dump her body in the river outside of Corynth. Problem solved, and she would never be found. The beasts of the Black Cauldron Ocean would eventually devour the remains.

Savis, on the other hand, was normally very good at finding things that wanted to remain lost, but his current target was almost a ghost. Months had passed without a sighting, not so much as a single rumour, since he had began the hunt five months ago. For most of that time, Savis had been following the Cethosian ArchWizard Giddeon Zirakus, hoping he would eventually lead him to his primary prey. However, following Giddeon's group had turned out to be exceptionally challenging, because the largest of the two warriors with them seemed to know they were being followed. Every single time he had gotten close enough to try to identify the people travelling with Giddeon, the swordsman would drop back and wait. Twice, he nearly tricked Savis into revealing himself. He never did get close enough to identify them all and as the months passed, the warrior became more suspicious, and that keen sense that alerted him to danger seemed to get stronger instead of easing. Once acquiring his primary target though, Savis had no further interest in Giddeon's group anyway.

As he stared down from the tree above the Elvehn woman's camp, Savis was unsure for the first time that he could remember how he was going to fulfil his contract. For days now, he had followed Kael and the witch named Kyah while trying desperately to keep the little girl Cassie in sight once she had arrived and began following them as well. Savis loved to use the trees, a lot of assassins did, and he even preferred to travel in them, if they were close enough together and large enough to hold his weight. But the little girl was using the trees to travel in as well, and he was positive that she was more squirrel than human. She practically flew through the trees, barely touching the branches with her toes and hardly making any sound. Thankfully she made just enough noise for him to hear her when she was close. Twice she blew right past him, travelling so fast she never even felt him or heard him, and the second time, he fell from his tree almost twenty feet in order to avoid her running right into him. The soft leaf mould covering the forest floor saved him from serious injury.

Savis had never feared death and he still didn't. He just preferred to carry on with living. But the longer he watched Kael, the more he was certain that his chances of surviving an encounter with him would be slim, should he attempt the assassination.

He had watched the massacre the previous night at the witch's camp with a professional fascination that bordered on awe, something he felt for no other being alive. He had never seen so much devastating magic and raw weapon skills be used by one person. The small clearing had quickly become an intoxicating bloodbath. Wounds that would have killed lesser men had not even slowed Kael, and when the little girl dropped from the trees at his side, Savis was sure she would become his next victim. Instead, when she spoke to him, he sheathed his weapons and fell to the ground unconscious, rift portals to several of the Nine Hells closed at the same time, pulling their demons back to Hell.

The determined little girl hauled his unconscious body out of the camp, but when Savis landed on the ground to follow, hoping for a chance to fulfil the first contract, he quickly realized that Kael had unintentionally left one of the witches alive. It forced Savis to deal with her because he had been visible. It had taken him too long to kill the stubborn witch, and by the time he had, the Elvehn matron had already returned with the little girl to help Kael. He remembered now why he hated witches so much. She refused to die quickly and was persistent about trying to poison him with her vile, filthy excuse for magic.

Witches always seemed to be a serious pain in Savis's backside, because the guild always used him when they needed one dealt with. He cocked his head, deciding it was a good thing though, because at least he knew how to kill them.

But now, Kael was almost completely healed, and Savis was back to figuring out how to stay alive and finish the job. He knew that Kael would not leave until morning so he slipped down from the tree without making a sound and headed for the river a couple miles back and to the west. Using his family's inherent ability at night meant that Savis was all but completely invisible. During the day, in bright light, he could be seen, though barely. At night, though, it was an advantage that allowed him to move like a phantom. In almost a hundred years, he had never been seen at night and only twice during the day. As he bent down at the river to wash his face and refresh with a mouthful of cool water, he had no fears of being seen by anyone.

"It appears to be a fine evening, Savis. Do you not think?" When he heard his name, Savis could barely move. His first thought was that Kael had sensed him and came to find out why he had been following him, but he knew beyond a doubt that his ability kept him hidden from magical senses.

Then again, he should be completely hidden by the dark night and yet someone could still see him. He looked around trying to find the voice, while at the same time grabbing a blowgun hidden in his wrist bracer that was loaded with a dart tipped in the poison of a Gyhreni Grandscorpion. The poisoned dart would kill a Human in less than five seconds. It was the last Gyhreni dart he had, but if it saved his life, it would be well worth using.

"If I was going to harm you, Savis, it would already be done, and I would not have felt the need to speak with you before I did so. Put your weapon away. I'm paying for your current hunt, and I promise, no harm will come to you."

"Who might you be?"

"You may call me Sythrnax. I have known Merethyl for many years. She told me who you started to follow for your hunt. It's how I found you."

"How can you see me? You shouldn't be able to," Savis asked, still surprised.

Stepping forward from the shadows of the treeline and to within three feet, Sythrnax shook his head. "My eyes are very different from your own, Human. I see many things that you cannot."

Savis stared at Sythrnax, noticing that his eyes were in fact quite different. They were solid black, but only where a Human's were white, a feathery iris, bright purple in colour, glared vibrantly against the black, and enhanced the red slitted pupils that looked similar to the large jungle cats' in Salzara. He had never seen anything like them before. It gave the hooded and masked stranger a surreal appearance.

"So I see," Savis said, with no intentional pun.

Sythrnax only grunted at the implication. "I would envision that you are exerting great effort and mental expense in trying to come up with a way to accomplish your task favourably, correct?"

"If you mean complete the kill and still remain breathing afterwards, then yes, I am. Why?" As Sythrnax put his hands together in front of his chest, about six inches apart,

Savis noticed the shiny black talons that tipped each one of the man's fingers. Extending at least an inch past his fingertips and curved inward, the nails looked sharp enough and strong enough to score polished granite. This job was getting extremely strange, even for him.

A few whispered words from Sythrnax caused the air between the black talons to shimmer and blur, words in a language Savis had never heard before. As he watched Sythrnax closely, Savis' hand slowly moved to the matched set of daggers he wore at the back of his waist, only stopping when he realized the shimmer between Sythrnax's hands created an image of the dagger his right hand was about to grasp. The swirling magic called forth a perfect representation of the Broken Blades' magical wooden dagger.

"As I am sure you are aware, assassin, the daggers you carry and the method the Broken Blade Guild employs is a confirmed method of killing a Kai'Sar," he reminded Savis.

"I am aware, yes?" Savis asked, not quite knowing where the stranger was going. Sythrnax waved his right hand over his left and whispered a single word that again Savis did not recognize, and the image of the blade disappeared.

Sliding his arms into the wide sleeves of his robes, Sythrnax continued speaking. "Then listen closely. I will provide for you the simplest kill of your career. Kael will continue heading north to Kazzador City. I know what he is after, my words have brought him this far. The entrance to the old Dwarven city has been cleared, and inside, he will find the means to discover a room deeper in the ruins. The room contains the monolith he is looking for. You will follow and observe. The ArchWizard from Cethos is also hunting him, and you must wait to see if he will do your job for you. Is that part clear?" he asked. Savis recognized the warning; it was not a simple question. Try as he might, he couldn't piece together what was going on, and suspected that he would rather not know.

"No problem so far. If Giddeon makes the kill, then let it be done, but do you think he will? Is he even capable?

It's a little outside his expertise, is it not?" he joked nonchalantly, not really caring either way. The contract was offered to him by Merethyl so he would be paid no matter who killed the target.

Sythrnax nodded as he continued. "By this time, Kael will not be a threat to your success, but should Giddeon fail to kill the target, you must see it done. By order of King Bale. Your secondary target can be killed at any time after the first, but there can be no mistakes. Even the smallest slip will result in you and your entire guild happily begging for your deaths. Is that clear, Savis Ephemeral?"

"Crystal." He watched the strange man return to the shadows. A flash of bright white light seared Savis' vision. It took several seconds to blink the glare from his sight and as his vision returned, he realized Sythrnax was gone.

"Curse the Ancients, what did I get myself into?" Savis whispered to himself while shaking his head and kneeling by the river once more.

Cupping the cool river water in his hands, he splashed his face repeatedly, hoping it would clear the hectic, confused thoughts storming around his increasingly sore head.

Chapter Thirty-Four

"Evil always seems to work its way into wherever it desires to be. It can insinuate itself into any group and begin spreading its vile purpose with the simplest of ease. The simplest comments and calmest gestures can lead to the biggest disasters. I know this better than most ever will."

Ella Navasha, the White witch From notes found in an alley in Argela, Ellorya, Date unknown

DWARVEN MOUNTAINS

The sun descended below the treeline of the forest by the time Giddeon and Ember had agreed it was time to stop for the night. They left Cairnwood in the morning as soon as the sun had crawled from the darkness onto the horizon of the eastern sky. They rode hard all day, only slowing to walk their horses and to swallow a bite to eat. They all knew that the months they had spent trying to chase down Kael were nearing an end. They guessed themselves to be less than two days behind Kael at the start of the day. Though they were not aware of it, they had managed to gain almost a full day on Kael and Cassie while he lay in a hidden camp north of them, recovering from his injuries.

Force of habit led them to find a campsite on the eastern side of the mountain path, the opposite side as Kael and Kyah had a couple of nights earlier, but farther north. Ember and Saleece prepared the camp for supper while Max and Kasik scouted the area for dangers. Their return would determine whether they could have a fire and a warm meal. The further into the Dwarven Mountains they went, the more cautious they had to be because of the increased amount of danger.

Still pulling the wagon they were given in Dasal, Giddeon and Yrlissa headed out around their camp to gather fallen wood for the fire. In a matter of a few days, the forest would thin and wood for fires would be scarce. Max suggested filling the wagon with firewood for when there were no trees. The idea was a welcomed one, and everyone had pitched in when they could.

Max returned a full hour before Kasik and reported finding no signs of life other than plenty of animals, mostly large rabbits and numerous turkeys, which he brought back with him. Removing the string from his obsidian bow, he immediately sat down on a fallen log to clean the four large rabbits and to pluck the feathers from the fifteen-pound turkey.

Yrlissa, having already placed several loads of wood she found into the wagon, sat down across from him and helped. Kasik's return came with the same news of no danger, so Ember started the fire and put a large pot of dried vegetables and water over the flames for the rabbit stew, while Saleece set up the spit in order to rotate the bird as it cooked. They were all looking forward to the warm meal after the day's long ride.

The remainder of the evening passed, quickly, everyone getting some much needed rest. Those on watch kept the rest safe while they slept.

The new day started early as Max and Yrlissa woke the rest just before dawn. Having taken last watch together, they fed and watered all the horses, before grooming and saddling them for the ride ahead. With everyone up and moving, a quick bite of cold turkey and hard bread served to break their fasts as they left the camp, heading for the northern trail once more.

The morning passed the same as the day before; the group rode as hard as they dared to push the horses. Shortly before noon, they slowed to give their mounts yet another rest, while Giddeon, Saleece, and Kasik rode out front about a hundred feet from Ember, Yrlissa, and Max. Having tied the wagon's draft horse lead to his saddle, Max was the furthest back when all the commotion broke out.

With the possible dangers present in the mountains, Kasik had recommended that they travel in two groups with some distance between them. Because of this, Giddeon's group, over a hundred feet ahead, disappeared from sight as they turned a sharp dogleg in the mountain trail. The moment they cleared the turn and came out onto a stretch of arrow-straight path, they could see almost a mile ahead.

The trail was lined with towering, ageless white birch trees. The paper-like outer bark had peeled back from their year long winter slumber. The breathtaking view was soured by a lone figure covered in dirt, blood and gore, slowly stumbling towards them. The putrid, sickening sweet scent of death drifted on the air, making their noses twitch and their breath catch in the back of their throats.

Kasik was the first to free his tongue along with his sword. "Tyr's blood Giddeon, it looks like a deadwalker."

"*Drepa aldrnari,*" Giddeon said lightly. The force of his words ignited long dancing flames in both of his hands. A quick command word would be all he needed to release the thundering balls of explosive fire at the stumbling zombie.

"By the Ancients, Father, stop!" Saleece yelled. Heeling her horse and pulling the reins, she forced it to jump in front of him. "She's alive father, look. She's hurt, not dead!"

She pointed as the woman fell, crying out for help. Saleece slid from her horse and ran to the young woman's aid. Giddeon extinguished his magic as he and Kasik raced after her.

Saleece had seen many mortal injuries in her life and had seen the effects of powerful magic when used against flesh and bone. The young woman she gently rolled over was one of the worst she had ever seen. She should have been dead. A quick assessment revealed her injuries were far beyond what normal magic could heal.

"Kasik!" she screamed. "Get Ember here as fast as you can. Hurry! There's not much time." Kasik nodded, vaulting back up onto his mount, he galloped back down the trail. The horse's hooves threw clumps of damp earth and grass high into the air as they vanished around the bend. Still thirty feet from Ember, Max and Yrlissa, Kasik yelled, continuing to ride hard.

"Ember, come with me. Hurry, we need you." Her confused look prompted him to shout. "Now!" He dragged the horse's reins back, forcing his mount to stop. He waited a brief moment to be sure she was coming, and then heeled his horse around. It bolted ahead once more. Ember was only seconds behind as she pushed her horse to catch up, not knowing what could have possibly happened in the few minutes the others had been beyond the curve of the trail.

Ember's agile young horse allowed her to take the corner with enough speed to easily pass Kasik on his larger mount. She arrived quickly at the spot where Giddeon and Saleece were already frantically trying to save a young woman. Pulling back hard on the reins to stop her galloping horse, Ember jumped from the saddle before it stopped running, landing easily on both feet, right beside the others. She nudged Giddeon over and knelt to help the young woman dressed in a tattered and scorched, long white dress. She quickly did her best to evaluate the countless numbers of injuries.

The most dire wound was above the young woman's stomach along her ribs, where she kept her arms clamped tight to her abdomen. Ember forcefully pulled the girls hands away and gasped in horror as her intestines and some of her internal organs nearly slid out. Any lower and she would have been completely disembowelled. Ember shook her head and gagged at the atrociously-infected wound, having no idea how the poor girl could still be alive.

"Oh my God, Giddeon." Ember heaved again, putting her left wrist up to her nose, trying to block the smell of the festering, maggot-infested wound. "You and Saleece have to hold her hands down," she snapped, clenching her teeth tight. "Hurry, or we're going to lose her." Knowing she had to work fast, Ember had already begun healing the girl deep inside, muttering the words to her magic as she tried to get through the insane fog of suffering the girl was going through.

"Water, Giddeon. We need to flush the wound, I can't sense what to heal through the mass of insect larvae." Not hesitating, Giddeon and Saleece both popped the tops off their water bags and began cleaning the wound. "Yrlissa!"

"I'm here, Ember."

"I don't know where to start. The wound runs from the backside of her ribcage all the way across her ribs and down to her hip. What weapon could do this? Where do I even start to heal her?"

"Focus, Ember!" Yrlissa snapped. "I can help, but only your magic can save her. Concentrate." Taking a deep breath, Ember gently pulled the girl's eyelids up and smiled as they tried to focus on Ember's face.

"That's it, sweetie," she said, softly. "We're here to help you. Look at me... Keep looking at me. That's it, now what's your name, hon? Think, all right, and tell me your name." Ember was doing her best to help the young woman focus on staying alive, all the while continuing to poke her healing magic into the dying girl, looking for a place to start repairing the damage.

"N-N-Niky, my... my n-n-name..." The young woman stuttered and shook, agony overruling all motor function.

"Niky?" Ember asked, as the girl nodded, unable to speak. Her breaths came in short gasps between whimpers of suffering.

"Gods, Ember. Can you not put her out and heal her?" Saleece asked. "You did it for me when were caught down south or like that little girl in Dasal." Ember's cheeks twitched with indecision as she sensed a partially torn artery deep within the young woman. Sliding her hand into the open wound she found the rupture and pinched it between her fingers.

"Quiet. Please." She took another deep breath and focused on the light pulse beating between her fingers. "I need the smallest needle and thread from my bag." Yrlissa handed her the small curved needle attached to a small length of sparkling thread.

Sewing the bleeder closed, she sighed and closed her eyes.

"*Aidora amaeh shalaness,*" she whispered. Vibrant pink and pale topaz magic flowed through Niky's body. The artery healed over the thread, becoming whole. "I don't know, Saleece," Ember answered. "I've never even seen wounds like these, and I don't know how to heal them. I'm doing the best I can, but I think she needs to be awake so she can fight. Her willpower has gotten her this far." She looked over as she felt a hand touch her shoulder.

"Stay calm, Ember. You're doing well," Giddeon said. To her surprise, he gave her shoulder a quick squeeze. "Just follow your instincts and let them guide you."

"Here," Yrlissa said, urgently. "She's still bleeding inside, inches above the one you healed." Ember nodded and pushed her hand back inside Niky's body. Repeating the process with the needle and thread, she spelled the artery whole once more.

Yrlissa quickly added, "Giddeon, you need to clean deeper inside her. We can't close her up like this. She'll die from the infection.

Nodding her head in agreement, Ember swiftly refocused, pouring her concentration into trying to help the dying girl. Sealing off and healing the second bleeder had significantly slowed the blood flow coming from her abdomen. With the area clean of larvae and dirt, Saleece used her other hand to gently clean the large wound as Ember's Fae magic slowly repositioned the girl's insides to where they belonged instead of having them slither out the raw opening.

"Max, we need more of that enchanted thread from Ember's medicine pack. Just bring me the whole..." Yrlissa said, stopping short as she looked over her shoulder. Having already anticipated their need, Max handed her the roll of sparkling thread.

"Dammit," Ember cursed. "I can't get her stomach muscles to bind together. My magic's not strong enough."

"Stay calm," Yrlissa prompted. "We'll have to stitch the muscle together. Hand me the quiani extract. I'll coat the thread with it. Hopefully it'll stop any internal infections. Ready, Ember?"

"All right," she said, taking the needle and thread. She stitched the stomach muscles together and mended blood vessels and nerves as best she could. Giddeon and Saleece helped her as she pulled the girl's flesh together and stitched the open wound closed. Using magic, Ember cleaned up the few areas she could.

Finishing up, she handed the needle and thread to Yrlissa when Niky arched her back and screamed, stopped abruptly and slumped back. Ember froze, positive the young woman just dropped dead. She looked at Giddeon, who had his fingers pressed to the side of her neck.

"She's all right," he said. "She just passed out from the pain."

With a deep sigh of relief, Ember finished wiping the girl's stomach, and applied a salve made from turrin moss and quiani extract. The wound would leave a wicked looking scar that she couldn't heal. The rest of the wounds didn't pose as great a threat as the abdomen and she was exhausted.

"Can you two finish up?" she asked, glancing Giddeon's way for a second. "I'm wiped out." There were still several deep claw marks and numerous large burns, some so severe the flesh on Niky's body was blackened and cracked, even oozing a clear liquid in places.

"We'll do what we can," Giddeon said smiling. "There's some balm to help the burns and Saleece can help me regenerate some of the cracked skin with our magic. She has a chance, Ember. Well done." Father and daughter continued working on the young woman as Ember sat back. She sighed again and closed her eyes for a minute when Saleece gasped.

"Ember? You should see this..." Yrlissa muttered. Sitting back up, Ember opened her eyes. Giddeon turned Niky's head to the side, revealing a second grievous wound she had somehow missed. The bottom claw of whatever attacked her must have caught her jawbone, just below her left ear. It peeled the flesh and muscle from her jawline all the way to below her chin. Ember winced at the sick sensation in her belly caused by what the poor woman must have experienced, yet still found enough willpower to walk for days looking for help.

After doing her best with the enchanted needle and disinfected thread to mend the ghoulish wounds to Niky's face, Ember sat back again and relaxed, letting go of the strength that had helped carry her through the horrifying ordeal. Rubbing her sore eyes, she helped the others carry Niky and place her in the back of the wagon. Covering her patient with spare blankets they brought with them, Ember climbed into the wagon so she could watch the woman closely. Sitting down beside Niky, physically and emotionally exhausted, she closed her eyes, trying to rest. The others pulled the wagon and horses off the path and had a bite to eat while waiting to see if all their work had paid off and Niky would survive.

Two hours passed as they waited for some sign of life to return to Niky's broken body. Max and Kasik patrolled an ever-widening route before eventually working their way back to the wagon. All was quiet for as far out as they went. Ember never moved from the woman's side, and for the first hour, she used fresh water and clean cloths to clean the girl's beaten and severely bruised body. She never once let her mind wander from the task of watching for complications. Well into the second hour, though, she was beginning to doze off, the expenditure of magical resources and the emotional drain causing her excessive fatigue. When Niky regained consciousness an hour later, Ember was wide awake in mere seconds, already casting what magic she could that might ease the lingering pain the woman woke up with.

Sparkling waves of soft flowing magic entered the woman's body, giving her a light feeling of euphoria that easily subsided a large portion of the pain she still suffered from.

"Thank you for your help," she rasped softly. "I had thought the earth mother had called me home."

"You were lucky we found you." Ember smiled as she laid her hand on Niky's head to feel how she was doing. "You would have died otherwise." She took Ember's hand so gently and with such kindness that she wondered what kind of animal could have hurt her in such a way.

The woman placed Ember's hand on her chest, added her hands to the top. "If it was the will of the goddess, then it would have been. No one could have healed me if it was not her will. Thank you for your part in it."

"Are you a priestess?" Yrlissa asked. "We assumed so by your dress..."

"Yes. My sisters and I serve the earth goddess, Mylla."

Giddeon listened to the conversation with an intent look on his face and naturally added his opinion. "I never mean to speak ill of the gods, Sister, but the mother Mylla had no part in you surviving. That was the magic and medical skills of young Ember here," he said, as he gently squeezed her shoulder. Still obviously exhausted, and her breathing laboured, the priestess did her best to respond.

"My thanks to you all. We must discuss such matters of faith later, Master Giddeon. I am not feeling well."

Surprised, he replied, "You know who I am?"

Nodding slowly, she took his hand. "I am Vesta Niky, from the Chapel of the Mother Mylla in Corynth. I know you, but we have not met... officially..." Saying no more, she closed her eyes and ran her tongue over her dry, cracked lips. Ember offered her some water, warning her to take small sips, even so, most of it spilled, running down the priestess' neck. Ember used a small cloth to dry the woman off and then gently spread some honey balm on her lips to moisten them as best she could.

Vesta Niky's smile of gratitude warmed Ember's heart. "Thank you. You have so much more than a healer's touch," she praised.

"Thank you. If you like, you may call me Ember." Niky managed a smile, but nothing else.

"Vesta Niky?" Yrlissa asked calmly. "What were you doing out here? What happened to you?" Yrlissa had not even finished her question, but it brought forth tears from Niky's eyes and a quivering fear trembled her lips.

"W-we... we camped... north of here. West o-of... I, I..." She could not finish. Her eyes rolled back in her head and her back arched off the floorboards of the wagon. Intense seizures racked her body. Yrlissa sprang up into the back of the wagon to help Ember. They both held her down.

"Kaisaney Vallanomin," Yrlissa barked, casting her magic into the ravaged young woman. The spell eased the convulsions as Ember gently put her into a deep sleep, knowing she needed rest more than anything if she were to recover.

"Thank you, Lissa. I wasn't sure what to do," Ember said as she looked desperately at her.

"I know, *nahlla*, convulsions must be calmed by using your magic on the nerves in the brain. The Dyrannai spell I used means 'calm body'. You must find the Fae equivalent within your memories. The girl has been horribly traumatized. She needs rest, not questions," she said, sternly eyeing Giddeon.

"All right, Yrlissa," he replied. "We'll find their camp and figure out what happened to them from there."

Yrlissa nodded and Ember continued to watch over Niky. "I'm going to make sure I didn't overlook something when we healed her before. I'll stay with her," she said, nodding to the others.

Giddeon wasted no time in gathering the others away from the wagon. Max approached the group last, having waited for Yrlissa to finish cleaning herself up.

"Well, Giddeon," he asked, his hands in the air. "What's the plan, or more importantly, what are we looking for? What could have done something like that? It sounds like there could be a significant number of bodies out there."

Saleece agreed, nodding. "Max is right, Father. There could be other survivors as well, if not some of these Sisters will have had magic. We can't leave them to rot."

"Agreed," Giddeon said, scratching the back of his head and tightening his ponytail. "As for what could have done this?" He shook his head. "I cannot even begin to guess. We must find their campsite and see for ourselves. Max, Kasik, the Vesta said they were west of the trail..." he stopped when Max gave him a strange look.

"Sorry, Max," he clarified. "A Vesta is a priestess or a vested sister, our lucky lady here is a vesta for the goddess Mylla. Their temple is across the road from my home in Corynth, remember?" When Max nodded, Giddeon continued. "All right, where was I? Oh, yes. You two take Yrlissa and see if you can track Sister Niky's trail back to their camp. Saleece and I will bring everything else, the wagon and your mounts. We'll follow at a safe distance and give you support if whatever did this is still around. All right?" They all nodded, knowing what they had to do.

There were very few people, if any, whether Human or Elvehn who could exceed Yrlissa's capabilities when it came to tracking in the forest, or anywhere else for that matter. Niky had left an easy trail of blood, disturbed earth and drag marks for Yrlissa to follow back down the trail and into the forest. The others followed not far back, and as always, Max was right by her side as she showed him what to look for. A blood smear on the far side of a tree, a deep, circular depression from a fallen knee, and splashes of blood as they splattered off her clothing or were flung from the tips of her fingers. Max had taken every chance he could to learn as much about tracking people and animals from her. Every group should have at least two trackers Kasik told him once not long ago.

An hour passed while Yrlissa and Max steadily followed Niky's trail back through the forest. Kasik followed closely, acting as their eyes against danger while their attention was focused on the trail left by the vested sister. The trees thinned considerably at the current elevation in the mountain range, but the uneven ground prevented them from seeing the campsite until they climbed the small rise before it. They crested the top and Max was the first to see the clearing campsite of the vested sisters of Mylla. The site was the equivalent to an open-air abattoir.

"That's... bracing when you're not ready for it," Max choked. "What could have done such a thing?" He coughed as the disturbing smell assaulted his nostrils.

"Nnnnn." Yrlissa merely grunted, even with the back of her wrist firmly to her nose, she still could not keep the abrasive stench of death and decay from making her eyes water. They both heard Ember gag and cough from the back of the wagon below the rise. The putrid air seemed to permeate the forest as a gentle shift in the wind's direction towards the east seemed to settle in, carrying the smell back the way they had come.

Giddeon, Saleece and Kasik approached the small hilltop, and stood looking at the carnage.

"You ever seen anything like this, Giddeon?" Max asked solemnly.

The ArchWizard nodded. "Yes, but only in the aftermath of war, not like this..." he explained as he swept his hand across the clearing that looked more like a battlefield. "You?"

"Yeah," Max said. "In Iraq, also during war. During the march to Baghdad, our heavy artillery bombarded the hot zones ahead of us. It left nothing but body parts and ruin."

"I can't imagine," Giddeon said, shaking his head. "I saw your world, briefly, the night I brought Kael there. The technology... I can't imagine the destructive capabilities of such advanced technology. It makes magic look small."

"In some ways," Max agreed, staring out across the massacre. "Yet magic likely did this..."

"Giddeon?"

"Yes, Kasik?"

"Perhaps it would be better if Max and myself checked the area? This smell could easily draw in unwanted attention."

Giddeon nodded. "You're right. Max, string your bow before you leave. If a troll or an ogre finds its way here, we're going to need it. Saleece, stay with Ember and watch her back. Yrlissa, come with me and let's see if we can figure out what happened here."

They walked down the slight depression to the camp when Giddeon turned back and added, "Kasik, you and Max stay reasonably close in case something decides to join us." Both nodded as they headed into the forest in different directions.

Arriving at the edge of the camp Giddeon glanced at Yrlissa. "Well, this is your area of expertise. What do the tracks show?"

Yrlissa looked back and forth across the camp, taking in everything she saw. There were the remains of seven tents, three to each side and one in the middle at the far end of the camp, directly across from where she stood. For some reason, the tent had been raised against the cliff. It did not sit right with her. It was where she would put a prison tent in case she had to blow it and its prisoners over the cliff. A concentrated blast of air from a lone wizard could easily do the job, but why would vested sisters of the earth goddess have a prison tent? They wouldn't, she decided, and dismissed the idea, contributing the tent's position to the priestess' lack of woodlands experience.

She moved on as the rest of the tents drew her attention. They were all destroyed, either ripped, burnt, or splattered with bodily remains. She could not be sure, but there appeared to be about twenty bodies, all were female and of varying ages, and all were dressed in the white flowing robes of the priestesses of Mylla. Most seemed to have been torn apart by creatures with large sharp claws, while there was no doubt that others had been killed by bladed weapons and magic. Magic whose trace residue Yrlissa knew all too well.

“Kael did this. Gods, but why?” she whispered.

Giddeon had slowly drifted over to the right from where she was standing. She glanced his way, but it was clear he hadn't heard her. Crouched down, he examined something on the earth. She was already positive she knew what he found.

"It's a hellrift, isn't it?" she asked.

"No. It doesn't appear to be a rift opening, it's shaped more like a tear. If I didn't know better better, I'd say something from the lower planes tore its way into our world," he said shaking his head in disbelief. "What's more," he paused, pointing all over the sight of the massacre, "is that there are dozens more spots just like this one. What the hell happened here, Yrlissa? Do you have any idea at all? Is it related to Kael? Is it possible he did this?" Giddeon stammered, clearly disturbed by what he was seeing.

Yrlissa knew without a doubt that the magical residue matched Kael's underworld magic. Sensing trace magic was a skill that had been lost many thousands of years ago, and it was the one skill only the Elvehn had ever really been blessed with. She suspected that there were still a rare few of her kin who were born with the blessing to understand trace residue magic and the ability to see magical auras, but it was something no one ever spoke about. It was a skill certain groups would enslave or kill to possess. What she could not understand was why Kael would have attacked a group of priestesses who would never harm anyone. Or why it looked like these vested sisters may have had a prison tent.

Confused, she stared at Giddeon. "Keep looking. I want to check out the tents. Something is not right here. In fact, something is very wrong."

"I'll be here. Maybe I can find some more clues on the bodies. I'll gather them together. Max and Kasik can help when they get back. We'll have to dispose of them. Most of these women and young girls were bonded wizards, which means..."

"Leaving them to rot or burying them will seed this meadow in death-flowers. We'll have to cremate them." Giddeon nodded as Yrlissa walked to the tent against the cliff's edge.

Managing to erect the front two poles so she could get inside to look around, Yrlissa was glad the large centre pole hadn't been smashed. It gave her room to move while inside the blood-soaked, charred tent. Once inside, she quickly realized the tent was bare of any furniture except for a sleeping area. Soft blankets had been laid on top of an even softer sleeping mat and then surrounded by velvet pillows. The arrangement was definitely Salzaran and a little extravagant for Mylla's vested sisters, but not abnormal. The only thing she did she see out of place was a small bundle of rope lying by the centre pole of the tent. Bending over, she picked it up to examine it closer. It was tattered and frayed where someone had used incredible strength to snap the fibres of the rope, possibly to free themselves. She looked over her shoulder out the door and saw Giddeon on the far side of the camp with Max and Kasik. They had just begun the gruesome task of collecting the dead for disposal.

Turning back to the rope, she closed her eyes and whispered. "*Savanomin ivey hanor.*"

The spell activated slowly, as it was meant to, so the caster could make sense of the colours, sounds, and feelings as they flashed through the mind. Yrlissa frowned as she concentrated with more intensity, and images began to appear in her mind.

She saw Kael, but the ferocity of his hatred and anger was insanely powerful and unlike anything she had ever felt. It knotted her stomach with fear. Another flash changed the images—women in long white gowns fled in absolute terror as demons stalked the campsite and tore several of the women to pieces. Dark cyclones filled with black icicles and razor shards of purple ice twisted through the tents, snapped support poles and flayed several of the youngest priestesses trying to hide inside. Yrlissa groaned. The girls could not have been more than ten years of age. Horrific visions of senseless slaughter filled her mind until she could handle no more. Releasing the power that supplied the mind's eye spell, one last image slammed into her mind. Stronger than the others, the scene stole her breath. The priestess they had saved, Vesta Niky, sat smiling on Kael's lap. He was tied with the frayed rope as he sat against the pile of soft pillows and she gently bumped her nose to his with the familiarity of a loved one, but her smile quickly turned to a savage grin of someone victorious. Yrlissa opened her eyes to find herself back in the tattered remains of the tent. She collapsed, rolled onto her back and stared up at the roof of the tent.

"What happened here?" she whispered to herself, more confused than ever.

Chapter Thirty-Five

"The months have passed slowly since I've been here. Talohna. The word is quickly becoming a synonym for suffering. Everywhere we go good people die or lose all they have. This world needs people who would put the needs of others ahead of their own. But I will probably die long before that happens. People are just as selfish here as they are on Earth. It's as if the human race can't help themselves, regardless of the dimension."

Kael Symes, Journal entry, 2025 PC

DWARVEN MOUNTAIN RANGE

Three black ravens sat side-by-side on a branch far above the camp full of dead women in white dresses. They watched intently as Giddeon, Kasik, and Max dragged and carried bodies to the centre of the clearing while Yrlissa tried to figure out what had happened. As if blessed with a superior intellect, the dark eyes of the large black birds followed the group on the ground, as if listening carefully to what was said, or perhaps taking stock for themselves as to what had caused the massacre in the clearing. After fifteen minutes, all three birds took flight and climbed high above the towering trees, flying to the north.

A half hour passed before the birds dove together, dropping through the trees and racing around branches before finally coming to a rest above a second camp. This one was occupied by the living—an older Elvehn woman and two younger Humans. One was male, his skin covered in detailed black and purple tattoos. A younger girl, no more than thirteen, bustled around the camp helping the Elvehn woman. The ravens listened for an hour, never moving, before they took wing and scattered in different directions.

Nekrosa Kohl's solid black eyes cleared, the whites pushing the black to the centre of his eyes until his bright silver irises reappeared and the black vanished within his dilated pupils. He glanced over at his wife, Sephi, just in time to see the black vanish from her dark gold eyes. With their control over the black ravens released, they waited several minutes before their trusted companion, Luthian Bathory, did the same. All three shuddered as their consciousness completely returned to their own minds. Sephi stared closely at Nekrosa, the memory of the massacre site still fresh.

"Do you think it's possible he did that to those women?" she asked.

"We haven't seen anyone else out here who could have," Nekrosa answered, "but where did the vested sisters come from and how did we miss them?"

"I couldn't even hazard a guess, your majesty," Luthian added. "But if Kael has lost control over his powers, then our problems have just multiplied."

"Several times so," Nekrosa agreed. "We have enough problems to solve. We don't need an insane DeathWizard in the middle of it."

"What do we do then?" Sephi asked, standing to stretch muscles that hadn't moved in well over an hour.

Nekrosa remained silent for several minutes before he finally spoke. "We'll have to wait and see. He seems to be fine now. If he'd lost permanent control, the young girl and the Elvehn woman would already be dead. We're getting closer to the information we need, as well as understanding what Kael hopes to discover about the Kai'Sar up here in the mountains. There has to be something in the old ruins of Kazzador City. It won't be long now. We keep following them all. Our answers are there, and hopefully an opportunity arises to prove to them that we can help."

DWARVEN MOUNTAIN RANGE, FURTHER NORTH

Kyah jerked awake in the back of an old wooden wagon. Pain ruled her entire being, but she quickly pushed it aside. Suffering was just another part of being a Dead Sister, let alone a Dead Healer. Catching a flash of red hair from someone who could only be Kael's wife, the memories of the last few days rushed back to her. She smiled, proud of herself that she actually managed to spit out the 'vested sister of Mylla act'. Considering her injuries, it was a serious accomplishment. Even better, it seemed that everyone believed her, and she was now firmly situated inside the ArchWizard's group. Most importantly, she still had a way to get to Kael.

"Giddeon, Yrlissa!" Ember shouted, facing the top of the rise. "She's awake." Ember quickly slid to the bottom of the wagon and dropped the gate so she could help Sister Niky down out of the back.

"Thank you, Ember," Kyah said and smiled as she gently stepped down onto the soft earth of the forest floor.

"Don't thank me yet," Ember replied. "We're at the site of your camp. We needed answers, but you were out cold, so we tracked your trail through the woods back to here."

Still smiling, Kyah asked, "You have very powerful magic with you, then?" She sat down on a fallen log, panting from the exertion.

"We do, but we also have an Elvehn tracker with us. There are few signs she can't read." Ember thought she saw a flash of panic cross the young woman's features, but when the sister groaned from the pain, she quickly passed it off as such.

Giddeon and Yrlissa walked over the small hill and down to where Kyah sat. Ember did her best to make formal introductions.

"Niky, do you remember? This is the ArchWizard, Giddeon Zirakus, and Yrlissa Blackmist. She's the one who followed your trail back to here."

Kyah nodded, offering a short bow to Giddeon. "I do, and thank you both. All of you," she said, turning to Ember. "It is good to see you again, ArchWizard Zirakus."

Returning the bow, he smiled. "Please, call me Giddeon. There's no need to stand on ceremony out here. You might as well stay here, Ember, we found no more survivors. I am sorry, Niky, but no one else made it out alive. No one we could find at least."

Tears slowly ran down Kyah's cheeks. She took a deep breath, as if trying to hold back more grief and appear strong in front of the others.

"I suspected as much when I woke after the attack. I did not expect to," she said, her voice wavering.

"What happened here?" Yrlissa asked. "What we saw up there makes little sense. Why would you set one of your tents against a cliff like that?"

Taking another deep breath, Kyah shook her head. "We always set the prayer tent as far to the west as we can. Our evening prayers to the goddess are spoken to the west as the sun's final rays caress the earth mother."

Nodding in understanding, Yrlissa continued with her enquiry. "Is that why there was nothing else in that tent but pillows and blankets, Vesta Niky?"

"Yes, mistress. The tent is often full of sisters for several hours during the evening prayers so we rest our knees on the pillows to ease the discomfort. Some sisters stay well past dark, the blankets provide warmth for those who do. We use that tent for nothing other than prayers."

"Elloryan silk pillows and weaved velvet blankets? A bit extravagant for vested sisters, no?" Yrlissa persisted.

"We have few personal belongings, mistress. When we travel, we are allowed certain comforts."

"I see," Yrlissa said firmly. "What about this?" she asked, holding out the bindings she found in the so-called prayer tent.

"I am not sure," Kyah said, looking closely at the frayed rope. "Perhaps it is the binding from one of our clay oil lamps. It must have been broken during the attack." Yrlissa frowned, and nodded.

"What were you doing out here?" Ember asked

"We..." Kyah coughed, wincing in pain. "The writings of our goddess tell us that one of her Ancient temples could be located here in the mountains somewhere. We were asked by the high priestess to see if we could locate any evidence to support the sacred writings."

"High Priestess Shanea has been looking for ancient Myllan temples for decades," Giddeon said.

"Shouldn't you have some protection with you?" Ember asked.

"I assure you that under normal circumstances, our magic and martial abilities are usually more than sufficient to defend ourselves."

"Clearly not this time," Yrlissa snorted. "Mylla's vested sisters aren't normally capable of producing the magical shit-storm that occurred over the rise."

"When one is fighting for your life, you manage..." Kyah swallowed hard, nearly gagging. "Sorry."

"Yeah," Yrlissa said, clearly still suspicious. "Sister Niky, tell us what happened. Take your time and in your own words."

Taking another deep breath, Kyah licked her dry lips, prompting Ember to hand her a water jug. She took a swallow before beginning.

"We had been camped here for about two hours and were preparing our evening meal. We'd found no evidence of any temples this far south, so we decided to make camp early and prepare a hot meal—we'd been on dry rations and light camp for days while searching. There were still two hours until the setting of the sun and our evening prayers were just about to start when two riders asked for permission to enter our camp. A young woman no older than twelve, and a man our age," she said, pointing to herself and Ember. "He had dark hair, it was spun into braided Salzaran dreadlocks and pulled back into a ponytail. A thin beard covered his face, like he had not shaved in a week. Some of the sisters were terrified of him—he was covered in frightening black tattoos. Writhing vines with savage looking barbed thorns, so real..."

"That has to be Kael!" Ember blurted. "Sorry, didn't mean to interrupt."

"It's all right," Kyah said, patting Ember's hand. "You are right. They introduced themselves as Kael and... Cassie." She paused, moaning softly as she held her ribs. "We... We never turn away travellers, so we asked that they join us in our evening meal. They accepted and we delayed our prayers so we could enjoy the meal together with them. They sat with us all as we ate... Seemed like a very nice young couple. She was quite young for a man's mate, but we don't judge other customs..." Kyah stopped, as if her tongue were stuck to the roof of her mouth.

"Hmph," Ember scoffed, frowning. Kyah looked at everyone as her eyes glassed with moisture.

"I... Sorry." She sniffed and Giddeon offered her a cloth to wipe her nose. "We thought... We didn't know..." she stuttered, clearly not knowing what to say. Ember took Niky's hands into her own and whispered softly, though the frown remained. A ripple of Fae magic gently trickled into the woman's body through her hands. The calming effect was instantaneous, and her eyes opened wide with surprise.

"How did...?" Niky asked.

"It doesn't matter," Ember whispered. "Please finish telling us what happened."

Wiping her eyes again, Niky took several slow, deep breaths followed by a sip of water. She appeared a bit calmer and pressed on.

"Very well. Thank you for whatever that was you did. The meal ended and we were getting ready to begin our evening prayers. It was nearly sunset, and as is our custom when we have guests, we asked if they would like to join us in prayer. Both blatantly refused, calling it a waste of time."

"That can't be right," Ember said, shocked by what she was hearing. "Kael has been extremely religious in the years following the shooting back home. He'd never be so disrespectful. Something is not right here, Giddeon." He held up his hand and nodded for Kyah to continue.

"I apologized for offending them and told them that we asked out of respect for them being our guests and nothing more..." she stopped speaking, her body shuddered.

"Please keep going," Yrlissa demanded gently.

"My sisters and I left them at the fire and went to begin our prayers. We had only just started when the woman, Cassie, yelled at us to stop praying. We cannot stop our evening prayer to the goddess once we have started, and the situation escalated greatly because of it. I don't know why, but the young woman went crazy, casting bright green magic at some of the sisters who were closest to the door of the prayer tent."

Yrlissa interrupted. "Please go on, Sister. I just thought of something." Turning, she headed back up the hill.

Kyah stared after her for several seconds before continuing. "Most of us ran, but a couple sisters stood their ground, casting fire spells. Some hit the young man. He went insane," she sobbed, shaking at the recollection. "He cast all kinds of dark magic. Black lightening cracked across the camp. Wind filled with slivers of ice cut my sisters down right before my eyes..." she cried. Putting her face in her hands, she pulled her knees up to her chest and said no more. Ember knelt in front of her, a blank look of horror on her face.

"I don't believe it," Ember whispered. "Kael would never do that," she said, louder. "It's not true! It can't be true! He would never do such things. He's my husband!" she repeated, yelling even louder. Hearing her distress, Max looked down the rise at what was going on.

Kyah regained control of herself as she looked at Ember with disgust. "Your husband?" she cried. "You're married to him? He did that!" She stood, pointing up towards where the massacred bodies had been strewn across the plateau. "Your husband killed my sisters, beautiful women I've known my whole life, and when they fought back," she screamed, her voice nearing the raged edge of insanity, "he tore open doorways to hell and turned loose savage Brethren that haven't walked this plane in ten thousand years! I watched demons tear my sisters to pieces as they begged for mercy!" she screeched at the top of her lungs. Finally, she fell to her knees in grief and pain.

Slowly backing away and fighting the urge to scream, Ember forced herself to calm down. She stared at the Sister and searched for signs of deceit. She saw nothing but a traumatized young woman, shaking with fear more than anger.

"What's happening here?" Ember sighed, forcing back tears that fought to surface. Refusing to surrender to despair, she added. "I don't believe you. Something more happened in that clearing." Max arrived at her side, wrapping his arm around her for support.

Still sobbing with soul wrenching sorrow, Kyah carried on with her detailed description of the events from two nights' past, though Ember could see that anger was quickly taken over from the fear. It was a puzzling change.

"Your gods-damned husband is," Niky hissed, "is a monster. A Kai'Sar. A wizard who revels in the death and misery of others. He used death magic to string me up like a prized hog and then used one of those sickening blades he carries to gut me like an animal. He is a monster. Why can't you see that?" Kyah groaned. Putting her head back down, she sobbed even more.

"No," Ember said. "Kael wouldn't do that... He wouldn't. This can't be him. I don't believe you," she said. Max kept his arm around her and led her away. Giddeon looked back and forth between the two women before staring at his daughter with a lost look in his eyes.

"Gods, Saleece. What in Inara's name is going here?" Giddeon asked.

"I don't know," she answered, "but we knew this could happen to Kael. We have to decide what to do."

"Later, maybe," Kasik added, descending the rise. "Right now, we have to get rid of those bodies and find a safe place to camp for tonight. Come, we have to burn the remains." As Saleece headed up the small hill to the camp on the other side, Giddeon walked over to Ember and knelt beside her.

"You can stuff your god-damned 'I told you so' up your ass, Giddeon. Save your breath for someone who cares to hear it," Ember snapped.

"I'm not here to gloat. I just wanted to know if you would be all right with just Max for now. Yrlissa isn't back yet from wherever she went, and Saleece and I need to burn the bodies." Ember turned away from the ArchWizard and looked up at Max. He wrapped his arms around her.

"It's okay," he said, nodding to Giddeon. "I don't believe it either, Ember. There's definitely something else going on here."

On her way down the hill, Yrlissa passed Giddeon as he helped Kyah up the rise to say goodbye to her sisters. "I'll come help in a minute," she offered. Getting a nod, she waited until he passed over the rise before turning to Ember.

"Your instincts are very sharp, *nahlla*. The priestess is clearly distraught, but something else happened here. She claimed the young girl with Kael used green magic by the prayer tent, yet there are no traces of demonic magic anywhere near there. In fact, the only demonic markers I found were on the camp's outskirts, on the north side."

"What does that mean? Why didn't Giddeon or Saleece notice that?" Max asked. Yrlissa glanced over shoulder to make sure Giddeon was out of earshot.

"Being able to detect trace magic is a skill long forgotten and one only the Elvehn normally had. I'm not sure what it means. There were demons on the loose in that clearing several nights ago, her memory could have been altered... Or..."

"Or what?" Ember whispered

"Or else she's lying about what truly happened here. Neither is a welcome consideration. You two have got to learn to follow your instincts now that you're here in Talohna, and stick by them. Ask questions and dig deeper when you have doubts. Take little at face value and remember that everyone has their own agenda. I must go help. Stay with Max. I'll be back in a few minutes." She left, climbing the rise to join Giddeon.

Max offered Ember his water bag and softly whispered into her ear. "I want you to listen to me. I know we are new to this world, and it's confusing at times, but we can never give up on Kael. Do you understand?" She nodded, but didn't look up. "This world is full of magic, Ember. It's everywhere, and things are seldom as they appear. In fact, things are never as they appear," he stated, laughing softly.

She stared up at him. "Do you know something, Max?"

Looking around for anyone else and seeing no one, he smiled. "No more than you, but do you believe for one second that Kael would murder all these innocent women and young girls for any reason?"

"Of course not, but why would the priestess lie?" she asked.

"If things aren't always as they seem... then?"

"Then maybe it wasn't Kael who was here that night."

"Or?" Max prompted.

"Or maybe the vested sisters aren't who Niky claims they are," she said, shaking her head.

"Believe in yourself and believe in Kael. Yrlissa and I will be beside you every step of the way, but never let anyone tell you something is true if your eyes have not seen it for yourself. Not in this world."

Sighing, she smiled, feeling better. "What would Kael and I ever do with out you, Max? You mean the world to us both. You know that, don't you?" she said, hugging him.

"I will always do my best to watch over you both. I promise you that from the bottom of my heart."

Ember let go of Max as Kyah's scream of terror rent the air. They raced up the small hill towards the clearing. Max grabbed his bow from his back, an arrow notched in place as they crested the rise and saw what lay below.

Two humanoid creatures had somehow crept into the destroyed camp without anyone noticing. Giddeon lay semi-conscious on the ground, dazed from the initial attack. Kasik fought to reach him. Unable to focus or commit to either creature, the beasts took turns trying to drag the ArchWizard away as Kasik's attention shifted from one to the other. The Northman was fighting a losing battle. The second he swung his greatsword at one monstrosity, the other slid in and grabbed Giddeon by a leg. At over seven feet tall and with unnaturally long arms, both creatures easily outreached Kasik's sword arc.

Ember gasped as she got her first good look at the creatures. Long, greasy black hair, crooked bulbous noses and jet black eyes dominated the features of both. The second beast, clearly male, had two sets of horns. The first grew upwards from above its eyes and curved outwards. The horns, the width of a finger, spiralled up to a point six inches above its head. The second set were thicker, but smooth. Several inches wider, they grew outwards from the creature's temples before turning up to a sharp point.

Completely naked, the female fought savagely, the ferocity of her attacks quickly forced Kasik to defend himself against the onslaught of razor sharp claws. He cursed as the second being dragged Giddeon closer to the forest.

The stench of rot along with the sight of oozing yellow slime and putrid drool dangling from their jagged black teeth reached Ember. Her already-queasy stomach flipped. That both the creature's sagging pale skin were covered in warts, growths, and lesions didn't help matters.

"What the hell are they?" she wheezed, just as Yrlissa reached her side.

Having taken Kyah back to the wagon, the assassin swore. "Bastard toldari!" Rapidly barking a spell, a wave of focused air slammed the male, rolling it back into the forest from where it came.

Yrlissa's spell arrived seconds after two obsidian tipped arrows from Max's bow sunk to the feather flights in the female toldari's sagging chest.

Yrlissa screamed. "Again, Max! Until they fall!"

The ear-wrenching sound of twisting, grinding glass announced the draw on Max's bow as the third arrow instantly whistled away, puncturing the forehead of the female toldari. Kasik took advantage of the chaos the arrows wrought by dragging Giddeon back to the rise and the protection of the others. Two more arrows whistled by overhead and the Northman glanced back in time to see each arrow enter cleanly through the toldari's eye sockets, punching through the back of its skull as two small pieces of hair and bone spun away. The creature finally dropped. With no signs of the toldari getting back up, Kasik finished dragging Giddeon to the safety of the group.

He spun to see the second toldari return to the clearing from the forest and rushed to meet it head on. The long, razor sharp claws of the toldari's left hand slid against his rune-forged greatsword. A piercing screech echoed across the plateau and a burst of colourful sparks danced along his blade as they passed each other in the middle of the destroyed camp. Underestimating the speed of the scavenger, Kasik winced as claws from the creature's other hand viciously raked across his back as it passed, tearing through his chain mail armour and lacerating his back. Stumbling from the shock, he cursed the tearing spasm of agony, but recovered abruptly as the Northman's seething rage tempered the pain. He pivoted. The toldari was right there, both of its claws spread wide for another attack.

A split-second hesitation by the creature gave Kasik an opening. Lunging forward, his sword punched straight through the monster's throat and out the back of its neck.

Kasik's anger brought forth an ancestral warcry as he powered the blade deeper into the toldari's throat. Back peddling from the massive thrust, the toldari retreated until the point of Kasik's blade sunk into the thick bark of a giant tree. The big Northman planted his foot on the creature's chest. Pushing the male toldari down the length of his blade, he pinned it against the tree. It clawed at his face and chest, hissing like a Ghyreni viper. A powerful twist of the corded muscles in his wrists, and the razor-runed blade, still lodged in the bark, flipped vertical. Wood snapped and popped. Taking a deep breath, Kasik forced the blade up, cutting through the neck and chin of the toldari, coming to a stop between its eyes.

With the beast still kicking and fighting for life, Kasik tore the sword from the tree. Ripping it through the creature, he powered the blade down through its abdomen and out between its legs, slicing it into messy halves. The toldari dropped dead, nothing more than an obscene pile of gore.

Only then did Kasik notice the four arrows buried deep in its back. The perfectly timed distraction he needed earlier had been provided by Max's unerring accuracy and power with his bow. He showed Max his thanks with a quick nod and stumbled from the wounds he received at the toldari's claws. Ember raced to help, but he dropped to a knee before she got there.

Ember immediately forced him onto his stomach as she separated the remains of his chain mail and examined the wound.

"Giddeon! Yrlissa!" she yelled. They came her way but she didn't wait, unbuckling the straps to Kasik's armour. She pushed the chainmail over his head and opened his leather shirt, yelling again. "Is there any chance those things have poison claws?"

"Just bloody great," Kasik mumbled. "Filthy bastard retches," he continued cursing.

"Please try and relax, Kasik. Keep your heart rate down, all right?" Ember said.

"Yes, mistress," he sighed sarcastically and closed his eyes to rest, like he had no cares in the world.

Yrlissa and Giddeon arrived and saw Kasik's back had four deep claw marks. Each had black worms of festering poison spreading from them, growing darker and longer as they watched.

"What the hell…?" Giddeon said, stopping suddenly. "Dammit. I know that poison; it's black burrow worm."

"Burrow worm?" Ember asked, "What is that?"

Giddeon pointed to Kasik's back. "Poison so called because it resembles black worms. It will eventually burrow its way to his heart and kill him."

"How would the toldari get their hands on such an exotic poison?" Yrlissa asked.

"I have no idea," he replied scratching his head.

"I have been an assassin for many times longer than you have been alive and though I have heard of it, I've never seen it, or seen it used. Ever," she explained.

Kasik opened his eyes long enough to mumble. "We have, haven't we, Giddeon? You know what you have to do, so get it done and get back to finding your son." He closed his eyes and continued to breathe slowly.

Ember's eyes grew wide as she began to understand what was happening. "There's no cure is there?" she asked softly as she looked to Giddeon and then Yrlissa.

"No, not anywhere around here anyway," Yrlissa replied to her question.

Giddeon rubbed his temples. "DormaSai would be the only country with a cure. Or the knowledge and means of making one anyway, and they would not help us even if we could get there. The king and queen are both practising necromancers. They don't exactly believe in saving lives," Giddeon explained. "This poison is one that only a necromancer can make. It's a mix of magical plants and physical essence stolen from the Void between life and death—a place only necromancers can go. The plants used to make it have magical elements that guard against a cure, especially magic healing. We saw another necromancer use it years ago. I wouldn't be surprised to find out that this stuff came from DormaSai. That country is ripe with some of the nastiest magic ever spawned. Azmerak killed several people with it during the necromancer rebellions, and by many other means before we stopped him." Saleece sat down beside Kasik and gently laid her face against his as they talked quietly.

Ember realized that they would have to watch one of their own die after everything they had been through. Panic lit up inside her belly.

"There has to be something we can do! Yrlissa? Giddeon?" she asked, glancing from one to the other. "This is Kasik we're talking about, he's one of us. There has to be a way... I could jump us to this DormaSai, just give me a picture of something there to focus on," she pleaded desperately.

Yrlissa put her arm around her for support. "I am sorry, *mai nahlla*. It is too far to realm-jump. What you're feeling is your Fae empathy. It is common knowledge that losing someone weighed heavily on their hearts and soul. Kasik is a friend, that makes it so much worse, I know. But there is nothing we can do, any attempts to heal him with magic will trigger the poison's acceleration effect and kill him instantly. I'm sorry, but there is nothing we can do." Ember shook her head, not knowing what else to say.

"Of course, there's something you can do," Kasik barked. Opening his eyes, he gave Saleece a kiss. "Stand me up, so I can face death like a Northman when you push that dagger into my heart."

Yrlissa's look of surprise made him laugh, he snorted. "What? You think these two should have to do it?" He chuckled, looking at Saleece and Giddeon. "Over twenty years we have fought, argued, and laughed together. I wouldn't ask it of either of them unless I had to. But you..." he hesitated. "Killing doesn't bother you. Guess I'm lucky we dragged an assassin along, huh?"

Bending over to help him up, Yrlissa nodded as the Northman regained his feet. "I understand. I'll make it as quick as I can. It'll still hurt, a lot," she smiled.

"Of course it will. Pain cleanses the soul. Just make sure you burn my body with the others before you leave. I will not miss my place at Tyr's banquet of heroes because you idiots can't burn a body right, got it?" he snapped, but it instantly turned into a laugh.

Ember shook her head, unable to take the banter any more. "This is insane. He's not dead yet. You can't do this, Yrlissa. The poison may not kill him. We don't know," she said.

Yrlissa ignored Ember's pleas and quickly placed her hand on her dagger, but her eyes remained locked on Kasik's. "You do not want to see him die of this poison, Ember, I promise you." The blade slid from her sheathe with a dull scrape.

Ember screamed. "No!" A burst of bright white light rushed out from around her, knocking everyone down. Kasik landed face down at her feet.

Time stood still.

The wall that held back the knowledge of Ember's Fae heritage crumbled within her mind. Only a few small pieces remained intact. She knew beyond any doubts exactly what she was and that she could save Kasik. The cost would be her own life. To those born of Fae blood, originally created by magic's purest light for the sole purpose of helping others, there is no choice when saving a life, even if it meant facing death. To heal others, to ease suffering, or to give your life to save another is what it is to be Fae.

Ember knelt over Kasik and placed her hands over the claw marks on his back as the others lay motionless on the ground. The burrow worm poison retreated through the Northman's body and he gasped from the pain. The poison broke through the surface of his skin. Curling around her fingers, the worms of poison quickly entered Ember through her skin and cored their way through her flesh, past her knuckles and hands, and up into her forearms.

Time suddenly caught up.

The long black worms of magical poison burrowed their way into her upper arms before disappearing under her clothing. Magic flowed back out of her hands uninterrupted and into Kasik's body, healing the damage done by the caustic effects of the poison.

Ember healed the last of the poison's damage to Kasik's body and fell unconscious as Yrlissa screamed hysterically.

"No! You stupid girl." The normally dispassionate assassin raced to Ember's side and gently lifted her head. "You stupid, stupid, girl! How do I explain to Kael if you die? He will need you, *nahlla,*" she whispered as she held Ember tight. "I knew you were going to do that. Fight it!" she screamed. "Do you hear me, Ember?" Yrlissa put her forehead to Ember's and her voice calmed. "You fight like you have never fought before. There is more at stake here than just our lives. We need you here in this world. Don't you dare give up."

With one lone exception ten years ago when her husband and little girl died, centuries had passed since Yrlissa had felt the desperate loss of someone so close. She had not cried in almost ten years and just like then, there was nothing she could do to help. Ember did not have the experience to fight through the poison's effects and live. Her Fae healing would only prolong her suffering.

Max knelt at Yrlissa's side. "How... How long does she have?"

Yrlissa shook her head. "She will die on this gods-forsaken mountain within the next four or five days." Looking up at him she added, "I can't help her Max. I..."

Kyah slowly made her way back over the rise and approached Yrlissa as she sat holding Ember. "I would like to help in any way I can... she did save my life."

"Thank you, Niky, but no. I will watch over her until... until..."

"I understand."

"Come," Max offered, bending to help lift Ember. "I'll take her to the wagon."

He carefully carried her back down the rise to the wagon where Ember had started the journey north from Dasal days before.

Kyah couldn't help but smirk to herself. Dead Healers could always turn a disadvantage around and infiltrate almost any group, no matter how smart the members were. The Dead Sisters always travelled dressed as the vested sisters of Mylla because it gave them free passage everywhere they went. This time the dress had saved her life and allowed her to easily insinuate herself into the ArchWizard's group. It helped her find out that Kael's little tramp of a wife was actually alive, a problem she could now easily remedy. If the stupid girl had not already killed herself, the smallest amount of magical healing would ensure her death and the Fae would cease to exist in Talohna once again.

Kyah's mind was a whirl of everything she had discovered. A DeathWizard married to the only known Fae. The irony was almost orgasmic. She knew some of the gods had a twisted sense of humour, but it was obvious they were all playing at something very serious in the mortal world.

Kyah smiled. She would make damn sure to be right in the middle of it when everything came to pass.

She smiled as she thought of the price her sister was likely going to pay for the ritual at the camp during the night of the massacre. Garz'x was expecting a heaven-bound soul. Unfortunately for Kyrce, Ember was still alive. It made for some interesting options for later. The powerful KiPara demon was not quite a god, but he was the uncontested overlord of the Nine Hells since he had killed the Archdemon Salotan. Besides Kael, Garz'x was the closest thing to a god the Dead Sisters had.

Kyah knew she wouldn't have to pay the price for Ember's soul not being delivered, so it didn't really matter to her. Her sister's body was not in the camp with the other Dead Sisters—neither was Voranna's or Ashea's. Kyah almost snorted out loud—the thought that three sisters, a ternion, had escaped Kael's wrath didn't go unnoticed. The irony was unbelievable. Fate? Perhaps, but more likely some gods' twisted sense of humour.

Kyrce would eventually come to kill her, but maybe Garz'x would take care of that little problem for her first. It mattered little now. The turn of events had ultimately spun back in her favour, even if she had lost Kael for the time being.

As Max and Yrlissa helped Ember to the wagon, Kyah watched closely as Kasik sat and rested and Saleece and Giddeon burnt the bodies from the massacre. Both had to use large amounts of their power to turn the bodies to ash so that no other predators would move into the area and so there was no chance a death-flower field would take root. The toldari Kasik had cut in half and the one that had been riddled with over a dozen of Max's arrows joined the pyre as well. Their tough hides required even more strain on the two wizard's magical resources. Kyah smirked; it would leave both wizards weak for at least the next two days.

Finally completing what they had started earlier, Giddeon and Saleece returned to the wagon. Kyah moaned from her injuries as she crawled into the back of the wagon with Max's help. Nodding her thanks, she sat beside Yrlissa and watched Ember closely as they headed back out across the trail and deep into the other side of the forest. They travelled several miles until they found a safe place to camp for the night.

Once their camp was set, Yrlissa checked on Kasik and told him he would recover most of his strength in a matter of days. Kyah stayed at Ember's side, but Max refused to leave the wagon until Yrlissa returned. Travelling or sitting still meant little difference to Ember's condition so they agreed to continue after Kael at sunrise.

Kyah frowned. Yrlissa refused to leave Ember's side and Max watched over them both through the night. Her frown quickly turned inward and became a smile. She had plenty of time to get to Ember. It would take but a whisper and two words to activate the poison's acceleration magic.

Yrlissa and Max had to sleep eventually.

AVELERA CITY
DEEP RIVER DOCKS

Kyro Yorcali leaned against the railing of the large wooden deck attached to the front of the harbour master's building and looked out over the huge docking district of Avelera City. The massive Deep River was one of Ellorya's most travelled waterways. Import and export vessels left and arrived by the dozens every day. Today, though, the sight was drastically different than any other. It made Kyro smile. Two hundred Elloryan Naval ships occupied or waited to occupy all fifty slips in the dock district. Supplies and two thousand blooded gladiators waited to board the ships to their new home—Dasal. It would take more than a day to load the two hundred and eighteen ships. The docks only held fifty ships at a time and getting every man on board for the sail north took time.

"That is a sight I never thought I would see, Master." Kyro turned to see two young men standing with Niko. He recognized one immediately, but the second did not look familiar.

"Kyro," Niko said. "This is Alec Terraine, and Caavis Varius. Caavis was elected by all the gladiators to act as ambassador for them."

"He was? Good. All right, Caavis, first rule. I am not your master and neither is any one else. You work for me, and once we arrive in Dasal, for my father as well. Because you work for us, you will be paid like any other army is. Housing, practise facilities, and meals will all be provided. I only ask that you make Dasal your home and help defend it if need be."

"You are serious?" Caavis asked, disbelief riddled every word.

"I am. I'm also not a fool, Caavis. I imagine there will be plenty of you who run the first chance they get. I only ask that you tell your people to come to me if someone wishes to leave. They won't be punished, and if they really want to leave, perhaps arrangements can be made to help them. Though, I promise you, most of you will love the city of Dasal, but I won't force anyone to fight for her." Kyro chuckled.

Caavis nodded. "I believe there will be few problems. You have already agreed to bring along the families of those who have them." Pointing to the line of men waiting to board the ships, Caavis smiled. Several gladiators were holding wives or children. "You have reunited some families who haven't seen each other in years. If you continue this treatment, this respect, almost every man will stay and defend our new home, and they will be happy to do it. Fighting for a worthy home is better than dying for the glory of the arena. Thank you, Master Yorcali."

"You are all welcome, but please, call me Kyro. You and your men are not slaves, Caavis. You have no masters, only employers, and I hope some day, friends. Go back to the gladiators. I want every one hundred men to have an elected leader. Preferably a man respected and looked up to in battle. It'll make things easier going forward." He shook Caavis' hand and turned to the other man. "Mr. Terraine. You were interesting to watch in the arena."

"Glad you found my death sentence intriguing," he said. Niko snorted as she covered a laugh.

"You misunderstand," Kyro said. "I was referring to your luck. I could tell by the look on your face you didn't know about the hidden blade in your shield. I was glad to see you figured it out in time. You're welcome."

"*Welcome*? How do you figure I owe you my thanks?" Alec asked testily.

Niko put her hand on Alec's arm. "The weapon room. How many shields were by the rack you were shoved into?"

"A couple. They were too heavy to use. The only one I could... was... the..."

"Exactly," Kyro said, smiling as he clapped Alec's other shoulder. "It was a long shot that it would help, but it was all we could do. Elloryan's are disgustingly honest for the most part. Getting that shield in there was tough."

"How did you...?" Alec asked. "Why?"

"That is the question, my friend. A certain merchant here in Ellorya has a noble relative, I believe you know him?"

"Yes," Alec hissed. "He destroyed my life, both of them."

"We know," Niko said. "It's why we tried to save you. We have thirty hours to track this man down and get the information he has. We're going to uncover what they're up to and make sure they're out of anyone's way."

"You don't mean kill..."

"No," Kyro said. "We don't. While killing two pieces of shit who prey on those less fortunate than them is an exhilarating feeling, arrested and convicted serves our needs much better though. Now where do we find the merchant who accused you of stealing gold that was actually your own?"

"He'll be in the upper markets, by the arena entrances used by the nobles and the powerful. If possible... if you see them, can you bring me one of the silver lockboxes. The names of my wife and children are engraved on the bottom of one. I'd like to have it back some day."

Niko raised her eyebrows, getting a nod from Kyro. "You know what to do, Niko. Take Caavis and another gladiator with you. I have to stay here, give us an alibi. Make sure you find out where that money's going. Grond's climbed pretty high in the thieves' guild here, see if his people can help you. Be back here in a day. I won't be able to hold the ships back for you three."

"Relax, Kyro. We'll be back, and it'll be done right."

He nodded as she pulled her hood up and quickly disappeared into the crowd.

"As for you, Mr. Terraine," Kyro said. "You're free to wander until my ship docks. You'll travel with us and help work with any documents Niko finds. Some day you will return here and my people will help you find the murderers who turned the blade on your family. You have my promise. For now, you will quickly come to understand that there are things that need to be done first." Alec nodded and turned away, disappearing within the crowd of people.

Chapter Thirty-Six

"A Broken Blade assassin kills. Only a fool talks to a corpse before it actually is one."

Fifth Law, Broken Blade Guild

DEEP RIVER DOCKS
TWENTY-NINE HOURS LATER

Kyro was exhausted. Twenty-nine hours had crawled by achingly slow. Finally, the last eighteen ships had been tied to the docks and were being loaded, four with gladiators, thirteen with supplies needed to feed everyone for the ten-day journey home. Kyro's own ship, *The Mongrel,* sat at the docks as well. Thankfully the Elloryan Navy had extensive experience sailing the SaltRock River, and it would cut weeks from their journey, saving them the trek over land by being able to sail straight to Dasal instead of docking at the port hub of Caleb's Reach in southern Yusat or risking the volatile Sea of Storms.

Kyro turned to look over his shoulder for the third time in as many minutes. Niko still had not returned with Caavis, and he was beginning to worry. The last ships would be loaded in less than an hour and he would be forced to ship out, so the merchant vessels that had been waiting just upriver for almost two days could begin unloading.

Turning for a fourth time to look for Niko saved his life. The wooden dagger missed its mark, slicing a shallow line along Kyro's neck. A blast of magic hammered his back before he could defend himself. Slamming into the railing of the deck, he realized he faced at least two Broken Blade assassins. Dock workers and merchants scattered. In a matter of seconds, Kyro was alone, facing two of Talohna's best magical killers.

"Boy, you bastards really don't give up, do you?" he muttered. Standing, he pulled his Elloryan scimitar from its sheathe and quickly slid his left hand into the pocket of his long coat. Removing his hand, the cestus hidden inside the pocket came with. Studded with overlapping bands of rounded and reinforced metal, the close combat weapon was a fierce addition to his impractical fighting style.

"Not even a word to tell me why you're here?" he asked. The first assassin attacked again, a flurry of blades came his way. Kyro's scimitar was light and fast, but much slower than the experienced killer and his short blades. Using his caestus to deflect a straight stab to his heart at the end of the flurry, Kyro broke the sequence by stepping back. Blood jetted from his left arm, below his elbow. He stumbled, pulling his arm close in an attempt to stop the flow of blood from the severed artery. A second cut bled from his ribs on the right side.

Both assassins closed on him as he backed up, trying to buy himself some space to breathe. The assassins lunged together, one on each side. Kyro threw his cestus-covered hand out, blocking the first blade of the assassin to his left, but the second dagger passed easily, stabbing his side. His scimitar deflected the set of blades from the assassin on his right as he stumbled backwards bleeding heavily.

"Fucking bastards, my crew and my father will see your guild turned to dust," Kyro barked, dropping to a knee.

The first assassin laughed. "Threats from the grave are no threat at all, little Yorcali. Your father already knows that." The man's head twisted sideways with a sickening crunch of bone. He collapsed immediately as Caavis let the body drop. The second assassin died almost as quickly as Niko hamstrung the killer with her long daggers. Stabbing the assassin a dozen times before he dropped, she kicked his body to the deck.

"You're late," Kyro mumbled as blood dripped from his mouth and he collapsed. Niko pulled the cloth from her hair and tied off his arm above the wound. Sliding the handle of her dagger through the cloth, she turned it to tighten the tourniquet, slowing and finally stopping the artery's blood flow. Packing the stab wound with her shirt, she tied it securely with her jacket, and with Caavis' help, lifted Kyro to his feet.

"The merchant and his noble?" Kyro growled through clenched teeth.

Niko smiled down at him. "Both were arrested a half hour ago, and Grond recovered the documents we needed. Both the merchant and the noble were funnelling money to supply the group raiding Blood Kingdom cities and towns. And there's more information in the other documents; we just have to find it and follow the money trail."

"I knew it," Kyro gasped.

"Your father was right," she added. "Coming for these gladiators was the right call, except it seems we've pissed off the Broken Blades or someone connected enough to hire them."

"Let's get him to your ship," Caavis said, "One of my gladiators... his wife is a healer. She is travelling with you."

"Good. She can patch the idiot up."

Semi-conscious, Kyro mumbled. "Not an idiot, Niko."

Niko shook her head as Caavis helped her carry Kyro to the ship.

"Most people run when they hear one Broken Blade assassin is after them. You stand and fight two of them, pretty much qualifies as the definition of stupid, Kyro."

DWARVEN MOUNTAINS

After taking the entire day Aravae had helped them in order to rest and heal, Kael was anxious to continue on even though he was still weak from the fight with the Dead Sisters. He could still remember nothing about the battle but the odd flash of violence and terror. Though Cassie had told him that the witches were all dead, he was still concerned for Aravae if Giddeon were to find him and Cassie with her. The next morning, they thanked her for her help and said their goodbyes before leaving through the forest and paralleling the northbound trail deeper into the mountains. Not knowing how far behind Giddeon and the rest of his group were, Kael decided to stay in the forest and off the trail for the next few days. He quickly realized he was far from travel-ready. The heavy blood loss and the months of constant abuse to his body were catching up and it slowed their pace, drastically.

After four hours of trekking through the forest and trying their best to stay even with the trail, they hiked up a small rise. The smell was the first indication that they weren't alone. Quickly dragging Cassie down into the brush, Kael looked down into the shallow, but wide depression making up part of a vast clearing. Looking on in disbelief, Kael realized he must have led them farther from the trail then he wanted. The forest clearing had been made to accommodate the large camp located below them.

As they watched closely, it became clear that finding a way around the camp would cost them at least a day, if not two, and once Kael got a good look at the camp's inhabitants, he knew trying to barter their way through the camp was tantamount to suicide. The creatures occupying the clearing were unlike anything he had ever seen. At seven feet tall and wiry thin, the pale-skinned beings all had black hair and black eyes. Their bodies were covered in warts or growths and oozing, open sores covered nearly every creature he could see. Savage claws, several inches long, adorned every single finger on both the males and the females.

The males had two sets of six inch horns. The creature's long, pointed teeth were shiny and black, just like their eyes. The entire camp permeated the forest with the stench of filth and rotting meat. A small cauldron on the side of the camp closest to Kael and Cassie gave off an odour twice as vile as the camp itself. Long, black strings of ooze dripped from the sides. Kael felt the colour drain from his face as he watched the strings of ooze writhe and wiggle like worms as if they had a life all their own.

"I don't imagine you know what these things are do you, Cassie?" Kael whispered.

"I'm not sure. They might be trolls, or toldari maybe. I have never seen either in real life," she guessed.

"All right then. I would imagine bartering our way through will land us in hot water," he smiled, trying to be funny.

Clearly not amused with his sense of humour, Cassie wrinkled her nose. "That's not really funny. Trolls eat people, you know."

Smiling even more, he chuckled. "Yeah, I guessed as much. I was trying to lighten the mood, but I guess my sense of humour leaves a bit to be desired, huh?"

Cassie nodded. "How do we get past them? There are no trees above and a cliff that way," she said, pointing to the left. "The forest to the right is too thin. We'll have to backtrack and walk for hours to get around this clearing."

He looked at her strangely. "Spend a lot of time in the forest, do we?" When she smiled with embarrassment, he said, "Well, I do have one idea, but I doubt you'll like it."

"You don't really expect to barter your way across, do you?" she asked, her nose wrinkled a second time at the idea.

"No," he whispered with a quiet laugh. "I was thinking more along the lines of magic. The forest on the other side of their camp is much thicker over that way," he said, pointing almost straight across from where they were.

Putting her hands up to shield her eyes, Cassie nodded. "I see where you're pointing, but how can we get there?"

"I was thinking that if you held on to my back, tightly, then we could shadow-walk over there," he suggested uneasily.

Looking from him to the dark patch of forest and back, she looked terrified. "You... Uhm... You don't sound so sure. Will I be safe?"

Taking a few minutes to think about, he nodded. "It should be. I don't see another way, other than losing a day or two, and then we run the risk of walking right into Giddeon. He has to be damn close by now. I've done it lots, it just makes you dizzy for a second if I'm not in the middle of a fight."

Confused, she stared at Kael. "You mean there is a difference?"

"Yeah, I guess there is, or else in the middle of a fight I've just never noticed it. Too busy trying not to die usually," he joked.

Cassie laughed nervously. "Okay. I trust you. Let's try."

Kael closed his eyes and took a deep breath to clear his mind. Nodding to Cassie so she could climb on his back, he turned to the dense area of forest across the camp. He felt her legs wrap around his waist and her hands slid around his neck.

"Ready?" he asked. The moment she answered him, he stepped forward, and disappeared into a swirling cloud of black.

Kael stepped out of a similar black miasma on the far side of the creature's camp, well inside the thicker part of the forest, exactly where he wanted to be. He sighed with relief at his success.

"You all right back there?" he asked, as Cassie's arms locked tight around his neck, tugging hard on his throat. A lot harder than a thirteen year old could tug.

"Cassie..." He choked.

"Help me! My foot." Cassie cried out, desperation straining her voice. She sounded terrified, but he could tell she was trying her best to be quiet, knowing the camp full of creatures were less than fifty feet away.

Kael loosened the death grip she had on his throat enough to turn and look at what was panicking the little girl. He instantly recognized the black and dark purple tear. Cassie's left foot disappeared into it.

"Hang on. I'll pull you out," he whispered.

"Something grabbed me. It won't let go," she cried, as tears ran down her cheeks. "It hurts. It's digging into my foot." Nearly panicking, and with Cassie still holding on to his neck, Kael slid his left arm around her waist. Arching his back, he pulled with every ounce of strength he had. Her foot slid out of the tear, and with it, the clawed hand of a monster Kael remembered all too well. The demon's hand was locked tight to Cassie's ankle and he watched helplessly as one of the long claws dug deep into her foot as the demon refused to relinquish its prize.

Cassie buried her face in Kael's heavy cloak and screamed in agony as he watched the claw dig deeper into her. Knowing he had to act fast or Cassie would end up losing her foot, Kael grasped his Vai'Karth with his right hand, and spun the handle, bringing about the blade. He swung it with everything he had. The savagely accurate swipe severed the demon's hand just above the wrist. A short howl of pain-filled laughter preceded the rift's closing as Cassie slammed into him and he fell on his back holding her tight. He rolled over and pulled the long claw from her foot. Biting her lower lip, Cassie grunted with pain as it slid free from her flesh.

Looking at her, Kael apologized. "I'm so sorry. That's never happened before. Ever. I don't..."

"I'm all right. Gods, what was it?" she asked, shaking.

"A demon of some kind. I must have done something wrong this time and allowed it to come to our world. I don't know. God, I'm so sorry. I can't even heal you, and I don't think you can heal yourself. Most wizards can't."

"Help me bandage it and I'll look for the plants and herbs that will help it heal. I learned enough from my aunt. I'll be fine," she said, shaking.

"Okay. Let's get out of here then, before something from that camp wanders this way," He bent down to wrap her sore foot.

She nodded in agreement, but he noticed she couldn't take her eyes off of the clawed demon hand laying in the weeds.

“Kael?”

“Yes?” He pulled a thing strip of rawhide from his travel pack and wrapped it around the cloth, securing the wrap around the wound on Cassie's foot.

“Do you think that really is a demon hand?”

“Very likely.”

“Wrap it up and bring it with us.”

“Why the hell would we do that?”

“My aunt used to tell stories to her patients about the alchemical uses of demon blood, hair, and even the claws. Maybe the hand will come in handy,” she said, and blurted out laughing at her pun.

He sighed at the sour joke and wrapped the hand in his spare shirt. “All right, worse case scenario, perhaps we can sell it for some gold before it rots.”

“Or we could cure and dry the hand when we make camp tonight. Keep your eyes open for rock salt and green quaini plants that still have some puffy leaves on them,” Cassie said.

Kael nodded and helped her to her feet. Once he was sure she could walk, they headed into the forest, moving to the north once more. Cassie leaned heavily on his shoulder. When the pain became too much for her, he hoisted her onto his back and carried her, even though he was utterly exhausted.

They had been walking for two hours, trying their best to head straight north of the toldari camp when they came across the first group of horses. Kael recognized them immediately as the mounts the Dead Sisters kept in a small pen on the north side of their camp. All four animals had the same painted symbol he had seen on the horses back at the witch's camp. An uneven line and two half circles that looked like a horizon with a sun above it and the moon below. It was painted on every horse the Dead Sisters rode.

The four horses were still extremely skittish from the creatures in the forest or the fighting at the camp, but there was nowhere for them to go because of the forest's dense brush between the sparsely growing trees. Even so, it still took them a half hour to catch all four and calm the scared horse's nerves enough to ride them.

Though they had no saddles, they managed to rig enough vines from the brush for two bridles and halters. After doing their best to curry the mounts with their fingers, the horses calmed enough to ride and they headed north within an hour.

Camping that night in the forest, Cassie showed Kael how to dry the demon hand with the rock salt and sulphur crystals they scavenged from a trickle of sour water weeping from the mountain's western rock wall. They also managed to find one green quaini plant to help cure the demon hand. It would still take days of being wrapped in salt and sulphur to dry it out.

They returned to the trail the next morning and encountered no more problems over the next eleven days. Cassie's foot healed well, and there was no permanent damage, thanks to the help from plants they found in the forest, but Kael was positive it would leave an ugly scar on the top of her foot.

They arrived at Kazzador City just before dark on the eleventh day away from Aravae's camp.

DWARVEN MOUNTAIN RANGE SEVERAL DAYS SOUTH

Giddeon's group continued along the northern mountain trail the morning after their fight with the toldari. Max drove the wagon, while Ember lay unconscious in the back wrapped in blankets to keep her warm. She had not regained consciousness yet and likely wouldn't. Yrlissa and Kyah rode in the back as well. Yrlissa refused to leave Ember unattended, and Kyah was still weak from her grievous injuries. Kasik and Saleece rode at the rear, grateful to be spending time together because of what Ember had done to save Kasik, though he still moved slowly from the pain caused by his torn back. Ember had slipped into the coma immediately after taking the poison into her body so she was unable to heal the vicious wounds caused by the toldari's claws. Yrlissa had done her best to close the wounds.

Giddeon rode out front. They encountered no problems of any kind and he continued riding out front for the next three days. Yrlissa remained in the wagon and kept an eye on Ember's failing condition. It was becoming increasingly clear that she was fighting a losing battle, and it was beginning to weigh heavily on Yrlissa and Max. Both grew quieter as the days passed by.

Giddeon slowed his mount until it was even with the wagon. He had just started to discuss finding a camp for the night with Yrlissa and Max when ahead on the straight stretch of trail they noticed a hooded traveller walking their way.

"She's Elvehn," Yrlissa commented as she pulled her hood lower to shield the glare of the setting sun. "And she's an elementalist."

"How could you possibly tell from this distance?" Giddeon asked with a touch of ignorance.

"Look closer, Giddeon," she replied. "You can't tell me that you have seen a Human with such physical features, and her magic? Look how the wind blows the grass and leaves everywhere but where she walks. Nature responds to her presence, she doesn't interact with it. I'm also pretty sure she's not Orotaq. Or would you like to argue that too?" She snorted at the indignant look she received as the ArchWizard heeled his horse and trotted ahead of the wagon.

Giddeon raised his hand with the palm facing behind him to let Max know that he should slow the wagon. Max passed the signal back to Kasik and Saleece. Urging her mount forward, Saleece rode to join her father. Kasik stayed behind to guard the rear from an ambush.

Continuing to ride along the trail, Giddeon smiled back over his shoulder. "You win, Yrlissa. She's definitely not Orotaq. Now that she's closer..." he trailed off, just as Saleece rode up.

"Father? What's wrong?" she asked.

"Come, let's go meet our fellow... traveller." His smile widened and they urged their horses forward at a faster pace, stopping only feet from the hooded woman.

Giddeon raised his arm. "Greetings. If you're alone this night, we would be honoured to share a meal in exchange for news from the north."

"I should hope so, my husband," Aravae said, as she gently pulled down her hood. "I should hope the least you could do was offer a meal." She smiled.

"Mother!" Saleece shouted, as she bolted from her horse. Landing on the ground, she jumped into her mother's arms. "I'm so glad to see you!"

"As am I, daughter." Aravae laughed as she returned Saleece's hug. Still holding Saleece tight, she looked up at her estranged husband. "Giddeon, you've been well I hope?"

"Well enough, Ara. You?" he asked.

"I have been all right. Thank you for asking," she replied.

As Saleece let go of her mother, a suspicious look flashed across Aravae's face. "Giddeon... What are you all doing up here, and why in all the gods forsaken places are you dragging a wagon with you?"

Giddeon sighed as he looked at her, his eyes weary. "Let's find a place to camp for the night. Once Max and Kasik can tell us it's safe, I'll fill you in, fair enough?"

"It will have to be, won't it? Come, I passed a good place to camp for the night a short way back," she answered, a confused look crossed her smooth features.

"It's a long story, Aravae."

Only a short way down the trail, they were able to get the wagon carrying Ember off the trail and into the woods. They stopped for the night about a quarter mile in from the lightly travelled mountain road.

With Kasik and Max out scouting for dangers, Giddeon brought Aravae to the wagon. Yrlissa was in the back, watching over Ember, even though there was nothing she could do.

"This is part of the reason we are here," Giddeon said, lightly touching Ember's saturated forehead. The dangerously high fever was out of control.

"Who is she?" Aravae asked. "She's very sick."

"I know. Gods, I don't even know where to start. I sent a letter to your family in Kyll'Darhen half a year ago to let you know, but I guess it never found you," he explained.

"I have been in Commune. You know that. One year for every year our baby would have been a child," she replied, shaking. He took her warm hands in his.

"I know, love. Sixteen or eighteen years depending on what your soul dictates. I had hoped your Commune was over, so I sent the letter, because... He's back, Aravae. About five months ago, Kael was brought back to this world…"

Aravae slowly shook her head, and out of nowhere, she slapped Giddeon, hard. The sharp report echoed across the camp site like the snap of a heavy branch. With watery eyes and ringing ears, he grabbed her hands, gently, so she couldn't strike him again.

For several minutes, she stared at him, shaking with anger. "A letter, you spineless bastard? Our son came back from another dimension and you sent me a *letter*? You deserve nothing less than to rot in the deepest, darkest hell that exists, Giddeon Zirakus. You should have come and found me..." she hissed. Her anger quickly fled, turning to disbelief. "But you didn't come find me because you were too busy hunting him. You're going to kill him, aren't you? Even now, you're all chasing him, aren't you?"

Yrlissa jumped into the conversation, placing her hand on Aravae's shoulder. "Not all of us hunt Kael, *Mynerha*. I do not intend to let anyone hurt him again."

Hearing the Dyrannai term used to offer the highest respect, Aravae studied Yrlissa closely. "You speak Dyrannai, young one, and with the proper accent. How is that possible?"

"I'm not so young, I promise you." Yrlissa smiled. "As for the other, I am a Blackmist. My family's blood was among the first born to the soultrees of the Dyrannai."

"And mine," Aravae answered. "The Valyndir family would have lived and died beside yours for many centuries. I wasn't aware another family had survived to the present day. My family knows nothing about those times, do you?"

Shaking her head Yrlissa lied. "No, mistress. I am the last Blackmist, I am sorry."

"Still, it is good to meet another descendant of the Dyrannai Forest, my dear. You on the other hand, you bastard," Aravae barked, turning back to Giddeon as Yrlissa headed into the forest to scrounge for firewood. "Do not think for a moment I will allow you to..." She stopped talking, as if all the pieces finally clicked together. "That *is* why you're up here. You're chasing him up the mountain. You're the one's who hurt him. That's why there were no Brethren markers on him. It was you! Which one of you tried to kill my son,

Giddeon?! Answer me, or I swear to all the gods, you will pay right here and now!"

"What in the Nine Hells are you talking about?" Giddeon demanded.

"Four nights ago, I found a young girl running through the trees looking for help for her friend. It was Kael, it was our son. Nothing about him..." She broke down crying. "I healed him and he told me his name was Kael, but I never even thought that it could be our Kael. Dammit, Giddeon. Why are you doing this? He's our son. How could you do that to him? He almost died!" she rambled on, confused and hurt. With no other option, Giddeon grabbed her and pulled her to his chest, fighting her attempts to break free.

"It wasn't us, Ara!" he yelled, holding her tighter. "I promise you, it wasn't us. We're not hunting him. At least not any longer, I don't think, anyway," he tried to explain.

She calmed down enough to look up at him. "What do you mean? I don't understand."

"Neither do I, believe me. Here, turn around, all right?" he asked, gently pulling her arm and looking down at Ember. "This sick young woman is Ember. She is Kael's wife. She and Max crossed over with Kael when the Dead Sisters brought him back. She is the reason we aren't really hunting Kael. She is Fae, Aravae, a pure and full-blooded young Fae woman. We have given her our promise to talk to Kael first before anything else. Though it seems we may be running out of time. The morning you found him, he attacked a group of Mylla's vested sisters. We burned the bodies, but it was a massacre. He is losing the fight for his humanity."

"That's not right, Giddeon," Aravae said. "The little girl with him said it was witches who kidnapped him and she helped him escape." Kyah's eyes shot up, focusing on the discussion.

"We know," Giddeon said stopping her. "The young woman with him is a young Dead Sister. She lied to you. You said yourself there were no marks of Brethren magic on him," he said.

"No, that's not right. The girl had healing magic. I watched her, I helped her heal Kael. There were only stab wounds and some electrical and fire burns, but she helped. Dead Sisters can't heal, Giddeon, they have no empathy. You know that."

"Then there's another explanation. You know what Kalmar Ibess believes about the Dead Healers. Maybe she was one. As desperate as they were for help, I imagine they lied to gain your trust or your pity, maybe both. These are not normal people. The Dead Sisters are cruel, beyond the darkest of evil. You know that as much as I do, Aravae. You helped for years with the research about the Black Sun phenomenon."

"Do not think for a single second that I am a coddled fool, Giddeon Zirakus. That girl was terrified, not being a thespian. It doesn't matter. How do we help Kael now?"

Shaking his head, Giddeon said, "I don't know. With Ember alive, we might have had a chance to talk him down, but it looks like she will be dead within a day or two..." Kasik entered the camp on the far side and waved Giddeon over.

"I'll be right back, Ara," he said.

Kyah stepped around the wagon, bowing to Aravae, as a vested sister would. "Mistress. Can you do anything for her? You have very strong healing magic for an elementalist."

"You're a priestess of Mylla," Aravae said, not asking.

"Yes, Mistress."

"Your group is the one Giddeon mentioned. The one Kael attacked?"

"Yes, Mistress. We tried to defend ourselves, but he was so strong and we weren't expecting it. They seemed so nice during our evening meal. I tried to calm him, but the man we shared a meal with was gone. The markings on his skin grew into his eyes..."

"How could you possible know that unless you were face to face with him?" Aravae asked. Frowning, she stepped closer. Kyah put her head down and slowly untied the soft, white belt that held her tattered dress closed. The dress parted, showing off the monstrous scar from the wound Ember healed.

"I was," she said, as Aravae gasped at the extensive scarring. "Right before he ran me through with the wickedest looking weapon I have ever seen..."

"I'm sorry..." Aravae began

"I survived, thanks to her," Kyah said, interrupting as she motioned towards Ember. "Can you heal her?"

"I can try, yes." Turning back to the rear of the wagon, Aravae placed one hand on Ember's head and one on her her chest, then closed her eyes to concentrate. "Gods, her aura is amazing. It is so pure. I can feel the poison in her, but it acts like its alive, retracting just from my presence," she explained as she continued examining Ember.

"Is there some magic you can try? Anything?" Kyah said, pushing harder as she watched Giddeon and Kasik's conversation come to an end.

"Perhaps. Let's see..."

"Aravae! Stop!" Giddeon yelled from the far side of the camp.

She frowned, turning. "Yes?"

"It's black burrow worm." Aravae's hand leaped from Ember's skin as if she had been burned as she spun towards Kyah, grabbing her arm. "Why didn't you tell me that? Magic healing will kill her," she lectured.

"I am so sorry, Mistress," Kyah said. "I did not know..."

"It's all right, Aravae," Giddeon whispered as he approached. Aravae released Kyah and gave her a stern look as she silently excused herself and went to sit by the spot picked for a fire. Giddeon continued. "She will die anyway. Maybe there is something you can do."

"I'm sorry. Maybe with a couple of months in the Ageless Library at Drae'Kahn, one might find a cure. If there is one. Only King Kohl would know how to help her."

"We already discussed that. DormaSai might as well be on another plane. The distance is too great to help. There is nothing else we can do." Aravae nodded her agreement and went to sit with her daughter while Giddeon waited for Max to return.

He knew in his mind that whether or not Ember survived, it was starting to look like his son was losing control of his sanity. He may still have to do what he had started out to finish so many months ago. He just wished there was a way for him to talk to Kael alone first. If he really had lost his mind, then Yrlissa, Max, and now Aravae, would all fight to defend Kael should the rest of them try to kill him.

His head hurt from the war of emotions and feelings that were fighting with his sense of duty, and he was running short of time to find an answer.

Chapter Thirty-Seven

"Eons ago, the gods blessed six families with magic drawn straight from their divine blood. These families quickly became known as the Elderblood Families. Each was granted a single god-like ability that was triggered by a single word. The power has been carried down through the blood of all the family's children. Invisibility, rapid healing, immortality, levitation, time and dimension magic, and the most powerful Elder power of the six: magical augmentation, the ability to drastically increase or change all kinds of magical power. Though several descendants still exist, only a single wizard alive today is known to have Elderblood with active magic. Master Wizard Seifer Locke."

Kalmar Ibess
Excerpt from annual lecture to new apprentice students at Inara's University of Magic Summer's Dawn, 4998 PC

DASAL

Seifer and his apprentice, Kittrix Dawn, scoured every piece of paper and written document they found in Lircang Yorcali's house and places of business, and they still had a mountain of boxes to go through. Everything was spread out in the barracks' lunch room and had been there for too long.

Kit sighed and leaned back in her chair. "Is everything this paranoid bastard wrote in code? How many codes did he need?"

"Apparently Lircang didn't want anyone to know what he was up to."

"The only thing not in code was what Dahlea told me during her interrogation," Kit added as she stared at yet another ledger written in a code they'd yet to decipher. "I'm sorry, Master. I don't know if we'll ever find out where Katarina might be."

Seifer frowned as the door to the barracks opened. It closed gently so he ignored it, concentrating on the stack of papers in his hand. "Then we'll keep looking until we do. It has to be here. Lircang Yorcali had a way of contacting Ella Navasha. I won't stop looking until we find a way to track down Kat and bring her home."

"I knew you would never give up," Katarina said from the entry way. With his back to her, Seifer wondered if his mind was playing tricks on him. Kit's voice told him it was not so.

"Blessed Mother Inara," Kit whispered. Seifer spun, the papers fell from nerveless fingers and drifted to the floor.

"Kat?" he asked, his voice barely a whisper.

"Yes, Seifer. It's me." He could see her lips trembling and her whole body shook. Afraid to approach her, he stepped forward slowly. It was all she needed. Kat ran to his arms and buried her face in his neck as he slowly embraced her.

"I... I missed you," he said, causing her to break down. He held her tight, refusing to let go as the barracks door opened again, and Ella the White walked in followed by a young woman with eyes cold as ice. Pulling Kat behind him, Seifer's right hand filled with fire as the words for his spell left his mouth. His left hand filled with a clear shimmering magic that instantly jumped to his right. The red and orange flames sizzled with the increase in power and quickly turned white hot as he prepared to roast the witch who took Kat from him so many years ago.

The witch smirked as Kat jumped in front of him. "No, Seifer!" she yelled. "Stop, please." Seifer felt his magic fade along with the feeling of excitement at seeing Kat again.

"Why?" he sighed, staring at Kat. "Why would you defend her? I know Lircang took you and sold you to her, he told us before he died..."

"Lircang Yorcali is dead?" Ella asked, moving closer.

"Yes, killed by assassins after he was caught trying to have a young man killed and his wife kidnapped. Now would someone please explain what the hell is going on? You have a lot of nerve stepping foot in my city, Ella Navasha."

"Perhaps," the witch replied. "But we need your help and I thought it was time that Katarina came home."

"*You* thought?" Seifer exploded, stepping up to her. "What about what she wants? You don't own her, no matter what a dead slaver says. You better start talking or that age-old argument about Elder Blood and White magic will be settled here, now."

"Do not threaten me, wizard," Ella snapped. "I came here out of respect for you. You are the only right-minded, University-trained wizard alive. Don't make me change my mind about you. There is more at stake here than the love between you two foolish mortals."

"She's right, Seifer," Kat said. "Please listen to her. We need your help."

Seifer shifted his eyes back to Ella. "No. It'll be a cold day in the Ninth Hell before I help you. How dare you ask for my help? Get out of my city, Ella, before I have you burnt at the stake!"

"You insolent little fool," Ella barked, snapping her right hand out. Sizzling white magic leapt away.

Seifer was ready. "*Auka vardas,*" he spat, the words to his spell finished first. Ella's magic slammed into Seifer's shield, and with a twist of his hand, bounced off, exploding into the barracks wall. A second spell followed immediately, and it shot away out the hole in the wall the moment it hit his shield. Two dozen guardsmen entered the barracks and surrounded Ella, half instantly trained their longbows on her.

"Stop!" Kat screamed. "Both of you, stop! She didn't come to fight, Seifer."

"Yet she attacked," Seifer said. "Like she always does. I used to feel sorry for you, Ella. Giddeon screwed you over, the king, even BlackSpawn's bastards. But you'll never change. What you can't get willingly, you take by force. Leave my city. Now." Turning to Kat, he added, "You go, too. It's clear you're with her willingly."

"Seifer..."

"Go, Kat," he said, turning his back.

"Seifer?"

"What, Ella?" he barked, without turning around.

"Help us and Kat can stay..."

"Mistress, no," Kat said.

"She doesn't want to stay, Ella..."

"I do, Seifer. There's more going on here than you know. We need to find the DeathWizard, and quickly."

"What?" Seifer said, not quite sure he heard properly. "What do you want with Kael?"

"I would be very careful how you answer that question," Kittrix said. Quiet and observant only to that point, Seifer's apprentice rose to her feet.

"Kael?" Kat asked. "You know him?"

"He came through here several weeks back. He was the one Lircang tried to have killed. Kael stopped a pirate attack on the city at the same time. Giddeon got here two days after Kael left and his group went after them. What do you want with him?"

Ella shook her head, the disbelief all over her face was a sight few saw.

"Strange days indeed," she said. "Kat told you there was more going on, Seifer. We were chasing after a crazy alchemist when I... felt Kael in distress. We broke off the hunt so we can find him and help."

Seifer snorted. "You're not known for your helping hand, Ella."

"Perhaps, but when the power of a DeathWizard falls into the wrong hands this world will suffer. I won't allow that to happen."

"Because that power is safer in your hands, right? Don't screw me around, Ella. You want that power for yourself, and that means killing Kael. *I* won't allow *that* to happen."

"I have no interest in killing Kael or taking..."

Seifer whirled, stepping face to face with Ella. His voice held a dark edge. "Do not forget who was at your damn side the last time you took power like that. I saw what was left of Sylestia when you ripped her power from her, and she was here to help us." His voice dropped even further as he took a deep breath. "You murdered an angel for her power, power you already had and you expect me to believe the same won't happen to him? I know where Kael is, but I will never tell you, and I will never boost your magic so you can find him." The barracks door opened, but Seifer didn't dare take his eyes from Ella.

"Then tell me," Kat pleaded. "I swear to you we don't want to harm him, Seifer. We don't want his power. Ella told me that even she couldn't control his magic. But someone else is after them..."

"She's right, Seifer," Kyro Yorcali said, laughing. "And I'll be happy to tell you who it is... Can't believe I'm saying that. Didn't this place get interesting while we were gone, eh, Niko?"

DWARVEN MOUNTAINS

The next night, with the sun just below the treeline, Giddeon's group stopped travelling a bit earlier in the day. Ember's condition had declined rapidly as the day wore on and Yrlissa was sick with the knowledge that she would likely pass from the living world by dawn. They all agreed to camp for the night and wait for her time to come, so they could do the proper ritual and send her soul to the higher planes of the after life.

Max was visibly upset at not being able to help her and immediately went to scout for danger in the surrounding area. As the others prepared camp, Kasik approached the wagon.

“Yrlissa, can I have a minute alone with her?” She nodded and hopped down. Giving him a hug, she left him alone with her. Not knowing what to say to the young woman who gave her life for him, Kasik stared down at Ember's still body for several minutes.

"Ember, my people believe that a person can hear what is said to them until their soul flees our realm for the afterlife. If you can hear me, then I want you to know that I wish you had let me die. You have this affect on people that changes the way we see things. Your life here in Talohna is... was... more important than mine could ever be. You shouldn't have done what you did. But then I guess you wouldn't be you. I promise you I will do what I can to keep Kael alive, even if it means protecting him from Giddeon.”

A small blade appeared in his hand. Kasik cut a length of his hair and tied it to the red locks behind Ember's right ear. “My Kreeda—my oath, my promise,” he said quietly. Measuring an equal length of Ember's fiery red curls, he used the knife to cut her kreeda for himself.

“Goodbye, Ember, and thank you. May the Valkyrie carry you to Paradise." He felt Saleece slide her arm around his waist. Neither said a word as she braided Ember's length of hair into Kasik's on the opposite side as his father's kreeda. She turned and he followed her back to where the others were preparing the campfire.

Max stalked through the forest with barely a whisper of sound coming from his movements. He didn't know whether he wanted to kill something or if he was going to be sick to his stomach. His promise to Kael that he would always take of Ember if something happened to him was eating him alive. Over the years, he had grown to love her like a sister, and his failure to protect her left him furious with himself.

She would always be the first to jump in and help someone in need. She had been like that her whole life. He never suspected she could possess such staggering power and strength of will as to give her life for another. Even though he knew it wasn't Kasik's fault, Max had to try hard to suppress the urge to choke the life from the big Northman. Ember would have given Talohna a small bit of hope, whether it be the increased power of healing or just the single life here and there she herself might one day have saved. Like the little girl in Dasal, who now had a long life to look forward to, instead of a painful single year of agony and a frightful death. His mind boiled with anger and thoughts he could not control, and his lack of attention to his surroundings allowed someone to sneak up on him.

Max stopped and took a deep breath, trying to clear the muddle in his head. A tear crept down his cheek as he thought about telling Kael that Ember was gone. The voice from behind him startled him for only a second.

"She's not dead yet, big man," she said. The voice was calm and soft, with no hint of threat. On instinct, Max whirled around, an arrow already released from the powerful Orotaq bow. He watched as the black, razor tipped arrow easily sliced into the forehead of a beautiful young woman. To his surprise instead of falling, the woman merely dissipated like a wall of mist in the breeze, and stepped out of the darkening forest almost a dozen feet to his right.

"Now, now. You seem a bit shaky tonight. Why would you want to kill someone who is here to help?"

"What the hell?" he said. He stepped back and pulled one of his swords.

"Please stay calm. It's not like you've never seen illusion magic before. Now would you like our help or not?" she repeated. Refusing to put his weapons away, he rested on the balls of his feet, facing the woman.

"If you wanted to help, why would you sneak up on someone and risk an attack?" he asked.

"Because... I needed to know that you were alone. You travel with people my husband and I don't like," she said sternly. Smiling, Max suspected he knew exactly who this exotic woman with the strange loops of braided hair, was not fond of.

He smiled wider. "Giddeon has that effect on people. You've earned a few minutes of my time as well as my attention... Miss."

"Oh, *Miss* is it? You learned some proper etiquette in your time away from our world haven't you... *Max*," she replied. He noticed the deliberate pause at the end of her sentence.

Slightly puzzled, he shook his head. "Don't know what you mean, but if you've come to help, I'm listening."

"Uh-huh." She smiled. "My name is Sephi Kohl. I am the queen of DormaSai, my husband, Nekrosa, is watching our discussion from close enough to make you regret any stupid moves you may decide to attempt. Are we clear?"

He nodded. "What do you want?"

"DormaSai is the only land to survive intact after Jasala's Cataclysm over five thousand years ago. Our country thrives on magic, and we have a library that was standing for countless millennia before the continents shattered. We know what is happening right now. We have access to written prophecies that the ArchWizard and Cortina's chapel don't. Giddeon Zirakus is a stupid, arrogant fool who refuses to listen to us because of the gifts we were granted by the gods."

"Oh, you mean that raising the dead and controlling people's minds thing? Yeah, he's way off-base there, isn't he?" Max hardly believed what he was hearing.

"I'm not here to debate magical ethics with you. If I were, you would lose," she said, glaring at him dangerously. Max thought perhaps he should just shut up and listen. Giddeon had told him the king and queen of DormaSai commanded fearsome powers when it came to the magic of necromancy, and that they deserved to die. But Giddeon felt the same way about Kael, too.

"Then why are you here? What do you want?" Max demanded, his patience at an end. Sephi put one hand up with her palm outward and nodded as she slowly slid her other hand inside the small pocket on the front of her dress. Pulling out a finger-sized black vial that sparkled from the rays of the setting sun that were still sliding between the trees, she offered it to him.

"This is the last amount of High Brethren blood in existence. It has been in my country's possession for thousands of years. It has a preservation spell on it that no one has been able to cast off the vial. It will cure any magical poison or disease, or so the records from that time tell us. Yet it will do nothing for a physical wound of any kind. We offer it to you freely, and all we ask in return is that when Giddeon and his group betray you, give us the chance to help you instead. We will continue to follow you, but you won't see us or find us should you try, but if you want our help, we will be there when you need it. Fair enough?"

Unsure of what to say, Max could only inquire about their motives. "Why? What's in it for you?"

Sephi stepped forward and handed him the vial. "I have already told you, Max. Our library has many ancient records. We know about the darkness within the earth. But we don't know what it is or what it will do, but we know to start protecting ourselves against it. There are those who work to free this darkness. If Ember dies and there are no Fae in the world when whatever this is rises, we will have no chance of retaining our freedom. Everyone will die, or be forced to bend a knee and become slaves to whatever power rises."

Taking the vial and holding to the light, Max frowned. "What do I do with this?"

"First and most important is to not let Giddeon know what you are doing. He will try to stop you. That being said, I do not expect you to trust my words without question. There is a very unique Elvehn assassin in your camp. She should be able to remove the preservation spell and verify this vial's contents. If she can, then you must somehow get your young Fae to swallow as much as she can. The blood will not last long after it is opened—perhaps a half hour—but she must drink as much as possible. All of it would be better, understand?"

Quickly putting the vial of High Brethren blood into a pocket he had Yrlissa sew to the inside of his leather shirt, he nodded. "Thank you for your help. I suspect we will be seeing you soon, won't we?"

Turning to leave, Sephi responded by looking back over her shoulder. "If Giddeon stays true to his ways, I believe we will be fighting by your side in a matter of days. Be safe, big man, and believe that I have given you the only means to save that young woman's life."

"Wait, Sephi," he called. "How did you know... everything?"

She smiled at the same time as a huge black raven flew in and landed on her shoulder. "We have eyes where we need them," she said looking at the bird. "This is the kind of mind control we practise. It helps us acquire knowledge we may need, not what Giddeon has told you." The raven opened its mouth and cawed as if agreeing with her statement. The bird's eyes held a human-like intelligence. "Go Max, and help her, for all our sakes. Please. The area around your camp is secure, return to her quickly," she said softly. Max looked down briefly as he touched the vial in his pocket, when he looked back up only seconds later she and the raven were gone.

Max worked his way back to camp and went straight to Yrlissa. She was at the wagon by Ember's side.

"Is she still alive?" he asked, slightly winded.

"Yes, but it won't be long. Two hours, less perhaps."

Chewing his bottom lip, he asked, "Do you know anything about the king and queen of DormaSai, Yrlissa?"

Taken completely by surprise, she answered slowly. "Um, a little. Why would you ever ask about them?"

Looking around to be sure no one was within earshot, he shook his head. "How about the Higher Brethren? Know anything about them?"

Frowning with confusion, she replied, "Angels? Again, a little. Why? Necromancers and Higher Brethren are far from a good mix in any conversation, let alone one I happen to be having with you."

Checking over his shoulder once more, he whispered, "I just had a conversation with the queen of DormaSai, or at least that's who she claimed to be." Pulling the vial from his pocket, he handed it to her and continued. "She said that Giddeon will eventually betray us and that she and her husband would like to help us when he does. She gave me this and said it was High Brethren blood. She claims it will save Ember's life, but only you could..."

"Remove the preservation spell," she interrupted.

Shocked, he replied, "Yeah, that's exactly what she said. How did you know?"

"Because Max, she was right. I can sense the spell and the blood. I guess we have nothing to lose, do we?"

"It doesn't look like it," he replied.

"Did she tell you what to do with it?"

"Yes," he said, hopping into the back of the wagon. "Once you remove the spell, she said we have to get Ember to swallow as much of it as we can, preferably all of it."

With a quick look around, and seeing no one else nearby, Yrlissa held the vial in her hand and whispered.

"Asravan moreina."

The black vial instantly glowed red but quickly faded to gold. Max gently eased Ember up off the bed of the wagon and held her on his lap. Yrlissa joined him and gingerly pushed Ember's head back as she poured the vial's contents down her throat a little at a time. Ember coughed and sputtered, gagging several times, but soon the entire contents of the vial went down, not a single drop had spilled.

"How long before something happens?" Max wondered.

"If she is still alive at dawn, we'll know it's working. I'm going to lay down back here and rest with her, all right?" Yrlissa asked.

Max nodded, exhausted. "I'll keep watch. If she slips away, you let me know."

Yrlissa reached out and grabbed his hand. "She'll make it, as long as they were telling the truth, and I believe they were." Peering over to the campfire, she added, "I'm still not sure about Giddeon and the others though."

Max affectionately squeezed her hand. "No, neither am I, but I do believe we should be watching for betrayal," he said. Letting go of her hand, he sat down against a tree, only a few feet from the wagon.

When Max woke at dawn, he jumped up and looked in the back of the wagon and was surprised to see Ember's chest still rising and falling steadily. She even appeared to have a bit more colour in her features.

Yrlissa smiled and nodded at him. "I think it worked." He returned her smile and went to help the others pack up the camp. Yrlissa called her recovery the miracle of being Fae. Max nearly snorted when Giddeon seemed to accept it as the truth. They were moving north once more an hour later. Ember was stronger, but had yet to regain consciousness.

DASAL, FREE LANDS

"What the Nine Hells do you know about this, Kyro Yorcali?" Seifer barked.

"A lot. Kael is being hunted by a... creature... called Sythrnax. An Elloryan merchant and his noble uncle through marriage believe he's a real, living Ancient, if you can believe they're actually that stupid. Crazy idiots. Care to call a truce with the witch and step outside?"

"You succeeded?" Ella said smiling. Kyro nodded.

"This makes me feel so much better," Seifer said, frowning. "Talohna's most powerful witch working with its most corrupt criminals."

"Just come on," Kyro said, leaving the barracks.

Seifer followed Kyro and Ella out of the barracks. Turning right, he walked for several seconds before his eyes caught sight of Fang Bay. Seifer stared, not quite sure what he was seeing. There had to be almost a hundred ships in the bay and just as many out in the Sea of Storms. A very distinct black ship was sailing out of the bay in the distance.

"Ella, is that the BlackSpawn Bastard sailing out of Fang Bay?' Seifer asked, disbelief riddling every word.

"Mmm-hmm. It is," Ella purred. It grated on his nerves. "Bauro was nice enough to offer us passage here. Don't worry. He's on the hunt, after a traitor. You won't see him again."

Seifer shook his head and refocused on the other two hundred or so ships threatening his city.

"Kyro Yorcali. What did you do?" Seifer asked. Kittrix whistled at the sight.

"My father and I called in the debt we were owed by Emperor Mero. Those ships hold two thousand Elloryan gladiators, all arena-experienced. Give me permission to bring them ashore and they will defend Dasal against further attacks."

"No." Slowly turning to Kyro, Seifer added, "You think I'd let you take over this city? No!"

"Go get Father, Seifer. He'll tell you that's not what this is—"

"Your father's dead." Seifer could see Kyro wince and grab at his side.

"Assassins? Broken Blade, right?"

"Assassins, yes, but there was no evidence it was the Broken Blades. Well, that's not exactly true. The assassin used Grandscorpion poison. I can't imagine anyone other than the Blades could get it."

"Grandscorpion?" Ella asked. "You sure?"

"Yes, I'm sure."

Ella sighed. "That's why my mark of rebirth didn't save him. He had no chance."

Kyro shook his head. "Yeah, well, we knew it was a risk. We just didn't expect to cross them in the process. They hit us twice in Ellorya."

"Almost succeeded the second time," Niko said. "Dummy here thought he was tough enough to fight two Blades on his own."

Seifer winced. "You don't have magic, you idiot, why didn't you run?"

"That's what I said," Niko said.

"It doesn't matter," Kyro said, pulling a letter from his coat pocket. "Here, Seifer, this is for you. Father said if anything happened to him to give it to you. Read it and then let us dock. We have their accommodations to get ready."

Seifer took the letter and sat down on the stairs leading to the lower markets and opened Lircang's letter:

Seifer,

If you're reading this letter, it means I'm dead, and you won. So, fuck you, wizard. There. Now that I feel better, on with business. By now I'm sure even your empty head has figured out that there's a lot more going on in this world than just what happens in our little corner. There's something heavy coming. You can't tell me you don't feel it.

All our differences aside, my son and I have done what we could to help you, though I apologize for the way some of them occurred. Ella doesn't believe she will survive the coming darkness, so she asked me to bring her a young woman with Elderblood, but no magical affinity. I am truly sorry, but Katarina was the only one who fit. The Desolla bloodline originated so many aeons ago. She must train with Ella until she is able to survive absorbing Ella's power of the White. You will need Ella's power, and Kat must learn how to use it before the next year is up.

And now for you, you ugly bastard. My son and I have joint control over the gladiators in front of you. You reading this means I cannot do it in person, so this letter will have to do. My half of control of the gladiators will pass to you, my written Legacy Will ensures. Kyro will defer to you in all military matters and with any concerns to Dasal's defence. The mountain canyon north of the city has already been prepared for their arrival and half my fortune will be left in trust to you through my Legacy so you can feed and train them to fight as an army.

I did this for the city we both love, even if it was in a different way than how you would have done it. Now, don't let Dasal fall to the enemy or be destroyed. Good luck, ya miserable shit. I'll be waiting for you in Perdition, Master Wizard.

Lircang Yorcali

Seifer stared at the letter, hardly able to believe what he read, even after a second pass. In forty years it was the only time Lircang referred to him as Master Wizard. "Fair enough, you fat Kariyan bastard—and thank you." He stood and looked at Kyro as the young man nodded. "Unload our army."

"Master?" Kittrix asked.

"It's all right, Kit. It seems these gladiators are actually under my control. Right, Kyro?"

"They absolutely are. It was always the plan, especially with Father..." He stopped and cleared his throat. "I'll act as liaison with the gladiator's ambassadors and my crew will arrange to feed them. Their accommodations are already built in the canyon. For the most part, all of Father's... *My* businesses are legit from this day forward. Most of it is tied up in pleasure houses, taverns, and upscale bathhouses—places that earn big money. We'll need it to feed our army.

You will have to find someone to train them to fight as units. They're only used to fighting on their own or with a second or third. Father thought you'd have some good ideas for their commanders."

"I have a couple of ideas," Seifer said. "I'll send missives with messengers in the morning. For now, get those men and families off those boats, settled, and fed. And... I'm sorry about your father Kyro. Truly."

"He knew the risks, Master Wizard, as do we all." Kyro and Niko both bowed and headed for the docks.

"Nice to see you've come to your senses," Ella said, smiling.

"If you're lying to me, Ella, and I find out that Kael died at your hands... I will use every one of these two thousand men and every Inari who will answer my call, to hunt you down and burn you alive." He turned and glared at her. "On my vow, as head of the Inari, I promise you."

"He'll be safe with us, love," Katarina said, taking his hand. "As soon as we know he's safe, I'll return here to be with you. *I* promise."

Seifer frowned, hoping he was doing the right thing. "I don't need to boost your magic, Ella. Forgive me, my friend, if I'm making a mistake... Kael went north to Kazzador City. That's all I know, but you'd better hurry. Giddeon was only two days behind when he left Dasal. You might already be too late."

Chapter Thirty-Eight

"The Dwarven people have been gone for aeons. Very few ruins remain, but each one that is found is always an outstanding discovery."

Kalmar Ibess, The Lost Cousins of the Elvehn 4920 PC

KAZZADOR CITY ENTRANCE

The trail leading to the old Dwarven Capitol of Kazzador City ended with no warning at a small square opening in the front of the towering mountain. Kael wasted little time and entered the doorway. Cassie followed right on his heels. Once past the entry, they found themselves in a large hall bare of any furnishings. Yet the walls were adorned in what was once incredibly detailed murals and writings. Walking around the perimeter of the room, Kael noticed that the paintings were sectioned into three areas on each side.

The west wall contained the painted mural of a massive battlefield, but age had faded the finer details. The writing was mostly still readable, but Kael only recognized one of the languages they were written in. The east wall's mural was in terrible condition and they were only able to make out the six-pointed star that seemed to have been painted onto a land mass, like some kind of map. The writings on the first two sections were not familiar, so Kael walked to the far end of the wall to see if he could recognize the last set.

Standing and staring at the complex language written on the last section, he realized that he was looking at a dialect he knew well. It was essentially English as spoken back home with slightly different inflections similar to the common tongue spoken everywhere they had been. It was the language he'd been able to read only days after his arrival through the dimensional bridge. The detailed diaries and historical accounts he found in the basement of Jasala's tower had been written in many languages, most of which he *could not* read. The Elvehn dialect from the Dyrannai forest was one he could, though he still had no idea how. The other was another derivative of the common tongue, the wall in front of him was written in the same and without conscious thought, he began tracing a finger along the words.

Cassie stood beside him and looked from the wall to Kael and back.

When he said nothing, she quietly asked, "Well? What does it say? Tell me," she whined. Frowning, he continued to trace the deteriorated writing while trying to glean a translation.

"I'm not sure. It says something about secrets or a secret sealed away below. After that it's too worn to read, but these words here say *births, black, and sun*, but there are words between them," he mumbled, while trying to understand what the missing words could mean.

"It sounds like its about your people, Kael," she suggested. Scratching his two weeks worth of beard, he shook his head.

"I don't know, the missing words could mean anything... yet down here," he said, kneeling. "There's clearly a warning, but there's not enough to know what they were warning about."

"What do we do now?" Cassie asked.

"I guess we go down below and see if there is any more information down there. Grodin said that any knowledge of my kind would be here, that Sythrnax was looking for it."

"Can you trust what he said?"

A darkness settled over his features. "Yes, Cassie. He was in no condition to lie to me at the time, I'm sure of that."

"All right," she said, smiling and full of excitement. "Then let's head down, the exit seems to be between those two statues."

Though he hadn't noticed before, the exit and entryway walls had no drawings or writing, but two marble statues instead, one male and one female. All four were identical to each other and looked like what Kael guessed the Dwarven people had looked like. The statues had a strong resemblance to features that were common among the Elvehn. Carved with long hair, slightly pointed ears, and though significantly shorter than the average Elvehn, the statues shared other features with the Elvehn people. Both the male and female statues had been carved with ornately braided hairstyles Kael had seen on several of the Elvehn. The male statues were also carved with flowing beards twisted into two thick braids.

Even though the statue was only five feet, two inches tall, it radiated physical strength with a finely corded muscle structure far beyond that of the Elvehn. The statues had been painstakingly carved into the raw mountain's marble and used for the exit's silent guardians. Kael wondered what the extinct people would have been like as they passed by the marble stonework and headed into the depths of the old city.

The stairs descending into the old ruin were cut into the raw bedrock of the mountain. Each step was layered in countless years' worth of dust and worn smooth by the amount of foot traffic that had clearly used the stairwell to travel into the city below, many long years in the past. Descending twenty feet at a time, the stairs turned at a ninety-degree angle and continued down another twenty steps where the stairwell turned again. This pattern carried on until Kael and Cassie arrived at the bottom of the column-shaped stairwell over an hour after they had begun.

Leaving the stairs behind they found themselves staring at the remnants of a huge underground city.

"Whoa," Kael exhaled, his mind swamped by deja vu as memories of the underground city below Tazammor Mountain came rushing back. This city, however, was a complete ruin. Cave-ins and earthquakes had collapsed all the structures, and everywhere were fissures several feet wide and too deep to see the bottom. Small amounts of sulphur laden steam rose from the wounded earth. But just like before, not a single body or decrepit skeleton could be seen anywhere he looked.

"This isn't natural..." He trailed off as he noticed scorch marks and electrical burns everywhere. Chunks of stone had been scoured by splashes of what could only be acid. "What the hell..."

"Kael?" Cassie asked.

"There was a battle here, Cassie. Aeons ago. Someone destroyed this city. There's evidence of magic every place I look."

"Hopefully they're long gone," she said, looking around nervously. Kael nodded and they set out to make their way through the ruins, skirting the deep cracks in the ground while keeping his focus to watch for possible threats.

It took a few hours to pick their way safely through the city even though it wasn't that far across. Kael was losing his patience, and his anger rose at the lack of anything left standing. He feared what he had travelled so far to find would be destroyed as well. As they reached the far side, they discovered a forged metal door with a huge locking mechanism on the front set into the raw bedrock.

To Kael's surprise and Cassie's amazement the door opened slowly the moment he touched it. Kael pulled his reaper-blades from their sheaths, ready for an ambush as he led the way through the receding doors and down six steps.

Ten feet in front of him stood a pillar of rock covered in writing from corner to corner. Kael smiled with relief. Shaped like an obelisk, the marble structure had to be the monolith he was looking for.

Approaching it slowly, Kael cursed. "God damn... I can't read it." He shook his head—another dead end.

"You're sure, Kael?"

"I recognize the lettering. It's the same as the letter Jasala left behind."

Kael knew beyond a shadow of a doubt that the writing was the same as the letter he carried against his heart on the inside of his Orotaq cloak. He removed the letter and double-checked it against the stone engravings. The characters were identical. His heart jumped with excitement as he realized the tablet had been written by his kind, or at least for them. Cursing quietly under his breath, his temper flared dangerously at the realization that he was still not strong enough to read so much information.

"Kael?" Cassie called, from the other side of the tablet. He left the stone monument, determined to return and read it some day and adding it to the list of things he was not yet strong enough to do. As he walked around the side of the carved rock looking for Cassie, he noticed the room flared out in three other directions, in the shape of a large Maltese cross. Thirty feet away in the middle of the room, Sythrnax was standing on a large symbol carved into the floor at the centre of the cross.

His hands were folded inside his sleeves, and he carried no visible weapon, though Kael knew from experience he could summon one in only seconds. The anger that had flared so easily seconds before was now obvious. Kael's innate hatred for Sythrnax calmed. He could control it more now. But it was far from gone. Cassie walked backwards, away from the creature who had caused Kael so much misery.

"Kael?" she said, her voice trembling with fear. Cassie refused to take her eyes from Sythrnax, as if doing so would provoke an attack. She continued to walk backwards to Kael.

"It's all right, Cassie, you're almost here. Just keep walking." He turned his attention to Sythrnax and asked, "Why are you here?"

"Come now, Kael, surely you must realize that my offer still stands. Let me teach you how to use all that power that is there just waiting to wreak havoc on the world," he chuckled. As Cassie reached Kael's side, he quickly pulled her behind him before answering.

"My answer hasn't changed. In fact, I would prefer to kill you here and now," Kael barked, shaking as his anger took off on him again.

Sythrnax burst out laughing. "Surely, you're not still angry about the death of that little vampyr, are you, Kael? Please. It wasn't me who killed her," he said, shaking his head. "Besides, they're vermin, a disgrace to the true DemonKind lineage. She was nothing more than a diseased, demon mongrel. You need to learn to play with the real power here, not the bottom feeders of the Lesser races. Choose the right side. Help me return this world to its past glory."

"Arabella said the exact same thing to me once, days before I handed her every ounce of pain she ever gave me. She died screaming. Be happy to show you how."

"You're stronger, Kael. I'll give you that, but you're still not strong enough. Not even close, child."

"We'll see," Kael hissed. "That vermin? Lycori? She had more soul than you could ever have. You'll pay the balance for her death, I promise."

Still laughing, Sythrnax mocked, "You remember what happened the last time we fought, newborn? What makes you think you will fare any better this time?"

"Because I know how to use my magic now," Kael said, with a smile, before spinning his reaper blades and disappearing in a cloud of black shadows, only to reappear behind Sythrnax. Both of his blades entered Sythrnax's back by an inch and then stopped as snake-like appendages slithered from under Sythrnax's hood and wrapped around Kael's blades, halting them from penetrating further. Kael vanished in a cloud of black as Sythrnax swung his staff behind him. The frost from his weapon sparked as it entered the black smoke left by Kael's disappearance.

"Seems you have a lot more to learn about my kind than you think," Kael said, re-emerging from swirls of black ten feet away.

"No. I don't. Shadow-walking? You little... *dosa*. Well done, you got close enough to draw blood," Sythrnax said, as he touched his back and pulled back fingers covered in purple-red blood. "Do you even know what you actually do when you use that type of magic? I doubt it or you wouldn't be so damn stupid. I cannot believe one of the Lower Brethren hasn't tried to pull your ass back into Hell after passing through their realm," he said, laughing again.

Cold tremors rolled down Kael's spine as he glanced over at Cassie. Fear grew in her eyes until Kael was positive she feared him more than Sythrnax. It was the same look he had seen in Lycori's eyes long ago, but it gave him an idea.

"Cassie, run, now!" Kael yelled, noticing her fear had her frozen in one spot. "Run, hide, and don't let him find you. Now!" he barked even louder. With a sigh of relief, he watched her turn and run, vanishing out the door and into the ruins.

"I have no interest in her anyway..." Kael smiled as Sythrnax trailed off.

"I know," Kael said. "I wasn't protecting her from you, but from me. You know why I can pass through Hell untouched, Sythrnax?"

"You can't, you just..."

"Because the demons of Hell obey my call." Though he had learned how to shut the voices out, once he relaxed his hold, Kael's mind was bombarded by offers to help.

"You bluff, *dosa*. Demons can no longer walk Talohna's surface." Kael's smile lessened at the creature's ignorance and he called out inside his head to the one demon he knew would help.

"Tusk, just you. Help me, and his soul is yours." His answer was immediate.

"The offered soul will suffice. We have a deal, dark wizard."

Kael's blade-filled right hand shot out, and he chuckled as the air to the left of Sythrnax rippled and tore. "You're a fraud, Sythrnax. You know less about my kind than I do. This demon proves it." A thunderous crack of power rocked the chamber as a rent widened and the demon who helped Kael in Dasal pushed his way through into Talohna's reality with the help of Kael's magic. Roaring like a big cat, the demon towered over Sythrnax by several feet, outweighing him by three hundred pounds.

"Incredible," Sythrnax gasped, glancing back and forth from Kael to the demon. "In fifteen thousand years, no DeathWizard has ever pulled a Demon Lord across, and you, a gods-cursed newborn, crack the fabric of the Ninth Hell with no training. Garz'x, old friend, you've been well, I assume?"

"Sythrnax," the demon growled. "With Salotan gone, the Nine Hells are very well."

"Good. I'm glad I could help you get rid of your ArchDemon." The demon bowed its head. Kael began to panic, wondering if his plan was about to backfire.

Sythrnax stared at Kael, his mask pulled up by the smile underneath. "You see, Kael, I do know. I know every single thing there is to know about you. I just didn't imagine you'd ever have the power to pull one low-hell demon through, let alone the Lord of the Nine Hells..."

"Lucky me," Kael said, his voice riddled with sarcasm. He could still feel Garz'x tethered to his magic. "Too bad your demon buddy is here for me."

"Oh, he's here for you all right, Kael. Garz'x, you know what I need done. Take Kael, cut his throat, and when he dies, drag his soul to Hell." Kael laughed. Sythrnax frowned as the demon joined in Kael's laughter.

"Funny thing, Sythrnax," Kael said, his laughter fading. "My death magic and that demon are controlled by my strength of will..."

"That takes centuries to develop, newborn..."

"Normally perhaps, but not after six months of torture at the hands of the Dead Sisters," Kael barked. "Garz'x, kill him."

"Sorry, old one." The massive demon laughed, jumping at Sythrnax and snatching at him. Sythrnax's staff rang through the chamber as it scraped against the demon's claws. Not hesitating, Kael disappeared among a cloud of black shadows, reappearing long enough to pass by Sythrnax as his left Vai'Karth sliced deep into both the creature's hamstrings.

"Enough, Garz'x, stop!" Sythrnax screamed. Raising his left hand, Sythrnax stared at Kael as the demon closed, again following only Kael's demands. A black energy pulsed from the stone within his glove. "You lose, Kael. When you can't control a demon, you banish it." Laughing, Sythrnax hissed, "*Aytto Asai.*"

The fabric of reality inside the chamber tore again, opening much faster than when Kael had done it. Garz'x roared with fury, lashing out with his long, spiked tail as Sythrnax's magic tried sucking the demon back into Hell. A tail spine sunk deep into Sythrnax's thigh, snapping off as the demon tumbled into the hell-rift. A second crack echoed through the chamber as the tear in reality winked from existence. The expense of magic and the embedded demon's spine dropped Sythrnax to his knees. Kael attacked immediately, crossing his blades as he stepped from swirls of black. Sythrnax laughed, slamming the butt of his staff into the ground, throwing up a wall of ice. Both Kael's Vai'Karth cut deep into the frozen barrier, but stopped short of his enemy.

Anger radiated through Kael as he screamed the words for more magic, fury and determination increased the power of his spell significantly.

"Hrinda Bal." Black and purple molten fire jumped from both his hands, running along his blades before ripping into the ice wall. Chunks of ice hissed and exploded outward as the dark energy quickly ate its way past the wall and shot through the far side, catching Sythrnax along his left hip. He grunted as Kael poured more power into his magic. Hatred fuelled the results. The flames hissed and spit, sparked and jumped, splashing into the walls around the chamber. The stone in Sythrnax's glove pulsed again, forcing Kael's magic to slide away, but not before burning a gouge two feet long from Sythrnax's hip and back.

Sythrnax cursed, limping away. Kael followed, stalking him as his enemy circled to the left, coming to a stop on the design at the centre of the Maltese cross. "You're stronger than I thought, Kael. You have no idea what I could teach you. My people invented the VosHain, the magical language..." Close enough now, Kael swung his left blade. Sythrnax was a moment too slow to block with his staff, and Kael's blade cut deep into his right shoulder.

"VosHain was created by the Ancients," Kael said, his voice emotionless. "You lie."

"Yes, Kael. It was created by the Ancients. Think! Use your small *dosa* mind!" Kael stopped, taking a couple steps back, trying to process what Sythrnax said.

He frowned. "You're not an Ancient, you're a fucking disease..." Kael vanished in a cloud of black. He materialized behind Sythrnax, spinning both his reaper-blades upwards and driving them into Sythrnax's back.

Kael smiled, savouring the feeling that only comes with revenge fulfilled as Sythrnax's body slumped into death on the end of his blades. Laughter echoed around the chamber and Kael realized he could not move a single inch. A light clapping came from behind him and Sythrnax's voice followed, muddling Kael's mind.

"Very, very, good, newborn." Still unable to move, Kael caught movement in his peripheral vision as Sythrnax stepped into his sight.

Staring at Sythrnax's body suspended from his blades, Kael realized his mistake. "God damn illusion. I was never fighting you."

Sythrnax laughed. "No, not really. I have heard about your skill with illusion, Kael. Waltzing right past all of Lircang's people in Dasal with their prized slave and they never even saw her. I almost hoped you would see through mine. It's... disappointing."

"Illusions aren't solid, Sythrnax."

"True. This is Ancient illusion magic and super-imposing soul possession, Kael. Real magic, not the bastardized nonsense wizards flick around in today's age. Technically, you were fighting me, but her body is so limited compared to mine—it is why you killed me... or her." His glove pulsed as he laughed. "Here, I'm sure you'd like to know who you killed?"

Kael stared in horror as Sythrnax's body suspended on his weapons shook with light tremors. The robe, the armour, all vanished, leaving a sparsely-dressed young woman impaled on his blades.

"Jesus Christ, Sythrnax," Kael cried out, guilt already eating at his soul. "She can't be fifteen years old. What the hell is wrong with you?"

"Me?" he taunted. "You killed her... You know, you really are a slow learner when it comes to magic. She sacrificed herself, willingly, for the betterment of our cause, our plan. Yet you're more worried about the dead girl hanging from your blades than the fact you can't move a muscle." As his eyes shifted to the floor under him, Kael finally understood that ignoring the symbol under his feet was another grievous mistake.

"Kin Atoll," Sythrnax barked, and the Vai'Karth were torn from Kael's grip, slicing through the young girl's body and snapping several fingers on both of his hands. The blades clunked as they stuck to the seal on the floor. When he realized he still couldn't move, Kael understood that he had walked right into whatever Sythrnax had planned, again. He

struggled against what held him. The seal on the floor under him pulsed. The magical trap exerted more force to hold him still.

"I am surprised you can't yet read the script written on the tablets here, Kael. It would have told you all you needed to know. They were carved by your people and their guardians for your future kind, many, many thousands of years ago," he smirked. "Perhaps you would like me to tell you what they say? Fill in a little of your past you so desperately want to know? What do you say? It seems we have some time to spare before the ArchWizard Zirakus gets here to kill you." Sythrnax broke out laughing once more.

"Either tell me what you want or kill me Sythrnax. Your big flapping mouth is starting to hurt my ears," Kael said, frowning.

"You have nothing to fear from me, Kael," he said, holding his hands out to his side. "I have no intention of killing you at all. In fact, I can't kill you. That seal you're standing on will open when your blood is spilled by a person other than my race. A betrayer to the Lesser races of Talohna. Though I must say, there are a handful of people entering the ruins right now who would be more than willing to do it."

"Why?" Kael asked, struggling against the magical bindings of the seal. "What does it gain you to have me killed here? Some Dwarven weapon to help you with your conquest of the world? If you want this world so bad, then take it, I won't stop you. There have only been two people here who have shown me any kind of humanity and one died at your witch's hands. You can burn this world for all I care. Just let me take Cassie and leave," he begged.

For the first time during either meeting, Kael quickly realized he had struck a weak spot in Sythrnax, though it was unintentional. Sythrnax flew into a rage. Unable to move, Kael could only watch as Sythrnax kicked the dead girl's body aside and grabbed his throat. Sythrnax's face twitched under his mask.

"You insignificant little pest, typical of you dosa. Do you think I have waited all these thousands of years just to conquer these two polluted kingdoms? My home lies to the north of the Blood Kingdoms, in the Ancient Kingdom. When your cursed ancestor tore the continents apart, she freed me from my prison, but also cut me off from my homeland. You stand on one of the many seals that will allow my people to return to Talohna and reclaim the power that has been kept from us for over fifteen thousand years."

Sythrnax's fury increased as he shook Kael repeatedly, almost crushing his throat as the seal held him firm. "You cannot begin to fathom how meaningless these petty kingdoms are to me. They are merely a very small means to an end. Four of the seals are here, and the countries supply me with warriors to do what needs to be done, but that is all. The races of these kingdoms cannot comprehend what this is all about. We will be free and we will take back what was stolen from us so long ago, I promise you that. Your blood will start it all." His anger spent, he released Kael's throat and stood back.

Coughing and gagging from lack of air, Kael could not believe what he was hearing. Everything he had been told of the DeathWizards made no sense against what Sythrnax had just said. As his breath returned, Kael hoped to get some answers from the creature whose face he had never even seen.

"Then if I'm gonna die," Kael rasped, "tell me why. What the hell can my blood do for you?" He watched the hooded and cloaked being for signs of more anger, but it never came.

"You really want to know?"

"Of course I want to know, you asshole. If I'm gonna die for some big cause at the hands of some creature who refuses to show me his face, then you owe me that much."

"I owe you nothing, pest, but I will show you and tell you anyway. After I prepare the seal. Jasala Vyshaan might have destroyed the world, but she reinforced the locks on this seal for five thousand more years. Curse her *dosa* soul."

Sythrnax bent over and slid the key he retrieved from Vexa into the top of the Animus Seal and turned the locking mechanism a full turn. The intricately designed grooves within the seal widened and spun, creating a spiral set of grooves that led to the centre of the seal.

"Done. For the better, I guess," he said. Standing, he reached up inside his hood and pulled his mask to the side. Kael gasped, surprised by the beautiful face underneath. Sythrnax's high cheek bones and complexion were flawless, his smooth skin more like that of a young child's. He smiled, showing a hint of sharp, serrated teeth behind thin lips. Even so, his blazing purple eyes still dominated his features. That quickly changed as he lowered his hood. He had no hair, instead dozens of long, silver-scaled appendages writhed their way free as if they were alive. Offset rows of the tentacles covered his head and thousands of small silver scales layered each one, shining as if actually made from silver metal.

Kael nodded slightly at the recognition that these tentacles, for lack of a better word, were what stopped his first attack against the illusion Sythrnax had cast on the young girl.

"Happy?" Sythrnax asked, as the scaled appendages slid back underneath his rising hood. He replaced the mask and stared hard at Kael. "The show is over. Now to the telling. Thirteen thousand years ago, there was a great war-"

"The DemonKind War?" Kael interrupted.

"DemonKind War?" Sythrnax asked, and laughed as if he had never heard of something so absurd. "The foolishness you speak of didn't even happen. Thirteen thousand years and a land cataclysm, along with the stupidity of your wizards, has a way of losing history. What did happen was a real war, one that involved every single race of the time. A magical war that we, in fact, tried everything in our power to avoid."

"Fact?" Kael huffed. "A fact is nothing more than the distorted reality of the one who experienced it, Sythrnax. I've seen what you consider to be fact." Sythrnax smacked Kael on the side of his head. With no give in the magic holding him still, the solid strike hurt like hell. "You should stick to listening, Kael, philosophy doesn't suit you. This great war was one that we were winning, until your kind came along. The dreaded Kai'Sar, the DeathWizards. Creatures who revel in the misery of death. We know you were created, made. Some kind of perversion of desperate, twisted magic. I know that you live a very, very, long time and that every offspring you breed is birthed like you were, during the Black Sun and with magical powers drawn from life and death. Eventually, there were six of you at one time. Those six each opened an Animus Seal, one of which you stand on right now. These six seals were all opened at the same time and every one of them was situated on or below a battlefield where my people were fighting. Your ancestors used their very life-force to pull my kind through the seal, and then they sacrificed their souls to close each one, locking my people away forever. After I was freed by Jasala, I learned that the few who remained were hunted and killed. It was the day the Ancients died." Kael shook with terror as the words sunk in.

"Jesus, my kind killed the Ancients," Kael whispered in a low voice.

"In a way, you did, yes. The good thing is that the dimension they... *we*... were sent to has a stasis effect on living flesh. When Jasala destroyed Talohna as it was five thousand years ago, it released me from this very seal. It has taken me five thousand years to figure out exactly what happened, what had happened after our disappearance, but more importantly, how to open it again and free the rest of the Ancients, my people. You see, once you are dead and my people are free, this land will become what it once was, a great and prosperous land for all. And a land free of the abominations that are your kind."

Sythrnax was talking about events during the time of the Ancients. A time people had told Kael they knew little about. The people of Talohna revered the Ancients, some countries even worshipped them and the Fae more than they did Talohna's gods. It was common belief that the Ancients helped the mortal races learn about magic and were thought to be fair in a world that prospered for all people, regardless of race.

Until they disappeared.

If Kael did not escape from the clutches of the magical trap that held him, he was going to die in order to serve a cause he knew nothing about, for a people who would be worshipped like gods upon their return.

And his executioners were only hours away.

Chapter Thirty-Nine

"To save the life of a Northman is to earn the favour of his or her entire clan. The Kreeda Oath is taken deadly serious by anyone born on Kastalborg Island. Even if it means their own death, a Northman will honour this oath until his or her last day."

High King Garnath Stormshield, 883 PC

APPROACH TO KAZZADOR CITY

Ember sat in the back of the wagon as it shook and rocked its way down the trail. Yrlissa helped her secure Kasik's kreeda properly and then braided the rest of her hair tightly so it stayed out of her eyes. Yrlissa had quickly filled her in on what had happened. Ember first woke on the seventh morning after taking the burrow worm poison from Kasik's body, and another three-and-a-half days had passed before she woke again, feeling only marginally better, but not as tired. It had taken almost three more days for her to wake for longer than what it took to eat a bite of food. Now, still weak, she continued riding in the wagon as she absent-mindedly played with Kasik's kreeda.

Too many thoughts rolled around in her head. Aravae had wasted no time introducing herself to Ember and explaining that she and Giddeon were Kael's birth parents. Giddeon's behaviour sickened Ember all the more with every word Aravae spoke. She came to admire the Elvehn woman, and her heart ached for Kael when she thought of the mother he should have had compared to the one Giddeon had left him with.

Yrlissa had also quickly brought her up to date about her real recovery when Giddeon and the others were out of earshot. The fact that the necromancer king and queen from DormaSai had saved her life and offered their help was puzzling. "Practitioners of death" Giddeon had called them. She scoffed; he had once called Kael a "prophesied force of death". The so-called death practitioners saved her life, which was far more than Giddeon had ever done. Even so, she couldn't understand why those so closely linked to death would save her—a Fae dedicated to preserving life, but she did not doubt for a single second that they also had their own agenda. It seemed everyone in Talohna did. Only Yrlissa had been more honest with her than not. Being able to trust Yrlissa had helped get her this far.

Ember frowned as she watched Kasik slide from his horse. Handing the reigns to Saleece, he jumped into the wagon and sat cross-legged across from Ember.

She stared at him for several seconds. "You gave me this?" she asked. He nodded. "Why?"

"My people are not Elvehn. A life-debt does not exist in Northman society. When you save the life of a Northman, though not mandatory, he or she is within their right to offer this oath of loyalty. We call it the Kreeda Oath. The lengths of hair we exchange are also called a kreeda. Both are a symbol of unbreakable loyalty in Northman society."

Ember nodded. "The kreeda you gave me is only nine inches, your father's is eighteen," she said, lifting Kasik's longer braid from behind his left ear.

"Yes. The longer braid and left side represent the solidarity of family and the strength of their protection. It is customarily a Northman's shield side. The right side symbolizes allies and the reliability of your right hand, your sword hand."

"You Northmen are complicated, Kasik" Ember said, shaking her head. "What does it ultimately mean?"

"I have already told you what it means for you when you were at death's door. You tell me." Ember closed her eyes. Several minutes passed before they snapped open.

"I remember. Like a hazy dream. You told me you'd defend Kael, even against Giddeon if need be."

He nodded and gave her a slight bow. "Were you not Fae, you could be of Northman blood," he said, smiling. Standing, he gently squeezed her shoulder and hopped from the wagon onto his horse as Saleece led the big mare closer to the moving wagon.

"Thank you," Ember whispered, as she lay back to rest.

Two hours later, and with the Kazzador City entrance visible in the light of the two shining moons, Ember felt much better, and her heart raced at the realization that Kael was likely only hours ahead of her.

They rode into the small clearing at the foot of the small passage's entry stairs, noticing two horses standing nearby. Though they were not tied to the trees, two of the mounts Kael brought with him and Cassie had yet to wander off.

Climbing down from his horse, Max walked over and examined them as they grazed on the damp grass.

"These must be Kael's and whomever is with him. They left nothing behind, Ember," he offered as she walked over.

"It matters little," Giddeon said, frowning. "Except for the fact it means we are closer than we have ever been before. Come on," he ordered, as the others grabbed their travel packs, readied their weapons, and entered the doorway to the city.

"Look, Father." Saleece gasped once they were inside. "These drawings and writings, what are they? I have never seen anything quite like it," she called back over her shoulder as she hurried to the west wall. Joining her, Giddeon and Kasik stood staring at the mural of a huge battle depicted on the wall.

"What is it, Giddeon?" Kasik asked.

"I'm not sure. I don't recognize the writing," he answered, looking to Yrlissa with a raised eyebrow.

"One is a rare dialect of the Dyrannai Elvehn," she replied. "The other two, I'm not sure of. Aravae, do you know them?"

"No," Aravae acknowledged from behind them. "I recognize some Elvehn in the one you were talking about, but the rest are unfamiliar."

"Can you read it?" Max asked Yrlissa, joining them.

"No," Yrlissa lied. "It hasn't been used by the Elvehn people for well over ten thousand years. I already looked at the other wall. It is written in only one I understand, an outdated vernacular of the common tongue. It's very old as well."

After stepping across the room and looking at the eastern wall alongside his wife, Giddeon rubbed the back of his head as if he knew there was no way he would be able to read any of the archaic languages.

"What does it say?" he requested.

Yrlissa had to think hard before answering. "Most of it is worn away as you can see, but it speaks of something sealed away down below," she pointed out, truthfully.

Nodding his head, Giddeon said, "All right then. We know where Kael went. If we are going to make any headway in talking to him like we've agreed, then we all need some sleep and clear heads. We should make camp here inside this hall. It will be easier to defend if we need to. Kasik, Saleece, myself, and Niky will cover the first set of watches, the rest of you can follow on into dawn, then we'll go see if we can talk to Kael without all of us dying."

"Okay," Max agreed. "Kasik and I will do a quick check below us to make sure we can sleep soundly. Kasik?"

"Lead the way," the Northman nodded. The others got busy setting up the camp, though they all agreed to go without a fire and have their late supper meal cold instead. It took Kasik and Max well over an hour to return, having reached the bottom of the stairway with the ninety degree turns. They found two sets of prints heading into a destroyed city, but no threats. Everyone quickly settled in and were soon asleep.

After waiting two hours for everyone to be in a deep sleep, Giddeon silently asked the others sharing watch to meet with him outside the hall in the clearing at the bottom of the entry stairs.

Once they all arrived, he began. "I think we need to discuss what our plan should be. I was all for trying to talk to Kael before, but with the massacre of your sisters, Niky, that changes things. It's pretty clear Kael's lost some of his faculty for rational thought." Saleece shook her head, disagreeing, but it didn't stop Giddeon from continuing. "We burned those bodies, Saleece, there were young girls, ten and twelve years of age among his victims. When he finds out we lied to him about Ember and Max, he's not going to listen to us, is he?"

Kasik stayed silent, as if waiting to see what the others would do.

"I'm not sure, Giddeon," Kyah said, carefully. "My sisters deserve justice, but the earth mother preaches patience and respect for all living creatures. We believe that forgiving your worst enemy is the path to true peace for one's soul, but *my* soul screams for justice for what was done to them. I'm not sure what to do, but I will go along with whatever you all decide should be the proper course."

"Fair enough," Giddeon said, placing his hand on her shoulder. "You are true to yourself to speak so openly. I think Mylla would be proud, and so would your sisters who died that night. Saleece, how about you?" he asked.

"I can't, Father. I would never have made it out of the Wildlands if not for Ember. I cannot betray her by doing this. I'm sorry, but I won't," she said sadly. Kasik put his arm around her in an attempt to comfort her.

"She has earned our trust, Giddeon, and we hers," Kasik warned. "If you betray that now, it will never be regained. I owe her my life, and I gave her my kreeda the night we thought she would die. I carry her braid now. I can't stand against her. The code of the Kreeda Oaths make that very clear."

"I understand, but we have to consider what he has already done. If given the chance, he could very well kill us all," Giddeon argued.

"*Could*, Father. The reality might be very different," Saleece debated, refusing to back down.

Taking a deep breath and sighing softly, Giddeon tried one more time. "What if there is another way? One where we can talk to Kael without having the others there?"

"What do you have in mind, Giddeon?" Kasik asked suspiciously.

Pulling a finger sized vial and a cloth from the pocket of his robe, Giddeon showed them. "I stole this vial from the Taktala herbalist I worked for when we were slaves in the Wildlands. It's full of their sleep poison. There is more than enough for us to hit every one who would defend Kael with it and then go after him by ourselves. That way we can decide whether he is the threat that I suspect he is. If he is, we can deal with it without having to fight Max and the others. I understand how you all feel. My wife will lay her life down before she allows us to hurt Kael. It is too big of a gamble to do it any other way," he stated firmly.

"Father!" Saleece exclaimed. "You realize you are talking about possibly creating the exact situation Zaddyk warned you about. If we make a mistake, all of Talohna will suffer for it. Are you sure its worth that risk?"

"What choice do we have?" he replied, as he looked at everyone with him. "I'm sure between all of us, we can make the proper decision, right Kasik?"

Kasik stared hard a Giddeon before answering. "Are you ready to accept that if we act incorrectly, then we will have destroyed everything we have tried so hard to save?"

"I honestly believe that if we take the others to speak with Kael, things will go very badly, very fast."

"We agree on that much," Kasik said nodding.

"Are we *agreed* then?" he asked.

Kyah merely nodded as Saleece answered. "Yes, Father, I think so."

"All right then, everyone take a dart and dip it in here," he instructed as he held up the vial of Taktala poison and unrolled the cloth, revealing a handful of darts.

"You better give me at least a half dozen, Giddeon," Kasik requested. "Max seems to shake off the first three or four."

"Good idea, hold them between your fingers and use a slapping motion. One at a time won't work, he'll remain awake too long. I almost forgot about his strange resistance. Remind me to tell you about a theory I have about him when we are finished with all this," he smiled.

"I will. I have nothing against him and he has earned my respect, but there is something not right with him," Kasik pointed out as he took the six darts from Giddeon and the others took their coated darts as well.

"Remember: the side or back of the neck works the fastest. I'll take Yrlissa," he offered. "She'll need two as well. Saleece, you want your mother or no?"

"I will take Ember. Sister Niky can have mother," she said. Turning to Kyah, she placed her hand on her shoulder. "Please, don't hurt her."

Kyah smiled and gently reassured her with a hug. "I promise, I'll be careful."

"All right then. Let's get this over with," Giddeon ordered, leading the way.

Using the poison-tipped darts worked perfectly as Ember, Aravae, and Yrlissa never even woke from their normal slumber.

Max woke up swinging the instant the darts pierced his neck. Floored by the first punch, Kasik crashed onto his back and slid over ten feet, dazed.

Only managing to get to his knees, Max cursed. "Bastards. I knews sit," he slurred before falling face first on his sleeping mat. Giddeon helped Kasik to his feet, a trickle of magic helping to clear the bright stars and bring him back to his senses.

Within only minutes, the two of them led the way down the stairs and into the city after Kael, leaving the others defenceless where they lay.

APPROACH TO KAZZADOR CITY

Nekrosa and Sephi Kohl had been running for over an hour when the dawn of the day's sun crested the eastern horizon. The group of warriors pursuing them were immune to nearly every kind of magic they had tried, if their magic managed to work at all. There were far too many to stand and fight.

Though they were not aware of it as they travelled, they quickly discovered that Sythrnax had left a large force of his men hiding in the mountain forest with clear orders to move forward and kill everyone they saw before dawn. They were to continue forward until the ruins were devoid of any life. The one warrior they had managed to catch alive happily told them his orders as he died smiling, convinced his fellow fighters would avenge him during the ruins' purge.

Luthian Bathory, Nekrosa's childhood friend and leader of his spy network, was out front leading the way and watching for dangers ahead. As Nekrosa and Sephi raced into the clearing leading to the Dwarven ruins of Kazzador City, Luthian was already deep into a ritual casting that would regurgitate three buried skeletons from the earth under their feet. Nekrosa recognized the tell-tale scent of death as raw earth burst up from beneath his feet. The DormaSain king jumped back and the skeletons crawled forth from the ground, clawing their way out of their ancient graves. The scent they brought with them told Nekrosa there were many more dead below where they stood.

"That's it, my lord," Luthian gasped. "The last of what I can draw from the Void before the enemy gets here went into these three," he offered, clearly exhausted from the hour-long fight and flight.

"Come on then, old man. Let's go. The bones can slow them down," Nekrosa said as he limped over and tried to drag Luthian onto the entry stairs. Sephi finished a second summoning as two more skeletons dug their way out of the earth. She grabbed Luthian's other arm and started to help as well.

"Stop, my lord. Please, my queen... Stop," he begged. "You go, both of you. I'll stay here and try to hold them off for as long as I can. It will give you both the time you need to get in there and make sure that young Fae stays alive. It is the least I can do."

"Stop talking foolish, Luthian," admonished Sephi. "We cannot leave you behind. I *refuse* to leave you behind. You are all we have left from our childhood. The war for the throne took everyone else. Now, come on," she said, her lower lip quivering with emotion.

He quickly stepped up and gave her a hug. "It's all right, Sephi. I'll be right behind you, I promise, but you and Nekrosa go finish what we came here to do. I'll be fine." He smiled, in a clear attempt to make her feel better.

Nekrosa limped over, and grasping Luthian's hand, he shook it. "Are you sure that this is what you want, old friend? You know I would never ask this of you."

"The fact that you would never ask it is the reason why I offer, my lord," he said.

Nekrosa grabbed him forcefully. "Cut that *lord* shit out right now, do you hear me? If you're going to say goodbye, then you do it as the brothers and friends we have always been, you understand?"

"Yes, brother, I do. Goodbye, my friend. You make damn sure you get that girl out of here safely, do you understand?"

With his eyes shiny from moisture, Nekrosa whispered, "I will. I promise you, I will."

Letting go and shoving Luthian behind him, Nekrosa yelled, "Now get outta my way so I can give you some help." Holding his hands out, Nekrosa stared at the earth, feeling for the touch of corpses that tickled his mind. Drawing massive amounts of power from the Void, he pushed his shaking hands towards the ground.

"*Na gravasay, corpagra nava*!" Nekrosa screamed with rage as he tapped more power from the Void, releasing waves of pulsating magic into the earth across the entire clearing. For seconds, nothing happened, but then the ground began to shake vigorously as a growl awoke deep beneath the earth.

Skeletal hands tore their way through the earth, surfacing everywhere in the clearing. The flat earth over the ancient battle ground gave birth to the walking dead, animated by the raw power of a prodigal necromancer as Nekrosa tried desperately to give his friend a fighting chance of survival. With Luthian and Sephi managing to summon five skeletons together and Nekrosa's horde of more than fifty, all of which were armed with the rusted weapons they had died with, Nekrosa had given his friend the only advantage he could. Luthian bowed to his King and Queen and drew both of his swords as Nekrosa tossed a small charm his way.

"The tether, brother. The horde answers to you," Nekrosa yelled. Luthian slid the charm around his neck and went to join his undead warriors, intent on granting his King and Queen the time they would need to save Ember's life from the forces that Sythrnax had left hiding in the forest.

Racing up the stairs and into the entry hall, both the king and queen of DormaSai nearly tripped over the bodies of Ember and her group as they lay there in a drug-induced sleep.

"What the Nine Hells..." Sephi cursed as she knelt to feel for a pulse on the side of Ember's neck. "Thank the gods. She's still alive, Nekrosa."

"Yeah, so is the big man," he added, as he started to stand back up. He only got half way as Max exploded back to consciousness, grabbing Nekrosa by the neck with his left hand

and in three big strides, slammed him into the mural on the western wall.

"What have you done?" he roared into Nekrosa's face. With his airway completely compressed and his boots a full three feet off the ground, the DormaSain king could only grunt as he struggled.

Sephi quickly drew her weapons and approached the two from the right, where she stopped just short of impaling herself on one of Max's Elloryan blades.

With a twitch of his blade he growled, "You have five seconds and then I snap his neck." His intense brown eyes seemed to stare into her soul, as she responded instantly to his demand.

"Max, it's me. Sephi, remember? I gave you the cure in the forest so you could save Ember. Remember?" she demanded as he shook his head. She could see that whatever was clouding his mind refused to clear. "I don't know what happened to you, Max, but this is my husband, Nekrosa. We've come to help you, just like I promised we would." She spoke fast, but her words slowly sunk into his disoriented and confused mind. He gently released Nekrosa and touched his own head.

Nekrosa coughed, wheezing in a panicked attempt to draw air into his deprived lungs.

"Are you all right, husband?" Sephi asked. He nodded, so she turned to Max.

"Where are Giddeon and the others?" she prodded easily.

"Giddeon?" Max replied. "Goddamn, that fucking son of a bitch. I am gonna wring his skinny wizard chicken neck. Oh, Jesus, my head hurts." He cursed as he sat on the floor holding his head.

"Giddeon did this? Are you sure?" Sephi asked, hoping for verification at the same moment a groan from across the room told them that Yrlissa had just woken up.

"Yes," Max snapped. "The fucking traitor stuck us with those stupid Taktala sleep darts."

Ember and Aravae woke at the same time, but it was Aravae who stated the obvious. "Oh gods, that stupid husband of mine did this, didn't he? I should have seen this coming. He never thought twice about taking our son through that gateway twenty years ago. I should have known he wouldn't have changed... Oh, I should have known," she whispered softly and slowly started to massage her pounding head. Yrlissa managed to slide over to Ember and help her to sit up.

"Yrlissa!" Aravae gasped. "Your tattoo. It's smaller."

Yrlissa touched the side of her face gently. "Gods, no. How much smaller is it?" she asked, as Ember touched her chin and turned her head.

"From your temple to your cheek," Ember said. "What does it mean? You said it was just a tattoo, for your family."

"It doesn't matter, we must hurry. Come on, Ember," she pleaded quietly. "You need to get it together and clear that poison from your system, then clear the others so we can get after Giddeon and Kael. You know what this means. He's trying to trigger Zaddyk's prophecy. Ember, we have to hurry."

Gently shaking her head to clear the dizziness, she nodded. "Yeah, okay. Just give me a second here," she asked. Closing her eyes, she whispered a spell and touched Yrlissa's head to clear the sleep poison.

Nearly back to normal after being choked by Max, Nekrosa overheard what Yrlissa said to Ember. "Hold on there, you two," he said, walking over, still rubbing his throat. "What prophecy are you talking about? We have most of them back home and we haven't heard of a prophet named Zaddyk, have we?" he asked looking at his wife. When she shook her head, he continued. "I did not think so. Perhaps you should explain. Quickly."

"Perhaps you should explain," Aravae said, stepping towards Ember protectively. "Your kind are not normally known for helping others."

Sephi snorted. "More northern prejudice. Your husband says the same about your son. I shouldn't have to tell an Elvehn elementalist that magic is a tool wielded by either a good person or a bad."

"We do not have time to debate this!" Yrlissa snapped. "They saved Ember's life. For now, that will have to be good enough. Max?"

"Yrlissa?"

"If either our new royal companions try anything stupid, kill them both. We don't have any time to waste. We have to go now."

"I'll watch them," Max said. Frowning at Nekrosa, he pointed at Sephi. "You have that chance you asked for, don't waste it." It earned him a bow from the DormaSain king.

Ember used the same quick touch to help Aravae. Heading over to Max, she did the same.

Nekrosa shook his head. "Very well, that will have to..." he stopped speaking in mid sentence and rubbed his sore throat. Ember gently pushed her way to him, whispering something and touching him at the same time.

"Thank you, young Fae," he said, realizing his throat no longer hurt.

She smiled. "Ember. My name is Ember. Now, please, hurry," she said, before joining the others on their way down the stairs to the old city.

Chapter Forty

"Those who get up after being knocked down will always thrive in life. It takes a strength of will that not everyone can find inside themselves. As hard as it may be to stand back up, to lift oneself from the devastation this world often deals us, is the sign of a true survivor. We have watched Talohna's worst knock Kael down time and again, and he always finds a way to get back up. I hope he fights as hard against the dark corruption racing through him. If so, perhaps Talohna will have a chance against the true darkness that is coming."

Yrlissa Blackmist, Date unknown

BLOODKIN CASTLE, DRAGON ISLES

Even though Shelaryx WhiteScale was using the magic of her mirrored table to keep track of the events unfolding at Kazzador City, she was still surprised when a bright light blazed through her private castle chambers and Eva ThornWing, the Fae Matriarch, stood beside her.

"We must go, Shel, before it's too late. The demon seal is active," she said, clearly out of breath.

"That's impossible. The room is shielded, I know, but I have been watching the ruined city outside the seal's room. No one has entered besides Kael and the little girl with him."

"There must be another way in from the back, an open fissure perhaps. The seal is active. I saw it myself before I left Vaenaria. It has to be Sythrnax. He must be there!"

Quickly turning from the mirror, Shelaryx asked, "You came alone so we could take more Kin, correct?"

Nodding calmly, Eva replied, "Yes, bring only six. I hope to return with my daughter and the others."

"I will gather our best and meet you in the throne room. We won't be long." She spun and left the bedroom at the same time Eva vanished in a flash of white light.

Eva's short realm jump took her to the far side of the crystal castle, knowing she would likely still arrive only seconds before the Queen. BloodKin castle was full of magic and secrets. The DragonKin could appear anywhere in the castle, whenever they so decided, and never had to walk from one end of the sprawling complex to the other.

Shelaryx walked into the throne room with three Talon warriors and three female Zephyrs, the DragonKin's most powerful magic users.

The DragonKin joined the Fae monarch and their own queen without a word and a whispered spell sparked another bright light as the realm-jump magic known only to the Fae whisked them away to Kazzador City in the Dwarven Mountains.

KAZZADOR CITY
DEATHWIZARD'S MONOLITH CHAMBER

Kael spent the next couple hours silently watching Sythrnax make preparations for whatever he had planned. Adding wards to keep others from freeing Kael and weaves attached to the seal that became invisible upon activation, Sythrnax worked non-stop in preparation for what was to come. Having worn himself out, to Sythrnax's great amusement, Kael gave up on trying to break free of the trap he stood on. Instead, Kael hoped to figure out a way to escape by watching and learning what Sythrnax was doing. When it became clear it was getting him nowhere, Kael could no longer keep control of his anger. The vines of his death-flower began to twitch uncomfortably with his aggravation, and soon the vines were on the move. But after only ten minutes they stopped coring through his body, even though his anger was still well beyond his control. It was disturbing that they had finally quit, but it only added more fuel to his anger.

"God dammit. Why the hell do you not just kill me, you coward, or at least fight me. What you're doing makes no sense," Kael yelled. He felt his rage climb even higher when Sythrnax laughed.

"Because your feeble young mind doesn't understand what I am doing doesn't mean it makes no sense. Your kind have believed for far too long that you are the dominant beings of this world, and that needs to change."

"God, and you say I'm stupid—use a mirror much? I don't know anything about my kind or this world, Sythrnax, and I don't care to. My wife is dead, my best friend is dead, and I killed Kyah myself after she revealed her true self to me. There is nothing here for me except that little girl who ran earlier. Why do you all not understand that? I'm not even from this world, for Christ's sake."

"I am well aware of that. I followed your life every way possible, and I orchestrated your return to this world so that you would come to be here, in this exact place, when I needed you to be. The others don't matter..." He stopped and held up his talon tipped finger. "Actually, I take that back," he said quickly. "They matter in the sense that they are needed to spill your blood upon that seal, and seeing as how it sounds as though they are coming, I will leave you for them," he chuckled and turned to walk away.

"You're just gonna leave me here? Defenceless? You really are a coward. I'll find you some day, Sythrnax. If I have to claw my way out of all Nine Hells, you will see me again!" Kael screamed at Sythrnax's back as he disappeared down a side tunnel still laughing.

As Kael's echoing voice reverberated down the tunnels and came to an end, he could hear the voices of others as they entered the sunken room with the seal. Giddeon, Kasik, and Saleece walked around the side of the carved tablet and saw Kael. He saw someone duck behind the tablet, but he didn't get a good look at who it was.

"I knew I heard someone yelling down here," Giddeon said. "Kael, we need to talk with you about some things you've done." Not bothering to struggle with the seal's trap, Kael tried to talk his way out. He had no other chance.

"You need to listen to me, Giddeon. You don't understand what is happening here. Please, you need to leave. Now!" Kael yelled, pleading with the ArchWizard to listen.

Shaking his head, Giddeon responded, "That's impossible," he said, looking at Saleece.

"This is it, Father, a wrong choice and you know what happens. We've triggered Zaddyk's prophecy."

Nodding, Giddeon continued. "We won't be leaving until we know whether or not you are a threat to this kingdom, so just answer what we ask, all right?"

"It's not as if I have a lot of choice," Kael replied.

"Good. Now, the most important thing we need to know is why you killed almost twenty sisters of the goddess Mylla roughly two weeks ago."

The timing couldn't be a coincidence, Kael snorted. "I promise you, Giddeon, I have never killed a priestess of Mylla. Ever."

"I see," Giddeon said. "Niky, come here please." Kyah came out from behind the stone tablet and walked up beside

Giddeon. "You see, Kael. You left one alive. Though it took a miracle to save her." Kael lunged violently at Kyah, but the seal's bond held him tight.

"Her living through that night will be one of my biggest mistakes, and the fact that you took her in and healed her? That will seal your fate some day as well. Sister of Mylla? That's a joke. And you, Sister Niky, now is it?" he said maliciously, staring at the young woman who had betrayed him so thoroughly. "We're not done either, Kyah. Her soul will be free if I have to go free her myself."

It didn't take long for Giddeon to notice that Kael couldn't move.

"What happened to you?" he asked. What Kael had said about Kyah was swiftly forgotten as the ArchWizard approached the seal to examine it.

Exhausted physically and emotionally, Kael sighed. "What does it matter, Giddeon? If you're going to kill me, then just do it already. I'm tired of running." Giddeon stood up and looked into the face of his son. With the exception of a questionable attack on the sisters of Mylla, Kael had done far more to help Talohna than he had ever done to harm it.

"I'm not going to kill you, son. I'm going to try and help you, but there are some things we need to tell you." Kael frowned as a voice behind him spoke.

"It's about damn time, old man," Savis Ephemeral cursed, as he materialized beside and slightly behind Kael. Reaching around, he grasped him by the throat. "Your king thought you might lose your nerve, Giddeon!"

He smiled and plunged his wooden dagger into the base of Kael's skull.

TAZAMMOR MOUNTAIN

Bauro BlackSpawn sailed into Izotan Bay on the western side of the Tazammor Mountain Peninsula to continue his search for the missing and presumed traitor, Dominique Havarrow. Twenty ships followed in his wake. Before dropping her off in Dasal, Ella told him that she could feel Havarrow's presence somewhere around the old Dwarven weapon foundry and prison called Arkum Zul.

"Land-sucking witch," he muttered, recalling the conversation. "Arkum Zul. No one has found this cursed place in aeons."

"Captain?" Talvira asked. Bauro glanced at his sorceress.

"Too bad you couldn't find things as easily as you can hide them."

"Sorry, Captain. Perhaps spread out the fleet so we can search both sides of the peninsula? We could try the east side." She pulled an old leather map from the navigator table. "Flatwater Bay has a small dock, perhaps we'll find answers there."

"Carwin," Bauro yelled. "Bring us about and head for Flatwater Bay. Tell our signaller to split the fleet. Hack's *Bled Trader* can lead the search here."

"Aye, Captain."

Bauro's ship turned easily in the stiff breeze and headed back out of the bay, remaining close enough to the shore to see any signs of hidden inlets or secret docks.

The hours passed slowly as Bauro paced the deck of his ship, and all his sailors kept their eyes on the shore. As the BlackSpawn Bastard rounded the last rocky point stretching out into the ocean and sailed into Flatwater Bay, all hell broke loose. A dozen of Sythrnax's ships attacked instantly. Fire-enchanted ballistae bolts roared as they leapt from several ships, slamming into both Bauro's escort ships.

"Return fire!" he barked, even though his men were already swinging the matching pair of catapults at the front of his ship into position. Dropping the lock pins, both men cut the catapults loose. The iron-heavy stones jumped away and slammed into the ship firing the enchanted ballistae. One last bolt let loose as the ship splintered under the barrage and broke apart. The flaming bolt landed at midships on Bauro's vessel, and swath of fire rolled out all the way to the captain's cabin below the helm.

"Water!" Talvira screamed. Without hesitating, Bauro's second mate kicked two barrels of sea water over, drenching the deck and putting out the fire.

"Good work, Kes," Bauro shouted, and turned back to his helmsman. "Turn the Bastard broadside so our ballistae can even the odds."

Carwin spun the wheel hard, and Bauro's ship eased to the right. Every ballistae thumped, releasing their bolts. Each hit a separate ship even with the water level. The boltheads compressed and four spring-loaded blades snapped out, shredding the vessels' side planks and coring through the ship and out the bottom of the far side. All three enemy vessels listed and began sinking, no longer a threat.

Several of Bauro's other captains followed his attack plan, and dozens of ballistae bolts and stones filled the air. The unique bolts cored through everything they touched, and another six enemy ships sunk to the bottom of Flatwater Bay. The final two enemy ships tried to run.

"Signal the other ships," Bauro barked. "Drag those cowards back."

As Bauro's signaller waved both flags, his ballistae operators pulled the spring-load bolts from their siege engines and slid in new bolts with ropes clipped to the rear. Several crewmen adjusted the sails, catching more of the wind, and Bauro's ship shot forward. In less than a minute, the *Bastard* was in range, and Carwin spun the wheel again as both ballistae let loose. The first bolt missed, landing in the ocean between the two escaping ships, but the second bolt hit the trailing ship, sinking deep in to the decking. Bauro's crewman grabbed the excess length of rope and ran to the front of the ship. Both catapult operators pulled the lock pins and slid the catapults to the side on greased tracks, making room for the crewman to feed the rope into a massive two-man winch. Each pirate turned the handles on their respective sides. The man on the left dropped a lock catch into the gear. It clacked as they turned the handles, pulling the two ships together.

It took fifteen minutes for the crewman working the winch, with the help of those manning the sails, to drag the fleeing ship to the *BlackSpawn Bastard*. The two ships came together with a crunch of wood. Already up the shrouds, Bauro's boarding crew were on the enemy vessel before the ships came together. Unlike most pirate captains, Bauro was one of the first to board the enemy ship, his hunt for its captain underway.

Sythrnax's crew fought relentlessly and several pirates died within minutes of landing on the ship's deck. Bauro growled as a young Elvehn man cut down one of his boarding party right in front of him. Not slowing, Bauro drove his cutlass into the man's back. Twisting the blade as he withdrew it, he kicked the mortally wounded enemy to the deck and moved on. He finally spotted the ship's captain standing alone on the helm deck. The big man held a shield and pointed his sword as he stared at Bauro.

Taking the steps up to to the helm two at a time, Bauro drew his long dagger with his left hand to offset the shield as best he could. The deck remained clear of other fighters, and as Bauro got his first look at his fellow captain, he understood the big man needed no one to help protect him. The Northman put up his shield and smiled, but didn't waste time with words.

Bauro lunged with his sword as the Northman stepped into his shield, blocking the blow and pushing Bauro back. Bauro tried again, but pulled his strike and sidestepped the shield, driving his dagger towards the Northman's stomach. His dagger was easily blocked by the Northman's sword. Trying to figure out a way past the well-trained shield, Bauro stepped back and three arrows whistled past, stitching the Northman from ribs to ear. He crumpled, dead, as Bauro glanced to his right. Kes smiled and waved from the enemy ship's far shroud. Bauro picked the big Northman up and heaved his body overboard.

Looking down to the main deck, he watched as his crew killed the last to oppose them. Four surrendered.

"Kes," Bauro barked.

Dropping from the shroud, she looked up to the helm. "Captain?"

"Get your new ship ready for battle and either execute the survivors or give them our mark."

"Aye, Captain."

As Bauro hopped the rail back to his own ship, he saw that three of his other vessels had brought the other fleeing ship to heel. He smiled and tallied the count in his head. Three of his ships were sunk in the battle, thanks to the surprise attack that sunk his two escort ships. With the two ships they captured, he was only down one. An acceptable loss in any battle involving so many ships.

"All right, everyone," he yelled out across his ship. "Let's find that traitor!"

MONOLITH CHAMBER

"No!" Saleece screamed, as the blade of Savis' dagger sank to the hilt at the base of Kael's skull. With a vicious twist, he broke the split wooden blade off inside Kael's neck. Unable to move or defend himself, Kael cursed as he felt the blade slide into his neck. He struggled to handle the pain that was tearing through his body, but when the assassin snapped the blades of his dagger off inside his neck, it was like a switch had been thrown. His legs buckled and eternity slammed his mind.

Savis held Kael's body upright as he pulled his second dagger and cut Kael's throat from ear-to-ear. Releasing his hold, Savis kicked Kael's legs out and smirked as he fell onto his back.

Blood pumped from his throat, running into the furrowed grooves of the seal's inset design.

Savis tried to recast his family spell and disappear into the shadows of the room's outer walls to escape down the tunnel Sythrnax went down. Dealing with the second contract was impossible. He started to speak the single word spell when he heard Giddeon's roar of outrage, and Savis was lifted from the ground and tossed against the far wall, knocking the breath from his lungs. Desperately trying to breathe so he could make himself disappear or defend himself with magic, Savis instead watched in fear as Kasik rushed across the room and rammed his greatsword, Still, into his stomach. Saleece rushed to her brother's side. Pressing her travel cloak to his neck, she tried to stop the blood flow as Kasik impaled Savis. The thrust buried Still almost a foot deep in the stone behind the assassin.

Shaking with fury at the thought of failing his Kreeda Oath to Ember, Kasik grabbed Savis' face and squeezed. "Why? Why were you told to kill him?"

"The king..." he started, but Kasik twisted Still with his right hand, the sword ground and popped in the stone, causing waves of agony to rip through Savis' abdomen.

"There has to be more to it than that," Kasik growled as Giddeon stepped up beside them.

"The guild," Savis gasped. "They... were asked to... do it... you failed..." He cried out in agony. "Just... kill me. Just... a job."

With his face twisted in anger and pain, Giddeon growled. "Gladly, assassin. I just hope and pray that the cursed Ephemeral Elderblood dies with you. Our kingdom has been trying to get rid of your damned family for far too long. Your blood has always done their best to destroy everything people hold dear. As the only ArchWizard of Talohna, I sentence you to death by termination of your cruus..."

"No!" Savis gasped. "Not... Kill me you... Fool."

"He was my *son*, assassin," Giddeon screamed back. Placing his hand on Savis's chest, he sneered. "*Sal qnd skera.*"

The spell activated immediately as a tearing squelch echoed inside Savis' chest. “Sentence passed,” Giddeon hissed.

The spell granted only to the authoritative office of the ArchWizard tore into Savis' very soul, shredding both the magical and physical sides of his spirit and collapsing his connection to the earth's power. Kasik forcefully pulled Still from the assassin's belly and let him crumple to the floor. Giddeon had used the spell only twice before. The assassin would die in an extreme amount of pain over the next few hours. Savis would barely have the clarity of mind to moan from the intense agony he was about to endure.

Kasik turned around in time to see Giddeon kneel before his son.

"Is he..?" he asked Saleece.

With tears streaming down her face, she sobbed, "Yes, he's dead. There's nothing I can do. I'm sorry, Father."

"It's not your fault," Giddeon said softly. "It's mine. I should have known something wasn't right..." He put his hand to his mouth and tried desperately not to break down. He would never be able to tell Kael that he was his father, that he loved him, and that he had done so many things wrong.

A vivid bright light flashed beside them and Giddeon looked over to see eight strangers appear out of thin air. Sliding around the corner of the massive stone cenotaph, Kyah hid as tears dripped from her chin. Recognizing one of the newcomers as the DragonKin Queen, Shelaryx WhiteScale, she did her best to stay hidden on the far side of the giant stone.

The DragonKin's Queen rapidly took in the scene before her. Seeing Kael's body, she scoffed with disgust.

"Giddeon Zirakus, you gods-cursed stupid Human. What in the Nine Hells have you done?" she roared.

Eva ran to Kael's stilled form on the seal and shoved Giddeon and Saleece out of the way. “Sheathe that damn sword, Northman,” she snapped up at Kasik. He obeyed immediately and his sheath smothered the silence runes. Fae healing magic flooded Kael's body, lighting the dimly-lit room with a myriad of bright colours. The open wound in his neck closed and she reached around his neck and tore the dagger blades free.

"Seize them all," the DragonKin Queen ordered. Before Giddeon and the others could react, they were surrounded and subdued, relieved of their weapons by the Talon warriors and Zephyr mages accompanying her. A third Zephyr dragged Kyah out from behind the monument by her hair, shoving her into the others.

"Shel..." Eva began. Looking back over her shoulder, she shook her head. "It's too late... He's already gone." Shocked and speechless, she stared up at the Queen.

"Gods, no...." Shelaryx stumbled and caught herself as Eva exploded off the floor.

Lunging at Giddeon, she grabbed his robe. A full foot shorter, she yanked him down to his knees with incredible strength.

"No! No! No!" she screamed, shaking him. "Not after everything we did, every sacrifice we made. You fool!" Staring him the face, trembling with fury, Eva hissed. Her eyes flared a bright green and slowly the outer edges darkened, the black eating its way into her green pupils. "You are the sole reason every race in Talohna will be slaughtered or forced to their knees in subjugation, you stupid, witless Human. And where is my daughter?"

"Breathe, Eva," Shelaryx said, touching the Fae matriarch's shoulder gently. "Control it." Giddeon stared into Eva's eyes with awe. Seconds before they became solid black, the small woman inhaled deeply and the bright green swallowed the encroaching darkness.

"I don't even know who you are, or what you're even talking about. We didn't kill Kael. An assassin did and not on my orders," he explained. Trying to remain calm, he pointed to the writhing killer on the floor. "Kael was my blood-born son. We came to help him." Looking at the DragonKin queen, he asked, "Queen WhiteScale? What's going on?"

Before she could answer, though, a female Zephyr stepped up beside the queen. "My queen?"

"Yes, Vyteera?"

"Sythrnax's forces have just entered the hall up top. They have nullification amulets. We need to leave before we are stranded and must fight."

"Yes, of course. Thank you," Shelaryx replied, pulling Giddeon from Eva's grasp as if he were a rag doll. "This is your lucky day, Giddeon Zirakus. If I had more answers, I would leave you here to rot with your son and that assassin. But I need to know exactly what happened here and why, so you will *all* come with us." Seeing he was about to object, she added, "Do not think for one second that you have a choice. As of right now, all of you are prisoners of the DragonKin and Fae. More importantly, you all hereby stand accused of sedition against the Lesser Races of Talohna and for murdering those born of a pure magical race. Eva, take us back to BloodKin castle."

"My daughter, Shel. We need to find her before we leave. I will not leave without Ember," Eva demanded.

Shelaryx looked at Vyteera. "Do we have time?" The Zephyr closed her slitted eyes for only a second before they snapped back open.

"No, they will be here before we could search even a small area." She turned to Eva. "I am sorry, Mistress ThornWing," she said, bowing.

"You will pay for this, fool wizard. We Fae still have Darklings imprisoned on Vaenaria. They will discover the truth of what happened here even if it means shredding your mind. You *will* answer for your crimes," Eva said, glaring at Giddeon as she waved her hands. "Everyone closer, unless you want half of your bodies to stay behind," she barked.

With a whisper from Eva, a crack of power and a flash of white light lit up the seal chamber. As the glare died away, the chamber sat empty, except for Kael's body, a suffering assassin, and Cassie, who had been hiding up on a rock ledge overhead.

Having slowly worked her way back to the chamber with the seal, Cassie had managed to climb up the eastern wall where the mountain rock had pushed through the chamber wall. She had watched all of what happened below, too terrified to even move, but with no one left in the chamber except for the man who had killed Kael, she gradually made her way down to where Kael had fallen.

Kneeling beside his body, she grabbed his hand as tears fell from her chin.

"I'm so sorry I ran." She sobbed. "I was afraid... I should have helped you, like you helped me in Cairnwood. I'm glad you came to Cairnwood that day. I'll never forget you, I..." She stopped as more voices echoed from outside the chamber back towards the ruined city. Having heard what the strange woman had said about forces on their way, she ran to hide behind the rock slide, below where she had hidden before.

Chapter Forty-One

"The Darkness within the earth will some day rise. It has been foretold since the day it was put to rest there. We will continue to fight against those who will try to release it. No sacrifice is too large when it comes to the safety of this world. I will pay whatever price is demanded of my soul in order to acquire the power needed to keep this threat buried where it belongs."

Ella The White, 5 PC

RUINS OF KAZZADOR CITY

With little time before they would be overrun by the forces that Luthian and his animated skeleton army were fighting against, Ember's group, along with Nekrosa and Sephi, moved through the rubble of the demolished Dwarven city as swiftly as they could. They slowed only when they came across the set of chamber doors standing open.

"What is this place?" Max asked.

Yrlissa frowned. "It's a place that should have remained long buried, dammit," she cursed. She had been increasingly more irritated the farther down they went.

Nekrosa stared with fascination. "You're the Guardian," he said excitedly. "That's the only explanation. You know what this is don't you? She has to be, Sephi, it makes sense."

"You two have no idea what you're talking about," Yrlissa barked. "Now come on, we have little time left." She led the way into the chamber with Ember right behind her.

Yrlissa ignored the engraved tablet and stepped around it, heading towards the centre of the room. Seeing Kael lying on the blood-filled seal, she gasped and nearly fell to her knees.

"Oh, no... No, no, no," she muttered, rushing to his side.

Ember realized a second later what was happening. "Kael?" she whispered softly, as if not sure whether it was him. A single step forward confirmed it. "Kael!" she screamed. Running towards him, she threw herself on top of him. "No, Kael. Not now." She lifted his head and pulled him close. "Don't, babe, please. Don't be gone."

"I'm sorry..." Yrlissa said.

Ember never heard her. "I'm here, babe, right here. We made it. You can't leave me after all we... after all this. Please don't go, please!" she screamed. "Aravae, Lissa, what do I do? How do we heal him? Tell me, please!" she shrieked. Aravae shook her head as she slowly collapsed beside her son.

With tears in her eyes, Yrlissa shook her head. "It's too late, *nahlla*. He's gone, there's nothing..."

"No!" Ember cried. Putting her forehead to Kael's, her voice faded. "I can't be here without you, Kael. Don't leave me. God help us, please." She sobbed, burying her face in his chest. Yrlissa knelt at her side, her hand on Ember's back.

Max could only stare at Kael lying dead on the floor. Clearly having a hard time deciding whether to comfort Ember or start back up into the city to find Sythrnax's men to vent his growing fury on, instead he stood where he was, smouldering in anger.

Sephi grabbed Nekrosa by the arm. "Try, husband. Maybe he is still in the Void. You can bring him back."

"It's too late," Nekrosa said. "He will have already passed through, and if he hasn't, his spirit will obliterate mine in the Void. I barely got out last time, Seph."

"We have a Fae this time. She can bring you back. You have to try. We need them all, especially now. This seal will open in less than an hour or two," she pleaded.

"All right," he sighed. "I'll try." Approaching Ember and Yrlissa, he said, "Let me try something, please."

"What do you think you are doing?" snapped Yrlissa.

"Trust me, like you trusted us when we saved her." He smiled as he touched Ember's shoulder. Ember failed to acknowledge his touch as she continued crying on Kael's chest. Yrlissa nodded her consent.

Very few necromancers have ever had the power to walk their spirit into the Void between life and death, and most who tried never returned. Nekrosa had done it many times, even returning when Kael had unintentionally trapped him there weeks ago when they were in Dasal together.

"*Na gravasay, spyratallis,*" he said softly as he placed one hand on Kael's leg, using it as a connection to find his spirit. The rush of the Void's power expanded as it entered Nekrosa's mind. He entered into the vastness of pure dark.

The Void between life and death was a friendly place for a necromancer of Nekrosa's talent, and it took little time for him to detect a spirit that had yet to pass through to the underworld. With only a thought, Nekrosa found the soul and with only a few thoughts more the spirit showed him what had happened. He opened his eyes to find Yrlissa staring right into them.

"You're a VoidWalker," she said in an accusatory voice, as the power of the Void cleared from his eyes. "Please tell me Kael was still there."

Nekrosa frowned, shaking his head. "Kael's spirit has already passed. He is gone, there is nothing more I can do. I'm sorry. That one, however," he said pointing to Savis. "He has not passed through yet. I don't understand why he is here and in the Void at the same time, but I do know he is the one who killed

Kael. I pulled his disjointed soul back to his body. You should be able to talk to him."

Yrlissa glanced over at the writhing killer and immediately recognized the broken blade still in his hand.

"What the hell is going on here?" she muttered, walking over to the man who took Kael's life.

She bent over and hauled Savis up straight so she could look into his face. "Who are you?" she asked. "Where did you get your broken blades?" She grabbed his hand and looked at the palm, recognizing the mark of the Broken Blade guild magically tattooed there. When she shook him and got only a light groan, she jolted him with a shot of electricity. His eyes popped open and he started laughing.

"Ah, I shoulda known you would be waiting for me when I died, High Commander," he giggled and wheezed.

"You're not dead yet, assassin, and I promise you I am very much alive," she said.

Surprised, he stammered, "That's impossible... I killed you myself..." He wheezed with pain a second time.

Yrlissa sneered, hatred rumbling through her voice. "You failed. I lived, and by the looks of what was done to you, you won't, not for much longer. Tell me why you did this. Why did you kill Kael, and why did you try to kill me?"

"Orders, Commander. Just orders... When you are given an order..." He coughed again, his breath coming much quicker. "Did your assassins ask why you gave their orders?"

"No, they didn't, but I know all of them. Every single assassin in every sanctuary in every country, except for you," she said, giving him a shake when his eyes closed.

"Merethyl..." he started to say, before his eyes rolled back into his head. His mouth slowly opened and he moaned lightly in pain, Yrlissa knew he would say no more. She dropped him to the floor and turned back. Everyone stared at her except for Ember.

Luthian stumbled into the chamber, fell and slid across the floor, leaving a smear of blood in his wake from three arrows in his back.

"Luthian!" Sephi screamed. She hurried to his side, snapped the arrows off and rolled him over.

"I am so... sorry, my q-queen, I tried..." His last words were an apology for not being able to do the impossible.

"You did well, my friend, as always," she said and then grabbed his shoulders and dragged him over to the seal by the others. Nekrosa rushed to the chamber doorway, his spell well under way as he tried to reanimate the thousands of remains hidden within the city ruins, but his spell sputtered and quickly died.

Limping back to the others, he gasped. "They're too close already. Magic won't work. We need a plan. If we go down that tunnel, the way Giddeon and the others must have went those warriors will overrun us or we'll be arrested by the ArchWizard," he said.

Yrlissa knelt beside Ember and took her by the chin. "Look at me, girl. We need your help and we need it now. You have to jump us out of here Ember, quickly."

Ember just looked at her. "You lied to me, Lissa. You know what's going on. You lied to me, and now he's dead. Why?"

Max took up watch just outside the chamber doors, and Yrlissa could hear him engage in combat against the first of Sythrnax's forces.

"Even if her magic works, where do we go, Yrlissa?" Sephi asked. "It's clear Giddeon betrayed you. There is nowhere safe now, and she can't jump us all to DormaSai. It will kill her. There are too many of us."

"There is somewhere closer we can go," Yrlissa realized. "Ember, look at me, please," she begged, trying once more. "Do you think this is what Kael would have wanted, for you to give up and for Max to die fighting a battle he cannot win? I promise you I will tell you everything once we are safe. Everything, *mai nahlla*, I promise," she pleaded as the battle outside the doors picked up in intensity.

Sephi looked back towards where Max was fighting, then stood and raced to help, the tempo of the battle increased the moment she arrived by Max's side.

"If you want my help," Ember said, her voice thick with hurt and anger. "Tell me the truth. Tell me something!" she screamed. "Tell me what was so fucking important to keep secret that it cost him his life!"

Her eyes full of tears, Yrlissa replied softly, "We have to take Kael home, do you understand? We have to take him to the Dyrannai Forest, *nahlla*. It is where others like him are buried and where I can give you all the answers you will ever need and a reason to keep fighting."

Wiping her own eyes, Aravae stared at Yrlissa. "That's north of the Black Kasym, Yrlissa. No one even knows if the forest still exists."

"The Field of the Fallen will still be there, Aravae. It has to be. It's our only hope."

Closing her eyes for only a second, Ember tried her best to hold back the sorrow of her broken heart and the tears that refused to stop running from her eyes.

"How do I jump us somewhere I have never been? It will kill us all."

"Listen closely, picture what I tell you, and we will get there, all right?" Ember nodded, and Yrlissa began.

"The Dyrannai Forest has a burial ground—the Field of the Fallen, and when you are facing north while standing in the middle of this field, you can see the mausoleum of the first fallen wizard of Kael's kind. Her name was Yvette Dasair. Her name is engraved along the mausoleum's top. The stone building is ten feet high and ten feet across with two stone pillars just before the sealed, black marble door. The pillars are unlike anything else in this world, Ember, focus on them. They are three feet wide and made from polished white ivory. Dark purple and black plants are engraved up the pillars. They match Kael's markings and the ones on my face. Picture his markings climbing those ivory pillars and take us home, *nahlla*."

"I got it. Call the others," Ember said, and closed her eyes to concentrate.

Yrlissa pulled her daggers and ran to get Max and Sephi, arriving in time to see a sword pierce Max, she screamed and lunged through the air, driving both her daggers into the neck of the warrior whose blade was stuck fast in Max's side.

She looked up from the dead man to see Sephi's flashing blue blades disembowel the last two enemies outside the chamber. With a loud grunt, Max tore the sword from his side.

"Ah, shit," he said, dropping to a knee. "Too many I guess." With dozens more of the enemy already within sight on the ruin's far side, Yrlissa and Sephi both slid under his arms and dragged him back into the chamber room.

"We have to go now, Ember," Yrlissa called as they rounded the stone tablet. "There are too many to fight. The rest will be in range with those amulets in minutes!"

With her eyes still closed, Ember nodded. "Close as you can everyone, I've never done this before." With the others crouched close, she held Kael tight and pulled his travel pack and weapons up onto his chest. "*Relamus Aidora,*" she whispered.

But nothing happened as a glass alchemy vial fell from the travel pack, breaking on the floor. It read B.B. Purge.

"It won't work," Ember cried, not noticing the vial.

"The amulets, dammit," Yrlissa cursed, too preoccupied to see the glass bottle. She jumped up and ran towards the door. "Don't wait for me," she yelled back over her shoulder. Exiting the chamber, Yrlissa stared at the mess of bodies before looking up to see more warriors less than a mile away.

"Not this time, Sythrnax. Fuck you and your amulets," she mumbled. With no other option, she glanced back to make sure she was alone and raised her hands above her head.

"*Ivey K'Sarahn,*" she hissed, lowering her hands as magic sprayed out in a fine mist. Flashes of bright light lit up the bodies of two dead enemy warriors, but Yrlissa wasn't done yet. "*K'Sarahn Asravan.*" With the magic dampening amulets lit up a bright white from the first spell, Yrlissa ducked back into the room as the second spell activated and the amulets exploded, destroying the dampening enchantment affecting Ember's magic. She raced back to the others, yelling, "Now, Ember. Hurry before the rest are in range."

Not hesitating, Ember tried again. "*Relamus Aidora.*"

The flash of white that normally preceded a Fae realm jump built slower than Eva's had earlier, and Cassie, who had been watching from behind the pile of earth and rock, was left with no other choice. She dashed out from her hiding spot and ran into the blinding white light as if hoping they would take her with them.

The moment Cassie entered the white light, Ember knew something was very wrong. She focused harder, concentrating on holding Kael's body and getting them to the building with the ivory pillars. Pain cut through her focus and her mind buckled under an explosion of white.

Ember knew no more.

DEEP EARTH

Dravik BloodPounder and his warriors of the Bulwark Host broke through the rock wall blocking the tunnel, arriving just in time to see Ember's jump spell fade away. They stared down at the blood-filled Animus seal from a small precipice forty feet above the floor of the DeathWizard's monolith chamber. The Animus seal that should have been under the protection of the DemonKind was deserted. They watched the active seal for several minutes before Dravik's younger brother, Draven, spoke.

"Any chance that blood belongs to a child of the black, brother?" he asked. Dravik, commander of the Host and general of the Dwarven Army, stood five feet two inches tall and weighed a hundred and eighty-five pounds. He never flinched in the face of fear, having fought nightmares of the Deep Earth for far too many millennia, but looking down at the pulsing seal below, real fear rippled through him.

Dravik knelt, eyeing the seal with close scrutiny. Seconds passed before the ornately designed, carved magical glyph heaved one last time, splitting with a crack of shifting rock. A second thunderous pop caused more fissures to race across the surface of the seal.

"There's your answer. The blood of the Lost has been spilled over an Animus Seal. We must return to prepare our defences," Dravik finally answered.

"Where are the DemonKind, Commander?" one of the newer members of the Host asked. His long, black beard swung freely, the beads on the braids clicked lightly as he looked from the seal below them, to Dravik, and then back.

The Host commander sighed. "I cannot answer that, youngun. This the closest we've been to the surface in almost thirteen thousand years. If the DemonKind were here, then they have failed, that much is clear."

"That tunnel, brother," Draven added, pointing to the dark passage that Sythrnax had used earlier. The experienced eyes of the Dwarf noticed what few others would. "We should investigate. The monolith chamber is supposed to be sealed. That shaft was dug by hand, and some years ago by the look of the pick scars. It may give us some answers."

Having naturally evolved in the Deep Earth, Dravik and many of the Dwarven people had developed many unique gifts. With the same ease a wizard accessed magic or an archer drew an arrow, Dravik shifted the lenses inside his eyes and stared into the dark exit below and to the left of where he stood. Even with his eyes tinted red and his vision enhanced for pure darkness, he could not make out whether or not anyone was hiding inside the tunnel. But the hairs on the back of his neck prickled to life and fear flooded his veins like chunks of ice racing down a swollen spring river. It was a fear Dravik knew well and one he hadn't felt in aeons. Try as he might, he couldn't shake the unnatural terror as it sent a shiver of warning down his spine. An ancient warrior was already free of the seal—it was the only explanation for his irrational fear.

"Izotan's ton-heavy gonads," the young Dwarf cursed. "What is this fear eating at my guts?"

Dravik grunted as his brother answer the young dwarf.

"One of the enemy is free. You were taught this, GreyRock," Draven said.

"I remember," GreyRock said, smiling as he shook his head. "The pheromones created from the silver scales rubbing together against the appendages. Still to overcome this..."

"You focus," a young warrior said. "Use your anger to push the fear aside. You need more time with the Mahala scouting parties. It'll help you master real fear. Then you overcome this."

Dravik nodded his praise to the knowledgeable youth and let his attention shift back to the chamber floor. Another explosive crack of power rocked the seal below. More fractures began to form in the rock, spreading out where thin cracks had been present only minutes earlier. One last snap of stone echoed down the tunnel, and the cracks opened wider, the fissures rocketing outwards beyond the edge of the seal's design and into the stone floor of the surrounding chamber.

"There's no time to investigate, Draven. We must leave. That seal will tear open the dimensional barrier within the hour. We cannot fight and win against a sixth of the enemy's race. Let's move it, Host. Now," Dravik barked, before standing up and turning to walk back the way they'd arrived. "Drop this tunnel behind us, Draven. We cannot afford for the Ri'Tek to follow us home."

The younger Dwarf gave him a slight nod. "Consider it done."

When the rest of the Host were far enough ahead and with Dravik standing a few paces behind him, Draven closed his eyes and gently placed both of his palms on the wall of the stone tunnel. With a simple invocation, Draven BloodPounder called on Izotan, the Dwarven God of stone.

Unlike Talohna's others gods, however, Izotan answered, with a fury worthy of a real god. Celestial energy channelled through the priest as Draven's hands slid into the rock of the tunnel walls as if they were entering warm mud. A concussive blast of power shot down the wall to his left and then spiralled up and around the passage as it rolled through the stone towards the entrance to the monolith chamber. A massive, outward explosion blasted dirt and large rocks from the floor, ceiling, and both walls, destroying the tunnel as it collapsed in on itself. Any evidence of the Dwarven Host and the passageway they had just used vanished under tons of mountain rock. One last word ushered from Draven's mouth and more energy poured into the wall and rushed into the rubble. Steam spurted in short jets, carrying drops of molten rock. The raw, pungent stench of sulphur hung in the air. As Draven eased his hands from the stone, Dravik watched the light of Izotan fade from his brother's eyes.

The priest stumbled with exhaustion for a second as fist-sized rocks from the collapse rolled to his feet, but Dravik dared not offer his brother a helping hand. The scars and missing fingers on his left hand caused by energy burns years ago reminded him never to touch a priest after one handled the power of their gods.

Draven turned and nodded. "They can't follow. The stone will solidify, making this tunnel impassable."

"Good. Perhaps it'll be enough to keep us hidden. Because of the Cataclysm, the Ri'Tek will have no idea where the rest of the seals now lie. Jasala Vyshaan gave her life to hide us all. Let us hope her death meant that much at least," the Dwarven Commander said, as he spun on his heel to lead his men on the long trek home.

MONOLITH CHAMBER

The collapse of the Dwarven tunnel twenty feet up the side of the Monolith Chamber did not go unnoticed. As the last stone tumbled from the shaft with a hollow echo, a set of vibrant purple eyes flared from within the tunnel at ground level. With a wry grin hidden beneath the mask attached to his hood, Sythrnax stepped from the complete darkness shrouding the entrance to the shaft his men had started digging twenty years ago. He chuckled.

"Funny. Five thousand years I spent searching for the Dwarves. Stop looking for them and they show up."

A young Elvehn woman joined him. "Master? Should we look for a way around the cave-in?"

"Not now, Marissa. The seal's opening. Join up with the main encampment. I'll come find you after the Vikress has risen." The woman nodded. Obeying without hesitation, she turned and disappeared back into the dark tunnel.

Sythrnax waited, looking down at Savis writhing in agony.

“You did do what was asked, didn't you?” Sythrnax asked, though the assassin was far beyond hearing. Sighing, he bent down and dragged Savis into the tunnel, propping him up against the stone wall. Pulling a small blade from within his sleeve, Sythrnax cut open the assassin's leather armour and shirt. Working slowly, he cut an ornate design into the assassin's chest and then removed the black crystal from his left glove. Setting it on the design, he placed his hand over top and activated the magic he had taken from Kael months before. A silent blast of dark power enveloped Savis, freezing his wound closed and forcing his cruus to bind back together. It made him choke as he inhaled deeply. Sythrnax plucked the black stone from the assassin's chest and slid it back into his glove. Coughing his way back to consciousness, Savis blinked repeatedly as he stared up at Sythrnax, his body quaking with tremors.

“Sy... Sy... Sythrnax? How?”

“Don't make me regret this already.”

“Yeah, a... all right.”

"Get your legs under you and retreat down this tunnel until you find Marissa. Tell her I said to get you a tent and for a healer to come see you. The wound in your belly will stay sealed long enough for you to get there."

"Yeah, sure. Thanks." Sythrnax offered Savis his arm and pulled the assassin to his feet.

Stepping further back into the tunnel as the fissures inside the chamber exploded under intense magical pressure, Sythrnax watched Savis stumble away. Slowly, he turned his attention back to the seal's chamber. Steam hissed from vents deep within the earth, and orbs of bright light in various colours floated around the monolith chamber. As the orbs slowly settled to the cracked, heaved stone floor, a massive tear in reality formed above the seal. Sythrnax stepped forward and raised his staff as a long, serrated blade clicked, dropping from the bottom. Driving the staff into the earth, he activated the magic within it.

"*Kin Atoll Frosai.*" Waves of freezing mist rolled off Sythrnax's staff, enveloping the entire chamber, as the magic raced towards the dimensional tear. Slamming into the magic created by the Animus Seal, the waves of frost locked the tear open. Pulling his staff from the stone floor, Sythrnax slowly stepped into the chamber room as a beautiful young woman walked out of the tear. Naked as the day she was born, the woman looked around the chamber and stretched. Her *tresa*, the appendages covering her head where most had hair, clicked and lashed about, as if excited to be free.

Sythrnax pulled a cloak free from his travel pack and approached the woman. He bowed, dropping as low onto the frosted floor as he could get.

"Vikress Illara D'Artagen, welcome back." The woman held out her hand and Sythrnax took it gently and rose, wrapping the robe around her naked form.

"How long, Sythrnax?"

"Vikress?

"How long has it been since we were banished from our world? Our home?"

Sythrnax hesitated for only a second. “I'm not exactly sure, Vikress. Somewhere in the range of thirteen thousand years. No one really knows.” A quiet fury radiated from the woman's entire body.

“I almost had him, Sythrnax. I had my hands around his soul... Who destroys their soul in order to seal such magic?”

“You mean, Aysa N'ahai, the Kai'Sar who closed this seal?”

“Yes,” The Vikress said. “We should have never have dismissed our spies when they spoke of the Lesser races using this magic. They were capable of it.”

“Yes, Vikress. They were. The Kai'Sar are capable of far more than we thought.”

“Much has changed in Talohna then?”

“Yes, Mistress. Our people are now worshipped like gods by almost everyone.”

“Interesting. And the Kai'Sar?”

“Hated and feared. They are killed at birth or hunted to the death.”

“Good. Perhaps Aysa and the others did us a favour. It'll make reclaiming our world easier and freeing our magic much simpler.” Sythrnax nodded, offering her his glove with the black gem sewn into the palm.

She stared at the glove with disgust as it slid onto her delicate hand. “Back to using this pathetic magic.”

“You might find this stone more accommodating. Arkum Zul is under my control. I found the Ethereal Device. That stone holds the essence of the Kai'Sar whose blood freed you.”

The Vikress smiled. “What of the Lesser races?”

“Nearly all are extinct,” Sythrnax replied. “Only the Humans. Elvehn, and DragonKin are left. And some of the Dwarves.”

“The Fae, the Dragon Behemoths, DemonKind? The true power of the dosa are gone?” Sythrnax nodded. “Excellent. Come, Commander. It is time for the Ri'Tek to reclaim our real magic and rule Talohna once again.”

MONOLITH CHAMBER
SEVERAL HOURS LATER

Ella Navasha stood outside the DeathWizard's Monolith chamber she helped build thirteen thousand years ago and stared through the open door. A door only a DeathWizard could open. The popping and shifting rock echoing through the Deep Earth told her everything she needed to know. It made her blood run cold.

"Kat? It's time."

"What! No, I'm not ready."

"You'll have to be. We're too late. Here, take it." Ella lifted an ancient amulet from her neck and handed it to her apprentice. Kat shook her head but took it and dropped it over her head. "Just remember what I taught you. When the power hits the amulet, let it into your body and don't fight it. Let it swallow you and become you."

"Welcome it," Kat said.

"Yes. Desiree?"

"Yes, Mistress?"

"You keep her alive at all costs and get her out of here the moment I fall. Kat will complete our deal, you have my word," Ella said, summoning a five foot long wooden staff from mid-air.

"I know she will, Mistress," Desiree offered, smiling.

"Good. Now, come, girls," she said, as both drew their weapons. "If Kael's dead, we have Ancients to try and kill."

Ella led the way forward, walking around the monolith stone she helped carve too many long aeons ago. As she approached the Animus Seal, she knew immediately that Kael's blood filled the deep channels. A bone-chilling cold still hung in the air.

"So, that's how you did it, you crafty bastard," Ella whispered as she bent down and touched the blood filling the trough-like designs of the seal. "Well done, Sythrnax." To her immediate right the dimensional rift shimmered, weakening as the air in the chamber warmed and the powerful chill spell thawed.

Katarina shook her head. "He used the chill spell to hold the rift open long enough to free them."

"I did!" Sythrnax said from their left. He laughed as Ella whirled to face him. "And thank you, Ella dear. Your praise makes it all the more worthwhile. I thought it was rather inventive. Seeing as how your sordid fanatical creatures used their souls to seal the first rifts, preventing them from opening for longer than a minute."

"We had hoped it was foolproof. You're not supposed to be able use magic that powerful."

Sythrnax laughed even harder. "It might have, had I not found the Ethereal Device. In reality, how can you make something fool proof when you are the lesser species? I knew what spell would hold the rift open long before I found the first seal. The Dwarven Gods' device just gave me the raw power to do it. We Ancients always find ways to use powerful magic..."

A woman walked out of the tunnel. Like Sythrnax, she wore a mask and hood, covering her features. Ella felt her blood turn to ice, an irrational fear gripped her heart. "You just wait, dear Ella," the woman said. "Until we find a way to free our real magic. You don't know what real power is, witch. You never have."

"Vikress Illara. The pleasure is never mine," Ella said, offering a mock bow.

"Still with that witless tongue. I had hoped over a dozen millennium would have made you smarter."

"No such luck, Illara."

"Fair enough, *Ella*. I think I've heard enough from it." Illara raised her gloved left hand and the black stone pulsed, tearing Ella's tongue from her mouth. It hit the stone floor with a sickening thud. Desiree and Kat jumped forward, but were held back by Ella as she reached her arms out. Blood poured from her mouth and she shook her head.

The Vikress cocked her head to the side. "Nothing to say, dear witch? Too much time has passed, I guess. You forget what the Ancients were capable of, and now we have access to your creation's magic." Looking at the black stone sewn inside her new glove, she smiled. "It truly is a remarkable feeling to use real magic again, even if it's not my own."

Ella did her best to hold Desiree and Kat back, and with no other choice left, she pushed them back with her magic and attacked Illara. Two blasts of blazing white energy jumped from her hands. The Vikress swept them aside with her glove.

"Again, Ella? I detest using stolen magic," Illara scoffed. Looking at the glove and black stone in her palm, she sighed. "But with this power taken from that... DeathWizard – I hear they are now called. I just might find it suitable." With no warning, black energy tore across the distance, striking Ella in the stomach. She folded over, dropping to her knees as the constant bolt of magic sliced through her chest and skull, finally bursting into black flames across her body.

Kat screamed as Ella's magic exploded from her burning body. Slamming into the amulet, the wave of white magic lifted Katarina from the ground, suspending her in mid-air.

"Stop her. Sythrnax!" Illara screamed, but he was already moving as his staff materialized. He met a flurry of wooden daggers as Desiree leapt to defend Katarina. Ella's magic passed through them both, leaving them untouched as Sythrnax tried again and again to get past Desiree's defences. Her daggers danced along his staff. Deflecting a strike, Desiree tilted her wrist and dragged her blade across Sythrnax's knuckles, nearly severing his first finger.

"Pathetic dosa," he cursed. Slamming his staff down, a wall of ice shot straight up. Desiree turned as Kat fell to the ground, barely conscious.

She picked her up and took her weight. "Let's go, Mistress. You owe me that favour before we both die."

Vikress Illara's voice followed after them. "Both of you may run. By the time she learns to use that magic she stole, it will be of no concern to us." Desiree glanced back in time to see both Illara and Sythrnax disappear into a tunnel on the chamber's far side.

"Thank Assani's dark ass," Desiree prayed, as she realized they weren't going to die. "You'd better figure out what Mistress Ella gave you, Kat, and quickly. How are we ever going to stop them if you don't?" Kat stumbled and dropped to her knees amongst the rubble of the ruins. As Desiree bent over, Kat glanced up, her eyes glowed white with Ella's power.

"I... I can barely hold her power, Desiree, I..." Without thinking about her own safety, Desiree gently grabbed Kat's face in her hands. Her flesh sizzled at the contact.

"Listen, Kat. Remember your lessons. Let the power consume you." Desiree winced as small whiffs of smoke curled from her fingers.

"I... can't. I'm afraid. It hurts!" Kat screamed.

"Because you're fighting it, Kat. Let in in. Now!" she yelled. Kat's eyes calmed and she nodded her head.

"Thank you," she whispered, and fell unconscious. Desiree peeled her hands from Kat's face, leaving pieces of her fried fingers behind. Wiping her burns with a salve from Kat's bag designed to help magical burns, Desiree wrapped her hands in clean cloth and lifted Kat onto her shoulder.

Heading back to the column stairwell out of the ruins, she muttered. "Let's go home, Kat. All we did was for nothing."

Out of nowhere, Kat exploded with uncontrolled violence. Desiree dropped her to the dirt before realizing she was having a seizure. She held her arms down until the shaking subsided. Kat's eyes shot open and she grabbed Desiree's bare arm.

Desiree heard a voice in her head. It sounded like her own and it took several seconds before she understood that she was the one speaking, her voice mixed with Kat's.

"It was not for nothing. The prophecy has come true:*...will see Black's poured blood, returned to times past,"* she said, reciting the final line of the Last Light prophecy. Caught in the throes of such strong angelic magic, Desiree translated the literal meaning as well. Her voice echoed, as if coming from some place far off.

"...Kael's blood has filled the Animus Seal. The Ancients have returned."

Chapter Forty-Two

"Home is the place where, when you have to go there, they have to take you in."

Robert Frost, The Death of the Hired Man, 1914

CORYNTH, CETHOS

The two hooded riders had been travelling as fast as their stolen mounts would carry them for weeks. The spare horses they had stolen from the small Taktala scouting party had died of exhaustion days ago, but it was small price to pay. They crested a small hill and were able to see the city of Corynth for the first time in almost a year. They raced to the gates, where they were forced to stop and submit to a search. Galen Vihr and Kalmar Ibess both pulled down their hoods and identified themselves, informing the guards of their standing at the University of Magic. Master Wizard Cradik Senne vouched for them both. As part of the increased security ordered by King Bale, Cradik was stationed at the Corynth main gate for eight hours a day. He smiled as he recognized his old friends.

"We thought you were dead. Welcome back," Cradick said smiling.

"Is the ArchWizard here?" Kalmar asked.

"No. Giddeon's not here. But the Wizard's Council will be happy to receive you. Here," he said, writing two quick notes and handing them each one. "You both look... different. Younger..."

"Thanks, Cradik," Kalmar said, turning towards Galen.

The guards called for the heavy city gate to be opened. Galen's horse refused to stand still, pawing at the ground and prancing back and forth. Its emotions mirrored that of its rider. Looking back down the difficult road they had travelled, he wondered how long they would have to prepare before the Wildland tribes began their forays into civilized lands. It was their duty to alert the University and King Bale of what they had learned about the imminent attacks, though they were unsure of when a full scale invasion would occur, only that it would. The Wildlands had declared war on the Blood Kingdoms for breaking the peace treaty. Galen and Kalmar had barely escaped the Wildlands with their lives. The tribes were no longer taking slaves, they were killing the enemy.

It was also paramount that they inform the representatives of the Blood Kingdoms about Kael and the threat they knew he would not be. Why his return was kept secret from the wizard community, Galen did not know, but it would take a lot of convincing to prove to everyone that Kael wasn't a threat. It was an argument he and Kalmar were happy to take up. One last look down the road before entering Corynth had Galen hoping that his friend was safe and that he had found some answers about who he was.

He missed Kael a great deal and would never forget what the young man had done to help them all escape from the horrific slaughterhouse prison of Arkum Zul.

ARKUM ZUL CAVERN DOCKS

"How are the retrofits coming along, Captain?" Sythrnax asked, as he stepped up beside Dominique.

"Good," the pirate said, raising his voice over the clanging of blacksmith hammers and the gasping wails of their massive bellows. "The last cannon is going in to the *Twilight Reave* as we speak. The other six ships are about a quarter way done."

"A couple months yet, then?"

"Eamon figures a month. If the crazy bastard doesn't bring the mountain down on our heads first."

"Marissa told me that the first two cannons from the mould exploded when test fired. It made my cavern bigger."

"Yeah. He said his black powder mix wasn't right. Says, and I quote: "Fecking Talohna, even the black powder is more effing powerful." Whatever in the Nine Hells that means. Every cannon since has held so we know it wasn't a casting problem. Crazy fucker always says it's better to use too much than too little. Seems backwards to me."

"Good," Sythrnax said. "Thought you might like to know that Bauro's here looking for you. I lost a dozen ships from the Flatwater Bay docks. My scouts couldn't get to them in time to warn them."

Dominique shook his head. "I didn't think he'd find us that fast."

"It seems he had help from a certain White witch who wants to eat Eamon alive."

Laughing, Dominique scratched the stubble on his cheek. "Bloody Eamon. He's the only hermit in existence who could piss off Talohna's most powerful witch without ever leaving home."

Dominique noticed Sythrnax turn his way. "Ella Navasha is no longer. I assure you. Talohna's only living White witch might as well be an infant."

"Your plans went well then? Your people are free?" Dominique asked.

"Some, yes. Five seals still remain. Everything went extremely well, and Ella the White learned what the Vikress is capable of."

"So, the Ancients have returned to Talohna. This world will welcome you with open arms, most of it anyway. You have my thanks, Sythrnax. As you can see, I wouldn't have stayed hidden from Bauro long enough to complete our original deal, let alone the time to complete the retrofits to my ship and the other six. Fucking Bauro. I had no plans to betray him. I was just trying to finish the job you hired me for."

"I understand. My spies in Dasal told me nothing of Bauro heading this way, only that he was hunting you. The loss of my ships and men does not fall on you. As long as you remember our agreement and never turn these monster ships on my people, this cavern will be yours for as long as you want it. You can convert as many ships as you like."

"From what we've seen of the effects of these cannons, six fully outfitted ships will be plenty for now," Dominique said.

"Well then, how about showing me what all the talk is about?" Dominique laughed and waved Sythrnax forward. Turning right at a dock intersection, Dominique took the lead, walking past the massive Dwarven forges. All three were working steadily as blacksmiths and helpers worked metal, made sand castings, and broke open cannon moulds. At the far end of the docks, tied securely was Dominique's flag ship, the *Twilight Reave.*

"You added a deck, Havarrow," Sythrnax said.

"Mostly to make room for the cannon operators, Eamon calls them cannoneers."

Sythrnax nodded. "You're running two levels of six cannons on each side?"

"Yes," Dominique answered. "Hence the extra level and other changes. And two chaser cannons at the front. They're bigger, too."

"Even surrounded, you'll be dangerous. Just might have to ask you for a favour some day, Havarrow."

"What are you thinking?"

"That once another ship is done, you head out and destroy Bauro BlackSpawn once and for all. If these upgrades prove successful enough to do that, I may just hire you to take my people home. Rumour has it you've been through the Jaws of Rock and Ice, the only captain to make it. Is the old kingdom still there?"

"From what I could tell. The beasts of the deep forced us to return before we made landfall, but the land was there. As far as the eye could see," Dominique said.

"That is good news. Then when we're ready, you can bring the Ancients home so we can begin our real work. The Sepulchre must fall."

ARKUM ZUL
DOCKSIDE HOLDING CELLS

Corleya Bale sat in her cell at the far end of Arkum Zul's cavern docks with her lady in waiting, Alia, sleeping beside her. Corleya stared out across the cavern and wondered if she would ever see home again. Almost three months had passed since she ran from the castle like a spoiled princess who did not get her own way. She shook her head at her own stupidity. The past three months had shown her a lot. Tribals, cannibals, spirit magic, pirates, and even a supposed Ancient being. She longed for the comfortable life at court her father wanted for her.

Heavy chains rattled to her left and she glanced over. Lycori occupied the cell beside theirs but she had said little in several days now. Bound by silver chains, Corleya knew that the simple act of moving caused her immense pain. Even though she was a vampyr, Corleya still felt sorry for Lycori. She had been nothing like the vampyrs she had learned about in school. Lycori was friendly and had tried to help repeatedly.

As he had done every day since they had arrived in the cavern, Damien Krass brought their noon meal.

"Up and moving, slaves," he said, banging on the metal bars. "It's time for swill and spit." He laughed as Corleya frowned. His description of the food wasn't far off. The watery gruel tasted worse than it looked. "You know," he added, "you two could leave that cage if you swear allegiance to Captain Havarrow. He's a good man."

Corleya snorted. "A good man who is helping a very bad man? Maybe in your messed up world."

"Come on, sweetheart. You made your point, you're loyal to the vampyr. Fine, I get it, but enough is enough. You can't sustain yourselves on this kinda food. It's worse than we got from the savages down south. All of Havarrow's men are eating roasted keske and broiled veggies. You could be, too." He slid the bowls through the cage. Corleya handed one to Alia as she woke. Focusing on her own food and her growling stomach, Corleya turned her back to Damien.

"Fair enough, sweetheart. See you tomorrow. Same time, same place."

Chapter Forty-Three

"The magic behind the Pillars of Rule is a puzzle to all, even myself. I understand the rituals, the language, and the results, but the magic itself is a definite mystery. The Pillars terrify everyone, noble or commoner, and I must confess they make the hairs on my neck stand on end. I have never seen them unleashed in order to save a king or his reign. I'm pretty sure I wouldn't want to."

ArchWizard Keenan Desolla,
Cethosian Royal Wizard. 3718 PC

CASCADE CITADEL, CORYNTH

"You *will* step down and surrender the throne, Joran Bale!"

Though the meeting hall was filled to capacity with nobles from all over the Blood Kingdoms, less than half cheered the demand made by Duchess Vakaran. "You have no heir. By the laws of the Bloods, you must pass the throne to the Grand Duke." Despite only recently being handed the title of duchess by her dying father, the inexperienced twenty-year-old was well-known and respected amongst the Blood Kingdoms' nobility.

"There is no need for the throne to pass," Grand Duke Sheering answered. "Not yet, especially seeing as we now face war with the Wildlands."

"Princess Corleya went south. Everyone knows the truth. She is the cause of this war!" the duchess said. "King Bale can deny it all he wants, but it means she's dead, or wishes she was dead if she's in the hands of the Wildlands' Tribes. We need a king not affected and influenced by personal loss leading the war efforts."

"My daughter is not dead, Duchess," the king responded. "So, no, I don't have to do anything, least of all surrender the crown that has been in my family for over a thousand years."

"Then you run the risk of starting a civil war," the duchess barked back. The clear threat brought four Pillars of Rule to their feet. The third Pillar, the Wizard, was the first to stand.

"You speak words of treason, Tania Vakaran," he said. "Be careful how you proceed. Inexperience is no excuse for your behaviour in court. The king has broken no laws and no terms of succession-surrender have been met."

The duchess refused to back down. "There is no heir in this court, Pillar. Therefore, the Bales cannot sit on the throne."

The second Pillar added her support for the king. "As Priestess of the Pillars of Rule, I can assure you that no laws of Man or the Gods have been broken. This monarchy is not in forfeit until the true heir's dead body has been produced. Missing is not dead, Duchess Vakaran."

Focusing her rage at the king, the duchess pushed harder. "You would rather risk war than step down from the throne, Joran? The law is clear, regardless of what your Pillars say. No heir, no throne. I am not alone. You wouldn't win a vote of succession..."

King Bale leapt from his throne, fury radiated from his very being. "I will not surrender this throne until I have seen my daughter's body before me and certainly not when the Blood Kingdoms are facing war! And if you yourself want to play war, little girl, then gather your bannermen and the other high nobles who will follow you. I fought and won two wars by the time I was your age, and I've fought against the most powerful necromancer who has ever lived, and not only survived, but won that war, too. I didn't order my bannermen to fight for me; they followed *behind* me right to the very front lines of the worst wars in this country's history. War is a game I know all too well! Decide, Duchess Vakaran, because this debate is over!"

The king's first Pillar, the Knight, drew his sword, wrapping his hands around the pommel. A hush of quiet panic permeated the Hall of Nobles. Holding his sword to his chest with the blade pointing down, the Knight descended the raised dais of the king's throne. Armoured in enchanted plate, his heavy boots struck the stairs with a hollow thud as he approached the Duchess. Swallowing hard as the mysterious knight came to a stop in front of her, the duchess went pale with fear.

"King Bale has issued a challenge of war to a high noble. Do you accept, Duchess Tania Vakaran?" The Knight gently placed the tip of his sword at the Duchess' feet and held the crossbar, offering her the handle. The assembled nobility watched with breath held as the Duchess chewed her bottom lip. Finally, she sighed, surrendering.

"No, Your Majesty," the duchess said. "I won't condemn our people to war with each other. Not now. I hope your daughter is alive, King Bale. I do. But it has been months, and the chances of her survival shrink every day. At some point you will have to step down, even if she's not found." The First Pillar lifted his sword. Re-sheathing it, the Knight returned to his seat at King Bale's side.

King Bale stared at the duchess, his eyes cold and emotionless. "You still make demands of your king? If you were not your father's daughter, I would have you executed at dawn for this treasonous debate. For the little bit of life left in Sterling Vakaran's body, I won't do that, but do not push me. I have more important things to deal with than this gathering you've incited. It could have waited until the nobles' court next week. If you are going to take over your father's lands and responsibility, I suggest you learn how to behave, Duchess, or else hand your Duchy to your younger sister. Now go home." The six Pillars of Rule stood, signalling the end of the gathering. As the second Pillar, the Priestess, raised her hands above her head in prayer, the Wizard and the Knight moved to the left and right hand side of King Bale.

"May the gods bless all your travels," the Priestess said, "so you arrive home to your families safely."

As the nobles cleared out of the main meeting hall of the Cascade Citadel, King Bale and the Pillars of Rule waited until everyone had left.

"It won't keep those against you quiet for long, Your Majesty," the Wizard said.

"I know, old friend. Let's just hope Giddeon returns soon, and with good news." The fourth Pillar grunted her doubt. The Spy had returned only moments before the gathering convened and had yet to report.

"If the Mistress of Secrets has something to add," the Corsair said, "then perhaps she should say it." The sixth and final Pillar of Rule's dislike of the Spy was more than obvious. It earned him a sideways grin from her.

"They are already moving," she said. "The wind whispers, but the Grand Duke refuses to meet with the conspirators. It is possible that he will remain loyal."

King Bale snorted his disagreement. "No one remains loyal when they have the chance to be king." Turning to the Spy, he added, "Is the Duchess at the head of the nobles who moved against us so quickly?"

The Spy shook her head. "I know not. I've yet to get someone inside the inner group. They're careful, Your Majesty. Very careful. Someone with power and intelligence is at the head of these traitors."

"If my daughter isn't found soon, they won't be traitors. They'll be well within their rights to demand that I step down."

King Bale rubbed his forehead, the stresses of the day showing clearly.

"I don't think so, Your Majesty," the Priestess said, frowning. "Tania Vakaran gains nothing if the Grand Duke takes the throne. She won't win the confidence vote even if she were considered. Pointless anyway. The law is clear. The Cethosian crown was granted by the gods on the agreement that a direct-blood descendant ensured the monarch's power. It says nothing about the heir having to be in court. Until the princess's body is recovered, we Pillars will ensure you remain on the throne of Cethos. It is why the gods created our positions and why the initiation ceremony kills one in three prospects. Once we are unleashed we will not fail to keep you on this throne."

Quiet and off to the side as if not really there, like the ranger he was, the final Pillar, the Hunter, nodded. "I have rangers stationed in every banner, Your Majesty," he said, quietly. "Several carry the black mask."

The Knight grunted, but said nothing.

King Bale shook his head. "We're not assassinating nobles. They have a legitimate concern, even if their claim for me to step down isn't," he said.

"It may come to that, Your Majesty," the Spy counselled. "You cannot surrender the throne with everything that is happening. A new monarch would be disastrous. The southern tribes will attack in force, which means war. There is a DeathWizard on the loose somewhere, and that may eventually mean war. If the creature named Sythrnax tells the truth and there *will* be war between Ellorya and DormaSai, the last thing Cethos needs is a change in leadership. Assassination of upstart nobles may be our only option."

King Bale sighed, rubbing his eyes. "Perhaps, Mistress Spy. But not yet. Right now, all of you focus on your duties and on finding my daughter. I can't imagine what she must be going through."

"My rangers, the Corsair's sailors, or the Spy's whispers will find her, Your Majesty, and all will risk their lives to see her home," the Hunter said.

"I know." King Bale sighed again. "It is why Cethos is the only country to still honour the Pillars of Rule. Take care, old friends."

The six Pillars of Rule bowed and left the Hall of Nobles, each with the full intention of doing what they could to ensure their king's reign.

The End

Acknowledgements

My son and daughter:

Thank you for the constant support and belief that I could and can do this. You both will always mean the world to me.

Stacy Jones:

For all your incredible support and enthusiasm for this series and the world of Talohna, thank you. As for all the hours you spent beta reading and proofing, or your help with brain storming and writing blurbs, I will be forever grateful.

Joel Lagerwall and Stefan Celic:

Thank you both for your amazing work on the cover art for Blood of the Lost. You are both incredibly talented artists.

Fiona Skye from Casa Cielo Editing:

Thank you for the countless hours of hard work and the constant support, but most of all for helping me to become a better writer.

Addison Winchester:

For taking on Blood of the Lost at the last possible minute and giving it that extra polish and typo check, thank you. I appreciate it more than you know.

To the members of the Facebook group The Dragon's Rocketship and their writing sub group called Speed Dragons, thank you for all the amazing support over the years. I wish you all the best in your individual endeavours.

To everyone else:

Thank you. I can't possibly name everybody, but you know who you are, and know that I do appreciate you all.

Please enjoy a sneak peek from the upcoming 3rd book from the Darkness Within Saga.

Coming soon:

The Darkness Within Saga:

Book 3

The Fallen Sepulchre.

Chapter One

"To my beloved Kael,

Today is the one year anniversary of your death. It's been a very long and difficult year. You would be sad to see what is happening to our surrogate home. Talohna has become a true, living nightmare for many people. The Wildland tribes have attacked Yusat and are now at war with the Blood Kingdoms and three months ago there was a Black Sun event. It was terrifying and surreal, but incredibly beautiful all at the same time. The eerie darkness lasted for four hours. The child wasn't found and we pray that there was only one because there is no one left to find him or her. The ArchWizard, his daughter, Kasik... all are still missing.

Max, Yrlissa, and I have taken refuge in DormaSai under the protection of its king and queen. Protection that was short-lived, for now we are threatened by war as well. Ellorya's emperor blusters and threatens while having the audacity to demand my hand in marriage. As Talohna's only living Fae, it was to be expected, I guess. Thankfully, King and Queen Kohl refuse to bend under his pressure and war will be the likely outcome. I will never marry again.

Nekrosa and Sephi's help inside Kazzador Mountain that dreadful day saved our lives, though not everyone made it out alive. I miss you more and more with each passing day, my love. Forgive me, Kael, please. We should have reached you in time. I failed you when you needed me the most. I am so sorry. I know I'll see you again some day, even if it is in the Hall's of Paradise after my own death."

Excerpt from Ember Syme's personal diary, 5026 PC

DORMASAI, SOUTHERN KINGDOM SUMMER'S DAWN, 5026 PC

Darkness settled over DormaSai's Capitol city of Drae'Kahn. Torches positioned throughout the city cast their light into the darkest alleys of the blackest neighbourhoods as music and sounds of revelling from the taverns drifted on the night air. Even though threatened with war, the city and those living in it continued with their lives.

Ember Symes, the last Fae in Talohna watched the flickering lights as the evening breeze peaked and she listened to the sounds of happiness while standing on the balcony of her room high up in BlackVoid Castle; the home of DormaSai's king and queen.

The previous king had been the vilest of tyrants and had eventually led his country into civil war. A war that Nekrosa and Sephi Kohl had won. Ten years had passed and DormaSai prospered under their rule, but Ember knew their lenient laws on magic would always make them a target for the rest of Talohna. Even though Nekrosa and Sephi had risen to power on a wave of blood and undead magic, Ember had never felt safer since arriving in Talohna than she had while being with the two necromancers.

Nekrosa and Sephi granted Max, Ember, and Aravae, along with Yrlissa and her daughter Cassie, official sanctuary after returning from the Dyrannai Forest where they had interred Ember's husband. Kael Symes had been murdered deep beneath Kazzador City's soaring mountain peaks by a Broken Blade assassin working for King Bale of Cethos and possibly his ArchWizard, Giddeon Zirakus. The running fight from one end of the old Dwarven city to the other had taken the life of Nekrosa's friend, Luthian Bathory, and left Max mortally wounded. Ember used her Fae magic and realm-jumped them to the Dyrannai Forest using Yrlissa's knowledge of the area.

Ember couldn't help but think of the chaos that followed during their months in the ancient Elvehn forest. Rumours that the DragonKin had captured the ArchWizard, Saleece and Kasik, along with a priestess of Mylla, Sister Nikki, just moments before Ember, Max and their new allies arrived at the Animus Seal ran with intense abandon throughout the cities and towns of Talohna. Wildly exaggerated tales that the Ancients had returned to Talohna were also spreading like an uncontrolled wildfire. Many of Talohna's citizens believed it was only a matter of days or weeks before it became public knowledge. After countless millennia of worshipping the Ancients as the founders of modern magic and civilization, the people of Talohna had real hope for the future.

Ember shook her head. She was beginning to doubt all she'd heard over the last year. Though she'd always remain loyal to Nekrosa and Sephi for their help, Yrlissa Blackmist's warnings were starting to fall on deaf ears. The woman who's words she once trusted over all others now seemed tainted with the lies and personal agendas of the assassin she was. But then, betrayal will do that, assassin or not.

A light knock rapped on the door to her room. Without even making a conscious effort, Ember's magic told her it was the Queen, she could feel the woman's powerful presence through the heavy wood and iron door. Ember's powers had grown in leaps and bounds over the past year, most of it during their time in the Dyrannai Forest located deep within the Ancient's abandoned kingdom. As if the enchanted forest had slowly eaten away at the remaining wall inside her mind that held back all that she was. She remembered everything. Her birth mother, grandmother and even where the Fae were hiding—a secret she'd told no one. Genetic memory Yrlissa called it.

"Come in," Ember called. Dressed in a flowing, sleeveless, white silk gown Sephi Kohl seemed to glide across the room's polished marble flooring without actually stepping on it before coming to a stop beside her on the balcony. Ember smiled as she felt the queen bump gently against her. Sephi Kohl was a warrior few could rival and an even more impressive friend.

"Are you ready, my dear?" Sephi asked, her voice tight with the edge of her station. "The Conclave is about to begin."

"As I'll ever be, I guess," Ember replied. Not making eye-contact, she continued to stare out into the city. Sephi put her left arm around Ember's shoulders and held her tight, her voice returned to the softness it normally held.

"I know the past year has been hard, hun. Kael's death was a senseless loss caused by ignorant fools. I am so sorry this meeting has to be tonight."

Using the back of her hands, Ember dried the moisture from her eyes and took a deep breath. "I miss him, Sephi. Death took him from me but it hasn't taken my love for him. We lost so much under that mountain."

The queen laid her right hand on Ember's shoulder with the softest touch. "We did and the biggest loss was Kael and Luthian, but we need to start making up for it, especially tonight. If Emperor Mero sees that you are not here against your will then he should stand down and we can focus on the things Yrlissa has told us about. Things of which you need to speak with her about, Ember. It has been eight months now since we've returned to Drae'Kahn from the forest."

"I can't, Sephi. If she had told us earlier what she knew... what she was. We could have done things differently. Had Max and I known, we would have left Giddeon behind and travelled faster. Kael would still be alive. I'm not sure I even believe her anymore. The Ancient's are worshipped by everyone in Talohna. They created so much beauty. If they have returned, how can they be evil like she claims?"

"I agree with you, hun, you know I do. She should have trusted in you and Max enough to be honest, especially after she found out you were Fae. But she didn't and it is the past. The secrets she kept from you... it was for the right reasons. Time and experience will show you that sometimes you must do things that will hurt your loved ones, especially if it keeps them safe. Had Giddeon overheard or suspected, or had you been captured; the Dead Sisters were a lot closer than we thought—ahead of us and behind us. It was a no-win situation for her. There was no right call, Ember. I believe deep down you know that."

"I disagree," Ember said, shaking her head. "You don't tell a trusted friend one thing and then keep your own agenda hidden. We had two chances to leave Giddeon behind. We could have travelled faster, used her knowledge to realm-jump to Kael. She never even mentioned such a thing was possible until her life and her agenda were in danger. Why? We could have jumped to him... The choices were endless, it's like she didn't want us to catch up to him... Kael might still be alive if she had. I will *never* forgive her for that!"

Sephi sighed. "You are hurt because she kept it from you and that is normal, but we must work together in order to push on. She has knowledge and skills we need. You know her secrets now, and you know what is coming."

“If what she says is true.”

“Because of the library below us, we know that some of what she said *is* true. And we must prepare for if the Sepulchre falls.”

"Fair enough, My Queen." Ember frowned as she bowed.

"Don't you dare," Sephi said, gently grabbing Ember's arm to interrupt the bow. "The Fae do not bow to kings and queens and what I just said to you is as a friend not a queen. Ultimately, Ember, you must decide whether you will forgive Yrlissa or not, but we still must work together towards our common goals.”

Ember nodded. With her heart lifted a smallest bit, she gave Sephi a hug. The two women walked from the room and headed to the peace conclave between DormaSai and Ellorya with the hopes of averting what could become the start of a Talohna-wide world war.

As they walked to the peace gathering, Ember tried to send her mind elsewhere. Anywhere would be better than worrying about threats of a forced marriage to a power-hungry emperor. She felt the magic inside her slowly wrap around her mind. The Fae ability was both a gift and a curse. With a part of their mind fractured off in the memories of the past, the Fae could relive those events with frightening detail. Ember had used the overwhelming Fae magic by mistake once after discovering it in the Dyrannai Forest. The wash of Fae-heightened emotions and crystal clear memories made her relive Kael's death and the days that followed as if it were the very moment it happened. Reliving the crushing loss a second time so soon after it happened nearly broke her. With a year passed now, she was no longer afraid of what she'd feel. Instead, she sought the strength the emotions would bring in the days ahead while dealing with the greedy emperor and a dishonest assassin or whatever else might find its way to DormaSai.

Part of her mind drifted back, one year, to far beyond the Black Kasym and deep into the long abandoned kingdom of the Ancients. No longer in DormaSai, Ember opened her eyes and saw the Field of the Fallen, the ancient burial ground where DeathWizards were laid to rest whenever possible. She recognized the memory. They had just arrived in the Dyrannai Forest, which meant...

Looking down she saw Kael dead in her arms and Max bleeding out at her side.

Made in the USA
Monee, IL
16 February 2020

21894720R00374